# Go the Distance

## A Twisted Tale

# GO THE DISTANCE

## A TWISTED TALE

JEN CALONITA

DISNEY • HYPERION
Los Angeles • New York

Published by Disney • Hyperion, an imprint of Buena Vista Books, Inc.

For information address Disney • Hyperion,
77 West 66th Street, New York, New York 10023.

Printed in China

First Hardcover Edition, April 2021
First Paperback Edition, September 2024
1 3 5 7 9 10 8 6 4 2
FAC-031939-24095
Library of Congress Control Number: 2020946065
ISBN 978-1-368-10401-2
Visit disneybooks.com

For Tyler and Dylan—
Always go the distance.

*—J.C.*

# PROLOGUE
## Some time ago . . .

"Excuses! Excuses! You give the same ones every week!"

"They're not excuses, Thea! It's the truth!"

"Truth? You expect me to believe you leave this house every day and go to *work*?"

Their voices echoed through the small home, inevitably reaching five-year-old Megara as she sat in the adjacent room at the window. She didn't flinch as their argument grew louder and more heated. As cutting as their words might be, Megara didn't understand them. Her parents' arguments had become as common as the sun rising in the morning and the moon shining at night. Even her mother seemed to anticipate them coming now, like she could feel an impending storm. As the sun began to fade each day, she'd move

Megara to the home's only other room minutes before her father would walk in the door.

"You wait here and play, Megara," her mother would say, sounding tired before the yelling even began. "Be a good girl now and keep quiet."

Her mother usually placed the *stromvos* in front of Megara to keep her busy. The top her father had once whittled her was the quietest of all of Megara's toys, though it had never been her favorite. That would be the *platagi*, but the rattle was deemed "too loud" by her father, and the *spheria* rolled all over the floor. One time her father had tripped over the marbles when he walked through the room and yelled so loud, Megara swore the walls rumbled. What she really wanted to play with was a doll with moving arms and legs like the ones she saw the girls at the market carrying, but somehow she knew not to ask for such an expensive gift. Most days her mother struggled to make enough from her mending to buy Megara milk.

"Where did you spend the money you made, Leonnatos? We need it for the rent! Maya will be here any minute to collect."

Megara rocked the stromvos back and forth between her thumb and index finger.

"I don't expect you to understand what it is like for me while you do nothing all day but sit here with her."

"*Her?* You mean your daughter? The child who is your spitting image? The one you all but ignore while I mend and clean for others to feed her, since you can't?"

Megara gave her fingers a small twist and watched the top take off, spinning wildly across the windowsill, the colors in the wood melting into one.

"It is hard enough to feed one mouth! You expect me to provide for three when there is no work in all of Athens?"

"You mean none that *you're* willing to do, Leonnatos. I see you when I bring Megara into the market. You stand around with those other louts all day laughing and doing nothing! While I fight to buy her milk!"

"Enough!"

Her father's roar reminded her of that day with the spheria, when he'd landed on his back after catching his foot on a marble. She momentarily looked at the door and held her breath, wondering if he would burst into the room and start yelling at her for doing absolutely nothing wrong, as he sometimes did.

"I can't do this anymore, Thea. I never wanted this life."

"Yet this is the life you have," her mother said sadly. "Rent is due today, the food is all gone, and there is a child in that other room who needs us."

"I have nothing to give her." His deep voice broke. "This is on you now. Goodbye, Thea."

Megara watched the top wobble as it neared the edge of the windowsill. If Megara didn't put her hand out to catch it, the stromvos would fall off.

"Don't you walk out that door!" Megara's mother shouted. "Leonnatos?"

The door in the other room opened and slammed shut.

Her mother gave a strangled sob, then was quiet.

The stromvos wobbled for a moment more before it fell onto the floor and skidded across the room, landing in front of the door. Megara turned to retrieve it, but the door opened first, sending the top back across the room and under a chair.

"Megara, get your things." Her mother swept into the room, gathering blankets and clothes and shoving them into a giant sack. Her pale face was tired and her brown hair was pulled high above her head in a messy bun held up by one of her sewing needles. "We're leaving, so move quickly."

"Are we going to the market?" Megara asked hopefully. Her stomach growled as if to remind her how hungry she was. They'd had nothing but a roll to split the day before. The money her mother made mending clothes never made it to the end of the week. By the last day, Megara would be lucky if she had one meal to sustain her. Megara recalled the jug with coins being empty that morning when her mother had peeked inside to see what was left. "Maybe today your father will bring home some pay," she'd said hopefully, but Megara had said nothing. Father never came home with money.

"We're moving," her mother said, not looking at her. "We need to get out of here before Maya comes to collect the rent. Rent we don't have because . . ." She exhaled hard. "Your father causes nothing but pain."

*Pain.* "Is he sick?" Megara asked, not understanding.

"Yes. Sick of us," Thea mumbled under her breath and then looked at her daughter. Her face softened, and she dropped the bag and knelt at Megara's side. "Look at me, child." She held the bottom of Megara's chin with a single finger. "Your father left us."

Meg blinked, unsure what to make of this statement. "Father went to work?"

This made her mother laugh, but the sound was bitter, like the taste of Kalamata olives. "No." She looked her straight in the eye. While Megara's deep red hair and pale skin resembled her father's, she shared her mother's unusual violet eyes. Their eyes were so magnetic a day didn't go by when someone in the street or at the market didn't comment on them. Today, her mother's eyes looked as if they were on fire. "No. Your father is gone and isn't coming back. It's just you and me now. I need you to be strong."

*Gone.* Megara blinked rapidly. He wasn't coming back. The way her mother was staring at her, Megara sensed this meant something that would change all she ever knew. Her eyes filled with tears.

"We will not cry, Megara." Her mother pushed a strand of Megara's hair behind her right ear. "We are better off without him. You'll see." She held her chin high. "Let this be a lesson, child. Don't ever let a man dim your light. In this world, you can't count on anyone but yourself."

Megara sniffled, but said nothing.

There was banging at their door. "Thea? Leonnatos? It's Maya. Are you in there?"

Megara and her mother looked at one another. Her mother put her hand to her lips. "Grab what you can and go to the window. We're going."

"Window?" Megara whispered. Their home was only one floor, so there was no need to worry about falling, but she'd never come and gone by window before. "No door?"

"No door." Her mother pushed her toward the window and opened it. "There's no pleading with that woman," she said as she dropped their sack outside. "You think she'll feel bad for us that Leonnatos left? That we can't pay to stay here and she's placing a child on the street? No. All she'll see is lost rent money."

"Thea? I know you're in there!"

"We will find somewhere else to stay," her mother told her as the banging grew louder. "I promise."

Megara looked around at the small home they had rented. The sparse furnishings, the tattered blanket on the bed they all shared, the small table where her mother sat to do her mending, the fresh orchids in the vase (the one luxury Thea allowed herself). None of the possessions being left behind were their own, but there was something about the space she'd lived in for five years that Megara somehow sensed she'd have a hard time finding again: a true home. Their world wasn't much, but her father had robbed her of it. Her eyes caught sight of the forgotten stromvos under a chair. That top was the one and only thing she recalled her father ever giving her. Instinctively, she went running back for it. Her hands closed around the top just as she felt her mother's hands on her back.

"Megara! What are you doing?" Thea hissed, pulling the child into her arms and lifting her up and out the window.

The stromvos slipped from her fingers as her mother dropped her over the side of the window. Megara could hear it hit the floor as she landed on the other side, but she knew not to ask her mother to retrieve it. Her father and the top were gone, and there was no use crying over them. Megara looked up to see her mother climbing out of the window behind her.

Maya appeared in the window looking angry. "You owe me your rent!"

Thea ignored Maya and reached for her daughter's hand. The two started to run.

"Thea!"

Megara could still hear Maya yelling from the window as they disappeared into the crowd at the end of the street.

If there was one thing Megara had learned in her short life already, it was this: love wasn't worth the trouble.

# ONE: In Thin Air
## Present day . . .

The view was spectacular.

That was Meg's first thought as Wonder Boy lifted her into his arms and a cloud carried the two of them into the air, high above the city of Thebes.

The second? Don't look down.

She wouldn't let her fear of heights ruin the moment. Hercules was beside her, his body awash in a golden glow that burned like the sun. Meg knew just from looking at him that he had finished his quest. Wonder Boy was now a god, and she was . . .

What was she, exactly?

Was she even alive?

In the last few years, Meg had been to hell and back—literally. She'd sold her soul to the god of the Underworld and spent her days and nights fulfilling Hades's every demand. While she still walked in the land of the living, her life was no longer her own.

Meeting Hercules had awoken something in her. Honestly, she wasn't sure what that something was, but she knew it felt *important*. Why else would she have leaped in front of a falling pillar to save him, causing her own demise in the process? That moment, and Wonder Boy's rescue of her afterward, was a blur now, like so many nightmares she tried hard to forget. The next thing she remembered was air filling her lungs as if she'd held her breath underwater for too long. Then there had been a crack of lightning, a flurry of clouds, and she and Wonder Boy were being whisked into the heavens toward Mount Olympus.

The city sat on a bed of clouds that shone like the sun burning brightly behind it. The majestic home of the gods rose high in the sky with peaks of clouds holding various buildings and waterfalls. As their cloud came to a stop in front of a massive staircase that led to Mount Olympus's pearly gates, Meg could hear cheering. Lined up on either side of the staircase, every god of Olympus was on hand to congratulate Wonder Boy.

"Three cheers for the mighty Hercules!" they shouted

as they threw flowers and blew kisses of gratitude into the air.

At that moment, Pegasus landed on a nearby cloud with Phil. The satyr caught a yellow flower in midair and began to chew happily as he surveyed the celebration.

"You did it, kid!" Phil shouted.

"Can you believe this, Meg?" Hercules said in wonder. "They're cheering for . . . me."

"You deserve it," she said warmly, because he did . . . but something was suddenly gnawing at her.

The fact that Phil was there made sense—he'd trained Wonder Boy on Earth, helping him achieve true hero status. But how had she gotten a front row seat to this party? Her association with Hades, and doing his bidding, had almost cost Hercules this moment. Did these gods realize the woman standing beside their newly anointed god had almost derailed his dream?

"Meg?"

She looked up. Hercules was offering her his hand. At some point, she must have stopped walking, because she was standing still as the cloud swayed slightly.

"Are you coming?"

Meg hesitated, looking from him to the crowd of admirers and those huge steps to the Mount Olympus gates. Her thoughts were coming fast, and not all of them were pretty.

Wonder Boy might have wanted her there, but it was clear a mortal didn't belong among the deities of Mount Olympus. Hercules was a god now. Where did that leave the two of them?

Mortals weren't allowed to date gods, were they?

Was this the last time she'd ever see him? If it was, she was just standing there, totally blowing it. She wasn't saying any of the things she wanted to say . . . which were what, exactly?

Well, there was the way he made her appreciate things in life she had never seen before—fragrant lilies in bloom, the way a kid in the market smiled. He had a contagious optimism that filled with her newfound energy. There were also those stolen moments between Hercules's hero training and triumphs, and Meg's awful meetings with Hades. The two of them would stroll through the garden, talking for as long as they could. They could not get enough of one another, drinking in each other's thoughts and observations like parched farmers reaching for brimming wells; Hercules brushing hair out of her eyes, Meg teasing him, making his ears redden so adorably. They had each challenged one another to see such vastly different points of view, to expand their worlds far beyond the reach of Mount Olympus and the Underworld. Those moments had been just for them . . .

or were they? Did the gods know about all the time they'd spent together? Did they care?

Okay, so it was clear there was a lot to unpack there, and Meg had no clue what the newly minted god in front of her was thinking. *That's* what she really wanted to know. But how did she ask Wonder Boy what he wanted when this was the moment he had worked so hard for . . . and when every god of Olympus was watching?

There was a sudden hush over the crowd and Meg followed the stares of the others to two figures who had appeared at the top of the stairs. Zeus and his wife Hera were a commanding sight: Zeus, a ball of blinding light with a long white beard and flowing hair, with muscles so large they looked as if they belonged to several men; Hera, a vison in pink, her curly hair and gown sparkling like gems.

Meg felt Hercules's sharp intake of breath at the sight of his parents. This was what he'd wanted, what he had been working toward his entire life. He glanced at Meg for a split second before rushing up the stairs to see them. She said nothing as she watched him go, staring instead at his bulging calves as he raced up the steps. Only one thought came to mind: *I should have taken the man's hand.*

*Way to go, Meg! Hercules asks if you're coming and you*

*just stand there like a Greek statue. Why didn't you talk to him? Why didn't you say, "Wonder Boy, I want you to stay. Don't become a god"? Because that sounds selfish, doesn't it? And what right do I have to ask him that after I almost cost him everything?* She could tell him the truth. *And what's that, Meg?* she countered herself. *How do you really feel about the boy?*

Meg looked at him as he reached the gates and her heart felt a sudden pull. There was only one thing she knew to say for certain.

"Don't go," she whispered.

He was too far away to hear her.

"Hercules," Meg heard Hera say as Hercules sank into his mother's open arms. "We're so proud of you."

"Fine work, boy!" Zeus punched him in the arm affectionately. His blue eyes that mirrored Hercules's own shone with pride. "You've done it! You're a true hero."

Meg suddenly felt Hera's eyes on her. Every other god in the joint turned to look at the single mortal among the clouds too. Meg shifted uneasily at the sudden attention of the immortals.

"You were willing to give your life to rescue this young woman." Awe coated Hera's voice.

Even Meg couldn't believe that Wonder Boy had almost

sacrificed himself to save her, of all people. And yet here they both were. *Don't go. Don't go.*

"For a true hero isn't measured by the size of his strength, but by the strength of his heart," Zeus told his son as he clasped a large arm around him. "Now at last, my son, you can come home!"

The gates of Mount Olympus opened, revealing a world beyond that Meg couldn't put into words. It was heaven, pure and simple. Paradise. It was a world not meant for a mortal like her.

She felt the shift as her heart—the one she'd only just gotten used to hearing beat again—stopped suddenly at the sight of it all. Any second now Wonder Boy would walk through those gates and never look back. She couldn't blame him. Zeus was offering him his dream come true—immortality, family, and home.

*Home.* That was everyone's dream, wasn't it? She'd never had a home of her own—not really. For years, she'd bounced from place to place, never staying long enough to even hang something on the walls. She'd never lived somewhere she longed to return to, where she felt loved, where she felt safe; a place she didn't want to leave.

Well, of course, she had felt that way once for a short while . . . and look how *that* had turned out.

The other gods crowded around Hercules, cheering

once more for the boy who was lost and found again. When Meg heard a cry, she couldn't help turning around. The god of love, Aphrodite, a vison in purple, was being consoled by a green god wearing a hat of leaves whom Meg didn't recognize.

"I can't believe we finally have our Hercules back." Aphrodite wiped away tears. "I'm just so happy for this family! Hera has waited so long to see her son again."

"Yes, well, she could have seen him sooner, but you know Zeus. He's so big picture," said the green god, and Aphrodite looked at her strangely. "Oh, don't mind me being dour on such a happy occasion. Just a bit of gossip I heard."

Aphrodite moved in closer. "Gossip away, Demeter."

Demeter was the god of harvest—someone Meg's first love had always prayed to when planting crops for the coming year. She strained to hear the zaftig god with the pink lips.

"Well, I heard that Hera was so inconsolable about Hercules being stolen that Zeus set out to find the boy, and he did. But once he found out the kid was mortal, he left him there. The Fates predicted Zeus's son was the only one who could stop the Titans eighteen years after his birth, so Zeus just waited the time out. Now he has the boy trained up, and strong enough to fight future battles."

Meg inhaled sharply as Aphrodite gasped. "No! He just *left* the child on Earth? Hera would be heartbroken to know that."

*Holy Zeus. Was it true?* Meg wondered.

Demeter shrugged and half-heartedly waved a palm leaf in the air in celebration. "Well, it's just a rumor, but I'll tell you something: if it were my daughter, I would never have left her sleeping in a cradle to be stolen in the first place. And I'd certainly never let her roam the Earth alone. If I knew where she was, I'd stop at nothing to get her back. Nothing."

Aphrodite patted her back. "We'll find Persephone. Don't you worry. I'm sure the girl is just off wandering meadows and farmland again as she likes to do."

"Maybe. But she has her harvest duties on Earth soon," Demeter said, her eyes on Zeus accepting praise for his son. "Anyway, all I know is I won't rest until I find her."

Phil rushed past the gods, separating Meg from them, with not even a greeting. He ran up the steps as fast as his small hooves would take him. Meg watched him, distracted. She couldn't get what Demeter said out of her head. Did Hercules know his father had located him, had known exactly where he was his entire life and never come for him?

Meg felt cold at the thought. She tried to shake the rumor aside, not let it get to her. She had enough to worry about—including saying goodbye to Wonder Boy in this,

his big moment. He'd opened up a whole new way of life to her—one where sacrifice was rewarded, and people could be good, and heroes could save the world. And now she was going back to Earth alone. There was nothing waiting for her in Thebes. Not anymore.

She had no one else to blame for her misfortune. What did her mother always say—never rely on anyone but yourself? It was true. After her father had abandoned them, she had lost her mother, and finally, her first flame. When would she learn that love was a dangerous game that she never won? Was it any surprise she was about to lose Wonder Boy, too?

Meg felt tears begging to come to the surface, but she refused to give in. She had no clue what she'd do next, but for now, she could stand on this cloud and watch Hercules till he disappeared beyond Olympus's gates. Hercules was home and she was happy for him—truly—even if she felt an urge to scream *don't go* once more.

"Congratulations, Wonder Boy," Meg said softly, giving him one last look. "You'll make one heck of a god."

She'd only made it a few steps before she felt someone grab her hand.

She turned around in surprise. Hercules was somehow standing beside her.

"Father, this is the moment I've always dreamed of," she

heard Hercules say, "but a life without Meg, even an immortal life, would be empty." He pulled her closer and stared into her eyes, making her heart quicken once more. "I . . . I wish to stay on Earth with her."

Her grip on his arm tightened. Had she just heard him correctly?

"What? How? Are you sure?" she whispered, still not believing her ears.

"I finally know where I belong . . ." he whispered back. "And it's with you."

Then suddenly he was kissing her and she was throwing her arms around him as he lifted her high into the air. She could hear the gods cheering, and this time it wasn't just for Hercules. It was for the two of them and their love that somehow defied logic.

Meg started to laugh and then thought she might cry. She stared into his blue eyes and didn't know what to say. But that was okay. She didn't have to rush her thoughts. Now they had time. Lots of time! Wonder Boy was coming back to Earth with her and they had a whole life ahead of them. Had something in her life finally gone right? It didn't seem possible, and yet Wonder Boy's lips on hers were proof. The gods approved. They were happy for them! They were—

"No."

*No?* At first, Meg thought she'd imagined someone

uttering the word and disagreeing with Hercules's wishes. But one look at Zeus's stern face and Meg knew—the gods' All-father was putting an end to their relationship before it could ever really get started.

# TWO: A Change of Heart

The air was completely still. No one spoke a word. Their eyes were either on Zeus or his newly god-anointed son. And he just looked downright confused.

"Father?" Hercules questioned, still holding tight to Meg.

"I said no to your request, my boy," Zeus repeated.

Meg noticed some of the other gods sense the friction in the air and start to move away. It was clear no one wanted to be in Zeus's crosshairs. Only Hera remained by his side, listening patiently to Zeus's reasoning. Phil quietly motioned to Pegasus and climbed aboard the horse's back, flying off without even a goodbye. There went her ride.

"We waited a lifetime to get you back and have you sit beside your mother and me," Zeus explained. "And now that you're here, you want to give that up and remain human?"

"No . . . but I . . . I want to be with Meg," Hercules said, running a hand through his wavy locks, as he did whenever he got nervous. "If I can't go back, can she remain here?"

"No," Zeus said again, laughter escaping his lips. "Mount Olympus is no place for *mortals*."

He said the word "mortals" as if they were the scum of the Earth. *We're the ones who praise the gods, make sacrifices and do their bidding, and we're not worthy of their company?* Meg thought, feeling suddenly defensive even though she had had a similar thought just moments earlier.

"Zeus," Hera started, but he blazed forward.

"Son, when you visited my temple, I was so thankful to know you were alive and well." He grabbed Hera's hand and smiled. "Your mother and I had always hoped and prayed you were out there somewhere and we'd find you someday. Instead, you found us."

Meg's eyes flickered to Demeter's. Her face was blank, but Meg felt her skin prickle. *He's lying,* she thought.

"That is why I sent you on a quest to become a hero," Zeus continued. "We wanted you to become a god again, and you did all we asked and more to make that happen. You fought every beast sent your way and won! You have proven yourself to be selfless and a fighter. You deserve to be a god again, child, and gods, as you know, belong here. You spent your time on Earth with the mortals, and I'm glad you enjoyed spending time with this one." Zeus's eyes flickered to Meg before he looked away dismissively. "But now your place is here with us."

Hercules let go of Meg. "But Father . . ."

Her body went cold. *I'm glad you enjoyed spending time with this one?* Was Zeus serious? Who was he to judge their relationship when he barely knew her? He didn't even know his son! If what Demeter said was true, Hercules had not needed to wait so long to prove his worth as a hero; Zeus had left him on Earth till he needed his help. He had abandoned Hercules, just like she'd been abandoned countless times over. And now he was dismissing Hercules's love for her as if it were nothing? Then again, why was she surprised? When her first love had lain dying, it wasn't Zeus who saved him. It was Hades.

Meg felt a flash of anger. If Hercules was going to stay on Mount Olympus, he deserved to know what his father had done, just as she had learned the painful truth about her own—they'd both been left to fend for themselves.

"Wait! Hercules, you deserve to know the truth!" Meg's voice was breathless. She felt a little dizzy now, the altitude finally catching up to her. "Zeus knew you were alive! Even before you reached the temple. He left you on Earth till you grew up and he needed you to fight the Titans!"

Meg heard gasps and saw Zeus look at her with disdain. She looked for Demeter, but she had suddenly disappeared from the crowd, as had Aphrodite. Smart move. Maybe she should have thought about revealing this news in front of an audience.

"What?" Hercules whispered, his pained expression making Meg's stomach twist.

"Zeus, is this true?" Hera asked, the anguish on her face mirroring her son's. Zeus looked away, his face turning redder.

"How do you know this?" Hercules asked.

"I overheard someone telling the story," Meg admitted, choosing not to reveal Demeter's name. Why have multiple gods mad at you? "You were mortal, so he left you on Earth, waiting till Hades resurrected the Titans so *you* could fight them for him," she continued, feeling the heat rise in her face as she thought of Hercules being a pawn in the god's game. "He only wants to keep you here now so that you can fight his battles." Hercules's broad shoulders sank. "I'm sorry. I just felt you should know what you're signing up for."

"Father?" Hercules looked up at Zeus, whose expression had grown even stonier.

Zeus glared at Meg. "Who are you going to believe, son? Me or this mortal?"

Meg's eyes flashed. "I'm not the one who let his own child be stolen while he slept."

The minute the comment left her lips, she knew she'd gone too far.

The other gods quickly began to dissipate. Hera stayed put, but Meg wondered if she was in shock.

Zeus's face turned almost purple as he seemingly grew three times his size. Behind him, the sky darkened like an approaching thunderstorm and lightning bolts crisscrossed the sky. Hercules instinctively stepped in front of Meg, putting one hand on her arm, but she nudged it away. She'd lived with Hades. She wasn't afraid to stand up to Zeus.

"You dare question my judgment, Megara?" Zeus thundered as the storm clouds rolled in around him. Lightning crashed dangerously close to where she and Hercules were standing. "You, the woman who worked to keep my son from completing his quest?"

On second thought, maybe she *should* be a little afraid of Zeus. Especially now that she realized he was well aware of what she had done.

"Oh yes, I know all about your life, too, Megara," Zeus said. "I suspect much more than my son knows."

Meg felt her cheeks flame. It was true she hadn't told Wonder Boy *everything*.

"You did my brother's bidding for him, trying to cheat Hercules from his rightful place at my side, and you think I should let him return to Earth with you?" As Zeus continued, Hera looked at her.

"I . . ." Meg wanted to explain herself, but Zeus was on a roll.

"You think turning my son against me will allow you to keep him?" Zeus bellowed. "You are not worthy of a god's love!"

"Father, she saved my life!" Hercules shouted. Zeus flinched and the lightning stopped.

"That may be true," he said, his size shrinking back down to normal again. "And it is also true that I could have come to you before, son." Regret laced his voice as he glanced briefly at his wife. "But I saw no point in disrupting your childhood when good people like Amphitryon and Alcmene could protect you and keep your identity hidden until you were old enough to learn how to fight for your right to be a god again. As that is indeed what needed to be done. Only a god can call Mount Olympus home, and you needed time to grow into that role. It would have been foolish and selfish to have rushed you." He narrowed his eyes at Meg. "*That* is why I sacrificed our time together—not because I didn't want you. *Never* because I didn't want you."

Meg felt her cheeks burn and she looked away. *Okay, that kind of makes sense. Nice one, Meg.*

"I was trying to protect you," Zeus added. "Can you, Megara, say the same for Hercules during his time on Earth?"

Meg looked at the ground. They both knew the answer to that question.

"I am sorry, son, but this mortal is not worthy of your love," Zeus added. "My decision is final. You will remain here and she will leave at once."

"No!" Hercules cried. Hera narrowed her eyes.

"Hermes!" Zeus thundered, and his faithful messenger flew to his side in seconds.

"You called, my lord?" Hermes hovered in front of him thanks to the wings on his hat. He rubbed at his fogged-up glasses to see them all better.

"Yes," Zeus said. "Take Megara back to Earth." He looked at his son and his expression relaxed slightly. "You may have a moment to say your goodbyes," he added hastily before gliding up the steps to the gates. The storm clouds slowly began to dissipate.

Hercules looked from Zeus to Meg. "I . . . you . . . Don't go anywhere. I'll talk to him." He ran after Zeus. "Father!"

Hermes flew to Meg's side. "Wow, you really know how to wind up the big guy! Ready to go?"

"Will you give us a moment, Hermes?" Hera appeared in front of her.

Hermes flew off and the two women stared at one another. Close up, Hera was almost blindingly stunning, the epitome of regal with her sparkling gown and rose-colored hair piled on top of the crown on her head. Small gold rings held up the draped sleeves of her dress, which ruffled in the light wind. Unlike Zeus, she bore an open, almost curious expression as she peered at the mortal before her. She held out an arm.

"I think we should talk," the god said simply.

Meg took a deep breath. "Look, about what I said before . . ."

"I will deal with Zeus later; that's not what I want to talk to you about. I want to know why you felt the need to tell my son about his father. Were you hoping to gain favor with him?"

"No, I just thought he deserved to know."

"Because?" Hera prodded.

"Because no one should live with a lie," Meg said.

"And?"

Hera was clearly fishing for something. Meg thought for a moment. "And . . . I owe him. He changed my life."

Hera drew closer. Now that she was getting used to the light emanating from the god, she realized Hercules had her wide eyes. Yes, Zeus also had the same magnetic blue shade, but there was a kindness in Hera's and Hercules's that instantly put her at ease. "And how did he do that?"

Meg closed her eyes and thought about Wonder Boy again. She pictured their rendezvous in a secluded meadow, a surprise picnic at the water's edge—these moments were some of the happiest she'd had in a long time. He had literally saved her body from the river Styx, her soul from Hades, but it was more than that. When they were together, she felt as weightless as the clouds beneath her. What she knew for sure was that she was content when she was by his side, like a piece of a puzzle had slid into place.

But could she say all this to his newly found mother? No way. Best to keep it simple. "He gave me my life back. A girl doesn't forget that."

Hera tapped her chin and looked thoughtful. "I see. Is that the *only* reason you wish for my son to return to Earth with you?" Meg opened her mouth and closed it again. "I assume you do want him to return to Earth, don't you? You didn't protest when he suggested it." A small smile played on her pink lips.

"I . . ." Meg looked back at Hercules, who appeared to be talking with his hands, winding them up as if he were about to throw a discus. "Of course, I'd like to spend more time with him, but if he's happy here . . ." She felt the lump form in her throat and couldn't believe this was happening. She would *not* cry while talking to Hera. "I want him to be happy. He deserves that."

Hera nodded. "And do *you* deserve to be happy, Megara? I suspect *you* make him happy. And if he stays here and you go back there, I don't think either of you will be." She looked up at her son and husband still arguing. "No, this arrangement of my husband's clearly won't work. We need to come up with a different plan."

Was the god of marriage and birth offering her an olive branch? Meg took a deep breath and tried to keep her words in check for a change while she deferred to Hera. "What do you suggest?"

Hera continued to look at her. "That depends. Are you in love with my son?"

"Love?" Meg took a step back. She immediately thought back to something she'd said to Hercules as she lay dying back in Thebes. *People do crazy things when they're in love.*

Was that what this was? Love?

Was she in love with a god?

No.

Yes.

Possibly.

How did one know for sure? Her track record when it came to love was tarnished at best, and she and Wonder Boy hadn't known each other very long. Of course, they had grown close, but in the moment she had uttered those words she thought it was the end of the road. Her experience with love up until then had been messy and painful; she had sensed things could have been different with Hercules if given the chance. But *if* was the key word. She had no clue what she would do next when she stepped off this cloud, and even less of a clue if her world didn't include Wonder Boy. Was Hera giving her a chance to change her fate yet again? Meg looked at the god. If saying she was in love would give her and Hercules time to figure their story out, what was the harm in saying it?

"Of course," Meg said firmly.

Hera clasped her hands together and smiled. "Wonderful! Then there is only one choice: you, Megara, need to become a god."

Meg wasn't sure she had heard Hera correctly. "I'm sorry. What?"

"You need to become a god," Hera repeated, as if it were as simple as buying figs at the local market. "It's the only logical answer to this predicament."

Meg's eyes narrowed. Gods didn't just offer the gift of immortality without reason. People prayed for such an honor all the time, but other than Hercules—who was born a god and lost his status when he was kidnapped—she could count on her fingers the number of gods she knew of who had started out as mortals: Psyche, Thyone, Ariadne . . . Dionysus counted since he supposedly had a mortal mother, but Zeus was his father. She had done nothing to help the gods like they had. All she'd done was anger Zeus. She looked up again at Wonder Boy still pleading with his father, who seemed as angry as ever. "And Zeus would be okay with this?"

Hera waved her hand dismissively. "Let me worry about my husband. Are you interested in what I have to say or not? We don't have much time."

Meg still couldn't believe what she was hearing. "What do I have to do? Let me guess. Save a pair of kids trapped in a chasm? Oh, wait. Hercules already did that when Hades set him up to fail."

Hera's smile faded. "Do you think I am trying to deceive you?"

Okay, maybe she'd overstepped. Again. A rumble of thunder in the distance made Meg choose her next words carefully. "Where I come from, offers like this aren't thrown around so easily. You'll have to excuse me for wondering what the catch is."

Hera's smile returned. "I like your spirit. And you

clearly care about one another. My son wouldn't ask to give all this up if that were not true." She stared at Meg. "I have a feeling you two would make a strong match, and that power is rare indeed—something that, in turn, could help the world. What good is one miserable god when there could be two extraordinary ones? That is why I want to help you. I assure you, this offer is no trickery. If you can prove yourself worthy, I can see to it that you are given the gift of immortality. There are special circumstances where mortals can become gods, and if that were to happen, then the two of you could be together." Her eyes flashed mischievously. "Whether Zeus likes it or not."

Meg was speechless. Hera wasn't joking. The god was offering her something that she'd never even dreamed of becoming. It took her a moment to catch her breath. "A god?" Meg repeated.

"A god," Hera said again. "*If* you can prove your worth."

Meg placed a hand on her hip and cocked her head to one side, her ponytail swishing. "And how do I go about doing that? Start helping kids cross the road and assist old men with their trips to the market?"

Hera actually laughed. "No. If you want to be with my son and become a god worthy of Mount Olympus, I need to see you understand love is a strength, not a weakness. That putting your trust in someone you love doesn't mean you can't stand on your own two feet. It means you know how to share responsibility and accept help when it is needed." She placed her hands on Meg's shoulders. "I want to see you know how to be vulnerable, Megara. And understand that love means opening your heart even if the story doesn't always end the way you want it to."

Meg crossed her arms. "I know all these things already."

Hera put her arms down and smiled at her kindly. "Do you?"

"Yes," Meg insisted, somewhat defiantly.

Hera continued to study her. "Then you've told Hercules about the loves you have lost, I assume. You told him about Aegeus?"

Just hearing Aegeus's name made Meg's lungs burn. The memory of crying and the screams that she associated with the name of her first flame came flooding back. As always, she attempted to block the noise out. "Of course," Meg said, which wasn't exactly a lie. Wonder Boy knew she'd been scorned before. How she'd been scorned, not exactly . . .

Hera's eyes glittered. "And what about your mother?"

# THREE: Life and Loss

## Before . . .

Thirteen can be a hard age for a girl.

Especially when that girl has to act like the parent.

Megara might not have realized how much her life would change that day her father walked out on her and her mother, but she learned quickly.

Forced to provide for her daughter in a society that viewed women as unequal, Thea couldn't own land or vote. Her place was meant to be keeping house, but since she had no house to keep and a daughter to feed, she had to figure out a way around the laws. Thea took mending work where she could get it, and when she couldn't find that, she'd clean the homes of men whose wives were too busy raising countless children to scrub a floor. (Megara would watch in wonder as her mother convinced men their wives needed an extra set of hands around the house. As harsh as Thea had always been with Megara's father, she was sweeter than nectar to these skeptical men, who almost always caved and gave her work.)

While her mother worked, Megara took care of their own life—cleaning their rented spaces, cooking so her mother wouldn't have to after a backbreaking day, and minding the money her mother brought home. If young Megara had learned anything from her time with her father, it was to hold on to her drachmas. She counted and recounted what her mother earned and learned to keep a budget for food so that they wouldn't go hungry if they could help it. And though girls weren't afforded school, Meg taught herself to read using the stone signs in the square, stealing Homer's works out of the school-aged boys' bags when she could. She watched the merchants in the market accept payment from shoppers, learning how to count coins and what each one meant. So when precious coins she kept in a jar went missing, she went straight to her mother to inquire where they went.

"Oh, Megara, it's just a few drachmas!" her mother would say as she lay on the bed they shared and tried to rest her eyes.

"Those 'few drachmas' were meant to buy eggs

for breakfast this week," Meg scolded. "Now what will we eat?"

Her mother sat up with a start, her eyes bright. "Who needs food when we have this?" Her mother opened up the sack by the bed and held out a tarnished flute. "This is for you!"

Meg stared at it unhappily. "I don't know how to play."

"You'll learn! Music feeds the soul. I always wanted to learn, but never had the opportunity. You, my darling Megara, do! Here. Try it."

Meg bit her tongue. Her mother was excited, but Meg still hated how impulsive she was. How could she think a rusty wind instrument was better than eggs that could feed them for a week? This was just like that time her mother had bought a vase said to belong to the gods, thinking they could sell it for a good price. (They never did.) Another time, her mother bought old copper wares hoping she could trade them for better goods. That didn't work out, either. Not to mention the fresh flowers she still bought every time she could. Meg was tired of it.

"Just think—the more you practice, the more beautiful the notes will sound," her mother said, trying again. She laid a finger upon a divot on its side. "It doesn't matter what the flute looks like. It's the melody you create, child, that can take you away from all this." She motioned to their small rental. "If you learn to play, people will want to hear you. I know it." She put down the flute, grabbed Meg's hands, and held them in her callused hands. "When I saw this instrument, it was as if the gods spoke out and said, 'Megara could be a great musician if you help her!' How could I say no?"

Meg shook her head. "But, Mother, the eggs . . ."

"Child, what do I always say?"

"Trust yourself," Meg repeated alongside her mother.

"That's right!" Her mother looked pleased. "When I saw this flute, my instincts told me that our money would be better spent on this flute for you than anything we could put in our bodies. Learning to play could change both of our lives." She picked up the instrument again and held it out to Meg. "I'm asking you to try."

Meg's stomach growled. How could she play when she could think of nothing but food? And how would she even begin to learn when her mother had never played, either? Why was her mother so infuriating? What if her instincts were wrong? Meg thought about speaking up and then saw her mother's face, so open and hopeful. She relented, taking the flute from her outstretched hands. She put her lips to the reed and blew.

The sound that came out was so dreadful, dogs howled in the distance.

Her mother smiled hopefully. "All you need is practice!"

Practice Meg did. Every time she saw that flute and thought of the lost money, she felt spurred on to make something good come out of her mother's impulsive purchase. While her mother did odd jobs, Meg taught herself notes, then eventually learned melodies. For inspiration, she would sit in the square and listen to musicians play. She tried to mimic them. After some time, Meg got better, which only made her want to practice more. Night after night, she tried new notes, new tunes strung together, experimenting with the placement of her mouth and fingers, with the strength of her breath. The first full song she learned was one about the plight of a white lily. She became swept up in its beauty, and in her ability to pour every bit of herself into it—her frustration at how difficult life had been for her mother and her, her ache for a permanent place in the world, her pride at how far they had come. Before long, her mother encouraged her to play for others.

"They will want to hear you!" her mother said, leading her along through the village square. Megara would never forget her words. "You are a survivor, like me. Remember that. No matter what happens, you can handle it. *Trust yourself.*"

Megara remembered being skeptical, but it turned out her mother had been right again. When she got lost in the music, people stopped what they were doing and listened.

A few even dropped coins at her feet and asked when she'd be playing again.

"Tomorrow?" Megara had said, looking to her beaming mother for guidance.

"Of course!" Thea said, picking up the coins and pocketing them. She put her arm around Megara as they left the square and looked at her daughter. "I told you, Megara, you are meant to shine, and look! You are shining, and you're being rewarded for it." Her mother looked around the village again happily. "I like it in this town. I think we should stay, and you can play here forever."

Megara tried not to get excited at the idea of putting down roots. No matter how smitten her mother was with a new village, the sheen wore off after a few days like on an old vase, just like it probably would here. Megara didn't blame her. Thea had been burned before. Sometimes it would be by a family that refused to pay after a backbreaking week of work or promises of long-term employment that went dry after a few days. Couple that with her mother's razor-sharp tongue and rash behavior, and Megara knew Thea's view of a situation changed like the wind. Thea trusted no one and always feared the little good that came their way was a ruse.

But Megara expressed none of this. Instead she just smiled and said, "I'd love to stay."

Her mother squeezed her hand. "Good."

One week later, her mother came through the door like a sudden gust of wind.

"Get your things, we're leaving!" Thea spun around the room looking for their well-worn travel sacks. She noticed them packed by the door and looked at her daughter suspiciously.

"Did something happen with Argos?" Megara asked innocently.

"Yes, Argos!" Her mother threw her hands up, forgetting all about the packed bags. "I don't trust that man!"

"That man" was the widower brother of Thea's current employer. The two had met the week before when Thea was mending shirts for the family, and Argos had inquired about giving her additional work. Megara had met him and his young son when they had run into them in the market. Megara had recalled Argos being soft-spoken and having long lashes covering his brown eyes. He had asked Megara thoughtful questions about her age and her birthday. Adults rarely talked to children about such things, in her experience. When he had noticed Megara eyeing the dried fruits that were far too expensive for them to even consider getting, he had bought her some. They had tasted sweet, like heaven. Thea had disapproved. "He's probably trying to get me to do his mending for free." Instead, as Megara learned through gossip at the market—which was always the best place to find gossip—Argos was looking for a new wife. Megara hoped against hope that her mother could be that person. And she prayed her mother wouldn't mess things up.

"Argos seems nice," Megara tried. "And his son is sweet."

"Yes, yes, but so young and needy as children are," her mother said dismissively. Megara tried hard not to take offense. Thea looked down, registering the expression on her daughter's face. "Oh, not *you*, Megara. But I have no time to play with the boy when I'm working, and yet, Argos keeps bringing him by! And then today he says . . . he says . . . he's looking for . . ." Megara noticed the fear in her mother's eyes. "It doesn't matter. He was just spinning lies. You can't trust a man. Never rely on anyone but yourself."

"I know," Megara said, knowing her mother's mantra well, "but Argos . . ."

Her mother shot her a look. "We don't need a man complicating things for us. Now we must go. Before he comes by. He said he'd be here in an hour."

"You're not telling him we're leaving?" Megara said, aghast. "Mother, that's . . ."

"Enough, child!" Her mother hoisted the sack over her shoulder and looked around the sparse room. "Let's go."

"Yes, Mother," Megara said and lifted the sack with

the coins in it. Thea hadn't even thought to ask if they had money for travel. Perhaps she already knew that if they had any, Megara would think to grab it. The vase her mother had briefly prized was left behind and all but forgotten. The only memento of their time in that town was the tarnished flute.

Megara kept her head down as they rushed out of the village and tried hard not to think about what her life would have become if her mother had accepted Argos's proposal. But dreaming of a life she'd never have was pointless. They didn't need a man when they had each other.

Until one day that changed, too.

The next town they landed in was no different than the half a dozen they had been to before. Thea still found work mending and cleaning while Megara counted their money and took care of the home and the cooking, practicing her flute in the evenings.

"Thanks for the bargain, Theos," Megara said to the young man in the marketplace who had given her a good price on day-old bread. "It's been a real slice." Then she turned with an expertly timed flip of her lengthening red hair—it was almost to her waist now—and swung her hips as she sashayed away. As Megara grew, she was learning that her charm was a tool she could rely on.

She was almost giddy as she thought about the things

she could make with two loaves of bread. Her mother would be thrilled when she returned from work that evening. But as she approached the home where they were staying, she saw the crowd gathered on the street. There was a lot of yelling, and some tears, but Megara couldn't see what was happening till she got closer. There was Thea, pinned beneath a horse and a cart.

"Mother!" Megara cried, dropping the bread and rushing to her side.

"I didn't even see her! She came out of nowhere!" the guy driving the carriage told anyone who would listen. "She wasn't watching where she was going!"

Men were trying to lift the carriage off Thea, but Megara knew it was already too late. Her mother was fading fast. "Hold on," Megara cried, starting to hiccup as she grabbed her mother's hand. "Don't leave me, Mother!" Her mother's face was white and her eyes were already closing. "Stay with me!" Megara begged. She was crying so hard she couldn't see.

"Megara, listen to me. You'll be all right," her mother whispered as she started to drift away. "Trust yourself. Remember, whatever happens, you can handle it."

Megara froze. It was as if she knew what her mother was going to say next. It was the same thing she always said to Megara when times were tough and it looked like the situation was impossible. Megara would always be the one in their relationship to worry, and her mother would be the one to crack the jokes. This time it wasn't funny.

"You're a big, tough girl," her mother said, her voice fading.

"No," Megara cried. "Please!"

Her mother's eyes closed. "You tie your own sandals and every . . . thing." Her mother's hand went limp. Megara threw herself over her mother's body. Thea was gone.

# FOUR: An Offer Meg Can't Refuse

## On Mount Olympus . . .

"You've made your point—I need to deal with the loss of my mother. What's that got to do with this quest?" Meg knew she sounded more aggravated than she should considering she was speaking to the mother of the guy she really cared about, who just so happened to be a god married to the All-father of gods.

Thankfully, Hera didn't appear ruffled. She quickly glanced at her husband and Hercules again. "You'll understand with time. For now, all you need to worry about is finding the lost aulos of Athena."

Meg wasn't sure she understood. "So to become a god, all I have to do is track down Athena's double flute?"

Hera smiled. "That's the *first* step."

Ah, there it was. The catch. Finding Athena's flute, which she had to assume wasn't just lost in a clearing or hiding under a rock, wouldn't be as simple as Hera made it sound. The last time she'd made a deal with a god, it had ended with her losing her soul. What would happen if she risked her life for this quest and failed?

Well, one thing was certain: Hades would never let her leave the Underworld again.

Meg shuddered at the thought. She did not want to return there anytime soon. Although, if she became a god, she wouldn't have to return at all.

She'd be a god. An actual god! And when she really thought about it, she'd make a heck of a great one. She wouldn't be all judgy and hurl angry lightning bolts like Zeus. No, she'd forgive people for their mistakes, like Hercules had forgiven her for the countless wrong decisions she'd made before he walked into her life. And as former mortals, she and Hercules would have insight on the world in a way these ethereal gods wouldn't. Together, the two of them could do a lot of good up on Mount Olympus. As she knew from her own experience, the gods didn't always get things right. Meg looked up at the gates to Mount Olympus again and wondered *what if.*

"You should know, I don't make offers lightly," Hera added, starting to sound impatient. "If you find what is lost and complete the tasks that follow, you will rise to Mount Olympus as a god and spend an eternity with my son."

*Eternity?* The word felt like a water nymph's punch to the stomach, instantly taking the wind out of her sails. Eternity as in forever? Her longest relationship had lasted a year, and look how that had ended. How did she know she and Hercules would even make it that long? Sure, she wanted them to have a chance to figure out their relationship without Zeus interfering, but if she did as Hera asked, could she spend an *eternity* with Wonder Boy? The gods were forever deceiving one another, fighting, and taking lovers. Is that what she and Hercules were signing up for if she did this? But then, what was the alternative?

Hera interrupted her thoughts. "I believe you're familiar with flutes, are you not?"

So Hera *did* know all about her past. Meg hadn't picked up a flute since Aegeus, but just the word evoked memories and music in her mind that she hadn't dared to think about in a long time. "Yes. I know how to play," Meg admitted hoarsely.

Hera nodded. "Good. Music will come in handy on your journey."

"And that's final!"

Meg and Hera looked up. Zeus was storming through Mount Olympus's gates, which closed firmly behind him.

Hercules's whole frame seemed to shrink in defeat, and Meg felt a pull at her heart. It wasn't just the way he always looked at her—with a mix of genuine joy and longing rolled into one—or his appearance, although he wasn't hard on the eyes with those rippling pectorals. She found herself drawn to those kind blue eyes and the hard line of his jaw, which moved when he was thinking. It was the dimples in his cheeks when he flashed her that magnetic smile, and the way his reddish blond hair had a single curl that was always falling in front of his eyes. But mostly it was that earnest nature of his, and his need to find the good in every situation, which was so different from how she viewed life, and gave her hope that the world could be more than she imagined it to be. All she knew was she wasn't ready to say goodbye to him.

Meg looked at Hera. "Thank you for the generous offer. I accept."

Immediately she felt something in her hand. It was an hourglass. Inside it, pink sand, the color of Hera, was piled high on one end. The other side was empty. Slowly, pink grains began to flow to the empty side of the glass.

"You have ten days to complete your quest," Hera said. "I wish you well, Megara." Then the god disappeared.

"Ten days?" Meg froze. Hera hadn't said anything about a deadline. What happened when the sand ran out? "Wait!

I have questions! Come back!" Meg cried just as Hercules reached her at the bottom of the steps.

"I'm so glad you're still here." He placed his arms around her. "Are you all right? What were you and my mother talking about?"

Meg buried her face in his chest and breathed in his scent. She had a sudden desire to stay right there in his arms and forget all about the hourglass. "Oh, you know. Nothing much. Your mother just gave me a quest."

"A quest?" Hercules repeated. "Why?"

So much for forgetting. Meg lifted her head and looked up at him, curious and worried, his brow wrinkling slightly. He really was something. "If I prove myself worthy and complete her tasks, she'll make me a god so that we can be together."

Hercules's eyes widened as he processed her words. Then his face broke into a wide smile. "That's amazing!" He lifted her into the air and spun her around. She laughed despite herself. He gently placed her back down on the cloud, keeping his arms around her.

"Yeah, wonderful for you. You don't have to go on the quest." Meg's fingers traced his ample shoulder blade. "I have ten days and counting." She showed him the hourglass.

"Ten days is a lot of time! You can do it, Meg," he said in

earnest. "You can do anything you put your mind to! I know it." He lifted her again and spun her faster this time.

She pounded her fists on his back, laughing. "Put me down. Didn't I just say I have a deadline?"

"Sorry." Hercules gently lowered her. "I'm just so excited! If you become a god, we can be together forever."

There was that idea again. Meg took a deep breath. "Quests aren't easy."

He looked at her. "Anything is easier than talking to my father." Herc sighed. "I tried to convince him how much good I could do on Earth, but he feels I belong here." He smiled wide again. "But now you can be, too. If my mother believes in us, we can't fail. Hera loves love and she loves me. She wants us to be happy." Hercules cocked his head, taking Meg's hand in his. "What does she want you to do?"

"She only told me my first step—I have to find Athena's double flute," Meg explained as a cloud drifted past them, shrouding them both in mist. "Any clue where it might be?"

Hercules's face darkened. "I heard it was stolen by a river guardian somewhere."

Meg relaxed. "A river guardian? They're not so bad!"

Herc shook his head. "Meg, they're huge and mean! Don't you remember Nessus?" She gave him a look. "Sorry. I know you can take care of yourself. I just don't see how Mother would give you a quest and not offer some sort of clue as to where to find the flute. It's a big world out there."

"That's true." *Come on, Hera, what am I missing?* Meg thought, looking at the hourglass again for clues. That's when she noticed something small etched into the top of the vial she hadn't seen before. It was a single word: KOUFONISIA. "Does this word mean anything to you?" Meg held the hourglass out to Hercules again.

"I think that's an island! It must be one of the Lesser Cyclades. That's right about here." He turned Meg toward the edge of the cloud and pointed to a large swath of blue below with a series of tiny islands peppered around it.

"Whoa! Not so close to the edge." She took several steps back before she got vertigo. If she did become a god, it would take some time to get used to this height.

"Sorry," Hercules said. "Hey! Koufonisia is kind of near Phil's island! You should take him with you."

"Oh, no." Meg backed away even more. "That red-faced mini menace hates me!"

"Phil doesn't hate you. He just thought you were a distraction." Hercules paused. "And he wasn't happy when he found out you were working with Hades, but that's all in the past! Phil likes you now, and he'd be a great guide."

Hercules might not have picked up on it, but she knew

there was no love lost between her and that satyr. "I like your enthusiasm, but I don't need help. I can do this on my own."

"I know." He nuzzled her face. "I just—I still wish I could go with you."

"We both know that's not going to happen," Meg said softly.

Hercules pulled away. "Maybe there is a way I *can* be there—at least for a little bit. I have an idea! Hold on!" He dashed to the other side of the cloud and returned at an impossibly quick speed. Meg couldn't believe he had been a mortal only a few hours ago. To watch him now, one would have thought he had been a god his entire life.

He came closer, gripping two small saddlebags in one hand, and holding out a bright fuchsia orchid in the other. "This is for you."

"It's beautiful," Meg said, taking the flower from him. She'd never seen an orchid like it. The color glowed like the gods.

"This orchid is powerful. Phil told me all about it once. It's as rare as ambrosia, and only grows on Mount Olympus. Think of it like having your own messenger to the gods. If you want to reach me, rip off one of the petals, say my name, and I'll be there."

"Well, I'll be." She gently pinned the stem to the clasp

on her gown. "There's only three petals on here. What happens if I run out?"

There was that crinkle in his brow again. "I won't be able to get another one. This was the only flower fully matured I could find." He touched her face. "But you won't need another. I know you can do this. Then we can be together."

"Yes." Meg tried to push her doubts aside. She'd died, been saved from the river Styx, and been offered the chance to become a god all in one day. It was a lot to swallow for any girl.

"You're my world, Meg." Hercules cupped her face in his large hands. "I can't imagine living an eternity without you. Be careful out there."

For some reason, his warning made her think of her mother. "I'm a big, tough girl. I'll be all right. I tie my own sandals and everything."

Wonder Boy smiled and leaned in for a kiss. His lips had barely grazed hers before they both heard a rumble of thunder.

There was a popping sound and Hermes appeared, the wings on his hat flapping wildly. "Greetings, lovebirds! Zeus sent me here to move the goodbyes along."

Meg could see the storm clouds rolling in again behind them. The last thing she wanted was another appearance by Zeus. She tightened her fingers around the hourglass. There was a trace amount of pink sand on the bottom of it already. "I should go."

Hercules held her tight. "Let me send Pegasus with you." She opened her mouth, ready to protest. "You'll be able to travel way faster with him than you can by foot." The horse trotted over and Hercules hung the two saddlebags on his back. Meg looked at them curiously.

"Supplies," he explained.

She inhaled, taking in Hercules's sweet scent one more time. "Okay." She smiled softly, placing the hourglass in one of the bags as he leaned in again to kiss her. At that moment, Pegasus bumped her from behind, swooping her up onto his back. He started galloping toward the edge of the cloud before Meg could even say goodbye. "WAIT!" she cried, closing her eyes and hanging on to Pegasus for dear life.

"Keep your hands on Pegasus's back at all times," said Hermes as Meg and Pegasus went galloping past him. "Enjoy your ride to Koufonisia!"

Pegasus plunged off the side of the cloud, and Meg's scream could be heard throughout Mount Olympus.

# FIVE: The Backside of Water

They were falling. At least that's what it felt like as Pegasus dove straight down and Meg clung desperately to his neck. She could feel the wind rushing past her, whipping her ponytail into her face as they continued to plummet.

*Don't look. Don't look. Don't look,* she told herself. *You went up. You have to come down. Everything is fine.*

The ride up to Mount Olympus had been almost peaceful. She was alive, she was in Hercules's arms, and he was suddenly a god. Just one of those things was enough to put her in a blissful state of wonder. But traveling with this flying beast was different. And why did she sense Pegasus was enjoying her panic?

Pegasus dipped again and Meg let out another terrified

scream. She squeezed his neck even tighter and opened her eyes against her better judgment. The horse was bobbing and weaving through clouds so fast Meg was sure she was going to be sick. She wanted off this ride.

"Hey! You!" Meg tugged on his blue mane. "If you don't want me to drag you down to Poseidon and make you a sea-horse, then slow down already!"

She heard Pegasus neigh unpleasantly, but he slowed to an acceptable glide.

"Thank you," Meg said, and Pegasus snorted softer that time. Meg loosened her grip on his mane and looked around. Koufonisia was growing closer. They were near enough that she could make out a few mountains and bodies of water on the island.

"Look, Peg—can I call you Peg?" Pegasus gave a half-hearted neigh. "I don't like this any more than you do. Hercules wanted me to take you on this quest." Pegasus quietly continued to flap his majestic wings. "The quicker we find what we're looking for, the quicker we can both go home. Wherever that is," she muttered to herself. "So let's find this flute and get out of here. Deal?"

Pegasus neighed louder, seeming almost happy. As he dipped again, the clouds cleared, giving way to bright sunshine and turquoise blue waters below. They glided so close to the water Peg's wings actually skimmed the waves. Finally they made it to the island's sandy beach. She climbed off Pegasus and patted his side.

"Nice landing there, Peg." She unhooked the saddlebag where she had tucked the hourglass and placed it on the sand. "Why don't you get yourself a drink and take a fly around this island before we explore?"

Pegasus neighed and took flight again, giving Meg a moment to look around. Koufonisia was pretty impressive at first glance. The sandy white beach surrounded a forest full of lush greenery, pink flowered bushes, and orange trees. In the distance, she could see a waterfall atop a green mountain. The sound of birds was the only noise she heard. There was no sign of boats or footprints or smoke. The island appeared to be uninhabited. Meg raised her eyes to the sun and felt the warmth on her face. Maybe Koufonisia was Elysium on Earth. Maybe she could hide out here and no one would even notice. There was no Hades around to torture her, no gods to remind her of her mother's loss or Aegeus's betrayal. Here, she could just *be*. Was it so wrong to want to skip the quest and spend her days lying on the warm sand, eating fruit, watching the waves?

But then there was Hercules to think about. *Do you love my son?* she heard Hera ask again in her mind. Meg looked at the saddlebag a few feet away. He had been so thoughtful, to pack her a few things even in the last few precious moments they'd shared together. She wanted more time with him, of that she was certain. And that meant she had a job to do.

Striding across the sand, Meg pulled the small hourglass out of the saddlebag. There was only a dusting of pink on the bottom of the glass, but grains were falling at a steady rate, almost as if they were taunting her. *You're already running out of time,* they seemed to say.

Turning her attention to the rest of the bag, Meg found fruit and water along with a smaller pouch perfect for holding the orchid and the hourglass. Slipping her hand in, she found something else tucked inside: a slingshot. The Y-shaped handle looked hand carved, while the tubing and the pouch were made from worn leather. Carved into the handle was a small fist, which she took to mean strength. Meg looked up at the heavens.

"Wonder Boy," she said softly, "you're full of surprises. Thank you."

Placing the hourglass and flower carefully in the pouch with the slingshot, she used the cord from the saddlebag to fasten it to her waist; she wanted to carry her most important items with her. Of course, she was kind of destroying the saddlebag in the process, but she could always put the food in Pegasus's other pouch when he returned.

Where was Pegasus, anyway? It didn't look like that big of an island. He could have taken a lap around and been back in a minute, and yet there was still no sign of him.

The hairs on the back of her neck stood up. Why did she suddenly feel like she was being watched? Meg stared at the water, which had gone quite still, then looked up toward the mountains now covered in the clouds' shadows. That's when she saw a speck in the sky. Peg was flying toward her. He swooped down over the beach and landed right in front of her.

"Am I glad to see you. For a second, I thought you abandoned me." Peg snorted in annoyance. "Yeah, I know, loyalty and all that, but you were gone awhile. Find anything good?" Peg reared up on his hind legs and neighed louder. Then he motioned with his head to follow him.

"You did find something, huh?" Meg trailed behind him across the beach, rubbing her arms, which were now cold. "Any chance it's the flute?"

Pegasus galloped ahead, stopping at the edge of a rocky part of the shoreline. Beyond it was a row of palm trees nestled among thick brush. Beyond that, she could hear a familiar sound coming softly from the woods. It definitely sounded like a wind instrument.

She hadn't even been on the island a half hour and

already she'd sort of located Athena's flute! Maybe this quest was going to be easier than she'd thought.

"Nice job, Peg." She patted the horse's side. "I think I'll keep you around." He snorted. "When you flew over the island, did you see the aulos or just hear it?"

Peg snorted and pawed at the sand with his front hoof. She watched as the horse shuddered. Something had unnerved him. She wished she spoke flying horse.

"Why don't you give me a lift so I can give the island an aerial view?"

Peg knelt down on his front legs, bending so that Meg could easily climb atop him. Once she was settled, he took off into the air. This time, she noticed Peg didn't jostle her or dive between clouds at a breakneck speed. Progress.

The flute was nowhere to be seen although she could still hear it, and it definitely sounded closer now than it had on the beach. She had to be getting warmer. Maybe it was on a mountaintop. She wouldn't put it past a god to accidentally drop a beloved instrument midflight.

"Peg, take a right," Meg said, hearing the sound of rushing water.

Pegasus flew lower and the waterfall she'd spotted from the beach came directly into view. The flute's melody grew louder.

Meg directed the horse to a patch of grass next to the waterfall. "Let's head over there. We've got to be close." As she dismounted, the sound of the water overpowered the flute, but Meg could still hear its music calling to her. Where was the wind instrument? Meg took a step closer to the mountain. "It sounds like it's coming directly from the water, as if that's possible. Unless . . ." Meg stared at the swift water collecting in the pool in front of her and wondered. "Maybe the flute is stuck on a rock or something." Meg moved toward the stones and spotted an opening. The waterfall concealed an entrance to a cave. She could just make out a small path. Meg lifted a vine covering the way and the flute hit a sudden high note, causing three birds in nearby trees to take flight. "Peg, the music is coming from inside a cave. The question is, where and *why*?" She paused. "I guess there's only one way to find out." Meg took a step forward and Peg rushed in front of her. "I know it's a bit scary, but I have no choice. I've got to go in there." Peg rose up on his hind legs.

Meg couldn't help thinking of Phil. The satyr would never let Hercules blindly go into a cave emanating mysterious music without a plan. "What if I take a weapon with me?" she suggested. "Hercules gave me a slingshot. I just need a few rocks." She grabbed a few and placed them in the bosom of her dress, afraid that if she added them to the pouch they would squash the orchid. "See? I'm completely prepared for anything now," Meg said, turning toward him. The rocks tumbled out. "Okay, maybe I need a Plan B . . ." She pinned the orchid to the inside flap of the satchel and placed the rocks in the pouch instead. "That will do the trick." Pegasus still looked uneasy, but he didn't protest as she headed toward the entrance again.

Suddenly the flutist started playing louder, the notes coming faster, like a wave, settling into a melodic frenzy. Meg froze. The tune was very familiar. A few more twisted notes sprang out from the water, and then it clicked into place: It was the first song she'd ever taught herself to play—"The Plight of the Lily." She clutched the slingshot firmly in her right hand and felt her pouch for the hourglass to make sure it was still there.

"Guess I'd better get this over with," Meg said to Peg, who started to follow. "No, you stay here." Peg neighed. "I appreciate the sudden loyalty, Peg, but I've got this. Besides, if we need a quick getaway plan, you're it." She held up the slingshot. "I'll be fine."

Peg pawed at the ground, but Meg gave him an encouraging smile. Still clutching her slingshot, she headed under the waterfall, pushing aside thick, intertwined vines. The back side of the waterfall was deafening, making it difficult for Meg to still hear the flute, but she kept shuffling along till the cave finally opened up in front of her—a chasm of rock and dripping water. From here, the flute's melody could be heard loud and clear again.

"Well, well, someone does live here," Meg said to herself as she stared at a series of lit torches lining the stone walls.

At the sound of her voice, the flute suddenly stopped and the torches dimmed, shrouding the cave in shadows.

"Games, huh?" Meg's voice echoed in the darkness. "That's fine. I know how to play games."

Having lived in the Underworld for a spell, she was not scared of darkened caves. Nor of the monsters that lived inside. What did worry her, however, was not knowing the type of monster she was about to face. She grabbed a dimmed torch from the wall and walked slowly, her eyes scanning the dark path in front of her. She didn't see any other tunnels. There was only one way into this cave, it seemed, and one way out. She started walking. When Meg finally looked back, the waterfall was just a speck in the distance. She could hardly hear it anymore. The only sound was the water trickling from the mossy condensation on the stone surrounding her.

In the distance, she heard the flute. It sounded far away again. *How big is this cave?* she wondered, quickening her step. The torches ahead of her roared back to life. The path was widening, too. She was finally getting someplace. The music was calling to her, beckoning her to come closer. And though every bone in her body told her she could be walking into a trap, she had to keep going. *The only one who can save you now is you. Trust yourself.* She was the master of her own destiny. Taking a deep breath, she held the torch in front of her and kept going.

She was not leaving without Athena's flute.

The music grew louder as the path curved downward and brightened. *Are my eyes adjusting to the dark, or is there really a light up ahead?* she wondered. As she turned the corner, she saw a path leading to a waterfall. Was it another waterfall or the same one she'd come from? Had she gone in a complete circle? She wasn't sure. She heard the flute again and turned around. This time the sound had come from the other direction. To her right was a second path. She made the turn and headed down it. At the end, she found herself in a large cavern where a beautiful woman sat atop a throne carved out of rock and played Athena's double flute.

Meg was mesmerized.

The woman was lost in the music, her eyes closed as she played the double reed pipe. Her head bobbed and swayed, her long jet-black hair sweeping around her bare shoulders. She wore a flowing peach gown with a train that swept across the length of the room, wrapping the space in fabric. Meg looked at the flute in wonder.

Legend had it Athena had thrown the flute away in disgust because playing it distorted her face and ruined her beauty. This woman, however, practically glowed as the notes escaped her flute. Meg listened with rapt attention, finding herself overcome with emotion. She played far better than anyone Meg had ever heard before. She felt a sudden pang. Whoever this woman was, she was meant to keep Athena's flute.

It took Meg a moment before she realized she had drifted closer to the throne to listen. Still, the woman didn't look up. Meg closed her eyes and let the tune take her to a different time and place—to that little village and the sound of her mother sleeping soundly in their bed as Meg practiced by the window. Meg was suddenly sleepy, too. Would it be so wrong to lie on the ground and rest for a spell? Meg started to drop to her knees.

*Megara!*

*Megara!*

*Be alert!* she heard a voice in her head command. Meg snapped out of her trance, opened her eyes, and gasped.

The woman was now standing inches from her face, the double flute of Athena held tightly in her hands. Her blue eyes were the exact color of the sea surrounding the island and her skin was a luminescent, milky white. She stared at Meg a moment before circling her slowly. Meg tried to remain calm. She felt so tired, like she could sleep for a thousand years.

"I . . . You play beautifully," Meg said, trying to focus. "I know that tune well."

"Yes?" the woman replied, and Meg noticed the word sounded almost like a hiss. Meg felt her heart beat faster.

"I used to play it all the time." Meg clutched the slingshot tighter in her right hand and prayed the woman didn't see it. The woman looked harmless enough, but every fiber of Meg's being told her not to believe appearances. She stood rigid as the woman's eyes swooped over her face.

"Have you come to play for me?" the woman whispered.

*Play?* Meg tensed. Hera had said nothing about her having to play the flute . . . had she? She had asked if Meg *could* play. But could and would were two different things. The last time she'd played—*no.* She didn't want to think about that moment. Here and now, she had a chance to get the very thing that would change her fate. She needed to focus. "Some say I play well enough to put Cerberus to sleep." The woman's blue eyes widened. "If you like, I will show you." Meg held out her hands.

The woman surveyed Meg curiously, clearly considering the offer. Finally, she held the flute out to her.

Meg felt her breath quicken. The double reed was beautifully made compared to the tarnished mess she had once owned. She pushed her doubts aside and locked eyes with the woman as she slowly moved her hand forward. Her fingers grazed the reed pipe.

And everything in front of her burst into flames.

# SIX: Escape

Meg felt the fire singe her forearms and she cried out in surprise.

This was no woman. Its gown had fallen away to reveal one bronze leg and one hoofed donkey's leg. Its black hair was engulfed in flames, burning bright red and orange as it moved toward Meg, mouth dripping with blood. It had scaly bat-like wings so large they couldn't even fully open in the cave. It was an Empusa. The vampiric beast was known to seduce men and feast on their flesh and blood, but when men were lacking, an Empusa was not going to let any other potential prey go unscathed. And Meg had walked right into its lair.

Meg stumbled, trying to get out of its path, but her arms were burning. She tried to move faster and heard a crunch beneath her feet. She inhaled sharply. What covered the cavern floor was not the train of a beautiful gown. It was a mountain of bones!

The Empusa sniffed the air. "Young blood. Blood so pure." It moved toward Meg, its arm outstretched. Meg watched as it tucked the double flute into a leather strap slung over its shoulder. "I haven't had young blood in a long time. What I wouldn't give for just a taste."

"Sorry," Meg said, climbing over the bones to escape. "I'm pretty fond of keeping my blood in my body." Meg picked up a rather large rock and threw it at the monster.

The Empusa kept coming. "Few come to this island," it said, gliding toward her. "Most realize what's here and leave before they even get near me. But you, child, came willingly, sent here to take something that is not yours."

"It's not yours, either." She pulled a rock from her saddle-bag, placed it in the slingshot, and threw it in the Empusa's path. "That flute is Athena's, and she wants it back."

The Empusa's eyes flashed. "If she wants it, she will have to pry it from my dead hands, mortal." The Empusa lunged forward, its long clawlike nails catching on Meg's gown.

Meg felt the nails sink into her thigh and she cried out,

falling onto her knees. The slingshot went flying, skidding out of reach. She lunged for it, trying in vain to find it again, but stopped when she saw the Empusa about to hook a claw into her shoulder. Meg tried to crawl backward on her burned hands and feet as she frantically searched the floor for a weapon. Her nails dug into the dirt as she tried to grab hold of anything that would aid her. Finally, her fingers closed around something large—a human skull—and she lobbed it at the creature's head.

The Empusa screamed and fell backward, one of its wings wrapping around to cover it. Meg grabbed two more large bones and threw them as well, hoping to keep the creature down.

*Get up!* she heard a voice in her head command, and Meg winced as she stood up and hurried out of the cavern. She tried to get her bearings. Where was she? Was this the main cave? Another path? Where was the waterfall? *What about the flute?* she thought. *It's the flute or your life! Go!* She staggered into the darkness, dragging her badly wounded leg behind her. Her only hope was to reach that waterfall and feel her way out before the Empusa caught up to her. She could hear it hissing. Meg whirled around and saw it rounding the corner, the flames of its hair whipping at the walls and setting the moss that grew in the cave ablaze. The cave quickly filled with smoke.

"I smell you!" the Empusa called. "You can't hide from me, mortal!"

Meg started to cough, her eyes welling from the smoke. She leaned on the rock wall to keep herself upright. Her leg was dripping blood, sending her scent and exact location to the Empusa, no doubt, and the skin on her arms was so badly singed it felt like it was still on fire. The cave was filling with so much smoke, she could no longer see.

*I failed,* she thought. *No flute. No way out. I'm going to die in this cave.* Meg's eyes started to flutter closed.

*Be alert, Megara!* Meg heard a voice say, and she opened her eyes and looked around. Still, all she saw was smoke. *Keep going! Hurry! You're almost there!* Meg took a step forward, covering her mouth with her arm and coughing wildly. She squinted through the darkness and saw a new shape in the distance moving toward her. It stopped right in front of her.

"Peg!" Meg cried as she clambered onto his back, fighting through the pain. "Am I glad you don't listen! We've got to get out of here."

Pegasus started galloping back the way he came.

Then she heard the scream. The Empusa was gaining on them, attempting to fly through the cave with its folded wings. It emerged out of the hazy darkness, its fangs dripping with blood.

Pegasus rounded a corner, and Meg saw light up ahead and heard the waterfall. "Move, Peg! We're almost there!" she cried. Then she felt the horse's whole body lurch backward.

The Empusa had grasped Pegasus's tail.

Meg fumbled for her satchel, reaching inside to grab another rock, which she lobbed at the creature's face. The Empusa cried out and let go.

"Faster!" Meg screamed. The horse flapped his wings harder, jerking from left to right to get away, but the Empusa came roaring back, catching the bottom of Meg's gown. Meg shook it off, wincing with pain at the sudden movement. "Peg!" she cried as the Empusa came back yet again.

With a final burst, Pegasus raced toward the waterfall, jumping straight through it and emerging on the other side.

The stream washing over her was just what Meg needed for a momentary revival, the water hitting her wounds and giving her a second's relief. She felt the clean air fill her lungs and blinked hard, trying to get the sensation of smoke out of her eyes. Then she heard the Empusa shriek.

It burst out of the waterfall seconds after them, taking flight on its massive wings and keeping pace with Pegasus. The horse neighed.

"I know! Get us out of here!" Meg cried, wishing more than anything Peg could whisk her away from this island

and take her . . . where? If she left Koufonisia without that flute, her quest was over. She glanced back at the Empusa and saw the double flute still hanging from the strap on the creature's chest. Was there any chance she could still grab it? *Think, Meg!* She looked around wildly for inspiration and spotted another cave on the edge of one of the mountain's cliffs. Above it were several boulders. That gave her an idea.

"Wait! Peg, new plan! Make a hard left to that cave!" Meg cried, and Pegasus started to snort and neigh angrily. "Yeah, I know we almost died, but I need that flute. I have to try!"

Peg continued heading toward the horizon, and for a moment, Meg thought he was going to ignore her. Then the horse dove straight down, Meg clinging to him before he veered left. The Empusa screamed and followed.

"Yes, it's following us! Keep that creature on its hooves!" Meg shouted.

Peg darted up and down, through clouds and around them. The cave was fast approaching. Meg held tight to Peg's neck as he flew toward the cave. She was just formulating her next move when she felt the jolt. Peg was bumped so hard he went sideways and almost pitched Meg off. She heard the horse scream and saw a gash in his side.

"Peg!" Meg cried as Pegasus started to spiral, falling fast.

Meg was sure they would hit the rock wall straight on, but the horse managed to pull up at the last second and glided unsteadily into the cave. Meg looked around. The cave had a wide enough opening. If the Empusa flew in, they could hopefully fly out at the exact same moment and—*BOOM!*

The Empusa barreled into Pegasus, knocking Meg clear off him and sending itself flying. Meg hit the ground hard and heard screams and Peg's nervous neighs. There was a ringing in her ears. The cave came in and out of focus. The Empusa, it appeared, had hit the cave wall and was knocked out cold. She forced herself to get up and was thankful to see Pegasus stumbling toward her. Meg knew what his neighs meant. *Let's get out of here. We won't survive a second attack.* He was right, but she couldn't leave without that flute. She lunged for the instrument still hanging from the creature's waist and her fingers closed around the reeds. Then she gave the strap a hard yank, and the flute came free. The Empusa immediately stirred, and the two locked eyes—violet meeting blazing red. Meg jumped up and started running.

"Peg! Go!" Meg screamed, running after the horse, who clearly wasn't sure if he should grab her or take off first.

Meg reached desperately for the horse's mane and felt the Empusa grab her gown. Meg screamed and Peg started to run with Meg clinging to his tail. Finally, Pegasus leaped out of the cave and took flight. He was slower with his injuries, but he still managed to pull Meg up out of the cave and then above it. But they weren't in the clear. Meg knew if she didn't get rid of that Empusa once and for all, it would keep coming back till it killed them both. She looked down and saw boulders. Meg didn't think. She just let go, knowing Peg would follow. The horse did, neighing frantically as he came down for a landing, but Meg was already dropping the flute into her satchel and pushing a large rock toward the edge.

"Quick! Help me!"

Peg used his snout, pushing on the boulder until it started to roll. Meg heard the Empusa's scream and knew it was coming.

"Keep going!" Meg shouted.

Her arms were burning, her leg was still bleeding, and Peg was losing blood, but together they rolled the largest of the boulders to the cliff. Then Meg stood at the edge, making herself a target. *Come and get me,* she thought.

Peering over, she saw the Empusa flying upward, its claws outstretched to grab her. The boulder had to roll off the ledge at just the right moment or it would miss. *Wait,*

Meg thought as it drew closer. *Wait,* she continued to tell herself as Peg looked to her for guidance. The Empusa was just a few feet away now and reaching out to grab her. "Now!" Meg screamed as she and Pegasus pushed the boulder off the cliff together.

The Empusa only realized what was happening when it was too late. Its red eyes widened as the rock hit the target, slamming the creature to the ground below.

Meg fell to her knees as she watched the Empusa's flaming hair burn out. Then she looked over at Peg in surprise and relief, her eyes welling with tears. With trembling hands, she pulled the double flute of Athena out of her satchel and held it up to the heavens, half expecting Hera to appear and commend her work.

Nothing happened.

Peg slowly walked over, looking the worse for wear. Meg slumped onto his back, her chest rising and falling fast. She was in so much pain, she could barely breathe. *Now what?* she thought. *The hourglass!* she suddenly remembered and pulled it out of her satchel. There was a layer of pink sand along the bottom that couldn't be ignored.

As much as it killed her to admit it, Hercules was right—she needed some guidance. She'd never survive another attack like this one on her own. Meg looked up at the clear blue sky and sighed loudly.

Peg looked at her.

She knew what she had to do, but she didn't like it. Not one bit.

"Pegasus? Take me to that cranky satyr before I change my mind."

# SEVEN: The Great Philoctetes

*Aaah . . . this is the life!* Phil thought as he lay in a hammock, putting his hands behind his head and letting his gut hang out for the rest of the island to see.

Truthfully, there was no one on this chunk of paradise but him, some goats, and a group of nymphs, but that would change soon enough. As soon as word got out that he'd helped Hercules go from a wet noodle to a superhuman to a god, everyone would revere the great Philoctetes!

Not to brag, but he was kind of a living legend, which is what he told those nymphs he'd been unsuccessfully chasing around the island for years. Forget Odysseus, Perseus, and what had become of Theseus. His work with Hercules would be what the world would remember. When the

Underworld finally got his goat, he'd wind up in Elysium for sure. And boy, would he have stories. How many satyrs actually got to visit Mount Olympus? He'd witnessed Hercules's glory and seen the mighty Zeus and Hera in the flesh. Sure, he felt a little bad about leaving before saying goodbye to the kid, but that business with Meg was not one he wanted to get roped into. Geez, Zeus looked hopping mad when the kid had asked to stay a mortal. And who could blame him? After all Phil and Zeus had done for the boy? The nerve! He was just going to try to forget the kid had ever made such a bad call of judgment. Zeus had said no, and his word was final.

Phil closed his eyes and was just drifting off when he heard the birds start to chirp madly. He opened his eyes with a start and looked around. A familiar white figure was flying over the Aegean Sea.

"Pegasus?" Phil scratched one of his ears. "What are you doing back—"

He spotted something slumped over the horse's back and froze. What was that? And why was Pegasus coming in at such a sharp angle and landing way too fast? Phil bleated, jumping out of the hammock seconds before Pegasus crashed into it and collapsed on the ground. The horse had a gash on his left side and was breathing heavily, which was alarming, but even more so was the woman he had been carrying with him. As soon as Phil saw the red hair, he knew who it was. That dame.

"Oh, no," Phil said, backing up. "No, no, no! What are you doing here? What do you want?" His face grew deep red to match his auburn bottom half.

That woman was trouble, and he'd had enough trouble to last three lifetimes.

Red lifted her head to look at him, and Phil noticed how pale her face was. She had bruises on her legs and burn marks on her arms. What trouble had she gotten herself and Pegasus into? Hadn't Hercules just saved her from Hades himself?

"Phil," Red said, her voice hoarse as she tried to dismount Pegasus. "I—"

"I don't want to hear it!" Phil cut her off. "I don't care what happened. This shop is closed, sweetheart." He looked at Pegasus. "I'll patch my friend up here, and then you two are on your way back to Thebes or wherever it is you were headed before you clearly got into some sort of scrape." Red didn't argue, and curiosity got the best of him. "What happened to you two, anyway?"

Red's eyes fluttered open, then closed. "Hercules told me to come find you first, but I didn't listen." She tried again to dismount and winced in pain.

Phil's eyes widened. "Hercules put you up to this? Wait

till I get ahold of that kid! Telling you where I live! Sending you with his horse!"

"He was right," Red tried again, pulling herself slowly off Pegasus's back. "I need . . . help." She stumbled toward him.

"Too bad!" Phil said. "Find someone else to do your dirty work, whatever it is. You caused me enough trouble. Why, I . . ."

Red reached for something in a satchel around her waist and pulled out a double flute. Phil's eyes widened with recognition.

"Wait a minute," Phil said. "Is that . . . Athena's?"

Before Red could answer, she collapsed at his feet.

What choice did he have after that? He couldn't let her just die again.

Okay, so maybe he considered it for a split second, but no one could fault him for that.

The two of them were in bad shape. He brought them home to patch them up, but his door was the size of a tack compared to the rest of the joint. Living inside the hollow head and shoulders of a statue had its challenges. He found Pegasus shelter under a cluster of trees nearby, and thanks to some TLC, Pegasus was recovering nicely. But the redhead was taking longer to come around. Red was out for a full day before she even started to stir, but at least by that point, his burn remedies were starting to work their magic. He'd had to deal with a lot of training mishaps over the years, so thankfully he'd gotten really good at emergency care. She'd be up and running soon. In the meantime, he could do some housekeeping and stick close by. The place certainly needed a good dusting.

He was just about to polish one of Jason's old swords when he heard Red gasp sharply, then start to cough. He made his way over to the bed with a glass of water.

"Drink this. You'll feel better."

Red took a long gulp, then looked up at Phil, confused. "Thanks. Where am I?"

"My place," he said, motioning around the oddly shaped room with artifacts piled almost to the ceiling. He was a bit of a hoarder, but how could he part with things like the mast to the *Argo*? It was proudly displayed, of course, hung on a rope from the ceiling.

Red's signature smirk made a quick appearance. "You felt guilty, huh?"

"What choice did you leave me?" Phil asked, his face growing hot. "When you barged in like that, bleeding all over the place, I couldn't just leave you there."

Her violet eyes widened. “Where is Pegasus?”

“He’s fine. Patched him right up. He’s already sailing around the island, taking some test flights. Good as new.”

“Oh no.” Red started frantically removing blankets and pillows. “Where is the flute?”

“Hanging right behind you, along with your satchel,” he said, pointing to the wall. “Got to say—I’ve been really keen to get an explanation about how you got it.”

Red opened the satchel and removed an orchid and then a small hourglass with pink sand. The bottom was a quarter full, and the sand on top was falling at a steady pace. “Oh no. No. No. No. No. *No!*” She looked at Phil in alarm. “How long have I been here?”

“A day, why?” He pointed to the hourglass. “What is that thing timing?”

Red slowly swung her legs over the side, noticing the bandages on her legs. “I’ve got limited time,” she said, sounding frustrated. “And I’ve now lost a whole day lying around here!”

“Hey. It’s not like you had an invitation! *You* showed up. You want to go? Go! I’ve got stuff to do.” He took the water glass away from her bedside and shuffled across the room.

“No, Phil, wait.” Red sighed and slowly tried to stand up. “I’m sorry, okay? If you hadn’t been here when Peg and I landed . . .”

Phil folded his arms across his chest. "You'd probably be on your way back to Hades!"

Red closed her eyes as if to block the thought. "You're right. I owe you one for saving us. And if I had just listened to Hercules and come to you first, I probably wouldn't have nearly died at the hands of an Empusa."

Phil fell to all fours. "You two faced an Empusa and survived? How?"

Red raised her chin defiantly. "Hercules gave me a slingshot and I improvised the rest."

Phil started to laugh hard. "A slingshot and wit? Against an Empusa? You needed fire-resistant armor! And at least three swords, and a bow and arrow to pierce its wings. And a killer escape plan." He waved a hand knowingly. "Those things lure innocents into caves and trap them there."

"Yeah, learned that the hard way." She paused. "Look, I'm not the best at asking for things." She flipped her hair back, and Phil immediately knew she was starting to feel like herself again. "But that's why I'm here. So I don't screw up again." She looked down at the floor, then back up at him. "Would you consider helping me?"

"Me? Help you? With what?" He shook his head. What was he thinking, even indulging her? "I can't. I am retired."

"Congratulations. Look, this wouldn't be a long-term

gig. We're talking eight days tops. The abridged version of whatever you did with Hercules."

Phil snorted. "Help you be a *hero*? In *eight days*? Not possible. No way. Sorry, lady."

Red threw her head back in disgust. "What was I thinking bargaining with a satyr? I'm out of here." She grabbed her satchel and flute and headed to the door.

"Good!" Phil snapped. Some thanks she gave him. Let her leave. Eight days . . . couldn't be done. Phil scratched his right horn. "Hey. Why do you only have eight days, anyway?"

Red stopped at the door, not looking at him. "I'm on a quest for Hera."

"You're on a quest for Hera?" Phil laughed hard. "You wish!" He turned around, grabbed a rag, and polished a gold shield. The aegis displayed Medusa's head, another one of his most prized possessions.

Red turned around, her eyes flashing. "It's true!" Phil continued laughing as she opened the door. "Just forget it. Pegasus and I are out of here." She made her way outside. Phil followed, watching Pegasus trot toward her. Red touched his mane, and he snorted softly. She attempted to pull herself onto his back, wincing in pain.

"Hey, kid, if you want to stay and recover longer . . ." Phil started to say, but Red shook her head.

"It's fine. Don't want to overstay our welcome. Thanks, Phil," she said as she tucked the flute into her satchel. She patted Pegasus's mane and braced herself to make another try at climbing onto his back. "It's time to go."

Phil suddenly realized that if she left now he'd never know what this all had been about. "Hey, this quest you're supposedly on. What is it, anyway?" Red didn't say anything. "Come on, I did patch you up. Least you can do is tell me what Hera asked you to do."

"Hera asked me to find her the double flute of Athena. Once I did that, she said the rest of my quest would be revealed, but I haven't heard a single thing." Red looked up at the sky for answers. "I guess I thought you were the guy to have by my side no matter what was next, so I came here. It was a stupid idea."

Phil almost fell over. Red had just paid him a compliment. "But what's the quest *for*?" he pressed. "Gods don't just go around asking for favors without giving you something in return."

Red pushed her bangs out of her eyes. "Hera said if I proved my worth, she'd make me a god so Hercules and I could be together."

Phil nearly fell over again. "Holy Hera."

Red nodded. "My thoughts exactly."

Phil slumped onto a crumbling piece of the statue he

lived in. "That means you and the kid could be together. Like forever." He thought he noticed her fidget. "No wonder you came to me for help. You can't do a job like this on your own."

Red gave him a look. "Hey, I did survive the Underworld without you, if you'll recall."

Whether she was up for the task or not, no one turned down a god, especially not one offering that kind of payoff. If Hera had given her a quest, maybe she saw something in Red that he hadn't. "Have you looked the flute over for any hidden messages or a note written on the strap?"

"No." Red retrieved the double flute from her satchel and turned it over in her wounded hands. "I don't see anything."

Phil thought again. "Have you tried playing it?"

A strange look came over her face. "I doubt that would help."

"How do you know? Can you play?"

Red hesitated. "Yes, but . . ."

"Blow a few notes through the thing," he said impatiently. "Maybe Hera has to hear it."

She sighed and looked uncomfortable as she stared at the instrument. "Fine. But don't expect much."

The first note came out rather loud and pitchy, but then she seemed to find her footing, quickly playing a few notes that were kind of nice. She didn't play long enough for him to get a sense of her skill. When she was done, she held up the flute and made a face. "Happy?"

"No."

Red, Phil, and Pegasus turned around.

Athena, god of war and wisdom, stood before them in the flesh.

# EIGHT: War

Meg knew it was Athena the moment she saw her. Like most Greeks, she'd seen many statues depicting the god, who appeared with an owl perched on her toned shoulders and a shield at the ready in one hand. She used her other to point directly at Meg.

"Where did you get that flute, mortal?"

Athena stood before them on the edge of the cliff, her back to the sun. Her lavender body seemed to glow, the silver on her headdress and gauntlets practically fluorescent. She wore an armored breastplate over her dress and a navy blue helmet that offset her sky blue hair. Her dark eyes looked anything but pleased.

Pegasus shuffled side to side restlessly and Phil was as still as a statue as Athena approached.

"I asked you a question: Where did you get my flute?"

Meg quickly came to her senses and spoke up. "I retrieved it from the Empusa who hid it from you on the island of Koufonisia."

Athena took a step back and it felt as though she were sizing Meg up. "You? A mortal stole my flute from an Empusa?"

Phil bleated involuntarily. "Hard to believe, Athena, I know, considering she had no training from me, the Great Philoctetes, but that is the story she gave me, too."

"Thanks, Phil," Meg said dryly. "It's true. Though as you can see, I could have used some help." She gestured with her bandaged arms. "Are you here to offer some guidance?"

"That depends," Athena said. "What is it you want, Megara?"

*She knows who I am.* "What do I want?" Meg repeated, unsure.

"Yes." Athena moved closer and looked her in the eye. "What is it that you want?" The god enunciated every word.

Meg thought carefully before answering. "What I want is to know the next part of my quest. Are you here to tell me?"

Athena sighed impatiently. "And *why* do you want to know?"

The god wasn't making sense. *So I can finish my quest,* Meg thought, but somehow she knew that was not what Athena wanted to hear.

"So she can be with Hercules!" Phil finally blurted out. He shot Meg a look. "How can you not understand the question?"

"Is that what you want, Megara? To be with Hercules and be a god as he is?" Athena asked, her voice tight.

*Say yes,* Meg thought. *But if she catches you sounding unsure, she'll know. She's a god. She knows everything.* "I think so." Phil slapped a hand over his eyes, but Athena looked surprisingly delighted.

"Finally! A real answer!" Athena's owl began to hoot. "I appreciate your honesty, Megara, but the truth will only take you so far." She pointed a finger at Meg's chest. "You are a mortal who does not know what she wants, and because of that you lack purpose. Where is your drive? How do you expect to complete a quest such as this one if you have nothing to fight for?"

"I have purpose and drive," Meg said grudgingly, folding her arms across her chest.

"Do you?" Athena asked almost mockingly. "Is that why

you played my flute so *beautifully* when given the chance? We both know you know how to play."

"You do?" Phil questioned. "It kind of sounded like you didn't. No offense."

Meg's cheeks colored slightly. "I don't play anymore."

"Not because you can't, but because you have lost your will," Athena pointed out. "Therein lies the problem."

"Why don't you play anymore?" Phil asked.

Meg brushed him off. "That's not important."

Athena's eyes flashed. "On the contrary, it's *very* important. You are going to war, Megara. And in war, one must have the will to fight for what they want or they will fall in battle as swiftly as a sword cuts through the air."

Meg stifled a sigh, careful not to offend the god in front of her. *What do I want?* she asked herself. *I care for Hercules, but we've just started to get to know each other. How do I know I want to be with him forever? And how do I actually know I'd even make a decent god? That's a pretty big commitment, too. When have those ever worked out for me?*

"Good!" Athena nodded appraisingly. "Finally, we are getting somewhere. Without questioning where you've been, you'll never understand where you must go."

Meg tried not to look too shocked. So Athena could

hear her thoughts. She supposed it made sense. She had prayed to the gods for answers before. One just happened to be standing in front of her now.

"Wait, did I miss something?" Phil asked.

Both women ignored him.

"But how do I know what I want without having the time to figure it out?" Meg questioned.

"War waits for no one," Athena said. "You have a deadline. To find answers, you must look to both the past *and* future for guidance."

Meg still wasn't sure she understood. How was someone supposed to understand something like love? How would she know what she wanted out of Hercules, out of *herself*? How could she be a god like Athena when she did not know the answer to those questions?

"Yes, like that!" Athena said, again seeming to hear her thoughts. "The more questions the better! I want to see fire in your belly, Megara. I know you have it, or you would not have been able to beat that Empusa." The god studied Meg. "Perhaps Hera was right to put her faith in you. If you do as I say, you'll do well on the journey ahead."

Meg inhaled sharply. The next part of her quest! "What do I have to do?"

Phil, Pegasus, and Meg looked at Athena. Her dress blew softly in the light breeze and she seemed to consider the question. Finally, she spoke. "You must go to the Underworld to retrieve a lost soul."

Meg felt as if the earth beneath her feet had dropped out from under her. Her mouth went dry. "The Underworld?" This had to be a cruel joke. Hera couldn't expect her to travel to the land of death and be able to return a third time.

"But we just got her back from there!" Phil sputtered.

*Exactly!* Meg wanted to cry, but she was too afraid to speak.

"Quests are not for the faint of heart," Athena said simply.

Hades did not just let souls come or go. Charon, the ferryman, only shuttled the dead, and even if one could get past him, there was Hades's three-headed dog, Cerberus, at the entrance to the Underworld to keep mortals out. This was an impossible task. Meg rubbed the bandages on her arm and tried not to let her fear show. "Do you know whose soul I'm looking for? The Underworld, unfortunately, is a rather large place."

Athena staked the tip of her sword in the dirt and squared her shoulders. "Her name is Katerina. I believe she captured the heart of someone you once loved."

Meg felt the world start to spin. "Katerina?" She reached out for Peg. Her knees felt like they might buckle.

"Katerina?" Phil repeated. "Who is Katerina?"

Meg wasn't sure she could answer that question without opening up an entire new can of worms. "He left me for Katerina."

Phil scratched his right horn. "Hercules?"

"No!" Meg felt herself grow impatient. Her chest felt like it was constricting, and it was suddenly hard to breathe. "Aegeus."

"Who is Aegeus?" Phil asked, but Meg couldn't speak.

Athena had to do it for her. "He's the one Megara gave up her soul for."

# NINE: Do or Die

## Years earlier . . .

*Adrift.* That's how Meg would later describe the years after her mother died. She was a ship lost at sea with nowhere to anchor, drifting from town to town, never staying in one place for too long. Her reasons for being nomadic weren't the same as her mother's had been. No, Meg found herself moving on anytime she noticed something that reminded her of her old life with Thea. It could be a song being hummed by women doing the wash, or the way a small girl with red hair called for her parents, or even the sight of fresh flowers in the market, but when Meg felt that pull, she couldn't stay a minute longer. She ran from her mother's ghost until she could run no farther, taking only one thing from her old life on her travels—the rusty flute Thea had given her.

She played that flute till her fingers callused and bled. She poured her pain and her grief into song, creating melodies that she played at dawn, midday, and in the middle of the night. The skill she had once turned her nose up at because it had cost her a week's worth of eggs suddenly became her most cherished possession. And it turned out her mother was right about one thing—music saved her. Meg was not one to take handouts or rely on the kindness of strangers. No. Her mother had warned her about living life that way. Instead, she used music to afford rent and food. With age and talent, Meg found herself getting more and more invitations to play her flute at performances with other musicians.

It was at one of those concerts she met Aegeus.

"You have a gift," she recalled him saying to her one evening as she walked off the amphitheater stage. "And a gift like that shouldn't be wasted playing alone. Play with me instead."

Meg remembered being ruffled by his words. She'd seen him earlier that evening. He played the lute like no other musician she'd ever seen, and she couldn't help being taken by his thick black hair and green eyes that shone against his tan skin. "Kind of forward, don't you think, Curly?"

He half smiled. "I had to say something to keep you from getting away." He held out a hand. "My name is Aegeus."

She hesitated for a moment before shaking it. "Megara."

The minute her fingers connected with his, she was adrift no more.

For the first time since Thea had passed, Meg found herself opening up to another. It had been so long since she'd shared someone else's company for any length of time that she'd almost forgotten what it was like to connect with another human. It wasn't long before they were playing music together on stage, and she found herself falling in love despite her better judgment. Her mother had said to never put her faith or trust in another, and here she was making future plans with a man she barely knew. But Aegeus wasn't like the father from her faint memories. He never raised his voice, and she'd only seen him cross once—when a merchant refused to pay them for a performance he had requested. Life with Aegeus was easy, and it didn't hurt that she now had someone to create music with.

"Your skills make me feel like an imposter," Meg lamented one night. Aegeus had played her under the table with a fast-paced arrangement on his lute, and she wasn't happy.

"You sell yourself short," Aegeus told her. "You're good!"

"I'm decent."

"You're masterful!"

"I'm your apprentice," she argued, as she nuzzled into his chest in front of the fire he had made for them.

"Don't say that." Aegeus ran a hand through her hair. "You don't become a master by acting like an—"

"Apprentice," Meg finished. It was one of his favorite sayings. "I know."

Aegeus picked up the lute again and his fingers plucked the strings so quickly, it seemed as if the instrument played itself. "You're self-made, Megara. You've never had a single lesson! Talent like that is a gift from the Muses. Who knows? Someday your skill may help you put Cerberus to sleep."

"And why would I ever need to learn how to put Cerberus to sleep?" she'd said with a laugh.

"Orpheus did," Aegeus reminded her. "When his beloved Eurydice died, he played so beautifully he tricked Cerberus into letting a mortal enter the Underworld to retrieve her soul." He reached out a hand and caressed her cheek. "If there ever comes a time when I have to do the same, my love, I, for one, will play like a master and sail by Cerberus as he sleeps to come find you."

She cupped his face in her hands. "And I would do the same for you."

Aegeus had mended her broken heart. What more could she ask for in life? She knew that soon he would ask for her hand in marriage—he hinted at it daily—and without question, she would say yes. Would her mother approve of the marriage, of her putting her trust in another? Probably not, but her mother wasn't always right. Was she? Aegeus would never betray her.

Though, of course, the rest of the world might.

One day, Aegeus fell gravely ill. Meg tried to get help, but she didn't have the funds for pricy herbs. She went to their fellow musicians, but they turned her away. "If he's sick, that's punishment from the gods," several said with a jealous tinge to their voices. They had never liked that Aegeus had outshone them on stage.

"And if he gets well, is that a gift from the gods?" she argued angrily. But she didn't wait around for their answer. Why would the gods punish Aegeus? He had done nothing but bring her joy and offer beautiful, moving music to the world. Despite her argument, she began to pray to every god she could think of to heal him. And yet, Aegeus grew sicker.

As he lay in bed, struggling for every breath, Meg found herself thinking of her mother. *I told you,* she'd say. *No one will help you. People are no good. You can't trust others.*

*But Aegeus is good*, she'd tell the voice in her head. *He deserves to live. I need him! Please, gods, save him!* But Aegeus's condition only worsened.

*Perhaps I am praying to the wrong gods,* Meg feared one night when she thought Aegeus was about to take his last breath. Their friends had abandoned him. Money for treatments had eluded them, and no aid came. But maybe there was another way. *Cerberus,* she mused, thinking of the Underworld. Her thoughts had turned dark and the path of darkness led to none other than the god of the Underworld. She placed her lips to her flute and played her most cherished tune—"The Plight of the Lily"—in his honor.

*Hades,* Meg silently prayed as she played, *if you save my love's life, I will give you anything you ask for. Just don't take Aegeus too soon as you did my mother. I'll give anything.*

*Anything?* a voice inside her head asked.

Meg looked up and stopped playing. *Was* this a voice in her head, or had a god finally answered her prayers?

"Anything!" Meg repeated, this time aloud. She held tight to Aegeus's hands to stop hers from shaking.

*Including your soul?* the voice said.

Meg looked down at Aegeus, so weak and pale she knew he wouldn't last the night. She loved him like she'd loved no other. He'd given her so much these last few months—a companion, inspiration . . . a home—she couldn't imagine walking the Earth without him.

"Yes," Meg said firmly.

It was the last word she spoke before she suddenly felt

her body begin to fade from Aegeus's bedside. She reached out to grab Aegeus's hand, but felt it slip through her fingers. Her flute clattered to the floor.

"Wait! Wait!" she begged when she realized what was happening. "I'm not ready to go!"

She didn't even have time to see Aegeus open his eyes.

She was falling, fast, into a never-ending darkness that made her scream die out before she hit the bottom. Her body went from cold to brutally hot. Her lungs felt like they were on fire and she was sure her skin would begin to melt, but instead she kept falling until she finally hit solid ground and felt dirt beneath her fingers.

The breath knocked from her stomach, Meg inhaled sharply, gasping for air. She sat up fast and looked around. "Aegeus! Aegeus, where are you?" she cried, her voice echoing in the darkness, but there was no answer. She blinked rapidly as her eyes adjusted. She was in a cave that glowed by torchlight. The air was thick and unbearably warm, and she could hear screaming in the distance. Suddenly, three hooded figures appeared out of the darkness and Meg screamed once more, trying to retreat farther into the shadows.

"Are you sure this is her?" croaked a tall, grayish being with empty eye sockets. She had a pointed chin and nose and long, spindly fingers. She held a pair of scissors poised against a string two others were holding taut.

"Because if it's not—*snip, snip*," said her short, squat companion. This one bore a pinkish skin tone and had a single eyeball in the center of her head.

"Every soul must be accounted for," said the third, who had empty eye sockets and a nose twice the length of her face.

"Who are you?" Meg cried. "Where is Aegeus?"

But there was no answer.

"You can back off, ladies," said a deep voice in the shadows. "This one is mine."

A god with a flaming blue head and hollow, deep-set eyes stepped forward. He smiled, revealing his razor-sharp teeth. "Hello, my little Meg-let. Glad you could make it."

"Hades," Meg whispered.

"In the flesh!" Hades bowed. "And hey, so are you. For the time being."

This shouldn't have been possible. She'd made a deal with the devil and he'd come to collect. Meg worried she was going to pass out. She was in the Underworld, and Aegeus was back on Earth dying. "Aegeus! Aegeus!" Meg shouted, feeling her way around the rock, looking for an opening so she could run straight for Cerberus and play her way out of there, except . . . she felt around, panicked.

The flute was not with her. She had left it behind with . . . "Aegeus!"

"He can't hear you down here. No one can." Hades folded his gray hands. "Well, except me, so can you cut it out? I'm not used to souls being all alive and stuff when they get here."

"That was your choice," croaked the one with the pointy nose.

"Who are you?" Meg cried.

"Meg, meet the Fates. Fates, meet Meg," Hades said. "She's going to be working for me for a while, as long as she behaves. Otherwise it's as they said." He made a cutting motion. "Snip, snip."

*The Fates.* Meg backed away again, her backside hitting cold rock. The Fates not only knew all, they *decided* all, and they were currently holding her life—literally—in their clawlike hands.

"But if you do as you promised, all will be fine, great, superb!" Hades said as he took Meg's string from them and pocketed it. The Fates shuffled out of the room. "Don't worry, Aegeus's thread stays intact." He clapped. "Yay! You got what you wanted. Your guy lives!"

Meg's heart was beating so fast she thought it would stop. "Aegeus is okay? He's going to live?"

"Yes, and so will you, technically and all that. It's kind

of a sticky situation." Hades waved his hand around and she noticed it turned into a stream of smoke. "Mortals aren't supposed to be in the Underworld. Against the rules and all that, which is why the Fates are all up in arms and eye and whatnot. But I can't do what I have to do on my own from down here." His eyes yellowed as he approached her. "I need someone up on Earth to do a bit of housekeeping, as it were. Big things are happening! Huge! It's exciting times down here in the Underworld!" He paused, staring at her expectantly. "Don't you want to know why?"

Meg met his gaze but said nothing. Her thoughts flew about wildly as she tried to comprehend what was happening. She was in the Underworld. She was in the Underworld. She was in the Underworld.

"Okay, okay, stop needling me for the dirt, you're embarrassing yourself. If you must know, I've got some business coming up with the Titans. They're making a comeback. *Hopefully.* And if all goes right, I'll be getting a promotion; we can save the details for later. The point is, I'm giving you a job!"

*Earth? Job?* "So I'm alive?" Meg repeated, unsure. *Aegeus. I have to get back to Aegeus.*

"Alive, yes. Can you see your guy at the moment? No." Hades's face darkened. "Your soul belongs to me, remember?"

Meg wiped the sweat from her brow. She was so hot she couldn't stand it. "But I'm alive, which means I can't *stay* here, right?"

Hades powered over to her in seconds in a haze and whispered in her ear. "Technically, if someone found out a mortal was here, things could get a bit dicey for me. But we're not going to tell anyone, are we?" His smile faded. "Wouldn't want anything to happen to Aegeus before you can repay your debt. That would be a real shame, especially after I just saved his life. So we're all copacetic. Anyway, I'm sending you topside to work, which means you will indeed get outta here."

*Topside? Earth? The land of the living? Aegeus?* Her next words tumbled out of her. "I'll do whatever you need to pay off my debt. Anything! I'll start right now. Please. I just want to go home." Meg hated how pathetic she sounded.

Hades looked at her. "Not that I don't admire the work ethic, but are you sure you even want to get back to this guy?" He whirled his hands around and shot smoke toward a fireplace she hadn't noticed in the corner. An image appeared in the sudden fire. "Looks like he's back on the market already."

"Aegeus!" Meg rushed toward the blue flames, then quickly took a few steps back as the heat sent a shock through her system. She stood, holding her arms, and found that through the flames she could see an image as clear as day. There was her love, rushing through the marketplace in their village. He looked well! A sob escaped her lips. Aegeus was all right. Hades had saved him! "Wait," Meg realized. "How can he be in the market? It's the middle of the night." She peered closer. "Is it daytime already?"

Hades shot smoke at the flames and the image disappeared. "Yep! Time travels fast down here. You want that boy to remember you, you better get a move on."

And so, Meg went to work for the god of the Underworld. The days marched on as she met with the nastiest of creatures all over Greece, creatures that usually never showed their faces in the light. She negotiated with river gods and harpies, a Nemean lion and a Minotaur, convincing them to join Hades in his quest to topple ol' Zeus, and she didn't feel bad about what she was doing. It wasn't Zeus who had come to her aid to save Aegeus; it was Hades. And besides, one more deed for the god down meant she was one step closer to returning to her old life, and to her love.

When she'd counted seven days in his service, Hades congratulated her.

"A week together, my little Nut-Meg," he'd said, throwing an arm around her. "And what a week it's been. You're good at your job, Meggie. You managed to get five new allies on our team this week."

"Yeah," Meg grumbled, turning away from him. "And I almost got eaten by one."

"The Minotaur? Nah. He's harmless. Just wanted to scare you. But, uh, you've performed far better than I thought you would, so I got you something." He reached behind his back, and through the smoke she saw something familiar floating toward her.

"My flute," Meg said in surprise, reaching out to grab the precious instrument. She clutched it to her chest and forced herself not to tear up. She wouldn't give Hades the satisfaction of knowing how much this meant to her. It would be just another thing for him to lord over her. "But how?"

Hades shrugged. "God of the Underworld, remember? I have my ways. I have to say, it's not much to look at, though. Rusty old thing."

Meg stared at it. "It holds a lot of memories."

"Of dear old Mommy, huh?" Hades asked.

Meg froze. She looked up at him, a wild idea popping into her mind, one she couldn't believe she hadn't thought of before. "Please . . ."

"Nope! Can't see her. Sorry. No good for her, and no good for you! I placed a veil as soon as you arrived so she wouldn't hear about your comings and goings." Meg started to protest, and Hades held up a long hand. "You have to concentrate, and Thea will just distract you. Besides, the residents would get twitchy if they knew there was a mortal staying among them. Unless . . ." He sidled up next to her. "If you wanted to stay for good. Then maybe I could arrange a reunion."

"No! You said once I paid my debt, I could blow this joint!" Meg's scowl returned, as it seemed to do more often than not in the Underworld. "Unless you want a certain someone to know I'm here," she threatened. "I haven't prayed to any gods as of late. . . ." That was about the only thing she could use against the guy.

"No, I know. I know. You want to get back to your love," he said, talking fast as he did. "You miss him. He misses you! Or at least he did . . . till he met *her*."

Meg whirled around fast, her heart almost leaping into her throat. "What her?"

"Oh, it's no big deal." Hades shrugged. "I shouldn't have even mentioned it. Hey, should we go over your schedule for tomorrow? I need you to go see a griffin."

"What. Her?" Meg repeated slowly and the god looked sheepish. "Hades!"

"Okay, okay. I wasn't going to say anything because I know you've been through hell and back—literally. Ha! But, uh, there's been a development with your boy." Hades motioned to the fire and a new image appeared. Meg walked over, flute in her hand.

Aegeus was standing near the ocean, his arms wrapped around a woman with long blond hair. She couldn't hear what he was saying, but they were talking closely as he nuzzled his cheek close to hers. The the woman planted a kiss on his lips.

Meg felt bile rise in her throat. "No. This is your trickery! Aegeus loves me! He was going to ask me to marry him before he became sick! You're just trying to make me crazy."

Hades looked forlorn. "Meg, I may be a lot of things—a bad guy, a cheat, a scoundrel, the leader of the Underworld—but what I'm not is a magician. This is real." He pointed to the blue flames again and Meg watched with despair as Aegeus lifted the woman in his arms and spun her around. The two of them were laughing. "I hate to tell you this, but the world is a cruel place. Didn't your mother ever tell you that?"

*Yes,* Meg thought miserably.

"You can't trust people, because they will always let you down. Aegeus has moved on, my little Nut-Meg. He's a guy. They can't stand being alone. It's in their nature."

In that moment, Meg knew Hades was right. This was no witchcraft. Aegeus didn't love her. If he had, he wouldn't have moved on to another woman a week after she'd sacrificed everything to save him. One *week*!

"Look, I know this hurts—you gave up your soul for the

guy, and this is how he repays you? Ouch! But this guy isn't worth it. You know it. I know it. Channel that anger into something we can work with and complete your sentence so you can get topside again. Isn't that what you want?"

*You gave up your soul for the guy.* Whatever hope she had left seemed to fade away like Hades's infamous smoke. "Who is she?" Meg whispered.

"Come on." Hades looked sad. "Does it matter?"

"Tell me her name!"

Hades sighed. "Katerina. Her name is Katerina."

*Katerina.* Meg looked down at the flute in her hands and squeezed it till her fingers almost bled. Her mother had been right. The only person she could rely on was herself. Love was for fools, and she had been played for one.

Meg felt a guttural sound emerge from her throat. She raised her hand and pitched the flute into the flames as Hades looked on in horror. Aegeus was dead to her.

It was time to get back to work.

Meg looked at Hades. "So tell me about that griffin."

# TEN: A Fateful Choice

## Back on Phil's island . . .

Meg knew one thing for certain: this quest was beyond cruel. It was vindictive.

Hera, it seemed, was poised to be the mother-in-law from hell.

*If* Meg even made it that far.

Athena and Phil stared at her, waiting for her to say something.

*Do I go to the Underworld to save the soul of the woman Aegeus left me for? Or do I refuse Hera and make an enemy of one of the most powerful gods on Mount Olympus? Great options here.*

"You okay there, Red?" Phil asked, looking worried.

Athena continued to stare at her. No doubt she would

report everything back to Hera. Meg could just picture the gods sitting around on a cloud laughing over her predicament. "The mortal will never survive!" they'd say. "You're so clever, Hera!"

Well, she wouldn't give them that satisfaction.

Meg had two options, and while neither sounded particularly appealing, the thought of backing down from the quest left a bad taste in her mouth. She might have been a lot of things, but she was not a coward. She thought back to something Hercules had said to her a few months earlier when they'd stolen away—her to secretly do Hades's bidding and get close to the would-be god; him from Phil.

"You know what I love about you, Meg?" Hercules had said. "You're not a quitter."

They'd been lying on a cliff overlooking the ocean for what turned out to be hours. Speaking earnestly with this sweet boy, getting caught up in his observations—she was breaking rules all over the place, but for the first time in a long time, she didn't care. There was something about this Wonder Boy, as she had grown fond of calling him, that drew her to him like a moth to a hunky flame.

"What makes you think that? You hardly know me."

He brushed a piece of hair out of her eyes. "You could have let me use my strength to get you out of that mess with

Nessus," he said, referring to the river god through whom they'd met. "But you wanted to fight your way out instead."

"I recall you calling me ma'am," she said pointedly, and his ears turned bright pink. "But you're right. I had things handled till you came along. I like a challenge."

"It's more than that, Meg," Hercules said softly. "It's the way you talk, move, act. You're a go-getter; you won't take no for an answer. Sometimes I think I need to be more like you."

Meg felt a twinge of guilt. If Hercules knew who she was working for, he'd feel differently.

Now, standing in front of Athena, Meg recalled Hercules's words in a different light. He'd said he wanted to be more like her. Did that mean she was worthy of being a god, too?

Could be.

Maybe this was her chance to finally figure out what to do with her life. She'd lost her mother, had lost Aegeus, had given up her soul, had been through hell and back . . . and yet she was still breathing. And now Hera was giving her yet another chance. She might have been less than thrilled at the idea of helping Katerina and Aegeus, but she still wanted to prove she could take whatever the gods threw at her. This quest was about more than just having an opportunity to be with Hercules. It was about proving to herself that she was strong enough to face a challenge as daunting as this one through to the end. And to see what she could become on the other side of it.

Meg could feel a new sensation coursing through her veins, one she hadn't felt in a while: determination. "Tell Hera I'll do it," she said to Athena as Phil gaped at her in surprise.

"She'd expect nothing less," Athena said simply.

"But I have a question first," Meg said. "What is it about Katerina that makes her worthy of another spin around the Earth?"

"Um, Red . . . people don't usually get to ask the gods those kind of things," Phil whispered, a bleat escaping his lips before he could stop it.

Just the sound of Katerina's name on her tongue made Meg taste bile. She might have moved on to a new and better (if complicated) relationship, but whenever Meg pictured the woman with her milky white skin, wispy blond hair, and tiny laugh, her gut still ached at the injustice of it all. "I feel like I have the right to know," Meg said, looking at Athena. "I gave up my soul for a man, which I'll admit was a dumb move. But then he fell for this woman in less time than the sun revolves around the Earth. And Hera wants me to save her? Why?"

Athena moved toward Meg, standing so close that their

noses were almost touching. Power radiated off her. "Listen to the satyr. You, mortal, have no right to ask such questions of a god," she said, her voice low and pulsing with anger.

Meg tried not to look afraid. She held her breath.

Athena's face softened ever so slightly. "But considering how you found my flute, I will forgive this one transgression. I suggest you focus on your journey. The Underworld is a large place and you don't have much time."

Meg sighed. Even if she *wanted* to save Katerina, the sheer vastness of the Underworld was a problem. It was made up of three realms, with most people resting in the vast Asphodel Meadows. The worst of the worst were in Tartarus, and the most revered were in Elysium. There was no way Katerina was living in paradise, which meant she was in one of the other two places; and they were tricky to navigate, even with a guide.

Plus, there were, of course, the relevant rules of the Underworld—that mortals couldn't enter or leave, and that Hades never gave up souls once they were there. Meg's debt to the god seemed to be a gray area that had made her exempt at the time, but Katerina was already deceased. Getting her out and back to the land of the living was impossible. Plus, Meg was supposed to pull it off on a deadline.

"How am I supposed to find someone I've never met?" Meg asked, changing tack.

"You will start your journey by visiting Aegeus and learning all you can about his wife," Athena replied.

*His wife.* Meg tried to brush aside a sudden chill. So the two of them had gotten married. And now she not only had to confront Aegeus, she needed to listen to him gush about Katerina, his *wife*? This seemed unusually cruel.

"You will find him in Athens near a bluff much like this one. He lives on a road anchored by an olive grove, in a humble home near the sea."

"I know the place," Meg said. The olive grove had been her and Aegeus's favorite spot in Athens. They would sit at the top of the bluff and play music and talk about the house they'd one day build there together—the one that would replace the tiny home they shared at the bottom of the hill.

"Well, now that we all know what Red here has got to do, I guess I'll be getting back to my retirement. Good luck, kid." Phil started to scoot backward toward his house.

Athena shifted her gaze, glaring while her owl hooted. "Where do you think you're going, satyr?"

Phil stopped, balancing on one hind leg. "You don't expect me to go on this quest with her, do you?" Athena didn't answer. He laughed nervously and a bleat came out. "You might have heard I've done a lot for Mount Olympus already and am now just trying to enjoy my retirement."

Meg moaned. Phil was the least of her problems. "Fine

by me! Go! I don't need you anyway. We're not exactly the closest of friends," she told Athena, who looked mildly amused. "If you'd just tell me how to get to the entrance of the Underworld, I'm sure I can get there on my own."

Phil bleated. "Oh, yeah, sure. Like you took care of that Empusa on your own."

"I did take care of the Empusa!" Meg snapped.

"You barely survived. And *I* healed your injuries," Phil said, eyeing Athena.

"Why, you arrogant little goat boy!" Meg seethed.

Phil turned bright red. "Did you just call me a goat boy? Why, I . . ."

"Stop!" Athena thundered, and they did as they were told. "Philoctetes, you are skilled in helping heroes on their journeys, so you *will* take Megara to the entrance of the Underworld via the river Acheron. Once you reach the river Styx, Charon will take Megara from the land of the living to the land of the dead. That is an order."

Phil's face drooped. "But . . ."

Athena lifted her chin. "You will leave this island together at dawn."

"Dawn? You expect me to help this one find the Underworld when she has no previous experience with quests or fighting monsters?" Phil's face was scrunched.

Athena didn't blink. "Yes."

"We're doomed," Phil said.

"Great," Meg said under her breath at the same time.

Athena strode forward, stopping to move a broken statue with her foot. "I suggest you both thank the gods for your gifts and fill your bodies with nourishment. Gather your supplies. Learn what you can from one another. This journey will not be easy."

"Tell me about it!" Phil scratched his chest and sighed. "I guess I'll start dinner." He pushed his way past some of the goats. "Coming through."

"Maybe I should help him," Meg suggested.

"No," Athena replied, surprising her. "Let us walk."

Meg stared at the god, who had turned and started heading toward the edge of the island. She quickly followed. When they reached a bluff overlooking the water, Athena stopped, holding out the double reed flute. "Play it for me."

Meg stared at the flute warily, its brass gleaming in the fading light of day. She had no desire to touch it, but was not about to further insult the god by refusing. She took the instrument from Athena's outstretched hands and felt the weight of it. Her flute was a piece of art, so carefully crafted, so different from the rusty one Meg had owned. And yet its notes would, in theory, be the same. Meg just didn't want to hear them.

"Is something the matter?" Athena asked.

"No," Meg said quickly, but the truth was she was afraid that the mere act of returning to this instrument would fill her with an aching sadness for the life she had once traded. But she couldn't deny Athena. She took a deep breath, then placed her mouth over the double opening of the reeds. Closing her eyes, she started with the first few notes of a familiar song almost instinctually—"The Plight of the Lily." The sound that emitted from the pipe was different from the one she was used to, but that seemed to be a good thing. It helped her separate the tune from her memories. When she was finished, she was relieved to hand the flute back to Athena.

Athena clapped, the wind blowing through her glowing hair. "Brava, Megara. You didn't miss a single note. And yet, I still can't help thinking something was missing from your performance."

"I'm sorry?" Meg faltered.

"Don't get me wrong. You are clearly a strong musician, child. One the Muses would be proud of, to be sure. But a true artist *feels* their notes in their soul." She looked at Meg. "You clearly have lost that desire along the way. You do not play as you once did."

Meg frowned, understanding dawning on her. "You've heard me play before?"

Athena smiled wanly. "At a concert in Athens. When true musicians play in honor of their gods, we come to listen from time to time. You were superb that night. Such a shame how lost you have become."

Meg felt her cheeks color. "Perhaps it is because this is not my flute. I'm used to my own."

Athena turned toward her. "And where is that one?"

Meg avoided eye contact. "In the Underworld." It was a half-truth, at least.

"I see." Athena turned away for a moment and looked out over the darkened sea. "Then you will take mine with you on your journey." She held the flute out to Meg again.

"I couldn't," Meg said. She didn't want to be responsible for the god's instrument, and all this talk about music had made her even warier. She had no interest in playing it again. "You've been without it for so long."

Athena smiled. "I suspect it will find its way back to me in the future. But for now, it will aid you more than it does me." She turned her head to the side. "Besides, I rather don't like to play the thing myself. It contorts my face in a way that is less than appealing."

Athena held the flute out to her again and this time Meg took it, knowing it was pointless to argue. "Thank you," she said. "I will care for it as if it is my own."

"I can see the thickness to your skin, Megara. You are tough. Courageous. Proud. I will assist you however I can."

Meg had heard tales of Athena helping those on heroic endeavors, but she'd never imagined she'd be worthy of such a thing. *"Thank you,"* she said again, with more feeling.

"But you must promise to open your mind and listen," Athena went on. "That is the best advice I can give you. You can complete your task if *you* believe you can. Don't fall victim to distractions."

Meg nodded. Athena sounded like her mother. The only person she would be able to rely on in the Underworld was herself. "Got it."

"Sometimes your head will lead, and other times it will be your heart."

An image of Hercules popped into Meg's head, her hand instinctively going to the satchel where the orchid was safely tucked away.

"Remember, the sands of time cannot be stopped," Athena warned, her voice deeper than it was before. "If you lose your way, you'll never see the light of day again."

Meg wrapped her burned arms around her chest. The wind seemed to pick up as night took hold, sending another chill through her. "Understood."

"You must ask Aegeus about Katerina," Athena insisted, and Meg felt her stomach begin to churn again. "What he knows about this woman could be the key to saving both your futures, Megara. Good luck." She squeezed her hands. "I'll be watching."

And then Athena faded away as the sun began to sink into the sea.

# ELEVEN: Home Sweet Home

Meg found the ride to Athens with Phil and Pegasus uneventful. They hardly spoke, and Meg wasn't sure if that was because neither was thrilled to be together or because the howling wind made it too hard to hear anything but the whistling past their ears.

Besides, it was difficult enough to focus on not falling off the flying horse. As Peg soared over Athens, the vastness of the city rose up to greet them, homes and temples dotting the landscape like trees. How had she never realized how large this city was? Athens was the last place she had called home . . . thanks to Aegeus.

"If we want to truly make music worthy of the Muses, we have to go where the action is—and the action is in Athens," he'd told her one night after they'd raked in a few measly coins for a performance in a little village.

"I don't know." Meg had hesitated. Her mother had never been a fan of being boxed into a big city. "Athens is so vast."

"Come on, Meg." Aegeus put his arm around her. "Would I ever steer you wrong?"

*Not sure,* she thought. *Would you?* There was so much she wanted to ask him, but sometimes the hard questions, the ones her mother had always warned her about, felt like marbles in her mouth.

"I love you, and I want a new life for us," he said, touching her cheek.

"Me, too." He'd already hinted at marriage. Starting their new life in a big city could be just the change she needed to finally rid herself of the ghosts of the past and move on with her life.

Meg looked around the square of the small village she'd been living in since she met Aegeus. There was the butcher arguing with Mr. Kostas over the price of meat again. Two doors down, the usual group of women watched their small boys play in a fountain. If she walked a few steps farther she knew she'd find the beggar outside the agora, where all the merchants were set up with their linens, spices from Syria, and dates. The crier would be shouting about the fresh fish that had arrived that day, and Mrs. Aikos would be trying to sneak all the samples she could before having to pay for her fruit. Meg knew the market so well she could navigate the area blindfolded. She'd lived longer in this village than she had lived anywhere since her mother died.

So much of her past she kept locked away in a part of her heart that she didn't share with anyone. Aegeus knew her mother had died when she was young, but he didn't know the details. It wasn't as if she thought Aegeus would look down on her. His life had just been markedly different from hers. Yes, he lived on his own, but it was because he wanted to, not because he had no one. Somewhere out there, Aegeus still had a mother and a father that he sent money to when he could. He talked often about his brothers and sisters and how he hoped they could visit someday. Aegeus had many lifelines, while he was Meg's only one. Maybe there was still a part of her that feared telling him too much could scare him away.

"You think we'll stand out in a place with so many people?" Meg had asked him.

Aegeus spun her around. "How could anyone not notice you, my love? You're extraordinary, and in Athens, you'll be a muse to the finest scholars! Not just Mr. Kostas."

Aegeus put her down and Meg looked at Mr. Kostas, still arguing with the butcher. "You've got a point there."

"So?" Aegeus's face was so eager his smile practically overtook his face. "Shall we start our new lives together in Athens?"

*Our new lives together.* It sounded so appealing, Meg pushed her mother's voice out of her head. She was making the decision to be with this man. She would still look out for herself, but now she could look out for both of them. "Yes," Meg said. "Let's move to Athens!"

Aegeus had hollered so loud the butcher and Mr. Kostas stopped arguing. They were so absurdly happy.

What a fool she'd been.

Meg felt Phil's elbow nudge her. "Hey! Red! Where are we landing?"

Meg touched her stomach, which was still sore from the Empusa injuries. "I could do without you punching me in the ribs every time you want to ask a question, Phil."

"Sorry! You see Aegeus's place anywhere?" he shouted over the wind.

"Peg!" Meg tapped the horse's side with her right leg. "Can you bring us in closer so I can look around for a landmark?"

Peg neighed and swooped down through a cloud, bringing them low enough that Meg could finally get a clear view of the city and the water beyond it. She and Aegeus hadn't had enough money to move into the heart of the city, so they had lived on the outskirts, using their funds to buy a small piece of land on a bluff. As Peg flew over the Apollo coast, Meg spotted the grove.

"That's it! Peg, land near those olive trees!" Meg shouted.

The home should have been at the base of the grove, but as Peg flew closer, all Meg saw was rushing water at the bottom of the hill. *How strange,* she thought. *Where is our house?* Meg searched the area and spotted a larger home she'd never seen before. Her heart gave a lurch. Aegeus had built their dream home for Katerina.

Peg came in for a landing on the cliff near the front steps. Meg helped Phil down, then lowered herself.

"Okay, listen up, Red. You need to approach this reunion a certain way," Phil said as he rushed to give Peg water and unload some bags. "Don't scare this guy off."

Meg was only half listening. All she could do was stare at the house she and Aegeus had talked about building. The single-story clay home had the long porch she'd so badly wanted, and several windows that opened up to the sea to let in the salty air. He'd built this home to her exact specifications. Aegeus had traded in their dream for one with Katerina. And though this was no longer her dream, it still stung.

"Hey, Phil?" Meg said suddenly. "Do you think this woman is worth saving?"

Phil shrugged. "What do I know? Never met her. The gods seem to like her, though."

"Unlike me," Meg said, "who no one noticed was missing from the world. No one fought for *my* soul."

"Hercules did," Phil reminded her. "He saw something in you I sure didn't. Maybe you need to do the same with Katerina." Meg couldn't help making a face. "Look, this conversation with Aegeus is going to be no picnic. But who cares that he dumped you for another woman?" Phil wagged a hoof at her. "You're working on becoming a god now! Use him to find out what you need to know and we'll be on our way."

Meg stared at the front door warily. Maybe Aegeus wasn't even home and they'd have to come back.

Phil crossed his arms. "We haven't got all day."

"I'm going." Meg strode toward the door, leaving Phil and Peg on the grass behind her. She pushed her bangs out of her eyes and adjusted the waistband on her dress. Her arms, while still bandaged, hurt less than they had the day before. She was growing stronger. She *was* strong. She was Megara. Someone Hera thought could be a god. She could have one little conversation with a spineless former flame. Meg reached the door and knocked.

"Is there someone at the door?"

It was Aegeus's voice. Her heart started to beat faster.

"Coming! We never get visitors! Who could it be?"

Who was he talking to in such a lighthearted manner? Katerina was in the Underworld. Meg's face began to burn. Had Aegeus moved on to another already? Unbelievable! Meg tried to stop herself, but she could feel her right arm pulling back and a fist begin to form.

"Red? What are you doing?" Phil called. "Red?"

Meg felt her heart speed up as she heard the door handle turn. The door creaked open. She had visions of her fist connecting with Aegeus's lying, cheating, unfaithful chiseled face. She lifted her hand as the door swung open.

It was Aegeus. "Me—Me—Megara?" The color faded from his face.

"Aegeus?" Meg's voice shook. Her hand fell to her side in shock. There was something rather large lying in Aegeus's arms.

It was a baby girl, no more than a few months old, her face round and chubby with eyes big and dark like Aegeus's. She had rolls on her legs and thighs and a tuft of blond curls on her head. She took one look at Meg and burst into tears.

Meg understood the feeling. She wanted to cry herself, but she wouldn't.

Instead, Aegeus did it for her.

# TWELVE: Hard Truths

"What did you say to him?" Phil came up behind her. "I told you to be nice!"

"Not a word," Meg insisted.

Phil covered his pointed ears with his hands as the baby's wail reached a fever pitch. That only made Aegeus cry harder. "Well, make it stop already. It's giving me a headache."

"You think I know how to make a baby stop crying? I know nothing about babies!"

"Well, you know him! Make him stop it!" Phil motioned to Aegeus, who had tears streaming down his face, his sobs so heavy his whole body was shaking.

Now she was worried he was going to drop the thing—baby—child. There was really no time for such added bumps in the road. "Aegeus?" Meg tried, but he kept crying, holding the baby to his chest as they both heaved great sobs. "Aegeus?"

He leaned back against the doorway and closed his eyes, crying harder. "Why, my gods? Why?" he railed to the heavens, and his arms looked like they might drop.

Meg swooped in and snatched the child from him just as Aegeus collapsed against the doorframe. The baby registered that Meg was holding it and started to scream louder. Meg held it under the armpits as if it might bite her.

She'd never held a baby before in her life. Aegeus had talked about his siblings' children and how much he wanted kids of his own, but truthfully, Meg had never felt that pull. Her mother's life had been hard and having a kid to provide for had made it even harder. Her own circumstances hadn't been much better. Even when she met Aegeus, they had gotten by, but they weren't wealthy by any means. She couldn't imagine bringing a kid into the mix. And now, here she was, holding Aegeus's baby in her arms—his, and, of course, Katerina's.

The child had her light hair and his eyes. As much as Meg had tried to deny it at the time, Hades had been right—Aegeus didn't love her. He hadn't mourned for her. He had moved on immediately and created a family with Katerina, forgetting she had even existed.

The truth felt as painful as the wounds still healing on both her legs. She wanted to wish the pain away, but it was currently in her arms, screaming. Could she put the baby down somewhere? Why was it crying so hard? How did she make it stop? Now its tears were plopping onto her arms. Her whole body felt numb.

Phil reached up. "Give the kid to me."

"Gladly." Meg handed Phil the baby and he cradled it in his arms, making a shushing sound as he rocked it back and forth. Amazingly, the child stopped wailing. The baby started to close its eyes, still sniffling as it was being rocked asleep. Phil marched past the sobbing Aegeus into the house. Aegeus and Meg followed.

"My child," Aegeus said through his sobs.

"Relax, Papa," Phil told him. "I have no interest in taking the kid. I just want it to be quiet. This baby needs a nap! Ah, here's what we need right now." Phil spotted a small wooden crib near the window and laid the child in it. Then he gave the cradle a rock for good measure. He looked at Aegeus. "Now you two can talk in peace."

"I need air," Aegeus said, wiping his eyes as he walked back to his front door.

Meg marveled at Phil. "How did you do that?"

"Satyr. We've got the magic touch. I was the oldest of

four; I looked after the little ones," Phil said proudly. "I've always loved babies."

Meg thought they seemed like a lot of work. "I was an only child," she said. "I looked after myself."

"Well, now you need to worry about that one." Phil motioned to Aegeus, who was walking ahead. "Go talk to him! And do it quietly so he doesn't wake the kid!"

Meg sighed and followed Aegeus out the door, watching as he moved through the gardens near the house. How was she going to get through this conversation when all she wanted to do was wring his neck?

"Aegeus?" she said as calmly as she could muster. "I need to talk to you."

"My child," he started to say, looking back at the house.

"The baby is safe with Phil," Meg said dismissively. "He's practically a nursemaid."

Her response only made Aegeus cry again. She, on the other hand, found herself growing angrier. How dare he weep at the sight of her? He was the one who had betrayed *her*, who'd repaid her biggest sacrifice for him by starting a family with another. She thought of her mother's words: *Trust yourself.* Perhaps if she had done more of that, she wouldn't be in this ridiculous mess in the first place; she would be asking some random man about his lost wife to complete Hera's quest. In any case, she would not allow him to waste the little time she had with false tears.

"Enough is enough," Meg said under her breath, spinning him around by the front of his chiton. "Aegeus! Stop it at once!" she shouted. As soon as they made eye contact, he rubbed the wetness from his eyes.

"How is this possible?" he asked, sounding shaken. "I'd say you were a ghost, but you arrived with a satyr and a winged horse. Am I dreaming this, Megara, or have you come back from the dead?"

"I'm alive," she said stonily. "No thanks to you."

Aegeus threw his hands in the air. "Thank the gods! The sacrifices and prayers I made have finally been answered! You are okay." He reached out to touch her face and she stepped back.

"What do you think you're doing?" Meg asked, outraged.

Aegeus shook his head, his eyes still brimming. "I'm sorry. I never thought I'd ever see your face again. I can't believe you've been returned to us after all this time!"

*Us?* Did he mean him and his *wife*, Katerina? What was Aegeus playing at? She knew Phil would tell her to stick to the script and get the goods on Katerina, but she couldn't help herself.

"Returned? Don't act as if you're happy that I've come

back. You *abandoned* me!" Meg shouted, and Aegeus winced. "The moment I was gone you moved on and got yourself a wife!" Aegeus flattened himself against an olive tree as if pushed by the force of her words. "I made a deal with Hades to save your life. You didn't wonder where I'd gone when you were suddenly well enough to rise from bed? You just followed the next woman who crossed your path? I gave up my soul for you!"

"What?" Aegeus gaped. "Meg, I—"

"And the moment I was out of the picture, you married Katerina!" Meg spat. "So much for wanting to spend your life with me. I saw it with my own eyes! Hades showed me everything!"

"Hades?" He shook his head once more and let out an anguished cry. "I don't understand."

She wouldn't be swayed by his pain. She had enough of her own to last three lifetimes. He needed to know how much he'd hurt her. She had given up everything for him. What a fool she'd been.

"And now to find you in our dream home with a child?" Meg felt hot tears touch her cheeks. "This was supposed to be *ours*! I saved every coin I had to help you buy wood and materials for this place! And the minute I was gone you went and built it for your new love? You aren't worth the dirt beneath my sandals."

"No, Meg! Please! Just listen to me," Aegeus begged. He reached for her hands, but again she pulled away.

"Why should I?" Meg snarled. "So that you can spin more lies? I'm the one doing the talking now." Meg paused, realizing she was doing the very thing Athena had warned her against—getting distracted. She took a breath, focusing. "Look, I am only here for one reason—for myself. I need you to tell me all you know about Katerina." It sounded ridiculous, even to her, but now that the true purpose of her visit was out in the open, she crossed her arms, waiting. The sooner she could get this over with, the better.

Aegeus's eyes widened. "Katerina? How do you know my wife?"

"She's the reason I'm here." Meg stood a bit taller. "Hera has sent me on a quest to retrieve her soul from the Underworld."

"You're going to bring her back?" Aegeus put his head in his hands and sobbed even harder.

She couldn't take this crying, the reminiscing, the painful reminders of her old life. She was clearly getting nowhere with Aegeus, and had no desire to comfort him. This sort of thing wasn't her bag.

She needed to think.

Before she knew it, she was racing out of the garden.

She heard Phil calling her, but she didn't care. She whistled for Pegasus and the horse landed at her side.

"Get me out of here," Meg said, climbing onto his back and taking off into the sky. She didn't look back.

# THIRTEEN: I Won't Say

Meg took a deep breath and inhaled the salty air as they took flight, letting it fill her lungs. The sound of the wind helped her heart slow, and for the first time she could remember, she wasn't squeezing Pegasus's neck. *Maybe this flying thing isn't so bad after all,* she thought. *Maybe I just needed to be in a panicked rage to enjoy it.* Of course, Meg was not about to look down, but she certainly felt calmer and more in control than she had on the ground. The farther they flew away from Aegeus and her old life on that cliff, the more she felt something else: freedom. With Pegasus, she could go anywhere her heart desired and no one could follow. Meg felt a primal roar rise up from inside her.

"YESSSSSS!" she shouted into the clouds.

Peg neighed nervously.

"I'm fine!" Meg patted his mane. "Better than fine!" She started to laugh. She'd never felt more free. She could kind of see why Hercules liked riding Pegasus.

*Hercules.* Her hand went to the satchel and the orchid tucked inside it. *It would be nice to hear his voice right about now,* she thought. *He is so much better at tapping into emotions than I am.* Maybe he'd know how to handle the conversation she still had to finish with Aegeus.

"Peg, can you land somewhere Phil and Aegeus can't find us?" The horse neighed again. "Not for good," she clarified. "Just so I can take a breath. All this feelings stuff is exhausting."

Pegasus seemed to understand, because he came in for a landing in a meadow blooming with hyacinth, orchids, and myriad other colorful blooms. The meadow was gorgeous and completely private. She didn't see another soul around. Carefully, Meg removed her orchid and held it up to the sun.

"Ready to see your friend?" she asked Peg, and he launched back on his hind legs in excitement. "Here goes nothing." Meg ripped the petal in half and watched as it blew away.

Seconds later, she saw a bright flash. She shielded her

eyes as a glowing ball started to form in the air. In a moment, Hercules was standing in front of her.

"Meg!" He ran to her, scooping her up in his arms and swinging her around before pulling her in for a kiss. "Are you all right? What's happened? Do you need my help?" He put her down and pulled out his sword in one swift move, his face darkening as he spun around.

She couldn't help laughing. "I don't *need* anything." The lug was cute when he was in protective mode. It suddenly struck her that she'd not even thought to call upon him during her battle with the Empusa. "Well, that's not exactly true. I could use your advice." She touched his blond curls. "Plus, I just wanted to see you. Is that enough of a reason to call?"

"More than enough!" He pulled her into his arms again. "I've missed you."

"I've missed you, too." She sank into his large glowing arms. She was still getting used to his being a god. They stood there for a moment, listening to the sound of the flowers rustling in the breeze and each other's hearts. Then she heard a neigh.

Hercules turned around. "Pegasus?" Peg jumped around. "Hi, boy! Have you been taking good care of Meg?" He patted the horse's side and saw the healing scar. "Whoa, what happened to you?" He noticed the bandage on Meg's arm. "And you!"

"You've missed a few things while you've been upstairs," she said, nodding to the heavens before quickly filling him in on their fight with the Empusa, finding Phil, meeting Athena, and her insistence that Meg talk to Aegeus. It was draining, rehashing it all. Maybe that's why she left the most important part of the story out.

"Meg . . . wow, I'm so sorry you had to go through all that alone." He held her even tighter. "Seeing Aegeus must have been rough."

"Brutal." She buried her head in his chest and wished she could just forget about the whole journey.

"Why did Athena want you to talk to him, anyway?" Hercules pressed. "Does he have anything to do with the rest of your quest? Which is what, actually? You never said what Athena told you my mother wants you to do now that you've found Athena's flute."

Meg sighed. There was no prolonging the inevitable. "You might want to take a seat for this next part." She patted the lush grass beneath their feet and Hercules looked worried as he settled in next to her. Meg sat up straighter. She wanted to appear strong. She *was* strong. Still, her lower lip trembled. "I am supposed to retrieve a soul from the Underworld—the soul of Aegeus's wife, Katerina, to be exact."

Hercules jumped up. "Meg, no, she can't make you go back there!" He tumbled over his own words. "Hades won't let you go again! It's impossible! And to save your former flame's new wife? That's mad!" Meg felt her heart warm. He really was something—immediately taking her side, not showing a shred of jealousy, even when they were talking about her ex. Then Hercules started to stride away. "I need to talk to my mother."

"No!" Meg grabbed his hand and pulled him back down. "You know you can't do that. This deal is between me and her, and besides, I'm not telling you all this so you can try to sweet-talk her on my behalf. I think I just needed to hear myself say the plan out loud." She snuck a glance at him. "It's as bad as it sounds, though, isn't it?"

Hercules didn't speak right away. "It's . . . well . . . it's not easy, but this is *you* we're talking about. You can do anything you set your mind to. I'll help you any way I can. Just say the word."

This was why she liked this boy—er, *god*. She squeezed his hand. "Thanks."

He leaned in and kissed her softly. "So what's your next move?" he asked, his lips still close to hers. "Did you talk to Aegeus about Katerina? Maybe he can tell you a bit about her that would be helpful in tracking her down in the Underworld. It's kind of a large place."

"Oh, I remember." She plucked a poppy growing near their feet. "I tried to talk to Aegeus, but our conversation didn't go well." She looked at Hercules. "I kind of bit his head off." Hercules's eyes widened. "I know! You don't have to say it. I need his help. But just seeing his stupid face again got me so fired up! You don't know what it's like to stand in front of someone you thought you loved who betrayed you. . . ." Her voice died out and they looked at one another. Hercules couldn't help a small smirk. Her cheeks began to burn. "Okay, I'm going to eat my own words now. It was just hard, okay?" She ripped the poppy into pieces that blew away in the wind.

"Of course it was," he said gently. "But you still have to face him if you want to learn about Katerina. And who knows? Maybe he'll surprise you." He touched her hand. "People can do that, you know."

Wonder Boy really was too good for this world. "True. But I'm not holding out hope for Aegeus. I was gone one measly week when he recovered from his illness, met Katerina, and completely forgot I existed."

"A week? How is that possible?" Hercules plucked a new poppy and held it out to her. "I can't imagine anyone forgetting someone like you, especially not in a week."

"You should see him now," she grumbled. "He's married with a kid and everything." She looked at him. "Not that I want those things with him, of course. It just sort of, well, *stings*."

But Hercules seemed distracted. "A week . . ." he whispered to himself, shaking his head. "It doesn't make sense." Meg looked at him. "I'm not defending the guy or anything, but a *week*? Meg, are you sure?"

"Yes!" She took her anger out on the flower again, ripping apart its petals as well. "Hades showed me them together seven days after I got to the Underworld. After that, he'd make me watch scenes of Aegeus and Katerina together at night, like it was some sort of performance."

Hercules sat up straighter. "Hades did that?" He looked out across the meadow. "Huh."

Meg sat up taller too. "What do you mean, 'Huh'?"

"I just mean, you believe him? It is Hades, after all, and he is the god of the Underworld. He's played some pretty dirty tricks on both of us. What if he was lying?"

"Lying?" Meg dropped the flower stem. "But he *showed* me them getting close, falling for one another. And they did end up getting married."

Hercules nodded. "I'm not saying they didn't end up together, but Hades has his ways of distorting the truth.

If you had to pick one person to trust, would it be him or Aegeus?"

"Neither!" Meg said, but she knew he was right. She hadn't even really questioned the tricky god of the Underworld. She threw herself back on the grass and looked up at the clouds in the sky and groaned. "My gods. Now I don't know what to think. Also, I pretty much just ripped Aegeus's head off. Like clear off, as if he were Medusa and I had a sharp blade."

Hercules lay down next to her. "I'm just saying, give Aegeus a chance to explain. Like I gave *you*." He squeezed her hand and she laughed.

"Okay, yes, you've made your point. I'll talk to Aegeus again." She ruffled his hair. "Thanks for the pep talk. This is why I keep you around," she teased.

He leaned his chin on her hand. "I'm glad you do. And just think: when you finish this quest, we get to be together for eternity."

Meg's smile fell slightly. There was that word again: eternity. That was a *long* time. But, she reminded herself, there was still a quest and a week left before she had to think about it. One thing at a time. "I'm glad you're here."

"Me, too." He kissed her again. "I know this task isn't as fun as mine was—beating up monsters and all that. But my mother must trust you if she gave you a quest as major as this one. There's a reason she wants you to save Katerina. The gods don't tell us everything. Or at least, that's what they're telling me in my Olympus training classes." He rolled his eyes. "There are so many dos and don'ts and rules to this god thing. I had no idea."

Meg put a hand to his lips. "Wait. Back up. What did you say about a reason?"

"You mean, the 'the gods must have their reason' part?" Hercules repeated.

"Yes!" Meg tapped her chin. "They must need Katerina for something. Do you know why?" He hesitated. "You *do* know!" She waved a finger at him. "Tell me!"

"All I know is what I overheard my mother telling Athena," Hercules admitted. "They mentioned the name Katerina the other day after you left. It sounds like she's important, but I'm not sure why. All I know is Father feels guilty about her death. I don't think they intended for it to happen. Mother said something about a flood."

Meg thought for a moment. "Flood, huh? Gods know, Greece has had a lot of those."

"Maybe that's how you handle helping Aegeus's wife," he suggested. "Keep thinking about how she wasn't meant to die."

"True." Meg ran a hand through her red hair and thought of that wailing baby. She was so young to be without her mother. Even younger than Meg was when she had lost hers. She closed her eyes and let the sun warm her face, then opened her eyes to look at him for as long as she could. A field of hyacinths swayed behind him. "I wish I could live here in this meadow. It's gorgeous."

"Yeah, it is," Hercules agreed. "That's Persephone's handiwork," he explained. "She's the god of vegetation."

"Demeter's daughter, right?" Meg said. "I heard Demeter talking when I was on Olympus. Something about not knowing where the girl had run off to."

Hercules nodded. "Yeah, Demeter keeps appealing to my father to find her. No one has seen her in months, and harvest will be coming before long." He touched one of the hyacinths with his finger. "Every flower has its season."

Suddenly Meg heard the distinctive chime of bells. She looked at Hercules.

He smiled sheepishly. "Uh . . . they're ringing for me upstairs."

*Poof!* Hermes popped up in front of them carrying a clipboard and a writing utensil. He stared at Hercules over the top of his glasses as his winged hat fluttered fast. "Hercules, your father wants you home immediately. Helios is threatening to walk off the job and refuses to race his chariot across the sky tomorrow. Something about lack of vacation time. Zeus wants you there to facilitate the argument."

"Okay, I'm coming. Let me just say goodbye to Meg." Wonder Boy turned to look at her. "Are you okay getting back on your own?"

"Of course," she said, sitting up and wrapping her arms around him one more time. "I should get back, too."

Hercules leaned in for one more kiss as his whole body started to waver. "Be safe, Meg! I love—" He disappeared before he could finish the sentence.

# FOURTEEN: Ugly Truths

Pegasus and Meg landed softly outside Aegeus's house as night began to fall. There seemed to be a fire glowing behind the house, creating shadows along the ground, but all was quiet except for the sound of the ocean in the distance. She'd been gone longer than she intended, but she felt much more prepared now. *Time to face the music,* she thought as she patted Pegasus and headed to the door. Before she could knock, she felt a tug on her skirt. She turned to find Phil holding a hand up.

"You stay right there!" he hissed.

"Phil, I—" Meg started.

"Shhh!" Phil shushed her. "Cassia is asleep!"

"Cassia?"

Phil rolled his eyes. "The baby? Took me an hour to get her to nod off." He grabbed her by the arm. "We're sitting out back so we don't wake her. Come on. You two still need to talk."

"I know," Meg said with a sigh.

"You don't have the whole story, okay?"

"I am starting to see that," Meg told him.

"Now don't clobber me for saying this, but Aegeus seems like a good guy, and that baby . . ." Phil got a goofy look on his face. "She's a cutie." His face hardened again. "I think you have to put your history aside and help the kid."

"That's why I'm back, Phil—to talk to Aegeus. Alone."

"Finally! Go, and make it snappy, okay? You only have seven days left."

"No need to remind me."

Phil motioned to the garden, where Aegeus was sitting on a log, staring into the flames. Meg hesitated. "What are you waiting for? Talk to the guy."

Meg cocked her head to one side. "Were you this bossy with Hercules?"

"Worse," Phil said. "Go! I need to wash a few of Cassia's things and clean up inside. That kid can make a real mess." Phil shook his head, a little grin playing on his lips, and walked off.

Squaring her shoulders, Meg walked toward the garden.

A soft hum of music reached her ears and she realized Aegeus had his lute. Hearing the melody gave her pause. Perhaps sensing her presence, Aegeus lowered the instrument and looked up. He didn't burst into tears, so that was an improvement.

"Don't stop playing on my account," she said, walking closer.

He smiled softly. "It would sound better if I had a partner. You have a new flute, I hear."

The satyr had been doing some talking, it seemed. "It's not mine. It's on loan."

"Would you consider playing something together?"

The thought was too painful to even entertain. Meg shook her head. "We still need to talk about your wife."

"Of course," Aegeus said, sounding sad. "And we will, but first, I think I must explain myself."

"Aegeus—" she said, attempting to cut him off.

"No, please." He put the lute on the grass beside him. "I need to understand what happened with us. Did you really make a deal with Hades to save my life?"

In the distance, Meg thought she heard Phil puttering about inside the house. "Yes. I gave up my soul for you."

His face twisted with anguish. "Why?"

"I couldn't let you die," she said, her voice breaking as she sat down on the log beside him. "You were so ill, and I couldn't imagine a world without you in it. I prayed to many gods while you were sick. Hades was the one who answered and made a deal with me. I just didn't realize he'd come to collect my soul immediately."

"Megara . . . I can't believe . . ." Aegeus's voice was so low she could hardly hear him. He fiddled with his hands. "Well, this explains why you were gone when I woke up."

She closed her eyes, reliving the moment despite herself. "Yes. I was gone, and you were free to move on with your life," she added bitterly, despite herself. "Which you did immediately."

He turned to her. "That is where you are wrong. When you disappeared, I searched for you everywhere. I assumed you had journeyed somewhere to get help, and when you didn't return, I feared the worst. I knocked on doors and put up notices for months. I couldn't sleep. Couldn't eat. I was desperate to find you." He looked at her sadly. "Megara, I searched for you for almost two years."

Meg's head whipped around. His words made her feel like she was in a free fall. "Two years? But . . ."

"Two years," he repeated. "When there was no sign of you after that time, I knew I had to accept the fact you were truly gone."

Meg felt a lump form in her throat. Had she lost more time than she'd realized? The Underworld was a place where that happened. She'd seen many a soul come through Hades's door, imagining they'd been dead mere moments when it had, in fact, been years. Was that what had happened to her as well—did the "days" that had passed actually equate to months? Years? Her hands were shaking. It all made sense now. For Hades to allow her back on Earth to do his dirty work, he had to be sure she wouldn't run to find Aegeus, and the only way to ensure she wouldn't search for her love was to keep her there for as long as it took for Aegeus to believe she was gone. And then to make sure she hated him, to make her think he'd committed the ultimate betrayal.

*Oh, Wonder Boy, you were right.*

"I was so consumed with grief that I built this house to stay sane, hoping you'd return to me," he said sadly. "This wasn't built for my new family. I built it as a memorial to you."

"I didn't know." Meg was still stunned. "I thought you moved on to Katerina in less than a week."

"I swear to you, I tried to find you," Aegeus said. "Finally I realized I had to stop living in sorrow, because you wouldn't want me to do that. I stopped working on the empty house. And then I met Katerina. Even after we married, I couldn't imagine living here. This home was your dream, and Katerina understood. I fixed up the house at the base of the hill instead and we started our new life together there."

"You did?" Meg felt her voice shake.

He closed his eyes for a moment. "I only moved in after Katerina died and our house was destroyed. The baby and I needed somewhere else to live." His eyes brimmed with tears again.

"I'm sorry. How did she die?" Meg asked as gently as she could.

"There was a storm unlike anything I had ever seen. The rain pounded the roof like Titans' fists. The wind was so fierce I thought Zeus himself was blowing on the house, ready to make it cave in. I feared the house wouldn't make it through the night, so I told Katerina we needed to get to the newer one. I knew that its framing was strong enough to sustain such conditions. Katerina handed me the baby and sent me out first, staying back to collect as many of our things as she could." Tears began to trickle down his face. "I had only started to head up the hill when . . . the house was swept away by rising waters." He let out a sob. "Katerina was gone."

Aegeus looked completely broken.

*A flood.* Wasn't that what Hercules had mentioned?

"And now there is suddenly a river where the house

stood. An actual river! It's a constant reminder of what I lost. It's like the gods themselves put it there."

*The gods themselves. A rain pounding like the Titans' fists.* Meg thought for a moment. "When did you say the river appeared?"

Aegeus's throat seemed to clench. "Only a few days ago."

Meg looked at the dancing flames as the facts started to click into place. The flood had occurred during the Titans' return, when the world had been thrown into chaos . . . before Hercules had saved it, of course. It was the Titans and the gods that had caused the disaster that took Katerina's life. *Maybe if I can save her, we can all finally find peace.*

"Do you really think you can bring Katerina back?" Aegeus's soft voice interrupted her thoughts.

Meg set her jaw. "I'm going to try." She shifted her attention back to him. "What can you tell me about her that could help me find her in the afterlife?"

"She was a lot like you, actually," Aegeus told her. "She didn't have much in the way of family nearby, so she did everything on her own."

*I can admire that,* Meg thought. "What else?"

"Her birth name was Katerina Aikos, but she took my last name when we married."

*Dimas,* Meg thought. She'd often wondered how

Megara Dimas would sound, but she'd never said the name aloud. Katerina Dimas actually had a better ring to it, anyway. "And?"

"Her parents live on the other side of Greece. She hadn't seen them in years, which sounds strange, I know, but she said it was too painful to visit them."

"Why is that?"

"Katerina had a younger sister. Layla. She died of illness when she was only seven. They were very close. Katerina always blamed herself for Layla's death."

"But if she was ill . . ."

Aegeus shook his head. "Like you, she couldn't accept that her loved one was dying. She begged the gods for help to cure the child of her illness, but they didn't hear her prayers. She didn't like to talk about Layla's death itself, so I mostly know how the girl lived. She was pure joy, Katerina always said. She was always making up stories as big as myths. And she loved to gather poppies, which she placed all over their home. Katerina loved them as well."

*Layla Aikos. Tall tales. Poppies.* Meg tried to commit the details to memory.

Aegeus smiled to himself. "I never saw Katerina without a poppy tucked into her hair. That's how I spotted her that day in the market—I saw the red flower. I must have looked haggard, because she took it out and gave it to me, saying something about how I needed a spot of sunshine more than she did. After that, we started talking every day that I came to the market. I started to make daily trips in the hopes I'd run into her. I felt we had something in common—we both had lost someone we loved, and that connected us. At first, all we talked about was the two of you."

Meg startled. "Me?"

"Yes." Aegeus looked at her. "Katerina wanted to know about the woman who captured my heart. She encouraged me to talk about you often, as if you were still around us in the very air we breathed. She talked of Layla the same way. She said, 'We imprint the lost on our hearts.'"

*Mother,* Meg thought. Katerina was right—while Meg's mother was gone, she knew she always carried her with her.

"Katerina was the one who actually inspired me to pick up my lute again," Aegeus went on. "She wanted to hear the songs we had created. She encouraged me to play for the public again in your honor."

"She did?" This Katerina was making Meg feel horrible for thinking so ill of her before. And slightly jealous. She just seemed so . . . perfect. *What is wrong with me?* "This is a lot to swallow," Meg admitted.

"I know," Aegeus said. "I guess I just wanted you to know you will always hold a place in my heart, Megara, even if the Fates led us in different directions."

Meg knew the end to their love affair was tragic, but it hadn't ended because they stopped loving each other. The Fates—or in her case, Hades—had intervened. She'd channeled her rage and hatred toward a woman she'd never met and a man who had truly cared about her. And yet, now that she knew the truth, that anger dissipated as quickly as a summer storm. As awful as that period of her life had been, the path had led her to Wonder Boy and given her the opportunity to truly find out where she belonged in this world. How could she be mad about that?

The sound of wailing wrested Meg away from her thoughts.

"Cassia is awake again," Aegeus said, standing. "She is not the best sleeper, I'm afraid. I should go to her. Phil has been a godsend, but he needs rest for your journey. He said you must leave in the morning."

Meg followed Aegeus into the house, where they found a bleary-eyed Phil rocking the crib.

"Why don't you two get some shut-eye and I'll sit with the kid?" Meg said, lifting the child from the cradle. This time the baby stopped crying, almost in surprise. She looked up at Meg with her big, dark eyes, seemingly wondering the same thing Meg was: *Are we going to get along or not?*

"You?" Phil sputtered.

"Why not?" Meg hoisted the child on her hip, straining a bit. Babies were heavy.

Aegeus and Phil looked at one another. "I won't break her, if that's what you're worried about. Get some sleep. Us girls will be fine on our own." Maybe the night air would soothe her. On her way out, Meg spotted a small wooden platagi and took that with her.

Meg walked back out to the fire and looked around for something suitable to sit on. Holding a baby on a log would probably not be the most comfortable. Then she spotted a *klismos* nestled in the trees. The chair had a curved backrest and tapered legs with a woven seat. Meg brought Cassia over to it and bounced her on her knee. The two stared at one another.

"Well, it's you and me, kid, for the next few hours at least."

At these words, Cassia started to whimper. Meg bounced her quicker.

"No, no—no tears. We've had enough of those today. Any more and this house will float away like your last one."

Cassia started to cry a bit then.

"Sorry. Okay, cry if you need to. I just mean we need some quiet. There's been a lot of heavy talk about things you'll never have to deal with. Hopefully. Unlike your father, mother, and me, maybe you'll meet someone nice and settle down without the Fates or the god of the Underworld pulling the strings."

Cassia began to cry harder.

"All right, no more talk of the Underworld or tragedy." Meg shook the rattle, hearing the beads move around inside. The baby saw it and her wailing stopped for a moment. She reached out with chubby hands and clutched the rattle clumsily in her fingers. Cassia shook the rattle so hard it hit Meg in the nose.

"A little less enthusiasm, please." Meg gently pushed the rattle down so that it wouldn't keep hitting her in the face. "But the sound is nice." When Meg had been young, her father had never let her use her rattle—he'd said it made too much noise. But Meg found she actually enjoyed the sound. *Shake it, kid,* she thought.

Meg started to hum along with the shaking rattle, rocking Cassia at the same time. The two of them stayed like that for a while. Eventually Meg saw the child's eyes slowly closing. She took the rattle from the little hands and rocked the chair as long as she could. Meg had never been happier for the quiet. She'd never been a fan of cryfests. Her mother wouldn't allow them.

---

Meg couldn't have been more than six or seven at the time, but she remembered tears coming hard and fast. She had found her mother just coming out of the forest with her bow and arrow and a sack, most likely full of birds or hares, fresh kill for supper. Meg raced into her mother's arms.

"Shush now, Megara. It's all right," her mother had said, placing her bow and arrow on the ground and hugging the child. But Meg had just kept crying. "What have I said about wasted tears? They don't help us. What is the problem? Together we will fix it. Now what's wrong?"

Meg had looked up at her mother with her slightly sunburned cheeks and the dark circles under her eyes that came from working the olive groves for hours. Her mother didn't have much, but she fought hard for everything they did have. Even at a young age, Meg knew telling her the truth would break her heart, but she'd already learned fighting her mother was pointless.

"They said I couldn't play with them," Meg said softly. "They said thcy don't play with beggars."

Her mother had held her close then. "You are no beggar, Megara. You are strong. You are clever and you are brave. You know friends like those aren't worth your time. Trust your instincts." Gently, she placed the bow and quiver of arrows in Meg's hands, urging her to try them on her own. "They won't steer you wrong. Remember that."

---

*Trust yourself; trust your instincts.* It was something her mother said to her over and over. She didn't need anyone but herself. And her mother had been right, of course, but Meg still couldn't help wishing the woman were still on this Earth to help her navigate this world. She held Cassia tighter, feeling tense as she looked down at her small pink face, hearing the tiny baby breathing. Cassia was so young. She hadn't even had a chance to know her mother like Meg had. Did she have any clue what she'd already lost at such a young age? How different would this child's life look if Meg could bring Katerina back to her?

*You can save her.*

Meg heard the words inside her head as clearly as if they'd been spoken aloud, and she knew then they were true. She would rise to this challenge and help this innocent child. Cassia didn't have to grow up as Meg had, feeling lost. Cassia deserved to see the world differently than she did. Tears sprang to Meg's eyes.

Cassia stirred slightly, her arms twitching in her sleep. Meg rubbed them gently and the child's right hand closed over her finger and held on tight. Meg didn't move.

*Who are you?* Meg wondered as she stared at the child's dreaming face. *Who will you become? You must be someone important for Hera to take interest. But even if you're not, I will help you,* Meg thought. "I won't let you grow up without a mother like I did, Cassia," she whispered. "I promise I will bring Katerina back to you."

At some point, Meg fell asleep, too. When she awoke, purple and pink swirls were racing across the sky and Helios was getting ready to start their day. Hercules had obviously worked his magic and figured out Helios's vacation time in some other way.

Aegeus and Phil appeared looking slightly in awe that all was still quiet.

Meg stood up with the baby still asleep in her arms. "We bonded." She placed Cassia in Aegeus's arms. "Tell her I'll be back soon and next time I'll have her mother with me."

Phil beamed. "Attagirl. One question: where are we headed next? We still have no clue where an entrance to the Underworld might be from here."

"I wish I could help you search," Aegeus said. "I barely leave the cliff. The new rapids at the bottom of the hill make it impossible to travel with Cassia."

Rapids. The new river—the flood that had been caused by the Titans and their war with the gods. Meg rushed to the edge of the cliff and looked down. The water below was rushing swiftly, debris and twigs floating past at a high speed. Meg's eyes followed the trail of the water, which headed in the opposite direction of the ocean. It seemed to move inland and then disappear near a mountain range. Her instincts told her this was the way.

"I think we should follow this strange new river," she said, turning to Phil and Aegeus. "My gut tells me this was made by the gods. Pegasus can help us sail over it until we get to the Underworld's entrance."

Phil walked over to the hill to look down at the water with her. "For mortals, the Underworld is only accessible by boat. If you think it's this river, we're going to need some sort of vessel."

Aegeus's eyes brightened. "That I can help you with! It isn't much. I only use it for fishing in the ocean, but it should take you where you need to go."

Aegeus and Phil trotted down to collect his boat while Meg continued to hold Cassia. She was determined to memorize every detail of the child's face so that she could tell Katerina about her. She walked around bouncing the baby and felt something hit her foot. She looked down. Cassia's rattle had rolled away when they'd fallen asleep. Meg picked it up, staring at Aegeus's woodwork, listening to the beads move. There was something about the sound that was very soothing. Meg wasn't sure why, but she opened her satchel and tucked the rattle inside it.

# FIFTEEN: Rising Water

Aegeus's caïque was a small, bright orange fishing vessel with a long, sharp bow and a sail that pulled taut in the light breeze. Pegasus was the first on board, stepping gingerly onto the wooden planks, which immediately began to rock.

Meg came right behind him. She handed Cassia back to Aegeus, then glanced at the hourglass before returning it safely to her pouch. She was alarmed to see it was more than a quarter filled with sand. Six days left. It was not a lot of time. "Coming, Phil?"

"I'm coming, hold your feta," Phil said, and she thought she heard him sniffle as he touched Cassia's cheek. "Bye, kid. You're going to miss Uncle Phil, aren't ya?"

"*Uncle* Phil?" Meg repeated, and she and Peg snorted.

Phil shot them both a look. "What can I say? Babies are cute and much easier to deal with than stubborn heroes-in-training."

Meg rolled her eyes.

"We will miss you, Philoctetes," Aegeus said. "If you ever travel this way again, please know you are always welcome here."

Phil looked like he might cry. "Maybe I'll drop in on my way home and see how you guys are doing."

"Please do." Aegeus's eyes moved to Meg. "You are welcome as well. I still don't know how to thank you."

"You can thank me when I've returned with your wife." Meg looked at the baby, who was reaching for her, and longed to say something she'd understand, but knew she couldn't. Instead, she silently appraised her. *Hang on, Cassia. I'm going to find her and bring her back for you.*

"We will be praying for your safe return, Megara," Aegeus said as he shifted the baby on his hip. "May the gods show you favor."

"They already have," said Phil proudly as he stepped aboard and cut the line holding them to shore.

They drifted away so fast Meg barely had time to turn and see Aegeus lift his hand and wave goodbye before the boat rounded a bend, rocking and swaying as it moved faster downstream. Meg felt her heart rate quicken. They were on their way.

"Buckle up, kid," Phil said as the boat jostled over a rock. "If you're right and this river leads to Acheron, this is going to be a bumpy ride, especially since you've never sailed before."

"Says who?" Meg asked as she dipped her oar in and steered them around a cluster of rocks ahead. Phil looked at her in surprise. *You can thank your boy Hercules for that.*

Months earlier, Hercules had gone from zero to hero practically overnight. He destroyed the most infamous monsters in Thebes day after day. Hades, on the other hand, was practically molten with frustration, and he was coming down on her and his other minions hard to try to figure out how to stop the Wonder Boy. Could she help it if she seemed anxious when Hercules showed up one afternoon wanting to see her?

"Let's go do something," she recalled him begging. "Anything you want! Maybe a ride over the sea on Pegasus?"

"No rides on that thing," she'd said quickly. "Look, I appreciate you coming by and all, but I'm not exactly in a sightseeing mood."

"Come on, Meg," he'd insisted. "We can do nothing but sit quietly and stare at our sandals if that's what you want. Let's just take a teeny-tiny break to spend some time together. Please?"

She knew she should say no, to protect his heart as well as her own; but he had that adorably goofy grin that was almost too big for his face and that earnest look in his eye. He'd even shown up with a bouquet of flowers, for gods' sake. How could she turn him down? "I guess I could slip away for an hour, but nothing more."

His smile grew even wider. "That's great! An hour is all we need. We can . . . well, let's see; flying is out, and we can't go anywhere Phil can find us," he rambled. "Ah! I've got an idea. Follow me!" He grabbed her hand and led her to a nearby lake.

"You want to go swimming?" she had asked, the disdain probably written all over her face.

"No, no, of course not." He ran behind some brush and pulled something large out from within it with ease. It was a small fishing boat. "We're going sailing!"

Meg remembered scoffing. "I don't sail."

"Why not? It's fun! My father used to take me." He pushed the boat into the water, then put one foot up on the bench to hold it steady and held out his hand. "I'll teach you."

She'd stared at his hand apprehensively.

"Come on, Meg! No one will find us out on the water. Don't you ever want to escape?"

"Always," she'd said without hesitation, and before she knew it, she was climbing aboard.

He rowed them effortlessly over a light chop to the center of the lake, his biceps bulging as he paddled with both oars. Then he handed her one. She looked at it for a moment. "I can row on my own, of course, but usually when two people each take an oar, it's a smoother ride."

"Why don't I just take a turn driving us?" she'd asked, grabbing the second oar from his hands and attempting to use both oars at the same time. Okay, it was way harder than it looked. She nearly lost one oar in the water as she dipped it into a wave. Hercules reached out and grabbed it.

"Here, let me show you." He carefully moved to the back of the boat and sat behind her so he could guide her arms with the oars. She was well aware of his body being so close, but she tried not to seem ruffled as he placed his hands on her arms and gently guided her through the circular motion. "Like that. You've got it!"

She could feel his breath on her neck. *How does he smell as sweet as nectar in this heat? Do I smell?* she found herself wondering. *Why do I care?* Their close proximity was definitely doing something to her.

"Okay, now you try it on your own."

He let go of her arms to let her paddle both oars, and instantly she felt the difference. Churning the oars through the water was tough, not that she wanted to let on, and the only motion she could make was turning them in circles.

"You sure I can't do one and you do one? There's nothing wrong with teamwork," he'd said.

"Fine." She passed him an oar. "But only because I don't want us stuck out here in the middle of the lake forever."

As soon as Hercules had taken an oar, they were able to paddle in tandem, and the boat began to glide over the chop, sailing at a clip across the lake.

"Nice, Meg! You're doing it!" he'd yelled as they moved faster and faster. "Isn't this great?"

It kind of was, though she hesitated to admit it. What wasn't to like about the sun warming her face, the breeze blowing through her hair, and the fact that she was alone on a lake with a guy who seemed to want nothing more from her than her company?

"You're a good boating partner, Meg," Hercules had said with a laugh.

"So are you, Wonder Boy," she'd told him.

*Partners.* She'd never been around a man who didn't

seem to have an ulterior motive. Her father had left when she and her mother got in his way. Hades owned her. Aegeus had turned out to care only about himself and the next woman on deck. With Hercules, things felt right.

Hercules was someone who challenged her to see the good in the world, while accepting her as she was. He was someone who never stopped surprising her, who could make her heart race with a mere look. But did that mean they'd work well together for eternity? How did she know for sure she was even in love with the guy? There was no guide for these things. It was a feeling, but what if she was wrong? Or what if she made a bad decision like she had in the past, one that would wreck them? Eternity was a long time to not screw things up.

Aegeus's boat lurched sideways, almost tipping them over, and Meg grabbed the oar and righted the boat. "Don't worry, Phil. I know what I'm doing here. This river will be the easy part of this gig."

"I don't know about that." But Phil moved to the left side with his oar while Meg navigated the right. Within minutes, they were steering in tandem without arguing. They were somehow making it work, jumping in to balance the ship, and maybe that was the point.

The same could be said for her and Hercules, couldn't

it? When the two of them worked together, each of them picking up slack and lifting the other one up, things felt right. Maybe there would never be some huge sign that he was the one. Perhaps it was a bunch of little signs, and she just had to decide once and for all to take that leap.

They hit a rock and the boat lifted off the water, then dropped fast and hit a sudden dip. Meg kept her oar steady as the river kept winding and turning. The dense vegetation along the sides of the river was so thick she couldn't get her bearings. All she knew was that she didn't want to fall overboard. That dark churning water beneath them felt uncomfortably familiar; it reminded her of the haunted streams in the Underworld—the ones teeming with lost, anguished souls. Her gut said they were on the right path, at least.

"Pegasus," Meg called out to him. "Grab an oar. We could use your help." The horse took one with his mouth as they all leaned to the left, hoping the boat would turn away from a tree trunk jutting out into the water. They narrowly made their way around it.

"Red, we're nowhere near the entrance," Phil yelled as he paddled faster around a floating branch rushing alongside them. "We'll never get there at this rate."

"How do you know?" Meg called. "Have you been to the entrance before?"

"No, but I . . . *rock*!" They leaned to the left and paddled to avoid it. "If it was that easy to find, don't you think everyone would be banging down the door to the Underworld to go get their loved ones back?"

Meg hadn't thought about it that way before. "Only if they've forgotten about Cerberus!" Pegasus snorted in agreement. "How will we know when we're getting close?"

Phil looked back at her for a second. "Believe me, we will know because . . . *tree*!"

They navigated the boat around the stump sticking out into the rapids.

"Because what?" she pushed. "I didn't arrive in the Underworld by boat before. Last time I was just dropped in Hades's lair." They hit another bump and both she and Phil fell backward. They scrambled to get up again.

"Really?" Phil momentarily turned to look at her. "Huh. Didn't think humans were allowed to chill in the Underworld. Chill. Ha! Get it?"

"Yeah, and they're not," Meg said as water splashed over the side of the boat. "Hades hid me, I guess."

Phil wiped water off his nose. The boat righted itself and started to move along more steadily, giving them all the opportunity to catch their breath. "They say the Underworld messes with your bearings. You sort of lose track of things—sense of place, time . . ."

"Yeah, figured that last one out. How does everyone seem to know all of this except me?" Meg asked.

Phil shrugged. "All I'm saying is hang on tight to that hourglass down there," he said as they began to round another bend. "That will help you remember, and—hey . . ." Phil stopped rowing. "You hear that?"

"Hear what?" Meg used the back of her hand to keep the ongoing spray of water out of her eyes. Peg neighed nervously as Meg tried to see what was up ahead. The river seemed to just end right beyond a row of trees. But that didn't make sense. The water was still rushing forward, almost as if . . .

She and Phil looked at one another at the same time. "Waterfall!"

"Hang on!" Meg shouted as she leaned back, pulling the oar's flat side through the water trying to slow them down. The boat kept barreling forward. Meg pictured a hundred-foot drop ahead of them. If that were the case, they would be done for. "We have to bail!" she said. "Pegasus, let's fly!"

"NO! You can only find the entrance on water!" Phil argued. "If we lose this boat, we're finished."

"Are you mad? If we stay here, we'll be smashed to smithereens!" Meg cried, her fingers itching to drop the oar and rush to Pegasus's side. "There's no way we'll make it!"

They were nearing the edge now. She could see the spot where the river just dropped off.

"We will!" Phil countered. "Trust me!"

*I don't trust anyone but myself,* Meg wanted to say. But she had little choice. "Fine!" she yelled as the front of the boat neared the edge and Peg started to whine. "If we die, don't expect me to play chess with you in the Underworld!"

"Deal!" Phil shouted. "Now lean back! Everyone! One, two, threeeeeeeeeee!"

The boat hit the edge and fell forward so fast, Meg thought they were going to plummet ahead of the boat to their deaths. Water rushed over them, making it impossible to scream. Meg felt Pegasus come flying toward her. She grabbed hold of the mast at the same time Phil did, and Pegasus wedged his body behind it. Meg held her breath, waiting for impact. The boat finally slammed into a wall of water, then bounced for a moment, water spilling into it, and righted itself again.

Pegasus collapsed on the deck of the boat in exhaustion. Phil fell over, clutching his oar. Meg sank to the floor and found a fish flopping on the deck next to her. She picked it up, disgusted, and threw it back in the river.

"Look! I can't believe we made it!" Phil looked back at the waterfall gushing behind them. "Yowza! That had to be a hundred feet!"

"What do you mean, you 'can't believe we made it'?" Meg said, trying to catch her breath. "You said we'd be fine."

"Well, we were, weren't we?" Phil spat more water out of his mouth. "You got to learn to trust people, Red."

"Yeah, because that always works out so well," she said under her breath.

"I mean it! Once you learn that the horse and I are on your side, we'll have you to the entrance of the Underworld and back with Hercules in no time. And then I can get back to relaxing." He wrung water out of his furry tail.

"Oh, sure. This has been a piece of baklava so far. What more could go wrong?" Meg pushed her wet bangs behind her right ear and looked away.

"Hey now, don't do *that*."

"Do what?"

"Doubt yourself." Phil stomped over to her, climbing onto the boat bench to look her in the eye. "I've had heroes-in-training do that before, and they are the ones who don't make it. It takes guts and faith to do what you're about to do."

The satyr sounded so smug she wanted to take his small body and throw him overboard. But then, who would help her steer?

"I know, Phil," she said with an involuntary eye roll.

"Do you?" he protested. "You've got to believe you can

take anything this quest throws at you, whether it's a waterfall or a harpy."

"Harpy?" Meg asked. "Why would we run into harpies?"

He sighed. "I'm just saying you've got to believe in yourself." Phil jumped down and grabbed a bucket to try to get some of the water out of the boat.

*Believe in yourself.* There it was again. But did that contradict what Phil had just said about trusting others? Her mother had thought so. . . .

"I believe, okay?" Meg fixed her ponytail. "If I didn't, I wouldn't be here risking my life."

The tingling of bells made them stop arguing.

"Hi there!" Hermes hovered above the back of the boat, his winged hat helping him navigate closer. He seemed out of breath, and his brow was sweaty. A handkerchief appeared suddenly in his right hand and he used it to wipe his face. "Wow, were you two hard to find! I was flying on and on and on! She said you'd be on the river Acheron and to bring you this gift, but then you weren't there yet, even though you don't have a lot of time left on your hourglass. So I thought, they can't still be back at Aegeus's, can they? But I made a pit stop there, popped into his house, and woke the baby. Whoa, can she cry."

"You woke the baby?" Phil groaned.

"Kid has some lungs! Boy!" Hermes held his head. "Aegeus said I should follow the river at the bottom of the hill, so I did, and then I saw the waterfall and thought, they're goners! But she said to keep looking, and I did, and found you down here." Hermes flew around the boat and then shot up high into the sky and came back down again. "Wow, you haven't made it that far, have you?"

Meg tried to be patient. "Hermes, you said you had a gift?" She hoped it wasn't that they got to keep the messenger for the rest of the journey.

"Yes, from her!" he said, his winged hat fluttering fast.

"What her?" Meg asked impatiently. "Hera?"

"Oh, no!" Hermes laughed. "She's not getting in the middle of your quest. You're on your own when it comes to her."

"Hit her where it hurts, why don't ya?" Phil muttered under his breath.

"This is from Athena." Hermes snapped his fingers and two sacks appeared on a seat of the boat. Meg opened the first sack and found a bow and arrow. "Ever use one of those before?" he asked.

Meg expertly nocked the arrow and pulled the bowstring back, then spun around, targeting Phil.

"Not funny!" He jumped out of the way and she laughed.

She used to practice archery with her mother. Her mom

had expert aim, and she'd caught them many a dinner this way. Meg hadn't held a bow and arrow in her hands in years, but the sensation came right back to her. "Yes. My mother taught me how to use one of these." She placed both items on the bench again and opened the second sack. Inside were two long pieces of metal held together with leather straps. "Is this an instrument?" she asked quizzically.

"A special kind of instrument," Hermes said. "Listen to the sound it makes."

Meg clapped the two pieces of metal together, and a terrible, high-pitched shriek emitted from them. Everyone held their ears. She could still hear a ringing even when the clapper was silent. Pegasus neighed miserably.

"Pretty dreadful, right?" Hermes asked. "Athena had Hephaestus make it for you. Said it might come in handy if you're reckless."

Phil snorted. "Reckless is her middle name." Meg shot him a look.

"Please thank Athena for me," Meg said.

Hermes looked farther down the river and whistled. "Will do. Looks like you'll need those gifts if you're headed that way."

"Why? What's up ahead?" Meg asked worriedly.

There was a chiming of bells again.

"I'm late!" Hermes cried and, poof, he was gone.

# SIXTEEN: Leverage

Meg stared at the bow and arrow and clapper worriedly. If Athena was suddenly granting gifts for her journey, there had to be a reason. Meg looked ahead at the newly calm waters and endless miles of trees and wondered, *What out there would cause me to be reckless?*

"I've seen that thing before," Phil said as she placed the instrument carefully inside her satchel. "I think it has a name. Rota? Rata? No. That's not it. Tala?"

"It's called a clapper," Meg said.

Phil scratched his left ear. "No, it's got an official name, I tell ya. It's on the tip of my tongue. It's a krotala!"

"What's a krotala?"

Phil's smile faded. "I forget. It's important, though. I think."

"Well, it looks like you have time to remember." Meg stared at the waterway. "We're barely moving." The water was almost stagnant now, the breeze nonexistent. Up ahead, the river grew narrower and the waters became almost turquoise blue. It was so shallow that she could see white sands at the bottom. Rocks rose to greet them on one side while thick vegetation and trees were on the other. There was no sign of life on the riverbeds nor another boat to be found. Eerily, she didn't even hear wildlife. For such a serene spot, it was completely deserted. Meg looked at the mast and saw it was split in half. "So much for this sail."

"Wouldn't work if it was whole anyway," Phil said, putting his hand on the split mast. "No wind, no current. Even the water doesn't want to go where we're headed. But at least we are moving in the right direction. If your instincts were correct, we've finally made it to the river Acheron. When we cross with the Kokytos and the Pyriphlegethon rivers, we should find your entrance."

"And Charon will be waiting," Meg said almost to herself. She'd ridden with the ferryman to the Underworld numerous times; Hades always traveled to and from the Underworld with the chauffeur, but she'd never ridden with Charon by herself before. She shuddered at the thought.

Phil did the same, though his chill seemed to be from

sticking a hoof in the water. "You feel this river? It's dead already. As cold as ice."

Meg dipped her fingertips off the side of the boat, and they grew numb after a few seconds. No wonder she saw no wildlife or other people here. Acheron might have *looked* beautiful, but it truly was the gateway to hell. She stretched her legs out on a bench and leaned back, her face to the sun. "So now what do we do? I don't have time to just sit here and wait for a breeze."

"Relax, Red! I'm sure a breeze will pick up at some point. In the meantime, we row."

Phil picked up an oar and Meg did the same. For some reason, as clear and pristine as the water looked, moving the oar through the river felt like pushing through sludge.

"It's not working," Meg said in frustration and put down her oar. She pulled out her hourglass. It was almost halfway empty. "I've got less than six days and the Underworld is a labyrinth. How am I going to find Katerina and get her out of there before the sand runs out?"

"You've got to be smart!" Phil said as he continued to row. "We both know Hades ain't going to be happy to see you again, so avoid him as long as you can. You said the place is a labyrinth, but you should know your way around there more than the average soul, no?"

"Kind of," Meg admitted.

"Good! Stick to the shadows and avoid Hades's minions. You've got to find Katerina before he finds you. Did Aegeus give you any clues that will help you find her down there?"

"Aegeus made her sound like a saint, so she's certainly not in Tartarus, but Elysium sounds like a long shot, too. My guess is she's in Asphodel Meadows, like most."

Phil scratched his chin. "That's still a large place. How are you going to narrow things down?"

Meg thought for a moment. "Aegeus said she has a younger sister, Layla, who died when Katerina was young. I'm sure she's with her."

"Good!" Phil's face lit up. "I mean, not that the kid's dead, but it's a clue to finding Katerina. What else?"

"I know Layla loved poppy fields—so did Katerina—and telling tall tales." Meg yawned. Suddenly she was quite tired. Were the events of the last couple of days finally catching up to her? "That's about all I know. We had a lot of ground to cover in a short amount of time."

"Yeah, yeah. Tragic love affair. I know. Stay focused and find that kid," Phil said, his eyes looking as heavy as hers felt. "We may have a plan to get you *in* the joint, but how are you going to get out?"

"I'm not sure," Meg realized as she settled down on the bench again. The boat was barely moving. "But Hercules did give me this." She pulled the orchid out of her satchel. "It allows me to call for him three times. Well, two, since I already used it once." Her cheeks burned.

"Then that's your ticket out of hell! Literally!" Phil said. "Don't waste those petals. Use them to have Herc get you out of there once you find her."

"Maybe." Meg stared at the flower. She wasn't the rescuee type. Maybe she could get out on her own.

Phil shook his head. "You really are stubborn, Red. You know that?" He yawned again.

It made her yawn once more, too. She tucked the orchid back in her satchel and stretched. Would it be so wrong to take a nap? Meg started to lie down on the bench opposite Phil, who was already drifting off. She sat up with a start. "Phil, I think this river is putting us to sleep!"

"Sleep?" he murmured. "Why would a river do that?" He curled up in a ball and started to snore.

"Phil? Peg . . . ?" She looked around to see that the horse was curled up on the deck, already fast asleep.

Meg's heart quickened. *Stay awake!* she told herself, but her eyes were closing almost of their own volition. This river had somehow taken hold, as if it didn't want them to see exactly where they were going or how to ever get back there again. And no matter how hard she fought it, within minutes, she had drifted right with it.

---

When Meg awoke some time later, she noticed the sun straightaway. It had moved.

No longer was it high overhead. It was now halfway across the sky, and shadows were stretching from the trees. It had to be late afternoon already, and it looked like they had barely moved. She looked over at Phil and found him still snoring away, along with Pegasus. She hurried over to wake them.

"Phil! Pegasus!" she said, and the satyr stirred. "The river put us to sleep."

Pegasus flapped his wings and blinked rapidly as if rising from a long slumber.

Phil rubbed his eyes. "What? No. How?" He yawned, stretched his hooves, and looked around. "How long were we out?"

"A while," Meg said with a groan. "And we haven't moved at all."

"No!" Phil rushed to the side of the boat and looked around. "These trees definitely look different. I think." He stood on the boat bench. "And look, up ahead. There's a meadow. We haven't seen a meadow yet."

"A meadow?" Meg joined him at the front of the boat to look. Something gold glinted in the distance and made her blink. What was that? The boat drifted closer, and suddenly a clearing appeared. Phil was right. The boat had moved toward a meadow dotted with trees full of low-hanging fruit. Were those golden apples?

*You haven't lived till you've had one of these, Nut-Meg,* she heard a voice in her head say. *They're to die for! As a matter of fact, many a man has! Ha!*

*Hades.* She remembered seeing him eating one once or twice, savoring every last bite down to the core. It might have been one of the few occasions she'd seen the god happy. Usually the only thing that did that was talking about his Titan takeover, or a large group of souls showing up to his realm at once. Those golden apples were an elusive bright spot in his life. If she could get her hand on just one of those pieces of fruit, maybe she'd have some leverage with Hades if they crossed paths.

Her eyes moved to the shoreline, where a short gate was all that stood between the apples and the river. There was even a group of baskets sitting on the ground near the gate, just begging to be used to collect fruit.

"Phil," Meg said excitedly. "We've got to steer this boat over to the shore. Those apples are Hades's favorite. If I bring some with me, I might be able to barter with the hellion."

Phil moved to the right side of the ship and frowned. "Yeah, no can do. That orchard looks like it could be on the Hesperides' land."

"The Hesperides . . . *hmmm* . . ."

Her mother had told her legends about the Hesperides, who guarded fruit said to give people immortality. No wonder Hades enjoyed eating them—he was already immortal, so taking that gift away from a human would be something he would relish. But this couldn't be the nymphs' orchard. The legend said nothing about it being near the entrance to the Underworld, did it? Why did she think there was a piece of this story she was forgetting?

"I don't like this, Red," Phil said. "Those apples are not meant for human consumption."

"Good! I don't plan on eating one," said Meg, rowing closer to the side. "They're for Hades if I run into him."

"See that gate? It means stay out. We can't trespass."

"No one is even going to know we're there!" Meg argued. "The orchard is deserted."

"Unless there's some sleeping dragon around there somewhere just waiting to eat us. I wouldn't put it past those nymphs to have an extra layer of protection around apples so rare." Phil tried to rush in front of her. "Don't do anything rash. Let's call on Athena, or Hercules if you want. I'm sure they'd tell you this isn't a good idea."

Meg snorted. Phil was being ridiculous. She gently went around him. "I'm not wasting their time on something like this. We don't need their help. Phil, I'm telling you, dragons are massive. If one was there, we'd see it." She pulled her oar through the water, turning the boat toward shore. "I'll be quick. I promise you." Meg jumped out of the boat as soon as she was close enough. That way Phil couldn't stop her. "I'll be back quicker than your hooves can get you off this boat."

"Red!" Phil growled. "You're being reckless! Remember what Athena said? Don't be a fool!"

Meg ignored him, stepping onto land and walking swiftly to the gate. It was unlocked. *Ha!* she wanted to say. *This was meant to be!* She pushed the gate open and walked a few yards to the first tree she found, her eyes darting back and forth for any sign of movement. There was none. *Phil is such a worrier,* she thought.

The trees were so full, the golden apples were hanging as low as Meg's head. They were practically begging to be picked. She reached up for the first shiny gold apple she saw and gave it a quick twist from the branch, hearing the small snap as it broke free.

She turned to Phil and Peg triumphantly. "See? No problem."

She'd barely gotten the words out of her mouth when she heard an ear-piercing screech. Meg turned and saw countless birds swooping over the orchard, angrily heading straight toward her.

# SEVENTEEN: Rash Doesn't Look Good on You

It took Meg a moment to comprehend what she was seeing. At first glance the birds looked like nothing more than tiny, tan specks on the horizon line, but as they flew closer, their size grew apparent. They were as large as humans, with sharp metallic feathers and bronze beaks, and there were hundreds of them all heading her way. She noticed something drop from the sky. Was that dung? The dark-colored substance hit the top of a tree and the branches surrounding it withered on contact, the whole tree starting to smoke. Poison!

Their ear-piercing squawking on approach made her instantly cover her ears, but the move did nothing. The sound was making her dizzy. She needed to get out of that orchard, but she was suddenly unsure of her surroundings. She turned toward the river and saw the boat.

"Red! Back to the boat! Red!" Phil called.

Meg dropped the precious apple and started to run, going no more than a few feet before she tripped over a root she'd failed to notice in the ground. She stumbled, but kept going, her eyes on the gate a few yards away. *Bang!* She was down again, her toes catching on a large root that seemed to appear out of nowhere, which was impossible, and yet . . . Meg sat up and spun around. Roots were growing up out of the ground all around her. She scrambled to get up again and felt a sharp root pierce her right sandal.

"Ouch!" she cried, dragging her right foot behind her as she kept moving toward that gate. Suddenly a root broke out of the ground right in front of her, rising like a tree. Meg stopped short, trying to change direction, but the vines whipped around her ankles, tightening and holding her firm. "Phil! I'm stuck!"

"Bat them away with anything you can find!" Phil shouted.

Meg spotted a large rock. She reached down and began bashing the roots with it. They recoiled, loosening their grip, and Meg burst forward, throwing herself at the fence.

"It's locked!" Meg cried.

"Pegasus, go get her!" Phil yelled.

Why didn't she think these things through first? Now she'd put the three of them in danger.

The horse took off from the boat, flying straight toward the gate, and Meg held her arms up, ready to grab whatever part of him that she could. Pegasus reached the fence and—*BOOM!* He bounced back as if he'd been struck.

"Peg!" Meg screamed in horror as the stunned horse flew through the air.

Phil saw what was happening and used an oar to turn the boat around just in time. Pegasus landed with a thud, half in, half out of the back of the boat, sending wood flying and breaking the sail completely off. Phil struggled to pull him back in.

*WHIZ! BAM!* The birds' feathers were launching off their wings into the air and hitting targets. Several feathers pelted the tree closest to her, slicing it in half. The tree fell to the ground, apples rolling toward the gate.

"Phil! Their feathers kill!"

"I know that!" Phil shouted. "Those are Stymphalian birds, Red! They aren't here for a picnic!"

"What do I do?" Meg cried as she pulled harder on the gate. She tried to get a foothold in the bottom and pull herself up and over it, but her sandals kept sliding. The fence was as slick as ice.

"Oh, now you want to listen—RED! Behind you!"

Meg dove to the ground as one of the birds attempted to hook its talons in her shoulders. It kept coming, Meg rolling out of the way before it could land. The bird hit the gate, denting it and stunning itself in the process. It shook its beak, trying to get its bearings, and Meg jumped up and ran farther down the fence line looking for an opening she could squeeze through. Feathers pelted the ground around her. A huge dung ball splattered the nearest tree and poisoned it on contact. The tree slammed to the ground, narrowly missing her.

Meg dove for cover, hiding herself in its branches. She gathered as many apples as she could around her to shade her from sight.

Phil saw what was happening and rowed in her direction. "I'm coming toward you!" he called from the boat, swatting at incoming birds with his oar. He batted one away and it landed in the river. "You need a weapon! Those birds can't pierce cork. If you can find some, it would protect you."

Meg could hear feathers slicing the ground around her as the birds squawked angrily. They were looking for her. She pulled herself in tighter, trying not to be seen, but the birds spotted her anyway, landing on the downed tree, pecking away. One pierced the fabric of her dress and slid right through. Meg screamed. She was a goner if she didn't find a weapon soon.

*Weapons.* Athena's gifts in case she was *reckless.* How did that god know her so well? If only she hadn't left the bow and arrow on the boat.

"Red, use the krotala!" Phil cried.

"What?" Meg pulled her legs tighter to her chest.

"The clapper! Use the instrument!"

*The clapper?* she wondered as a bird grabbed hold of her dress hem and started to pull. *What is that thing going to do? Do I throw it at them?* Meg pulled the instrument out of her sack and looked at it skeptically, ready to question Phil, but then she thought better of it. She had to have faith he knew what he was talking about. She clapped both pieces together, hearing the sharp sound it made. Several birds shrieked in agony and flew off. *I can't believe it!* she thought with glee and struck it again. The birds on the tree disappeared and Meg crawled out. "Phil, it works."

"Good job, Red! Take that, you bronze metalheads!" Phil reached the shore and was holding her bow and arrow.

"Phil, watch out!" she screamed.

A bird swooped in low on the boat from out of nowhere, lifting Phil and the bow and arrow into the air. Meg ran out into the open and threw a golden apple, trying to strike the bird down, but missed.

"Aaah! Red!" Phil cried, trying to kick out from the bird's grasp as he was pulled higher and higher.

*You are not taking my satyr.* She picked up another apple and threw it as hard as she could. She hit the bow and arrow, which dropped from Phil's hands. Meg bolted out into the opening, placed the krotala in her satchel again, and grabbed the weapon, quickly placing the arrow in the bow and aiming at the bird's wing as it climbed higher. She had only seconds before Phil's height would be too great to let him fall. She squinted into the sunlight and aimed, then let the arrow go. It pierced the bird's wing and Phil fell, screaming, into the top of a tree.

"Phil, stay hidden in that tree or the birds will—aaaah!" Meg felt the back of her dress lift as she was hoisted in the air by one of the birds. She could see other birds headed her way to get their piece. With no arrows left to nock, she used the bow the only way she could—to whack the bird holding her. The bird instantly let go, and Meg went tumbling several feet to the ground. Vines instantly wrapped around her legs and arms and slammed her face into the dirt. She tried to kick herself free and felt something grab her by the shoulders again. That gods-forsaken bird was back and tugging on her upper body while the vines tried to claim her lower half. She felt like she was being split in two.

She punched the bird's talon with her right fist and its grip loosened just enough for her to reach in her satchel for the krotala again. She clapped it fiercely and the bird immediately let go of her. Then Meg used the krotala to bash the vines till they receded. She kicked out of the vines and threw herself forward, the krotala slipping from her fingers in the process. Her reaching hand had just grazed the instrument when she felt herself being lifted in the air again.

"Nooo!" Meg cried and turned and punched the bird again. It dropped her and she started running.

"Red, it has Pegasus!" Phil cried as he started climbing down from the tree.

"Phil, stay there!" she shouted. "I'll—aaah!" Two new vines tightened around her legs, winding higher and higher around her body till they squeezed her chest so tight she was afraid she'd pass out. She felt her eyes start to close. She had lost the bow and arrow. She'd misplaced the krotala. Pegasus was just a dot in the sky. She didn't have much time to save him or herself. And what about Phil? *Stay awake!* she told herself. *Fight!*

Phil appeared out of nowhere, running as fast as his hooves would take him as he hurled apple after apple at the vines. He didn't see the bird come up behind him till he was hoisted in the air again.

*No!* She tried to cry out, but her voice was gone. She was being squeezed tighter and tighter. With the only thing free being her hands, she dug her nails into one of the vines and it recoiled. Meg did it again and again till they retreated enough for her to get her arms free. She reached out to grab the leather straps of the krotala and felt a bird yank her back, lifting her body off the ground again.

*Concentrate, Meg,* she told herself. *You're a big, tough girl. . . .* Meg kicked out hard and felt a vine holding her leg tear away. Arms flailing, she wound back with her free hand and socked the bird in its chest. *You . . . can . . . do . . . this.* The bird shrieked and instantly let go.

It would be back in moments, but a moment was all she needed to kick-start her plan. Meg launched herself forward again, trying to reach the krotala. If she could just reach it, she could scare the birds, then run for the bow, find the fallen arrow and aim it in the sky to make the birds drop Peg and Phil, and then . . . and then . . . okay, she'd have to figure out how to catch them, but she had the start of a plan. Plans were good. She needed to remember to make more of those before she sprang into action. But the point was, she was fixing things on her own.

Meg reached for the clapper again and her fingers closed around it just as the bird landed on her back and two more vines latched onto her arms. There was a loud snap and Meg was able to see a cluster of the birds breaking the bow with their razor-sharp beaks before the vines wove around her chest and squeezed. Meg felt herself start to lose consciousness. *You can do this, Meg! Fight!* she told herself. She had started to tap the clapper ever so slightly when there was a sound like thunder, followed by a crackle of lightning. Hercules burst from the sky dressed in what looked like a suit of armor made of cork.

It all happened so fast. Hercules landed two punches on the birds holding Pegasus and held on to another for dear life so that he didn't plummet to the ground. The bird released Pegasus and the horse began to fall, waking just before he hit the ground. With a giant flap, he tore up to the heavens and Hercules leaped for him, climbing onto his back and racing toward the bird carrying Phil. Pulling up alongside him, he punched the bird in the chest and it let go of Phil, who fell onto Pegasus's back. The three quickly descended, heading straight toward her. Meg barely had time to inhale before Hercules had jumped from Pegasus's back and landed on the bird holding Meg. He picked it up and launched it into the river with a flick of his wrist, then picked up the krotala and clapped it together so hard, every bird around took flight, flying away till they were nothing more than specks on the horizon.

# EIGHTEEN: Control

"Meg!" Hercules ran toward her, ripping off the vines still wrapped around her with his bare hands. "Are you okay?"

Meg rubbed her arms, staring at the rope burns from the vines that had replaced the burns lingering from the Empusa. Her ears were still ringing from the sound of the krotala, so his voice sounded muffled, and her legs were weak from being stretched and pulled, but the birds were gone. She tried to stand and Hercules offered her his arm. She didn't take it.

"How did you know I was here?" she said, her voice hoarse from all the yelling.

Phil and Peg were racing toward her.

"I heard you were in trouble." Hercules fixed his headband, which was askew and covering his right eye.

She bristled. "And you thought I needed rescuing?" Meg leaned against a tree to catch her breath. She was covered in grass stains, had cuts from the branches and vines and possibly a gash in her back from all that pecking, but she was still in one piece. "You didn't think I could take care of myself?"

Phil interrupted them, practically jumping on Hercules in his attempt to reach up and rub his golden hair. Pegasus hopped along excitedly beside them. "Am I glad you showed up, kid! I thought we were goners!" He hung onto Hercules's massive biceps, sitting on it like a chair.

"I saw my mother and Athena looking toward Earth from their cloud, and when I heard them mention Meg's name, I rushed over to see what was going on." He looked at her sheepishly. "As soon as I saw you were in trouble, I came running."

"Good thing you did," Phil agreed.

Meg's cheeks warmed with embarrassment at the thought of Athena and Hera watching her mess up. "This is just swell. Athena is probably furious with me."

"Actually, I think she's mad at *me*," Hercules admitted with wide eyes. "She said to let you handle things on your own, but I couldn't just stand there when those birds were trying to tear you apart."

His confession made her bristle once more. "I had it

under control," Meg said, hearing the edge in her voice. The men looked at her skeptically. "I did!"

Phil turned to Pegasus, who snorted, then back to Meg. "You're delusional. The birds had us, vines were pinning you to the ground, and there was a bird on your back. If Hercules hadn't been here to save our butts, your quest would be over! All because you wanted to bring Hades an apple."

Hercules did a double take. "You wanted to bring Hades an apple?"

"No! I mean, yes. I mean, it's hard to explain," Meg said, getting frustrated. "It doesn't matter now!"

"Wait, Meg, are you angry with me?" Hercules looked confused.

Meg tried to bite her tongue, but she couldn't hold back. "Yes! I was this close to using the krotala and finishing off the birds myself when you swooped in to do the whole hero thing. Athena gave *me* these gifts to use, not you."

"You wouldn't even have needed that krotala if you had just stayed on the boat and listened to reason in the first place!" Phil chimed in. "Now you've cost yourself even more time!" Phil bleated, and it set her off.

"This is my quest, remember? Not his." She pointed to Hercules. "And not yours. It's mine to do what I want with or screw up. I didn't ask anyone to butt in."

"I wanted to lend a hand," Hercules said. "I thought you needed me."

"I can take care of myself! Why can't any of you see that?" Meg stormed off toward the fence.

"Meg." Hercules ran after her. "I really didn't mean to step on your toes. I was just trying to help you."

The whole innocent farm boy routine was too much for her to handle at the moment. "I don't need your help. I do things on my own. Always have, always will," she said, thinking of her mother. "This is my quest, and it will only work if I rely on myself."

He looked unsure. "But why? You can count on me. I thought you knew that. When you called for me last time, you wanted my help figuring things out. Didn't you?"

"Yes! I mean, no. I just wanted to hear myself think!" she cried, starting to get confused herself. "I wanted you to be there for me. Not take over. There's a difference." Thea had taught her never to be indebted to anyone, and she'd already screwed up once when she went to Hades for help. She wasn't about to do it again.

"I thought we were a team," he said.

"Team?" She didn't like feeling helpless, and for some reason, that's how he was making her feel. "We're not a team! You're a god and I'm a mortal. How can we be a team if I only earn my own spot on Mount Olympus if I complete this quest? Your life isn't on the line here."

"Meg." He tried reaching for her and she stepped back.

Angry tears sprang to her eyes. She didn't want to hear what he had to say. "No. When this boat finally reaches the entrance to the Underworld, it won't be you or Phil or Pegasus who has to keep going. It will be me. I'm the one that has to convince Hades to let me take Katerina back to the land of the living. I'm the one who has to survive another brush with death." She was shaking. "How am I supposed to face Hades and whatever beasts await me down there if every time I'm in trouble, the mighty Hercules swoops in to save me?" For the first time, he didn't contradict her, and for some reason, that made her realize something. "You don't think I can do this, do you?"

"Meg, no . . . that's not true!" Hercules said, but she could see the fear written all over his face. "I just want you to know I'm here when you need me."

"Well, I don't." She just wanted to put an end to this ridiculous argument. "I can do this on my own, and I'll prove it." She pulled the orchid out of her satchel.

"Meg, what are you doing?" Hercules looked panicked.

"Red!" Phil's voice sounded like a warning. "Think about this! Red!"

But she didn't want to think. She hurled the orchid into the water. It floated for a few moments before sinking in front of their eyes.

"Meg . . ." Hercules looked forlorn. "I can't get another one of those. I . . ."

Bells chimed, and Hermes appeared. "Hercules, your mother wants to see you."

*Of course,* Meg thought.

"Can you tell her I just need a moment?" Hercules started to say.

"Nope! You're needed now. Something about a bird? Let's go, lover boy!" He grabbed Hercules's right biceps.

"Meg, I . . ." Hercules's face was pained.

She turned away. This part she was familiar with—he was going to leave her like everyone else did. "Just go."

Hercules stared sadly at her as he started to glow brighter.

"Goodbye, Wonder Boy," Meg whispered as he disappeared from sight.

# NINETEEN: Second Thoughts

"Are you nuts?" Phil cried, rushing to the edge of the boat to look for the orchid, which had disappeared below the surface. "You needed that flower!"

"I don't need anything," Meg said defiantly, but inside she was already regretting her impulsiveness. *What did I just do?*

"Not to mention letting him leave without having him get us down the river," Phil continued to rant. "We've got no sail at all, if you haven't noticed, and there is still no wind! We're basically stuck here!"

Meg hadn't thought about that. She stared at where the mast used to be and then looked around for the paddles. In the chaos, they, too, had been lost. The air was sickeningly hot and sticky and completely stagnant. Meg looked up, hopeful for signs of an impending late afternoon storm, but there wasn't a cloud in the sky. She sat down on the cracked bench and stared miserably at the spot in the water where she had hurled the flower. That was not smart. She'd really laid into Hercules, too. Also not smart. This wasn't really his fault. She'd just gotten so mad. She placed her head in her hands. "This is a mess."

"Yep," said Phil, sitting down next to her. Pegasus looked at them, forlorn.

"I'm sorry, Phil," Meg said, patting his hand. "I've doomed us, haven't I?"

"Pretty much. The day is almost done and you'll have one less day in the Underworld, *if* we can even get you there at this point." He gave her a look. "What were you thinking?"

"I don't know!" Meg groaned. "I started thinking about Hera and Athena watching me screw things up and laughing about it, and I got *so* angry. I hate the idea of them thinking I can't do this quest without Hercules's help. What god can't get things done on their own?"

"A lot, actually," Phil admitted. "Why do you think they're always teaming up on things or looking to mortals for help?" Meg paled. "It's okay to not always have all the answers on your own, you know."

The oars. Teamwork. *Right.* "Oh, Phil," Meg groaned. "I just imploded the best relationship I ever had."

He patted her back. "Chin up. You can't scare that kid away. He loves you."

"Sounds like a bad decision on his part."

"Is it?" said a voice.

Meg and Phil turned around. Pegasus jumped.

A god was standing on the ship, aglow in magenta, with rosy pink lips, long lashes, and the bluest of eyes. She wore a single-shouldered gown held together by a heart-shaped pin. Meg instantly remembered where she'd seen her before—on Mount Olympus talking to Demeter.

"Aphrodite," Meg said in surprise. "What are you doing here?"

Aphrodite smiled from ear to ear. "Athena sent me, of course, and it looks like I'm just in time if you were about to give up on love after one argument." She looked at Meg pointedly. "I didn't think a girl as tough as you would be willing to throw it all away so easily."

Meg stared at the god, flabbergasted. How did she know that? "Are *all* of you on Mount Olympus watching me screw things up down here?"

"No," Aphrodite said with a laugh, but the glint in her eyes said otherwise. "Let's just say many of us are invested in you, Megara, and we want to see you succeed, which is why aid is given when needed. Athena has declared herself your guide and as such, she's sent me to help you get past this unfortunate bump in the river, so to speak." Aphrodite looked out over the bow of the boat. "Such a beautiful river to lead to such a sad place. What a shame." She turned around. "And it's unfortunate that your mast is broken and there is no wind to move you along. How are we going to fix that?"

"We?" Meg repeated and looked sideways at Phil. "I guess we could start by patching the sail, but I can't do anything about the lack of wind. That's Notus's territory." Her mother always prayed to Notus in the hot summer months, hoping the god of the south wind would bring along a thunderstorm to cool things down. Hades had always commended the god's penchant for hurricanes.

Aphrodite's sparkling eyes seemed to cut right through her. "Oh, dear. Athena was right to send me. Of course we can do something about this wind—by working *together*, as this satyr was so right to point out." Phil puffed up his chest. "Gods and mortals do so all the time. There is nothing weak about that."

Meg felt her cheeks flush. "It's just not the way I was taught to do things."

Aphrodite sat down on the boat bench. "I know. Your mother did the best she could, but her life was hard. Thea taught you to use your instincts and rely on yourself to get by, and there isn't anything wrong with that. But don't you see? When you find someone worthy of your love, letting them help you is also powerful. Just as you, in turn, have helped him. It doesn't have to be all or nothing. You have found a true partner in Hercules. Love means it's okay to lean on one another."

Meg recalled something Athena had said. *Sometimes your head will lead, and other times it will be your heart.* "I just don't want him to think I can't handle this quest on my own."

"He doesn't think that!" Aphrodite sounded surprised. "Hercules knows you are a strong, confident woman. It's one of the things he loves about you, just like you relish his big heart and ability to see the world in a bright way. You've opened yourselves up to each other, which is a beautiful thing! But it's important to remember that when you let someone into your heart, you allow them to see all sides of you—even the vulnerable side. Loving someone does not make you any less strong. It means you trust in another and they trust in you—that you can give and you can take. No one is keeping count," she said softly. "When you love someone, you want to give them the world."

Meg placed a hand over her eyes. How could she have been so narrow-minded? Aphrodite was right. Wonder

Boy wasn't trying to take away her power; he was just trying to be there when she clearly could have used a hand. "Great. Now what? I tossed the orchid in the river, and I can't even call on him to say I'm sorry." He had given her a one-of-a-kind gift and she'd thrown it away so cavalierly.

Aphrodite smiled. "I have a feeling you two will be just fine—*if* you complete your quest on time. So why don't we focus on that? Put your faith in the journey and the rest will follow."

"Trust in the journey. I can do that." Meg rubbed her hands together, happy to move forward. Maybe she could fix things, one step at a time, starting with the boat. "First, we need to fix this mast." Using every bit of strength she possessed, Meg pulled it out of the water and drenched Pegasus in the process. "Maybe if we anchor some more wood to it, we can hold it together to get down the river." She grabbed some of the debris from the boat. "Phil, do you know if Aegeus left any supplies on the boat?"

Phil reached below a floorboard and pulled out a small box. "He left some fishing things."

Meg opened the box and pulled out the fishing wire. "This should work."

Within a half hour, they had fixed the mast, anchoring it with an assortment of fishing wire and fabric that had been ripped off the sail. They'd fashioned new oars out of driftwood, and Meg had used the wood carving skills she'd once seen Aegeus use on their instruments to smooth the edges of the wood that would pull them through the water. There were still holes in the sail of the ship, but enough was intact that the sail could still catch wind, if there was any.

"Ship is ready again. Now what?"

Aphrodite handed Meg a daisy that appeared in a trail behind her. "We trust Notus will answer our prayers."

Meg's stomach gave a lurch. Trust in prayers? They hadn't worked when she'd tried to save Aegeus. That's why she had called on Hades.

"Sometimes we must take a leap of faith," Aphrodite said kindly.

She'd never get used to the gods reading her thoughts. *A leap of faith.* Just like the one she'd taken when Wonder Boy wanted to slip away with her to row on that lake, or when Phil wanted to go over the falls. She had to open up and learn to just jump. "Okay. Let's call on Notus."

Phil grabbed a giant palm leaf and placed it over his head. "That god is brutal. How do we know he won't send a storm that will blow us all away? Notus destroys crops all the time."

"Yes, but this time, Meg is asking to return somewhere

Notus finds favorable—to the Underworld." Aphrodite looked deep into Meg's eyes. "Concentrate and believe he'll hear you, and I know he will."

Maybe Aphrodite was right. In addition to hurricanes, Hades was always singing Notus's praises for causing famines in the heat of the summer or wiping out an entire field of grain. If anyone would help a boat reach the Underworld, it would be him. "Let's think positive, Phil. At least the rain will cool us off." Meg closed her eyes and channeled all her energy into connecting with Notus.

*If you can hear me, God of Wind, the Great Notus, send your rain and wind down on the river Acheron so that this boat can move swiftly to the entrance of the Underworld.* She opened her eyes.

Phil frowned. "Still sunny."

"Keep going," Aphrodite encouraged.

Meg thought for a moment. What would Notus respond to? What would he want that she could offer him?

*Notus, I promise you, the passenger on this boat is one that will win you favor with Hades. Send your rain down on us and you will be rewarded.*

She paused. The gods seemed to like being in favor with one another, especially the powerful ones. Maybe Notus would appreciate the chance to show off for Hades.

*Bring all you have! Wind! Rain! Thunder! Shake the*

*heavens with your storm! We can take it! We need it and want it now! I beg you, Notus!*

She wrung her hands, trying to channel all the blind faith she could that this would work. And that's when she heard it—a low rumble of thunder.

"Red, I see clouds ahead! *Big* clouds! Look!" Phil jumped up and down and pointed to the dark clouds moving in fast, much as they had that day on Mount Olympus when she had incited the wrath of Zeus. Within seconds, she felt drops of rain, and there was a rustle through the trees as the wind picked up. The boat started to rock. Pegasus neighed with excitement.

"How can I ever repay you?" Meg asked Aphrodite.

"I knew you could do it." The god smiled. "Continue to open your heart to help and to new possibilities, Megara. It won't lead you astray." Her body started to glow brighter. "We are watching over you from above, praying for your safety, and guiding you on this next chapter."

There was a huge clap of thunder and then gigantic drops of rain began to fall. The boat took a fast dip and lurched forward.

"I should go," Aphrodite said and started to evaporate. "Be well, Megara."

Meg reached for her suddenly. "Please, tell Hercules I'm sorry."

"Tell him yourself when you see him," Aphrodite said, and she reached into the water and swirled her fingers around. "Oh, and watch the waves," she said as the water grew choppier and lightning flashed. "You never know what the water will dredge up."

As if in answer, the newly churning river splashed over the side of the boat, and Megara saw a flash of something bright white—the orchid! She reached out and snatched it before it drifted away again.

"Holy Hera," Phil whispered.

"Look at that," Aphrodite said as she started to fade away once more. "A flower as rare as this deserves to be cherished, don't you think?"

"Thank you," Meg said, trying not to get emotional. The rain was coming down in sheets as she quickly placed the flower in her satchel.

There was a huge clap of thunder that seemed to shake the boat loose. The rain was coming down so hard Meg and Phil had to squint to see as they both grabbed paddles and took their positions. Then the boat began to move at top speed.

*We're on our own again,* Meg thought. *But not really.* Then she stuck her oar in the water and plowed onward.

# TWENTY: The Unknown

The storm raged for what felt like hours, lightning crackling across the sky and wind rampaging. The thunder was so loud, the trio didn't speak. They just rowed and continued looking at that mended sail, wondering if or when it would crack under the strain of the wind.

*It will hold,* Meg told herself, trying her best to believe. *This boat will get us where we need to go.*

When their arms had begun to ache terribly from continuous rowing and their bodies started to shiver from being so wet, the storm stopped and the boat began to slow down. The sky was still dark and gray and thunder rumbled in the distance, but the storm was pulling away. In its place, a low-lying fog began to roll in, blanketing much of the landscape. Phil and Meg wiped the water from their eyes and looked at one another.

"We're alive!" Phil said as he wrung water out of his fur. "I'm not sure if we'll ever dry out after that storm, but look!" He pointed off the bow of the ship. "The river seems to be widening again. That must mean we're close to the crossing of the three rivers and the entrance to the Underworld." He looked at Meg in awe. "You did it, Red. You got Notus to bring a storm, and it carried us the rest of the way here!"

"I did, didn't I?" Meg said, feeling pleased with herself as she squeezed the water from her ponytail. The river definitely looked like it widened up ahead, but it was hard to see much of anything in this thickening fog. *Notus,* she thought. His sometimes-wicked storms seemed to also bring in a lot of fog, shrouding the river completely in mystery.

Meg pulled the hourglass out of the satchel and Phil peered over her shoulder. The glowing pink sands in the lower chamber had climbed higher since she'd last checked.

"Halfway full," Phil said somewhat glumly. "Looks like we lost about half a day between the birds and the lack of wind pushing our sails."

Meg tucked the hourglass away again and tried to think

positively. "Five days is still a lot of time to find Katerina . . . right?" She looked at him.

"Oh, yeah," Phil agreed quickly. "Think of all you've done in five days already!"

It was true. How had it only been five days since this journey started? In that time she'd been to hell and back, left Wonder Boy on Mount Olympus, fought an Empusa for Athena's flute, gained the god of war and wisdom's trust, made peace with Aegeus, almost killed them all with her jaunt to get a golden apple, and gotten a pep talk from Aphrodite. *And* she'd fought with Hercules. Meg closed her eyes, wishing to block that last bit out. What she wouldn't give to tell him how sorry she was for the way she treated him.

She had to believe she would see him again. But for now, she had to concentrate on the journey ahead. This next part was going to be the hardest of all.

"We should see Charon any second now," Phil said, sounding anxious. "Sorry. Just the thought of that guy gives me the creeps. But it's going to be fine," he added quickly. "Are you ready?"

Meg patted her satchel and motioned to Athena's flute, which was hanging from her waist. "As ready as I'll ever be, I guess. I know what I have to do. First step is getting past that three-headed mutt."

Phil nodded. "Steer clear of Hades as long as you can and get to Asphodel Meadows."

"Got it!" Meg repeated, taking deep breaths.

The current beneath them was starting to pick up, bringing her closer and closer to the river Styx. The end of their time together was fast approaching, which meant that soon she'd be alone. Meg's heart started to beat more quickly. The only time she'd traveled the river Styx before was with Hades. She'd never been in Charon's boat by herself. She and Phil looked at one another. She had a feeling they were thinking the same thing.

"Phil, I don't know how to thank you for getting me this far." There was so much she wanted to say, and not much time to do it. "I know I'm not your favorite person . . ."

"You weren't," Phil admitted, "but you are now. What you did back there with the birds to save me—that took guts." He swallowed hard. "You're going to do this thing, Red. I can feel it."

"Thanks, Phil," Meg said, feeling her throat tighten.

They looked at one another as the fog overtook them. Meg could hardly see the hand in front of her face. The air grew cold; the sound of the birds on the river disappeared. The boat seemed to stop moving, and then it started to spin.

"Hang on!" Meg said as the boat moved faster and

faster, twirling round and round till she couldn't tell which way was north and which was south.

Finally, the boat shot forward, gliding through the mist and coming to another halt in the middle of a lake where the fog began to fade. A charred wall of rock began to appear in front of her. The mountainside was dotted with dead trees that looked like they had been destroyed by fire. Near the base of the mountain was a cave with a river running through it. The entrance to the Underworld.

A small boat emerged and moved slowly toward them. It was ferried by a skeleton-like creature. Hades's minion who ferried the dead to the Underworld made her anxious. Meg placed one hand on Athena's flute to steady herself. *You can do this,* she told herself, standing quietly as the boat approached. *Trust yourself.*

Charon paused and sniffed the air as he approached. "Mortals, you may not enter here."

"We can pay, Charon," Meg said quickly, and he glanced at her curiously.

"We can?" Phil repeated.

"Yes, give him a drachma," Meg instructed.

He looked at her blankly. "I don't have any drachmas."

"What do you mean you have no drachmas?" she hissed. "You knew you were getting me to the entrance to the Underworld. Everyone needs a drachma to get there!"

"Right." Phil scratched one of his horns. "I forgot about that part."

"How could you forget?"

"Hey, Red, we had some other pressing things to worry about, like getting you here in the first place, and in one piece."

Meg groaned, unable to believe they hadn't discussed this before. "Well, what do we do now?" she asked.

"I don't know!" Phil started to pace. "If you don't have one, they say Charon makes you wait, and we don't have a day to spare! Where am I going to find a coin?" Phil started overturning everything on the boat in his search, but Meg knew he wouldn't find one. Aegeus would never be as careless as to leave a coin behind.

Where could she get a drachma fast? *Think, Meg.* She didn't feel right calling on Hercules for this. But she could call on her guide, couldn't she?

Meg looked up. "Athena, god of war and wisdom, guide to heroes and caretaker of those on journeys, if you can see us or hear me now, we could really use your help here," she whispered. "I need a drachma." Nothing happened.

A low growl emerged from Charon's mouth. "Do

you have payment or not? I have many souls to transport today."

"Please, Athena." Meg tried again. "I will take your knowledge and your gifts with me to the other side, but this I can't do without help." Meg thought for a moment about what might sway her. "Someday I will thank you in person and play your flute, and when I do, you'll feel my music with your heart. I promise."

Meg and Phil looked to the sky, both imagining a coin falling from the clouds. Nothing happened. Meg was starting to join Phil in his panic when she felt something cool appear in her right hand. She opened her palm. It was a silver drachma.

"Smart move, kid!" Phil cried. "We have a drachma!"

"Yesssss?" Charon hissed, reaching a skeletal hand out for payment.

"Thank you, Athena," Meg said solemnly to the sky. "I guess it's time for me to go."

"Wait," Phil said quickly. "What if you asked Athena for two more coins?" He eyed the cave ahead of them. "We could go with you, you know. Maybe we could be of some help down there."

Meg smiled wanly. She couldn't believe what Phil was offering. Even though they both knew that he couldn't follow, it was a touching offer nonetheless. The fact that she was heading back into the Underworld, a place mortals did not leave, let alone escape twice, was starting to feel ever more real. "You're going to miss me that much, huh?"

He rolled his eyes. "No. I just don't want you getting yourself in trouble without me."

They looked at one another, and Meg hesitated. "Phil, if I don't make it back . . . tell Hercules—"

"No," Phil cut her off. "I'm not giving any messages. Tell him yourself when you get back."

"But if I don't," Meg insisted, "promise me you'll tell Hercules that I . . ." She swallowed, still unsure of the right words. "Let him know that I . . . Just tell him I'm sorry."

Phil met her gaze, his face as serious as she'd ever seen it. "Okay."

Meg moved toward the edge of the boat. She felt her satchel for the krotala, and her waist to make sure the flute was still attached. She rubbed Pegasus's nose and he neighed sadly. Meg felt a tug on her heart. "And Phil, one more thing?"

"Anything," he said.

"If I don't return, make sure Hercules moves on from all of this," Meg said.

"Meg . . ." Phil swallowed hard.

It was the first time he'd called her by her actual name.

She tried to put her spinning thoughts into words. "I don't want him wasting his immortality on me. He's a good guy who gives so much of himself. He deserves to have someone do that for him in return. Got it?"

Phil looked at her. "Wow, you really do love the guy, don't you?"

Meg didn't answer. She handed the coin to Charon, and he motioned for her to step onto his boat. Then she turned around and looked at Phil and Peg again one more time. "See you on the other side," she said, hoping she sounded surer than she felt.

"You will!" Phil said, but tears were streaming down his face. Even Peg looked upset. "I know it. I'll see you in a few days. Hey . . . you know what? I'll wait for you at Aegeus's. Gods know he could use some help. I'll meet you there."

"Deal," Meg said. Charon immediately started to row away. She held up her hand in a wave.

Phil did the same, and they silently watched one another for as long as they could. Then a shadow crossed Meg's face. They had entered the cave.

A low moan came from somewhere in the darkness, and then another. Meg felt a bump underneath the boat and a tug on her dress. She jumped back. Something had just reached up and grabbed her. No matter how many times she rode in this boat, it was a feeling she couldn't get used to.

"Keep your limbs inside the boat, mortal, or they'll pull you down with them," Charon said in a gravelly voice.

Meg swallowed hard and tried not to imagine the river beneath them filled with thousands of lost souls who would do anything to get out. She pulled her arms and legs in and sat down on the narrow bench, peering into the darkness surrounding her. The moaning continued, as did the boat's swaying while the dead tried to climb aboard. "How long is this going to take?" Hades had always been too busy talking her ear off for her to pay attention to how much time passed, but she didn't remember the ride being this long.

Charon slowly but surely steered them forward. "The land of the dead is a large place and not a quick journey. It's meant to give you time to process all you've lost."

Meg closed her eyes, trying to block out the cries, but it was near impossible. *Don't look at the water. Don't look at the water!* She thought about how she had lost track of time in the Underworld before, about Phil's warning not to lose her bearings. It would be so easy to get pulled into the darkness, to give up hope as those shrieking beneath her were demanding she do. *Think of something happy,* Meg told herself. *Think of something good so you aren't pulled under.*

*Wonder Boy.* Meg smiled to herself as she recalled the one and only chance she'd had to cook for him.

---

"You did all this?" he'd asked when she'd convinced him to meet her one afternoon at the lake where they'd gone rowing. She was supposed to be scouting a Minotaur to add to Hades's cause, while Hercules was supposed to be throwing discuses to keep his hero skills sharp. But she figured they needed to eat anyway; no one would miss them for one measly hour.

"What do you think?" she'd asked, motioning to the blanket on the grass and the assortment of foods. There were nuts and dates, warm bread and cheese that she'd gotten at the market, and center stage was a fish roasting over a small fire.

"No one's ever cooked for me before," Hercules said, heading over to admire the blackening trout. He looked at her sheepishly. "Except my mother. And actually, Phil, but he's terrible. Don't tell him I said that," he added quickly and she laughed.

"Your secret's safe with me, Wonder Boy." She motioned to the blanket. "Sit down. Eat something. We'll have to get back before long."

Hercules seemed like a kid with a new toy as he ripped off a piece of bread, pairing it with a hunk of cheese and some dates. "The fish smells delicious. I didn't know you could cook."

"There's a lot you don't know about me," she'd said lightly. "I taught myself, actually. My mother was always working and exhausted when she came home at night, so I helped by making our meals. I'd spend hours in the market talking to the different vendors and pestering them with questions about cooking fish and what cheeses to pair with what meats and how to roll grape leaves and . . . by the time my mother got home she had a full spread waiting." She checked the fish again. "It was the one time of day she didn't look tired." She stopped herself when she heard her admission and glanced over at Hercules. He was listening with rapt attention. "I'm boring you, aren't I? I don't usually tell anyone my life's story." She'd never told anyone that particular anecdote, actually. Not even Aegeus.

What was she doing? Cooking for the man that Hades wanted to take down?

She felt Wonder Boy's hand on her shoulder. "You can tell me anything, Meg. I want to hear it all. I want to know everything about you."

"Are you sure about that?" she couldn't help saying.

"I'm sure," he'd said, and then he'd leaned down and kissed her. His lips tasted sweet like the dates he'd just eaten. She'd kissed him right back.

---

Meg saw a flash and looked up. Torches were coming alive along the cave's path, and she suddenly remembered where she was again.

"Get ready, mortal," Charon said. "You may have gotten by me, but Cerberus won't be so forgiving."

# TWENTY-ONE: Cerberus's Lullaby

The end of the cave suddenly opened, pulling apart like someone was parting overgrown vines. Quickly Meg saw what was on the other side: Cerberus.

The massive three-headed creature was as black as coal, and as large as the first monster she had lured Hercules to fight when she was still working for Hades. She watched as one of the heads snored, its mouth opening and closing, revealing teeth as large as the columns on a building. Drool puddled around its massive mouth and oozed into the river. The creature was collared and tethered to something on the ground, but it could certainly move its heads. There was no sailing past the thing without being swallowed whole. To make matters worse, the area around the animal was littered with hundreds of bones and skulls that she could only assume were the remains of other foolish mortals who had tried to enter the Underworld with their lives intact.

She needed to get ready to face it. She quickly began unhooking Athena's flute.

"Could you slow this boat down?" Meg said, but Charon kept his steady rowing pace. She cursed herself for not using her time on the boat more wisely. She had mere seconds to prepare, and she wasn't even sure what tune she was going to attempt with Athena's flute, let alone if she could remember how to play it. Athena had sensed her heart was not in it. Would Cerberus be the same? If she couldn't produce a solid melody for the beast, she was done for.

A low howl rocked the cavern and Meg looked up. Cerberus's right head was fully awake and alerting the other two of the mortal before them. The three heads sprang up and the creature lurched forward, filling up every available space in the cave. Its eyes were bloodred and its snouts were as large as Stymphalian birds. Spit flew from each mouth, landing inches from the boat as the dog chomped at the air. The sound reminded her of bones being snapped. She tried hard to ignore it.

*You play so well you could put Cerberus to sleep,* she thought. But the phrase didn't make her think of Aegeus this time. It made her think of the challenge at hand

and what it would take to return to Hercules. *Put this beast to sleep and get Katerina so you can leave this dreary place,* she told herself. She was about to play for her life. Literally.

"Goodbye, mortal," Charon said with an air of glee as the boat neared the creature. He'd clearly seen how this story typically ended.

*He won't see it again today,* Meg vowed.

She lifted Athena's flute to her lips and blew a few quick notes to get the beast's attention.

The right head immediately snapped to attention while the other two looked around.

*Good.* Meg blew into the flute again, hitting several high notes in a row that even made her wince.

The other two heads stirred and sniffed the air. Their growls momentarily stopped.

*Now I have your attention,* she thought. Her hands were slippery from sweat, but she held them steady and placed her lips on the reed. Once again, she returned to "The Plight of the Lily."

The left head spotted the boat approaching and started to growl, and the center head roared in response. It wasn't working. Meg removed her lips from the reed and exhaled slowly. Her hands were shaking. *Concentrate,* she reminded herself. *Remember why you used to play.* Meg started the melody again.

This time she noticed the change right away. The second head snapped back, listening, then the third, and then the first. She focused on each note, her fingers running along the reed as the notes came to her from the stores of her mind. She tried to forget about the creature and just focus on giving her best performance. *Forget he's there,* she told herself. *Just play.*

After a few seconds, Meg felt a thick stillness. She opened her eyes ever so slightly. The boat had moved closer to the creature, but its heads weren't moving. Its eyes had drifted shut and the creature was slowly sitting back. It lowered itself to the floor. She heard the first head snore and her stomach began to relax. She kept playing as Charon passed by, not stopping her tune until Cerberus disappeared and the cavern closed behind them.

"Impressive, mortal," Charon said as he rounded a corner and the cave opened up again, revealing a massive structure in front of her. "You've earned passage to the Underworld."

She breathed a sigh of relief. She'd passed her first test!

The Underworld rose to greet them, the landscape in front of the boat looking like a howling tree with a city atop it. Building after gray-stoned building was piled on top of each other, climbing haphazardly into the sky. Below them were two cavernous eyes that seemed to lead in different directions. And below that were two bone-like columns holding the whole thing up. Meg knew what she'd find between them—Hades's lair.

"Stop!" Meg said quickly.

For the first time, Charon stopped rowing. "Yesssss?" he questioned, an eerie grin on his skeletal lips.

"I . . ." Where did she want to go? Which way was Asphodel Meadows? She stared again at the large structure that led to each realm of the Underworld. The fire of Tartarus was a dead giveaway as to which way *not* to go. But which part held Elysium and which one contained Asphodel Meadows? How was she going to find Katerina there? And without being seen? "I want to get off," Meg said suddenly. "Please pull over."

"At the end," he said and started to row again. "There is only one way in and one way out."

"But I want to go to Asphodel Meadows," Meg protested as the boat neared a familiar spiral staircase leading to the structure above it. It was lit by flaming blue torches. Meg had taken those steps many times before. Her eyes darted around for a sign of Hades. She needed to get off this boat before he knew she was there.

"Don't they all?" Charon said, steering to a platform near the stairs and stopping. "There is only one way to reach all paths of the Underworld, and this is it. The end of the line, so to speak."

Meg sighed and stepped off. She approached the stairs. "Thanks for the ride. Any chance you know which floor to get off on?"

Charon looked at her. "No." Then he turned the boat around and headed back down the river, lost souls nipping at his bony heels.

"Helpful. Thanks." Meg looked around. The cave was eerily quiet except for the sound of licking flames. Meg took a deep breath and began to climb, rushing past the first two floors she knew to be Hades's home. She'd never had a need to go above them before. All her work for Hades had taken place on Earth, so most of the Underworld outside his lair was a complete mystery. Meg took the steps two at a time, staying close to the wall to avoid falling off the other side. When she reached the first landing, she was relieved to see signs chiseled into the stone walls.

TARTARUS–DOWN

ELYSIUM–UP

ASPHODEL MEADOWS–MIDDLE GROUND

Beneath the signs was a ticker that read: OVER 5,000,000,001 SERVED (AND COUNTING!)

"The Underworld, helpful as always." Meg looked around.

Well, she knew which general direction she wanted to head, anyway—up. Out of the darkness sounded like a good idea. Meg started climbing the never-ending staircase. She felt like she was walking forever. She wound around bend after bend looking for an exit to Asphodel Meadows, but there were no off-ramps. After ten flights, her legs were burning and her breath was ragged, giving her no choice but to stop for a moment. And just a moment. The fear of Hades appearing was enough to make her push on. She leaned against the wall for a second and looked up. She was high enough now that she could actually see a light among the stacked towers. Was that blue sky she saw, or an illusion? Could that be the land of the living or Elysium? She wasn't sure, but she knew she had to keep moving . . . so long as she didn't have a heart attack from all these stairs.

*Ping!*

Meg peered at the peculiar object that made the noise. Chiseled into the rocky wall were hand-carved double doors. They were so seamlessly part of the rock, she would have walked right past them if they hadn't chimed. As she stared, the doors opened. Meg ran down a few steps to hide.

"Going up?" asked a droll voice.

Meg peeked around the corner. The space behind the doors was empty. Who was the voice talking to?

"Asphodel Meadows on level two!"

*Asphodel Meadows?* Meg tentatively approached the open doors. Could this contraption take her up faster than the stairs? She peered into the small space. It was empty.

"Going up?" the bodiless voice prodded again.

Meg looked inside. There were four buttons: ELYSIUM, ASPHODEL MEADOWS, TARTARUS, and HADES'S PALACE. If this thing meant she could avoid more stairs and slip by Hades, it was worth trying. "Oh, what the hell." She stepped in and pressed the button.

Maybe using the word *hell* was her mistake. The doors closed and then opened again, filling with smoke that wound its way around her shoulders and down her body before she could react. She found herself being pulled forward.

Hades's face suddenly appeared inches from her own. "Hello there, Meg-let. Miss me?"

# TWENTY-TWO: Hades

As god of the Underworld, there was one thing Hades was not—a fool.

He knew Meg was back the second Charon rowed into the cave.

Scratch that.

He knew his little Nut-Meg had returned the moment Notus came calling about a redheaded mortal begging for some wind to get her boat to the entrance of the Underworld. She wasn't the first one to try that move, and usually he said no to these types of requests. Or, if he was in a generous mood, he'd let Notus do his thing, and the boat would be knocked around so badly, everyone aboard would perish and he'd get a few new souls without having to work for it. And they'd get what they'd wanted anyway—passage to the Underworld, just not quite the way they had pictured. Either way, it was a win-win.

But while the thought of Meg trying to sneak back into the Underworld made his blood boil, he was also intrigued. His most prized servant had betrayed him and run off with that beefy half-brained god, ruining everything he had spent the last eighteen years working for. For a move like that, it should have been *her* soul floating in the river Styx for eternity. Instead he'd had to climb his way out of the swirling river as those nasty beasts clung to him, begging for second chances.

He didn't give second chances, of course. Didn't they know that by now? He'd only given a mortal a second chance once, and look where it had gotten him. Meg had traded up, literally, and gotten out of her contract with him in the process.

Which was why payback was in order.

"So, Meggie, what brings you back to this neck of the woods?" Hades asked as he pulled her back out of the elevator, his smoke winding around her body and squeezing.

She managed to choke out a simple sentence. "I thought I smelled a rat in this dump."

Hades shot her into the air and let her hang there in his smoky cuffs. "My little flower, my little bird, my little

Nut-Meg, as lovely as it is to see you again, I have to wonder what brought you back so quickly. Did things go south with your muscleman already?"

Meg struggled against the smoky bonds. "Hercules is fine—no thanks to you."

"Hmm . . . then what brings you here?" he wondered, enjoying this a tad more than he thought he would. "You're not dead, sadly, so you're trespassing, which means you want something. What else is new?"

"I don't want anything," she said, her voice weakening as the smoke tightened.

"Are you sure?" Hades picked at the skull clip on his chiton, refusing to make eye contact with the temptress. "Kind of feels like you do, or you wouldn't have dared show your face here, since"—his body erupted in blue flames as his rage took hold—"you tricked me out of keeping your soul and helped Hercules defeat me!"

"How is that any different from how you tricked me?" Meg snapped.

"*I* tricked *you*?" This was an interesting development. His smoke disappeared. Meg started to free-fall as he walked away to think about what her statement meant. Then he heard her scream. If she died so quickly, this would be far less interesting. He snapped his fingers and his smoke caught her inches from the ground. He used it to bring her straight back to him.

His face came close to hers again. "Care to explain?"

Meg grit her teeth. "You lied to me."

"Me? Lie?" Hades asked, and his smoke disappeared. "Does that sound like me?"

Meg fell a few feet and hit the landing. She quickly jumped up and dusted herself off. "You made me think Aegeus moved on after I'd been gone days. I was here for *two years*!"

She'd caught on to that trick, had she? Hades scratched his chin. "Who? Sorry. Name doesn't ring a bell."

"You made me think he left me for someone else right away so I'd forget him and do your dirty work for eternity."

"Really? That cannot be true," he said, feigning innocence. "I am burning up at the thought."

"I paid my debt." She shook her head, her ridiculous hair bouncing about. "*You* made the deal with Hercules to change that. So actually, you should have no beef with me."

"True. True. True. But guess what?" He bared his teeth. "I am mad!" His whole body erupted in flames again. "So are you going to tell me why you're here or are you going to make me dump you into the river Styx with all those other useless souls?" He sent his smoke slowly toward her again.

Meg backed away as the smoke started to wind its way around her feet, then her lower body, and lifted her up again. "Fine! I'll tell you, okay?" she said hoarsely. "Just put me down."

He waved his hand and she landed on her hands and knees. "Go ahead. Spill your sob story. I could use a good one. There hasn't been anything good to watch down here in weeks."

"I've been sent on a quest to retrieve a lost soul."

Hades looked at her and blinked twice slowly. Then he dissolved into laughter, the flames on his head nearly reaching the next landing. "You're kidding me, right? This has to be a prank!" He looked around. "Who put you up to this? Hercules? Athena? Poseidon? He loves a good fish tale. Who?"

"Hera," Meg said calmly.

He laughed harder. "Zeus's little wifey-poo? Hilarious! No one leaves the Underworld once they arrive. No one!" His laughter died out. Smoke shot out of his hands and wound around Meg's waist. "Especially not with you." The smoke carried her over to the side of the stairs again as she struggled.

*Ping!*

"Uh, Magnanimous Lord of the Underworld?" The little demons Pain and Panic nervously shuffled out of the elevator. "The Fates are here to see you, Your Darkness."

"They can wait!" Hades roared as he prepared to toss Meg over the side.

Panic cleared his throat. "They said it's about the Underworld stowaway."

Hades dropped Meg without thinking and heard her scream as she disappeared over the side of the staircase. "Stowaway? Tell them I'll be right there." Hades joined them on the elevator, which shot down at breakneck speed and opened on the first floor. He strolled out, leaving Pain and Panic to go on ahead and deliver his message. He waited till the doors closed to exhale.

It was a pity not to hear Meg explain more about this Hera thing, but a fall like the one he'd just sent her on would kill her instantly. He supposed he could learn the details about her failed journey once her soul settled into one of his realms. He had bigger issues to deal with at the moment.

"Per? You can come out now."

A figure slowly emerged from the shadows. "Are they gone?"

"No one is here," he reassured her, his voice dropping to a new calm at the sight of her.

She was exquisite. He loved everything about her, from the crown of silver flowers she wore in her black hair to the dark eyes that offset her tan skin. For the first time ever, he even noticed clothing. He couldn't help admiring how she favored cobalt blue for her gowns over drab browns. Today's dress was clipped at her waist with a floral silver belt.

"What did the Fates say?" she asked, sounding timid for the first time since he'd met her. She was anything but a wallflower. She was fiery. He loved that about her most of all.

He glided over and put his arms around her. "I'm on my way in to see them right now. I don't want you to worry. I thought you were going to go do that thing to take your mind off all that."

"I am," she said with a smile. "You're going to love it."

He doubted that, but he wanted her to be happy. "In any case, we'll make sure the future is in our favor. Even if we have to burn the whole world to the ground."

She nodded and wound her arms as far as she could around his ample waist. "I'm not going back, Hades."

He had a fire coursing through him now that was different from anything he'd ever experienced before. He couldn't put his finger on what the feeling was. It wasn't anger, it wasn't hate, it wasn't even envy. Was this what all those lovesick souls were always talking about? Was he in love? It sure felt like it, and if that were true . . .

He was done for. And yet—he could not deny how nice it was to have someone to talk to after all these years, someone besides his ridiculous minions or the sniveling souls or the needlessly confusing Fates. She was interesting and lively. She went toe-to-toe with him when she disagreed on something, which was fun. And she made his future seem brighter, which he thought would have been impossible after the Titan plan failed.

"I know," he said, his hand caressing her cheek. "I won't let anyone come between us. That is a promise."

# TWENTY-THREE: Asphodel Meadows

She was falling. *Again*. Meg had her arms out in front of her, flailing as she struggled to grab hold of anything to keep her from plummeting dozens of stories to her death. She felt her hand hit something hard and she grabbed on, her body slamming against the rocky surface.

*Ow,* she thought, all the wind knocked out of her as she dangled by one arm off the edge of the staircase. She looked up, half expecting Hades to come roaring after her. Strangely, the god didn't appear, but she wasn't about to complain.

Panting, she grabbed hold of the ledge with her other hand and winced through the pain, pulling herself up to the steps to shimmy back onto the stairs. She needed to get going before Hades realized his mistake.

Taking the stairs two at a time again, Meg rounded corners fast, not paying attention to the number of levels she was ascending. She passed the floor with the bizarre lift contraption, bypassed the hot-zone turnoff to Tartarus with its unbearable screams, and kept moving, praying Hades was so busy with the Fates he'd forgotten all about her. Where was Asphodel Meadows already? She needed to get lost in that level fast.

She'd never been to that part of the Underworld before. No one went to Tartarus by choice, but she had visited Elysium one time when Hades made her deliver a message to Achilles for him. Elysium was like one large party—the finest food, the perfect weather, homes as large as Greek temples, and endless laughter. All they seemed to do was sit around all day and tell their hero war stories. Meg almost had to wonder if they remembered they were dead.

She had caught sight of Asphodel Meadows once, and at the time it had reminded her a lot of Earth—on the outside it was perfectly lovely, but upon closer inspection, things were definitely flawed. Maybe that's why Hades barely bothered with the souls there. If there was ever a place to get lost, it was in the Meadows.

Meg took another turn, and that was when she finally saw the sign carved into the rock:

**THE MIDDLE: ASPHODEL MEADOWS**

Meg moved to the door fast and turned the knob. It was unlocked. She took a deep breath and slipped inside.

At first glance, it looked like she'd stepped into the village where she'd spent the first few years of her life before her father had left. There was a square surrounded by small buildings, all quite plain, but nicely kept. Small flower boxes dotted the windows, each box containing strangely just one flower. There were the sounds of hammering in the distance and of birds chirping incessantly, even though none were in sight.

Meg tugged at her dress. The air was muggier here than it had been in the stairwell—not hot, not exactly cold, just a bit warm. The sky was filled with a smattering of clouds that kept passing the sun, as if the weather couldn't decide what it wanted to do for the day. She moved into the village, walking over patches of green grass that had a few dead spots in it. Other than the hammering and the birds, she didn't hear anything, and she didn't see a soul.

*Is this the right place?* she wondered. *Souls do live here, don't they?*

Finally, she heard talking and turned around. A group of women was walking toward her dressed in chitons and robes in various shades of tan. One wore a wrap on her head, reminding Meg of someone.

She felt a sudden pang. *Mother.*

Thea had to be here somewhere. Meg knew that from her digging last time she was in the Underworld. Of course, back then Hades had blocked Meg's mother from knowing Meg was there so Thea wouldn't try to find her daughter. But this time, she wasn't sure if Hades had thought to place a veil over Thea. Did that mean Thea had been able to learn of her arrival like other next of kin souls did when someone entered the Underworld? Would she look for the daughter she hadn't seen in almost two decades? Meg's heart gave a lurch. Was there time to even try to . . . *No.* Phil had been clear—stick to the quest. That being said, if Meg and her mother crossed paths in Asphodel Meadows, she knew she wouldn't be able to just walk away. There was so much she wanted to say.

If only she had more time. The breeze picked up and Meg felt her hand go to the satchel. She pulled out the hourglass and looked at it with dismay. It was almost two-thirds full. How could that be? Hadn't she just arrived in the Underworld hours ago?

*Time moves differently down here,* she reminded herself. *And I'm running out of it.* She had to focus on the task at hand.

Meg looked at the women again, their nameless faces coming straight toward her. She stepped into their path.

They were talking hurriedly, and one was laughing. It was good to know people in the Underworld still smiled.

"Excuse me," Meg interrupted them. "Do any of you know Katerina?"

They stopped short. "I'm sorry, love. Katerina who?" one asked.

*How silly of me. There must be thousands of Katerinas here.* "Katerina Dimas," Meg clarified.

The women looked at one another and shrugged. "Sorry, dear. We don't know anyone with that name," said one with gray eyes.

"Are you new here, dear?" asked one with a scarf wrapped around her head. "You speak rather loud for the dead."

"And your gown is purple," said the shortest, sounding wistful. "Oh, how I miss wearing vibrant colors. These tan gowns are quite dull."

"And never fit exactly right," said the first woman. "Mine is just an inch too long."

"While mine is a bit loose around the waist," said the one in the scarf.

"That's from a lack of overeating," said the short one. She looked at Meg. "We eat well here, not to worry, but it always feels as if we could go for one more bite, you know?"

"Or an extra sip of wine," said the gray-eyed one with a sigh. "The glass is never entirely full."

"But it could be worse," the short one reminded her. "We could be roasting."

"So true," they all agreed.

"You look lively, dear," said the one with the scarf. "Your skin is still glowing."

Meg knew she couldn't say she was alive. That would certainly cause a commotion in the Underworld that she didn't need. Hades would find her in seconds. "That's because you're right. I'm new."

"That explains it," said the tallest to the others. "Then you're in the wrong place, dear. You'd be with the new recruits. That's in the Evergreen, south of here."

"What?" Meg asked as the sound of hammering increased.

The one in a scarf huffed. "I swear, that construction is around the clock! I'm so tired of hammering!"

"And birds!" said the first woman.

"And bees," said the second. "But they beat the hammering. So many people moving in, the construction is never-ending. Such a headache."

"I said, go south to the Evergreen," the tallest repeated, speaking loudly and enunciating to be heard over the hammering.

"How do I get there?" Meg shouted.

"Follow the path," said the shortest. "But hurry. The

welcome party is only a few hours a day, and you don't want to miss it—all your relatives are usually there waiting."

"It's so much fun!" said the short one.

"And the one time you'll find the wine flowing freely," said the one with gray eyes wistfully.

"What is your name, in case anyone we know inquires about your whereabouts?" asked the tallest woman. "Word travels fast when a loved one arrives."

Meg hesitated as the clouds passed over the sun again. "Megara Egan," she said softly. "Daughter of Thea."

"Thea," one said, her eyes widening. "I think I once met a Thea with a daughter. If I see her, I will let her know where to find you!"

"Thank you!" Meg said, wishing more than anything she could stay and look for her mother herself. *That's not why you're here,* she reminded herself. *Keep to the quest.*

She hurried down the path, walking for what felt like an eternity, passing village after village that looked identical to the first she'd arrived in. They all had various names that sounded vaguely alike with buildings labeled things like ASPHODEL B-1,000. She wondered yet again which one could possibly be her mother's.

At least now she saw people outside. Some were sitting on blankets chatting. Others were taking walks or playing musical instruments. She heard laughter and singing.

People genuinely seemed content, although there was the occasional complaint to be heard about the mugginess of the air, or the hammering, or even the abundant bird population.

"What lovely coloring you have!" remarked a woman on a walk with her husband. "It's almost as if you're still alive!"

"Don't be silly," snapped her husband, giving Meg a look. "Why would the living want to come here?"

Meg smiled uneasily. It wouldn't be long before someone alerted the powers that be that a mortal was in their midst. Meg quickened her pace when she saw a meadow peek out over the next hilltop. As she got closer, the sun seemed to pull away from the clouds and the grass under her feet turned a bright green. She heard definite sounds of a party in the distance and quickened her pace. The air started to smell sweeter. Were those apricots she smelled? Or figs?

And there were trees again! She hadn't realized how much she missed them till she saw them growing there along the path. They had perfect little green leaves and flowers budding on branches. And at the side of the road was a woman kneeling over a garden tending to a bed of hydrangeas blooming in rich fuchsias, blues, and whites.

"Those are gorgeous!" Meg said in surprise. They

were the most colorful things she'd seen in the Underworld and the vibrancy warmed her heart for a moment. "I can't believe anything like that grows down here!"

The woman looked up at her and smiled, her eyes dark yet warm. "Thanks. I wasn't sure if it was possible myself, but with deep rooting and some good soil, it seems anything is."

"You planted these?" Meg said in awe.

The woman looked pleased as she glanced at the colorful beds of blooms in the nearby meadows. "You could say that. I love the *drama* of it all—the seeds being sown, the elements working for and against them, the flower erupting against all odds, then the death of the bloom. *So* much more exciting than my old life." She looked at Meg as though just remembering she were there. "But it's probably best if you don't tell anyone you saw me here."

"Oh." Meg made a motion to seal her lips. "No problem there. I'd rather you not tell anyone you saw me, either." She briefly wondered about the Underworld rules for changing the landscape—Hades probably would not take kindly to that.

"You've got a deal," Meg said.

"I didn't even expect to be here this long," the woman admitted, wiping her tan hands on her cobalt blue dress. "But time moves fast."

"Too fast," Meg agreed, taking another admiring look at the garden the woman had cultivated.

"And I refuse to let anyone control what I do," she said, a new fire in her voice. She ran a hand through her black hair. "I'm not sure why I'm telling you any of this."

"It's nice to have someone to talk to," Meg said. She never would have thought she'd miss Phil, but she did. Not to mention Wonder Boy . . . "It gets me out of my head."

"Exactly," the woman agreed. "As does gardening." She frowned. "Except this batch is extremely frustrating. This is my third time tending to these hydrangeas this week and the leaves are still dying out." She held out a yellowed stem for Meg to see. "I've never had this problem before."

Meg leaned down for a moment, taken by the sweet scent and the beauty of the blossoms. "Does this area get enough sun? Kind of feels like nothing in this place gets enough, but this spot in particular is kind of especially shady, don't you think? Hydrangeas do best in full sun in the early part of the day and then partial sun the rest." Meg looked around the area for a moment. "This bed might need to be moved farther down the road, where the sun is brighter."

The woman rocked back on her heels. She looked at Meg with interest as she pushed her black curly hair to the right side of her neck. "You really know your hydrangeas."

"My mother loved them," Meg recalled. "No matter

where we moved, she always splurged on flowers to spruce up the joint." Her heart tugged at the thought of Thea being so near. "She taught me how to prune them and make them grow."

"They are one of my favorites," the woman admitted and stared at Meg again. "What is your mother's name?"

"Thea," Meg said, realizing it felt good to say her name aloud again. It suddenly occurred to her that she should say it more often. *We imprint the lost on our hearts,* she thought. Aegeus said Katerina had liked to say that.

"Thea," the woman repeated, inhaling deeply as she said the name. "She will be happy to see you, I'm sure. You're new, I take it?"

"Yes," Meg said quickly, and felt a wave of panic. "Which is why I should probably go. You know, to go find her."

"You're lucky," the woman said wistfully, seemingly not wanting their conversation to end, "that you can be with the person you love. That's why I'm here, too, but it's not easy."

"No, it's not," Meg agreed. "Love is complicated."

"Exactly!" The woman shook her head. She sighed and plucked one of the flowers at her feet. "Living in shadows is exhausting, isn't it?"

Meg nodded. Then she heard the music growing louder in the distance and knew she'd already been there too long. "It was nice meeting you."

"Good luck with your mother!" the woman said.

Meg continued down the path, the flowers growing almost fluorescent, they were so bright and plentiful. Buildings came into view next, and Meg immediately noticed they were as vibrant and varied as a rainbow. In the middle of a large courtyard were several fountains spraying full streams of water high into the sky. And that was before she noticed the people.

Unlike the other villages, this square was flooded with people dancing, hugging, and crying happy tears. People were dressed in radiantly colored chitons (that appeared to fit perfectly) and still looked almost rosy in appearance as if they were still alive, even though they weren't. Meg didn't hear the incessant chirping of birds or hammering. She only heard the sound of laughter and light. Meg felt her stomach relax for a moment, reinvigorated by their joy. The Underworld could make a person feel like the weight of the world was on their shoulders.

It could also make people think no time had passed, when it clearly passed much quicker down here. It had been less than a week since the Titans' attack, but who knew how long that time had felt to Katerina? Would she still be partying and rejoicing at connecting with her family again? How long did people live in this in-between? There was only one way to find out: she would need to ask for help. *What would*

*Aphrodite say about this development?* Meg wondered with a small smile. Then, *What would my mother say?*

Meg hurried forward, joining the crowd of people who still looked a lot like her. The sound of the flute made her turn around. A group of men had gathered to play music while others danced, reuniting with some who were wearing tan and were grayer in appearance. A woman danced by her and Meg touched her arm gently. "Excuse me. I'm looking for someone."

"Sure! Who can we help you find, dear?" The woman's smile was still bright, her eyes still flecked with color.

"Katerina Dimas."

The woman thought for a moment. "I don't recognize the name, dear. When did she arrive? Was she on the ship that sank off the Greek isles today? There's a large group in the south of town from there."

"No." Meg shook her head. "She would be here a few days. She died during the Titans' attack last week."

"Last week?" the woman said in surprise. "That occurred a few months ago."

"No, it was only a few days ago," Meg started to say and stopped herself. But of course. If time moved differently down here, then the normal rules wouldn't apply. Katerina definitely would have moved on if she'd been here a few months. Where could she be? "I'm sorry. You're right.

Where would she move to after the Evergreen, then? Is there a directory I could look at to see where she lives now?"

"Directory!" The woman laughed. "Oh no, dear. Can you imagine how big it would be and how often we'd have to update it? I'm afraid not. You'll have to ask around, unless one of her relatives is here among the newly departed. Or she signed on to be a guide, like me. I get to stay here for eternity—and keep my rosy, alive glow, which is lovely." She looked at Meg again. "But you *do* look familiar." Her eyes opened wide as she scanned her up and down. "Are you Megara?"

Meg looked at her in surprise. "Why, yes."

"Your mother was just here looking for you!" the woman said. "She was told you arrived today and gave me your description, but I hadn't seen anyone with hair as bright as yours, so I sent her to Asphodel Unit A-6,985. That is where most of the new recruits were sent in the past few days. Maybe you can catch her."

Meg felt a deep pang of longing. Her mother was looking for her. "I wish I could, but I have to find Katerina first. Are you sure you don't have any suggestions about where I might find someone who has been here a few months?"

The woman pursed her lips. "I wish I knew. The only people that stick around the Evergreen for any length of time are children, and the adults looking after them tend to stay, too. Hades never bothers to make them move on. Someone has to take care of the young'uns, after all."

Meg felt a flicker of hope. *Layla*. "All children? What if they're here alone and later reunited with an adult?"

The woman thought for a moment. "We always send the adults to them there—they have the most beautiful seascape and mountains and glorious weather. It's gorgeous! The adults always fall in love with the area when they see it. Aside from Elysium, it's the nicest place in the Underworld to be."

"Where is it?" Meg asked eagerly.

The woman pointed toward the sun beginning to lower on the horizon. "The fields near the water. Sometimes you can also find them at the poppy fields."

Meg felt her heart begin to rev. "The poppy fields? Where are they?"

"Same direction, dear," the woman said, and Meg was already pushing past the dancers moving by her. "Good luck!"

"Thank you!" She was finally getting somewhere, and a lot quicker than if she had not bothered to ask. *Thanks for the tip, Aphrodite.*

Meg ran toward the water in the distance. As she ran, she noticed the path widen, and flowers sprang up from the cracks in the road. Trees grew fuller and flowers more colorful than she ever remembered them on Earth. Even the air felt different in the Evergreen. The mugginess was gone, replaced with a comfortable temperature and a sun that shone brighter. And that was all before she heard the wonderful sound of children laughing.

As she crested the next hill, she could see them. There were kids of all ages running and playing in the massive poppy fields along the rocky shoreline. Meg stepped onto a rock to get a better look at them. Some children were alone and some with adults. The question was, which one was Layla? Meg had to hope she looked something like Katerina, whom she'd seen in Hades's flames.

Meg jumped off the rocks, wincing in pain, and started searching, but it was like looking for the ripest grape in a huge vat. Children were running in every direction, playing, and picking poppies that seemed to grow back instantly. From a distance, they looked identical. Every one of them was dressed in beautiful vibrant colors and was carrying baskets of poppies. Some had flowers in their hair, while others walked hand in hand with parents who watched them play; but still, this offered her no clue to finding the girl.

Meg pulled the hourglass out of her satchel and sighed. The bottom of the jar was now more than three-quarters full. Somehow walking through Asphodel Meadows had cost her almost a day, which meant she had only two left. If it took her just as long to locate the pair in the poppy fields, she was doomed.

*Please let Katerina and Layla be here,* Meg prayed to the gods as she walked among families young and old, searching for anyone who might have Katerina's golden hair, pale skin, and dark eyes. *Please. I'm running out of time.*

The field seemed to go on for miles. Many women she came across had blond hair, but were older or younger than she imagined Katerina to be. Others had longer hair, or hair so short Meg knew they couldn't be her, and after a while, Meg wondered if she'd ever find the woman at all. At last, Meg saw someone who fit Katerina's description exactly. She was standing with a small child about Layla's age. Meg touched her arm.

"Katerina?" Meg asked hopefully, and the woman turned around.

A woman with green eyes stared back at Meg in confusion. It wasn't her.

"Sorry." Meg moved on.

The same thing happened over and over again to the point where Meg thought she'd never find her. It was if she could hear the grains of sand in the hourglass falling. *There's almost no time left!* they'd say. *Move faster! Faster! Find Katerina!* She spun around in desperation, her eyes searching the large field of poppies again. And that's when she heard a familiar melody.

*Aegeus,* she thought immediately.

The tune drifting across the meadow was one he had played for her the first night they met, and then a hundred times more over the course of their courtship. She knew the chords and notes as well as if she'd written them herself. Meg rushed toward the sound, trying to find who was humming the melody. She moved between children and mothers and babes in fathers' arms and whirled around, hearing the melody play on the wind, but still she saw no one. How was she going to find them?

What if she played the same tune on the flute? Yes. If she did that, maybe the person would come directly to her. Her hand went to Athena's instrument.

If she played, would she give her location away to Hades?

She had no choice. She had to risk it.

Hands shaking, Meg took Athena's double flute from the strap around her waist, put it to her lips, and started to play Aegeus's song. Two notes in, she hit a wrong note and then one way too high. It was as if the past was rising up to meet her, and she didn't like the memory. The tune made her feel restless and uneasy and she had to fight the urge to put the flute down and forget the song even existed; but she knew she had to keep trying. She took a deep breath and rushed through the notes, trying not to link the music with memory. When she was finished, a small girl with dark brown hair, holding a basket of poppies, was standing in front of her.

"I know that song!" said the girl with a laugh.

Meg held her breath. "You do?"

"Yes. I once heard Medusa play it to her snakes, and they all fell fast asleep," the child said with wide eyes. "All of them! At the same time!"

"Really?" said a small boy, listening to the story.

"Yes," the girl said solemnly. "I was secretly watching, but when Medusa caught me, she woke her snakes up, and that's how I wound up down here."

*Layla likes to tell tall tales,* Meg reminded herself.

"Layla?" Meg whispered.

"Yes." The child smiled. "How do you know my name?"

# TWENTY-FOUR: Lost and Found

Meg inhaled sharply. She didn't want to scare the girl away. "I know your sister. Is she here?"

"She's sitting right over there. Katerina!" Layla called and skipped a few feet away to approach a woman sitting quietly with her legs outstretched and her head facing the warm sun.

*Katerina.*

Meg paused. This was the person Meg had spent so much time thinking about: first, in anger and bitterness, watching her and Aegeus's love story in Hades's fire. Then, as the object of this quest, learning more about a woman who was not all that different from herself, someone who seemed to have been caught in the cross fire of the gods' affairs. It was strange to finally see her in the flesh (so to speak), sitting and drumming her fingers casually against her leg.

She had hair the color of wheat and skin as pale as the sand. Her eyes, Meg noticed, were deep brown, and there was no mistaking that distinct round nose. The baby had one just like it. As she drew closer, Meg could hear Katerina was humming Aegeus's song. She took a deep breath. This was it.

"This woman was looking for you," Layla said, bounding ahead. "She was playing that song you like to hum."

"Layla," the woman warned, giving Meg an apologetic look.

Layla turned to Meg. "Sorry! I meant to say, 'What is your name? Are you new here?' My sister says we should always help new souls."

The woman smiled, the corners of her mouth producing dimples in both cheeks. Cassia had them, too. "Much better."

"My name is Meg." She looked at the woman again, unsure how to explain everything succinctly. The faster she could impress upon Katerina that she was her ticket out of there, the better. "I'm looking for Katerina Dimas. Is that you?"

"I'm Katerina." Katerina's smile faded slightly. She

sat up on her elbows and stared at her. "But my last name is Aikos."

"You mean your maiden name was Aikos, right?"

"Maiden?" Katerina looked confused. "Oh, I am not married."

"Katerina!" Layla admonished, giggling. "That's not true! When you arrived, you said your new last name was Dimas. Remember?"

"I . . . Did I? I don't remember." Katerina reached for the child's hand and smiled up at her. "All I know is I belong with you." Layla leaned over and nestled into her sister's shoulder. Katerina looked up at Meg again and shook her head. "I'm sorry I'm so distracted! Forgive me. Do we know one another?"

"That's a complicated question," Meg admitted, "and it's not one I have time to explain in too much detail, unfortunately." She eyed Layla. "Do you think we could talk in private? It's important."

Katerina gently whispered something in Layla's ear. The child beamed at Meg, then took off racing across the meadow with her basket in hand. Katerina kept smiling till Layla disappeared from sight. Then she looked at Meg and her face hardened.

"If this is about my leaving the Evergreen, I'm not going," Katerina said, her eyes suddenly burning with a fire

Meg could respect. "I won't leave my sister here alone, and from what I hear, she'll be happier here than she'd be anywhere else. The two of us are staying."

"This isn't about the Evergreen—" Meg tried to interrupt, but Katerina kept going.

"She's been on her own far too long already," Katerina said firmly. "If you have a problem with it, then bring me to Hades and I'll take it up with him. I won't leave this child again."

Meg held her hands up to surrender. "No one is going to see Hades. At least I hope not. This isn't about Layla. It's about you. I'm here to take you home."

Katerina blinked. "Home?"

"Yes," Meg said breathlessly. "I'm here on direct order of Hera to get you out of the Underworld," she whispered. "Your husband, Aegeus, and daughter, Cassia, need you in the land of the living."

Katerina ran a hand through her hair, clearly flustered. "Daughter?"

"Yes! And your husband, Aegeus," Meg repeated, her voice rising with excitement. "You weren't meant to get caught up in that flood."

"Flood?" Katerina echoed again.

Meg stared, wondering if she wasn't being clear enough. "The one that you were lost in. I believe the gods didn't mean for you to die. In any case, they've sent me here to retrieve your soul. I'm to bring you back to your family, but if that's going to happen, we have to move quickly before Hades finds us."

Meg couldn't blame her for being overwhelmed. No one got an offer like this. Meg took Katerina's hand, finding eye contact to make sure the woman was registering what she was saying. "Do you understand? You can leave the Underworld!" A shadow fell across Katerina's face and Meg noticed eerie dark clouds start to gather in the sky. "But we have to go immediately."

Katerina pulled her hand away. She started to breathe more heavily. "I think you have the wrong person. I don't know an Aegeus or a Cassia. I don't have a child! I'm sorry. Good luck in your search." She stood up and started to hurry away.

Meg was dumbfounded. *How can Katerina not remember her own daughter?* Did the dead forget the living when they crossed to the other side? No. That couldn't be possible. If it were, the families around her wouldn't have been reunited. The people celebrating at the Evergreen village wouldn't have been reconnecting. So why didn't Katerina remember Aegeus or Cassia? Of all the problems she'd imagined having in the Underworld, Katerina not wanting to live was not one of them.

"Katerina," Meg started again, following her. "That song I heard you humming when I found you—it's Aegeus's tune. Your husband wrote it. You must remember him."

For a split second, Meg thought she saw Katerina's face flicker with some sort of recognition. But in an instant, it was gone.

"I don't remember where I learned that, actually. All I know is Layla likes it."

Meg stumbled over a rock, panic rising in her throat. She reached toward the retreating woman. "I know this must be confusing. But you have to understand: this is a once in a, well, *never* offer. You'd be a fool not to take it. Don't you want to live again?"

Katerina spun around. "I am living! In a way—with my sister here in the Underworld." Her voice was sad, but her eyes were firm. "She's who I choose to spend eternity with. Please respect that and just leave us alone."

Katerina hurried over to Layla, who was picking more poppies. Meg felt her heart stir at the sight of the two of them together. It was only then that she realized what she was asking this woman to leave behind.

*Don't leave me, Mother!* She heard her own voice in her head and winced at the memory. *Stay with me!*

*You're a big, tough girl. You tie your own sandals and everything.*

Thea and Meg's time together had been too short and much of it was difficult, but Meg still wouldn't trade it for the world. She couldn't begin to imagine what it would be like to say goodbye to a younger sibling. No wonder Katerina felt so conflicted.

"I lost someone I loved when I was young," Meg said, approaching the pair carefully. Both Katerina and Layla turned to her. "My mother." She looked at Layla. "She died when I was just a girl, and then I was on my own. Life was never the same after that. I miss her terribly every day."

"I miss mine, too. Missing is a part of living and dying," Layla said quietly. Katerina took her hand and Layla perked up. "Do you look like your mother?" she asked Meg.

It struck Meg that a child this young seemed comfortable talking about death. "Yes," Meg said, leaning down to her level. "We had the same red hair and we both loved music. My mother liked to listen to it, and I loved to play it. She taught me to trust my instincts and be strong. I am all that I am because of her."

"She sounds nice," Layla said wistfully. "Is she here, too?"

"Yes," Meg said, and her heart twisted at the thought.

"I'm sure she misses you," Layla added thoughtfully. "She'll be happy to see you when you find each other again.

And in the meantime, I'm sure she is okay. We're okay here, you know."

"Thank you." Meg gave her a soft smile. What an extraordinary child Layla was. She wondered if it was an effect of being in the Underworld so long, or if that was just who she had always been. She looked up at Katerina. "My mother had a tough life, and raising a kid on her own was difficult. I'm sure if she had the chance to be a mother again, she'd wish things were different."

Katerina said nothing.

Meg smiled at Layla. "Even now, though we're apart, I carry her with me." Meg looked at Katerina and repeated the words Aegeus told her Katerina favored. "Someone once told me we imprint the lost on our hearts."

Something flashed across Katerina's face again. It quickly disappeared. "Layla, look! A butterfly!" she cried. "Why don't you see if you can catch it?" The child grinned, then dashed into the field to chase it. "I'm sorry about your mother," Katerina said. "But that means you must understand my feelings on the matter."

"I do." Meg nodded and looked at Layla a few feet away. "No child deserves this fate."

"No, they don't. That's why I can't leave her," Katerina whispered. "I don't remember a lot from my recent life, but I remember my early memories. Layla's passing always haunted me. My parents never said it, but I always felt like her death was my fault." She closed her eyes and Meg saw her pink lips start to tremble. "I turned my head for a moment at her bedside and then she was gone." She covered her face with her hands.

Meg put her arm on Katerina's. "Aegeus told me that Layla was very ill. There is nothing you could have done to save her." She paused. "But you do still have a chance to be there for Cassia." Katerina opened her eyes and looked at her curiously. "Your daughter. The one you had with Aegeus," Meg tried again. "I've seen her, and she's a wonderful baby. She has the same color hair as you, and dimples in her cheeks."

Katerina seemed to be concentrating on something—maybe even a memory the corners of her mind wouldn't let her reach. Finally, she shook her head. "I'm sorry. I know I would remember my own child."

Meg furrowed her brow. She had to get through. "She has the sweetest laugh when she's not crying, and wow, can the kid eat! Layla didn't get a chance to grow up and experience the world, but Cassia will. Don't let her do it without you."

Tears began to stream down Katerina's face. "Please stop. I don't remember her. . . ."

But Meg couldn't stop now. She was close to getting

through to Katerina. She could feel it. "Cassia will miss so much," Meg continued as the wind picked up and the clouds gathered. In the distance, she saw a flash of lightning. "She needs you, and I'm here because Hera has given me a chance to bring you home to her."

Katerina put her hands to her head and started to pull at her hair. Was she finally remembering?

Meg felt her own buried regrets bubbling up inside her. "You've been given a gift that no one receives. Ever. I wish my own mother had once been in your shoes. Come back with me while you have the chance."

Katerina shook her head. "I don't remember . . . but . . ." She hesitated.

"Yes?" Meg leaned in, holding her breath.

Katerina bit her lip as a gust of wind blew through the fields, tilting the poppies sideways. "If what you say is true, will Hera let Layla return, too?"

Meg looked at the innocent child playing and felt her heart break all over again. "I'm sorry. That wasn't part of their offer."

"But you could ask," Katerina pushed as thunder rumbled again, sounding closer than it had before.

"I don't think . . ." Meg wasn't sure what to say. Layla had been gone a long time. The gods could do some miraculous things, but bringing someone back from the dead so many years later seemed impossible, even for them. "I don't think they can do that."

The anguish written on Katerina's face was almost too much for Meg to take. "Then I'm staying here." She turned to leave just as a blaring roll of thunder sounded.

Meg felt her heart stop. "Wait!"

"No!" Katerina snapped, and children everywhere looked up, worried. "I'm sorry." She lowered her voice. "I don't mean to be ungrateful. This is a generous offer from Hera, but without Layla, I can't accept. Please leave us in peace."

She hurried after Layla and Meg stood there for a moment, stunned. She was losing her. Meg racked her brain. *What convinced me Aegeus had moved on?* And then she realized: *Seeing him with Katerina! That's it! I need Katerina to* see *what she's missing. For it to be in front of her, undeniable.* But how could she do that?

*The orchid.*

Meg reached for the flower in her satchel. It was a tad crushed, but it was still there, just waiting for a moment to help. Her heart started to beat rapidly again.

"Wait! Please! I know how I can help you reclaim the memories you've lost!"

Katerina turned around. Layla stared at the two adults curiously as she swung Katerina's hand.

"This flower was a gift from a god," Meg explained, holding the orchid carefully in her outstretched hand. "I can use it to call for help. Perhaps if you are able to see the family you left behind when you came to the Underworld, you'll realize what you're giving up."

"You have a family?" Layla said excitedly.

"No," Katerina said quickly, glancing at the flower. "Don't listen to her, Layla."

"Please," Meg begged. "Give me a chance to show you what you lost." Meg took a deep breath and pulled off the second petal.

Katerina snatched the petal from Meg's hands. "Enough!" She ripped it into pieces before it could start to glow.

"No!" Meg cried, dropping to the ground to try to catch the fragments.

"I don't want to remember what I lost!" Katerina said angrily. "Please." Her voice broke as tears streamed down her face. "Just leave us alone! I'm begging you! Come on, Layla."

The child looked back at Meg sadly. "Good luck finding your mother."

Raindrops began to fall and children began running in different directions, laughing and screaming with delight as the orchid pieces blew away. She'd wasted a petal for nothing. There was only one left now.

*Don't lose them!* a voice in her head instructed, but Meg ignored it. She sank into the grass, ready to give up. Even if she caught up with Katerina again, what could she say to convince her? If she tried to use the last petal, Katerina would just tear it up again. She pulled out the hourglass. The sand was higher than ever. By her calculations, she had a day and a half left at most. She was running out of time.

*Clink!* Meg felt something hot clamp down on her arm. It was a glowing red cuff. She looked up in horror.

"Gotcha!" said Panic excitedly as he stood alongside Pain. "Hades wants to see you."

Then Pain snapped his fingers and the three of them disappeared.

# TWENTY-FIVE: Ultimatums

Meg reappeared seconds later in Hades's throne room. An extra-large furnace—a gateway to Tartarus—was pumping off heat while Hades's music of choice—low sounds of moaning and wails—created an ambience of gloom. Pain and Panic deposited her in the center of the room, where she found Hades sitting on his usual throne of bones. He pointed to her.

"You're alive."

"Appears that way," Meg said. Her foot twitched. She needed to find Katerina before time ran out.

"My mistake." Hades snapped his fingers and smoke unfurled toward her. "But that can be easily fixed."

Meg needed to think fast. "Don't you want to know why Hera sent me here?" The smoke stopped in midair.

"Let me think about that a second. Nope!" The smoke started winding its way around her legs. "Just like I could care less about your mother."

"My mother?" Meg looked at him as the smoke tightened and lifted her into the air.

Hades rolled his eyes, and with a flick of his wrist, Meg flew toward the furnace. "Came by when I was with the Fates—interrupting my meeting, by the way—crying about how she needed to see you this time. Blah, blah, blah."

*"This time?"* Meg repeated. "You always said my mother didn't know I was here last time!" Being so close yet far from Thea had been torture when she had been in the Underworld doing Hades's bidding. "She knew the whole time?"

"Maybe I forgot to actually place a veil and she was alerted, okay? Big deal!" Hades huffed. "You didn't stick around anyway, so what was the use in telling you she lived in Asphodel Unit C-23,762?"

Meg's jaw dropped. Had she passed that building today?

The yellow of Hades's eyes blazed. "Hey, it's all good. Now you can bunk next to her! Have a good reunion, Nut-Meg!"

The smoke pulled her to the door of the furnace. It opened on its own and Meg could feel heat licking at her heels. She was toast unless she did something. "I told Katerina everything!" she blurted out.

The smoke paused. "And who is Katerina?"

Meg gritted her teeth as flames singed the hair on her legs. "She's Aegeus's wife!" Hades didn't say anything. "My former . . . er . . . *flame*?"

"Former flame . . . former flame . . ." Hades muttered. "Knowing you, you have a lot of exes out there . . ."

"You know which one I mean! Katerina's death was an accident; not part of the cosmic plan. Hera wants her back. If you don't do as they ask, you'll . . . you'll . . ." What could she threaten him with? "There will be consequences!"

"Consequences, huh?" Hades zipped to her in seconds, his sinister face inches from her own. "I've already faced consequences! That's how I wound up *running* this place. And now that I am, there is nothing *they* can do to me down here. I literally let the Titans out to wreak havoc and run amok, and look who's back wheeling and dealing in the Underworld. *I'm* in charge of the souls that come here," he roared. "Not my brother or his wife!"

"Why doesn't Katerina remember her old life, then?" Meg tried a new tack. "Did you make her forget?"

"Forget?" Hades's smoke loosened slightly. "Why would I do that? Because her life was abysmally boring? I don't make people forget the past. Their pain feeds me, babe."

Meg didn't understand. "Why doesn't she remember her family, then?"

"Who knows?" Hades said. "I'm not a therapist! Maybe she was so upset her brain blocked it out? Or maybe it was a divine mistake. It happens."

*A divine mistake.* If Katerina had been killed in a flood created by the gods' battle, maybe her memory loss was an inadvertent side effect. That could be another reason why the gods wanted to undo their mistake.

"Either way, I don't go around erasing people's memories, kid. I am a nice guy when I want to be."

*"Nice?"* Meg spat. "You refuse to let go of her soul so she can reunite with her loved ones."

Hades shrugged. "Yeah, well, love is a fickle thing, isn't it? One minute you have it, the next it's gone . . . or someone is trying to say you can't be together because you live in different zip codes." He bared his teeth. "No one said life or death is fair!" The furnace roared bloodred, as did Hades's head. "Bye, Meg-let!" The smoke prepared to drop her into the flames just as the doors to Hades's throne room flew open.

A woman with dark hair came running into the room. "I couldn't stay away any longer! What did they say? Did you convince them to—Hey." She noticed Meg about to be thrown in the furnace and stopped talking. "It's *you*!"

Meg did a double take. "And you!"

"Do you two know each other?" Hades cut in. "My

love, I was just about to burn Meggie-kins at the stake. Can this wait?"

"Burn who?" The woman put her hands on her hips. "Her? No! You put her down this instant."

Hades looked from Meg to the woman in surprise, and Meg noticed the flames on his head flicker. "No, Per, you don't understand."

"I don't care if I understand! Put her down. She saved my whole bed of hydrangeas this afternoon. You're not tossing her in the furnace."

Hades hesitated. "But, Per . . ."

Meg stared. She had never heard him this docile before.

The woman pursed her lips. "Put her down, Hades, and just talk to me."

Hades sighed. "Fine." He flicked his wrist and the smoke uncoiled. The furnace's flames dropped to barely a flicker. "Just know she had it coming."

Meg fell to the ground with a painful thump. She really hated when he did that.

The woman walked over and offered her a hand. "Thank you for the help earlier," she said with a smile. "I'm Persephone. And you are?"

Meg accepted her help. "Persephone . . . you're Demeter's daughter!" she realized. "You're the one the gods on Mount Olympus are looking for!"

A look of panic came over Persephone's face. "Who are you?" She looked to Hades. "Who is she?" she asked, her voice rising.

Hades smiled smugly. "*This* is who you just interrupted me from roasting: Megara. You know—the one who ruined my plan to overthrow Zeus?"

Persephone spun around and stared at Meg. *"Her?"* She started to back up. "That means you're with Hercules, and you're alive. Which means when you leave here, you could tell the other gods where I am." She moved farther away. "My mother will find me and take me away!" With that, she ran to Hades and grabbed his hands. "We'll be done for."

"Hey now, it's all right," said Hades as he brought her in close. "We won't let her."

Meg gaped. This wasn't like Hades at all. Sure, he was still threatening her life, but he seemed to actually be concerned for someone who wasn't himself.

"What did the Fates have to say?" Persephone whispered.

Hades's face was grim. "I don't want you getting upset."

"I'm already upset!"

"They don't know *everything*."

"They *do* know everything. What did they say?" Hades hesitated, and Persephone put her hands on his cheeks. "Tell me."

Hades sighed. "We're not exactly seeing eye to eye on things. In fact, I thought about making sure they never saw anything again."

*"Hades . . ."*

"I know. I didn't. I'm just saying I thought about it."

"So what was their prediction?" Persephone searched Hades's face. "Is there a future for us or not?" Her lower lip quivered.

"They said some riddle about the Earth being the only hope for you." Persephone gasped. "But who cares what they think!" Hades said, his voice rising. "No one knows you're here. We're safe." He looked at Meg, a smile spreading across his gray lips. "At least we were before Meg here showed up."

Persephone looked at her, and Meg started to back away. Whatever bond they had formed in the meadows was clearly not enough to save her now.

"Why do you think I was about to get rid of her?" Hades asked. Persephone folded her arms. "Your mother is part of the Olympus crew! If we let Meg out, she's going to go running to that beefy boyfriend of hers, and Papa Zeus and Demeter and everyone else will show up to take you away."

"No," Persephone whispered, eyeing Meg worriedly.

"I wouldn't tell anyone," Meg swore.

"Who are you going to believe, Per?"

Persephone looked intently at Meg. "Toss her in the fire."

Hades grinned and smoke began to seep out of his hands again. "With pleasure, my love."

Meg had only seconds to make a decision. "I can help you stay together!" The moment the words left her lips, she knew the cost might be too high, but it was her only move left to play.

"Stop!" Persephone said and Hades's smoke disappeared.

"She's just stalling," he complained. "How could she help us?"

"I heard Aphrodite and Demeter talking about you when I was on Mount Olympus," Meg appealed to Persephone. "Your mother is desperate to find you. She's worried."

"Yes, because she doesn't understand my love for Hades. She wants me harvesting solely on Earth, and I want to be here with him." Persephone put a hand on his fleshy gray arm. "If she finds me, she'll take me away."

Meg licked her lips, which felt dry in all this heat, and thought fast. Persephone had been *gardening* in the Underworld. She clearly missed at least a portion of her old life, even if, for some unfathomable reason, she wanted to be with Hades. What if there was a way for her to have it all? "What if you compromised? Offered to spend half of the year tending to the gardens on Earth, and the other half here in the Underworld with Hades?"

Persephone and Hades looked at one another.

"Why would Demeter agree to that?" Hades asked.

"Because she wants her daughter to be happy," Meg said. "Demeter would still get to see Persephone, Persephone would still get to be with you, and Persephone could have everything she loves. It's a win-win-win . . . if the gods agree, that is."

"So, what? You want me to pray?" Persephone rolled her eyes. "Prayers don't always work—especially when it's one god praying to another god."

"Maybe not, but what if I could make a god appear here so we could appeal to them in person?" Meg pulled the orchid out of her satchel. "This orchid makes whatever god I call on appear. There's one last petal, which I can use to call upon Mount Olympus and appeal on your behalf."

Persephone's gaze flickered to the flower. "And what do you get in return for doing this for us?"

"She wants to bring a soul back to the land of the living," Hades explained, looking troubled. "As if I'd ever let *that* happen."

"Who is it?" Persephone asked, curious. "Which soul?"

Meg took a deep breath. "Her name is Katerina Dimas. She's the woman my first love left me for."

Persephone's eyes flashed. "Tell me everything."

# TWENTY-SIX: Wheeling and Dealing

Meg didn't waste time. "She died in a flood created by the gods in their battle with the Titans, but it seems she wasn't meant to perish. She has an infant daughter on Earth. Hera asked me to bring her back to her child."

Persephone glanced at Hades. "Can you do what she's asking—allow a soul to live again?"

"It's a gray area," Hades said, sounding uncomfortable. "She hasn't been gone long, so it's technically possible, but if I do it for Meg here and word gets out, every soul will want a get-out-of-hell-free card."

"He has a point," Persephone said.

"No one has to know," Meg replied quickly. "Just give me a chance to convince her to come back with me."

Now Hades grinned. "*Convince*? You mean she doesn't want to go?"

Meg paled. Why had she let that slip? "She will. She just doesn't remember her family on Earth at the moment. But I can fix that and get her back to Hera on time."

Hades's grin widened. "Hmm . . . interesting. You're on a quest, so you must have some sort of deadline. When does your time run out?"

The heat in this place was making her sloppy. But it was too late to backpedal. Meg pulled the hourglass out of her satchel. The sight made her stomach drop. The sands were almost to the top. "About a day."

Hades laughed. "You'll never make it!"

"Then what do you have to lose?" Persephone's eyes flickered to Meg's for half a second. "Let her help us, and then Megara can try to help this woman before her quest is done." She took Hades's hand. "I want to be with you forever, but we can't keep hiding. We should be free to enjoy our lives here without fear of losing one another." She paused. "What was it the Fates told you? The riddle?"

Hades sighed. "Something about the Earth being your only hope. I don't know, it's hard to get a straight answer from the all-knowing. They talk in circles."

"But she's technically from the Earth," Persephone continued, pointing to Meg. "What if they mean *her*?"

Meg leaped at the opening. "The Fates are never wrong. And I'm offering help. Let me at least try."

Hades looked at Persephone and put both hands in hers as he stared into her eyes. They stood that way for a while. Then he sighed, lowering his voice. "Make the call."

Persephone nodded once.

Inhaling slowly, Meg tore the petal in half. As she did, it and the stem disintegrated and drifted off into the air. She absently wondered if it would actually work to call a god other than Hercules, her stomach twisting at the thought of losing out on a chance to talk to him. Meg shook her head, trying to stay focused. There was only one god who could make her suggestion for Persephone happen. Someone who not only believed in marriage, but who could talk the All-father into going for such an unusual arrangement. "I wish to speak with Hera, please."

A warm orange and pink ball began to form in the center of the room. It grew larger and larger till it burst into a ray as bright as the sun. Hades and Persephone shielded themselves from the bright light. Slowly, the outline of the god began to appear. She was dressed in the same magenta gown Meg had seen her in atop Mount Olympus and wore the same crown, which was glistening despite the dreary room. Hera spotted her and looked around at her surroundings in surprise.

"Megara?" Then she did a double take. "Hades." Her eyes narrowed when her gaze found the woman standing next to him. "And Persephone! So *this* is where you've been hiding. Your mother has been looking for you everywhere!" She looked at Meg again. "What is the meaning of this? Why have you summoned me? *How* have you summoned me?"

"I apologize for being so bold," Meg said as Hades and Persephone watched the exchange. "Hercules gave me an orchid that allowed me to call on him if I was in need."

Hera pursed her lips. "I see. And yet you call on me instead of him?"

Her tone was frosty at best. This was not the way to win over one's potential mother-in-law.

"Only *you* can help with what needs to be done . . . and that is to allow Hades and Persephone to stay together," Meg said. Hera stared. "I know it may sound strange, but these two . . . well, they are in love." She looked back at the pair. "I've seen them together, and they actually seem to suit one another. When he's burning, she cools him down. And she has added much-needed beauty to the Underworld that Hades never would have allowed before." She paused, thinking out loud now. "I think that's because she's inspired down here with him. Maybe they're inspired by each other. In any case, they wish to be together. And besides," Meg realized, "it couldn't hurt to have a happy god of the Underworld, could it?"

"That would be a plus," Hera admitted. "But Persephone has responsibilities. The Earth's harvest, for instance . . ."

"That's why I'm asking you to appeal to Zeus and Demeter to let Persephone stay with Hades in the Underworld for half the year. She would spend the other half on Earth for the harvest. Everyone wins." *Including me,* Meg thought. She thought of Layla and her heart began to ache. *Maybe not everyone.* Though they would all be reunited again someday, she knew it wouldn't lessen the blow of Katerina leaving Layla now.

Hera looked at her sharply. "*This* is your request, then—what you really want your last appeal to the gods to be?"

"Yes," Meg said firmly. "I believe helping *this* love will help others."

Hera seemed to consider this. "Then I will grant your request, Megara, and I will talk to Zeus and Demeter." She looked at Persephone. "You will be the first god allowed to travel back and forth regularly from the Underworld."

"Really? Thank you, Hera! Thank you!" Persephone cried. She and Hades held on to one another.

Meg almost couldn't believe it herself. She'd done it! She'd negotiated with Hera! Maybe she could go toe-to-toe with a god after all.

"There are stipulations, of course," Hera continued. "Spring is upon us, and the grains of the land must be replenished. Persephone, you will come back and do your duties to the Earth now, and when the summer has faded, you will return to Hades for the fall and the winter."

Hades and Persephone looked at one another.

"We'll make it work," Hades said as much to Persephone as he did Hera.

Hera went on. "A boat will arrive in the next few hours to take you back to the world of the living. But know this: once you board, you cannot look back at the Underworld or at Hades. You should concentrate on your work on Earth and trust you will be returned to Hades when your time is over," Hera stressed. "If you turn back for any reason, the deal will be broken. No one is meant to travel back and forth between worlds. This is an exception made only for your . . . unique situation."

"Thank you, Hera," Persephone said. "I won't let you down."

Hera's eyes flickered to Meg's. "You've done well,

child. I do not say that lightly." Then Hera faded away as quickly as she'd come, the glow from her lingering embers drifting up into the cavernous ceiling. Meg was on her own once more.

As Hades and Persephone embraced again, Meg looked back at the hourglass clutched in her hand. There were only a few grains left, and she still had to convince Katerina to come with her as well as figure out their own way home. As Hera had said, no one was meant to travel between worlds.

"I need to find Katerina," Meg blurted out. "What's the quickest way to Asphodel Meadows?"

"The stairs," Hades retorted, not taking his eyes off Persephone. "And don't forget—I will only turn the other cheek until your time runs out."

Meg groaned. She'd climbed almost a hundred staircases and walked for miles to reach Katerina the first time. She'd never make it.

"Hades, a deal's a deal," Persephone chimed in. "At least give her a shot." She snapped her fingers and Meg's feet flamed, shooting her straight up the stairs at lightning speed.

She could still hear Hades shouting as she zipped around staircases faster than light: "Good luck, babe! You're going to need it."

# TWENTY-SEVEN: One More Song

Meg was moving so fast, all she saw were greens, golds, and yellows as she whizzed through Asphodel Meadows. Finally, the sky in front of her started to come into focus and she saw a welcome sight: poppies. She wasn't sure how the flames knew where to stop, but she was grateful they dropped her in the familiar field. By her calculations, she had less than a day, but in the Underworld, that might feel like an hour.

The grass was still damp from the recent storm, but people were out in droves again, already laughing and playing once more. Meg searched the field frantically for Katerina, silently praying she'd still be there. She felt a tap on her back and heard a child's familiar giggle. She turned around.

"You're back!" Layla held her hand out to Meg. "Are you looking for my sister again?"

Meg nodded, a lump forming in her throat as she thought about how she was trying to take Katerina away from her. "Yes."

Layla's small face clouded over slightly. "Did you find your mom? Thea?"

"Wow, you've got some memory," Meg said admiringly. "But no, sadly, I keep missing her."

Layla plucked a poppy and handed it to Meg. "That's too bad. I'm sure she misses you, since you're her child. Even though you're no longer a child." She laughed. "Everyone likes kids."

"Sure." Meg never thought she'd agree with that statement, but she had been taken with Cassia, and Layla was pretty special herself. "I lost her pretty young, though."

Layla's face scrunched up. "My mother didn't get to be mine too long either." She concentrated on the poppy in her hand and plucked off a few of the petals. The motion immediately made Meg think of the orchid again.

"It's not fair," Meg said softly.

"No," Layla agreed and looked up at her with big, round eyes. "Did you come back to try to bring Katerina home to her baby?"

Meg knelt down. She couldn't lie to her. "I'm going to try."

"You should. She would be a good mother, and I know we'll see each other again one day."

"Yes." The kid was wiser than her seven earthly years. Maybe that came from having been around so much longer than that. "But I don't want *you* to be alone, either."

"It would be nice to have someone," Layla said thoughtfully. She broke into a grin. "But maybe I can."

The child whispered something so quickly in her ear that Meg asked Layla to repeat it, just to be sure. She could feel her heart drumming and vibrating with anticipation, and unbelievably, *hope*. She leaned down and whispered back. Layla nodded.

Now she just had to convince Katerina to go. This time, she had to get this right.

Layla held tight to Meg's hand. "Here comes my sister."

She saw the woman rushing across the field toward them and steadied herself.

"You!" Katerina looked upset. "I told you not to bother us! Layla, get away from her."

"Katerina, please," Meg said, letting go of Layla's hand. "I just want to talk to you."

"Listen to her, Katerina. She can help you get home," Layla said, and Katerina looked startled.

Katerina put a hand on Layla's head and looked at Meg. "Look, I appreciate what you're trying to do, but I am staying here. I don't remember these people you speak of."

"But—" Meg tried to interrupt as Katerina cut her off.

"No matter how many times you try to describe them to me, that won't change," she said, her voice softening. "I know this isn't what you want to hear, but I think you should go. Come along, Layla."

"Katerina." Layla frowned as her sister pulled her away.

"Layla, come on!" Katerina insisted.

Layla looked back at Meg, tears in her eyes. Meg tried to smile reassuringly, but hope was leaving her as well. She pulled out the hourglass again and her despair deepened. There was only a pinch of sand left. She was not going to make it.

She wasn't the crying type, but if there was ever time to let go, this was it.

She had failed her quest.

Meg sank down into the wet grass and closed her eyes. She was not leaving the Underworld again. She would not become a god. Cassia would grow up without her mother, just like Meg had. She'd never again get to see Hercules's face or apologize for the way she acted the last time they were together. Her last words to him had been cruel. How could she have wasted the time they'd had worrying about whether they were meant to spend eternity together? Why couldn't she have realized how great things had been between them in the moment? She didn't even have the remains of the orchid to remember him by.

Absentmindedly, her hand went to the satchel where she had kept the flower and her fingers brushed across something wooden. Meg pulled it out: Cassia's rattle. The beads inside began to jangle around.

"Katerina?" Meg jumped up and rushed over to the retreating woman. She held out the rattle. "You should have this."

For once, Katerina didn't fight her. Her fingers closed over the rattle in Meg's outstretched hand. Then she turned and walked away.

Meg watched her and Layla disappear into the field, all her hopes carried along with them. Maybe she hadn't been sure of herself at the start of this journey, but as she got closer to reaching Katerina, she had started to believe she could complete her impossible quest.

The old Meg definitely wouldn't have trusted anyone else to help her, would never have believed in leaps of faith. She also would not have been so successful at bargaining with Hades and winning over gods like Athena, Aphrodite, and Persephone. Even Hera had liked her resolution for

Hades and Persephone's love affair. So how could she have come so far and failed?

A breeze picked up and Meg ran her hands over her legs, rubbing them to keep warm. Her fingers grazed Athena's flute.

Unhooking it from the strap, Meg stared at the instrument she'd saved for a god. *You do not play as you once did,* Athena had said, and it was true. Meg's love of music had been wrapped up in her mother and then Aegeus, and after losing them both, she didn't have the heart to play the way she used to. But now she looked at the flute and wondered. Her life was over. Would the flute disappear because she had failed her quest? If it did, would she ever get the chance to try it again?

Meg decided to place the reeds to her lips one last time. As the melody she played took hold, she thought about all this quest had taught her and all the things she'd never do again. The tune shifted into the first song she'd learned for her mother—"The Plight of the Lily." It morphed into the song she had played with Aegeus, the sweet notes lifting into the air, and then the tune changed again. She thought about Hercules's unwavering belief in her, about Mount Olympus and Katerina and this quest, and the notes unfurled into a new song altogether. She let the music take her to another place and time, and for a moment she continued with complete abandon. When she finally took a breath and opened her eyes, Katerina was standing in front of her.

Tears streamed down her face. "That was Aegeus's song," she whispered. "And you're . . . ?"

"Meg—Megara," Meg supplied, her heartbeat quickening.

Katerina sank down on the grass, still clutching Cassia's rattle. "I was married. I had a baby." She looked ashen. "She was so young when I wound up here." She grabbed Meg's hands, her eyes widening. "Her name was Cassia and she already had wise eyes and a playful heart and a cry that cut deep into your soul."

Meg felt her heart stop. "Yes!"

Katerina let out an anguished sob and held up the rattle. "Aegeus made this for our child when I was expecting." She started to cry again. "I remember. I want to go back to my life. I want to see my baby." She looked at Meg in horror. "Am I too late? Can you take me to her? I . . ." She turned around, startled, seemingly having forgotten her sister was standing behind her. "Layla . . ."

Layla reached for Katerina's hand. "You have to go to Cassia. I'll be okay, as I have been before. And we'll see each other again. I can't wait to meet your baby."

Katerina stood and hugged the child fiercely, her face crumbling all over again. "Are you sure? Layla, I . . ."

*"Go,"* Layla insisted. "I promise you, I won't be alone." Layla glanced at Meg before kissing Katerina. Then she ran off over the hill without a second goodbye. It was probably better that way.

*That kid really is amazing,* Meg thought.

Katerina looked at Meg. "What do we do now?"

Time was running out, and there was no Persephone to speed up the journey. *Persephone.* Meg squared her shoulders, a new thought dawning on her—they needed to get to Persephone. Hera had said she was sending a boat for Persephone's unique *situation*, but she hadn't said the only passenger could be the god of vegetation. Could they hitch a ride? Their stories were entwined, after all.

"Persephone, don't leave without us," Meg prayed. Then she reached for Katerina's hand and prepared to tell the woman to move her legs as fast as she ever had before. But before she could even utter the word *run*, the pair disappeared.

# TWENTY-EIGHT: Last Chance

Meg and Katerina materialized at the edge of a dark, rocky dock alongside the river Styx. A voice came to them in the darkness.

"I heard a prayer you wanted to join me on this boat," Persephone said, her eyebrows raised. "So I thought I'd give you a lift. We're leaving soon."

Meg would actually have hugged the god if she didn't think it would offend her. "Thank you."

"Now we're even," Persephone said. She noticed Katerina clinging to Meg's arm. "So is this the ex's new wife?"

Meg nodded. "This is her," she said, but her focus was on Charon rowing his boat toward them, his presence especially eerie in the glow of the torches along the river. She wished he would move faster.

"Where are we?" Katerina trembled as she eyed the large cavern. The stalactites hung precariously above their heads, and the vast cities of the Underworld lay behind them, perched on top of one another like an overgrown tree in need of pruning.

It occurred to Meg that Katerina might not remember this place, let alone even arriving in the Underworld, after all she'd been through. She held tight to the woman's hand, fearing she might bolt. "This is the entrance to the Underworld," Meg told her, "and that boat is coming to take us out of here."

Katerina squeezed Meg's hand as she watched the lost souls swirl about in the dark water. A low layer of fog rolled in. Meg could feel Katerina shaking harder now. *Go faster,* she willed the boat, picturing the last grain of sand shift in the hourglass. *Faster!*

"Hades isn't coming to say goodbye?" Meg asked anxiously. If he appeared, they were done for.

"Oh, no, he'll see me off." Persephone held up a hand to show an ornate snakelike silver band wrapped around her ring finger. "He asked me to marry him." Her dark eyes glowed almost yellow in the darkness, but it sounded as if she was smiling. "My mother is going to flip."

"Congratulations," Meg said, hoping she sounded sincere even as she wished Hades would miss the boat. *Come on, come on,* she begged Charon, who was only feet away. Once they stepped on board, they would be free, right? She didn't want to think about the alternative. She'd gotten Katerina this far. She had to see her through to the end.

Katerina's breath quickened as Charon's boat knocked up against the landing. He held out his oar to hold the boat steady and Persephone climbed in. She turned around and held her hand out to Katerina. Meg practically pushed the woman inside, then jumped in after her.

*"Uh, uh, uh."*

Hades's voice echoed through the cave. The god of the Underworld was gliding toward them on a bed of smoke, his hands folded calmly.

"Not so fast, Nut-Meg. Per has a get-out-of-jail-free card, but as for you two, I'm pretty sure the time for your little quest is up by now. Which means you've failed, and we have no deal." The yellow in his eyes glowed. "You two belong to me."

Meg's heart thudded. "If we *had* run out of time, we wouldn't even be here, would we?" she said as evenly as she could muster. She could see Persephone watching from the corner of her eye, and she wondered if the god would reveal the truth. "We still have some left."

Hades held out his hand. "Prove it! Show me the hourglass!"

"Fine." Meg swallowed, the thick heat making her ache with thirst. Her fingers trembled as she reached into her satchel for the glass jar. *Please let there be sand left,* she prayed to the gods. *Please! We're so close!* Meg's fingers closed around the vial and she pulled it out, her breath catching in her throat as they all turned to look.

"HA!" Hades roared.

The last sands had fallen to the bottom. It was over.

"You're not going anywhere!" Hades's voice was laced with triumph. Smoke sprang from his hands and headed toward them.

Katerina grabbed hold of Meg once more. "What does he mean? Megara, no. Please, no!" She burst into tears.

Meg stiffened. *Nope. I'm not going out like this.* She grabbed Persephone's arm, instantly regretting the move as Persephone looked down at her hand in surprise. Meg had been rash with a god before, and her mouth had gotten her in trouble. But this time, her words were the only thing left that could save them. She let go and tried to channel calm and diplomacy with every word. "Would you talk to him? He'll listen to you." Persephone frowned, but Meg continued before she could refuse. "We're so close to the end of the journey. I can't send her back now." They both looked at Katerina, who was sobbing. "Please? We're on the boat already. Can't he just let us try to get out of here?"

Persephone pursed her lips. "But if your time is up, the quest is over, no? Even Hera wouldn't let you leave the Underworld if you failed."

"I haven't failed yet," Meg corrected her. "If Hera hasn't stopped this boat from leaving with us on it, she must be looking favorably on us, no?"

Persephone thought this over. "Maybe. Or maybe she doesn't realize what's going on yet."

"I think it means we have an opening," Meg argued. "*Against all odds.* Like your flowers. And if we have an opportunity to get out of here, I am taking it. But I need your help. I gave up my last chance to reach the gods to help you. Can't you do the same for us?"

Persephone looked from Meg to Katerina and was quiet for a moment. After what felt like an eternity, she turned to her fiancé. "Hades, I'm taking them back with me."

Hades's face froze. "Wait—WHAT?"

"I'm taking them with me," Persephone repeated slowly. "Whether the hourglass is full or not, they're already on the boat, so Hera must be allowing it."

"Or she doesn't know what's happening!" Hades's head erupted in blue flames.

*They really do think alike,* Meg realized.

"Either way, there is no harm in letting them try to leave," Persephone said calmly. "Megara helped us stay together, my love. Shouldn't we offer the same courtesy to her? Doesn't it make for the better story?"

Hades glared at Meg. "No!"

"Well, *I* want to help her," Persephone announced, and Hades's flames died out. "At least let her try to travel to the end of the river Styx. If Hera doesn't allow her reentrance, you'll know. She'll be back." Hades crossed his arms and looked away, his head starting to erupt in flames again.

The sound of water dripping was interrupted by Charon's shifting bones. "Well, are we leaving or not?" he asked, his oar hovering above the water. Meg saw a soul reach for it and Charon swatted it away.

"Hades?" Persephone tried again.

"Fine!" Hades said, sounding annoyed.

Katerina wrapped her arms around Meg and began to weep again. Meg finally exhaled.

"Thank you, my Hades," Persephone said.

Hades's resolve seemed to weaken slightly. "You're welcome, love. I'll see you soon." Hades looked at Meg and his eyes flashed. "As for you, Nut-Meg, the same rules Hera gave to Per apply to you, too—either one of you looks back at the Underworld on your way out, and you're going nowhere."

"Believe me, nothing would make us want to look

back at this place." She glanced at Persephone. "Sorry. No offense."

Persephone shrugged and turned to Charon. "Go already, or my mother will have my head." She sat on the bench and stared straight ahead. "Goodbye, my sweet!"

"See you soon, my pet!" Hades started to laugh. "You too, Meg-let. Now that I think about it, probably in no time at all."

"What does that mean?" Katerina asked, adjusting her seat so that she was facing forward like Persephone and Meg. The ferryman shoved off, moving slower than seemed possible.

"He's just trying to scare us," Meg assured her.

Hades continued laughing. "Wait! Don't you want to say goodbye to your loved ones before you duck out?"

Meg's stomach filled with dread. *What are you doing?* she wondered. She raised her eyebrows at Persephone, who shrugged. "Hey, I just asked him to let you go. He's not going to make it easy. It's not his way." She sighed with a lovestruck, faraway look in her eyes, and Meg inwardly groaned.

"Layla—" Katerina started, but Meg cut her off, taking her hand.

"No matter what happens next, don't turn around," Meg told her firmly.

"But . . ." Katerina said, her voice cracking. "She's so young. She shouldn't be on her own."

"She'll be okay," Meg assured her. "I promise."

Katerina's small nose scrunched up with worry. "How can you promise that?"

Meg attempted a small smile even as her heart started to thud. "Ask me again when we're out of here. Just try to focus on getting home to your baby. Don't listen to anything he says."

Meg felt the boat begin to rock as the souls from the river moaned and begged to climb aboard. Katerina pulled herself in tight, squeezing Persephone, who looked less than thrilled at the loss of personal space. The women remained quiet. If Layla showed up, Meg wasn't sure Katerina's willpower would hold strong. Finally, Charon approached the area where two gigantic bony hands that served as walls opened to reveal Cerberus, who lay still. Katerina gasped.

"Relax. He's out cold," Persephone assured her. "Hades made sure of it." One of Cerberus's heads snored loudly.

The boat glided by and Meg felt her stomach unclench slightly. *It's going to be okay,* she told herself as the guardian's area closed off behind them. Up ahead, she could swear she saw a small light begin to form. *Maybe Hades's threat was just a scare tactic. Faster!* she silently urged Charon, who did not seem to be bothered by their painstaking pace. *Faster!*

"Megara! Megara! Where are you?"

As soon as Meg heard the voice echo through the cave, her blood ran cold. She swallowed. "Mother?"

"So many have told me you're here, but I can't find you," her mother cried out. "Please, let me see you. I've missed you so much!"

Tears flooded Meg's eyes. *How could Hades be so cruel?* Meg couldn't ignore her. "Mother, it's me!" she cried out.

"What are you doing?" Katerina whispered. "Megara, no!"

"Megara! I've found you! Where are you, child? Let me see you!"

"Be strong, Megara," Katerina said, squeezing her hand. "Don't turn around. Think about what's at stake."

Meg's heart beat faster as her tears continued to fall. "I love you so much, but if I show myself, Hades will trap me here forever, and I'm free to go, Mother. I'm free! I have a chance to do something pretty extraordinary with my life. Please don't tempt me to go back and find you, because I love you so much that I'm pretty sure I will." Her voice cracked. An excruciating silence followed. "Mother?"

Had Thea heard? Would she understand? Was she

all right? Meg gripped the bench, tears streaming down her face.

"Mother?" she tried again, more forcefully.

"I understand, my child!" her mother yelled with an anguished sob. "You cannot come back. Be strong and brave like I taught you, my love. You're a big, tough girl. You tie your own sandals and everything."

Meg let out a sob of her own and wrapped her arms around herself to try to remain calm. "I love you, Mother!" she said, but this time there was no reply.

Katerina squeezed her shoulder. "Megara, look."

Meg lifted her head and saw the light.

# TWENTY-NINE: The End of the River

"Almost to the end of the river," Persephone announced.

Meg took a few shaking breaths as Katerina patted her back. *Enough tears now, Meg,* she told herself and squared her shoulders. She lifted her head higher. *You need your strength for whatever comes next.*

Meg watched as Charon's boat approached the large opening. Beyond it, she could see the fog that covered the lake at the entrance to Earth. The fog thickened as they neared, and the souls below them began to quiet.

Would Hera let them pass? Or were she and Katerina about to be returned directly to a triumphant Hades? Meg had missed her deadline, but she'd also fought her way out of the darkness and won. Even if she couldn't become a god and be with Hercules, Katerina deserved to be returned to

Aegeus and Cassia. *Please let her live,* Meg prayed to Hera as the boat reached the end of the river. *I understand now what you tried to teach me with this quest. If one truly wants to live, they need to open their heart to others, and I have. No matter what comes next for me, I know now I loved and was loved in return. I will carry that thought with me for the rest of my days if you let me. Just please allow us to pass.*

Charon broke out of the cave into the lake, and Meg felt Katerina's hand slip from her own. Meg watched in wonder as the woman's pale form began to brighten. Katerina's hands and arms started to glow orange along with the rest of her body. Her tan dress faded away, replaced with one as yellow as the sun. Color returned to Katerina's cheeks and then, finally, the woman inhaled sharply, air filling her lungs for the first time in months.

She cried out and looked at Meg in surprise. "I'm alive?"

"You're alive!" Meg shouted, and the two women embraced as Persephone watched them, her eyes sparkling.

*And so am I,* Meg thought. *Thank you, Hera. Thank you!* She inhaled deeply. The smells of burning and decay were gone. In the distance, she could swear she smelled pomegranate seeds.

"We made it," Katerina said. "Oh, Megara, how can I ever repay you?" She reached out for Meg and started to cry again.

As Meg hugged Katerina, she couldn't help thinking about the fact that she was embracing the very person she'd resented for far too long. Now they were both free. Katerina would get to live her life and be there to watch her daughter grow up. Meg had helped make that happen.

"This is the end of the ride," Charon said as the boat came to a sudden stop.

"Thanks, Charon," said Persephone. "See you in a few months." The ferryman shrugged his bony shoulders. Persephone looked at Meg. "And you. Thank you. For helping Hades and me. And for making things infinitely more interesting."

"You're welcome," Meg responded. "And thank you for making the case for us to leave."

Persephone smiled and held out her hand. "Good luck, Megara."

"You, too," Meg said. "But, um, any chance you can get us to shore before you go?"

"Not a problem." Persephone snapped her fingers and the three of them found themselves on dry land.

Meg felt the grass beneath her feet and the feel of solid ground again and whooped with happiness. The fog started to fade. The river Acheron, where she had toiled for days, started to appear through the mist. She and Katerina hugged again.

"I'm off to see my mother and show her my ring,"

Persephone said, her voice gleeful as she admired it in the light. She looked at Katerina. "You take care of that child of yours. A seedling needs proper love and care. You hear me?"

"Yes," Katerina said. "I will love her with my whole heart."

Persephone nodded, and with one final look at the two women, she snapped her fingers and disappeared.

"Who was that, by the way?" Katerina asked, and Meg couldn't help laughing, realizing with all that had happened, she'd never gotten the chance to explain.

"That was Persephone, the god of vegetation."

Katerina's eyes widened. "We were riding with a god?"

Meg laughed harder. It felt good after ten tough days. And yet, she still couldn't help thinking of what she'd lost during that time, too. She might have been freed from the Underworld, but it looked like she would be staying Earth-side. Hercules was hers to love no more. "Come on. Let's get you home."

She looked around, wondering if they could fashion themselves a boat. It was too far to walk. The river had more trials than it did triumphs, and the thought of the Stymphalian birds was enough to make her want to stay at the edge of that shore permanently.

Suddenly she heard a neigh and looked up. Pegasus was flying toward them.

# THIRTY: Reunion

"Peg!" Meg cried, rushing to the horse's side as he came in for a landing next to them.

The horse seemed as happy to see her as she was to see him. She patted his mane, smoothing his blue hair and nuzzling her face against his.

"Can you give us a lift to Aegeus's?" Peg snorted again. "We have a ride," Meg told Katerina. "Climb on!"

Peg quickly took to the sky again and Katerina and Meg held on as the horse soared away from that dreaded lake and river and carried them from the mouth of death. With each flap of the creature's majestic wings, Meg breathed a little easier.

*Last ride,* she thought a bit sadly. After this, Pegasus would return to Hercules, and she . . . she wasn't sure where she'd go, actually. Wherever it was, it most certainly wouldn't have this view.

Meg chortled softy. Could it be after all this time, she actually *enjoyed* soaring above the clouds? She looked down, trying to commit every detail of the flight to memory—how the trees looked like specks and the lakes like splats of blue paint.

Pegasus neighed loudly and they started to dip down between the clouds. Katerina held on tight to Meg's back as they came in lower. Meg could see the coastline up ahead and she felt her breath quicken as Peg dove faster, racing toward the small dot on the hill on the horizon. Finally, he swooped low, his neighs filling the sky as two small figures came running toward them. She could hear their cheering as Pegasus came in for a landing.

"Katerina!" Aegeus cried as he and Phil ran from the house.

"Aegeus!" Katerina sobbed. She scrambled off Pegasus and ran toward him.

Meg watched as Aegeus and Katerina threw their arms around each other and kissed. Seeing them together, she was thankful her heart no longer felt envy. Her heart swelled instead with the joy that came from celebrating someone else's triumph, a love reunited. Who knew such a feeling was even possible?

"Red!"

Meg turned around.

Phil was practically jumping into her arms. "You did it, Red! I can't believe it, but you did it! When you didn't appear on the riverbank on the tenth day, Pegasus and I feared the worst. . . . I kept sending him back on flights to look for you and now here you are." He suddenly looked misty. "I'm so proud of you."

Was the satyr really going to make her tear up again? "Thanks, Phil."

"So tell me everything," he continued, now talking a mile a minute. "What was Cerberus like? Bigger than a Titan? Hades? Does he really burst into flames? How'd you track down Katerina?" He stepped back. "Hey. Why aren't you glowing like Hercules was? Aren't you a god now?"

Meg exhaled. "Phil, there's something you should know."

"There's a lot I need to know! Did you call for Hera yet?" He poked Meg in the arm. "Maybe you need to square things up with her, and then they'll take you up to Mount Olympus."

"Phil . . ." Meg pulled the hourglass out and showed him the gathered sand. "I failed."

Phil looked at the glass bottle and blinked. "Failed? No! You're here!" He looked back at Katerina still embracing Aegeus. "And she's here, too." His face reddened. "How are you here if you failed?" he demanded. "Is this a joke?"

"We got out of the Underworld, yes. But I didn't make it in time." Meg filled him in on everything that happened from the moment she entered Charon's boat: Cerberus, her interactions with Hades and Persephone, what happened when she found Katerina, and how she entered Charon's boat a second time only to find that the last grain of sand had fallen. Phil's jaw dropped when she told him about hearing her mother's voice calling to her on the river Styx. And somehow, Hera had allowed them to return to the land of the living.

"Aww, kid, I'm sorry." Phil shook his head. "I thought you had them beat. I really did." He touched her arm. "Either way, you did good. Real good. Look at those three."

Meg and Phil turned around. Aegeus was holding Cassia out to Katerina. Meg watched as the child hesitated for a split second before reaching for her mother, nuzzling close as if no time had passed. Katerina held her daughter close, and the child laughed and pulled at a lock of her hair.

"Katerina gets to live and Cassia has her mother back," Meg said. "That's what's important. And who knows? Maybe someday Aegeus and Katerina will tell her about the woman who went to the Underworld to reunite them."

"Of course they will." He patted her arm. "Who cares about timing? You finished the race all the same. You're a god in my book, Red."

"Thanks, Phil. I just wish I could see Hercules one last time. His love inspired this whole quest in the first place. And because of that, I was able to get through to Katerina and beat Hades at his own game." Now she felt like she had a lump in her throat. "I don't think I realized how much I really loved the guy till I lost him."

"Maybe you should tell him that."

Meg and Phil turned around. Athena and Aphrodite stood behind them.

"Great gods!" said Aegeus, and he and Katerina knelt down as Cassia continued to wriggle in her arms.

"You have done well, Megara, and acted as a true hero," Athena said. "Even when the path was murky, you found your way."

"And it is clear you have learned what true love really is," added Aphrodite with a bright smile. "Give-and-take, sacrifice, learning to trust in others—it's all a part of it, as you now know."

Meg looked at both gods. "I am thankful for all your guidance."

"As am I."

A third god had appeared on the hillside.

Meg inhaled sharply. "Hera."

"What you did in your hour of need did not go unnoticed," Hera said. "You fought your way to Katerina and never stopped until she remembered the truth about her loved ones. Even when faced with adversity and the choice to save the orchid for yourself or use it to help others, you chose their needs over your own." She tilted her head and looked at Meg curiously. "I thought I had you figured out, but clearly I was wrong. That is why I am here to offer you a gift." Meg looked at her. "Even though you failed to complete your quest before the sand ran out, I will allow you to see Hercules one last time."

Before Meg could even comprehend what was happening, Wonder Boy had materialized in front of her.

"Meg!" he cried, racing toward her and pulling her into an embrace. "You're back!" He kissed her fiercely and lifted her up into his arms.

Meg placed her hands on both of his cheeks, blinking through new tears. "Wonder Boy," she whispered. "I thought I'd never see you again."

He grinned and placed her back on the ground. "I knew you could do it. I just knew it, Meg."

Her smile faded. "But I didn't. Not in the time I was given to complete the quest."

Hercules's brow creased. "But you're here. . . ."

"Yes. It's a long story, but that's not important now." She held him tight, and would as long as she physically could. She had to speak while she still had a chance. "I need to apologize," she said, rushing the words. "I'm sorry for yelling at you when you tried to help with the Stymphalian birds. I was wrong to not accept your help."

"Meg," he tried.

"No, listen to me," she shushed him. "I learned something along this journey. I know now that love means showing up for one another and trusting that the other person always has your back. It means asking for help sometimes, and not thinking that means you look weak. Love means opening your heart to another, no matter the consequences."

"Meg," Hercules said, pulling back to look at her. "What happened down there?"

She smiled sadly. "A lot, and I did good. You'd be proud of me. I saved someone else's love story at the sacrifice of my own." She thought again of baby Cassia and Katerina and Persephone and all those she'd managed to help, even though she couldn't help herself. She felt her voice tighten. "People do crazy things when they're in love."

Aphrodite let out a sob and leaned her head on Athena's shoulder. The other god did not look amused. Even Phil started to cry again. This was it. The end of her love story with Wonder Boy. She knew she'd never find another like him.

"Meg, I don't understand—" Hercules started to say.

"You don't have to," Hera interrupted before Meg could explain further. She walked over to the two of them, beaming. "I can see my son is truly happy with you, and you have more than proven yourself worthy. You have given us what matters most—Katerina." She looked at the babe a few feet away. "Cassia will flourish under her father and mother's tutelage and one day will become a great hero, with Philoctetes's help."

Meg's eyes widened. So that was why the gods had been so keen to get Katerina back to the land of the living.

"My help?" Phil repeated and puffed up his chest. "I guess I could hold off on retirement a *little* while longer."

A dove fluttered into view and landed on Hera's shoulder. In its beak was a small glass bottle, which resembled the hourglass Meg had carried for ten days. Hera took the bottle out of its mouth and offered it to Meg.

"Drink this," she said. "It's ambrosia, the nectar of the

gods. One sip and you will be transformed into a god." Meg couldn't hide her surprise. "I know you didn't complete your quest in time, but gods always find a way to help when a hero shows a true heart." She touched Meg's face. "I have seen yours, Megara."

Meg took the bottle from Hera's outstretched hand and drank its contents without hesitation.

A warmth flooded her as the liquid slid down her throat and spread to every limb. Her body started to glow thistle in color until light emitted from every inch of her. She could feel Aegeus, Katerina, Cassia, and Phil watching her along with the gods, but she only had eyes for one other at that moment.

Hercules stared at her, speechless. "Meg . . ." he started as she continued to transform.

She knew where she belonged now, and it was by Wonder Boy's side. Together, they could do great work.

She put a hand to his lips and smiled, unable to contain her happiness. "Tell me once we're home, Wonder Boy."

# EPILOGUE

## A few months later . . .

She was getting used to this god business.

There was a learning curve, to be sure, but each time Meg heard a mortal call out for help, her purpose became clearer. Hera had named her the god of vulnerability, and it suited her, even if she bristled at the title at first.

As Wonder Boy kept telling her, she had a knack for hearing a mortal in need, more so than the others. When doubt raised its ugly head, or a mortal acted too proudly, she stepped in and tried to steer them in the right direction.

And Holy Hera, was the feeling rewarding when the mortal actually *listened* and accepted her aid.

Even ol' Zeus, who was less than thrilled to see Meg back on his turf, had to admit she was good at her job.

She seemed to make Hercules deliriously happy, and the feeling was mutual. All the gods were talking about a Mount Olympus wedding, but she and Hercules were taking their time.

She still had some unfinished business she wanted to take care of before she thought about the next part of her own story. And that business took her back to Earth.

Meg appeared there suddenly one afternoon while Katerina was working in the garden, Cassia tucked safely in a basket at her side.

"Hello, Katerina," Meg said.

"Megara!" Katerina stood up quickly in surprise, dropping her trowel.

Cassia screamed with delight at the sight of her, or maybe it was just the fact that she was glowing. Aegeus came running.

"Megara!" he said, looking on in surprise. "To what do we owe this honor?"

"Aegeus, you can forget the formalities. I may be a god, but I'm still me," she said, sitting down on their garden bench and picking up the baby, whom she bounced on her knee. The child had gotten bigger—and heavier—since she'd last seen her. "I am here with some news for Katerina."

"News?" Katerina said, confused.

"Yes." Meg smiled and put Cassia back down in the

basket. "I know the guilt you have about leaving Layla still torments you, especially in the evening when the moon is high."

"It's true," Katerina said, her face crumbling. Aegeus quickly put an arm around her. "I am so grateful for all you have done for me and our family, and I can't imagine not being here to see Cassia's every breath, but leaving Layla is still one of the great regrets of my life. I worry for her."

"I know," Meg said, "which is why I wanted you to know that I was true to my word when we left the Underworld—I promised you Layla would be okay, and she really is. As a matter of fact, why don't I let you see for yourself?"

Meg walked over to the small pond in their garden, and Katerina and Aegeus quickly followed. Meg flicked her wrist and the water in the dark green pond began to swirl. Suddenly an image, much like their own reflection, shone back at them. It was Layla, and she was waving to them.

"Layla!" Katerina cried out and let out a sob on Aegeus's shoulder. "That is my sister," she explained.

Layla held up a basket of poppies to show them, then waved to someone out of sight who stepped into the frame. Meg's heart felt like it might burst at the sight of the two of them together.

"Who is that with her?" Aegeus asked about the woman with the long red hair.

"My mother, Thea," Meg said softly, and the pair looked at her. "Layla and I spoke of my mother in the Underworld, and when she gave you her blessing to leave, she asked me where she could find someone who, too, was looking for love and nourishment in the Underworld. I gave her my mother's location and have since gotten word that the two are inseparable." She looked at Katerina. "Layla has found the surrogate mother she needed to thrive, and my mother finally has the chance to be the parent she never could be on Earth. Persephone checks in on them both, in fact, now that she's returned to Hades, and I'm told they are both quite happy. I thought you'd want to know."

"Yes," Katerina said, smiling through her tears. "Thank you, god of vulnerability. Thank you for this gift!"

They heard a squeal and turned around. Cassia had wriggled out of the basket and was crawling toward them. Katerina scooped the child up and faced her to the fountain so that Layla and Thea could see her.

The image of them looking at one another was one Meg knew she'd never forget.

She heard the tinkling of bells, and Hermes popped up beside her.

"Come along now, Megara! Hercules and Hera are waiting. Meeting starts in ten," he said, fluttering alongside her.

Meg turned toward the family she had helped put back

together and smiled. "I must go, but know that I'm always a prayer away if you need me." The image in the pond disappeared as Meg began to fade away.

The next thing she saw was Wonder Boy waiting with outstretched hands. "Well? Did it go okay?" he asked.

Meg stepped into his arms and kissed him. "It was absolutely perfect."

# UNBIRTHDAY

## A TWISTED TALE

# Unbirthday

## A Twisted Tale

Liz Braswell

Disney · Hyperion
Los Angeles • New York

Published by Disney • Hyperion, an imprint of Buena Vista Books, Inc.

For information address Disney • Hyperion,
77 West 66th Street, New York, New York 10023.

Printed in China
First Hardcover Edition, September 2020
First Paperback Edition, September 2024
1 3 5 7 9 10 8 6 4 2
FAC-031939-24095
Library of Congress Control Number: 2020002213
ISBN 978-1-368-10403-6
Visit disneybooks.com

For my sister, Sabrina.

We are not Mathilda and Alice but have moments of each.

I forgive you for that time you tricked me into eating
a fancy chocolate with a hairball inside.

Sort of.

*—L.B.*

# A gentle note, Dear Reader:

*As you are probably already aware, this book is a work of Nonsense.*

*That being said, it behooves us to remind you that the Mad Hatter is a fictional character and doesn't conform to the strict rules of our own world.*

*To wit:* mercury is deadly poisonous.

*Hatters really were said to have gone mad in the nineteenth century because of exposure to mercury in their hat-making processes: in effect, they suffered long-term mercury poisoning.*

*You cannot eat the fish from many rivers and lakes of America even today because of the deadly mercury that lies on their muddy bottoms eternally, the result of toxic industrial pollution.*

*In this book the Hatter drinks mercury.*
*You, dear reader, cannot.*
*It will kill you.*

*—L. Braswell*

# Alice as You Remember Her

# Chapter One

Morning sunlight waved a cheery hello on the papered walls of an equally cheery bedroom. It had rained overnight, a proper rain—hard with big droplets—and the day came fresh scrubbed and eager. The air that drifted through the open window was chill and sharp and had a bit of a kick to it. A flock of little sparrows who had been nest mates barely a week earlier chirruped excitedly back and forth in a way that would eventually result in either a sudden flight en masse, or feathery fisticuffs.

Even the hammer strikes of Mrs. Anderbee's solid heels against the floor downstairs sounded springier and more energetic than usual.

The girl lying so peacefully in her brass-frame bed,

thick golden hair spread around her head and neck like the resplendent halo of an angel, was coaxed from sleep to wake at once by the abundance of all these cheerful noises. Her eyes snapped open, the long lashes on her lids waving like wheat with the suddenness of the motion.

"Today," Alice declared, "is a perfect day for adventure!"

She grinned and basked in the glory of her decision for a moment, then shot out of bed. Dinah, a cat both grumpy and unwilling to see the day for what it was, stretched once in place (where formerly her mistress's warm feet had been), then closed one elderly eye to the day and was asleep again seconds later.

"Sorry, old girl!" Alice said, giving her a kiss. "But *tempus fugit*, you know; time waits for no one!"

Of course, this being the time and place that it was, adventurers couldn't just run out the door in their chemises. It would be scandalous. And so Alice began the tedious process of donning all the layers necessary to going out into the world as a respectable young English lady. She had:

*Drawers* that went down to her knees.

A *crinoline* that looked like a cross between a bee skep and a cage. It was basically a series of steel hoops in diminishing circumference that circled her lower body from her calves to her waist. This held the skirts worn on top of it out from around her like a giant bell with her legs the clapper.

*Corset.*

She didn't tight-lace, despite the fashion and the pressure from friends. On this one thing Alice and her sister agreed: it was pure foolishness. Her waist was fine as it was, thank you very much, and she left the corset to its main job: keeping her back aligned and her womanly attributes smooth and in place.

*Petticoat.*

*Petticoat.*

*Actual dress.* A nice summer-weight gingham in blue and white.

*Jacket* and *hat.*

And finally, *camera* bag.

Alice hurried through all of this as fast as she could and then nearly skipped like a girl much younger than eighteen as she ran down the stairs . . . only remembering to try to keep her footsteps silent at the very last—and far too late—minute.

*"Alice!"* a strident female voice cried out. Mathilda, her sister. Of course.

Well, since she had been heard, she might as well have some breakfast.

"Good *morning*, Mother, Father, Sister," she said grandly, sweeping into the dining room. Her family was gathered at one end of the long table like refined squirrels, cracking soft-boiled eggs, spreading jam on toast, sipping tea and coffee, and generally looking completely at ease in the formal and bric-a-brac-filled room. Her mother turned a plump, still-pink cheek for a kiss and Alice obliged. Her father's face was mostly hidden behind the newspaper, but she managed to get in a quick peck, not quite on his muttonchop.

She patted her sister on the shoulder dismissively, as if brushing off some dandruff.

"Married yet?" her father asked from behind the paper.

"No, Papa."

"In the stocks yet?"

"No, Papa."

"Hmm. Good." He shook his paper to facilitate the turning and folding of a page and then continued reading about things happenings in foreign places, his favorite type of story.

"Are you *sure* it's good, Papa?" Mathilda asked. She was severe, beautiful in a slightly off-putting way, dark eyes and lashes and hair where her younger sister's were light. Her somber dress was as drab as Alice's blue-and-white one was gay and summery. But if they had ever really made an effort to go out together—and if Mathilda ever made an effort with her appearance beyond brushing her hair—they could have owned all of the town of Kexford.

Not that Alice wanted to own Kexford. But it would have been an absolute gas for one party at least.

"She's eighteen, you know," Mathilda prodded, spreading jam on her toast most seriously.

"And I believe you're twenty-six," her mother observed.

"*I* have prospects!"

"Yes, yes you do," her mother said quickly and soothingly.

"I'll keep my baby girl Alice for as long as I possibly can," her father said from behind his paper. "Don't go interfering with that."

"My dear friend Mr. Headstrewth has a friend—Richard Coney," Mathilda said, turning to Alice and ignoring her parents. "I believe I have told you about him a number of times. I think you may even have met him once? Very bright young man. Handsome. With a great future before him—he's already working on Gilbert Ramsbottom's election campaign. I have invited him—"

"Oh, he sounds *lovely*, yes, thoroughly interesting, fantastic, do keep me informed of his doings, absolutely! Good morning, and goodbye!"

Alice winked at her mother, who tried very hard not to smile.

Then she grinned and spun away, and it wasn't until Mathilda turned back to her breakfast with a huff that she noticed her carefully buttered and jammed toast was missing.

Walking down the sunny road, Alice thoroughly enjoyed her purloined breakfast, so expertly buttered and jammed. After wiping her lips and cheeks with the back of her hand like a cat she raised her face to the sun, enjoying its warmth as it hit her skin. For only a moment, of course, before it did any real damage. She adjusted her hat and—

"Oh dear."

She had forgotten her gloves.

"Oh, my fur and whiskers," she sighed. "Not respectable at *all* today."

A momentary feeling overcame her. It wasn't *sadness* exactly. But it wasn't just nostalgia, either. There was a golden drop of happiness in the feeling, whatever it was, as warming and delightful as sunlight. A memory of old dreams that had worn thin like the comfiest pillowcase one couldn't bear to throw out.

*Wonderland.*

The details had dimmed long ago but the feelings remained: adventure, magic, fascinating creatures. True, not all her imagined adventures in Wonderland had been fun or safe. And not all the people had been particularly nice or polite. Some of the flowers in Wonderland were downright violent.

And the Queen of Hearts! She had wanted Alice *dead*! "Off with her head!" The phrase still sent shivers down Alice's spine.

But . . .

She hadn't had another dream like that one since.

"Stuff and nonsense," Alice declared, shaking her head. "It's a gorgeous day! Let's go find the magic right here!"

*Right here* was, of course, Kexford, a shining little town of university professors, ancient halls, glorious green parks, and glittering canals. There were gleaming white walkways, ancient stone buildings, and gardens so tiny and bright they practically sparkled like jewels. Everything was ordered and perfect and old in these hallowed grounds—even down to the properly wrecked, robed students hurrying to class after late-night partying or discussing Petrarch.

(Alice's house was just north of the university area, a fine large place with gardens and a lawn; not too long a walk to where the action was downtown, but not close enough to hear "Gaudeamus Igitur" being belted out at three o'clock in the morning.)

After waking from that magical dream ages ago, little Alice had devoted all her free time to searching the town for anything that reminded her of Wonderland. No place was safe from her explorations: every bell tower she could sneak into, every alleyway she could slip down when her parents' backs were turned. Top to bottom, high and low, nary a stone unturned.

(Mostly low: rabbit holes and mushrooms, tiny caterpillars and large spiderwebs, dumbwaiters and surprisingly small doors in other people's houses she really ought not to have explored and opened.)

Her wooden treasure box had contained rather more than the usual number of strange trinkets children tend to collect: tiny brass keys, tiny glass bottles, leftover halves of unusual biscuits, a left white glove, a right off-white glove, scraps of paper with the words EAT ME and DRINK ME laboriously written over and over again as she tried to match her flourishes to memory.

Alice hadn't been a morose girl—far from it—but she wondered sometimes if the reasons she never again dreamed of Wonderland were just a little bit her fault.

*"Of all the silly nonsense—*
*this is the stupidest tea party*
*I've ever been to in all my life!"*

*"Well, I've had enough nonsense.*
*I'm going home—straight home."*

*"Oh no, please. No more nonsense."*

*No more nonsense.* There, she had said it herself. And her subconscious had obliged and kept her nightly excursions to a world with little nonsense in it at all.

So Alice had tried her hand at drawing the few things she remembered clearly from her dream (the Cheshire Cat, the White Rabbit, a pretty little golden key) or the curious things she saw while she was out exploring (a student with surprisingly pointed ears, an interesting clump of moss, part of a stone wall with vines that looked like they could be pushed aside to reveal a hidden entrance to somewhere fantastic).

"Hmm," her father had said, looking over her sketches.

"We don't have much artistic ability in my side of the family, either," her mother had commented.

"She *does* notice many . . . obscure things. Even if she can't . . . reproduce them."

"Yes, she spends quite a bit of her spare time *noticing* things. Perhaps she needs some sort of focus for that—er, besides drawing, I mean?"

And that was where Aunt Vivian had come in.

*She* couldn't draw, either, but she could sculpt a fair piece, hosted literary salons, was occasionally involved in rather scandalous doings, and wore trousers like a coal-hauling pit lass. Her house was running over with fringed lamps, art made by her friends, incense burners, and velvet.

She was not married. In fact, she was just about everything a family could hope for in a black sheep.

And she helped her brother and his wife (and their daughter) by fulfilling that role perfectly: she bought her niece a camera.

One of the latest models, a Phoebus box camera. It was a beautiful little thing and extremely portable, requiring neither a tripod nor bellows. It fit very nicely into a medium-sized case and could be brought out to quickly capture whatever took Alice's fancy—provided the light was bright enough.

(Aunt Vivian already had a darkroom sufficient for developing its glass plates; she was famous for the costumed tableaus she took at her salons with a much more traditional and giant-sized portrait camera.)

Alice was delighted. There was something inherently Wonderlandy about the whole process: light and shadow and mirrors and glass and lenses and images appearing magically.

A side effect of the new hobby was spending a lot more time with her aunt, which relieved her parents (who were concerned about her wandering the streets of Kexford by herself) and worried her sister (who believed Aunt Vivian was a terrible influence; not so much *modern* as *profligate*). Mathilda need not have been overconcerned, however; Alice loved her aunt, but she was now eighteen and had her own agenda—which had nothing to do with artists or vermouth or poppies or trousers.

Alice of course used the camera to document anything the remotest bit mysterious. She spent her days on what she called "photo walks": looking for objects and people that hinted at a hidden, fey, or wild side, which she would try to coax out with her camera. Once she found a potential subject she worked long and hard composing the shot, sometimes with additional mirrors or a lantern if it was in a dimly lit alley. She developed these images in her aunt's darkroom and then laid them out around her own room, studying them and trying to conjure a world out of what she saw there. Sparkling dew on spiderwebs, gloomy attics, a pile of bright refuse that might have hidden a monster or poem. The elfin qualities of a child, her eyes innocent and old at the same time.

She never told her parents (or her sister) about her visits to thc lcss storybook parts of Kcxford. But it was whcrc things weren't kept quite as neat or perfect or orderly that she felt magic and nonsense had a chance to bloom.

And that was where she was headed on this glorious day.

Down the road and south . . . and then east, away from the pretty campuses and annoying students. She chose her route to pass Mrs. Yao's tea shop. Really it was too beautiful a day for a cup of oolong and gossip, and she was still full from her stolen bread and jam for a sweet bun. But she turned down the tiny twisty street anyway and contented herself with a smile and wave to the woman behind the window. Mrs. Yao smiled and waved back. She served her customers out of brightly mismatched cups and plates from England, China, and even Russia—which was magical, and felt a bit like Wonderland.

Just past the tea shop, under a rainspout, was a tiny, delicate fern that had not been there the week before. Alice's questing eyes immediately spotted its out-of-place bright greenness, its patterned and gracefully uncurling frond. *Definitely* magical. She gauged the light then pursed her lips sadly. The narrow street was dismally dark, she had no lantern or mirror, and only a few more film plates left. None to waste on potentially terrible shots.

"Apologies, young master fern," she said, giving it a little curtsy. "Maybe next time, when you've grown a bit."

Or *opened up like a telescope*, really.

Following the twisty street around, farther into a tangle of old buildings, she stooped through a low archway and finally emerged at her real destination. At one time the little open area had been officially called Wellington Square but was now known as simply *the Square*. As in *the Square* where many of the local children met up and played, often the sons and daughters (or orphans) of immigrants who weren't necessarily welcome in the nicer parks. Alice took their portraits and listened to stories of their homelands and travels to England—some of which, especially with the younger sitters, were mixed up with fairy tales from their mother countries.

Today several of the children had a ball and were playing with it in a corner, scuffing up the dirt. In another corner three girls were playing a counting game, effortlessly switching back and forth between English and Russian and Yiddish. Alice took out her camera and began composing possible images in her head.

"Oh, look, it's the famous English girl come to take photographs of the poor but pretty foreign children."

Alice spun around, affronted by both the words and tone. A young man not much older than herself leaned lazily on a worn statue of a cannon and gave her an indecipherable smile. His clothes were very different from the rest of the crowd here: they were adult, for one thing, pressed and clean and grey and professional. His jacket was spotless, his waistcoat well fitting. He didn't have a watch, but his purple cravat looked expensive and silken. His hat was carefully brushed. Under it was red hair so dark it was nearly black, trimmed very neatly around his ears and neck. His eyes were a light hazel that was nearly orange. His cheeks glowed a healthy shade of rose.

"Tell me," he continued, reaching down to pet a stray cat that quickly disappeared around the corner, "do your patrons enjoy weeping crocodile tears over portraits of the other half, and how they live?"

"I beg your pardon," Alice replied coldly, straightening her spine—until it cracked. "These photographs are for my personal use, and the occasional private viewing with my aunt to a select and discreet crowd. I am not some sort of terrible charity vampire preying on the sorrowful state of others."

"Oh? And how much do you know about their *sorrowful state*? How much do you know about them at all?" he pressed.

Alice regarded him coolly for a moment.

"That girl over there, in the jacket with the large bone button. Her name is Adina. She is from a shtetl too far from St. Petersburg to be safe from the pogroms. Her mother is dead; her father and her aunt Silvy are her only family in the world." She gestured at another child. "That's Sasha. He is probably five years old and prefers cheese to sweets. His mother sews piecework and his father collects rags for the paper companies and his sister is dying of tuberculosis, although he doesn't really understand that yet.

"I never speak to them patronizingly and I never bribe them to pose with coins or candy. If I bring anything it is enough for all of them and it is just because it pleases me to give. I treat even the littlest one with the same kindness and respect I expect out of *every*one." She said the last bit pointedly, glaring at the stranger.

"All right, all right." The young man laughed easily. "I apologize. I accused you without knowing whereof I spoke. I was a cad and a scoundrel."

He gave a bow, and it wasn't ironic at all.

"You are forgiven," Alice said, polite but still distant. "May I know whom I have the—*pleasure*—of addressing?"

"Katz," he said, taking his hat off. "Abraham Joseph Katz, Esquire. Barrister at Alexandros and Ivy. But you can call me Katz. At your service."

"I'm—" she began to introduce herself.

"Oh, everyone knows Alice and her camera around here," the man said, waving his hand. "The one and only Alice. But seriously, you have to understand, these children—even those of us who have grown up here—have not had the greatest experience with your fellow countrymen. Either it's spit and sneers, or cold charity and exploitation. There's rarely a middle ground."

"Us? You sound—you look—" Alice faltered, wondering if she was being rude. "British."

"I was born here. My parents were not," he said with a shrug. "They worked hard and I studied hard. Now I help out when I can with a little pro bono work. Sometimes someone with legal power needs to step in and save a child from the poorhouse or a parent from jail. Or worse. Sometimes a *patron*—say, with a camera—takes a child they fancy away entirely. For display, or ostensibly for charity, or for . . . things best not spoken of."

"That's dreadful," Alice said with feeling. "I am deeply, deeply sorry for all of it. All the same you can't blame me for the actions of a few of my terrible countrymen. That would be just like me treating you all poorly because of one bad apple that came in from Russia."

"A perfectly fair point," he agreed immediately. "In that case, I offer my stunning visage in case you ever decide you want to come back and take a portrait of *me*. I am an adult and a child of immigrants—and can legally agree to fair usage of my likeness, should it come to that."

There was nothing untoward in his tone. He did not wink at her or enunciate any word suggestively. He smiled and it was innocent; he did not even tilt his head dramatically as if posing. Alice felt neither flirted with nor threatened.

It was a little strange.

"Your English is better than that of many of my

'country-men,'" she said slowly while she tried to work out what that meant. "My neighbors, at least."

What on earth was she talking about? Was that rude? He had grown up here—he'd just said that! Of course he could speak English perfectly well!

"Ah, well: barrister, remember? I know Latin as well as Russian and English. *Quo usque tandem* and all that. I should probably learn French, however, so I can at least pronounce the wines."

Alice felt the world spin a bit like she was tumbling down a rabbit hole. What a strange man to meet in such a strange way! Normally she either avoided the young men pushed on her by her sister, or quickly forgot the ones she somehow met herself. Most were dull and unlikely to be found in this forgotten square. They all made unamusing and lewd jokes and references to Roman scholars they thought she wouldn't get.

She never had a desire to take a picture of any of them.

Unlike Mr. Katz.

"I didn't bring enough film today," she lied. But she *did* have lots of film already exposed at Aunt Vivian's waiting to process. Really, that's what she should have been doing instead of spending the day adventuring. "I was just realizing that when you approached me."

"Oh, I was joking about the picture. It's just that I have nothing besides my handsome good looks to offer you, to make up for my insults. I should keep a packet of sweets on me at all times. Remember that—always keep a candy around for emergencies. Someday it may save your life.

"Or, if you have any rats around your house, I could get them for you. I have a friend who is an expert at it."

"That won't be necessary," Alice said quickly. "I'm fairly certain our gardens are rat-free."

"I don't know. Rats are pretty sneaky. Sometimes they even make it into elected positions. Sometimes if you let them get out of control they even become mayor."

Alice couldn't repress a smile at that, and it almost became a snicker. He was very obviously referring to Ramsbottom, the candidate her sister and the boring Mr. Headstrewth so fervently supported. There was only one other person running, and for the life of her Alice couldn't remember his name (he was quite forgettable since he had no party affiliation and didn't write letters to the *Kexford Weekly* about building workhouses for the poor, kicking out foreigners, and giving the police bigger clubs).

"Well, I should be off, then," Alice said, putting her camera firmly back in her satchel and closing it up.

"Come back soon," Katz pleaded. "You're the most interesting person I've talked to in ages."

Not *you're a bright light in a dark corner of the world*, not a *fair face in a gloomy neighborhood*, not a *muse* or a *nymph* or an *angel with a rosy smile to bestow on her willing supplicants*. None of that nonsense verbiage men usually offered her. He asked her to return, very simply, because he wanted to talk to her.

Alice curtsied, because it was always good to curtsy while you were thinking of a reply, then hurried off, unable to think of one.

# Chapter Two

She found herself walking quickly away from Wellington Square—more quickly than before, and far more quickly than was strictly necessary. She forced herself to slow to a more ladylike stroll and concentrated on adjusting her breathing (not that hard with a corset already restricting her deepest breaths). Her cheeks felt warm and were probably a beautiful rosy shade.

It wasn't *entirely* a lie. She really *was* heading straight to Aunt Vivian's now to develop her pictures.

She remembered herself enough to cross to the other side of the street so she could peep into the window of Willard's Finest Haberdashery. His sign had gold letters and silver flourishes and the hats in his window were stacked artfully on top of each other like a carnival act, complete with fancy plumes and ribbons and spangles. It was delightful—and also felt somehow familiar. In fact, Alice had made friends with Mr. Willard because he reminded her a bit of someone she once knew in a dream, someone she couldn't quite remember.

When *he* shared a cup of tea with Alice, the cups matched, they sat quietly, and he discussed the advantages of an economic system in which the common people controlled the means of production—or at least regulated it—and medical care and legal help were free to all. Also advanced schooling and university would be provided gratis.

While this was a trifle boring, it was also quite mad, and his hair was white and wild. He and her aunt had hit it off splendidly—not romantically, but they were bosom companions at once and he became a fixture at her salons.

Today he wasn't at his worktable but standing outside his shop, eyes closed and face turned up to the sun like a flower, enjoying its rays.

"How do you do, Mr. Willard?" she asked, curtsying. He opened his eyes and smiled at her, his cheeks crinkling into a thousand happy lines.

"Oh, my dear, I am just enjoying this day. The sun is still free for everyone—never forget that. We can *all* enjoy its life-giving warmth as much as we want."

"Absolutely true, Mr. Willard. As is the clear blue sky."

"Quite right, my girl! Say—did you develop that portrait you took of me? Not that I'm vain or anything—all right, perhaps I am. A silly old man indeed! But I would dearly like to see it and show it to my friend Mrs. Alexandros. She is fascinated by photography but not perhaps as brave as you to take it up as a hobby."

"Why, I'm just on my way to Aunt Vivian's right now, Mr. Willard. I shall have it developed directly."

"Oh, excellent. And say hello to your aunt, would you? Tell her I have a hat I think she will absolutely love. Also a pamphlet concerning scientific principles that may prove once and for all that alloparenting—the act of a non-parent helping to raise a child, a niece or a nephew, say—is not just normal, but in fact *integral* to our evolution as a higher species! Not everyone need have a litter of kittens to be part of the great human cycle, I mean."

"Alloparenting. Kittens. Yes. I shall, Mr. Willard. Good day!" Alice said, curtsying again.

"Good day, Alice!"

She strolled happily down the road filled to a surfeit with the bonhomie of the moment, the sun, and a day full of the possibility of everything. Of course there was also that young man she had just met. . . . *He* certainly added a certain sense of wonder and potential to the air.

She forgot herself, pondering this, and cut through the market: sometimes a place for wonderfully interesting photographs and sometimes a bore, full of gossips who had very strong feelings about Alice and her prospects. She started to duck and hunch over before she caught herself.

"Alice," she told herself in a patient but chastising tone, "you are eighteen years now, fully grown and an adult, and you can no longer be ordered around or bullied by other adults. Please behave as such."

She took a deep breath, thanked herself for the reminder, and straightened up, proceeding past the stalls of cabbages with her head high in the air.

*"ALICE!"*

She slumped.

"Hello, Mrs. Pogysdunhow," she said as politely as she could. "Good morning, Mrs. Pogysdunhow."

The short and red-faced woman (*Piggysdunhow*, as Alice used to call her to Dinah) pushed her way over to talk. She looked exactly the same as when Alice had been of the age to run away from her at first sight: flat grey hair pulled back under an old-fashioned bonnet, dark old-fashioned dress with nary a crinoline or fancy stocking. Despite being the mistress of the rather respectable house up the street from Alice's family, she dressed and spent like a skinflint from a previous century—and screamed like a tavern matron from a previous millennium. Despite this, or possibly because of it, Alice's parents had occasionally employed her to look after Alice and her sister when they were younger. Her food was terrible and her breath worse. Somehow she was also always with babies, either children or grandchildren or other young, innocent, and heretofore harmless members of her extended family.

*"ALICE, HOW IS YOUR MOTHER?"*

She had a baby under her left arm right then, rather like a ball, tucked and restrained despite its desperate squirms in the name of freedom.

"She is fine, Mrs. Pogysdunhow. Thank you."

*"DID SHE GET OVER THAT BIT OF GOUT SHE WAS EXPERIENCING?"*

"Er, yes, Mrs. Pogysdunhow. She's quite well now, thank you."

*"COMES FROM TOO MUCH MEAT, YOU KNOW,"* the older woman offered confidentially, which meant lowering her voice to mere half-scream volume. *"IT'S ALWAYS WISE TO TEMPER A ROAST WITH A FEW DAYS OF PORRIDGE OR HASH AFTERWARD. A GOOD TURNIP HASH WILL CLEAR IT STRAIGHT UP!"*

Alice tried very hard not to shudder.

"That seems reasonable, Mrs. Pogysdunhow. Excellent

advice. But if you'll excuse me, I'm on my way to see my aunt now, and to develop the portraits I took last week. Including the one of you."

The other woman shook her head. *"OH, YOUR AUNT. WELL THERE'S A BLACK SHEEP IN EVERY FLOCK AND THERE'S A PLACE FOR BLACK WOOL IN EVERY SHAWL, I SUPPOSE. GIVE YOUR MOTHER MY REGARDS—AND YOUR FATHER MY SYMPATHY."*

"Yes, Mrs. Pogysdunhow. I shall."

Relieved almost to the point of fainting at such an easy escape, Alice tried not to rush away. While their relationship had improved somewhat since Alice had the dowager sit—with several babies—for a portrait, she was still mostly an unpleasant, cabbagey woman whose habits had involved making young Alice and Mathilda read long, archaic passages about the importance of . . . well, things Alice couldn't even remember. She shuddered at the memory of endless hours of endless sentences in books that made no sense.

*And which probably cost the good woman no cents,* Alice added thoughtfully, knowing well her tightness.

Down the hill now, she entered the more bohemian section of town, a poor area with pockets of strangely upbeat residents. Some were truly penniless philosophers who would rather read than eat; some were artists who spent every last coin on supplies and refused all patronage. Some were of semi-aristocratic descent, enjoying the decadent atmosphere around their artistic friends (and sometimes even actively contributing). Aunt Vivian was one of the latter.

She had a whole building to herself instead of just a flat, perhaps in slightly better shape than those around it. Alice rang the bell and let herself in; the door was never locked. She immediately began to cough. Besides all the usual apparatus of an artistic lifestyle (half-silvered mirrors, enough silk fringe draped everywhere to curtain a small theater, great and terrible paintings hung on every square inch of wall, etc.) her aunt was a big believer in *incense*. There were braziers everywhere, and blue smoke hung heavily in every room like a scratchy wool canopy. Alice gulped several mouthfuls of air through her fingers, trying to get used to it before her aunt appeared.

*"Alice."*

Her aunt strode in from the hallway with her usual drama and even clapped her hands. She wore soft trousers that came down to her calves, exposing a pair of shiny, chic boots. A thick tunic of velvet made for a shirt, and this was protected with a small apron. She also wore a small pair of gold-rimmed glasses and had her light brown hair back in a bun, which meant she was sculpting.

The two women embraced, and her aunt gave her a very Continental kiss on each cheek.

"You have a bit of a backlog in the darkroom," the older woman said a little accusingly as Alice carefully took off her hat and removed her satchel. "We shall have to work together, overtime, to get everything developed. It's a good thing I ordered all those compounds from the chemist—I knew we would be doing heaps. . . ."

Alice wasn't really listening. She was looking at the various portraits around the room she had seen a thousand times: farmers, actors, politicians, laborers, midwives, a princess, boys, girls, babies, all in rich and luscious tones. Photography captured someone exactly as he or she really was, but left out the color in the cheeks. If she were to take a portrait of Katz, it wouldn't capture him completely unless she used some pink pastel on his face afterward. And some gold for his eyes.

"Hello? Alice? Where are you?" Vivian demanded, narrowing her own pale grey eyes. She shook a finger at her niece. "You are not here. You are entirely elsewhere. What are you thinking about?"

"Oh, the difference between the arts of photography and painting. . . ."

Her aunt regarded her silently.

"I just met someone, that's all," Alice finally admitted, waiting for her face to flush, but it didn't.

"A boy?"

"A young man. A barrister. He was with the children at the Square. He helps out the families there sometimes. His parents were immigrants, too."

"Oh. A Jewish boy. Your parents are going to *love* that," Vivian said with a wicked grin. She grabbed Alice's hand and pulled her farther into the house, into the basement where the darkroom was.

"No, it's not like that. . . ."

"No talk. No lies. Just work. Work and art!"

Vivian took a burning joss stick from a brass holder as she went by and waved it before her as if clearing the air.

After putting on (bigger) pinnies, the two women were nearly silent for the next hour. The darkroom was tiny and smelled of fresh chemicals and magic. Well-practiced in what needed to be done, each worked as if she knew the other's movements beforehand: Pour this solution into that pan. Dip the dry plate in it. Dip the plate in the stop bath. Carefully set out to dry. Repeat.

Most of the ones they were working on were Alice's (although a few of the photographs were her aunt's, one a particularly detailed large-format re-creation of *The Death of Socrates*). She couldn't wait to take a look at them under real light; in the dim glow of the lantern with the red filter, she could barely see anything even when she tilted them back and forth and squinted.

Eventually they finished, tidied up the spilt chemicals, and left the plates to dry on a half dozen pressed and clean tea towels.

"I'm going to have a bit of vermouth and see if I can't get Monique to make us a light lunch," Vivian said with a heavy sigh, as if they had spent the last hour lifting weights. She crankily stuffed a piece of hair back into her bun and disappeared into the smoky rooms beyond.

They were supposed to wait an hour or so before handling the plates, but, always impulsive, Alice couldn't help herself. She snuck one into her palm, knowing that if she was caught her aunt would lecture her about how Patience and Time were the lost twin sisters of the other muses, the extra ones no one ever talks about (as compared to the more showy ones like Terpsichore and Urania). Alice quickly made her way to the little solarium off the study, where the brightest light in the house would be.

The portrait she had grabbed was of Mrs. Pogysdunhow; she caught a glimpse in the photo of the settee from the staging area where she had taken it. Alice couldn't remember if the sitter had been scowling or grinning with her two weirdly wide rows of tiny white teeth. Maybe it would be a masterpiece of artistic realism, or maybe just a horrible mockery that she would never be able to show the poor woman. The babies had been squirming. The exposure time had been approximately half a second—too slow to freeze the little tots; they would be blurry around the edges. But then weren't babies a little blurry around the edges all the time anyway, with their drool and blankets and fuzzy hair?

Alice slipped into the bright sun of the solarium and anxiously tilted her hand around, trying to get a good look without glare.

Her eyes widened when she saw what she really held.

It wasn't a portrait of Mrs. Pogysdunhow at all.

It was the Queen of Hearts.

# Chapter Three

Alice stared at the piece of glass in her hand, slick and thin and flat like a mirror, and tried to convince herself that she was wrong.

"'Tis a trick of the light," she murmured aloud to make it true. Too scared to believe.

It was a smudge, a drip, a chemical defect. A distortion that was her fault somehow for not making sure the solutions were properly mixed and properly spread. There was a bubble in the fixative.

But when she held the negative up to the blue sky beyond the panes of window glass—also rectangular, like her photo plate—there was no mistaking it. The horrid, imp-like thing gawping in the middle of the picture had too massive a head, too vicious a grin even for Mrs. Pogysdunhow. And there were no babies.

Also she was wearing a crown.

A tiny, strange angular distortion of a crown—the sort of crown you'd give a playing card to wear if it had come alive. The Queen waved a fan (in the shape of a heart) at the viewer as if to say, *Yes, it's really me, don't look away, you horrid girl.* Her hands and feet were tiny. Too tiny for her barrel-like body.

Alice realized she hadn't breathed in several seconds.

Wonderland!

*Exactly* from her dream.

But—

It was . . . real?

Alice wondered if this was what other girls felt like when they claimed they felt faint. The air in the tiny solarium *was* a little close. But instead of suffocating her, the warmth from the sun felt alive and rich on her hands, her skin soaking up its power with relish.

Yet even that, and everything else—the sky and brightness and the whole beautiful day—had become drab and unreal next to the strange grey-and-black image on the plate.

Alice peeped at it again almost from the corners of her eyes, afraid it would be gone, afraid it was a momentary hysterical delusion now replaced forever with a picture of a sadly all-too-non-fictive person. The Pogysdunhows of the world were too real to deny.

But no, the Queen was still there.

Alice laughed aloud and almost danced in the tiny confines of the solarium. Her smile and tossed golden hair put the glorious day outside to shame. She had Wonderland in her hand!

"Fancy that!" she breathed.

And yet . . .

Alice examined the picture more closely. There was *hate* in the negative-bright eyes of the Queen. Her smile was triumphant and cruel and looked like it could eat cities. True, the Queen of Hearts was malevolent and, in modern parlance, *unbalanced* in her constant sociopathic desire to take off everyone's heads, but she had said and done everything with the callous antipathy of any unpleasant child playing with dolls. Not with any real feeling about the situation.

"Alice!"

She jumped at the shout. Her aunt was looking for her, swishing in and out of rooms with languid yet efficient movements, pant leg wiffling against pant leg.

"Yes, Aunt Vivian?"

She let herself back through the solarium door, the tiny brass doorknob reminding her of other things: tiny keys, tiny glass tables, tiny doors. . . .

"Oh, getting a little sunlight, hmm?" her aunt asked appraisingly, looking at her over the tops of her glasses. "Probably quite healthy after the darkroom. Opens your pores. Here, these just came for you in the morning post."

Alice took both the cards with surprise. Who had possibly known where she was, who was so formal and needed her? Which *two* people?

Breathlessly she cracked the first one open. In her excited state she wondered dizzily: Would it say EAT ME? Or DRINK ME? Or be some sort of invitation to a playing-card ball? Anything was possible!

But the handwriting was immediately—and sadly—recognizable as her sister's.

*My dearest Alice,*

*You did not let me finish speaking at breakfast in your haste to go running off to Our Aunt's.*

*You will be delighted to hear, I am certain, that Mr. Headstrewth will be visiting with us during receiving hours. More than that, however, he will be bringing his good friend Mr. Richard A. Coney, whom I was also telling you about at breakfast.*

*Let me refresh your memory on the fine attributes of Mr. Coney in case you have forgotten: He is a very educated, intelligent young fellow destined for great things in our Party and the world in general. His hair is a brilliant platinum to your golden and I am certain you two will get along famously.*

*We will be receiving them at noon; a light tea will be served.*

*Ever yours,*

*Mathilda.*

"No," Alice said, her disappointment so severe it felt like gastric distress. Or perhaps that was merely the mention of Coney. "Absolutely not."

"I don't blame you," her aunt said, having read the note over her shoulder. "Sounds ghastly and bourgeois."

With something like feverish desperation Alice cracked open the other card. In the best of all possible worlds, there would be a tiny etching of a rabbit on it.

There was not.

*Alice dear,*

*Please do not bother yourself in making up an excuse that we would never believe anyway.*

*Come or we shall never hear the end of it from your sister.*

*—Your Loving Mother.*

Vivian let out a terribly unsophisticated bark of laughter. "She's got you there."

"Bats and cats," Alice swore, crumpling her hands into fists. "Bloody—"

"Aha, language," her aunt said, tsking. "You had better go. Otherwise I doubt you will ever be allowed over here again."

"But the other film plates!" Alice cried desperately. "I want to see them! They're almost dry. Let's do just have a peek first. . . ."

"They shall be waiting for you when you're done. Or no—I can send them over in the late post. Or by errand boy. Along with your camera. Come along, you'll have to hurry if you want to make it home in time. And you must never let them see you run, of *course*."

But Alice did run. She ran as fast as her leather shoes, corset, and crinoline let her. She felt strangely naked without her camera satchel but at the same time light and free—the only thing she carried was the glass plate of the Queen of Hearts (it didn't *quite* cut her hand as she gripped the sharp edges). Her hair tugged in its hastily reassembled chignon. Her arms spread out behind her like wings for a moment, memories of the freedom of chasing a white rabbit and thinking of nothing else but catching him.

As she rounded the corner to her house she slowed and adjusted her breath, slowing it as well. She swept her hands back over her hair to neaten it. Not that she *really* cared, but she didn't want to hear her sister making nasty little remarks about it.

Sedately and calmly she strolled up the cobbles and let herself in.

Everyone was already in the sitting room and looked up at her expectantly as she approached. The men stood. First and foremost was Corwin Headstrewth, Mathilda's "young man"; older than her by seven years, a smidgen overburdened with health and wealth. He was overall light brown in his jacket, trousers, waistcoat, hair, skin, and eyebrows. Like a happy rodent. Obstinate lips rested uneasily when they weren't moving (which was almost always).

Next to Headstrewth was a younger man, almost his direct opposite. He was so pale as to be milky, with light blue eyes that would have been gorgeous had they not been framed by red lids and nearly invisible eyelashes. His hair, an extremely acceptable shade of gold, had so much pomade in it that it looked crunchy.

"We were just expecting you," Mathilda said pleasantly. She was wearing the medium blue dress with rosettes at the neckline that she thought was especially fetching on her—and was that a hint of powder on her face? On *Mathilda*?

Alice looked to her mother, the only person in the room worth looking at. She had on a bright smile and confused eyes, perhaps a shadow of the old woman she would someday become. For now it was less dementia and more like *Well, I'm here, but wouldn't I be better off somewhere else—with my sewing or in the garden, perhaps?* Alice's father was nowhere to be found. He didn't like young men coming after his girls and had decided the future could be avoided by avoiding young men in general.

"Yes, of course," Alice said. "How do you do." She extended her hand politely to Headstrewth's friend.

"Richard Coney," the man said, bending over and kissing her hand instead of shaking it. Alice gave her mother another look; her mother covered her mouth with her fingers, hiding a mischievous smile that hinted at the girl she once was. Alice groaned inwardly: she would get no help there. "Your sister has told me so much about you."

"Really," Alice said neutrally. "How positively of her."

No one noticed the lack of adjective: quite rightly, she assumed each would fill in whatever he or she thought sounded most appropriate.

"Oh, let us have some tea," her mother said, ringing the little bell next to her. "And I know it's a bit early for a heavy bite, but Mrs. Anderbee just made a tray of macaroons."

"That sounds delightful, Mother," Mathilda said.

Alice didn't say anything: she was trying to sneak another look at the glass plate in her hand. Here she was stuck having tea with two of the most boring men she had ever met—she assumed—when all of Wonderland was out there waiting for her!

"What do you have there?" her sister asked. "Might you not share it with us?"

"Oh, it's just a picture I developed at Aunt Vivian's. It didn't come out the way I had expected," Alice said, holding up the glass and trying to tilt it back and forth specifically so no one could focus on the image.

"It's Mrs. Pogysdunhow," Mathilda said, her sharp eyes seeing it immediately. "And her two grandnieces. What an odd subject. I salute you for your charity."

Alice frowned and looked back at the plate. No: for her it was still just the singular Queen of Hearts. Fascinating!

"You're one of those 'photo fiends,' eh?" Coney said, not even bothering to take a look. "Snapping pictures of everyone everywhere?"

"I beg your pardon. I always ask permission. I would never invade anyone's privacy."

"*Richard* has a hobby, too," Headstrewth said broadly and awkwardly, perhaps competing in some unknown competition for *worst segue ever*. "He helps print up and distribute pamphlets for Ramsbottom's campaign—he is the campaign manager, along with Quagley Ramsbottom. He's even organizing the big rally next Tuesday!"

"Do tell," Alice said, not even trying *not* to sound bored. She turned her attention to Mrs. Anderbee, who had come in with the tea tray. Her mother didn't offer to pour, looking distractedly out the window, probably thinking of birds.

"Ramsbottom is the man to go with. England is changing," Coney said, taking up the new topic excitedly. "We're in a time of great upheaval. Factories everywhere, new technologies, unparalleled growth—why, the very definition of *labor* is changing. It's a tremendously exciting time to be alive. But with all this change it is vital to make sure we keep England—you know, *England*. English values, English ideas, English *citizens*."

Alice wondered if the sudden pain in the top of her nose was the beginning of the same sort of headaches her mother developed when her father grabbed his toolbox and claimed he could fix something himself.

"This tea, I believe, is from India," she said aloud, taking a delicate rose-covered cup from Mrs. Anderbee with a nod. "This cup, China. The fabric of Mathilda's dress is from Paris. My locket was made in Italy. There are no doubt more countries represented in this room than there are actual English *citizens.*"

*As well as one from Wonderland,* she added to herself.

"That's all very well and fine," Coney said, eagerly rising to the argument. Mathilda and Headstrewth gave each other nauseatingly familiar and knowing smiles. "As long as the locket makers stay in Italy and the tea farmers in India. If you know what I mean."

"I am sure I *don't* know what you mean," Alice said with a deceptively innocent face.

"Oh, but look at some of the lovely photos Alice has taken of the children in the Jewish quarter," her mother said unhelpfully, pointing out to Coney a pair of pretty silver-framed portraits. Alice was particularly fond of those; she was close to the two young sisters. When the family had moved to York, they continued to stay in contact by post.

"Wouldn't you rather be handing around lovely pictures of your grandchildren?" Headstrewth asked her mother with a knowing smile.

"Are you and Mathilda setting a date, then?" the older woman replied innocently, taking a prim sip of tea. Mathilda gave her a nasty look. Alice almost snorted her own tea out her nose.

"Yes, yes, these are very picturesque," Coney said. "And I'm sure—in their own way—these orphans are very appealing."

"They're not orphans, they're—"

"Yes, yes, I'm sure. You have it in your head to save them; that's very charitable of you. But look here, why not come to the lecture we're doing as a fundraiser for the rally? It will be quite intimate and fun, just for Ramsbottom's closest supporters. He'll give a little talk—short, I promise—and then take questions. See it from our side—it might open your eyes a bit. You could be my guest."

"Oh, that would be fun," Mathilda said excitedly. "We could make it an outing. A foursome!"

"Oh, that does sound lovely," Alice said. "An evening taken up by an informative disquisition on xenophobia with, no doubt, an aside or two about the benefits of being a Luddite. But I am sorry to say I have a previous engagement that day."

"We haven't said what day yet," Mathilda said, narrowing her eyes.

"Yes," Alice agreed sunnily.

The bell rang; Mrs. Anderbee went to answer it.

"So many visitors," Alice's mother said. "Perhaps I should be around to receive them more often.

"Or . . . perhaps move further away from town," she added reflectively.

But Mrs. Anderbee came back without any additional

guests; instead she carried Alice's satchel and a small packet tied with ribbons.

"My photographs!" Alice cried, leaping up joyfully and taking them.

"Children today," Headstrewth sighed. "Always checking the mail, too anxious to hear from friends who aren't actually present, or what the news is—so busy with such intangible communication. . . ."

"I beg your pardon," Alice said, dipping a curtsy like the child she was accused of being. "I have been waiting for these. A pleasure meeting you, Mr. Coney."

"Alice, you're not leaving?" Mathilda said incredulously.

"I am afraid so. This absolutely cannot wait. Good luck with—whatever." Alice nodded at the men and rushed up to her room. Would there be Hades to pay later? From her sister, and, reluctantly, her mother?

*Who cares?* Alice thought resolutely.

She sprawled on her bed and ripped apart the neatly tied velvet knot.

There were three photographs: one supposedly of Mr. Willard, another of a little boy named Ilya, and a third of a pretty wind-shaped pine from the park, by the river.

Mr. Willard, standing behind his desk, a pile of hats

on either side, was most assuredly not himself. Instead he was . . .

"The Mad Hatter!" Alice practically screamed in delight as the memory came rushing back. The tea party, the songs! The riddles! And there he was, just as she remembered him: short, with a nose that took over his entire face and a head that was the size of his tiny body. He wore a giant top hat with an equally giant tag that said IN THIS STYLE 10/6. He must have been standing on a chair, because he loomed over a desk, his hands firmly placed on it as he leaned forward.

But . . . he was turned, as if something off camera had caught his eye. He didn't look so much Mad as suddenly worried about whatever it was he saw, as if he was just about to entreat the viewer, beg her for something, when he was interrupted.

And while that was strange—even for a strange land—Alice quickly flipped to the next plate, eager to see what else there was. Ilya had become a spectacle-faced bird in his photo, one of those that had taken pity on Alice when she felt her most lost and alone in Wonderland. The boy had a sensitive face in real life; the bird in the picture looked equally empathetic despite the lenses for eyes and very sharp shaft for a beak. He was running, his feathers blurred.

"This is truly astounding!" Alice said in awe. "The

camera somehow sees through the real world and channels *Wonderland* through its lens instead!"

There were of course crackpots who used new photographic technology to claim they could capture ghosts or fairies or the auras of people, "scientifically": with chemicals and light and mirrors. This was obviously not that. Alice had complete control over her equipment, the process, and the plates. And there was nothing hazy, indistinct, or unbelievable about these images.

The tree in the last photo turned out to be a flower.

A swaying flower the size of a house (or perhaps the camera and artist were shrunk small) with lips at the end of her petals. Alice wasn't even sure what kind of flower it was; certainly nothing as easily identifiable as a rose or a jonquil. Even a rose or jonquil with eyes.

"Oh, I bet she can sing!" Alice cried. "This is fantastic! My dreams were all *real*! Here they are right before my eyes!"

But why had they chosen to make themselves known now? Why couldn't anyone else see them? And if it was all real, where had Wonderland been for the past eleven years? Alice hadn't found a single hint or peep of it—and she had been looking ever so hard! She had *dozens* of photos of cherubic children and many interesting personalities from around town, several years' worth at least. Also walls and flowers and designs in the cobbles and a few even at the beach—and up until today all the pictures resembled their subjects.

"Best not to question the magic," Alice decided. Whenever she had questioned anything in Wonderland from her last . . . *visit* . . . she had never received a straight answer; sometimes people became even ruder to her as a result of her asking.

So: the Queen of Hearts, the Mad Hatter, a spectacle-bird, and a singing flower. Every single one of her plates was a glimpse into Wonderland.

"Is it a world that mirrors ours? Hidden somehow? I wonder if everyone—if every*thing* has a double, like a reflection," Alice said thoughtfully. "Curiouser and curiouser!"

Well, there was really only one way to find out.

She repacked her camera bag and checked her film—there were four dry plates left. Only four! Time to order or make more.

Dinah, who had quite profitably spent the morning on the end of Alice's bed and hadn't moved an inch since, watched her mistress with one lazy half-open eye.

"Dinah! Of course you! I'll bet you're the Cheshire!" Alice cried, nuzzling her nose into that of the grande dame. Then she carefully set up the camera to take a long, slow shot of the cat because the room was dusky. She needn't have worried, however; the old kitty fell asleep, or pretended to, and didn't move a muscle until she was done.

Or after, either.

Alice then carefully changed film and ran downstairs and was on her way out the door again—before she remembered her hat.

"Oh, my ears and whiskers," she swore cheerfully, going into the parlor where she had left it. Once there she saw that Headstrewth and Coney were taking their goodbyes formally at the front door. Mathilda had her own hat on, and a shawl; perhaps she was going to escort Mr. Headstrewth into town.

"Saved by a hat," Alice said with a deep breath of gratitude, touching it to her head reverently. Such a thing seemed like perfect Wonderland nonsense, too. She tiptoed back the way she came and left out the kitchen door instead.

With only three plates remaining, Alice had to choose her subjects very carefully. She tried to find Mr. Katz—just for laughs, just to take his portrait, mind you—but none of the boys and girls at the Square had seen him since that morning. So she took one of Adina instead. Then she made Aunt Vivian pose, despite her aunt's weak protests of lethargy—and that she had done one already. Vivian seemed, however, to find the energy to fetch a turban with a long feather and a cape of gold and donned both. She draped herself across a cushy couch, and held an incense burner in each hand like some sort of unknown tarot card.

And then . . . Who for the last plate?

Alice knew even before she picked up the camera. In the back of her mind she had known all along.

She carefully set it on a table, aiming it at the opposite wall. Then she took one of her aunt's ivory-handled walking sticks, stood very still in front of the wall, and set the camera off by stretching her arm and lightly tapping the shutter button with the tip of the cane.

Her first—her only—self-portrait.

Developing the film was agony.

Her hands shook. She wanted to get it done quickly but had to be extra careful. It took too long. She wanted it to be perfect. She wanted . . .

She made herself leave the darkroom and take a walk while the plates dried. She would not look at them when they were imperfect and wet, encouraging wild speculations and guesses. She nibbled on a couple of cucumber sandwiches and a slice of cold Welsh rarebit (the cheese had solidified and was a little chewy, just the way she liked it). She wondered what a picture of *it* would result in: a plate of iced biscuits with the power to cause sudden growth? Or did some real-world things remain just that—things in the real world?

Finally, unable to delay any longer and driven mad by her own thoughts, Alice ran back and looked at the plates against the sitting room window.

Dinah was . . . Dinah. Just a cat.

Alice bit her lip in disappointment. She'd felt *certain* Dinah would turn out to be her beloved Cheshire, the strange smiling beast who sometimes helped, sometimes hindered her travels in Wonderland. The kitty before her looked just as normal and sleepy and grumpy as she always did; no hint of a smile at all.

Well, that answered that question: some objects or people (or cats) were *this* world things alone, without doubles in Wonderland.

Unless . . .

What if the magical moment was over? What if Alice was back to taking pictures of real, normal things now—things that remained real, normal things?

She flipped quickly to the next plate.

All her worries were immediately dispelled when she saw what was there: Adina was a bird with a delicate neck and a mirror for a face. Without eyes it was hard to tell what she was thinking or feeling, but there was no trace of happiness around the beak. Her head was tilted, regarding the viewer a trifle too intently considering that there was nothing where its face should have been but a ghostly reflection of the camera itself.

Alice hurriedly put that one aside.

She looked at the next and couldn't at first remember who or what it was originally; all elements of the real world were pushed to the edges or erased entirely. The creature who starred in the portrait was large and segmented—and not a little terrifying—until she suddenly remembered who it was.

*The Caterpillar* reclined languidly on his giant mushroom top, clouds of vapor twirling around his uppermost appendages in thick, almost recognizable shapes. Alice was torn between delight and annoyance. He had the same unhelpful, obnoxious smile on his face as when she had first met him. Very disagreeable.

On the other hand, he was really there, resplendent in detail down to his nose and little golden slippers.

"Oh my goodness! He's Aunt Vivian!" she suddenly realized. His short arms were spread the way Vivian's long ones had been, to either side, and the mushroom top was almost like a couch. Alice giggled, putting a hand to her mouth despite being the only one there. "I had no idea you were so polypedal in your soul, Auntie Viv."

Then, knowing who was left, she slowly pulled out the last plate.

And immediately grew cold.

She had no preconceptions, no idea what to expect; visions of bright-colored creatures and toddling oysters of course flickered through her mind as possibilities, but all she really thought she would see was . . . Alice. She was the only Alice in all of Wonderland, as far as she could tell. Alice in the real world and Alice over there.

But . . . this . . .

This other Alice, this Wonderland Alice, on the other side of the glass, was someone very different.

She had dark hair, for one; stringy, long, unkempt. The rest of her features were hard to distinguish because a thick, ratty white blindfold was tied around her head. Streaked and streaming down her cheeks from beneath it was thick black blood. Her lips were cracked and also bleeding, her bare neck and shoulders smudged with dirt.

Alice swallowed. She had never seen anything like it. Even at the theater the blood was bright red and flowed easily and didn't cake up so. This was not a tableau; this was not fake blood. It was all too real—like something out of a scene of war, of a horror story, of a nightmare worse than any Alice ever had.

And then the picture moved.

Suddenly the other Alice was either screaming or grinning—impossible to tell which with her teeth outlined in more blood, her lips pulled away from them. She was holding up a banner that was delicately penned despite the poverty of her apparent surroundings.

***MERRY UNBIRTHDAY***

# Chapter Four

Alice almost dropped the plate.

The image didn't move again.

She was frozen, that other girl, screaming or grinning eternally with her hideous missive.

Alice's heart thudded loudly within its double cage of ribs and corset. The house around her was silent and the light didn't change, but somehow she felt that everything had shifted when she wasn't looking. Opposite versions of the same emotion pulled in her belly: fear that the house had transformed into an expected nightmarish or Wonderlandy version of itself—and fear that it hadn't. She looked around.

It hadn't.

On the walls the pictures were all the same, on the floor the rugs were the same, the furniture . . . everything the same, same, same.

"Merry Unbirthday," Alice breathed.

In spite of the hideousness of the image as a whole, it was obvious the reason for it—perhaps the reason for all of the Wonderland images—was this written message. A message for her, real-world Alice, from this wretched counterpart. Who was she, exactly? Alice closed her eyes and tried to remember. Who looked like her, even a little, from the other world?

She recalled something about the White Rabbit, the one who had started everything. He *never* let her catch him. And he didn't even seem to see Alice as a distinct human being: he always confused her with someone named Mary Ann. *That* girl seemed to be his servant, and responsible for the white gloves he was constantly missing.

Was this she? Was this Mary Ann?

Alice ran a finger along the bottom of the picture, the edge of the banner, thinking about Unbirthdays. The Mad Hatter had said that she had only one birthday a year, so that left three hundred and sixty-four other days to celebrate Unbirthdays.

*But what has that to do with anything?* Alice wondered. It wasn't the Mad Hatter greeting her, nor anyone else from the tea party. This was someone she didn't know, and no tea was involved, and it certainly didn't look merry. It was a mystery.

"Or a puzzle, rather," she said thoughtfully.

Weren't there puzzles in Wonderland? Getting yourself the right size to fit through a door, eating or drinking the right thing for the intended effect?

Alice knelt on the ground in front of the sofa and took out all the photographs, laying them carefully next to each other on the soft velvet surface like a very slow game of solitaire.

*All* the Wonderland residents looked upset. Nervous. Scared. The birds looked particularly spooked. It was a little hard to tell with the Hatter, because he wasn't even looking at the camera—but *why* wasn't he? The flower seemed as if it was ducking its head, trying not to be seen. And the Caterpillar didn't look as smug as Alice initially thought; she had been rewriting the image with her own memories. His eyes weren't haughty; they were sad, and old. And wait. . . .

She squinted at the clouds around his head and hands. The *almost* recognizable shapes. There was something very odd about them. . . . If she had a decent projector or enlarger she could have had a better look, but that was one piece of equipment her aunt hadn't acquired yet (and Alice, always a good girl, didn't like to push). She jumped up and ran to her aunt's secretary and dug around its drawers and compartments frantically. Somewhere Vivian had a beautiful magnifying glass with a rosewood handle and cabochons of jet set around the outside—but it wasn't there. The closest thing Alice could find was an old monocle left by one of her aunt's more dapper friends.

So she dutifully put it on as best she could.

It was actually quite astonishing how well it worked!

Hazy shapes resolved themselves into letters, as they had when the Caterpillar had been teasing her so mercilessly. She could almost hear his voice again.

***HELP***
***US***

The clouds seemed to swirl; Alice couldn't tell if it was the magic of the Wonderland pictures or just her eyes tearing up from the use of the monocle.

"Unbirthday . . ." she murmured. "Help us. . . ."

She rubbed her head and scratched her eyebrow above the monocle. Help them *what*?

Sitting back on the floor, she looked out the window at the sky and the day as if to find an answer there. The afternoon was developing into a luxuriously warm and sleepy early-summer hug. While she was in a darkened, smoky room worried about creatures she had thought were just from a dream, there was probably a girl out there in the park happily weaving a daisy chain into a crown. Just like Alice had when she . . .

"Oh!" she suddenly cried. "It was a day very much like this when I fell asleep and dreamed of Wonderland!"

She went to her satchel and fumbled around until she found the journal in which she kept her film and exposure observations. It was a slim leather-bound notebook printed with all sorts of useful information in the front, including a nearly perpetual twenty-year calendar (as well as recipes for homemade salves and lotions). The tiny numbers on the mostly decorative calendar were nearly impossible to decipher. Once again the monocle proved its use.

"I do believe it was May when I went to the park with Mathilda for my lessons, years ago. Early May. It was a Thursday. I remember that clearly because I wanted to tell Mother and Father all of what I dreamed, the adventures that had happened to me, but they had gone to dine with the Ruthersfords as they did every Thursday. So I had tea in the nursery and had to tell Mrs. Anderbee about it instead, the poor dear. And Dinah, too." She squinted and finally found the date. "Oh, my stars! It *was* today! Exactly today! Eleven years ago!"

She wrinkled her nose—a habit both her sister and her

mother tried to break her of, but Alice swore it helped her think, like calisthenics for her brain.

"Eleven . . . that's a prime number, and a strange anniversary. Why didn't they come to me at ten, or five? That would have been far more traditional. But of course . . . this *is* Wonderland we're talking about."

She regarded all her old acquaintances laid out like cards. They looked back at her, scared and miserable. And the Queen of Hearts looked insane and triumphant.

Alice shuddered, remembering how terrifying the tiny little woman had been. Despite her size and ridiculous behavior—really, quite unacceptable and inappropriate behavior in any adult, much less a member of royalty—she was terrifying. Because whatever she said actually *happened* if her kinder, gentler husband king wasn't around to stop it. Her servants and card soldiers did whatever she asked. Everyone trembled in fear when she approached.

"Something is happening in Wonderland, something bad. *That* is why they are seeking me now. And it's to do with the Queen of Hearts," Alice said slowly. "And it is so very bad that they need my help. The—other—me seems to be quite . . . indisposed. They're coming all the way to the real world to fetch me."

To fetch Alice, the little Alice who had been chased and mocked in Wonderland, the girl who had tried and cried, who sang with the locals but was never really accepted as one of them. Who thought about them for years after she woke, and then slowly forgot them.

*They* remembered *her*, apparently, and thought she could do something.

*I must save them,* she decided. She squared her jaw. *I must somehow* go *to Wonderland. I will . . . find the rabbit hole again, or the rabbit, or someone else strange and furry to chase.*

She would return to the park. That was the first thing to do. She would find the tree she had climbed while her sister droned on and on from that terribly boring book without any pictures.

Of course she was an adult now, and without a chaperone, so things might need to be done a little differently. She grabbed her aunt's golden cape from a chair and stuffed it into her satchel for spreading on the ground, as if she were just there for a solo picnic. And maybe she would pack a few snacks, both to make it more believable and also to fortify herself for the quest.

"Well! That's different!"

Her aunt was suddenly standing in the doorway of the drawing room, an accusing finger leveled squarely at her niece.

Alice jumped, knocked out of her thoughts and strangely

scared that she and Wonderland had been discovered. Did her aunt suspect something odd was afoot? Did she notice anything was amiss with Alice?

Was she upset about Alice borrowing the cape?

"The monocle," her aunt said, shaking her finger at it. "I *love* it. A monocle on a girl. Absolutely subverting the whole masculine dandy gestalt. Oh my, you may start a trend. I wonder if I have another one. . . ."

And with that she spun on her heel, and the forgotten monocle dropped ironically out of Alice's eye, dangling on its long black velvet riband.

Alice betook herself to the park posthaste.

But the memory of the sunny day, that golden afternoon on which she first glided to Wonderland, was not as precise, detailed, or complete as she hoped. There had been the smell of moisture and sweetness of sun-loving flowers, the floating of insects and dust in the heavy yellow light, the drowsy feeling of all the earth taking her children into warm, comforting arms. There had been the drifting river, the bending reeds, the trees and the grass, her sister, the boring book, the rabbit.

But which was the right tree? *Where* had she first seen the rabbit?

As she stood on one hillock after another, peering at

the landscape between the prams, painters, and picnickers, everything seemed different.

"Well, of course everything seems different, because I've opened up like a telescope since then," she said, sighing. "I'm over a foot taller. Everything *would* look different." Unlike the speed with which she changed size in Wonderland, the creeping of time and aging in this world had come upon her slowly—and yet she was still strangely unprepared.

She tried getting down on her knees for a more childlike view. Awkward and unseemly. Also it didn't seem to help.

*Maybe I should start with the sort of place a rabbit would* like. *An open meadow, with tasty flowers and buds, next to a thicket, a safe place for running into.*

With this idea in mind she straightened her hat, adjusted her bag, and strode off like an intrepid adventuress down a game path in deepest Africa.

Two hours later there was still no rabbit, no rabbit holes (or at least no occupied ones), no Wonderland. Only a red and breathless Alice with painful feet and aching shoulders.

"You're *here*, I know you are," she shouted, uncaring who heard her. "I've seen the pictures! You're real! So come out already! Where *are* you?"

"I beg your pardon? Did you take secret photographs of me after all?"

Alice spun around.

Regarding her curiously from farther back on the path was Mr. Katz. He had a faint smile on his lips, but his eyes showed a real concern for her odd behavior. His jacket was thrown carelessly over his shoulder and he had taken his hat off in the warm weather. He hadn't loosened his bright purple cravat, however, and it blazed like the breast of a young, strange robin.

"No, I wasn't talking to you, I was . . . Oh, bother." Alice shook her head. "It's complicated and a little mad."

"Well, now you have me curious. May I accompany you on your perambulations for a bit?"

"I'm rather done in, actually. I've been *perambulating* for almost three hours now looking for a rabbit. Or a rabbit hole. Or a place where I saw a rabbit once. With my sister. I also sat in a tree—was it this tree? Fie on it, I just can't remember!"

She sat down wearily at the base of the questionable tree, a lovely oak with long spreading branches like outstretched arms, amusing and useful for little girls to sit on (unlike the tight upright oaks along Pelgrew Street that made such tight and narrow acorns). This very well *could* have been her tree.

In her sweat and exhaustion and under Katz's gently amused look, she realized she had completely forgotten about her clever ruse with the blanket and fake picnic.

Now she remembered the little sandwiches and fairy cakes she had packed. She reached in and pulled out a cake, only thinking to break it in two and offer a piece to her companion at the last moment.

"Thank you." He took it very properly and popped it in his mouth, but it seemed more out of politeness than real desire. He squatted on his heels, his back up against the tree—apparently unlike the otherwise proper girl next to him, he was unwilling to sit in the dirt.

"But what are *you* doing here, Mr. Katz?" Alice asked curiously.

"A friend of mine asked for help for a friend, in the friendliest way. . . . That sounds like a riddle, doesn't it? But I cut through the park—a *long* cut, mind you, not a short one, because it's such a beautiful day. Eventually I shall have to follow through on my promise. For now, however, tell me: what is so special about this rabbit, or hole?"

Alice chewed the cake thoughtfully. What had the little treats in Wonderland tasted like? Sweeter, she thought. Would they be too sweet now? Besides growing *up* and *out*, there were other changes in her. Given a choice between a fondant-covered petit four and a bit of fat from a juicy roast, she would choose the latter.

"You wouldn't believe me if I told you. But I simply must find him. Soon. It's imperative. After a brief rest."

"Well, all right, then. You grab a kip and I'll ward off thieves and suspicious magpies," he offered chivalrously.

"What about your promise to your friend? And I'm not going to sleep," Alice insisted. "I absolutely shouldn't sleep. I feel I wouldn't wake up for hours and hours."

"Oh, I keep all my promises," Katz said with a reassuring smile. "Never fear."

"Keep me awake, then, if you don't mind delaying your errand for a bit. Tell me something interesting, Mr. Katz. Tell me a story about your life. Tell me about your parents' lives. About coming here, and then having you, and you becoming a barrister. That's quite a lot."

"Ah, well, I suppose it's interesting enough to some people, but I doubt stories about studying law would keep you awake. How about instead I tell you stories I'll wager you've never heard, about a fantastic city called Chelm, full of fools and madmen?"

"That sounds *perfect*. I must in fact find a bunch of madmen," Alice said eagerly before she remembered how silly she sounded.

"Well, as the English are so fond of saying, *Once upon a time*"—and here he sat down on the ground, finally.

It was a little improper, perhaps, having the young man so close to her, but they weren't touching and there wasn't anything stupidly fantastic and romantic happening like her slowly falling asleep, overcome by the day, and leaning up against him. He didn't offer his coat to keep her warm. It was all fine.

"In the great city of Chelm in Poland there were many wise men who spent their days debating everything from the number of angels who could dance on the head of a pin to how best to save the moon from drowning in the lake at night.

"One day, the town baker came to the rabbi with a perplexing question. . . ."

Alice listened as best she could: he spoke clearly with an educated, academic accent and sounded like one long accustomed to telling stories.

But the day was working its slow magic on her and she found it hard to concentrate. Instead of keeping her awake and engaged, the story was lulling her dangerously toward a dreamy loss of consciousness. She watched the ducks playing on the edge of the water in the reeds with a diminishing sense of interest in the goings-on of the baker of Chelm and all his in-laws.

*What pretty rushes the ducks are playing in*, she thought as Katz continued his story. *I gathered some very sweetly scented ones once, while we were rowing. Who was in the party? Mathilda? I cannot remember. But what are the ducks eating? Frogs? Roots?*

*Look how the river reflects the sky. The water close in reflects the ducks. The sky and the clouds do not change for being reversed, but the ducks are upside down. Look at that one funny upside-down duck glaring at me like it knows something. Like it knows* anything *at all. Silly duck. Well, of course, a duck on the other side of the reflection might know something. Ducks on the other side would be different. All the world is made wise and strange in the surface of the river—oh!*

She sat up suddenly. The mirror duck was staring right at her. Through the water.

"Help us," it said, rather less *beseechingly* than *peevishly*.

"I heard that!" Alice cried. "That's it—the river! It reflects the opposite of everything—contrariwise!"

She leapt to her feet and, with energy she hadn't had a moment ago, went racing down the hill toward the ducks. A small part of her was concerned that Katz would stop her; obviously these weren't the actions of a sane girl. It probably looked like she was suddenly bent on drowning herself, an English Ophelia.

But if he was chasing her, he was too slow and too silent.

"I see you! You duck there! Don't pretend!" she cried—and threw herself into the water.

# Chapter Five

She fell, fell, fell, dragged down deep by her petticoats and crinolines and stockings and shoes, arms and legs tangling amongst the reeds and rushes and pointy, sticky things that tried to grab and drown her.

Self-preservation finally kicked in, and so did Alice's legs. A thought occurred to her as she thrashed and spun to push herself upright with her head pointing at the sky and her toes down below toward the depths: the water by the edge of the river hadn't *seemed* that deep. The bit off the bank she had been watching ducks swim around was little more than a few inches, just enough for frogs to slip away in quickly when you came too close. There was no way she could float suspended in the water and kick and still not touch the bottom with her feet.

And yet she felt the empty weight of limitless liquid, an ocean of it, in every direction. She hung for one unbreathing moment in this place before propelling herself reluctantly to the surface.

Alice gasped as her head exploded out of the water, her hair an unbunning mane that shed droplets and rivers. She was sitting, of course. Spraddle-legged and awkward. In a shallow pool.

It was a decorative, rectangular pool as might be seen in a book about ancient Roman villae. There were some decorative plants—reeds—tucked in the corners in a naturalistic manner. They were red.

Everything was red, actually.

Alice pulled her arms out of the water with a cry, thinking she was covered in blood.

As diamond-bright drops flew, she realized that only the pool itself was red: its tiles and the walls and floor around it. The water within was normal and clear, but refracted very, very red.

"Curious," Alice said, but a little sickly. She stood up and the water peeled off her; had she been paying attention she might have noticed that she dried quite a bit faster than was strictly natural.

"I did it! I'm not dreaming at all! I'm awake and alive and in . . . Wonderland?"

She was *in* what looked very much like the rest of a Roman villa, but all exploded and flat, or perhaps drawn by an uninspired and talentless student of the classics. The mosaics below her feet were set into what must have been different pictures and patterns, but they were all red. A single wall with a single doorway appeared before her, also red. Through the door in the distance she could see the beginnings of a lush forest—strangely drippy at the edges, and very red.

(Though if Alice squinted she could just make out organic shades here and there: a little bit of green or brown peeking through.)

The wall before her was redolent and moist.

She squished toward it, feet still heavy from the copious amounts of water sloshing around in her leather shoes. Putting out a single finger, she delicately touched the wall. Red came away on the tip. She brought it to her nose.

"Milk paint," she murmured, not entirely surprised.

Beyond the open door to nowhere was a pretty little orchard of orange trees, each and every fruit a perfect round red. Like picture-book apples. She felt very unsettled and anxious, as if something terrible had happened or was about to happen, like descriptions she had read of the battlefields in the American Civil War when brother found brother in battle, wearing the opposite side's colors. Things were familiar but horrible. Everything was red and terrifying. If photographs came in color she was sure her picture of the Queen of Hearts would have been in all these shades of red as well.

Suddenly there came a terrible noise, horrible and loud and utterly uncategorizable. Alice flinched, covering her ears and hugging her head to try to drown it out (and probably getting red paint in her hair). The sound was a bit like a pile of something crashing—but a *giant* pile, a gargantuan stack of pots and pans. It was also a bit like a gong, like the tiny one in Mrs. Yao's tea shop, but multiplied by a thousand and played by a thousand miniature mad monkeys.

She closed her eyes and fell to her knees, praying for silence.

Eventually the noise stopped and the echoes faded.

Alice unplugged her ears and saw that the sound had some effect on the otherwise empty landscape: beyond the grove of orange trees, figures were now hurrying, hunched over, along the base of a high red wall that had just appeared and was a slightly different shade of red from everything else—a little whiter and dustier, as if it was older. A portcullis slid open just wide enough for the creatures to slip through before it slammed down, locking them in.

Then everything was still and silent again.

"This doesn't seem very Wonderlandy at all," Alice

observed. The landscape was empty of movement now; not a single creature gyred or gimbled out in the open or the shadows; not a mome rath, or mouse, or bandersnatch or any of the hundreds of other creatures that normally crowded the paths and byways of Wonderland. There weren't even any woken flowers.

("Mome rath! Bandersnatch! I remember all of them now, and all the funny names, too!" Alice realized with joy.)

She felt very unsettled and anxious, as if something terrible had happened or was about to happen, like descriptions she had read of the battlefields in the American Civil War, when brother found brother in battle, wearing the opposite side's colors. Things were familiar but horrible. Everything was red and terrifying. If photographs came in color she was sure her picture of the Queen of Hearts would have been in all these shades of red as well.

She walked to the portcullis—for this was Wonderland, despite its strange new mood, and what else was there to do? You went to the obvious thing, the thing that provoked your interest, following whatever intrigued you like a child. That's how *things* progressed.

Her body remembered trotting across the grounds of Wonderland with little-girl excitement; her adult legs were a little less prone to such movements. Still she strode quickly and threw in an occasional half gallop when she could resist the urge no longer. Whether it was her perspective or her imagination or Wonderland itself, the wall grew taller much more quickly than it should have as she approached, suddenly looming over her like a cat about to pounce upon a helpless ball of yarn. Its façade was smooth, of course, except for lines and bumps where stone blocks met, and the occasional heart-shaped decorative keystone. There was no portcullis anywhere.

"Of course," Alice muttered.

The door had disappeared, as doors always seemed to in dreams when someplace didn't want to be found.

But a man had appeared in its place, as if he had always been there, and at this too Alice was unsurprised.

He was all in black, the tired worn black of a high-end suit bought at a secondhand market by a farmworker who harbors some misplaced notion about impressing his peers with an outfit ill-suited to outdoor toiling. Fashionably wide trousers were tucked into high, hard leather riding boots. His waistcoat was crisscrossed with nautical-seeming belts that held muskets and bullets. The short jacket he wore seemed very proper, except that the golden fob clipped to a pocket led to a dagger, not a pocket watch. The man's hat was a dusty old bowler but had a giant black plume sticking out of it like that of a child playing dress-up.

His face was so real Alice did a double take; there was

nothing dreamy or hazy about his narrow, sharp nose, the pronounced ridges above his lip, the tired crow's-feet around his eyes, or the sharpness of his dark red pupils. If she had any doubt at all that she was awake, this cleared it up immediately.

He held a scroll and a pen and was going over what was written there very closely—and seemed utterly unsurprised that Alice now stood in front of him.

"All the VIP seats for today's teatime executions have been filled," he said, looking up only at the last minute, and then myopically, as if he were gazing at her over a pair of glasses. "Come back tomorrow. There are sure to be more then."

"Executions?" Alice asked in shock. Although from the terrible sounds and the hunched movements and the general redness of the place, this development wasn't entirely unexpected. Plus—the Queen of Hearts and all.

"Beheadings, you know. 'Off with his/her/its,' et cetera," the man said, casually swiping his finger across his neck. "If you haven't shown your patriotism yet this quarter, I suggest you appear posthaste for the standing-room-only section. There's a waiting list that opens up at thirteen-thirty."

"I beg your pardon. I feel I am a bit confused. May we begin again? I am Alice." She performed the tiniest curtsy, feeling like a child again. "And who might you be?"

"I'm the Knave of Accounts," the man responded with dry surprise.

"The Knave of . . ." Alice blinked. "But why . . ."

"I know, why am I out here acting like an overglorified usher?" he agreed with a shake of his head. "Dashed useless waste of my skills—but on the other hand, I *am* also in charge of the schedule, so maybe it all makes sense. Speaking of which, you look like a VIP. Can I pencil you in for tomor—oh, no, no executions tomorrow. It's Cricket Day. The Thrumsday after next?"

Alice hated to disappoint; he seemed so eager. She was the only living thing within sight and very possibly the only one who ever actually took a moment to talk to him. Did he stand here all day, waiting?

"I'm sorry, but who's to be executed today, if you don't mind me asking?"

"Oh let's see, that would be . . ." He rolled and unrolled the scroll, lines of illuminated red hearts sliding in and out of the margins like a zoetrope. "Ah yes, the Hatter, the Dodo, and the Dormouse. Quite an A-list lineup, if you ask me."

"The Hatter! The Dormouse! The *Dodo*?" Alice cried. "To be *killed*? No! That's terrible!"

"That's very funny," the Knave said, squinting at her again. "Most people, after I read off the names, say, 'What did they do?' It's treason, probably, if you want to know. That's usually the reason given."

"But the King—or something—always intervenes!" Alice protested. "No one is ever actually killed!"

"Yes, tell that to all the corpses swinging in the rose garden. As for the King—well—I don't suppose you're from around here, then, are you?"

Far from it. She would definitely follow up on the King business later. As for now, she had friends in trouble.

"I should say not. But please—when are they to be executed?"

The Knave pointed his right boot; at the tip of it was a watch Alice hadn't noticed before. On the left boot was a brandy glass.

"In about a quarter hour," he answered.

"Oh, do let me in! I must stop this travesty at once!" she said, desperately putting her hands out to find where the portcullis had hidden itself.

"There's no use," the Knave said sadly. "The VIP section is full."

"But what about standing room?"

"Oh, that's the first to go so people can make their quota. Also full, obviously."

"Mezzanine?"

"Filled with ladies of the court, I'm afraid."

"I am trying to rescue my friends about to be killed. I'm about to commit what you would probably also call treason. And you still insist I need a proper ticket?"

"There's rules about these things," he said apologetically.

"I'm afraid I left my gloves under my seat, from yesterday," Alice said through gritted teeth. "In the excitement and blood I simply forgot. I'll just nip in and fetch them."

"Well-behaved girls don't lie," the Knave said accusingly.

"Please do not attempt to inform me what well-behaved girls do or don't do, or assume I am well behaved or wish to be well behaved, or even if I am a girl. I am eighteen now, you know," Alice said frostily, drawing herself up to her full height, which was still a good deal shorter than the Knave of Accounting. "If being naughty saves the Hatter, I will be the naughtiest, most rascally woman you ever laid your unfortunate eyes on. Now *open that door*."

The Knave blinked at her silently for a moment.

Then he buried his face back in the scroll.

"Perhaps there is a rule allowing patrons in to check for Lost Property."

"Oh, for goodness' sake. Let me have a look," Alice said, humphing. And on a whim, perhaps because the Knave seemed to have issues with seeing himself, or because it gave her hands something to do, or maybe it was just an Alice fancy—she would never be able to say for certain later—she pulled out the monocle and popped it in.

"*Oh!* I didn't realize you were in Accounting, too!" the Knave cried, looking at her in surprise. He held up a monocle as well—one he didn't use, apparently. Not as fine-looking as Alice's, it was trimmed in rusty grey metal and hung on a largish chain. "Or Legal. My apologies. Please allow me. Professional courtesy."

He swept a bow and at the same time the portcullis appeared, creating itself downward and then drawing itself back up.

"*Thank* you," Alice said with as quick a polite curtsy as she could manage. With her head held high—and while trying not to drop the monocle—she went through.

# Chapter Six

Alice went pale when her mind finally managed to make sense of what it saw.

Half the scene was dreamy Wonderland nonsense. There were bleachers and seats in tiered rows made from all sorts of inappropriate things: a sofa on legs that was in imminent danger of growing bored and walking off with its sitters still on; wicker thrones with silk parasols attached; chairs sat on the wrong way, upside down.

The standing-only area was fenced off with giant wooden forks and should have been as raucous as similar sections in Angleland at cricket matches or political speeches—especially considering the miniature elephants, large-mouthed ants, and strangely shaped humans all pushing each other for a view.

But no matter which tier they were in or what manner of creature they were, the spectators were all—quite rightly—subdued. Unlike Alice's previous visit, when the Queen had just shouted *Off with her head* wherever she went—croquet court, alee in the gardens, parade grounds—this was a place that had been custom made for her gruesome orders.

The focus of attention was a large, strange pile that haunted the center of the arena. It was made from rubbish and junk and all the detritus of a fantasy world: teapots and tiny castles, golden eggs and garbage bins, locked trunks and suits of armor that didn't seem like they were quite emptied out of their owners yet.

Balanced precariously on top of this was a stage stained a different shade of red than the red with which everything else had been painted. Darker. More permanent.

The castle in the background was the same as Alice remembered from her dream, such a dark red as to almost be black, but now it was the tallest thing in any direction of a flattened, red-rubbled land. Ominous black smoke poured out of its loops and murder holes. Everything smelled faintly of burnt tarts.

On a strange little pavilion to the left of the pile was a gigantic puffy red heart. Standing (carefully behind a railing) on the ramparts atop this were a pair of old familiar faces: Tweedledee and Tweedledum. They grinned, their mouths practically splitting their ridiculous faces, and waved to the crowd as if they were the main attraction at the event. Tweedledum wore a giant pin that said BEST BOY. Tweedledee wore a giant pin that said BOY, BEST. Below each of these was a second pin, large and glittery and tacky: a ruby red heart.

"Well," Alice said to herself, "it's safe to bet whose side *they* threw their lots in with. But where is the Queen herself? Shouldn't she be overseeing this business?"

A horn sounded: a long, beautiful golden horn with red banners trailing from it that would have been achingly lovely had not what it summoned been so horrible.

(Also, it sounded itself; there was no horn player present.)

Prisoners were marched out, bound up and miserably shuffled along by something Alice decided was a kind of ogre, as well as a grumpy-looking elephant who stood on her two hind legs. Alice caught her breath. Hatter, the tiny Dormouse, and the Dodo looked so sad. Not terrified, as she would have expected. Exhausted and dirty and dried-out and somehow ancient, too old for their time. The Hatter gazed at the crowd with a face that didn't beseech, only wondered *why*.

Behind them came what had to have been the method of the execution and the executioner all in one: a giant creature with a black hood over its eyes and ears and top of head, its snub-nosed, razor-toothed muzzle wide and ready to snap heads off.

Alongside this gruesome parade came the soldiers. Hundreds of cards marched stock-straight at attention, eyes unreadable and sharpened swords all identically at the ready. Were Alice to charge them, it would be death by a thousand paper cuts.

"Most decks only have fifty cards—fifty-two at the most, surely," Alice breathed.

"Oh, she's been building her ranks again, haven't you heard?" an old gossipy sheep said, shifting her knitting aside to look over her glasses at Alice. She lowered her voice to a raspy whisper. "Playing rummy and a new one called Spite and M'alice to maximize her offense."

"But where is she? Where is the Queen?"

"Oh, she don't come to executions anymore. Too many of them," the sheep sniffed. "I suppose we watch them *for* her."

"Is that what it is about, the quota? Does everyone have to be here for a reason?"

"You must be from the Outer Board—or as dumb as a hat on a tove. *'Course* we have to be here, at least once a quarter, or it's treason. Beg pardon now. I don't want to lose my seat." The old sheep passed Alice into the middle tier, where she held up a heart-shaped ticket to an anteater usher and was then escorted to a church pew.

"And they all just come and watch the executions?" Alice asked wonderingly.

How on earth would she save her old friends? If the soldiers were countless and the crowd unlikely to rebel, terrified for their own lives, what could *she* do?

There had to be something. There was always an answer in Wonderland, if you just knew where—or how—to look.

And then she spied it.

In the VIP section was a prettily set table with refreshments for the upper crust. There was tea, punch, tall crystal glasses of what could only have been champagne, delicate sandwiches shaped like hearts, and trays and trays of tarts and biscuits.

(Ironically, the other sections also had food—pie and cider and the like—but these were *sold* by vendors. The refreshments for the rich were free. "More Wonderland nonsense," Alice thought.)

But she was drawn to one particular stand made of delicate gold wire and glass. It held trays of fondant-covered petits fours delicately iced to say EAT ME.

"That must do something!" Alice cried. "It will either allow me to grow tall and step over all the soldiers, or tiny so I can slip between their legs!"

So she pushed her way forward to the gated VIP entrance, where a fox in a dashing cap stopped her.

"VIPs *only*," he purred politely.

"But I'm a knave," Alice said quickly, popping in the monocle again. "In Accounting," she added, rather more hesitantly.

"Oh, quite right, then," the fox said, stepping aside and opening the gate for her. He whispered: "And about bloody time, too, if you ask me! Women have a lot more to contribute than just as queens and ladies-in-waiting. I've a kit would love to be a Foxen Spy if she were only given the chance."

Alice nodded politely, afraid that saying anything else would give her away.

She was dimly aware how bad it looked, her diving right into the refreshments instead of exchanging pleasantries with the pig-nosed marquesses under their parasols, the nearly extinct dukes, the viscounts and vultcounts. Everyone here was also subdued and stern, and they spoke to each other sotto voce, and the dresses were large and lovely. But time was ticking.

Alice plucked a lovely vanilla-looking square with lavender bits on the top and was about to pop the whole thing in her mouth but remembered at the last moment to nibble.

"Last time I ate too quickly, my neck lengthened until

I looked like a serpent—and scared the wits out of that poor bird!"

She swallowed. And waited.

Did her toes feel tingly?

Were her fingertips itching?

Was the ground suddenly farther away—or a great deal closer?

No. None of it.

Nothing happened.

Another horn blew. Alice watched in dismay as the prisoners and their executioner were led up a rickety ladder onto the platform. An officious-looking creature that seemed to be half pangolin took out a megaphone (really, a toucan held by its feet, beak propped open) and began shouting out a list of what were presumably their crimes, but between the noise of the crowd and the laziness of the toucan it was impossible to hear what precisely they were.

Alice anxiously—but cautiously—nibbled a bit more of her petit four.

The Pangolin on the platform bowed and stepped away, finished with whatever trumped-up charges he had announced. The elephant and the ogre prodded the prisoners forward to the front of the platform and then down to their knees. The Executioner scampered behind them improbably on its four large paws.

Alice still didn't grow.

Or shrink.

She stuffed the rest of the cake down her throat and grabbed a teacup in each hand, throwing back the pleasant lemony liquid like a drunken sailor.

NOTHING!

Nothing at all happened.

"What am I to *do*?" she wailed.

"Cut back on your between-meal snacks a bit, I'd say, lassie," said the servant bear who quickly replaced the treats she had scarfed down.

The Executioner opened its wide mouth. A surprisingly cute pink tongue, acres in size, lolled to the side. There was nothing cute about its teeth, however; ivory-colored, sharp as death, and springing out of pitch-black gums. It bent over the prisoners. . . .

*"STOP!"* Alice cried out, unable to think of anything else to do.

And everyonc *did* stop.

Everyone.

They all turned to look at her.

"Stop this nonsense at once!" Alice ordered, trying to sound regal. But her voice was shaking.

The prisoners spotted her, and the Hatter made a face that broke her heart: his exhaustion melted into a relieved *smile*. Nothing Mad about it at all. As though—as though Alice was here now and everything would be all right.

"What in blazes is this?" the Pangolin demanded from below, his voice perfectly audible without the toucan (the poor bird now hung forgotten at his side). The crowd looked at him with delight. "This is highly unusual. Out of the ordinary."

"Release the prisoners at once!" Alice demanded back, pointing. It was very rude, but these were dire circumstances.

The crowd craned their necks to look back at her—rather like they were watching a tennis match.

"Release the *prisoners*?" the Pangolin cried. "They are enemies of the state. They are treasonous, foul miscreants. Didn't you hear their crimes? *Gathering with the purpose of undermining the Queen's authority*, *spreading spurious lies about the Queen*, *stealing tarts*, *redistributing property properly seized by the state and eminent domain* . . . It's all there, and you want me to release them? Don't be mad."

"We're all mad here!" Alice shouted. "Has there even been a *trial*? With a judge and jury and barristers and tea?"

The crowd began to murmur and talk to each other, nodding like this was a good point.

"The Queen doesn't require a judge," the Pangolin said haughtily. "She's the Supreme Authority."

"Well!" Alice said, uncertain where to go from there.

"I hardly think so. Now release them before I come down there and do it myself."

"Are you a knave or . . . a queen?" the fox guard whispered in awe. "You're certainly not a pawn."

The Pangolin, meanwhile, was snorting himself into a fit. The crowd quieted in wonder while he guffawed, choked, and made other terrible noises with his nose. He bent over with his arms crossed in front of his stomach.

*"You?"* he finally managed, the apparent laughing fit over. "Against Her Majesty's army?"

"They are just cards," Alice said, stepping forward—but slowly. "Shan't be a problem at all."

The prisoners weren't wasting a moment while everyone was distracted; they were conversing quietly amongst themselves and untying their bonds.

"Get on my back," the Dodo ordered the Hatter.

The Hatter scooped up the Dormouse with one hand; with the other he grabbed the Dodo's neck and swung himself aboard.

"Be off with you!" Alice shouted at the soldier cards, making sweeping motions with her hands. "Shoo! Or I shall scatter you directly and let the maid sweep you up. You'll all be replaced with a nice fresh pack of clean, well-behaved cards."

She moved forward menacingly. Worried spectators moved out of her way.

As was always the case with perspective in Wonderland, it switched quickly; in no time Alice was down at the level of the field and realized she was no taller than the cards. Though she remained a good deal thicker round the middle, one of them could easily curl itself around her like a rug and finish her off by squeezing—without even having to touch his sword.

"I'm going! I'm going!" the Dodo shouted.

And indeed he was.

Alice, the spectators, the card soldiers, the Pangolin, and the fox usher all watched in awe as the ungainly bird flapped madly and took off into the sky. The Hatter grinned triumphantly and waved like royalty to the crowd.

(He waved with the hand holding the Dormouse, which seemed a little unfortunate for the poor queasy thing.)

"I rather thought dodos couldn't fly," Alice said in wonder.

"Might as well, since he's extinct," the knitting sheep said with a sage shrug.

As soon as the fugitives disappeared into the sky, all attention was turned back to Alice.

*"You're responsible for the prisoners escaping!"* the Pangolin spat in a frothy fit of rage. The soldiers all flexed, almost as one, with eagerness and anger.

"Seems more like it's those two?" Alice suggested,

pointing at the ogre and the elephant. The guards looked at each other in surprise. The Executioner was bored and had taken to chasing its own tail round and round for a bit.

*"Idiots!"* the Pangolin raged.

"If you'll just excuse me," Alice said politely to the people in front of her, stepping around them.

*"Don't let her escape, too!"* the Pangolin cried.

And then Alice ran.

# Chapter Seven

Alice could hear the *fwip fwip fwip* of the cards running after her. How she longed to be huge, to turn around and gather them up and shove them in her pocket like the naughty little things they were.

If she died in Wonderland, did she die in real life?

She pushed people and creatures (and creature-people) out of her way and dove through the portcullis out to the other side. She had a vague vision of the Knave of Accounts looking surprised somewhere on her right but barely registered it. Wonderland had rearranged itself a little during her time in the arena, as was its wont, although this didn't impact Alice's escape plan for the very good reason that she didn't really have one. She just hove hard to the right and kept close to the wall on the slim hope that the soldiers would assume she had actually dashed straight ahead and into the plains beyond the castle, back through the orange grove.

The wall surrounding the arena split off and became two walls, and then three, and then joined into a number of smaller and thicker walls at strange angles. These were in turn soon replaced with boxwood and topiary. With a flash it came to Alice: she was now in the horrid maze that had nearly entrapped her forever last time in Wonderland!

It was even more ominous now, all painted red. Drippily, thickly, large gobbets of paint clumped on top of curling and dying leaves.

Alice risked a glance behind her.

The soldiers had not been fooled. They *fwipped* closer, legs matching gait perfectly and arms held up identically, short spears at the ready. Where were the silly cards of before? The bumbling buffoons mis-painting roses and acting as croquet hoops? It wasn't their alien build or the general wrongness of inanimate objects consciously attacking her that was the most terrifying; it was the perfect synchronicity with which they did it.

But they were without a non-card commander or lackey. The Queen was still absent—which relieved Alice a bit, to her surprise. Everything seemed more *survivable* and less confusing without her constantly shouting death threats.

"You win," Alice growled at the maze. It might lead to problems later, but right now it was her only hope for losing pursuers.

She chose her route at random, left right right left and up a little ramp. The paint had pooled underneath the bushes into thick, goopy lines on the ground, an ugly mess of red sludge over dust. Her hair was entirely undone now, and when she cut a corner too close it whipped against the wall and came away heavy and sticky.

Sound echoed strangely amongst the high bulwarks of red bushes and trees, and just like last time, it was unclear if the sky above her was the same as it was outside the maze or just a very high ceiling. But the noise of the cards grew quieter behind her, and Alice began to feel a little safe: as safe as a mouse in a maze escaping a cat. Out of the frying pan and into the laboratory.

She slowed her pace, and her own footsteps grew loud. Loneliness increased exponentially as a function of time away from the entrance of the labyrinth.

She swallowed an incipient sob and nearly choked on the dust and her own dry throat. Her ears rang with the beats of her heart. Her breath came in short gasps.

"When I return to Angleland, I really must engage in a routine of physical exercises and calisthenics," Alice told herself, focusing on being out of shape rather than lonely and scared. "One never knows when one will be forced to run away from an army of playing cards. Or angry dogs."

She turned down a path at random, because what did it matter? She crossed an intersection. At the end of one of the paths was a figure: a strange fellow, mostly human, wearing a bell-shaped garment of bright red that went to the ground and a sort of matching upside-down bell-shaped hat. The stitches were large and obviously hasty. Alice was pretty sure she saw a bent nail or two put to use in holding it together in place of pins.

"Bless you, my child," the strange man said, making a gesture with his hand.

"Beg pardon?" Alice asked politely.

"We are all pawns hoping to make it to the end of the Game."

"Pawn? You look more like a bishop," Alice said, pointedly looking at his hat.

*"We are all pawns,"* the man repeated, also pointedly. "We arrive at the end equal and unafraid. Actually very, very afraid. All hail the Queen of Hearts!"

"What game?" Alice said, advancing on him. "*Not* cards? Is it chess? Or have we wandered off into entirely different realms now, like pachisi or quoits? Does this have something to do with the executions?"

"May She be the last standing!" He looked around nervously. *"Say it,"* he urged her in a desperate whisper.

"Why?" Alice also whispered.

"Everywhere they are listening, *you* know that! *SAY IT!*"

"I don't want her to be the last one standing. I don't want her anywhere at all, much less standing in it. She seems to have grown completely out of control since the last time I was here. Wonderland looks like it was razed to the ground by a terrible cyclone or other act of God. Now I repeat: what game, what ending, and why has her murderous behavior suddenly become so—rigorous and systematic? And why is everyone just kowtowing to her whims? She's ridiculous. Together you needn't be afraid of her."

The man saw something past her, over her shoulder, and went pale in despair. "Look! They heard me! Here they come!"

Alice spun around. There was no one.

When she turned back the man was gone.

"People come and go in the most curious ways here," she said.

"You never answered. *Are* you for the Queen of Hearts?" came a whispering voice from inside the wall next to her head.

She peered in between the thorny, desiccating, and blood-colored branches. Therein crawled a tiny serpent, pale green with large black eyes. It looked adorable and utterly harmless, but Alice had read several cautionary tales about snakes from Africa whose poison was so strong it could kill a man in ten steps after he was bitten.

Also, the Bible and all.

"I can't be for anyone or anything unless I know the full situation," Alice said politely. "But I would say probably not. Are you the reason that poor man disappeared? Are you the one listening for the Queen of Hearts?"

"Why does a silly girl need to know the *full situation*? And anyway, I work for the White Rabbit, not the Queen. It's a simple question: are you for her, or against her?" He pulled a twig aside to get a better view of Alice: she was fairly certain he didn't even have his pale, almost translucent front appendages before.

"Oh, put a sock in it," she said crossly. "A serpent in a walled garden indeed. Very subtle. I doubt the devil was so rude."

"I shall record your recalcitrance and reluctance to respond posthaste!" the little thing screeched.

"Do. Please. I insist," she said, letting the branch snap back. The cry of the flung lizard grew immediately softer as he fell into the shadow depths of the bush.

Alice sighed and set off again. "Now, how to best get out of here and find my friends?"

As she wandered down a long narrow path, she thought about how strange that was; the term *friends.* None of the three creatures she'd helped save was precisely her *friend*, much less even polite to her. Yet she thought of them as such—dear old friends she missed and hadn't seen in years and was very anxious to become reacquainted with. Which was strange, because until the photographs, she had forgotten most of them. It was obvious that whatever note their relationship had ended on before—Alice stomping angrily out of a mad tea party to which she hadn't even been invited—the Hatter, at least, thought of her the same way: with hope and nostalgia. She had seen it in his eyes.

Thank goodness they *had* managed to get away, despite Alice's failure to mount a dramatic rescue. It was unsettling the way the tiny cakes and Wonderland tea had no effect on her whatsoever. The last time she was here she couldn't eat or drink a single thing without something happening. Mushrooms, elixirs, cakes . . . even smelling perfumed gloves had altered her physical self dramatically.

Was the Queen of Hearts responsible for this change as well, somehow? She seemed to have literally taken over most of Wonderland—did she now have sway over its rules and effects?

"What terrible things have happened while I was gone," Alice thought sadly.

Of course the denizens of Wonderland had been afraid of the Queen of Hearts before, but not in the crazed sort of way the Red Bell Man was, or the beaten-down crowds who came tiredly on demand to watch the execution of their fellow fantasy citizens. And what was all that about being the last one standing?

She explored the maze a little diffidently, no goal in mind beyond avoiding the soldiers and trying to find the Hatter and get to the bottom of things.

*"But you were never supposed to* be *gone."*

Alice whirled around: there was nothing there.

She waited impatiently.

She crossed her arms and tapped her foot.

Eventually a mouth full of teeth appeared, but its smile wasn't the moon-sliver grin of old; it was wry. A pair of eyes eventually appeared above it, more resigned than mad.

"Cheshire! About time. What do you mean, 'I was never supposed to be gone'?"

"You were saying—oh, you were *thinking* " The rest of the cat appeared in the air and twisted languidly there like he was rolling on a particularly soft and tufted couch. "I have it out of order. It's a problem with hypercativity. In your head a while ago, not aloud just now. But it's just as true as it ever was. You were never supposed to be gone, the both of you."

Alice had to resist reaching up to scratch his neck the way Dinah would have liked. One probably didn't touch sentient creatures without their express permission—at least not on first meeting. She wondered if there was a children's book in Wonderland somewhere full of useful rules of etiquette and proper Wonderland behavior for good girls and boys.

"But whatever do you mean, I was never supposed to be gone?" she asked. "I didn't ask to leave, although I was terrified for my life—the Queen wanted to kill me. I just, as you know, sort of woke up."

"Yes, but you woke up too early. You didn't see it to the end, because Mary Ann didn't end it then."

"Mary Ann—the White Rabbit's Mary Ann? But she was the one with the message about the Unbirthday! She—called me here!"

"Like calls to like," the cat said, now bored. "One or the other. You save, she saves, he she it saves, we all save. In Latin it's *pipsquo*."

"It isn't, either. But . . ." Her last memories of being in Wonderland were of chaos: a large-headed queen screaming bloody murder and *off with her head* and soldiers and everyone running which-aways and Alice wanting to shout and cry. "Mary Ann was supposed to save you? But—why wait for *me*, then?"

"Why not you? You're not from here, but you were there. You're Alice from another Land—Angleland. Not as good as Mary Ann, but you tried. You rose to the occasion. Literally."

"But I cannot rise at all now," Alice protested. "Not like bread or anything. I had the Eat Me cakes and the drinks and nothing at all happened to me."

"Well, of course." The cat twisted again, but only his striped purple-and-orange body: it rolled all the way around while his head stayed fixed and his eyes on hers. "You're finished shrinking and growing now. You're at your tip-toppiest. You can't be taller than your tallest, my Alice."

"That's an assonance," Alice pointed out smugly. "Of course I'll help you—and Mary Ann—if I can. But what precisely is happening here? What game is the Queen of Hearts playing at?"

The words, the tit for tat, came rolling off Alice's tongue as if they had been waiting all her life for someone else's dialogue to play with. It felt like a game, a grown-up one, and she hadn't played for years. It felt *good*.

The cat regarded her with an eyebrow raised.

"'Hands she has but does not hold; teeth she has but does not bite; feet she has but they are cold; eyes she has but without sight,'" he recited.

He fell to the ground—feetfirst, of course—and looked up at her inscrutably. Like a normal cat.

"Oh, you're no help," Alice said crossly. "All recrimination and riddles."

"You're not much help yourself. You're certainly no Mary Ann. She's the real hero. If you want my advice . . . you'll figure out my riddle, and find her. The *her*o."

It looked like it physically pained the Cheshire Cat to speak so plainly. He went green and chuffed and coughed up a fur ball—which opened bright pink eyes and then went running off into the bushes.

"Fair enough." Despite a strange incipient jealousy of this superior girl, Alice had to focus on the fact that whatever kind of hero she was, she was in trouble. She needed help. All of Wonderland did. "But how do I do that?"

"Ask around . . ." the cat said, drifting up into the air again. He yawned and put his head on his paws. "Keep your ear to the Grunderound, if you please."

"Grunderound?" Alice asked. "What? Where? How? Oh—he's gone."

The smile remained, inanimate, in the air.

"Of course," Alice sighed.

"The answer is *doll*, by the way," she added, sticking her tongue out at the smile. "Oldest one in the book. Are you saying the Queen of Hearts is a doll? That Mary Ann is?"

Then a distant squawk caught her attention.

In the glary sky above her an undiminishing speck resolved itself into a large awkward bird and its larger-hatted rider. They bobbed and burbled as they went. Someone from the castle must have finally found a suitable antiaircraft weapon and was firing giant crossbow bolts at them. Alice flinched, but the heavy things, made out of dark orange cheese, all fell far short of their mark.

"Hatter! Dormouse! Dodo! I'm coming!" she cried, and took off after them.

# Chapter Eight

Alice tried to keep an eye on the trio flying above her but soon lost them behind the high walls of the maze. She paid little attention to the twists and turns now, ducking in and then out of the cul-de-sacs haphazardly and not bothering to memorize the changes of direction she made as a result of this. Things crept behind her and pattered away in front of her, and she paid them no mind. All she really *did* mind was the length and breadth of her skirts, which impeded her speed and occasionally caught on curlicued signs that pointed to nowhere.

At some point the maze happily disappeared.

The sides of the labyrinth were replaced with thick and wild shrubs that poorly mimicked the boxwood. A spectacle-bird, perched with its giant toes wrapped around a low branch, eased from one foot back to another as if guarding—or perhaps merely watching—the imaginary entrance to the labyrinth.

"Pardon me, but have you seen the Mad Hatter?" Alice asked it politely.

The bird thing looked at her inscrutably, not an iota of kindness, interest, or curiosity in its strange eyes. And this was the most alien thing of all. The last time she had been here Alice was gently accosted by all sorts of odd, harmless creatures—curious fauna who wanted to play with her, or run away from her, or perhaps loom menacingly over her to keep her away from their territory. But never had they displayed this frigid disinterest.

"I wonder if I am entering the Tulgey Wood again," Alice said with forced casualness, turning away from the bird and feeling strangely embarrassed, as if she were the cause of some Wonderland faux pas.

(*Tulgey Wood!* She remembered it so clearly, the name and the place. But if asked what street she lived on back home, she would have said, "Baxterflashenhall!" And then, "No, that's not right at all. . . .")

It might indeed have been the forest from her previous visit: the trees were thick-trunked with storybook branches, and darkness grew under their leaves like a living, breathing entity. Ghostly green moss glowed and flowed around roots. Little flowers—eyeless, mouthless—poked star-shaped blossoms up from the forest floor. Strange pastel lights flickered off and on at unpredictable distances. It all felt very familiar.

And yet.

Once there were signs everywhere espousing nonsense: THIS WAY or THAT WAY or OVER HERE, nailed several to a tree, roughly carved into pointing shapes. The signs were still there, but in place of the friendly and useless words were bloody hearts painted slapdash upon them. Thick, ugly drips of red ran down their fronts like tears.

"'All ways are the Queen's way,'" Alice repeated to herself with a shudder.

She walked into the woods.

The first thing she noticed was how silent it was; the beeps, warbles, burbling streams, and qworking duck-bulbs were silent. There were of course no paths and she had only a vague idea of which way her friends had gone. It was like chasing the White Rabbit all over again.

"And where *is* the White Rabbit, anyway?" Alice mused. "He wasn't at the executions. Usually he's right up front with the Queen and other important people. But of course the Queen wasn't there . . . so perhaps he is out with her, wherever she may be. What did that lizard thing say?

That he *worked* for the White Rabbit? What does that even mean?"

Suddenly Alice spotted something at the base of one of the gloomy trees: a little flash of unnatural color. She bent down and saw a single mome rath, a bright pink one, desperately trying to pretend it was a flower.

"Excuse me," Alice said gently. "I understand that you may not be able to tell the difference between regular people, especially girls, but I am not at all associated with the Queen of Hearts. And I could really use your help. If you please."

The little tufted head lifted up just a smidgen so that the tops of two large and innocent eyes could gauge her trustworthiness.

"Really," Alice said as patiently and calmly as she could. "You can see there isn't a spot of red on me. I just freed my friends from the Executioner, and now I'm looking for them. It's the Hatter, the Dodo, and the Dormouse. Although if you knew anyone else who was left the March Hare, for instance—I would love to see him again, too."

The mome rath raised itself up out of the ground on a pair of purply-pink and cautious legs. Keeping both of its large eyes on hers, it tottered, unconvinced, around her feet. Alice stayed perfectly still, resisting the urge to scrunch and unscrunch her toes away from it.

Finally the tiny thing made up its mind and went whirling into the woods. Alice wasn't entirely sure if it had decided to help her or was off on a mission of its own, but she followed nonetheless.

"I thought you fellows always traveled in crowds," she said to make conversation. "When I was here last, I only saw you in packs. Or flocks, rather, or—what *do* you call dozens of mome raths? A herd? A murder? A blessing?"

The creature stopped long enough to look back at her with sad, baleful eyes. Then it spraddled its legs out and fell to the ground, eyes closed.

"Oh. I see. They were stepped on," Alice said softly. "I'm so sorry."

The mome rath gave her another look that was impossible to interpret without a mouth or other point of reference. Then it leapt up and toddled on. Alice followed, continuing her conversation—but with herself this time. That way there was no more chance of her accidentally saying something hurtful to the other party.

"Eleven years later and I'm still mucking things up," she chastised. "I used to laugh at little Alice for telling the Dormouse all about Dinah. What an improper thing to do, bragging to a mouse about a cat! And now here I am in a war-torn land asking about the Queen of Hearts' latest victims as if they were no more than a—background image, a picture or illustration with no real feelings. Naughty Alice. Be more careful! Think before you speak! Remember what happened last time and learn from it!"

She opened her mouth to say something nice and soothing to the little creature, but the mome rath was gone. It had just faded out of consciousness as if it had never been there at all. Alice found herself beside a small brook that broke apart and foamed over rocks into a lovely little pool below—but it was all absolutely silent. *Impossibly* silent.

"No, none of that. Nothing is impossible in Wonderland," Alice said with a sigh, dipping her hand into the water and whipping it around with her fingers. Even that made no noise.

Then she heard the faintest bit of *something*. A song that was started and then stopped suddenly . . . a chorus? In the middle of the woods?

"Oh, that's rather mad," she said, cocking her head and listening.

*"Oh!"* she said again, realizing what the music reminded her of. "It *is* Mad! Mad as a Hatter!"

Cautiously Alice picked her way to the sounds. It was far harder than it should have been: the Wonderlandians' now very recognizable voices grew louder for no good reason and then suddenly shut off like a door had closed. She had to stop, wait, then turn around and try different directions.

She suspected that it was the trees. They scattered sounds they didn't like or didn't want to hear, or perhaps translated it into something closer to *tree*.

She rounded a particularly large oak and the source finally revealed itself. It nearly broke poor Alice's heart.

The escaped prisoners had found the perfect camouflaged hiding spot: a small clearing between trees so large that their branches knotted around each other overhead.

(Literally—Alice found herself suspecting that some of the tangled branches didn't actually come from the trees at all and had just grown ex nihilo in place.)

On the ground were several large, flat boulders suitable for sitting. Between them, tuffets of tall grass had been quickly and inexpertly plaited together to make a kind of a flat surface. This swaying, delicate top was set with a number of unlikely objects: a couple of broken teacups; a shell; a flat, concave stone; a snuffbox. All were filled with water and rested on broad leaves.

Two of the old friends slumped tiredly on the big rocks. But the Mad Hatter kept his back straight, shoulders back, elbows close, and pinkie out as he picked up the snuffbox with one hand and used the other to hold a leaf beneath to catch any spills.

Besides his familiar green top hat with the label sticking out, the Hatter now sported a much tinier one over his left eye. Alice gasped when she realized that the doll-sized velvet hat was there to cover up what was probably an empty socket; there were terrible scratches around his lid and cheek. The bags under his right eye had bags. He was gritting his teeth.

He also seemed to be taller than last time, almost normal height, and his head of a more conventional size. *Normal* and *conventional* being the operative, and therefore terrifying, words.

"No, properly now, let's, and . . ." he was saying with a forced smile.

The Dodo, missing his wig and a number of feathers, picked up his own "teacup," the concave rock, with a resigned look on his face.

"This is where he would start to sing," the Hatter prompted sotto voce. "The March Hare. He would sing: *Ohhhh, a very merry . . .*"

"'Fraid I don't know the words—but I could learn 'em if you want. Or can we run a race instead?" the Dodo suggested. "That might cheer us up! A good old-fashioned caucus race!"

The Dormouse lifted his head up out of the snuffbox the Hatter was just about to sip from. He, too, looked exhausted, but his eyes were wide and unblinking and he shivered a little.

"TWINKLE TWINKLE LITTLE BAT," he screamed. "IF I WERE A BAT I COULD FLY LIKE THAT ALL AWAY FROM EVERYTHING!"

"Sssht!" the Hatter said, snapping the snuffbox shut desperately. As water squirted out its sides, he suddenly realized the danger to his friend and snapped it open again. The Dormouse popped back up like a jack-in-the box—wet, but with the same wild look in his eye.

"Oh dear oh dear oh dear!" Alice cried, stepping forward, unable to watch any longer.

She probably should have restrained herself a little. The Hatter leapt up, pulling the snuffbox close to his chest and holding his other hand out to—what? Fend off an attack? With nothing? It was a crushingly valiant gesture. The Dodo stumblingly turned around and tried to hiss like a lizard or something far more dangerous. And while he wasn't at all a dangerous creature, he *did* have the mad look of someone, no matter how awkward he seemed, who had definitely had enough.

"Alice!" the Hatter cried. And again that change of expression on his face: the softening, the relief, the desperation, shot right into Alice's heart. It was the least Mad she had ever seen him.

"Alice? What's an Alice?" the Dodo asked, patting himself down for a pair of glasses or something he obviously no longer had. "Oh, I know you—did you ever wind up getting yourself dry, my dear?"

"Yes, thank you, I have," she answered. "I'm so glad you managed to escape!"

"Yes, *we* did," the Hatter said, his face falling again. "Yes, we did," he repeated softly.

"Please, tell me what is happening," she begged. "I received your message, your cry for help. I am here now. What can I do?"

"It's monstrous. *She's* monstrous," the Dormouse sighed in his quavering voice, swaying in the snuffbox like a cobra entranced by a flute.

"A pox on the Queen of Hearts and her caucus bans!" the Dodo said, trying to pound his fist—wing—onto the tabletop, which resulted in nothing but the grass bending and being crushed under his force. The shell of water slid precipitously toward the ground. "I'll drink to her removal!" He grabbed up his own concave rock, toasted everyone, and took a sip. "Fine vintage," he observed.

"But what exactly is the Queen hoping to accomplish? What is the scope of her operations? What is it her intention to *do*?"

"*Do?* Intention?" the Mad Hatter said, suddenly fixing Alice with bright aqua eyes that were clear for just a moment. "What a question! Does it matter? She is sweeping her armies across the entire land and burning everything as she goes. She is throwing everyone into prison. She is seizing everyone's property. She is executing anyone who dares ask why or stands up to her. *Executes* them!

"*Why?* I have no idea why. Ask the eye I no longer have. Ask the friends who are no longer here. She . . . just . . . wants it. All. All the cake. Whatever."

"Ooh, a nice bit of cake would go well with this port," the Dodo observed.

"It's tea," the Dormouse corrected gently, as if the Dodo were mad and to be handled with care. "But do try the chestnut pudding. It's delightful."

And with that he hurled a prickly cocklebur at the bird's head: it wasn't even a horse chestnut, much less pudding. The Dodo caught it in his rock cup and gulped it down, which of course resulted in a fit of choking and coughing as the little hooks grabbed the inside of his throat.

Alice closed her eyes and counted to ten. They were all Mad here. She had to remember that.

"But mightn't it help if we knew what her eventual goal was? Croquet and cards—it's always all about *winning a game*. What is she looking to win? The rule of all Wonderland? Alone?"

"Rule?" the Hatter scoffed. "Rule is for rulers. And protractors. And perhaps slides."

"Well, one *might* just as well ask what the use of War is," the Dodo said philosophically. "There is no purpose. You just pull out your cards over and over again, and whoever has the most at the end wins."

"There is no purpose," the Hatter repeated darkly. "You just put your soldiers out over and over again, and whoever has the most bodies at the end wins."

Of course it did make a strange sort of Wonderland sense: in the end the Queen of Hearts was nothing more than a card grown too big for her britches. Alice used to play War—or Battle—all the time when she was little. Mostly against Dinah or her dolls, since grown-ups and Mathilda found the game random, tiresome, pointless, and silly. It made Alice blush to remember how sometimes she used to secretly stack her half of the deck with all the royal suits to give herself a leg up against the opponent kitten.

Still, it seemed a little strange that the Queen was so energetic and directed in her undefined violence. Something didn't quite fit.

"So for all we know, she is just rampaging until she destroys all of Wonderland?"

"Or until the Great Clock ticks its last," the Hatter said with a weary sigh. He scratched distractedly at the tiny velvet top hat over his left eye.

"Yes, what you have seen in Heartland is just the beginning," the Dodo said with a sigh. "A view of what's to come."

"All right, we have a mad Napoleon on our hands," Alice said briskly. "I'm not sure what I can do to help—she has an *awful* lot of soldiers on her side, and as you saw, I can no longer shrink and grow as I used to."

"You cannot grow because you have decided you have stopped growing," the Hatter said diffidently. "You haven't grown in ages and you've lost the knack."

"Well, I beg your pardon! In *my* world you don't get to decide whether or not to stop growing. My mother is rather short, my father is not overly tall, and I believe I am about average for an English lady."

"You 'believe,'" the Hatter mused. "'Twas a time you used to believe six impossible things before breakfast, if I'm not mistaken."

Alice started to retort but then sat back on her heels and considered: she was the odd man out here, so to speak. These locals knew the realities and rules of their own land. Perhaps she *had* decided to stop growing. It seemed possible, since she had such a ready and pat answer about her parents.

"You haven't done much growing up at all actually," the Dodo said, a trifle rudely. "*Except* for your height, I mean. You've stayed the same, in the same house, trying to do the same things you've always done."

"Excuse me!" Alice said, frowning. "I have a passion for photography now and am finished with my schooling. If you had contacted me earlier, perhaps I could have come sooner and prevented some of this mess."

*"Mess?"* the Hatter said wryly. "I wonder if that's what the March Hare would call this, rest his poor long-eared soul."

"Oh . . ." Alice crumpled.

Everyone was silent. The Dormouse swayed sadly.

"I am so very, very sorry," she said softly. "I did not mean any disrespect to the poor thing." She took a deep breath. "*But* if we are to prevent such horrid occurrences from happening to anyone else, we must strategize. Work together. Plan. Isn't that why you wanted me here? To help you stop this?"

"*Mary Ann* wanted you here," the Hatter said moodily. "She was trying to stop it all. She had the odd notion you could help."

Mary Ann thought *she* could help? Alice tried not to let this thought distract her. But how could this other girl know anything about her?

"Mary Ann!" the Dodo squawked. But not like one would imagine a dodo squawking, or any bird at all; he squawked like an overdramatic man. "Now *she's* the tardigrade's petard!"

"The—I'm sorry, I haven't any idea what that means," Alice said, not trusting herself to repeat the confusing phrase correctly.

"Tardigrade's petard. The echidna's phalarope. You know."

"I'm afraid I don't know. I suppose it's a good thing?"

"A *good* thing? A rare thing indeed!" the Hatter snorted. "Have you ever seen so tiny a petard that would suit a tardigrade? The Dodo's a bit dim at times, but he has it on the knuckles there: Mary Ann could fix everything up."

"All right," Alice said uncertainly. It was strange and a trifle naughty, but she couldn't help feeling a *bit* put out at the constant lauding of Mary Ann, this other version of her. The first time she had been in Wonderland, with all the growing and shrinking, she had wondered if she was still Alice at all afterward. She even considered the possibility that she had become another girl entirely. Including specific girls she knew who had terribly boring lives full of lessons and empty of toys. How dreadful that would have been!

But here Mary Ann was the savior of the fantasy land, Alice the Anglish girl who had led a comparatively boring, normal life until called for help. Well, that was a turnaround! And a bit painful for the ego.

"Really, dear girl," she reproved herself. "Even if this

Mary Ann turns out to be more vexing in person than she is in stories, she is the one who seems the most able to save everyone. Set your childish thoughts aside and do what is right!"

Aloud, she said:

"How did she do it? Contact me, I mean?"

The Hatter shrugged. "She had to wait for your Unbirthday. The proper one, I mean: the eleventh anniversary of your first visit. I suppose there was nothing else to do in prison but wait and hope and wish."

"That explains why she appeared the way she did in the photograph," Alice said, remembering the blindfold and the wounds and shuddering a little. "She certainly looked like she was in prison."

"She traveled to you by photograph?" the Dodo asked curiously.

"She *appeared* in a photograph. Of me. Actually, quite a few of you appeared in place of the pictures of people I knew. I suppose each of you is reflected in a real-world—excuse me, Anglish-world—version of yourself."

"Really? Whatever do you mean?"

"Well, Hatter, in my world you are—well, a hatter."

"Really?" he asked, looking delighted for the first time since she had arrived. "I'm a *hatter* in this other land? How exciting! And what kind of hats do I make?"

"All sorts. Especially large fancy ones for ladies."

"Think of it! Ladies' hats!" He took a dreamy sip from the snuffbox, forgetting about the Dormouse. The mouse seemed more curious than upset.

"But Mary Ann is no longer *in* prison, now," the Dodo said. "She's free! I rather thought because of what you said that maybe she escaped by photograph."

"Really! How wonderful!" Alice said, clapping her hands. "I think the best thing to do, then, is for us to find and join her."

The Dormouse swayed dreamily. "It's said she is hiding out in the Back of Beyond. . . ."

"*I* heard she went all the way to Helenbach," the Hatter added casually, sipping his water as if they were discussing where a friend was spending the summer.

"I heard she was drumming up a resistance, gathering revolutionaries and mendicants," the Dodo said confidentially.

"I heard it was flutes," the Hatter mused.

"FLUTY WOOTY DRUMMY DUMMY DONE-Y," the Dormouse whistle-sang before slumping to sleep in the water, splashing a little out.

"*Regardless* of whether it's drums or flutes," Alice said quickly, before they went off on another Wonderland tangent, "could she be someplace called the Grunderound?"

Everyone looked at her in shock.

"How do you come by this intel?" the Hatter asked suspiciously. "Nobody knows exactly where she is!"

"The Cheshire Cat told me," Alice said, not seeing any point in hiding the truth.

"Ah. Well, he *is* nobody," the Dodo conceded, nodding. "Most of the time. And nowhere at all the rest of the time."

"What *is* the Grunderound, if I may?" Alice asked timidly.

The Hatter tapped his teacup impatiently. "You know—when you're looking for secrets, or where you've hidden that last lump of sugar, or where the thieves go to sell their stolen tarts. You *grunder around* looking for the right wrong thing."

"Of course," Alice said, putting a hand to her head. "Grunderound. That makes loads of sense. Anyway, how do we get there?"

"Generally by walking," the Hatter said with a shrug.

"I prefer rocking chair myself," the Dodo mused.

"Haven't been flocks of those around since the Red Doom," the Hatter said, shaking his head. "I wonder if she's killed them all—or thrown them into her mews."

"Faster by bottle anyway, since the Sea of Tears," the Dodo said with a significant, accusing look at Alice.

"All right, can we shrink somehow? To fit into a

bottle?" Alice asked hastily. She had created the Sea of Tears herself years ago, when as a giant girl she had cried about her situation. It had flooded the place—and made a lot of Wonderland inhabitants grumpy and wet.

"No, but it's always up to me, isn't it?" the Hatter said grumpily. "Not allowed to be Mad even a quarter of the day now." He leapt up and began patting down his jacket, searching his pockets.

"It's true," the Dodo whispered to Alice. "The poor chap had the Nonsense knocked right out of him along with his eye. Hasn't been the same since."

"Oh my," Alice whispered back, concerned. That would explain his normal height and head; he was becoming sane.

"He keeps *trying*. To be Mad, I mean," the Dodo went on sadly. "It just doesn't come naturally anymore."

But the Hatter succeeded this one time, at least: he pulled an enormous umbrella out of his waistcoat. With a flourish he snapped the black and arabesque-y thing open. A shower of raindrops fell out from underneath until he shook it dry.

"I don't—" Alice began.

"You never do," sighed the Hatter.

And so saying, he tossed it, handle up, into the stream that Alice had dipped her hand in before (and that must have provided the "tea" for their party). But she was fairly certain it hadn't been *right next to them* until just now. Yellow cowslips smiled up from the banks—literally, of course. Their heads nodded and waved cheerfully, as Alice always imagined the wild happy flowers would. With a courteous bow—and another flourish of his hands—the Hatter indicated for Alice to get into the umbrella.

"Thank you, dear sir," she said with a little bit of a curtsy and, trying not to show any reluctance, stepped in. Whether she finally shrank or the umbrella grew mattered in the end not at all; the *getting into* it was not carefree and graceful as one might imagine in a fairy tale. It tipped just like it would in the real world, and Alice had a very hard time, swaying and balancing, not upsetting the whole thing. The Dodo half fluttered in next to her, more like a delicate canary than a large (mostly) flightless bird. The Hatter leapt in between them.

And the umbrella began to drift downstream.

# Chapter Nine

If their quest had not been so urgent, Alice would have truly enjoyed travel by umbrella. It was restful, and all three escapees from the Queen looked grey and exhausted and absolutely filthy where there weren't streaks of blood. They could have slept for a week, it looked like.

The Hatter scratched thoughtlessly under the tiny top hat covering his eye socket.

"If you don't mind my asking, Hatter," Alice asked, knowing she shouldn't. But she was always a curious girl. "Whatever happened to your eye?"

He looked over at her, and she was startled by the moment of lucidity in his good eye.

"Jubjub birds," he said bleakly. "She threw me to a nest

of them she kept hungry just for such a purpose. Wanted to know where Mary Ann was. I never told. I wasn't the one who betrayed her."

"Oh, how very brave of you," Alice breathed. "I'm so sorry."

"Bravery is for kings and wingless pigs. I'm just a Mad Hatter. Well, I was, once upon a time."

Everyone lapsed into silence again. The umbrella twirled and the landscape rolled by, a little too slowly for Alice's liking.

"I haven't heard any poetry yet," Alice eventually ventured. "There is always ever so much poetry in Wonderland. Has the Queen of Hearts done away with that, too?"

"Poetry! I say! Poetry!" the Dodo said, pounding one wing into the other. "Just what we need a spot of. Dormouse, wake up. Dormouse! Some nice refreshing poetry! Come, come!"

Dismissing without wages the usual sleepy stages between unconsciousness and consciousness, the Dormouse immediately stood up, straight-backed, in full recital mode.

*A dog and a cat and a droll wombat*
*Ran off to the Similung Sea*
*The sun shone fair in the immutable blue*

*'Twas as daylicious as a day could be.*
*"I spy a fish!" said the critical cat (who liked*
*trout fried in salt pudding).*
*"We haven't a pole!" the little dog barked*
*as the 'bat was sticking a foot in.*

*A flunder leapt up and glared at the three*
*"Our kind is not for your pleasure!*
*Go back to the sands of old Angler-land*
*On the beach you'll find great*
*. . . numbers of shells and something really sparkly and nice to take home and put in a cabinet, maybe."*

And with that the Dormouse fell straight forward onto the handle of the umbrella and began snoring.

"Oh," Alice said, trying to work out what she had just heard. "That didn't end properly."

"I beg to differ. It ended *most* properly," the Dodo said, flicking a bit of lint off his cuff. "They left the fish alone and found some lovely thing like a pearl or an oscilloscope to bring back to Mother."

"But, but—oughtn't it have ended, 'On the beach you'll find great heaps of *treasure*'? That makes sense, and moreover rhymes with *pleasure*, the way the other stanzas have the second and fourth lines rhyming."

"You asked for poetry," the Dodo pointed out. "*I* certainly didn't ask for a poetical lesson. Next time recite something yourself. Actually, this *is* the next time, because you're next. Up, girl, recite."

"Oh, I shouldn't," Alice said quickly. "Everything I ever try to say here comes out all wrong."

"Try something really easy," the Hatter said casually—but there might have been a twinkle in his eye. "Your national anthem, for instance."

"Oh! Of course! I know 'God Save the Queen' back and forth," Alice said. "My sister and her silly man friend sing it all the time, even before they go to one of their ridiculous rallies."

"Only forth, please," the Dodo said hurriedly. "I don't think we have time for back as well."

"I can't stand in the umbrella without tipping it," she said, shuffling her feet. "I hope no one is offended." Then she cleared her throat and sang the familiar tune:

"*My country, 'tis of thee*
*Sweet land of liberty*
*Of thee I sing. . . .*

"No, wait, that's not right," she said, frowning. "It doesn't even mention the Queen."

"I rather like it," the Hatter said. "That's what we need right now, anyway. *Liberty.* And no more queens. *Ever.*"

Somehow the trees had fallen away without her noticing; the cozy forest had been replaced by what seemed like endless silver water that rippled and waved randomly. Alice dipped a finger in and tasted a drop; it was indeed salty, perhaps even saltier than the North Sea. And much, much warmer. *Body* temperature, one might even say. They had come to the Sea of Tears.

"Does this leave us off in the hallway with the keyhole?" she asked.

"Only in March. Everyone out!" the Hatter ordered.

The Dodo scooped up the Dormouse and stepped forward; the umbrella, now somehow washing up onto a tiled floor, was much more stable, and he disembarked with great aplomb. Alice followed and the Hatter came last, pushing his umbrella back out into the water.

"Aren't you taking it?" Alice asked.

"No, it has filled out its term of service. Time for it to be free." He took off his (large) hat and waved goodbye. The umbrella handle uncurled and waved eerily back. Then it sort of pointed itself and dove underwater like a sea serpent, its cloth and spine splitting into two rear fins.

The black-and-white tiled floor they now trod on continued on an uphill slant away from the water, occasionally making sharp slanted turns into still wave shapes—it took Alice a moment to realize they were *dunes*. The squares changed size as required to fill in properly, but never curved or altered their straight lines and angles; the resulting mosaic was dizzying and impossible to focus on. Beyond this they came to a well-grazed monochrome sward, and beyond that a lovely little English village.

At first glance, any rate, it *appeared* to be a lovely little English village: there were houses, a main street, a horse fountain, people hurrying about at market. All the colors were right; all the movements seemed normal.

But the houses were built one on top of another. Literally. A large family house painted bright yellow with an airy porch and slate shingles was balanced on the roof of a lovely flag- and river-stone one-room cabin, and squarely on top of that was a narrow three-floor brick town house. A green witch's delight with round towers and intricately decorated eaves supported a solid farmhouse, perfectly symmetrical with three windows on the upper floor and a door between two windows on the bottom. The chimneys had to stick out sideways, of course, because this abode had what appeared to be a seaside shack—complete with a bathing machine—atop.

The fountain or horse trough in the market square didn't seem to be working and was moreover too high for horses.

A stone pillar held up a wide concave disk filled with water. When someone wanted a drink, he or she perched on the rim and bent over, taking delicate sips.

And therein lay the biggest surprise (or perhaps not so much, considering it was Wonderland). The people of this village had somewhat avian tendencies. Most sported beaks. Many had feathers, though the women often kept theirs under caps or oiled up into fancy designs and curlicues that looked like hats at first. Wings were used like hands and unshod feet had claws.

"What the blazes is going on here?" the Hatter asked, blinking at the sight.

Alice looked at him in surprise: surely *he* couldn't have found anything particularly unusual in the scene? This was his native land, and strange was normal, the odd the everyday to Wonderlandians.

So she looked at everything again, trying to imagine she was a local.

*Then* she saw it.

The inhabitants moved as if haunted. They slunk in the way birds shouldn't, hunkering down so their wing bones made it look as though they were hunchbacked. Their heads turned quickly this way and that, birds' eyes taking in the view in quick and feral glances.

Everywhere signs had been hastily amended with

splatters of paint: the symbol of a rabbit added to a sweets shop, a butcher, a tailor. Sometimes it was a red heart, but mostly a rabbit. Sometimes the rabbit was red, but mostly he was white.

In the market around the birdbath was a large, ugly, and hastily made statue that looked like it had been hammered together from spare bits of wood. Like a giant shrine, its base was covered in offerings of all sorts of food. But Alice couldn't figure out *what* the statue was at first; boards stuck out of it willy-nilly.

Then, as she was cocking her head and stepping back, it suddenly came to her all at once:

It was a rabbit.

"Hatter," she said, nervous but unsure why.

"No I don't like it no no no," the Hatter said, sort of agreeing, but it was clear he was finally a little Mad and of absolutely no help at all. He even seemed to have shrunk a little. The Dodo was busy washing his wounds in the bath, and of course the Dormouse was asleep. So Alice screwed up her courage and approached one of the lories hurrying by with a market basket on her arm. It was not, as Alice would have guessed, filled with seed. Instead there was a mound of luscious-smelling soft hay and three beautifully washed carrots.

"Pardon me—oh *my*."

It wasn't the giant hooked orange beak or gorgeous yellow-and-blue chignon the matronly woman had that shocked Alice; it was her hastily tied headkerchief. The two long ends were starched and twisted up a bit *to look like rabbit ears.*

"What is going on here? Why all the rabbits?"

"There is only the one rabbit!" the woman angrily hissed and whistled. "If he comes by we're ready. We like rabbits here. All bless the Rabbit and keep him and his mistress safe. *And out of our business.*"

"We're a good town, we are," a budgie in a morning coat and bowler insisted as he walked by. There was a bit of white fluff sewn on his rear for a little tail. "Absolutely loyal. We gave up immediately, we did."

"To whom? The Queen of Hearts?"

"Never! To the Rabbit's men. *He's* to be trusted, of course. If he says that's what the Queen wants, that's what we'll do," the lory said with a determined air and a sniff. "You tell 'im that if you sees 'im. Whatever he says goes with us here. Mayhap he'll put in a good word to the Queen. Maybe she'll skip us on her next raid."

"But of course, whomever the Rabbit follows, we're right with him," the budgie added quickly.

Alice knew there was a song about this sort of thing but couldn't quite remember it just then.

(In fact, she was thinking of "The Vicar of Bray," but when she tried to remember the lyrics about the man who changed sides for whoever was in power, all she could come up with was *"Whatsoever," sings the train, "Still I'll be quicker in May, Sir!"*)

"Alice, I don't like it here," the Hatter said forlornly. "Let us move on."

"Look right there," the lory said, pointing proudly at a rapidly growing pile of produce, offerings, at the feet of the rabbit statue. "A *pile* o' lettuce. That's from me. Much as it pleases him."

"And peases for him?" the Dodo asked interestedly.

"It appeases him," the budgie agreed sagely.

"Wait, that's not right," Alice said, but she wasn't really paying attention any longer.

For as strange as it was to see a town of birds be suddenly taken over by a fawning loyalty to rabbits, something stranger still managed to catch her eye. A shawled figure was adding her—his?—own offering to the pile of rabbit treats; he or she was entirely covered with robes and capes and cloaks and hunched over even more than the others. He gripped the edge of the cloth tightly with claws that weren't wingy at all.

Alice rushed over and grabbed the shawl and yanked it away.

"Aha!" she cried.

(Wondering—vaguely, in the back of her head—when she had decided it was all right to act like a seven-year-old ruffian again.)

Spinning out of the linsey-woolsey fabric wasn't a bird, although he did indeed have some birdlike attributes: a beak and wings certainly allowed him to hide out amongst the townsbirds, but his ears and tail and lion hindquarters had to stay firmly under cloth to pass. He let out a fearsome yelp, exposing teeth within his beak—again, certainly not birdlike at all. Then he curled his arms together quickly as if protecting something.

"Oh," the Hatter said, as if nothing untoward had happened. "Hello, Gryphon."

"A gryphon!" Alice cried out. "I've always thought you were imaginary and fantastic beasts!"

"Well, there's a fine how'd'ye'do," the Gryphon said a little wryly, looking left and right and trying to protect whatever it was on his arms. "I don't suppose there's any use in telling you that as of this moment you are the only little girl in Wonderland, and just as imaginary and fantastic?"

"She's not little anymore," the Dodo pointed out, still preening.

"But what about Mary Ann?" Alice asked.

"Hush!! Hush!" the Gryphon said desperately, putting

one clawed paw awkwardly over her mouth while keeping the other one curled around something protectively. "Do you want to get us all killed?"

"What's that you've got there?" Alice asked (somewhat muffled), unable to contain her curiosity and reaching for his paw. She pulled back with a cry when something horrific and tentacle-y extended and retracted itself. Whatever it was snaked quickly up the Gryphon's arm and under the voluminous cuff of his coat, reappearing as a lump at the nape of his neck.

After a moment the capped head of a timid green thing with golden eyes peeped out.

"Oh!" Alice cried in relief. It wasn't, as she had feared, the horrid thing from the maze at all. "Bill! Poor old Bill the gardener!"

But rather than being equally excited by this reunion, the little lizard fainted dead away, mumbling something about her being "even bigger this time."

"I don't understand this at all," Alice said, frowning. "I'm the same size as these townsbirds, who ought to be small, like real birds, oughtn't they? But I'm normal-girl-sized compared to Bill. Are we all small, or are the townsbirds large, or has something happened to Bill?"

"Leave it to an Alice to be talking about the general size of things when we're all about to be killed," the Gryphon said mournfully. "Silly, fantastic creatures, these little girls."

"Actually, we're on our way to join with *M-A* right now," the Hatter said with meaning.

"Come join us," the Dodo whispered. "We'll travel to the Grunderound together."

"*She'll* never fit in there. She's far too big!" the Gryphon squawked in a whisper.

"Now which fantastic imaginary beast is wasting time talking about my size?" Alice demanded, hands on hips. "Oooh—look at that."

A shop had opened and folded out one of its horizontally shuttered windows, locking it so it formed a shelf. On top of this, a baker set out pies to cool—caramel black thistle and ginger worm—along with tiny square seedcakes that smelled amazing. Not that Alice had ever *smelled* a seedcake before or known beforehand what a good-smelling one smelled like; perhaps time in the bird town was changing her. EAT ME was spelled out in pine nuts upon the top of each cake.

"Let me just try one of these. Perhaps I shall shut up like a telescope," she said, taking one and nibbling at it. The baker's wingy hand slapped ineffectually at her, but there were no other ramifications. The cake was nutty and buttery with a distinct hint of grasshopper.

All five of them waited to see what would happen: the Dodo, the Hatter, the Dormouse, and even the Gryphon and Bill, holding their collective breaths.

Nothing.

Alice gulped down the rest of the cake, barely chewing—which seemed a waste, it was so delicious.

Still nothing.

"Perhaps you really have forgotten how," the Dodo said.

"I can't imagine that's so," Alice said. "I remember exactly what it felt like. . . ."

"Remembering isn't the same as knowing," the Gryphon said accusingly. "You've been schooled terribly if you think that's so."

"That's it!" the Hatter cried. "You've filled your head with all the wrong things since you left. You pushed all the good things out. You need to unlearn them. *Unremember* them."

"You with your uns," Alice said fondly. "Like Unbirthdays. But everything I have learned is necessary, in my world. . . . And anyway, I couldn't *un*learn it all if I tried."

"But you haven't even tried. What's nine times ten? Forget it!" the Hatter shouted.

"What is the capital of Cumbria? Forget it!" the Dodo shouted.

"What is the airspeed velocity of an unladen sparrow?

*FORGET IT,*" shouted the Gryphon, apparently also forgetting that he was hiding from anyone or anything.

"I beg your pardon," said a passing sparrow, unladen except for a small briefcase.

The four travelers (Bill was still passed out) began to sing:

*"Forget the cheese and forget the fife*
*Forget the flies a-buzzing*
*Forget the one about the pair o'*
*brick-red Bristol cousins*

*Forget your name and forget your meat*
*Forget the Earl of Plumbing*
*Forget the time and forget the words*
*And all commence with humming!"*

And of course they hummed the last stanza, whatever it was.

"We shall take her to the Forest of Forgetting!" the Hatter cried. "Then she'll forget all the silliness of the other world and start again with shrinking and growing and become a powerful weapon—and then we can get to the Grunderound and we'll find Mary Ann and we'll all have tea!"

"I'm not sure I like the idea of forgetting everything," Alice said uneasily. "Or being some sort of powerful weapon. But if it's for the good of Wonderland, I suppose it's worth a try." She had been suspicious of the shrinking and growing the first time around as well but rapidly—well, grown used to it. Maybe this would be the same.

And the Hatter was, at least, beginning to act like his old self. A little more logical than he ever was, but shouting nonsense and songs and poetry. His head did seem a trifle bit larger, too.

"Let us go, then you and I—" he began, taking her gallantly by the hand.

"No! No dramatic, subtextual, free verse poetry now—stop, we're done with that. Rhymes only," the Dodo said, dragging him away by his ear.

As they walked out of the village and through the bright sunlight, Alice observed how strange it was for her companions to be *staying* with her. Generally in Wonderland she spent only a little while with each creature or person—or both—before everything changed and she moved on to the next thing. But they were a little marching band now, the Hatter even pumping his arms like a drum major. The Gryphon mostly walked upright beside him but sometimes dropped onto all fours and trotted like an absolutely enormous dog with wings. The Dodo chuckled to himself, and Bill had consented to ride on his beak, keeping one wary and distrustful eye on Alice. The Dormouse slept in someone's pocket.

The landscape did that thing it always did: seamlessly and silently roil into something entirely different. The vague seaside air with its accompanying grasses and black-and-white-checkered floor became more of a golden meadow, which, as often happened in late afternoon, wound up in deep, lush shadow from some hill or knoll no one could see. A lovely forest sprang up rather suddenly, like a fog had disappeared and revealed what it hid: soft pine and cushy oak and dappled spots of sunlight like a painting by Corot. A ridiculously straight-running brook—almost a canal—bordered it, but was apparently natural, insomuch as anything in Wonderland was natural.

"I'm remembering it all now," Alice mused to herself. "Everything here changes unexpectedly . . . but somehow you always wind up right where the next thing, the next bit of action is. When I was little I just *went* and *did* and followed my impulses and wound up at the next place. I should keep that in mind. Wonderland knows where it's taking you. I should trust that."

There were only two off notes to the otherwise perfectly Arcadian scene. One was a whiff of smoke that came from somewhere beyond the forest. It wasn't from a wood fire and smelled foul.

The other was a sign hammered up on an otherwise innocent oak, whitewashed and red painted:

**FREE OF TRAITORS**
**INSPECTED BY W. RABBIT**
**WEDNESDAY**

A crude symbol of a rabbit was hastily daubed on at the bottom.

"Which Wednesday, I wonder," the Gryphon mused, scratching his chin. "One from the last batch, I assume?"

"I think the next ones are all full," the Dodo said, pulling out a pocket watch.

"Is it still always teatime with you, Hatter?" Alice asked curiously.

"Oh, Time and I made up a long time ago," the Hatter said moodily. "He wanted to make amends before he went. And with the Queen of Hearts in charge, there is never tea anymore. For anyone."

"Isn't it funny," Alice said, reaching out a hand to tentatively touch the sign. "Last time I was here, all I wanted to do was find and chase the White Rabbit. And this time, no matter how hard I try to avoid him, his presence is everywhere."

"All right, here we go, then!" the Dodo said, puffing out his chest and reaching with one large and awkward foot to step over the stream.

"Not you, foolish bird!" the Hatter cried, pulling him back. "We need to fish out clean Alice on the other side, when she's back to the way she was. An empty girl. We can't do that if we've forgotten who *we* are and what we're about as well."

"Empty girl?" Alice said. "I don't think—"

"Off you go!" the Gryphon cried gamely and pushed her over the stream.

# Chapter Ten

She stumbled and fell against the trunk of a comfortable tree but nearly lost her shoes in the stream.

"Dear me, what just happened? I tripped over—wait, is this the forest I'm supposed to be in?" she wondered, taking her shoes off and tipping the water out of them. "I've forgotten . . . where . . . I was going. . . ."

She put her shoes back on and looked around. The stream seemed wet so she went the opposite way. The grasses she trod on were sweet and the pine woods she entered also smelled lovely. A bread-and-butterfly flapped languorously by, proboscis out, looking for weak tea.

"Do *you* know where I was going or who I am?" she asked, half addressing the insect. She was not the least bit worried, only a little perplexed. "I'm fairly certain I'm a girl—from my dress, I mean. And, well, I just *feel* like a girl. Oh, but wait! What if I am a lizard or a satyr going to a fancy-dress party? How frightening that would be to discover—only because I can't remember my life at all. . . ." She spread one hand before her and felt her head and face with the other. "No, smooth and lovely. No scales. No horns. Wouldn't that be a horror, to have forgotten who I was and then found out I was someone else entirely."

She ducked under the bread-and-butterfly and skipped a little. "Well, I suppose that now I can be anyone I want, since I am no one at all. I can *do* anything I want as well. And no one shall be able to chastise me later: How *dare* you do this or that; don't you know who you are? And I shall say: But I *don't* know who I am. So it's hardly fair.

"I wonder what I always wanted to do that I couldn't do before, before I forgot everything. Fly? Could I fly now, I wonder? Or grow a moustache?

"If I *am* no one now, that means I could *be* anyone. Perhaps I get to choose. Let's see: I could be queen, I suppose. But I think despite all the parties and parades, it would mostly be boring and stodgy and I would have no time for myself.

"I could be married with a sweet little husband and some enormous strapping children in a cottage with a garden and painted eaves. That would be lovely, if a bit dull. Perhaps someday.

"I suppose what I would *truly* like to be most of all is myself, whoever that is, and have all sorts of adventures in wonderful fairylands when I wanted. But not *all* the time. I would need days to think about them and tell my stories to friends and strengthen up for the next adventure—oh!"

She had been really enjoying herself and this flight of fancy when she nearly stumbled over another inhabitant of the otherwise empty forest. He was a lazy-looking, thin fellow stretched out at the base of the tree. But he must have been someone a bit fancy, for he wore a lovely sharp hat with long feathers and a beautiful bloodred velvet tunic over black breeches. There were crumbs on his lips and what looked like a hint of raspberry jam—or blood—on his cheek.

"I beg your pardon. How do you do?" she said politely.

"Haven't the slightest," the man said with a smile. She was struck by the light in his eye and the ironic yet plaintive expression on his face. "I can't seem to remember either *how* I do or *what* I do at the moment."

"I can't, either. Did you have a pie?" Alice asked interestedly, pointing at his face.

"A tart, actually. Raspberry," the man said with relish. He still wasn't getting up, which was a trifle rude. "I found several of them with me when I ran in here. I would offer you one, but I ate them all."

"Oh, how gluttonous!"

"I suppose," he said with a casual shrug. "There was no one else here at the time. If *you* had been here, I would have shared, of course. They were quite tasty."

He leapt up rather suddenly springily—on account of his pasteboard thinness, Alice supposed. Crumbs fell out of the rich fabric on his lap and he brushed off the remainder with artistically graceful and narrow fingers. His fine feather bobbed and swayed with a life of its own, matching the arch of his insouciant eyebrows.

She found herself quite taken for a moment.

He wasn't at all like—

—like—

"Mr. Nobody of Nowhere," he said grandly with an intricate bow wherein he touched his middle with one hand and threw out the other behind him and then immediately somehow took *her* hand and brought it *almost* to his lips, but not quite. "At your service."

"Miss Nothing of Neverbeen," Alice answered with a smile and a curtsy. "Shall we walk on together?"

"*Nothing* would give me greater pleasure," he said without a wink, and she found herself laughing.

She took his proffered arm and they strolled down a

little path, tan and dusty between the pine needles. Everything was delightful. She wasn't even concerned about her inability to remember anything. It was like . . . a holiday for her brain. She did wonder vaguely what was happening in her life that meant her brain required a vacation. She looked down at her clothes and skirts again to see if they would reveal her occupation, but couldn't come to any conclusions. They were cleanish and well sewn and mostly comfortable, though a little restricting.

"Just being by your side is utterly pleasant," the man next to her said eventually. "I'm sorry to not be making conversation, but I seem to know and remember Nothing—and Nothing is more pleasant than you in my sight. So there isn't much to say, is there?"

"'Lovely weather,'" she remarked wryly. She gave his arm a squeeze. It was fine and hard. "This is quite all right. Let us do just . . . *be*."

Too soon, or after many hours, or somewhere in between, the trees came to a sudden halt as if ordered by a mean sergeant. A narrow stream ran by at the trees' edge that was inhabited by chunky golden fish who stayed solidly on the bottom, waddling only a little hither and thither on their fins with great effort. On the other bank, sitting with their backs toward the strolling couple, was an odd collection of creatures warming themselves in the sun. They made black silhouettes free of fine detail—which only accentuated their strange shapes: tall heads, long beaks, too many legs.

"Wait—" she said vaguely as the gentleman made to cross the stream.

"Whatever is the matter?" he asked, concerned.

Alice frowned, trying to think. "I feel as though once we pass over, everything will change."

"Change isn't always a bad thing," he said, patting her arm for comfort. "There's no adventure without change. And no buying sweets, either. Have you ever tried to buy a lolly with a thousand-pound note? Disastrous."

"I suppose—" Alice said tentatively. His point made cents, although it didn't seem to apply specifically to *this* situation. Clutching his arm, she made a wide step over the water. . . .

"I'm Alice!" she cried. "Always and forever Alice!"

For some reason the thought cheered her immensely. She was a young woman from Angleland with nice hair from a nice household who had a lovely camera and aunt and boring sister and everything was generally good. "And I *do* have a lovely home to return home to, and Wonderland adventures! Isn't that just perfect!" she cried.

Her gentleman friend had a similarly joyous reaction: he leapt over the stream with as much grace and skill as

Jack o'er the candlestick and landed with triumph on the other side.

"Well, what do you know!" he cried, laughing. "I'm a knave! How fortuitous!"

The shadowy figures on the berm beyond had heard the shouts and leapt up. Alice ran forward to meet them.

"No! No more this way, no further," the Hatter implored. "One or two brooks is fine, but then you cross another or another, and then after the eighth one you're no longer our little Alice, you're a queen. . . ."

"I think I'd make a rather good queen," Alice said, her desire to gather her friends in a great reunion hug tempered by his words.

As her memories came back, they took a faster route than normal, as when one is trying to push through a crossword puzzle and can't remember the right word. Empty Alice became full Alice in less than a minute; she saw, through new eyes, her nearly adult height and all the changes and growth she had gone through in the last eleven years. All the subtle things that made her who she was today—which her Wonderland friends couldn't see. Subtle wasn't a function of Wonderland.

"But not yet," the Hatter begged.

"Alice! Step away from that man!" the Gryphon cried, hissing at the pretty fellow who ate tarts, and grabbing her with his talons. He could have done with a good trimming, Alice thought peevishly as they pinched her skin through her dress.

"Oh, alarm clocks and bearbells!" the Dodo said, shaking his head. "Alice, do you not know who you're standing with?"

"Knave of Hearts, at your service," her companion said with a bow, this time doffing his beautiful hat and winking at her.

"He's a shill for the Queen!" the Hatter whispered far too loudly to do any good. "He'll report us all!"

"Oh, I don't think so, not anymore," the Knave said with a sigh, dramatically brushing more crumbs off his waistcoat. "I'm on her wanted list now. I stole all her tarts, the ones she was saving for tea."

The Hatter raised an eyebrow skeptically. "*You* stole the *Queen's* tarts? But why? You were her favorite, her second-in-command."

The Knave shrugged. "They were delicious."

"And she made them herself, didn't she?" Alice said, remembering the rhyme:

*The Queen of Hearts, she made some tarts*
*All on a summer's day*
*The Knave of Hearts, he stole the tarts*
*And took them right away.*

"Fancy her having time to make tarts with all her wars and killing and executions," the Dodo said, tsking. "But no wonder you ran away. She would have your head on a pike, she would."

"No—the King would beat him," Alice said. "That is all, and he would return them. According to the rhyme, anyhow."

"Alice, the King has been dead or imprisoned or otherwise out of commission for over a fortnight. . . . Have you not been paying attention?" the Hatter asked, exasperated.

"Well, I can't very well return the tarts anyway, now can I?" the Knave said with a sigh. "The Dodo's right—the Queen would have my head and then decorate her ramparts with it. Silly of me to run into the Forest of Forgetting. I forgot and ate them."

"You could have at least saved one," Alice said, vexed. "I could use a tart to see if I could grow again."

"Oh! And how do you feel, little Alice?" the Hatter asked, dancing. "Fresh and new? Ready to start all over again? Are you unremembered now? Can you shrink and grow as the moment requires?"

"Please don't call me little. At least not until I shrink. You and I are about the same size," Alice pointed out. "And I am full-gr—ah, an adult now. Just like you. I am not your little *anything*."

"Bah, sounds like she still knows her maths and all," the Dodo said. "Failure!"

"Well, we shan't know until we find a treat of some sort. And anyway, one might just as well assume that life experiences and knowledge gained over the last eleven years have taught me to grow or shrink even better than I did before."

"And yet grow and shrink you don't," the Hatter pointed out. "Q.E.D."

"This is all a waste. We may as well go on to M—" the Gryphon started to say, but the Hatter took off his hat and hit him.

"Where are you off to?" the Knave asked, catching on immediately that there was a secret.

"None of your business, Queensman," the Dodo said haughtily.

"I told you, I'm no good to her now," the Knave said, hands out and open in supplication. "I'm a dead card walking if I show up anywhere near the castle. So you might as well take me with you. Perhaps I can even help, if you're—you know, planning something."

"Are you good with a sword?" the Hatter asked.

"Or a bootlace?" the Dodo added.

"Both, and both would be dedicated to—the cause," the Knave said with a bow. "Or at least to your lady here."

"All right, but you'll have to carry Bill, then," the Dodo said, putting his wing out so the little capped lizard could scramble over and up the fancy card's sleeve. The Knave's painted face seemed to blur for a moment into a look of disgust but soon smoothed out. Alice couldn't fault him that. She wasn't sure she would particularly want a strange lizard suddenly so close, crawling on her skin.

"Maybe after we had been properly introduced and chatted a bit it would be all right," she said to herself.

The group set off in a direction that was argued about several times before everyone managed to agree on it. The air seemed sunsetty—the sun, however, was feeling tardy and hung in the sky high away from bedtime. The moon sulked on the eastern horizon and turned away from its sibling, who always seemed to hog the attention.

In that light, the grassy plain quickly became a cozy landscape of tangled scrub bushes, old apple trees, and an abandoned hazel copse whose woody residents preferred to grow their new shoots in spirals like a little girl's hair gone wild and unruly—very hard to pick around. The mirror-birds loved them for roosting, however, and Alice couldn't help stopping now and then to see how she looked just for the novelty of the types of frames they sported. Some of the reflections even changed her hair and lip and skin color! Her friends hurried on ahead, chatting amongst themselves and listening a little too raptly to stories of the royal court in its current deadly phase, as told by the Knave.

Alice lingered at one particular mirrorbird whose reflective face gave her image freckles. The fashion in Angleland was of course to try to minimize tanning and other effects of the sun, at least for young women of breeding, by use of either powder or sun hats. But she rather liked the healthy, friendly look they gave to her otherwise clear face.

"I see Alice has *spotted* herself," said a musing voice from behind her. Since Alice knew who it was, she didn't turn around immediately, preferring to give herself one last nose wrinkle to see how witchy she looked with the freckles.

The Cheshire Cat was of course lolling on a spiral branch behind her, like a series of circles himself: upon the circular branch, his head and his body wrapped around and around, and his eyes seemed to bounce a little in his face as if to emphasize the conceit.

"How very original of you," Alice said dryly. "But I still like cats, however jejune they appear—fortunately for *you*. Kittens as well as mangy old striped things." She scratched him under the chin to soften the words.

"Mmm . . ." The cat rolled his body and thumped his feet, obviously enjoying it. But his head stayed in the exact same position, of course: impossible.

"Why don't you come with us, instead of just popping up now and then?" Alice suggested. "I really would like your company, and I think you might help the Hatter regain a bit of his Nonsense. You could sit on my shoulders, if you like, or I could carry you."

"Oooh, and be petted the whole time by the Great and Powerful Alice," the Cheshire said saucily. He twisted so she could get to his belly better, but his head popped off for a moment to give her a wink. "At least until we get to Mary Ann."

Alice stopped petting him and glared.

"All right, all right, I'll bow quietly out when she takes over you lot. I'm not a leader, or trained in the ways of rebellions or civil disobedience. I don't have much to add to your side. But I will still take comfort in seeing the Queen of Hearts dethroned and punished for her actions so everyone can return to their normal—ah, absurd—and safe Wonderland lives. So come with us, rather than making jokes, and help!"

The Cheshire Cat gave her an inscrutable look. Then he feigned fatigue.

"I *am* helping. . . . You don't know how hard it is to keep a straight thought in a place like this." His body suddenly became a series of sharp angles and squares, from rectangular ears down to his long looping tail that was now a spiral of not-quite-ninety-degree turns. He stood out in orange-and-purple starkness against the coiling organic growth of the trees behind him.

"Time is running out on you. He didn't even pay his portion of the bill."

Now he stood and made a triangle with his paws above his head; his head then began to drain into his body like sand in an hourglass. "Beware what churches and suits and jails all have in common."

"Is that another riddle?" Alice demanded. "Is it—oh, he's gone."

Of course the cat faded out of view, eyes last, which rolled up into the now invisible head. Then they bounced and rolled through the spiral branches like tiny croquet balls.

"Bother! How people *still* come and go in this place!" She allowed herself exactly one *humph* and stamped her foot exactly one time like the seven-year-old she once had been, and then ran after her friends. They were chattering nonsense at each other, not having even noticed she was gone. The cat's puzzle reminded her of another one from Wonderland, long ago.

"Hatter! Hatter! Do you remember your old riddle? The one you told me the last time I was here?"

"I don't own any riddles," he responded, pulling out his pockets to show how empty they were. Needles and pins fell out. They scurried to the side of the path to not be trod on. "I borrowed one once—but I doubt the March Hare will ever be able to collect on it now."

Alice took a deep breath.

"Why is a raven like a writing desk?" she prompted.

"I don't know, why?" he asked gamely.

"No—you asked *me* that, last time. I never figured out the answer myself. But I asked everyone when I woke up—er, came back to Angleland, and even read a great many books on puzzles and riddles to try and solve it. So now I have several answers. So tell me which one is right!"

She began counting on her fingers.

"One: because they both have quills dipped in ink."

Her audience just looked at her gravely.

Alice hurried on to the next.

"Two: the American author, Mr. Edgar Allan Poe, wrote on both."

The Dodo and the Gryphon looked at each other and shrugged helplessly.

"And three—my friend Charles came up with this—because each can produce a few notes, tho' they are very flat!"

She sat back on her heels, much pleased with herself, and waited for a reaction.

The Hatter took her gently by the hand. "Ah—it doesn't *have* an answer, my dear girl. That is the point of a riddle."

"That is *not* the point of a riddle!" Alice almost shrieked.

*"I think the heat has gotten to her,"* the Dodo whispered badly to the Gryphon.

"But I just gave you *three* answers!"

"Well, you had better take them back, they would best be used elsewhere. Here, there they are," the Hatter said graciously.

Alice regarded them all silently for a long moment. "I'm remembering this from last time," she finally said. "*Nothing* gives satisfaction in Wonderland. You always think you say the right thing, do the right thing, figure the deuced thing out—and you're always wrong. *Always!* The key is too far away. You're too short. The rules of etiquette are all skewed. The rules of *croquet* are insane. It's like the most beautiful and yet worst sort of dream where everything is upside down consistently and *could* be beautiful and perfect but instead just drives one to fits!"

*"Definitely the heat,"* the Gryphon whispered back.

"Well, what is it like in *your* world?" the Dodo asked politely.

"In Angleland, if you learn the rules, and follow them correctly, you generally get where you want to go or receive what you want to have."

"Seems boring," said the Dodo.

"Seems easy," piped up Bill.

"No matter who you are? No matter what your height is?" the Hatter asked curiously.

"It doesn't at all matter what you look like, or . . ." Alice paused, thinking about the children of the Square. "Well, perhaps it is a little easier if you're Anglish. Born in Angleland."

"And what if you don't have the luck of that?" the Hatter asked. "Can you change it?"

"Where you were born? Of course not!"

"Seems a bit arbitrary to me," the Hatter said. "Sounds *harder* than here, where you merely have to run twice as fast to get anywhere. At least you can choose how you run."

Alice rubbed her temples. He wasn't wrong. For a brief moment she had a vicious wish that all her Wonderland friends could spend a week in London, figuring out the trains and how to get a cup of tea they had to pay for, talking to alley cats and dormice who didn't speak back.

"Well, anyway, forget *my* riddle. Perhaps you can help me out with a new one."

("I thought she said it was the Hatter's riddle," the Dormouse whispered to Bill. The two tiny things nodded knowingly at each other.)

"We're already out, and there's no place to go *in*," the Gryphon said testily. "Speak plainly, girl."

"Call me *girl* again and I'll have you on a leash before you can say *bandersnatch*," Alice snapped. The Gryphon's eyes widened and he shrank back behind the Dodo. That was the other thing she remembered about Wonderland;

the random, abject cruelty that was constantly threatened. Well, when in Rome . . . "What do churches and suits and jails all have in common?"

"Oh, that's a good one! I don't know! What *do* churches and suits and jails all have in common?" the Dodo asked eagerly.

"I—don't—know," Alice said through gritted teeth. "I was told this riddle but not its solution, and it might be important to our mission."

"That's a trifle rude," the Knave spoke up. "Demanding the answer to a riddle you have no answer for."

"Try out one of the other answers that you kept," the Hatter suggested eagerly. "Poe wrote on both, perhaps?"

"It doesn't . . ." Alice began. "Besides, there are three things there, not 'both.' "

"Does a church produce notes?" the Gryphon asked the Dodo.

"If its bell tolls, or it's Lutheran," the Dodo said sagely.

"All of 'em have quills dipped in ink?" Bill joined in enthusiastically.

"Oh, forget it!" Alice cried. "I'll work it out myself. You're no help at all with your nonsense. Let's just keep going to Mary Ann."

The Knave's eyes widened when she said that, but he said nothing.

# Chapter Eleven

The denouement to their search was dreary and disappointing. Even in ancient Greek plays, the deus ex machina was a fellow let down in a basket draped in flowers and cloth of gold or whatever so that everyone could tell a god had come to save the hero at the last minute. It was ridiculous but glamorous and made good theater.

But our traveling heroes had merely made their way to an even less Wonderlandy place than usual: a scrubby edge of nothing. There were dead leaves and duff, unraked, in ugly drifts. The sharp-edged green grass that thrived here was interspersed with many dead yellow companions. The bushes and hazel had small leaves, smaller than they should have, and looked generally unkempt. The whole place resembled an abandoned park in a bad part of town.

*That's* what it was, Alice realized; the place looked *real-world* unkempt. Not "mysterious etching of a romantic moor" wild or "carefully contrived, abandoned and folly-filled gardens of the wealthy" wild. *Bad* wild. Ungoverned, and possibly with bears.

"There it is!" the Hatter cried. Then he looked around, alarmed. "There it is," he whispered.

Alice finally saw it, too: a worn and weathered sign whose bright colors had faded to the dim shades of the vegetation around it, saying: GRUNDEROUND THIS WAY. It pointed to a plain hole in the dirt whose edges had grown smooth and hard with roots over time. It was not unlike the rabbit hole Alice had first fallen down, except that it was even smaller.

"Oh, what are we to do?" the Dodo moaned.

"We could dig it out," the Gryphon suggested, holding up his claws.

"You know the defenses are prepared for that," the Hatter said accusingly.

"What defenses?" the Knave asked casually.

The other three gave him silent, frosty looks.

"Let the little ones go first. Bill and the Dormouse," Alice suggested. "Perhaps they can tell those below to let us in—somehow. Or at least see the lay of the land."

The Hatter shrugged and lifted off his hat. The Dormouse, who had been sleeping on its brim, tumbled down the Hatter's arm and neatly rolled like a billiard ball into the hole without so much as a peep. Alice wondered if the fall had even woken the poor thing up. Then the Knave plucked Bill off his chest like an oversized military medal and dropped him, rather quickly and perfunctorily, into the hole after the Dormouse. He too tumbled, feet over feet, but at the last second whipped his tail and landed, clinging to the side of the entrance. Despite his sleepy and anthropomorphic expression (and cap), he scuttled off *most* lizardlike into the darkness.

"Well, here's a fine mess. And you not even able to shrink," the Hatter said, then crossed his arms and sat down in a huff.

"And what about *you*?" Alice demanded, pursing her lips. "How were you, the Dodo, and the Gryphon supposed to be able to get down?"

"Oh, we're not important, you know that," the Hatter said grumpily, waving a hand at her like a ninety-year-old granny.

"So this is the hideout of the infamous Mary Ann," the Knave said with a sniff of distaste, kicking some sand into the hole. He took out a tiny flacon, unscrewed its tiny gold cap, and prepared to take a swig. "No wonder the rebels are losing. To the Queen!—Er, Queen's defeat, that is," and he made to drink it down.

"No! Give it to me!" Alice cried, forgetting herself and

all her good manners ("Ironic, that," she observed; she had been out of the Forest of Forgetting for a while now). She grabbed the bottle from the Knave's hand and without a word of apology or excuse tossed the entire contents back. It burned in a cardamomy, cinnamony, peony sort of way.

"Surely this will do something," she thought. "It *feels* strong!"

"I say," the Knave said, a little dismayed that his quaff had been quorffed.

Only the Dodo and the Gryphon looked hopeful. The Hatter just turned away and rolled his eyes, grumbling.

Alice stood, arms out, legs spread, body parts removed from other body parts, fingers and toes splayed and nothing touching itself, waiting for the magic to come.

Nothing happened.

"You see?" the Hatter said sourly. "You're too grown. You . . ."

"Oh, shut *up* already," Alice snapped. "Do you know, I'm really *growing* weary of your constant comments about me and my physical relation to Wonderland. Why should *I* grow and shrink, anyway? Why should *I* remember or forget according to what you think will work? 'Get small to fit in the tiny door, Alice.' 'Get big to get the key, Alice.' Get too big and scare the birds. Shrink, and the birds and mice walk all over you. I'm tired of being something else for everyone else.

"It's long past time Wonderland started changing for *me*."

And, not quite sure she knew what she was doing but full of red and rage, Alice marched over to the hole and pulled it open.

It was a bit tricky and didn't budge at first, like a cold piece of leather, but after a tug or two and an unladylike groan she managed to stretch the hole several feet across—quite large enough for herself, the Knave, the large-headed Hatter, the hexaped Gryphon, and the portly Dodo.

Everyone blinked in surprise.

Alice recovered herself quickly and tried not to look surprised, too.

*She did it.* How had she known she would do it? *Had* she known? It was and yet wasn't like a dream where you realize you have to do something and somehow it works. In dreams everything was fuzzy with no clear beginnings or embarrassing ends; here she could have failed spectacularly and just wound up clutching dry dirt.

She had just trusted in herself, and Wonderland, and . . . it worked.

"Remember that," she marveled to herself. "Trust in yourself and Wonderland."

The Hatter whooped in delight, taking off his hat and whacking the Dodo with it. "She did it! Alice did it!"

"Alice always does," the Dodo said proudly, like she was his daughter.

"But never in the way you expect," the Gryphon added, also like she was his daughter.

Alice rolled her eyes at them. "All right, I'm first. Here we go—"

And she leapt into the darkness and unknown, for that was what Alice always did.

But she did not land in an abandoned hallway with a charming door leading to an even more charming garden. Nor was it a forest, nor a castle, nor an oversized banquet, nor a bucket on a sea of tears.

It was like nothing Alice had ever experienced before.

It was *loud.* Dozens, perhaps a hundred or two hundred different voices muttering and cursing and wailing and soothing and talking and sighing with the occasional strident laugh. Creatures of all stature and make sat, stood, padded, milled, or lay on benches in—well, in some sort of building. Something large and cavernous with a vaulted roof. From the smell—hoppy—and the size of the place—infinite-seeming with shadowed corners—Alice thought it might be a tavern, or perhaps a Viking longhouse, or something she had no name for in which people of all ages gathered but that wasn't a church and stank a bit.

"Wounded in the bedrooms, please," a long-necked duck told her tiredly. His hat was beaten about the brim and his bright yellow neckerchief was spotted with blood. He held a clipboard and what Alice couldn't help noticing was a quill pen—but black. Dipped in ink. Someone else's feather.

"A raven's, perhaps," she mused.

But before she could focus her thoughts on what was actually going on, the Hatter hit her squarely in the head in his tumble from the skylight (which was dark, of course, and opened onto absolutely nothing at all). She fell aside and managed to just avoid being landed on again, by the Dodo this time. The Gryphon spread his elegant wings and coasted to the top of what looked very much like a bar.

"Dear me, this place has changed a bit," the Hatter said, swallowing.

"Don't tell me you frequented this notorious joint," the Dodo said with a wink and an elbow in the ribs.

"When I was younger, and a little less Mad," the Hatter said with dignity, pulling out his cuffs and straightening himself. "But there were more refreshments then. And fewer . . . wounded . . ."

The duck had decided that the newcomers were fine and wandered off, checking in on other recent arrivals.

"But who are all these people?" Alice asked as what

looked like an overgrown hedgehog and three baby brushes woefully waddled past her. The mother—Alice assumed—clutched a pathetically small bag of possessions and had a bandage around one broken arm, which didn't really work because of her spines tearing up the wool.

"People with nowhere else to go," the Hatter answered with a shake of his head. "I thought the Grunderound had just become a place for conspirators to meet, for the resistance to convene, but it looks like word has gotten out. These are all refugees from the Queen of Hearts' War."

"My *doll*! They took my *doll*!" one of the baby brushes cried.

Alice frowned.

*Hands she has but does not hold. . . .*

Nothing in Wonderland was a coincidence. Especially not with the Cheshire Cat helping her.

"*Who* took your doll?" she asked as gently as she could, kneeling down to look her in the bristles.

"The soldiers, of course," the mother snapped, pulling her child back protectively. "They took Earnest's cup and ball, too! Ruffians! Thugs!"

"But you still have your bag . . . and a necklace . . ." Alice said, confused. "Why would they bother with toys and let you keep your valuables?"

"Who knows? But their father is missing and we have

no home. Doll's the least of our problems now," the mother said, trying very hard not to cry by frowning and marching away.

"Odd," the Hatter said, which for him was also odd.

"Let's find Mary Ann," Alice said, swallowing as she saw a—well, hard to say what it was. Something long and furry and bound entirely from head to hoof in one long bandage. Its blue mouth let out a groan as a pair of pigs tried to carry it gently over to a bench. "Perhaps she can clear up this mystery for us."

"They would be in the back room, in the hidden casino," the Hatter said, pointing. "Behind the false cabinet."

How he knew that was more than Alice wanted to consider at the moment. She pushed her way through the crowd and around to the back of the bar, someplace she never in a thousand years imagined she would ever find herself—either in the real world or Wonderland. There was a point in her childhood when she assumed that the men and women who stood behind bars in pubs had no legs at all but were merely puppets who moved back and forth behind their wooden stage as they magically produced glasses and froth.

She squeezed herself along the large set of wooden shelves that at one time must have been full of bottles of whatever passed for imbibables in Wonderland. There were a few tiny brown jars of bitters and cordials that remained, dusty, on a lower shelf; these Alice hastily grabbed and stuffed into her sleeve. DRINK ME said one, VIOLETS said the second, HOURS said the third.

She tried pulling the cabinet away from the wall as if she were opening a normal, if oddly shaped, door. It didn't budge.

"Not another Wonderland puzzle," Alice moaned.

"*Slide* it, you silly girl!" the Hatter said impatiently. "Have you never been in a secret room before?"

Alice pushed, and the whole thing simply slid away from her with very little effort. She allowed herself exactly one Wondersecond of chagrin. A cold, dank wind blew from the slim rectangular opening as if it were trying to escape whatever was within. Reluctantly she stepped in, taking the Dodo's wing and Hatter's hand and pulling them behind her.

(The Gryphon stayed behind. When she last looked, he had been allowing a sick person to be loaded onto his soft, furry back to be better examined by a doctor magpie.)

The room they entered looked just like Alice would have imagined the hidden base of a secret rebel cause: cold and dark but for one candle on a crate being used as a table. Filling the darkness was the smell of stale sweat and exhaustion, sour at one end of the scent spectrum and earthy and moldy at the other. Four bone-weary creatures huddled on sacks of supplies: a large muskrat, a man all dressed in newspaper, a ruby-eyed white bird, and a—

"Caterpillar!" Alice cried.

He was not as the Caterpillar should have been. The arrogant, plump morsel only too perfect for a bird to snap up was now skinny in the wrong places and flabby in the others, as if a caterpillar without the right things to eat or think shrank into itself like a sponge. There were deep bags under his eyes.

Alice wondered for one wild moment whether, if she gave him a big juicy leaf or glass of lemonade, he would puff back up again into his former glory.

At least his bearing was the same: he turned a desultory head toward her and regarded the girl with exhausted, world-weary eyes.

"Of course it's you," he drawled. "*Who* are you?"

"I'll tell you who she's *not*," the muskrat snapped, voice rasping and almost cutting out entirely. "She's *not* . . ." But the Caterpillar surprisingly and deftly clapped a stubby foot over his mouth.

The white bird began to flutter and coo. It shook its wings and head, and feathers flew out from under its arms.

"Where is Mary Ann?" the Hatter asked, looking around as if he expected her to leap out and shout *Surprise!* from behind a barrel or shadow. "We've come to join her and you. I believe Alice—that is her name, you know. *Most* girl children have them. Names, I mean, not Alices. She was summoned here by Mary Ann specifically to help us against the tyrant."

"None of us knows what you're talking about," the muskrat muttered, looking away.

"Oh, for heaven's sake!" Alice cried. "You're in a *hidden* room in a *hidden* place called the Grunderound. You're tending to the wounded and frightened out there, and in here you're plotting your next move against the Queen of Hearts. Mary Ann came to me—she *called* me here to help. And so did you, Caterpillar! So please, produce her at once!"

"Produce her," the bird cackled hysterically. "Turn her into produce. Yes, yes. A pumpkin or an egg. That would be much, much improved. Compost."

"Well, that's very rude!" Alice said. "To say that about your leader."

"No—you don't understand. We're just no good without her. We're lost," the man in paper said sadly, watching the bird. "Her words were worth a thousand pounds a letter."

"Yes, I can see that," Alice said, taking a deep breath and trying to remain patient. "Where. Is. She?"

The bird cackled again. "Where is one when not

in Wonderland? When the other's won and you're Undone?"

"I don't . . ." Alice began, but she began to suspect.

The man in paper looked at her with gentle, doleful eyes.

"Mary Ann is dead."

# Chapter Twelve

*"What?"* Alice gasped. "No! In the picture, when I saw her . . ."

Well, if truth be told, and Alice tended to tell the truth, at least to herself, the girl did not look well in the photograph. She seemed to be incarcerated. There was blood and a blindfold. But she had been alive.

"Where was that?" the muskrat demanded.

"Don't you mean *when*?" Alice asked shakily. "How long ago it was?"

"Time is meaningless, unless he's offering to pay, you know that," the Hatter said, but the words were thin and scratchy, and his heart wasn't in it.

"She was being held against her will somewhere. But I thought she had escaped!"

Alice wrung her hands and twisted her lips to avoid tears. Why was she so distraught? She had never met Mary Ann. Not even during her first time in Wonderland. Mary Ann had always seemed like a figment, a ghost just out of reach, a white rabbit. Now she was beyond Alice's grasp forever.

She hadn't felt anything when the other girl had died, had she? Some sort of tremor, or echo of feeling? If each resident here had a counterpart in Angleland, surely there was some connection she would have severed when she passed away? A phantom pain in Alice's own neck?

For surely—

*Off with her head—*

"The Queen of Hearts," Alice murmured. "She did it, didn't she? She found and executed Mary Ann."

"Less execute and more *murder.* Less capitalism and more capital *punishment*," the Caterpillar said sourly.

The Dodo sat down suddenly next to Alice, collapsed, like a human boy rather than a bird, feet splayed out and a dumbfounded look on his face.

"She didn't come back here—she didn't want to draw the Queen's attention here, to have her find out about us and the refugees. We had hoped she made it to the Unlikely, but she didn't," the muskrat said woefully.

"Mary Ann *always* gets away," the white bird trilled. "She always gets away with it somehow."

"I guess her luck ran out with the postman," the man in paper said sadly.

Everyone was silent. This had been Alice's one lead, her one goal, and it was gone.

She voiced the thing everyone was thinking.

"What are we to do now?"

"Why, you're to take over the resistance and lead us to victory in her place, of course," the Hatter cried. Then he scrunched up his face in pain and pulled his giant hat down over it. "Oooh, it hurts to make sense!"

"I haven't an ounce of tactical or military knowledge!" Alice cried. "You would be foolish to put your and everyone else's fate in my hands! Apparently I can open holes—that's my singular talent here now. I can't—"

"Hush!" the muskrat hissed.

"I shall not!" Alice cried. "*Listen* for once! You need a leader with experience. Wonderland always puts one in the most ridiculous positions—judging caucus races, choosing between identical brothers . . . But this time it is deadly serious! I have just learned that a poor innocent girl has died, and now you have me taking up arms like a centurion! I was to take you to Mary Ann, not *take her place*."

"But Mary Ann thought you could do it," the Dodo said softly. "She brought you here."

"No, *hush*; do you hear that?" the muskrat repeated, cocking his head.

Everyone immediately grew quiet, but to Alice's ears there was nothing but the rise and fall of the chaos outside.

"Hatter, Dodo, let us find the Gryphon and Bill and the Dormouse at once," she said after a moment, trying to bring some semblance of order to her thoughts. "And the Knave. Sadly, you are the closest thing I have to an advisory council. Somehow I must make sense of all this."

She made herself stand up and went back through the secret door, desperate to get out of the dank and suffocating room full of sad people.

For, despite her protests, Alice was already moving past the sad revelation of Mary Ann's death. Her arguing with the Hatter was merely an instinctive reaction. She had promised to take them to Mary Ann, and she had done her best. Now there was another job to do. She had no idea *what* to do or *how* to do it, only that she must. It was inevitable and solid as a boring granite statue of some bewigged leader of yesteryear at a park. In the same way that as a child she had just *done*, she would just *do* now. Maybe it would work out. The deceased Mary Ann had apparently put all her hope in Alice. What other choice was there?

The question was, what *could* she do? She wasn't a native of Wonderland, well versed in its rules and laws and shifting geography. She had no great military knowledge, having ignored all her sister's boring lessons when she was a child (fancy that actually coming back to haunt her!). She had never actually been engaged in any sort of job or organized anyone else to do anything.

Then again, the poor Wonderland creatures couldn't get themselves together even when actively trying to help one another. Back in the secret room, the leaders of the rebellion were just sitting around grieving and waiting for another Mary Ann to come along and save them. And outside, in the temporary hospital ward . . .

Alice watched as a mole ran around with a nice sterile bit of moleskin in his paw, shouting "I've got it I've got it!" and, like the answering call of a mated duck (a midwife duck, in fact), came a quack back, "I need it I need it! Where is the moleskin?"

Who else, in the end, *could* save them?

Only Alice.

"There's the Gryphon," she said, spotting the creature, who was kindly giving a few lost tots a ride on his back to cheer them up. "I don't know how we'll ever find the others, they're so tiny. *BILL! DORMOUSE!*" she shouted, hands cupped around her mouth.

"Have you seen a lizard, about yea high?" the Hatter asked an owlet. He still had his hat down over his face but was somehow making the correctly sized motions with his hands.

“A small Dormouse, probably asleep in something,” the Dodo explained to a goose-necked lamp-goose.

“And the Knave, let us grab him, too.” Alice looked around, surprised when she couldn’t see him. Surely he would have stood out in his immaculate red velvet doublet and hat. Actually, he would be the only person in here at all with a fancy matching suit.

*Matching suit.*

“A knave in a matching suit,” she said to herself. “Why does that ring a bell?”

But it was hard to focus on the beginnings of what seemed to be a fairly important thought: a low vibration began to thrum across the Grunderound, irritating and disruptive.

*Ba-Boom. Boom. Boom.*

It wouldn’t stop, working its way into Alice’s bones in a very upsetting way, along with the thought she couldn’t quite complete.

“Hatter,” she said slowly.

*Boom.* The vibrations grew louder, like a giant was striking the earth with a mighty hammer.

*Boom.*

*Boom.*

“There he is,” the Hatter said, jumping up and down

and gesticulating at a chandelier onto which the Dormouse clung. The tiny creature was strangely awake and pointing desperately.

Alice turned to look. At the far end of the great hall was a vaulted ceiling and multi-paned rose window, which taken together made it all look like the apse of a church. The thin glass shuddered with the strange vibrations, bowing in and out with the force of the thumps.

"Funny," she said to herself, "if that really is the apse, then the tavern bar is the chancel! And the place I fell into is like the nave. . . .

"Oh," she said as it all came together in her head at once.

*Boom.*

*Boom.*

*Boom.*

Everything rattled; creatures were screaming.

*Matching suit.*

"Hatter!" She took his hand, which surprised him into stillness: he looked at it as if the whole idea were outrageous. "What do a church, a jail, and a suit all have in common?"

"Alice, this is hardly the time for riddles—"

"*Knaves*, Hatter! Knaves!"

The Hatter blinked.

"Churches have naves, jails hold knaves, every suit of

cards has a knave! He's gone! I don't know if he even came down with us!"

"*He went back to the Queen,*" the Hatter said, swallowing.

"Oh, the Cheshire *knew*! He tried to tell me . . ." Alice lamented. "We must leave this place immediately—I don't know what is going on, but it can't be a coincidence that he's gone and now this is happening. . . ."

"Quickly, out the back door," the Dodo said, nodding.

"We're in the *Grunderound*!" the Hatter cried. "There is no 'back door.'"

"Of course there is. This is Wonderland," Alice said fervently. "There's always a tree with a door or a hole in the floor or a door in a door. Come on. We'll find it and then—"

And then the booming stopped. So did everything else in the Grunderound: for one magical moment all the chaos was still, every eye and antenna frozen, every beak, muzzle, pair of lips, and snout open but quiet, everyone immobile, waiting.

And then the walls caved in.

"Just like a house of cards," Alice observed a little crazily. "Or a really cheap pasteboard house, or one of the paper balloons your uncle likes to fold out of a discarded magazine."

There were no real bricks behind the brick walls, no stone or log to hold them up—not even dirt, as one might expect underground.

The edges of the building folded down, thin and flimsy, and soldiers marched over the crumpled remains.

Not that the soldiers were much heartier than the Grunderound itself, but there were so many of them: tens, nines, eights, and aces, all in bloodred armor. They wielded short, ugly swords and viciously sharpened axes. Row upon row came over the ruins of the old tavern, crushing it into dust under their feet and flowing over the rubble in a relentless flood.

"Run!" Alice cried. "Everyone, run! *Run!*"

This time she stood her ground.

She had no idea how big she was compared to the cards; the sight of them was so terrifying she didn't even stop to see if she could put them in her pocket. Like mad ants, like nothing she had ever imagined, they filled every bit of free space and attacked every Wonderland creature in their path.

"No!" she shouted.

She flung her hands out in front of her, unable to think of anything else to do.

"*No!* It doesn't end this way! *NO—*"

# Chapter Thirteen

And then, of course, she woke up.

# Alice as She Is

# Chapter Fourteen

"Easy, steady on!" a voice was saying.

A voice that had a smile in it—but no matter how friendly it sounded, a voice that irked Alice entirely. Wrong tone, wrong time . . .

She continued to struggle and strike out with her hands, but her waking mind already knew the indisputable truth of where and when she was.

"No! You mustn't! I must go back!"

"Back where?" the young man asked with faint amusement.

Alice stopped her pugilistic feints and sat up. She was under a tree—the big spreading oak she had fallen asleep against so many years before, as apparently she had done now. The ground was hard and a little chilly, even through the golden cape she had put down. Katz had carefully laid his coat over her. It smelled faintly of an aftershave with warm and pleasing lower notes of moss. There was, an idle part of her mind noticed, a single piece of purple thread or hair stuck on the back.

In her hands were dead leaves, left over from last year perhaps, crunching like flimsy cards.

Katz was smiling down at her, a little confused but not concerned.

"You know, *back*," she snapped. "I have to go back to—to . . ."

But there she paused, feeling as lost as her body was. Already her latest adventures in Wonderland were dissipating, spun on a breeze back to wherever they came from, too fragile to remain long in this world. The urgency she felt had the urgency of any nightmare upon waking. Real—but not.

"I have to find a way back there," she said helplessly. "They need me. I've left them again."

"If you were anyone else I would ask if maybe you were overindulging in laudanum," Katz said, offering his hand to help her up.

"Not at all, I'm afraid." She sighed, taking his hand, and creakily rose. She wished she could tell him everything, even if it would be just like telling a dream. It might keep the memories in her head a little longer, and it would be nice to finally share the stories with someone.

"That would be a most convenient excuse," she said instead. "The laudanum, I mean. If a terrible revelation. Here is your coat back—I'm afraid I've rather crumbled some leaves on it."

"Oh no, leaves, heaven forfend," he said mildly, and the space under his arched and solid brown eyebrows made two little sunrises of skin; he was a man who could smile with every part of his face and not have to move his lips at all. He took the coat and threw it over his shoulder carelessly.

Alice busied herself with patting her dress down and carefully shaking out the cape and folding it back up while she flushed, trying not to look at him.

She had to figure out how to get back to her friends and save them—because they *were* in trouble, weren't they? It was all soft and blurring now. The Queen of Hearts was involved somehow. . . . She had to be defeated. . . . Right?

But Alice *also* had to get home before anyone had a fit because she had been gone so long. There was the sun finally yearning for the horizon, its rays stretching out to the west as if it couldn't wait to be there.

The two walked in silence for a while, for which she was supremely grateful. Katz seemed to sense she needed a little quiet time. He wasn't asking her questions and demanding the due diligence of a sexist etiquette that usually came with these sorts of situations: *There, I watched you and loaned you my coat, now you owe me conversation at least.* In some ways, being with him had the ease of being with a Wonderland resident. As a two-time and now experienced visitor, Alice realized that for all their frustrating mannerisms, at least one didn't need to feel indebted or obliged to follow the commandments of social customs there. It was like tea with a toddler: messy but without guilt or rules.

(Although, *un*like Wonderland folk, Katz was fully human and had lips the same color as his cheeks, only several shades darker.)

"What the—*what in blazes is going on here?*"

Alice looked around the park, expecting some sort of crime or other shenanigan being perpetrated. But there was nothing. Before them on the path was a governess and her two young charges who ran back and forth happily. Beyond them a hunched-over and ancient couple wandered up a hill hand in hand. The scene was as serene as it could be.

*Behind* them, however, was Mr. Coney—really, of all the bad luck!—striding quickly to catch up. Now he wore a moderately trendy milk chocolate suit with wide trousers, long jacket, and a crisp straw hat. This sat almost perfectly down on his voluminous, macassar-oiled hair; Alice wondered if he had to put it on while still styling his locks. If she didn't imagine how it smelled or felt, it came across as very stylish.

She heard the wisp of a sigh from Katz, but that was all: his smiling brown eyes crystallized into stoic blandness.

"Who are you? Is this man bothering you? Stop harassing this lady at once!" Coney ordered. "Leave her in peace."

The children playing up ahead giggled at his behavior. It was more than obvious that Katz and Alice were friendly and no one was bothering anyone.

Alice felt bad for everyone involved in or watching the situation, even Coney—but mostly she wished he would disappear. Down into a rabbit hole, perhaps.

"In peace?" she asked dryly. "From what?"

"I hadn't realized my appearance was so frightening. Unless you already knew I was a barrister," Katz said easily with a mocking little bow.

"Now that I see you up close, I realize I *do* know you. You're the one who is always engaging with all the street rats and rabble from Wellington Square," Coney said accusingly. "You visit with pretentions and airs of doing good—but really with *schemes* and *questionable motives*."

A shade of rose deeper than normal came and went over Katz's face like a single ripple across an otherwise still pond. It left nothing in its wake, disappearing entirely.

"No pretentions, good sir; I leave that to those who have time for leisure and stylish hats. The children of the Square and their families are often at the mercy of a system weighted against their favor—I should know. I just help even the odds a bit."

"Mr. Coney," Alice said as politely as she could. "How pleasant to see you again. Where are you off to?"

She hoped he understood the not so subtle hint. *Off to.* As in, away.

"I am in fact hurrying to a meeting specifically about saving our country from these—those—pestilential parasites," he replied with an impressive amount of hauteur. "Before they wind up staying here permanently, agitating to destroy England as they are trying in Russia. They have no patriotism, you know, even the so-called citizens who were born here. They have no loyalty to anything save each other and their—their—*golden coins*."

"Shekels, I think you mean to say," Katz offered politely.

"They are trying to unseat the tsar!"

"Are you *kidding* me?" the other man said, finally losing his composure. His face showed a mix of genuine disbelief and a terrible tiredness; for a moment the edges of his eyes made him look far older than his years. Somehow this distinct *lack* of rage and the intelligence behind it, sparkled in his eyes like a treasure, ancient and precious.

Alice felt her chest tighten. It hurt and felt wonderful at the same time.

"That story is just that—a *story*. It's anti-Semitic filth. My people have been suffering at the hands of the tsar and our fellow countrymen—not the other way around."

"Of course you would say that," Coney said, moving forward into Katz's space, glaring down at the slightly shorter man.

Katz gazed back at him impassively.

Alice wondered, perhaps for the first time—although certainly not the last—if all human conflicts were started by men who thought they were doing it for a woman.

"I'm not *entirely* certain why you're concerned with the fate of Russia's tsar," she said, interrupting what appeared to be a heavy-breathing match, "but I do think you're being rather unforgivably rude. Mr. Katz and I are friends, and we just happened to bump into each other in the park. Rather like you're just bumping into us, now. He was offering to walk mc home."

Katz blinked at this unexpected statement and smiled stupidly before recovering himself.

*"Indeed?"* Coney said on a long inhale. "Well, I shall relieve him of that duty. I was heading that way myself to meet with Corwin and then pick up your sister. We are all attending an organizational meeting for the Ramsbottom

fundraiser tomorrow night. I am in charge of the souvenir pins."

"Oh, of course you're supporting Gilbert Ramsbottom. That xenophobic troglodyte," Katz said, rolling his eyes. "I wonder whom you will get to scrub your floors and fetch your coal and wet-nurse your babies once he has kicked out everyone *not* named Harold or Arthur or William. I shall bid you good afternoon, then; have fun shaking your fasces at the rabble. Alice."

He gave her a quick bow and sauntered off into the late afternoon, whistling. She watched him go with wonder: somehow he had exited the scene without appearing to have lost the conversation.

*"Alice?"* Coney demanded. "He has the gall to call you by your Christian name?"

"Oh, do shut up," Alice said, at the last minute trying to put a droll spin on her words. If she had been a true Wonderlandian, of course, she wouldn't have bothered. "If you're going to walk me home, let us hurry, at least."

And she set off grimly to the park's exit.

She had hoped to shake the terrible young man loose before actually approaching the door of her house; if he was seen by one of her parents, or God forbid, her sister, he would no doubt be invited in, and then she would have to bear even more of his now-loathsome presence. She put what appeared to be a delicate hand on the brass doorknob and gripped it with a strength that rivaled a carnival strongman's.

"Thank you, Mr. Coney, good evening," she said, opening the door as narrowly as possible.

"Alice? Are you home? Who is that?" her mother called from the foyer.

"Is that your mother?" Coney asked.

"Not at all," Alice promptly lied. "Good evening, Mr. Coney."

She sidled her way around the edge of the door to the inside in the most unladylike, serpentine manner and slammed it behind her, leaning against it as if to keep all the Visigoths out.

"Unwanted suitor?" her mother asked kindly.

"Would you please tell my sister to keep out of my affairs? Forever?" Alice demanded. She made to go upstairs—there were other, far more important matters on her mind to sit in private and consider than this nonsense with boys.

Her plans were derailed by a single mild, infinitely vexing statement from her mother.

"She means well, you know that."

"But who does she mean well *for*?" Alice cried, whirling around. "She has set ideas in her head that will not be changed for anything despite the fact that the entire rest of the world doesn't live in that same head, with that same head's rules. What if *I* tried to introduce her to someone *I* thought would be a lovely boy? A painter, perhaps? Or a boatman?"

"You would never do with a painter yourself, Alice," her mother said with a mischievous smile. "You have more imagination and buoyancy than a hundred young artists. Now a boatman, who could take you on trips down countless sleepy rivers—and earn coin while he did—I could fair see that. Your father would be disappointed, of course, and worry about your financial future, but perhaps not if he could fish a bit from the prow."

"As long as I had a good, solid, loving husband, it wouldn't matter?" Alice prodded, pretending she didn't fully understand why this question was suddenly so important. "It wouldn't matter at all who he was, or what he did? Or who his family was?"

"Not at all. As long as you are happy, unlike your—" And here her mother's eyes whisked away and back.

"Unlike my aunt," Alice finished softly. "She *is* happy, you know. And financially her future is fine."

"But what would you know about that? The finances, I mean, not the happy part," her mother said quickly, not wanting to dwell on whatever unconventional things made her eternally single sister-in-law happy.

"Oh, never mind. I'm exhausted from my present 'buoyancy.' Would you mind having Mrs. Anderbee bring me up some warm milk? I think I shall go to bed early tonight and miss supper."

"And also miss your sister at the table?" her mother asked archly.

Alice pretended not to hear her.

Twice she had actually gone to Wonderland and not just dreamed about it. But twice she had come *out* of Wonderland by waking. Perhaps sleep was merely the door, the way back in.

She ripped off her many layers of clothes as fast as she could and donned her warmest, snuggliest chemise. She grabbed Dinah where the poor thing was just having a quiet lie on the windowsill in the sun and brought her into bed with her, tangled in with her own blond hair. Dinah didn't resist and even curled around her head, purring into her ear.

Mrs. Anderbee came up with the milk and a suspicious frown.

"It's no' the right time for your *flowers*," she said in her thick Northern accent. "Tha'd better not be getting ill."

"Thank you for keeping so close a track on my health," Alice said with faint amusement, taking the milk. *Flowers* was such a lovely metaphor for it. "But I do definitely feel a bit of malaise."

"Girls today with their *humors* and *mal-ays*," Mrs. Anderbee muttered. "In my day you strapped on what rags you needed to and got on with work. Farms wait for no swoonin'."

"Thank you, Mrs. Anderbee," Alice said around a smile and a mouthful of milk. *At least if you were outside leading a dray horse around a field,* she thought, *you wouldn't need to worry about accidentally bleeding on a prized needlepoint cushion.* The old servant showed herself out and closed the door as quietly as possible. She did care beneath her hard exterior. You just had to ignore what she said and pay attention to what she *did*.

Warm milk down, Alice found herself sliding into sleep most delightfully, as if she hadn't spent half the afternoon napping under a tree in a park.

# Chapter Fifteen

But of course she woke in Kexford.

# Chapter Sixteen

While Alice didn't make it back to Wonderland that night, she had come very close; of that she was certain. There was a feeling of liminality when she awoke, like her dream-self had just touched whatever skin separated England from that other place.

*It's very similar,* she thought with a strange premonition, *to an old person dreaming of youth.* Not quite young again in reality, but near enough that upon waking there existed a certain confusion as to which version of age inhabited the current body.

She had a nightmarish glimpse at the strange bodies of Wonderland creatures tumbling over each other as they fled the card soldiers. Beaks and tails and crazed inhuman golden eyes and people with strange hats. There was the *smile of the Knave*—ooh, how she wanted to slap it off him.

There was blood dripping from roses. *Not* red paint.

Also a glimpse of a placid castle in a remote valley that seemed important somehow. Did she know it? Was it familiar? What did it mean?

If only she could have reached out and pressed through, somehow!

"Oh, wake up, you lazy thing!" said a voice that wasn't Alice's. "You have been asleep for ten hours, easily! This is what comes of not having a real project or even a suitor or *anything* to occupy your time."

Alice kept her eyes closed, hoping the voice would go away, trying to keep the few moments she remembered distinct. The castle was important. The wounded, fleeing creatures were important.

Everything was important except for that irritating voice calling her away from Wonderland.

"*Really!* I'm talking to you, Alice. Open your eyes at once! I can tell you're awake."

"Do shut up," Alice told her sister as she scrunched down into the covers further and put a pillow over her head. Mathilda had to disappear. If Alice could just have a few moments to herself, maybe she could remember everything and figure out what it all meant. "You're very rude to come in without knocking. I'm quite busy at the moment. Go away."

"I will *not*," her sister said with some amusement.

Alice opened one eye and saw the severely bonneted Mathilda regarding her with a raised eyebrow and *almost* a twinkle in her eye.

"Please. Leave," Alice said as seriously as she could. "I am trying to remember something very important and you're making it impossible."

"What nonsense. Trying to remember a dream? That is not being *busy*. I must speak with you."

Alice took the pillow off her head and just looked at her sister, uncomprehending. There she was, utterly composed, utterly *smug* in her position, perching on the end of the bed. As if the only proper way the universe could run was when older sisters with ideas they thought were important could barge into rooms unasked, to wake up happily sleeping people, to correct them of their (presumed faulty) personal lives and routines.

*That* was what really irked Alice about Mathilda, she suddenly realized. Besides the unasked-for lessons when she was younger, the unwanted introductions to terrible young men now that she was older, the constant and unrelenting sermonizing aloud of her beliefs and politics—besides these things, underneath it all was an unshakable smugness, an undefeatable certitude in all things she did. Which she did without hesitation or question. There was only one world-view possible, and it was Mathilda's. It wasn't even that she rejected other people's beliefs; she literally didn't see them.

"You have two minutes," Alice said levelly. "And if you ever so much as come into my room without asking again, you will wake up the next morning with a blancmange dripping down your face."

Mathilda's brown eyes widened in extremely satisfying shock. "This is precisely the sort of thing that I wanted to discuss with you, Alice," she said, a little more shrilly than she probably meant.

(Another unbearably irksome thing was her constantly calm, patronizing tone. Her losing it was a little *tick* of winning in Alice's game-board mind.)

"You were exceedingly rude to my friend Mr. Coney yesterday."

"*He* was *extremely* rude!" Alice shot back. "He acted horribly—like an uncle or an older brother or zookeeper in charge of the Alice beast. He said some horrible, really filthy things to *my* friend Mr. Katz. And he did so first, I might add."

Mathilda was shocked into momentary silence. She had obviously not been told the whole story by whichever tattle-tale passed it on.

But she did not question what Alice said.

"Well, but Mr. Katz isn't . . . known . . . to us . . ." she began instead, sounding apologetic. It was all too obvious what *isn't known* really meant.

"He could be a satyr or a demon and it still would behoove an Englishman to behave with a modicum of politeness if no insult to his person has been made," Alice said frostily. "And as Mr. Katz is neither, but a barrister moreover, perhaps he even deserves a modicum of respect."

Mathilda sighed and then nodded, looking this way and that, almost nervous. She smoothed the front of her dress out. "You are right, of course. I just . . . Coney is a close friend of Corwin's, and Gilbert Ramsbottom's right-hand man."

Alice jumped a little at that: Mr. Headstrewth was *Corwin* to her sister now. That was a step!

"He will have quite the political future, perhaps not as an actual elected official like Ramsbottom himself, but as a person more behind the scenes. An organizer, a doer. None of which matters, of course," she added quickly, seeing the look in Alice's eyes. "It's just that he is making things a trifle difficult for Corwin right now because of your . . . interactions yesterday. It has put me in a very difficult position. Perhaps I never should have introduced you the way I did, but now . . . He cannot seem to take a hint, or let you go—like a bulldog when its jaws are locked."

Alice wondered both at this strangely vivid metaphor from her otherwise dull and placid sister and the *almost* apology that came before it.

"Corwin understands that you don't want anything to do with Coney—I think a passing pigeon would notice that—but the man is his friend. Could you—I'm not asking you to *see* him as a favor to me, but could you perhaps . . . perhaps leave your relationship on less of a sour note than a literal door slammed in his face?"

Alice wanted to scream. And not just because of the imposition she was being forced to endure—which was all a result of her sister's initial nosiness. Silly Mathilda was wasting her time rambling on about boys and friendships and relationships and what was little more than gossip while an entire world was on the brink of some sort of disaster.

While the fate of her friends was on the brink.

Yet with the hours that had come and gone since she was expelled from Wonderland—even with the dream-reprieve of the past night—the urgency of the situation had lessened even further, at least emotionally. The feeling of desperation was fast becoming more like wishing to return to a book whose plot has just reached a climax when one is rudely torn away by workaday matters. The devout reader is anxious to return to those pages . . . but the need to do so is not felt as strongly as, say, the need to make sure there's enough milk for the baby.

When Alice focused back on her sister, she saw a fretful young woman who was worried about her relationship with her suitor—whom she obviously loved—and her friends. And she had basically just admitted it to her young, "silly" sister. She had admitted weakness.

All of which was touching, but Alice still had to get her out of the room as quickly as possible.

"Fineallrightwhatever," she said grumpily. "I will speak to him one last—*last*—time with you and *Corwin* present. But no longtime commitments and nothing intimate like a carriage ride or dinner at the club. Also something that has a definite terminus."

"Splendid! I have just the thing!" Mathilda cried, eyes lighting up. She did not, however, say *thank you*, Alice noticed. Instead she pulled out one of her loathsome pamphlets. Alice's heart sank. "Tonight is the fundraising lecture for the rally. Mr. Ramsbottom is giving a talk to his biggest supporters. There will be light refreshment. The four of us shall attend—and that way I also get you to actually come to one of my meetings."

"Great yes fantastic you win now get out," Alice said, scooching like an inchworm back into her covers and putting all the pillows back over her head. She felt the bed shift and the pressure in the air change as her sister stood up and left the room.

"Clubs," Alice said for no good reason, and resumed trying to dream.

But she never got close to leaving England or even falling asleep. And somehow, remarkably, as the day progressed, Wonderland slipped away so much that she forgot it entirely for minutes at a time. Bathing, getting dressed, attending to what little correspondence she had, and avoiding any more contact with her sister took up most of the afternoon. When she found out that Mathilda had invited Mr. Headstrewth (*Corwin*) over for a spot of tea before the lecture, Alice slunk out of the house entirely with the message that she was going to fortify herself for the evening as well—but at Mrs. Yao's.

(Also there were several specialty teas in her stock that were conducive to sleep: lavender, chamomile, valerian root, etc., which Alice thought she might avail herself of.)

This day wasn't half as glorious as the previous ones. It was misty and dark—practically begging for a good lie-in. A *duvet day*, as one of Alice's closer girl friends called it. Certainly not one for attending hateful and boring lectures.

"Then again, perhaps I shall be *so* sleepy and dull at the talk tonight that I will simply doze off . . . just as I did when my sister was reading to me so long ago—and thereby make my way back to Wonderland!"

That thought put her into a much sunnier mood, at least until she turned the corner and saw the tea shop.

Its dainty window was smashed to bits, its sign cracked in two.

"Good heavens!" Alice cried, rushing through the door. The bells that jingled merrily upon her entrance had at least not been ruined.

Mrs. Yao sat slumped at her counter with her lower lip sticking out sadly. But she broke into a smile as soon as she saw Alice and quickly busied herself measuring out the right quantity of Alice's favorite tea and pouring hot water from a constantly bubbling kettle over it.

"No, stop," Alice pleaded. "Let me do something—you look a wreck."

"Being busy keeps me from being sad," Mrs. Yao said with a wry grin. "Also, I have to pay for the damage somehow. Can I sell you on two biscuits this time?"

"You may sell me a half dozen. What has happened? Was it a bird?"

"Sure. If birds sank like stones from the air," the proprietor said sourly. She lifted up the stone in question from where it had sat in an icy-looking puddle of cracked glass. It was smooth and fist-sized and unlike something you would pick up from the wayside or a cobbled road. It was a beach stone, its origins far from Kexford. A string was tied tightly around it, attached to which was a surprisingly neatly and prettily written note:

*go back to whence you came*

"Oh dear," Alice said. "That's terrible!"

"I know who did it, too," Mrs. Yao said, going back to working on the tea service. "That wretched little Danny Flannigan. But I don't think it was his idea. He can't write. Or read."

She presented Alice with a pretty tray holding two teacups and mismatched saucers, a couple of fancy nibbles, and an enameled pot whose steam smelled divine.

"Has this sort of thing happened before?"

"Oh, you can't live here and look different from everyone else and not hear things like that from time to time. Breaking the window is new. But I have been told worse."

"I'm so sorry," Alice murmured. "I had no idea."

"Why would you? But I appreciate your sympathy, I really do. It's nice to think I have an ally—with good taste in tea."

Alice smiled and poured a cup for her friend and then for herself, breathing in the lovely-scented steam issuing from the pot.

"You should talk to Danny's parents. Even if the boy can't pay for a new window, he could help fix it or run errands for you until you're square."

"I am certain he was put up to it by someone else. He's not this clever. He's just a brat." She smiled mischievously. "We had brats back in Nanjing, too—and they *also* only targeted Chinese shop owners."

Alice sighed. "I just wish there was something I could do. Oh!" Her face suddenly brightened with an idea. "Can I take a photograph of you? Next to the window? Holding the rock? I could submit it to the newspaper. 'The scene of a hateful crime!' It might not do much, but it would shed a light on this sort of thing, and might also act as an advertisement for your business."

"Oh, that's an interesting idea! But I don't want Danny's name in the paper. I don't think he's the real villain—and anyway I'm fairly certain his father would beat him for it."

Alice spent the next hour setting up the shot. It was a tricky business because of the backlighting from the window itself, but she needed the shards outlined. Also, Mrs. Yao wanted to smile for the camera; Alice had to keep telling her to look stern or sad.

But as she worked, she couldn't help thinking:

*I wonder if* she *has a Wonderland double, and who it might be. . . .*

# Chapter Seventeen

After she left the tea shop, Alice spent what little afternoon there was left looking for hints of Wonderland everywhere and taking photographs of anything—or anyone—she thought might be a likely prospect for a double in the other world. Then she tried napping again, faintly hoping the world would end before she woke.

Evening came despite her best attempts to avoid it. Soon enough Mathilda—hair specially combed, more of that powder on her face!—appeared at her bedroom door. She looked a little disappointed at Alice's outfit, unchanged since the morning. It wasn't a formal dinner they were attending (and Alice didn't *want* to go, anyway) so her rather plain dress with red diamonds seemed just fine. She had shined her shoes a little to get the dust off and combed and restyled her hair, but that was all.

"Ready?" Mathilda asked, visibly restraining herself from commenting on Alice's clothing choice.

"As I shall ever be."

"That's not—you're not bringing your camera, are you?"

"Of course I am. Why, will your party members do something they don't want me to take a picture of?"

"No, no, of course not."

Mathilda shook her head swiftly, more like a dog than a person, unsubtly trying to reset the conversation. "Isn't this fun? We're going out—on the town—together!"

"*Très* droll," Alice responded, not quite rolling her eyes.

Downstairs, Corwin Headstrewth was sharing a brandy with Alice's father. Coney was meeting them at the lecture. *That* was something, at least.

"How delightful!" Headstrewth bellowed, beaming. "I shall have a sister on each arm tonight."

"You may only have the permanent use of one," Alice's father said with far less humor than that sort of joking statement should have accompanied. "And that I grant most reluctantly."

"We should take a picture to remember this happy occasion," Alice said, and only her father picked up on her tone. He hid his smile behind the snifter of brandy he held.

Mathilda made a few negative sounds but Headstrewth was tickled pink with the idea. He brushed down his front, carefully moved a stray tress on Mathilda's forehead (such an intimate touch!), and proudly held her in front of him.

*Definitely a pair of bandersnatches,* Alice thought. She couldn't wait to see what would develop.

But on the walk over, even she had to admit that Headstrewth could sometimes be charming—if loud. He didn't mention the lecture or Ramsbottom or Coney at all, but kept up a fairly amusing dialogue about the shops and people they passed and even the street itself.

*Mathilda must have schooled him on what subjects to avoid,* Alice thought with a faint snicker.

Aloud she said, "Oh—did you know? Mrs. Yao's tea shop had one of its windows smashed—by a small ruffian with a stone."

"That's a pity," Mathilda said sympathetically. "She's a lovely woman."

"It was one of those little foreign thugs, I assume?" Headstrewth interrupted, more matter-of-factly than maliciously. "That gang from the Square?"

"Not at all," Alice said through gritted teeth. "It was

one of the Flannigans, but egged on and abetted by someone who writes with a pretty hand. I took a photograph of Mrs. Yao and the note. Perhaps if it is printed in the newspaper someone will recognize the handwriting and we can get to the bottom of it all."

"Indeed!" Headstrewth said like this was the most brilliant, heady thing he had ever heard.

Alice fumed and focused her attention on the gutter, where all her goodwill to the man beside her had just flowed.

The venue for the lecture was a large and lovely house, much grander than Alice and Mathilda's, with a special room off the library just for gatherings like this one. In it there was a stage with a lectern and space for at least fifty seats. Red, white, and blue bunting had been draped around the windows, but any potential festival air was squelched by the intense conversations of the attendees, who all had serious eyes and grim mouths. A gaunt young man with a close-shaved beard stood at a table offering buttons and ribbons that said RAMSBOTTOM FOR MAYOR. There was also a small pile of the sort of pamphlets that Mathilda was so fond of.

*Not even the least bit droll.* Alice sighed.

"Oh! I'm so glad you could make it!"

Mr. Coney approached the trio delightedly, arms spread to encompass at least the *idea* of Mathilda and Alice and

Headstrewth. Alice marked the look in his eye: it was delight, to be sure. But it wasn't *rapturous* delight, the sort of emotion one might expect from a young man infatuated with a young woman—one who had seemed to allow him into her good graces once again.

*I wonder how much he actually likes* me, Alice mused to herself, *and how much it would merely be good for his career to be married to Mathilda's sister. Mathilda and Corwin, Alice and Richard, going to lectures and promoting mayors and taking the Grand Tour and making their way to London gatherings of like-minded political folks. . . .*

Mathilda and Headstrewth were exchanging a quick, *very* familiar look, like an old couple. Worry/hope/dismay/fear-of-embarrassment.

"Wouldn't miss it for anything," Headstrewth said aloud.

"We absolutely endorse Ramsbottom, as you know," Mathilda added.

"I brought my notebook," Alice said, pulling out her journal. "So I could take notes. And my camera for after."

"Splendid!" Coney said enthusiastically. "I have saved us four seats up front. Normally I would be up there, with the pins and buttons, you know. But I wanted to spend this time down in the trenches, as it were, with you."

Alice, unable to think of anything to say that wasn't sarcastic, dry, or ironic, said nothing at all. Apparently satisfied with her silence, Coney led them to their seats and traded chuckles with Headstrewth.

It turned out that Quagley Ramsbottom was the grim fellow subbing in for Coney at the table with the pins and pamphlets. Apparently the two brothers were twins. But aside from their political theories, they had little enough in common, at least physically: Gilbert, the politician, was broad, friendly-looking, prone to smiles.

"Gentlemen Tweedles Dee and Dum, I've no doubt at all," Alice murmured, taking out her camera quietly and setting up a shot.

"Thank you all for coming out tonight," Gilbert began. Alice noticed he had a RAMSBOTTOM FOR MAYOR pin on his lapel. Was that normal or egotistical?

She heard him say very little else after that and was elbowed only once by Mathilda for too obviously sketching the Hatter in her notebook, which was the real reason she had brought it. Words and phrases would occasionally make their way into one of her ears and thence to her mind: ". . . everybody, of course, but focus on the real backbone of England: its own children . . ." ". . . darkening our doorsteps . . ." ". . . exotic philosophies, and religions, and even food, anathema to our traditions . . ."

Alice looked up at Mathilda at the last one. *"Food, too?"* she whispered.

Her older sister looked a little chagrined but shrugged, lips tightened.

Mostly what Gilbert said *sounded* upbeat and positive—on the surface at least. He touched on how sad immigrants must be, so far from the shores of their real homes. Women and men alike in the audience murmured in sympathetic assent over this. He talked about the need to take care of them (though this sounded ominous rather than charitable) and how the planet had conveniently put giant bodies of water to separate the various races of men. The audience ate it all up.

When it was over Alice did not applaud.

"There's a question-and-answer session," Coney told her with a winning smile. "Won't you stay for it?"

"Oh," Alice said, "I think I have all the answers I need, thank you. And what I need now is a cold drink."

"Absolutely! I'll join you outside in a bit!"

*I will be long gone by then,* Alice promised herself but did not say aloud. She made for the exit as quickly and discreetly as she could, without waiting for her sister. Outside the lecture room there were refreshments and people milling about, speaking more animatedly than before, their spirits awoken by the hateful, upbeat nonsense of the would-be mayor. Alice wished she had brought a fan. It was hot and she wanted to leave at once—but it would be rude without her sister. She found the punch bowl and dipped herself a mug, then stood in the corner to drink it as guiltily as a child sulking with a cup of milk who wishes to remain unseen.

But then she saw something that nearly made her choke on her first sip: *Aunt Vivian.*

She, too, was by herself and sipping punch! But she did it somehow without looking lonely; she held herself like she was the queen of the room, vaguely bored, waiting for some dullard to approach her. Her dress consisted of layers of emerald velvet and silk and tassels, topped by a small but exquisite polygonal hat.

"Aunt Vivian!" Alice cried, approaching her with more gratitude than she could contain.

Her aunt's world-weary eyes widened.

"Alice, dear, whatever are you doing here?"

"I'm with my sister and Mr. Headstrewth. And Coney," she added after a moment.

"Oh, that's right, your sister buys into this nonsense. I keep forgetting that; she is so levelheaded in every other aspect of her life."

"But what are *you* doing here? Do you support Ramsbottom?"

"Heavens forfend! I'm here as a favor to Willard," she said with a spin of her wrist and a roll of her eyes. "They won't let him into their little gatherings anymore—not after the last one. Gave Gilbert quite the what-for, and all his nasty little cronies. I am to report back on the latest developments! But sadly I do not have much to tell aside from the usual hate-mongering drivel this crowd eats up."

"Perhaps if Willard is so inclined against Ramsbottom, *he* should run for mayor," Alice said a little archly, thinking of the Hatter and his constant search for other people to lead the way. Mary Ann, herself . . .

"What an idea!" Vivian said, shocked. "I absolutely love it. Ooh, hush, hush, dear, *They* are approaching."

She nodded over Alice's shoulder. Gilbert himself came up to them, flanked by Coney and Quagley. The would-be mayor was nodding and grinning and his little helpers were clearing the way, Coney practically hopping up and down with excitement. Mathilda and Corwin followed.

"You're looking lovely as ever, Miss . . ." Ramsbottom said, nodding at Vivian. "It *is* still Miss, is it not? There's no Mister in the picture?"

She could have said "I'm afraid not," or "Not yet, sadly" but instead she looked him in the eye and said simply, "No."

"Oh, but you come from such a good, strong family line, English to the core," Gilbert said with a smile, this one with his fleshy lips closed over his teeth, just the corners of his mouth turned up. "We need good women like you to make sure there are future generations of such."

"But there *is* another generation," Vivian said calmly, putting her hand on Alice's shoulder. "I wouldn't trade my nieces for the world."

"I have a law in mind for situations such as this, should I ever be so lucky as to make it into a higher office than mayor," Ramsbottom went on with pleasant menace. "A law about . . . *unwed* women. Preventing the sort of dissolute lifestyle that not having a stabilizing marriage to a man generally encourages."

Alice didn't react; she was too busy watching Mathilda and Headstrewth, both of whose eyes widened in shock.

"Oh, well, it's a free country, Gilbert," Headstrewth managed. "Vivian's no burden to the system. She supports herself."

*Apparently even they have a limit,* Alice thought.

Coney said nothing but grinned like both his master and his friend had said the cleverest things in the world, and he was anxious for a fight betwixt them.

"Well, hopefully women will get the vote before your law is discussed seriously," Vivian said, tossing the rest of her drink back. "*All* of us women get the vote, I mean, including the ones you fear are invading our country. Alice, do come home with me—it's early yet and past time you started earning your keep in my darkroom. I have a friend who wants a portrait of her own pretty little *English* niece. But she could be Welsh, or even French, so don't quote me on that."

And with that Aunt Vivian turned with the grace of a goddess and sauntered out of the room, Alice practically giggling as she followed.

She took giant gulps of the cool night air and enjoyed the feeling of her flush departing. The close smells of the party were replaced with moisture and horses and evening greenery. It was quiet on the street. Alice felt herself unfurling like the fern.

Then a trio of men exited the club next door, talking loudly and laughing uproariously, in fine—if raucous—spirits.

"Oh, look, there's Ramsbottom's stupid event tonight," one of the older men said, pointing his silver-handled cane mostly at Alice and her aunt, though meaning the building behind them. "I say! Let's crash the party!"

"George, yes, let's do!" another otherwise distinguished white-haired gentleman agreed enthusiastically. "I hear they have quite the spread. Oh, it would be so fun to tweak the nasty little start-up—he daren't order us out! He would just have to take it, hoping for our support!"

"Perhaps not, gentlemen," the youngest member of the

party said soothingly, with patience and humor. "We should really call it a night. . . . *Alice?*"

She had a terrible premonition just before he turned, she really did, of who it would be.

(Terrible?)

(Or *hopeful*?)

It was A. Joseph Katz, Esq., of course, and those were most likely Alexandros and Ivy, also esquires, the partners in the firm where he worked.

Any excitement she might or might not have admitted upon seeing the young man was immediately tempered by the look in his eyes: they flicked over to the house she and her aunt had obviously come from, and his face fell in disappointment when he realized why they were there.

"I hadn't realized you were so political after all," he said with a forced smile.

"I'm here because of my sister," Alice said quickly, without even the courtesy of a proper greeting, too eager to correct his assumption. "I owed her a favor. That is all."

"*Vivian*, it's been too long!" George (Alice assumed) called, waving his cane. "What the deuce are you doing at Ramsbottom's?"

"Stealing the silverware, of course," Alice's aunt quipped. "How is your wife?"

"Oh, she's a fighter! She's doing just fine, the old lass!

She'll be up and about soon, and we'll take that trip to Italy I promised her the moment she's better! The air there will do her a world of good, I'm sure of it!"

The other lawyer was still looking a little myopically at Alice and Katz, who were silently looking at each other.

"You know this young woman, Katz?" he asked.

"We're acquainted," Katz said shortly.

"George, walk with me? Ahead? With your partner?" Vivian suggested, tilting her head at the younger people, giving her friend a knowing look.

"Absolutely! Always willing to help out a damsel in distress!" he said, pulling Mr. Ivy after him.

"But *I* should like to steal some silverware," the other barrister said longingly. "Or at least a glass of port."

The three older people strolled ahead, and Alice and Katz, somewhat embarrassed, followed. Alice put her hand on his arm. They walked in awkward silence.

"I think Ramsbottom is just terrible," Alice finally blurted out. "He is loathsome. I don't know why my sister supports him—she is many things, but not stupid. Anyway, I have paid up my debt to her and will not be returning for an encore."

"I'm glad," Katz said with a smile.

"Are you glad I do not support Mr. Ramsbottom? Or

glad I will not be mingling with his supporters, perhaps?" she asked, a mischievous twinkle in her eye.

Katz didn't respond, at first looking chagrined and then smiling at his own obviousness. Alice felt a funny little thrill when he gave her a sidewise, conspiratorial look: *oh, you got me there!*

"Both, if I may be honest. But did *you* ever resolve whatever park-tree-rabbit-friends issue you were having?"

Alice laughed and it was perfectly natural, light peals that took a thousand stones off her shoulders.

"No, I did not, Mr. Katz. I did not. And as mad as it all may seem, it still worries me. It's all riddles and mysteries and things I'm beginning to quite forget, even though I really shouldn't. None of it makes a lick of sense. Do *you* like riddles, Mr. Katz?"

"Do you know anything about our legal system?" he responded wryly. "You *have* to love riddles in my job. Actually, I heard a good one the other day from a dear friend who—like me, like you—loves riddles as well."

"Oh, let's hear it!"

"All right. Who knows—maybe solving it will help you work out your own problems. They work like that, you know. Expand the brain or exercise the mind or something. Make you think differently about things. Here goes:

*"I have mine and you have yours*
*It's needed in a painting*
*But in the end none agree on*
*The meaning of the thing."*

"Oh, that's a tough one," Alice said, thinking. "It could be anything. Value? Color? What is it?"

"You must figure it out yourself," Katz said with one of his maddening little smiles.

They had stopped walking and were right in front of Aunt Vivian's house.

Alice had the sudden thought that he was going to tweak her nose, or do *something*—when suddenly one of the senior partners noticed them again.

"I say, is that a camera?" George asked, looking owlishly at her obviously technical satchel. "I've been thinking about getting one for myself or the wife—oh! Be a dear and take one of us three old codgers, would you? And print me up a portrait? I want to see what it will do!"

"Of course, but the light . . . oh, you're not listening anymore," Alice sighed, feeling this was somehow familiar. Somehow Wonderlandy. The two old lawyers were utterly ignoring her, running hands over their hair and straightening their ties. Vivian gave her niece a sympathetic smile and carefully led them as close to a gas lamp as she could so the flames could illuminate their features at least a little.

For a moment Alice wondered what Wonderland creatures they would be. And then she was taken suddenly by the thought that these three were old friends, all still getting along marvelously without all of Mathilda's silly rules about what was proper behavior for men and women. She took the picture, trying to remember the Hatter.

"Where does the picture come out?" the other lawyer asked interestedly.

"Oh, don't be ridiculous," Vivian said, shaking her head and giving him a hug about the shoulders. "We must go inside and *develop* the plates. Actually, we must go do that after we take another portrait I have promised. Alice?"

"Good night, Mr. Katz," she said regretfully.

"Until next time," Katz said with a bow. "And Alice—*do* figure it out. I think you will find the solution may help you. And I depend on your answer!"

"Oh, bother," Alice said, for many reasons, not the least of which was the three older people watching them.

# Chapter Eighteen

*Charlie* was the name of the terrified little six-year-old Alice was meant to do a portrait of. She had beautiful, overcoiffed ringlets of black hair and a perfect little white dress with a blue sash such as Alice herself had worn at that age. With soft words encouraging the exploration of Vivian's rather extraordinary bric-a-brac, Alice eventually managed to coax a smile out of the serious girl. She supposed the aunt wanted a proper old-fashioned pose, as was done with the large-format cameras in studios with velvet backdrops, but she also took one of the girl giggling and hanging off the divan upside down, the paintbrush tips of her thick black locks just brushing the floor.

*A hundred years from now,* Alice thought as she

developed the pictures, *someone will see* this *photograph and* really see *Charlie. He won't just wonder about the frowning little girl with the composed hands and face in the other photograph. He'll have an idea of what she was actually like.*

She was a little surprised when the "fun" picture, once revealed, remained the same—Charlie upside down—but the *serious* photograph revealed a Wonderland umbrella bird. "I suppose all children make up the little creatures of Wonderland," she said as the plate dried, thinking of Adina and how delightful that was. Although the umbrella bird in question seemed to be hiding behind a tree and peeping out from behind it nervously.

Alice also developed the photo she had taken of Mrs. Yao and the deadly stone. But instead of an incriminating newspaper showstopper, the scene was of a person tall and stern, with dark skin and a dark circlet of black baubles upon her hair. She held her arms crossed over her chest and stared directly at the viewer with an appraising look. A strange weapon was gripped in her right hand, one with three bells or spheres at the end of its shaft.

"A club?" Alice wondered aloud.

*Mrs. Yao was in the suit of clubs in the other world.*

But why?

There had been nothing in her adventures so far that involved any suit besides hearts.

She thought back to two girls on a stifling summer day, long heavy curtains drawn in the study but seeming to hold the heat and dust *in* rather than keeping things cool. A pack of cards, divided, lay between them. Alice had a drooping red bow in her hair; Missy Fedgington a pretty little black bonnet that had fallen to the floor. Their fathers were friends, but these two were united only in boredom and age. Each flipped a card, and despite the extreme lassitude of the afternoon Alice couldn't quite let go of the sting of defeat each time she lost a bout. . . . Little red and black queens, trading cards endlessly in a game neither much cared about.

The memory came back to Alice with force, like a suddenly recalled dream.

*You just pull out your cards over and over again, and whoever has the most at the end wins.*

She looked at the picture. The black baubles almost looked like a crown the way Yao wore them.

That was it!

In Wonderland, her double was the Queen of Clubs!

"*There's another queen,*" she murmured. "There's another queen in Wonderland! As powerful as the Queen of Hearts, and almost certainly her enemy. Maybe she can help us!"

Alice studied the image in the photo. The woman in it seemed a bit severe and stern—but she didn't seem mad.

Or at least not frothing-at-the-mouth mad. Someone who maybe could be reasoned with.

Well, it was the start of a plan, if Alice could ever get back to Wonderland. She cleaned up quickly, leaving the rest of the plates to develop another time, and practically ran out of the house.

"I'm coming," she promised the Hatter as she ran through the streets.

"To sleep!" she declared, bursting into her house and running up the stairs to her room. "On the nonce!"

(Which really wasn't that hard; it had been an extremely tiring day.)

But she woke the next morning with nothing more than a few half-remembered dreams of pink cheeks and wise eyes.

So she tried napping in the large chair her father preferred to snooze in after dinner.

She tried it on the couch, gazing at the image of the Queen of Clubs before closing her eyes.

She tried it in the garden on a blanket in a warm corner.

She even had a bewildered Mrs. Anderbee recite long and rambling stories about growing up in Yorkshire until she drifted off. The old woman was flattered, and Alice's daydreams were full of berries and furze, clear cold spring water and turkey for Christmas. But there was no entrance to Wonderland.

She might have been seeing things, but at one point it seemed like the Queen of Clubs in the picture had turned slightly to look at her. As if to say, *Well, are you coming?*

Time was ticking, whether you were friends with him or no.

"All right, let's look at this logically," Alice said, thinking about her friend Charles and his math.

The first time, she had chased a rabbit into the other world; the second time, she had been pointed there by a duck. Perhaps sleep wasn't the answer at all; perhaps *animals* were the interlocutors of Wonderland: the Nikes, the Charons, the Castors and Polluxes, the psychopomps. All she had to do was find the right one!

This, of course, resulted in situations that went from mildly amusing to downright shocking. Despite never really having cared about what others thought of her, Alice still had to bear with comments from her family about the fox she chased into the garden, the Scottie dog she *swore* was looking at her funny, the rat that nearly made her usually stoic sister scream.

(Rather than carefully avoid the furry monster the two sisters spied in the street, which is what sensible adults did when encountering the fat urban unafraid-of-humans variety of rodent, Alice knelt down and tried to reason with it. And when the right-thinking rat decided that *this* human was mad and therefore potentially dangerous, and tried to escape, she ran after it.)

There was also the bright blue tit in her mother's garden that she had merely wound up taking a picture of.

*All right,* Alice said to herself. *Perhaps I shouldn't rely on randomly finding some animal citizen of Wonderland. I should take the situation in hand myself. What else has my crossing over involved?*

Her quick and analytical mind—which had resulted in many a triumph over her father at chess—picked through the things she knew about Wonderland and crossing over, and fanned them out for review: sleep, animals, Unbirthdays. She had been called to Wonderland the second time; had the first time just been chance? What else was there?

*Aha!* Two people had been present when she had dreamed herself to Wonderland. The first was her sister; the second, Katz. And while her sister was downstairs and extremely easy, at least physically, to talk to, Alice didn't imagine the conversation would go very far.

"Excuse me, Mathilda, could you pause your pamphlet-folding for just a moment to cast your mind back to over ten years ago and remember exactly what I was doing before you woke me under the tree that time in the park?"

Even if Mathilda didn't dismiss it immediately as nonsense, the rest would still prove awkward and unhelpful.

Katz . . . on the other hand . . .

This was not, she told herself, also an excuse to see him (it was).

He would *not* be compelled to discuss with her such nonsensical-seeming things merely because he felt about her a certain way (he obviously did).

She was only doing any of this because it was vital for her return to Wonderland to save her friends (mostly true).

There were two problems with her plan. One was that she didn't have an answer to his riddle, and the other was that showing up randomly at his office might seem impetuous and a little desperate—especially to outside observers.

So she would start at the Square, where apparently he spent some of his time.

On the way there Alice stopped at the little fern (now a few inches taller and more unfurled) and paused to ask if it could help her.

It remained haughtily silent on the matter.

The Square was also strangely silent. There were fewer children than usual, and those extant were quiet and subdued.

"Hello," Alice said gamely to the closest boy. "Is Mr. Katz here, by any chance?"

The boy shrugged. "Katz hasn't been here today. We was hoping he'd come. Josh . . . they took Joshua away. And a bunch of others. Maybe Mr. Katz could have stopped it."

"Took Joshua *away*? Who did? Where?" Alice demanded.

"The police and someone else with them. They said they committed a crime—broke a window or something. Josh owes me a turn with his ball. He owes me a turn with his ball and he was going to let me *this afternoon*."

He said it with the timbre of righteous anger but his eyes were wide and wet.

"Broke a window? But that can't be. It was Danny Flannigan. I don't understand this at all. Tell me everything," Alice said grimly, kneeling down to put her face even with his. That was the thing of dealing with children: you didn't lie to them and you didn't treat them like lesser beings. Alice had managed *excellent* results with her little models by being as respectful and polite as she would to a vicar.

"Two cops just came and grabbed Josh and three of his other friends. Filthy orphans, they said. Josh is no orphan. He's got a sister and a cat."

"Of course. Don't worry—they are probably just down

at the police station," Alice said. "I'll go find Mr. Katz and we will have this sorted immediately."

*All right, maybe that part was a lie*, she thought as she straightened up and hurried back out of the Square. She wasn't sure he shouldn't worry. She wasn't sure they could have it all sorted immediately. She wasn't even sure where Katz's office was. But she would find it.

Alice hurried down the alleys and twisty little streets, picking up her skirts, heels pounding the cobblestones, foot strikes echoing off the walls. She knew a shortcut that would let her out almost directly on the high street where all the important businesses were; she was as at home here as a rabbit in its labyrinthine warren.

She tried to sort through crazy thoughts and priorities as she fought for breath and ran. First she would try to see about Katz and tell him about what was happening with the children. Hopefully he would be able to do something about that. *Then* she would take the photograph of Mrs. Yao to the newspaper. Or maybe to the police. She wasn't sure which. Then she could turn her thoughts back to Wonderland.

So much to do—and how was it suddenly all up to her to fix things? She had no experience in social justice, newspapers, the police, or politicians. It was all ridiculous. Nonsense, really.

Once again she passed by the little green fern and,

looking at it instead of the cobbles ahead of her, almost tripped over the curb.

A strong arm stopped her fall—and then grabbed her around the neck, a gloved hand over her mouth.

*"HAND IT OVER!"* rasped a muffled voice.

Alice tried to tear herself away from her assailant—whose face, she saw, was covered in a scarf to conceal his features. His coat was on inside out to hide any details.

He wasn't trying to strangle her, she quickly realized; he was just trying to hold her still with one hand while he fumbled for her bag with the other.

"Get away!" she shouted, her voice muffled. "Villain!"

She writhed and flailed trying to shake him off.

*"JUST GIVE ME THE BAG!"* he . . . pleaded?—still in a fake, raspy voice.

She gave the satchel one hard yank.

He let go.

She went flying back, smashing into the stone wall of a house behind her.

As the world went dark, Alice noticed that just beyond the little fern she had so admired was a green and gloriously exuberant garden.

# Chapter Nineteen

Gardens weren't at all unusual in Kexford—except in this part of Kexford, and this kind of garden. Anyone would have blinked twice and fallen in love with it; the perfection of detail, the exuberance of the flowers, the color of the leaves, the precise yet natural placement of the vines, the bright paint on the house, the neat little cabbages in their artfully dishabille cold frames. Alice immediately saw it for what it was: Wonderland.

And familiar Wonderland at that.

"Why, it's the White Rabbit's house!" she declared.

She put her hand thoughtlessly to her neck, and then head—had they hurt a moment ago? Had she suffered a headache? Whatever, it was all gone now.

And then seven-year-old Alice remembered she was now eighteen-year-old Alice, and this was no harmless little white rabbit: he was a Queensman. "But then again," Alice said to herself, "he didn't seem so harmless back then, either. Why, when he ordered me to fetch his gloves, thinking I was Mary Ann, I went and looked for them just like that! *Scared* to disobey."

But there were other differences in the two visits besides Alice's age and attitude: red heart card guards marched around, looking important and deadly in helmets that revealed only glowing red points instead of eyes. Fortifications had been erected around the house that were not there last time; a new wall here and a sandbag there, all befitting someone important and indispensable to a queen at War.

"Why am I *here*?" Alice wondered.

She had thought that if she made it back to Wonderland she would be returned to the place where she had been plucked so suddenly and horribly from her friends—the battle at the Grunderound. She had prepared herself to go back and face whatever had happened, to rescue those who hadn't made it out—and seek vengeance for those who didn't make it out alive.

Here, except for the soldiers and the walls, all was bright sunshine and peace: no real clues or revelation about the War currently being waged.

"Also, the last time I was here, I was the size of a rabbit, or a lizard, and then suddenly the size of a giant, and became stuck in the house. Poor old Bill! I hope he didn't get captured by the cards. He always has the worst luck."

Alice looked down at herself and then back at the house: she seemed to be about the right size to enter it. Old Alice wouldn't have thought twice about this, but now-Alice wondered if this was on purpose—if she was *meant* to go into the house. Or were there soldiers waiting for her inside? Old Alice also would have gone up the front steps immediately and knocked—or even entered directly without knocking, perhaps feeling a little naughty but mostly adventurous.

"I think I'll at least evade the guards," now-Alice decided.

This proved to not be very hard at all.

Much like Tweedles Dum and Dee fighting over a rattle, despite *looking* scary, the guards were very close to being useless. They marched stylishly and loudly around the house clockwise and widdershins and occasionally slammed into each other—perhaps because it was almost impossible to see out of their fearsome helmets.

Alice waited to make her move until a collision occurred on the side of the house away from her (she couldn't see it but heard the clang of the helmets and muttered swears). Tiptoeing quickly she let herself through the kitchen door—which was almost heartbreaking in its fine carpentry and snugness. There was a tiny heart-shaped window set in the middle, glazed in red glass.

Inside there were cookies freshly iced and sitting on a pan with the words EAT ME piped on them. More out of habit than anything else Alice grabbed a couple and stuffed them into her pockets. The murmurings of a housekeeper or chef rose and fell from the pantry, so Alice quickly moved on.

She still wasn't entirely sure what she was looking for. Gloves? Bill? War plans she could steal and thus figure out some sort of counterattack? Unlikely. Alice had no experience in the military, as said, and she was fairly certain Wonderlandians didn't work in such a logical, tactical fashion anyway.

What she *did* find was the Dodo.

He was chained up in a small study, certainly not the most uncomfortable of prisons. There was a soft rug and a cheery fire. It was as if the White Rabbit had no real idea of the proper way to go about treating treasonous criminals. The poor bird was perched on the floor, legs drawn up under him, looking bedraggled and tired. There was a gash across one of his eyes, and his wings were folded tight against his body in a far more avian fashion than the creature generally held himself. He had lost some tail feathers and his jacket was torn and missing buttons.

"Oh, Dodo!" Alice whispered in dismay, rushing over to him.

"Alice!" The Dodo brightened. "I knew you would come! I said so. And here you are."

"Shh. Let's see if we can get you out of this," she said, pulling at the cruel iron chain. The cuff was solid enough and sized perfectly for the Dodo's leg, not too tight but not able to slip off, either. There was a heart-shaped keyhole on the side that would of course require the usual Wonderland search for an iron key (with a heart on it as well, no doubt). Alice would bet her camera that the key would be hanging around the Rabbit's neck on a tiny and delicate version of the iron chain around the Dodo's leg. Or dangling from a high bookshelf, or . . .

"We haven't time for that nonsense," Alice murmured, pulling out one of her purloined biscuits and gulping it down. Then she put a hand on either side of the iron cuff and gently pulled her hands apart.

The metal expanded under her touch, and the wondering Dodo easily slipped his foot out of it.

"Astounding!" the Dodo said, shaking his legs out.

"Where's the Hatter?" Alice whispered.

"I don't know. He ran a different direction than I. There was quite a flummoxing when the cards—"

"Is there anyone else locked up *here*?" Alice pressed,

not wanting to get into a long Wonderlandy conversation while they were in danger of being discovered.

"No, just me. I was the only one they brought here," the Dodo said, a little mournfully. "I insisted on parole—on meeting with the White Rabbit. Bill was with me at first, but the housekeeper helped him get away."

Well, that made a certain amount of sense; he used to work here, of course. And poor old Bill certainly deserved a break after all he had been through.

Alice looked out the window. The guards were changing. She cursed herself for missing the advantage of the very ritualized moment that was taking up so much time.

"We'll have to sneak out the *front*—immediately, I'm afraid. Come on." Alice took the Dodo's wing and led him as quietly as possible down the hall. The house, she couldn't help noticing, was just the right size for her in her present form, but not proportionately; it was built for a rabbit's movements and habits. Doors were fatter, rounder, and shorter. There were lovely paintings of carrots and dill artfully arranged on the lettuce-print wallpaper along with the usual long-eared silhouettes. Lovely little velvet King Louis chairs were more like tuffets for resting on with all (four) of your legs pulled up under you.

They passed a delicate set of curling wooden steps, and Alice could have sworn she heard a whimpering from upstairs; a sad, mournful sound much like the Mock Turtle had made.

"There's another prisoner," she whispered to the Dodo. "You go on ahead. I'll meet you by the hedgerow just outside the gate."

The Dodo saluted and Alice had the funny thought of replacing his long-lost wig with a captain's hat.

She tiptoed up a flight of stairs that were honey-colored and thick and didn't creak at all. The part of her that still liked dolls ached for a house like this. Every decoration was well thought out; care had been taken in each last detail. The tiny window on the stairwell hadn't a speck of dust and the paint was recent.

She remembered the bedroom where she had searched for the Rabbit's gloves, and where she had grown too big and become stuck—that seemed to be the place where the sobbing was coming from. She stepped forward as quietly as she could and peeped around the doorframe.

It was the White Rabbit who sat there, weeping.

"Mary Ann," he moaned over a pair of white gloves. "You didn't deserve that. Oh, Mary Ann . . ."

Crying was a tricky business for the White Rabbit: tears rolled out of his eyes and then got caught up on his whiskers, sometimes flowing down them, causing them to droop and then spring up in an undignified fashion when the tears finally splashed to the floor. But sometimes they flowed back toward his face and matted down the fur there.

The gentlemanly little rabbit, still in the fancy waistcoat—now he also had an armband with a heart patch on it, and what looked like a tiny medal of valor—looked a damn mess.

"I should throttle you where you sit," Alice found herself saying aloud, despite her surprise at his reaction to the girl's unhappy fate.

The Rabbit looked up at her with the mindless surprise of a normal lagomorph: red eyes wide and dead, ears up, paws down. Just like one of his wild cousins right before it decides to bolt.

"I should have your skin for a muff," she added, shocking herself but meaning every word as she advanced. Fury freed her from any fear of stupid card soldiers and consequences.

The White Rabbit seemed to regain his sentience; he settled back into a slump of despair.

"I would deserve it," he murmured.

Alice blinked in surprise.

"I was only trying to do what was best. I was only trying to *end* this nonsense, this madness. The sooner it's all over the better," he said, waving a tired paw. But his voice had regained some of its irritating officiousness. "I didn't think she would get involved. She only need have waited for the

End of Time. I was speeding the Queen along. We already had so many toys. . . . The end is so close—"

"So many toys? You mean like dolls?" Alice interrupted. The Cheshire's riddle . . . and the brush-child-thing at the Grunderound . . . Dolls and toys and more dolls! "What are you going on about, Rabbit? The Queen is destroying everything in Wonderland and taking all the toys for herself? *Why?*"

"She wants all the toys, the most toys, of course. What else would you expect from the Queen of Hearts?" he said miserably. "I am helping her . . . acquire them. Sometimes there is resistance."

"What a terrible rabbit you are," Alice said, wondering if these words had ever been said in English (or any language) before.

"Take the Dodo and go," the White Rabbit said tonelessly, not paying much attention to her. He stroked the little white gloves. "I shall have to call the guards soon enough."

Alice backed out of the doorway, a little shaken by his strange words and behavior. But before she left she saw that she had been right: there was indeed a fine black iron chain around his neck, on which hung a key with a heart-shaped bow on the end of its shank.

---

The Dodo, bless him, was right where she told him to be. It was strangely surprising.

"All right then," Alice said, hunkering down in the hazel next to him. "Tell me what happened back at the Grunderound when I disappeared! Was anyone else captured? Was anyone hurt?"

"Oh, there were many people hurt," the Dodo said mournfully. "Although perhaps rather fewer than could have been. The soldiers were very surprised by your sudden disappearance. So surprised, in fact, that they sort of marched into each other and fell into a terribly messy pile. Cards, you know. Terrifying in numbers, especially the higher suits, but a bit of a disaster at times."

"Oh, I'm so glad," Alice said with feeling. "I never meant to leave you, you know—I was pulled away. Just like last time, when I thought it was all a dream."

"I know," the Dodo said, a little sadly, looking up into her eyes. "You have a whole other world to worry about, besides our little Wonderland."

"Well, I don't know if . . ." Alice started to correct him about her importance in that other world, much less this one, and then decided it wasn't worth the conversation right then. What a funny idea the creatures here had of her, though! It seemed like they could only think of Alice as a silly, useless girl who knew none of the rules of living here—or as some sort of replacement savior. Nothing in between. "What happened to the Hatter? And the Gryphon? And the Dormouse?"

"The Gryphon fought, raking his mighty claws at the enemy," the Dodo said, eyes lighting up at the memory. "Gosh, he was glorious. I think he tore several cards clean in half. The Dormouse was still on the chandelier, I believe, when it fell. The Hatter—"

Alice's heart clenched.

"The Hatter tried to get all the wounded and children to safety," the Dodo said with a sigh. "I don't know what happened finally, but he was leading a group to the exit. Had a dish and spoon riding on his shoulders last I saw.

"But I knew you would need help assembling your army, now that you're our leader."

"Indeed," Alice said, kissing him above the beak. "Good, loyal Dodo. Thank you so much for your perhaps undeserved trust in me—but *how* did you know I would wind up here?"

The Dodo shrugged.

"You . . . Mary Ann . . . the White Rabbit. You're all tangled."

Alice sighed. Of course. Wonderland logic.

"I don't think I have any of the skills the poor departed Mary Ann had for organizing Wonderland creatures and calling them to arms; it was utter chaos in the Grunderound just taking care of the wounded."

"We are all very independently minded," the Dodo said with a sniff. "When you identify as a Dodo, you are Dodo all the way. Auks just can't understand things from your point of view. I mean, they *can,* better than, say, whales, but they still do not truly know what it is like to be a Dodo. We have our own special needs and issues."

Alice rubbed her head. Perhaps this was what Coney was really afraid of—Kexford being overrun with a thousand different exotic ideas and votes. Caucus races, indeed. Still, it was a democracy; all viewpoints were supposed to be welcome.

"Except for the cards," he added darkly. "They are all too easily organized into nasty packs."

"Yes," Alice said with a sigh. "If only we could harness that for good."

Then she suddenly remembered: the picture of Mrs. Yao! The queen, dark and beautiful, bearing a club. *A queen of clubs.*

"Dodo! Tell me about the other suits—the Queen of Clubs, in particular."

"Oh, she is a fierce and respectable ruler," the Dodo said, preening his chest a little in thought. "She and the Queen of Hearts have come to blows a thousand times—border skirmishes—but they always manage to avoid a serious game of War in the end. It would be bloody indeed if they didn't."

"Do you think she would help us?"

The Dodo looked dubious. "The Queen of Hearts is conducting a campaign against her own people. Why would the Queen of Clubs get involved?"

"Because she's a good card?" Alice suggested hopefully.

"Well, I don't see much other choice," the Dodo conceded. "And we don't have the Hatter and his good sense to guide us. Since he lost his Nonsense, I mean; it really was a bit of a silver lining."

"Hatter . . . ? Good sense . . . ?" Alice said wonderingly. Imagine a world where the Mad Hatter was considered a reasonable and wise fellow! But perhaps in his own way he had a keener idea of what worked and didn't in Wonderland. "Dear old Dodo. Let us go find the Queen of Clubs, then."

"Dance, dance!" the Dodo suddenly cried, leaping up and cavorting away without even looking back to see if she were coming.

"What! What are you doing? Have the guards found us?" Alice asked in fright, running after him.

But . . . it wasn't proper running.

It was *like* Alice was running, but at the same time it

was all too sleepy and dreamy to be running. She watched the shape of her legs under her voluminous skirt with something like wonder: they pumped and moved the way they should have had she been actually running in fright, but so slowly . . . like she was moving through treacle.

She looked around and the landscape seemed to lean forward a bit, objects closer to her blurred as if they really wanted her to run, to be caught up in her tailwind, to finish the reality that her feet were suggesting.

And yet she hadn't moved an inch from her place.

"That's no good!" the Dodo scolded as he bowed and did a pirouette. *"DANCE!"*

"But we're not getting anywhere!" Alice complained. She risked a look behind her. A four and seven of hearts had just noticed the attempted escape and were reacting—very, very slowly.

The Dodo began flapping his left wing while clutching his chest with his right one. "Dance! Or we're done for!" he panted.

Well, running wasn't working and this was Wonderland, so why not dance?

Alice spun, feeling a little ridiculous, hand up as if an invisible partner were leading.

The Dodo's footsteps beat in time.

*One, two, if I were you*
*I'd pick up bricks and put 'em in the mix*
*A chair, a doe, an isinglass bowl,*
*Dance the Hob to pay for the toll*

*Three, four, dance till you're sore*
*Waltz on nubs to the Queen of Clubs*
*A mile, a road, we won't be slowed*
*Until we get to the Queen's abode!*

The Dodo was also spinning now, opposite her. She grabbed his wing tips and the two pirouetted along, faster and faster until the force of their spinning flung them apart and sent them tumbling down a hill.

# Chapter Twenty

Alice was laughing like a little girl, feet flying overhead, rolling harmlessly through warm, soft grass. *This* was Wonderland at its finest. Dancing from danger and potential death and winding up enjoying a perfect summer day from childhood. She sat up and looked around: of course the White Rabbit's house was gone. The Dodo was carefully getting up and dusting himself off very punctiliously, picking prickly seed heads out of his jacket.

"Can't travel like I used to," he was mumbling to himself. "Age requires more first-class treatment. Carriage boys and service gnats."

"Are you all right?" Alice asked solicitously.

"Far better than our old companions, presumably," the

Dodo replied, for just a moment morose. Then he shook himself out, preened a couple of feathers into place on his neck, and straightened his shoulders. "Come, then! To the Queen of Clubs! It's a bit tricky from here on out, so be on your guard and careful we don't get separated."

Alice stepped cautiously into the grass and looked around. They were in a gently rising meadow at the end of a wide valley of some sort. Grey cliffs like bulwarks bounded either side of the view. Far ahead, dark strips of foliage could be seen weaving in and out of the mild hills. The occasional patch of trees might have hid monsters or jubjub birds, but nothing in the landscape seemed immediately threatening or dangerous.

"There's nothing to worry about here. There's no one around—it's safe as houses," she protested.

"But how safe are those?" the Dodo asked. "They burn down and get exploded by young ladies all the time."

Alice decided not to argue with this, especially since she had been a young lady who had in fact exploded one.

They walked up one hill and down the other side. Over here the grass was grainier and dark green. Just ahead was a beautiful prairie blanketed with little white flowers, which Alice bent down to smell.

"*Oy*, get yer nasty knows away from us," one of them shrieked. "'Oo nose where it's been?"

"It's like they never been smelled themselves," another one said, sniffing. "If they 'ad, they would think twice about doin' it to others, they would."

"For shame!" a third cried, pulling a tiny bud safely away in its protective leaves. "Stinking away at such a wee one. You . . . *hussy*!"

"Right," Alice said, standing back up again. "I deserve that."

And so they kept walking.

This hill grew steeper and steeper until eventually it became the green skirt of a small, perfectly square tor—which Alice was fairly certain she hadn't seen before, and should have, considering all had been mellow and field-y with near infinite sight lines a few minutes ago. Just when the way became impossible and nearly sheer, a convenient set of steps appeared, carved into the cliff. Rocks jutted out at helpful locations for placing a hand for balance.

"Of course," Alice said. "How perfectly Wonderland. It always provides—just not in the way you expect."

She self-assuredly clambered up, remembering with ease the movements from a childhood of climbing trees.

At the top was a delightful alpine heath with short golden-green grass and scads of beautiful pink and purple flowers that Alice decided not to study more closely. *Even though* at second glance it became obvious that the glorious sunlight wasn't sparkling off their dew but the petals themselves: each blossom was a jewel, or maybe glass, and chimed gently in the wind.

The Dodo came up close behind her, huffing a little.

"Oh, you can practically see the Queen of Clubs' demesne from here," he said, pulling out a tiny telescope and looking through it the wrong way. He winced when the eyepiece touched the gash across his lid. "It's very tiny, but gets large enough once you're close. See it glitter?"

And there in the distance far below them, like a shiny beetle, was a blob of something black and unsuitable for the world they currently seemed to be in. Unnatural and man-made. The Queen of Clubs' castle!

Alice felt like skipping; maybe it was the air or the height (heights had never bothered her, and they still didn't). She was giddily happy as they walked along what turned out to be a plateau and not a single mountain after all. A little stream trickled out of some decoratively set boulders. Beside it was an old worn sign with bright gold letters that said YOU MAY DRINK ME, IF YOU PLEASE.

"Oh, I do wish we had brought a picnic," Alice said, kneeling down to take a sip.

"You didn't—" the Dodo began.

The ground gave way and Alice tumbled, far less pleasantly this time.

She banged back and forth in what seemed to be an open-topped tunnel. It was hard and cold and so slick and slippery that she couldn't slow herself down despite the hexagonal tiles that tessellated its brown-and-yellow surface. The grooves in between them were too slight and shallow to dig her fingernails in.

She kept falling.

She tried making her whole body stiff and using friction to slow her descent; that resulted in a skinned elbow and her dress tearing apart at the knees.

She hit the bottom with a *whump*.

A tiny cluster of white flowers inches from her face glared at her dubiously as she lay still (in much pain) for a moment.

*Whump!*

The Dodo landed right beside her.

"Alice! We were doing so well!" he scolded. "And then you had to go and bungle it."

"*Bungle* it? Bungle *what*? What did I do?" she cried, attempting to rise. She ached all over.

She tipped her head back to see where they had come from. The thing she had slid down on was . . . well . . . a slide. A brown-and-yellow one that snaked back and forth up the side of the hill to the top with the stream.

"You took the spring's water. You just *drank* and didn't

say please, naughty girl. What kind of leader and savior are you, anyway?"

"I'm not . . . But I've never had to say please before!" Alice cried. "This is Wonderland—everyone does just precisely as he, she, or it *pleases*. Without even a modicum of polite and civilized behavior. The sign said Drink Me, so I drank!"

"No, it said You May Drink Me, If You Please. *Very* proper and polite. You are *here* now, in the vicinity of the Clubs," the Dodo said primly, taking out a pince-nez and polishing it with a thumbfeather. "Rules are rules. And the Queen of Clubs has quite a few of them keeping her safe from the rest of the land. All the border areas around her castle are strict about that sort of thing."

"All right, I can sort of understand that," Alice said thoughtfully. The Queen of Clubs was sounding more and more like a reasonable, normal person every moment. Like Mrs. Yao.

She peered closely at the slide they had come down. Through some trick of her eyes or the hypnotic pattern of the tiles, instead of looking hollowed out it suddenly became the very opposite, curvy and full.

The end of it, or rather the head, pulled itself up and hissed at Alice, baring two fangs and a large forked tongue.

"Oh!" Alice said, falling back in fear at the green slit eyes. But the head did no more than weave back and forth as the rest of the creature stayed glued to the side of the hill.

"A giant snake! What in heavens . . . *OH!* I understand now!"

She stood up and looked around, carefully inspecting the miniature dell they were now in. There were neat squares of darker grass ahead and to either side of them. On their left was a tree with steps hammered in a spiral up around it, leading to somewhere above the treetops.

"It's a giant game of Snakes and Ladders!" she cried.

"Well, of course it is," the Dodo said simply. "Now will you kindly follow my lead, since you apparently do not have a real enough understanding of the game—or good enough breeding—to proceed properly? If you were actually familiar with Snakes and Ladders, you would remember that traits like Frivolity and Greediness slide you back spaces, sometimes quite a bit. Habits like Kindness and Pity advance you. Your Impolite Behavior before nearly sent us back to the beginning."

Alice was outraged. First of all, she was an absolute master of games of all sorts in her household. She had been playing this one almost since before she could count.

On top of that, she was nothing *but* proper behavior. She

always said please and thank you and curtsied when she was trying to think of what to say. One could complain about her lack of respect for social convention when it came to her camera, friends, or her occasionally mannish walking habits, but in conversation at a polite dinner party she had few equals.

"I beg your pardon! Do you remember the caucus races? And . . . the tea party? I was polite while everyone else was *extraordinarily* rude!"

"There is a Time and Place for everything," the Dodo said. "And Time is winding down. We could wait for him here, to wrap everything up, or we could proceed to the Queen of Clubs and save whoever is left of our friends. Being Quarrelsome, you know, slides you back five spaces. And so does having too much Pride."

Chastened, Alice flushed—and deservedly so.

"You are quite correct. I am most sorry, Dodo. Please lead the way."

"Take whichever way you like," the Dodo said magnanimously. "Take two if you so desire. It's what you do with them where I shall set the example. You see—Generosity. We should be advancing quite soon enough."

Alice curtsied—*very politely*. "After you, Mr. Dodo."

"Thank you kindly, Miss Alice," he said, also curtsying,

which was strange. His tail feathers flipped up and his legs sort of squatted to the side.

Alice decided not to say anything about it. She wondered if *Tact* was an approved—and useful—trait in this game.

# Chapter Twenty-One

As it is assumed that the reader has more than passing knowledge of Alice's previous adventures, we can cut to the chase a bit—because otherwise you would be doing nothing at all this chapter except for watching a rather slow game being played by a young woman and an old bird.

They avoided a square in whose center was a bright pile of all sorts of fancy treasure heaped up on a glass table: crowns and coronets and scepters and rings and other gaudy trash. But Covetousness was not the way to win the game.

Alice asked the Dodo to forgive her for setting them back several spaces and apologized profusely for it, and so they climbed a rapidly appearing, oddly lonely set of steps (for Penitence) that seemed to lead to nowhere but actually put them on the other side of a fast-moving and deep creek impossible to cross any other way.

She vaguely remembered another stream of water like it—or maybe it was a river—that she had rowed down once and nearly fallen into.

Alice bit her lip at the reminder of her other life. Of course she had to save an entire world here, but she had emergencies waiting for her when she returned to Angleland as well. What precisely thay were she couldn't quite remember. Something about children and tea and windows and . . .

"Catch it over here," a voice said behind her.

She spun around: the Cheshire Cat was on his back in the grass, playing with a daisy. Literally, of course: one claw was patty-caking with the leaves of the young bud.

"What am I to catch?" Alice asked politely.

"Your mind. It wandered off the game board entirely. That's dangerous in Wonderland, you know." He flowed up into a sitting position and the stripes on his tail moved a bit, winking on and off. Alice put out a hand to stroke him; his fur was warm from the sun. How long had he been there—or anywhere, really—watching her?

The Dodo was distracted, muttering to himself, investigating what lay beyond the border of their current square on the sides adjacent to the river.

"I was thinking about how it seems like I have *two* worlds to worry about now," Alice said with a sigh. "A real one and this one. I can't help thinking about the mess I left back home—children taken into custody . . ."

"Are the ones being thrown in the Queen of Hearts' dungeon and plundered of their toys any less real than your little ragamuffins?" the cat asked, as lazily as ever.

"Well, don't you suddenly become clear as crystal when something ticks you off!" Alice snapped, withdrawing her hand from the cat and putting it on her hip. "Perhaps I misspoke, but I have spent all my life in that other world and only been in this one a few times. And this world . . . it vanishes or fades from my memory over there, like it's a dream and not real at all."

"Only *this* one disappears?" the cat asked, his hind legs walking up a flight of invisible stairs and then falling down over its edge and down his face. "Tell me about your other . . . your 'real' world. What is the name of your aunt?"

"Hatshepsut," Alice said promptly. "Auntie Hatshepsut." She frowned.

The cat waited patiently.

"No, that's not right, is it?" she said with a sigh.

"And what is it that so upset you about your sister?"

"Why, it's her magpie, of course. It's always a bother,

always in my personal things, a real nuisance, carrying her voice. . . ."

Alice *kept* talking, hoping some sense would come out eventually. But it grew worse and worse as she spoke.

The Cheshire Cat said nothing, for once behaving like an English cat, staring at her with large, unblinking eyes as she realized the truth for herself.

"It's like the real—I mean, *my* world erases Nonsense from my memories . . . things that shouldn't just fade away. . . . But Wonderland replaces real—ah—*my* world's things with Nonsense."

"Very deep," the Cheshire Cat said. He curled himself around, forming a perfect circle with his body. Through it was a well, dark and endless. Alice leaned over and peeped in but couldn't see the bottom. The cat stretched and walked down the tiny spiral steps along its walls (on his own body!) until finally his hind feet followed. "Very . . . deep . . . indeed . . ." his voice echoed back.

Suddenly his face popped out of the sky, upside down, inches from her own.

"One wonders—*why* you go back and forth. Why you bring what little you carry from one world over to the other. And what that thing is, and how useful it might be."

"I have no idea what you're talking about," Alice said,

shaking her head. "Not a single word this time. And it's not even a riddle."

"A riddle, you say?" the cat said, suddenly frozen in delight. "But I simply *love* riddles. I'd run many a mile to tell a puzzling tale to a receptive soul. But *you're* running *away,* from Time, and the White Rabbit is running *to* him. And the Queen of Hearts bakes her tarts out of the tears of children. While you're off looking for unreliable help, he's sent you, oh, some friends to play with. . . ."

"Unreliable help? What do you mean? The Queen of Clubs is our only hope!"

"When has Wonderland ever been about anything besides Alice?" the Cheshire Cat asked, but not accusingly or sadly. It was more like a statement. "For Alice, I mean."

"I beg your pardon—I am not thinking of myself at all here. *Others* have suggested that I must lead armies against the Queen of Hearts—which really is ridiculous. I know my limitations, and I am not a queen myself—*or* a Mary Ann, apparently. But I am doing my best to help out in any way I can—which is not that much, I admit! But what do you mean the White Rabbit is running to Time? And what friends did he send? To play *what* with us? A greater game? A—meta game?"

But the Cheshire Cat had faded from view, and all she was left with were two slitted black pupils that fell with a tinkle to the ground like stones once the rest of the cat was entirely gone.

"You and your stupid riddles!" Alice said, disgusted. Although he hadn't actually told her one this time.

But *wasn't* there another riddle? A real one, that she had to answer? One that someone had told her she must answer? Soon?

"I think we should proceed, with haste, Miss Alice," the Dodo said, hurrying back to her. "The next squares are clear. No sense lollygagging."

"Are there other players?" Alice asked. A question she realized that she should have posed at the beginning of this particular adventure. No games were played alone except for Solitaire.

"Of course!"

"And where are they?"

"I don't know—around, I suppose," the Dodo said vaguely.

"Aren't we playing *against* someone? What do we win? What do they win? What is the point? Who gets to the Queen of Clubs first gains her support, or the like?"

"Perhaps?" the Dodo responded, a little desperately. "This isn't the area of my expertise, dear girl. I know about Tortoises and Impeachments. Do let us go, perhaps before we find out the hard way—as losers of the game."

A fair point. Alice picked up her skirts and strode quickly alongside him.

Things were quiet for a few more boring squares—no Snakes *or* Ladders to contend with. On the fifth square she finally saw someone else on the board.

Some*thing* else, actually.

Several some*things*.

At first it just looked like a scene directly out of a picture book on nature: a herd of strange deer cavorting in the field ahead of them. They were beautiful when they leapt, glittering like glass or fragments of something shattering in slow motion. But once they were back on the ground, their running seemed awkward and disjointed. Despite the fact that they had a formidable lead on the Dodo and Alice, she found herself wincing whenever one of them tottered and seemed about to fall. Finally one did, and it had a very hard time picking itself back up again. It rolled, and stuck out its long legs, and rocked, and . . .

"They haven't any knees!" Alice realized. That was why they looked so unreal and graceful in the air and terrible on the ground.

"What don't? Who? *Oh!*" The Dodo put up a pair of opera glasses (again, the wrong way around) and then shrieked, dropping them. "*Bonetalopes! Run!* Have they seen us?"

"They have now," Alice said dryly.

The delicate creatures turned their long ears toward the two. They pawed their tiny, sharp hooves into the ground and lowered their graceful necks so that a dozen pairs of terrifyingly metallic horns were all aimed at Alice and her friend. Then they cantered awkwardly into a menacing arrow formation with a leader in the front. He (or she) emitted a strange noise—like the honk of a horn but also the call of a bull, with a little bit of a mockingbird trill at the end.

The creatures charged.

Alice shrieked.

The bonetalopes suddenly fell back, snorting in frustration. They had hit the border of their square and could go no farther.

"Whew," the Dodo said, pulling a—still clean!—white handkerchief out of his pocket and wiping his forehead. "We're safe!"

"That's what the Cheshire meant! These are emissaries of the White Rabbit sent to stop us. But they are playing by the rules," Alice said slowly. "They can only go forward."

"Well, that's a relief, then," the Dodo said.

"Yes, as long as we stay here. But we have to *win*."

Her mind began to race—just as it did when she was playing against her sister or a male companion at any sort of strategy game. It was as if dozens of little Alices broke off from the main Alice of her mind and went running around in all directions, looking for an answer or a way out. Twenty heads were better than one.

"Sometimes," she reminded herself, "you have to dance when you need to get somewhere." Or do the thing that didn't seem to make the most sense.

"Look!" she said aloud, pointing. "If we go up a square we can Quarrel, and then slide down that snake over there." She pointed, grabbing the Dodo's arm.

"But that's preposterous. My dear girl, we can't go *back*. . . ."

"No, do you see? Two squares up from there is *Pity*, whose ladder takes us one square ahead of the, ah, bonetalopes."

"Lose on purpose—go *backward* so we can go forward? I suppose it will work," the Dodo said dubiously, looking the wrong way through his glasses again.

"Come on!" Alice cried. "Let's do try it!"

This felt right and Wonderlandy, and she nearly skipped with eagerness to test her theory.

The Dodo, however, being a bird—even an ancient one—was, like all birds, not overfond of snakes or serpents. The idea of *purposefully* mounting one to slide down its awful, scaly back was almost inconceivable. He pulled an old colander out of one of his pockets and put it over his head to blind himself.

"Coo coo," he said echoingly from inside.

They stepped into the next square, wing in hand.

"Oh, I'm sick of it!" Alice declared, trying to figure out a good Quarrel. "All of your . . . talking! And Nonsense! And . . . setting me up with young gentlemen I don't at all desire to have a conversation with, much less marry!"

"Eh, what?" the Dodo asked from inside his colander.

"Stay out of my life, you ridiculous thing! Imperious sister! Keep to your own banal little life, with your ridiculous views on what is and isn't right. Get married to that big wooden block of a sheep and leave the rest of us out of your idea of what a perfect Angleland should be like!"

"I beg your pardon," the Dodo said, echoingly, yet with some dignity. "I don't really care a huffle's ruffles about your Angleland, and I do not take kindly to your tone, Miss Alice. . . ."

"Choose a side, you ridiculous bird! You don't even know my sister or her magpie, but you know *me*! I cannot believe you would defend her! Impudent avian!"

The poor, mostly extinct bird was having a difficult time indeed with his end of the made-up row.

"Er . . . *you*!" the Dodo tried, thinking hard. "Then! Go take a . . . long walk . . . off a, let me see, very short couch! Yes!"

"*Go stuff it!*" Alice cried, grinning.

And so the snake, with a dull, confused look in its large golden eyes, tossed them into the air and onto its back, and the two went sliding down back a number of squares.

They landed with a double *thump*, right next to each other this time. And, having been prepared for the slide down, Alice wasn't injured at all and managed to leap directly up again.

After rising, the Dodo put his colander away with specific movements and affronted dignity. "Well, I'm not surprised that your sister wants to rein you in a bit. You do seem like a bit of a Monster."

The square they were in was greener and moister and cooler than the ones around it. Little trees and bushes cast some much-needed shade on the otherwise open landscape of the game.

"Oh, a tea rose, most excellent," the Dodo said, delightedly taking in their surroundings. "Just what we need."

Alice was about to admonish him for his nonsense, but of course the tea rose had fat buds that, when closed, made perfect teacups, complete with steaming, delicious-smelling tea within. Actually, a nice cuppa didn't sound too bad right then.

"All right, on to the next square, and Pity," Alice declared.

"Why is it a pity?" the Dodo asked, a little dumbly.

"No—it's the 'Pity' *square*. We have to get ahead now."

"I already have a head," the Dodo squawked, outraged. "You were the one who seemed to let your mind drift back there. And you've lost your mind completely if you think the ground is pitty; seems like it's fairly flat and even to me."

"Never mind," Alice muttered. *"Nonsense."*

They stepped to the next square, where a beautiful, swaying ladder as light as mist rose into the air just out of their reach. Its other end dangled languorously on a moss-covered stone just beyond the bonetalopes.

Alice closed her eyes and summoned the faces of the spectaclesbird and mirrorbird taken away by the policebirds.

"I Pity the poor children, snatched from the Circle, to who knows where."

"I Pity your sister," the Dodo muttered. "Your temper is formidable."

The ladder unrolled slowly and deliciously into Alice's outstretched hands. The frustrated bonetalopes whickered and whinnied in frustration a square behind them. They really were beautiful in their own fragile, clumsy way.

But Alice still had to resist putting a thumb to her nose and waggling her fingers at them.

As she climbed onto the next square, she saw a funny white cloud hovering directly above them. One didn't have to look very closely to see its strong resemblance to a rabbit, and of course it was all fluffy and white. As the winds blew it, a paw seemed to drift to a fob and pull out a watch—and did the cloud wink at her? A younger Alice would have been delighted. An older Alice watched it uneasily and wondered what the Cheshire Cat meant when he said the Rabbit was running toward Time.

Just then a little spiral snout poked its head over a stump, and sparkling black eyes regarded Alice unblinkingly.

"Hello!" she said to it. "I'm very much afraid I don't have time to talk, but . . ."

A second curlicue snout popped up.

"Toves," the Dodo observed. "Slithy ones, at that."

"Are they dangerous?" Alice asked.

A third snout popped up. The three creatures seemed to confer, somehow rubbing their corkscrew snouts along each other's without getting them tangled.

"Not when taken singly," the Dodo said thoughtfully.

A fourth and a fifth tove crept around the bottom of the stump. Their paws were a little too large and strong for Alice's liking, claws a little too curved. Much like a badger's. Which, if Alice remembered correctly, was also relatively harmless when encountered singly, and as long as one didn't back it into a corner.

Now there were a dozen.

And they started creeping closer.

"Dodo," Alice said uncertainly.

Pinned to the fur on the breast of these beasts were tiny ruby-red hearts.

She grabbed the old bird's wing and ran, pulling him after her.

The toves brayed and launched themselves forward.

Alice felt a sudden pain in her ankle: she hadn't moved fast enough! One of the creatures had successfully connected with her flesh. She tumbled to the ground and the force of her fall knocked the horrible thing off—but not before she had felt it actually turning and squirming, trying to work its horrid, dangerously sharp snout farther into her skin.

With a moist-sounding snarl another leapt forward. Its claws raked furrows into Alice's side, slicing her clothes into a thousand tiny ribbons.

She scrambled up off the ground as best she could with the searing pain in her ankle. The toves hissed and lunged at her. The poor Dodo whimpered, surrounded by six toves lowering their heads and getting ready to drive their snouts into his belly.

Alice desperately felt around in her pocket for one of the biscuits she had taken from the White Rabbit's house. Swallowing it all at once without chewing was, of course, Mildly Impolite. A small snake slithered up and around her and the

Dodo and pulled them down—right to the square with the bonetalopes.

"Out of the frying pan . . ." she moaned.

"How dare you even speak of such a thing! Some of my grandbirds were murdered in a hot skillet with crusty breading!" the Dodo shouted at her.

But the biscuit's effects were working their way through her system.

Alice looked around for something to do. The Queen of Clubs' castle was in view but far ahead of them: a beetle-shiny square of blackness nestled at the base of the distant mountains, behind a formidable river.

She reached over and—*pulled.*

The game board stretched and distended like an India rubber ball. Alice's stomach felt like it was doing the same thing. Nevertheless, she hooked her thumbs into the best hold she could—the far riverbank—and heaved it mightily to herself.

"Come on! Run!" she told the Dodo.

"That's cheating!" the leader of the bonetalopes cried. She sounded and bugled, a fearsome beast with no fewer than six sharp knife-horns sprouting from her skull. The fierce thing lowered her head and galloped madly, nearly breaking her slender kneeless appendages in fury.

The Dodo leapt up onto the tongue of stretched land

and ran down to the castle, getting immediately smaller like a trick drawing or an illusion.

A tove rammed itself into the meat of Alice's calf and began twisting around, working its spiral deeply in.

Alice screamed.

She had never experienced pain like this in all her life. She could *feel* the sharp and deadly tip moving through her flesh, cutting sinew and muscle.

The bonetalope leapt.

Alice let go and fell. The land snapped back away from her. She grasped desperately at the riverbank, but instead plummeted into cold, wet blackness.

# Chapter Twenty-Two

Alice awoke.

A light breeze brushed her cheeks; it smelled dry and sweet. The bed she lay on was soft and giving in all the right places. A thick, clean linen sheet that had been draped over her body protected her just enough from the air to keep her warm without overheating. The light was unobtrusive. Nothing sounded of clangs, honks, shouts, horseshoes on cobbles, large wheels over ruts, the cries of deliverymen or women, or students getting their exams back. Nothing smelled of coal. Everything was peaceful and serene.

She awoke, but not in Angleland.

Alice's first real emotion that pushed through the blackness of recovering from collapse was *relief.*

The very last thing she had thought before passing out was how she was just going to wake up at home, yet again losing the immediacy of the dangers in Wonderland while being forced to deal with the problems in her own world.

(Only to return at a later time, perhaps, with things having gone from terrible to even worse.)

Alice's second emotion was—nothing.

Not joyous or sad or scared or angry. Just peaceful.

There was no one else in the room and she could, for the first time in a long time, just pause and think and *be.*

She pondered what would have happened if she had died in Wonderland. Would her spirit be trapped—freed—there? *Here?* Would she die in the real world? Was there a God and Heaven for Wonderland? Was He as full of Nonsense as His creations? Would she never have to return home to boring reality and stodgy sisters and flowers that stayed firmly silent . . .

. . . and young men with rosy cheeks . . . ?

Could she remain forever in a world where your words were constantly twisted? Where nothing and no one behaved properly? Where it was all Nonsense all the time, whether you liked it or not?

"I should like a world in between, I think," she murmured to herself, finally stirring a little. "Fancies and whimsies who don't quite know their place, but don't try to kill you, either. They remain delightful or annoying but small and easily dealt with. And same with the real world. Small problems and some sort of consistency.

"No, that sounds more like a wish for an end to all problems than a real world for living in. Very lazy of you, Alice. How about . . . large, eventually solvable problems in a world with rules that may not make sense, but at least stay consistent? And with friends and creatures and places that are occasionally prone to Nonsense?"

She sighed and sat up. Her hair had come completely undone and fell a little lankly around her shoulders. Her dress was gone but her underclothes remained. With only a little bit of aching, she managed to push herself up into a sitting position, resting her back against a positively enormous pile of pillows.

She wasn't in a proper room at all but more of an open space symbolically delineated by airy stone arches that dipped from the ceiling almost to the floor—but then broke off suddenly as if they had grown bored by the whole process. Beyond the arches on one side was an outer wall with giant (strangely indefensible) open windows. On the other side of the bed, wide corridors—or perhaps other connecting rooms—continued onto infinity, with interior walls angling in and out here and there.

Everything was pale grey stone, vaguely pearlescent, like a shell Alice might pick up by the sea and spend several long moments gazing at before deciding to keep or toss. The inside of a purple mussel, perhaps, fascinating in its silveriness that might have been the beginning of a gem—or just a stain from the mud in which it lived.

All of which made her question: had she won the game? Was she in the Queen of Clubs' castle? Because it didn't look very black, as it had from the outside. . . .

Alice's worries were somewhat relieved when a giant stoat, black as night (including her pinafore and apron and little nurse's hat) came quietly padding in on hind legs. Her neck was curled and crooked so she could carefully watch and balance the items on the shiny black tray she carried: a little black cordial bottle that said, of course, DRINK ME in silver curlicue letters, a glittering obsidian cup, and a black digestive biscuit that Alice at once decided she wouldn't put anywhere near her mouth no matter what it said on it. It looked eminently inedible and very disagreeable.

"How's the patient? Took quite a nasty fall there," the thing rasped in a voice far more deep and masculine than Alice would have expected.

"I'm right as rain. I feel marvelous," Alice said, obviously stretching the truth, quick to block any suggestions to the contrary.

But a shooting pain up her leg caused her to wince despite her best efforts.

The nurse carefully set the contents of the tray down on a little nightstand Alice was fairly certain had not been there before. Then she gently pulled the sheet off Alice's lower half. Her left calf, where the tove had pushed its snout fairly far into her muscle, was bandaged tightly and redolent of some sweet-smelling salve. But the flesh pulsed and throbbed with an almost unbearable magnitude when she pointed her toe or moved it at all.

"Toves is difficult critters," the stoat clucked sympathetically. "They pick up all sorts of nasty things from livin' under sundials—poisons and bad humors. Your leg is infected. We cleaned it out best we could, but not sure we got all the charms and nasty beasties out."

Alice was about to open her mouth to correct this outdated notion of science and medicine; thanks to Monsieur Pasteur, everyone knew that infection wasn't caused by magic or spirits or creatures of the usual kind. Merely tiny, microscopic . . .

And then a small blue thing, less a bug than a sort of star with too many legs, pulled itself up out of her bandage and looked around warily.

The stoat snapped out a paw faster than Alice could react (and anyway her reaction would mainly have been to scream in horror).

Triumphantly the nurse held up the thing and crushed it between her claws.

"Got 'em!"

Alice turned away, worried the nurse would pop it into her mouth.

But the stoat was far too professional for that and daintily put it back on the tray and covered it with a cloth.

"Most likely that'll be one of the last of them, don't you worry," she said soothingly. "Now drink your medicine."

Alice dutifully took the tiny—very heavy!—cordial glass after the nurse filled it to its rim with a thick, viscous black liquid. She was a little vexed at the amount and tossed it back as quickly as she could, uncertain whether to expect the nasty codfish-oil taste that came with real-world medicinal draughts—or the sort of complicated, delicious concoction that was the specialty of Wonderland.

It tasted of nothing.

Literally.

It was like . . . thick water. Sort of refreshing, but hard to swallow.

Immediately Alice felt a lovely warmth relaxing all the hard bits inside her, unknotting them, loosening the pain, unraveling the things that oughtn't have been tangled, burning out whatever evil creatures remained in her leg.

"Your wee might be a bit lavender for the next week.

Pay it no mind," the stoat advised, and then padded away, her long tail bobbing in the air.

Alice, feeling much better, rose out of the bed that was so oddly placed in the middle of nowhere and saw more things that she hadn't noticed before—that probably hadn't even *been* there before. Most apparent was a dress hanging from the air that was obviously meant for her. It wasn't at all like her old dress; it was shorter and had what looked like wide trousers instead of a proper skirt. The sleeves went only three quarters of the way down and were finished in knitted ribbing rather than a proper cuff. The material was a very flattering herringbone grey that looked like it might sparkle a bit in the right light.

Over the right breast was pinned a glittering brooch: three black and sparkling clubs held tightly together. As from a deck of cards.

"So I did indeed make it, and this really *is* the Queen of Clubs' castle," Alice murmured, pleased and perhaps just a trifle bit smug. "I don't fancy wearing her sigil, though. We haven't treated yet—nor even talked. I can't go around wearing a queen's favor without knowing where she stands on certain issues."

She smiled at herself in gentle mockery as she spoke. On the one hand, she sounded like a little girl trying to seem as if she understood the world and politicians and all that occurred between them (as Mathilda's magpie did). On the other hand . . . she did, a bit. She knew about the nasty Ramses' party line and the coming mayoral elections and the problems with antisemioticism.

(No, that wasn't quite right. But the feeling and basic thrust of it was.)

So maybe she wasn't an ambassador or spy, but she knew enough to ask: what was the Queen of Clubs' position on the Queen of Hearts' waging war on her own people, and would she help?

"Funny that," she said thoughtfully. "It's like what the Cheshire Cat said: I *do* carry a bit from the real world over here. Just enough sense or something to help me out. What do you call that? That little thing, that angle? That way of seeing something differently from someone else?"

Sighing at her funny memory in this funny world, Alice carefully unpinned the brooch and put it on the pillow on her bed, and only then donned the strange outfit.

She wandered the halls of the castle a little shocked by her own freedom. Certainly there were a number of strange courtiers and servants who gave her stern looks as she passed, but when questioned they directed her reluctantly to the Queen.

(The only ones who didn't respond at all were an

ordered column of creatures that might have been nuns or anhingas; it was hard to tell. They walked with padded feet and bowed heads and crossed wing tips, wearing either headdresses or feathers.)

Club guards stood at attention outside certain "rooms" or paraded in twos down the hallways—but did little more than give her a once-over.

The castle was also a little too free in its own architecture, Alice thought; she passed through rooms where private meetings between councilmembers—and one assignation—were apparently going on.

Decorations looked careless and hastily done, although they all matched. Asymmetrical tapestries on the walls and rugs on the floor were black or grey. Tiny occasional tables up against the walls would have a single piece of grey or black bric-a-brac, sometimes a vase holding a flower that looked just-picked and often droopy.

Some of the windows that looked out onto the world outside shouldn't have, as they were on interior walls. Alice stopped by one and stood on her tiptoes to peep through. Clearly depicted like an early Renaissance painting was the entire board of Snakes and Ladders. The game spread out in the plains beyond the snug little valley where the castle sat, guarded by its silvery moat. Cards and other creatures were fixing the bank of the river that Alice had accidentally ripped out when trying to save herself and the Dodo. She felt bad about that, of course, but wondered at the richness of the loam thus exposed, and the bucolic nature of the scene. It was the thematic opposite of her coming upon the cards painting the roses red or the dying boxwood maze; these creatures were working together quietly to repair nature, and, for all it seemed, happily.

Alice hurried on and eventually found—well, if not the throne room, then at least the Queen's sitting room. For the Queen herself was there and sitting on an elegant, tall chair. The Dodo was also present, relaxing on a tufted couch with a cup of tea and an owl of state perched uneasily nearby, craning his head around on a long accordion neck. He kept the nearly extinct bird fixed in his sight with large unblinking eyes. A little white dog chased both its own tail and a shiny black ball on a grey shag rug. A low table was set with all manner of nibbles and treats—though none of them was sweet. More of the black biscuits, some bright orange cheese, and finger sandwiches that were black with bloody red filling of some sort. Nothing looked appealing in the slightest, though it made a pretty picture. The Dodo, Alice noticed, wasn't actually sipping his tea.

"Your Majesty," Alice said, dipping into a low curtsy.

The Queen turned an elegant head slowly to look at her.

She was tall, very tall, as tall as the Queen of Hearts

had been short. She was serene, reposed, and had eyes that were black all the way to the edges—no whites at all. Her cheekbones were high and sharp as a stylized statue's and her hair was black and shiny and intricately swept into rounds and balls around a headpiece of similar construction, so it was hard to say where one began and the other ended. A long, draping golden veil hung from her crown over her shoulders and down her back. The rest of her dress was a familiar mix of checks, six-pointed stars, and club insignias in dark blue, black, and gold.

"More like the real card," Alice thought.

"Alice! So glad you're well!" the Dodo cried. "Bit of a close call there!"

Alice stuck out her leg—the bandage and wound were utterly revealed by the scandalously short dress thing. The pain wasn't too unbearable. She wondered what would happen when the black drink wore off.

The Dodo went pale upon seeing the scope of the damage.

Even the owl hooted, unable to help himself.

"Congratulations on winning the game," the Queen said formally, bowing her head a little bit. "You'll want a prize, of course. Here."

She nodded, and a thing that looked part hedgehog, part jay shuffled forward with a small wooden chest, which it opened with great ceremony. Inside was a strangely familiar pile of gaudy junk, though not, obviously, really junk: there were giant sparkling jewels hung on golden cords, bangles covered in silver bells, teeny tiny diamond crowns on hair clips, and all sorts of chunky, tacky dinner rings.

Alice selected a pretty little wristwatch whose large dial had pearls marking the numbers. It was the most tasteful thing of the lot, and anyway Alice had always wanted a wristwatch. It would leave her hands free for her camera while she was timing exposures and the like.

"Thank you, Your Majesty."

"I chose a tiepin." The Dodo preened, showing a golden stick that had NUMBER ONE WINNER engraved on it with diamond stars like fireworks all around.

"You risked life and limb to come and see Ourself," the Queen said in a resonant, deep voice. "Almost no one tries the game, much less wins it, these days. Especially after that nasty little rabbit let all those nasty, dangerous creatures into it. Very curious—normally toves don't attack people so immediately and so viciously."

"Yes, but my leg would tend to disagree with that," Alice said with a wan smile.

"Really? What do you have to say for yourself?" the Queen demanded of Alice's leg with interest.

For a moment Alice was terrified her leg was going to

answer back. She didn't know what she would do if that happened.

"I think both I and my leg are most grateful for the ministrations of your servants," she answered quickly with another curtsy.

The Queen seemed to like that, sniffing a little.

"We—I mean, my leg, the Dodo, and I—have come here to beg Your Majesty to help an ailing people . . ." Alice began, clearing her throat.

"Oh, we weren't expecting that," the Queen said, a little nonplussed. She patted herself all over and found a single coin—golden, shaped like a club—and tossed it at Alice. "You don't seem like a beggar."

"No, Your Majesty, if you please." Alice curtsied again, but honestly couldn't keep her eye off the curious golden coin. It was very shiny and intriguing. "I've come to ask for your aid against the Queen of Hearts."

The Queen of Clubs' eyes widened at that. Then she laughed. She shook up and down, stiffly, like an old man in a corset pretending to find a joke funny. "Why do you need our aid against her? We have *been* against her, with all our clubs and soul, since the beginning of Time. We have played War against her over and over."

"And who wins?" Alice asked politely.

"Sometimes we do, sometimes she does. More often

ourself," the Queen said, perhaps lying. She looked a little sly. "I grew tired of it. It's boring."

"Some say it's not a proper game at all," the Dodo put in, trying to be part of the conversation. "Because the cards are random, but set at the beginning of the game, and there is no actual choice or any additional random elements during play—you just flip cards and the outcome is predetermined. . . ."

"Don't be absurd," the owl cooed.

The Queen held up her hand impatiently. "We have no time for Nonsense right now, Dodo. We sense this girl has urgent matters on her mind. Now, have we answered your question?"

"I beg your pardon?" Alice said, blinking.

"We have told you: we are always *against* the Queen of Hearts. Is that all you wanted to know?"

"Ah—no, Your Majesty," Alice said, dropping into yet another curtsy while she thought, confused. "I was wondering if you would be—ah, *actively* against her. As in, help her subjects overthrow her."

"Help her subjects overthrow their *queen*?" the Queen of Clubs demanded. Her mouth went square, or maybe trapezoidal, her upper lip dipping down and the corners pulled taut and outward in disgust.

Alice could see how that idea might seem a little controversial, at least in another queen's eyes.

"Your Majesty, she is out of control, executing and murdering and locking up and torturing her own people, many of them for seemingly no reason. And taking all their toys," she added. She still felt it sounded foolish, but the Dodo nodded seriously and the owl let out a low whistle of shock.

The Queen's face froze as if it was on its way to another expression but she had forced it, by will, to stop.

"Taking . . . all . . . their toys, you say," she said slowly.

"Yes. But also ravaging the countryside and executing people and—"

"They are . . . *her* subjects. She may rule as she wilt." But even with her formal, toneless voice, Alice could tell she wasn't convinced by her own words.

"Do you know Mary Ann?" Alice tried.

"Of course. Who doesn't?" the Queen said, rolling her eyes. Probably. It was hard to tell without any whites.

"The Queen of Hearts had her killed, after torturing her first. I think—I think she blinded her, or ripped her eyes out, or something of the like." Alice trembled as she spoke, picturing the photograph.

The Queen went pale—perhaps. Her skin didn't change color but gave the impression of changing somehow.

"Mary Ann?" she whispered. "The White Rabbit's—the *Rabbit's*—girl?"

"Yes, and it's horrible. But I've seen similar things done

to people you might not have heard of. Children and lizards and most of the Hatter's tea party. The Hatter lost an eye to one of her jubjub birds. She's killing and maiming everyone who wants to stop her from taking all the, um, toys."

The Queen tapped the armrests of her chair with long and pointed black fingernails.

"And it doesn't even make any sense—or Nonsense, either," Alice said, more to herself or the world than the Queen. "I don't know what she expects to gain from any of it."

"Why, she wants to win, of course," the Queen said in surprise. "The girl who has the most toys when she dies wins. At the end of it all, of course. Everybody knows that."

Alice thought about it.

"So she means to die? To—what? Gather all the toys in the world and then . . . ? At the end of all *what*, do you mean?"

"The End of Time, you silly girl. She is going to bring about the End of Time, and the End of Wonderland."

# Chapter Twenty-Three

Alice had thought herself a sensible girl—outside Wonderland, of course—but for some reason she just couldn't make her normally logical, aphorism-stuffed mind chew through what the Queen of Clubs had just said.

"But—" Then Alice decided to shelve her follow-up question and move on to the next-most-obvious piece of information that seemed to be missing. "*What* does she win? If Time itself ends, if it's all over, if Wonderland itself is over and everyone—including herself—is gone, what is there left? To win?"

"She just *wins*. Everything. What can't you understand, girl?" the Queen huffed impatiently. "She is the *winner*. If she has the most toys. When we all die."

"Does she—does she then alone get to live through the End of Time?"

"It's the End of Time, you little fool," the Queen said, leaning forward to look her in the eye. "We don't know how Time works in *your* world, or what he works *at*—"

"Perhaps he's a druggist," the owl suggested.

"Perhaps a druggist." The Queen nodded. "Or a cobbler. But *here* the End of Time is what it sounds like. He—and everything—*ends*."

"But then," Alice said, reluctant to anger the Queen but unable to let the confusing issue drop, "if the Queen of Hearts . . . along with everything else . . . ends . . . what is the point of her winning anything?"

"Because she *wins*. Because she—Is there something wrong with this girl?" The Queen turned in desperation to the Dodo, who shrugged and gave a mild smile like the grandfather of a particularly dull but pretty granddaughter.

"All right, all right," Alice said hastily. She would just have to accept it; this was Wonderland, and their world-view was simply not her own. Winning was important even though you weren't around to enjoy any of your toys or acclaim or spoils. The End of Time was indeed the end of everything, but apparently not enough to whip immediate panic and terror into the hearts—or clubs—of the locals. That's just the way it was.

"So she wishes to acquire all the toys, or most of the toys, and then bring about the End of Time quickly so that she may be judged to be the winner," she said as slowly and clearly as she could.

"Finally the girl is making some sense," the Queen didn't really whisper to her owl. "It took an awfully long Time for her to do so, however."

Alice thought hard. She had won Snakes and Ladders; she could figure this out, too. Right?

Her "plan" up until now had been to throw herself on the mercy of the Queen of Clubs—a feckless and rash thing, considering the general self-interest and irrationality of all the Wonderland natives. She needed something that had much more tooth, much more appeal to a Wonderland type.

"Do you think all the toys of all her subjects would be . . . enough . . . for her to feel comfortable about her chances of winning? Or might she decide it's not *quite* enough, and she should seek beyond her borders for other kingdoms' toys as well?"

The Queen of Clubs narrowed her eyes and looked thoughtful.

"Aha," Alice thought. "*That's* got her attention."

"We do not know. This is a thought normally only given to queens to consider because of its political ramifications.

From the likes of *you*, this sounds like a tactical question, child. As if you are looking for ways to draw Our Royal Self into Hearts' ridiculous folderol."

Alice was surprised at how quickly the Queen saw through her cunning and, yes, manipulative plan. The ruler of the Clubs was much cleverer than many a Wonderlandian.

"Well, yes; that's why I came here," Alice admitted, holding her hands out. "To seek help from you in any way I could. The Queen of Hearts is destroying her own kingdom, plundering it and killing and torturing and locking up her subjects without stopping. I *had* hoped you would help stop this travesty out of the goodness of your heart—"

"Our *WHAT*?" The Queen stood up on her little footrest, which made her taller still. She seemed a mile high, and a trick of the light caused her eyes to look depthless and terrifying.

"Your *clubs*, I mean, Your Majesty, forgive me!" Alice immediately jumped off the couch and curtsied as low as she could, bowing her head. Her golden hair fell around her shoulders and sparkled in the sunlight. Perhaps that nudged the Queen's judgment positively. "The goodness of your clubs, I meant to say."

"You are forgiven," the Queen said haughtily, and sat back down.

". . . but even if you were unmoved by their terrible plight, perhaps you might choose to get involved to protect your own people and their, ah, toy resources."

Did that sound wise? Academic? Clever? Alice had a vision of herself and the Queen dividing up a globe while intently discussing the Doll Mines of Eastern Europe or the Toy Boat manufacturing centers of the Outer Hebrides.

"But of course," the Queen said, narrowing her eyes so dramatically to look down on Alice that they almost entirely closed. She smiled and said with warmth: "That is what a queen does—protects her subjects. Why do you think we put our castle here, at the end of a terrible game on one side and open to the Unlikely on the other?

"We are very much protected in this narrow valley. If the Queen of Hearts ever chose to turn her armies toward us and invade, she would have a hard time of it indeed.

"Our toys are safe."

The Dodo was blinking long, feathery eyelashes at Alice, obviously still keeping all his faith in her but wondering what to do next, where to go from here. His trust and loyalty were frighteningly endless. Alice steadied herself under his avian eye.

The Queen continued on blithely:

"We will not involve ourself in the domestic affairs or troubles of other queens. We have no proof of what she is doing, or if it is out of the normal way she reigns." She sniffed.

"Oh, you have evidence enough, I'd wager. I wager you have spies—knaves and the like—who keep you informed," the Dodo said unexpectedly. "If the Queen of Hearts keeps her eye on you, you most certainly do the reverse, and contrariwise," he added, sipping his tea a little too smugly through his long beak.

Then he coughed, ruining the effect, obviously having forgotten he hated the black stuff.

The Queen of Clubs darkened—really darkened, her skin going shiny and black like onyx. She glowered.

"*Please*, Your Majesty," Alice begged. "The Queen of Hearts is a monster—maiming, executing, and torturing even those once loyal to her! *You* wouldn't do these things, would you?"

"No, but We are a good queen." More than a little self-congratulatorily.

"To her own people," Alice thought angrily. Of course . . . if this were the real world and she were arguing with a real head of state of Europe, she could almost see some logic behind the Queen's thoughts, as backward and uncaring as it might have seemed. The Queen of Clubs was indeed a "good queen," but if she interfered in another queen's rule over her own people . . . what was to stop someone else from doing the same thing to her? What if a king thought that being made to wear little pins of clubs was malicious and coldhearted, and invaded to "save" these people? Because *he too* thought himself good?

Alice could argue about the plight of the Heartlanders until she was blue in the face, but Clubs here wouldn't do anything that might eventually jeopardize her own rule.

"Now, if her subjects actually rose up against her, *lots* of them, we mean," the Queen of Clubs said softly, "that would be a different matter altogether."

Alice blinked, slowly processing what she said with a mix of suspicion and intrigue.

"If a majority of people judge they are ruled by an evil queen, a vindictive, Heartless, cruel tyrant, and they have had enough, and they make that known—why, we would be more than happy to step in and lend them a hand. Perhaps even a flush or a straight."

The owl craned his head on his long accordion neck around in surprise at his mistress's words.

"We would do it out of the generosity of our own clubs," she continued serenely. "And only take as our fair reward in the end any toys our soldiers seized from the deposed despot."

Aha. *There* was the Wonderland angle. Alice strongly resisted rubbing her forehead in exhaustion. She wasn't sure it was a faux pas before royalty, but it seemed like the sort of thing that might be. She also tried not to sigh.

"So," she said instead, taking a broad, shallow breath, "if we can adequately demonstrate that the subjects of the Queen of Hearts are all—or mostly—resisting her efforts to mow them down and seize their property and bring about the End of Time and all of Wonderland, that they are ready to overthrow her themselves, then we may count on you for military assistance?"

"You may *count* on anyone you like," the Queen said generously. "Even our dog, if you wish, although there is only one of him, so it would be fairly short counting. We will commit troops. Pairs of troops, even."

Alice had no idea how to do what she had just proposed. From the savage and brutal drumming her friends had taken to their inability to organize for even the smallest, slightest operation, the task of organizing a revolution seemed hopeless. But at least there was a chance now. She would take it.

"This is just the sort of thing Mary Ann would have been so good at," the Queen said a little sorrowfully. "She knew just what to say, and she knew everyone, and she knew what to say to everyone when she met him."

"Also, she knew the heart of the Rabbit," the owl agreed, bobbing his head up and down. "And all his plans. And therefore . . . all the Queen's plans."

"Yes, upon considering it, we are . . . unsurprised at the removal of Mary Ann by violent means," the Queen agreed. "It was very efficient of the Queen of Hearts, we will give her that. But we can't imagine it endeared her to the White Rabbit."

Why did their talking about Mary Ann *still* irritate Alice, even a little? The poor girl was dead, had died trying to save everyone. She deserved to be thought of as a hero, not an impossible ideal to live up to.

Alice was ashamed of her inner self, and promised Penitence later when she had time.

"I shall depart at once to rally the people," she said aloud, getting up to curtsy again. "How will you know when . . . enough people have decided to throw in together against the Queen of Hearts? Even with, ah, spies, they can't be everywhere at once."

"Take this."

The Queen nodded to her owl.

He heaved and coughed and coughed and heaved most terrifyingly. Alice looked over at the Dodo for confirmation that this was normal Wonderland business—owls coughing up fewmets or pellets in public at the will of the Queen.

But the Dodo looked horrified and embarrassed and uncomfortable and started nodding his head back and forth as if he too were about to be sick, or were looking for a place to hide or excuse himself to.

Finally the owl reached a crescendo and leaned over. The Queen put out her hand. He promptly coughed into it a small and perfect ivory-colored egg.

Alice blinked in surprise. Wasn't the owl a boy? But, and also, was that how eggs came in Wonderland? And . . .

The Queen smiled, satisfied, and turned the egg over with her long black fingernails. On its shell, raised just a bit, was a perfect set of black clubs. The Queen extended it to Alice, who took it with both hands as carefully as she could.

"Take this with you. Keep it safe at all times. Reveal the will of the people to it. If all is as you say, we shall come when it is expedient to do so, with our army."

The Queen stepped down from her chair. Somehow she was now wearing a thick black cape with a long train that extended out of the room. It appeared just in time for her to turn and have it elegantly and dramatically swirl out around her as she left.

"You will exit out the back door, of course," she said, not bothering to turn around. "The bonetalopes were following you to the front—and the snakes didn't get *all* of them."

"Thank you, Your Majesty, Yes, Your Majesty," Alice said, leaping up and curtsying, although she wasn't sure it was necessary since the Queen wasn't even looking. Even so, there was a pair of black cassowaries who now stood guard on either side of the door through which the Queen had exited, with rather mean looks in their eyes. So perhaps it was just as well, for form's sake.

An all-black mome rath with particularly large and heartbreaking eyes and a platter balanced on its head bumped into Alice's leg, obviously encouraging her to put her used tea things on it. She didn't have any, of course, because the tea and its accompaniments looked disgusting.

"Well, this is exciting," the Dodo said (pensively, not excited-sounding at all) as they followed the creature through the halls. "Actually, everything has been rather *too* exciting lately. This is less exciting than some of the previously exciting things. This is *more* than usually exciting but *less* than recently exciting. And less violent too, with any luck."

"What is?" Alice asked, trying to pay attention. But they were passing what looked like a miniature bakery crammed into one of the castle's strange room-alcoves, and tarts and cookies had been set out to cool on an open window that hung from the ceiling. She couldn't help sneaking a couple, just in case. The cookies were pink and sandy and said EAT ME on them in little nuts that might have been pecans, but she wasn't certain; Alice had never seen them before.

". . . the Unlikely," the Dodo was saying. "I haven't been there since I was a fledgling."

"And what was it like?"

"It was *Unlike* anything else, you silly goose," the Dodo said, rolling his eyes. "The Queen is right—you *do* take a long time to get things through that head of yours."

This, of course, made Alice feel a bit glum. Especially since she had failed in the one task she had set herself once they had begged her to take over from Mary Ann: to secure help from the Queen of Clubs.

"Dodo, do you have any thoughts about how we are to go about this? I'm afraid we haven't had much luck with gathering the forces of good so far."

"You gathered the tea party," the Dodo said philosophically. "And brought us to the Grunderound. And you came back and rescued me. So there's two of us now."

"Oh, I really had thought to be able to turn the whole thing over to Mary Ann when we found her!" Alice said, trying not to whine. "I'm afraid the Queen of Clubs is quite right. I'm really not a very good savior, in comparison to her."

Was she hoping for him to disagree? Just a little? She peeped out the corners of her eyes to see his reaction.

"Well, there's no one like Mary Ann," was all he said.

"There's no one *like* anyone else in Wonderland," Alice muttered. "Not you, not Bill, not the Hatter—oh! That's what we'll do!" She clapped her hands. "We will talk to and rally all the Heartlanders we see along the way, of course, but *first* we shall find the Hatter! Assuming, of course, he made his escape and isn't . . . well, gone.

"Without his Nonsense he seems to have moments almost of clarity and purpose, and he certainly knows how to talk to all Wonderlandians."

Suddenly Alice was afraid she might have insulted the Dodo. Dear, kind, kind-of-ridiculous Dodo, who was loyal to the point of waiting on the enemy's very stoop for her to return. Who stayed by her side through Snakes and Ladders and the toves and meeting the Queen.

But he didn't appear to notice any undue compliments given to his friend, or rather, did not seem to be bothered by it.

The black mome rath indicated the end of a long corridor with a careless twitch of its leg and then scooted back the way they had come, bouncing off the walls back and forth as it (he?) went.

The ridiculously long hall narrowed down to a ridiculously tiny end, but of course by the time they made their way along it, everything had shifted and they stood at a giant blank wall in the middle of which was a drab, unremarkable little kitchen door. A giant sign above it said EXIT, with an arrow indicating the door just in case the reader didn't quite get it.

"All right," Alice said, putting her hand on the—slightly greasy?—knob. It swung open, crookedly, like one of the hinges wasn't fastened properly. The light was so bright after the dark, cool halls of the Castle of Clubs that the Dodo blinked and squawked and Alice shaded her eyes.

They stepped outside.

Alice expected many things: a forest made of broccoli, a vast plain that dissolved into a hazy swamp, a brightly colored and garish market town with blue onion domes and flying desk chairs. But what she saw instead was . . .

Home.

*Her* home.

# Chapter Twenty-Four

"But . . . But . . . I don't understand!" Alice cried.

The house wasn't actually, but *seemed*, much larger than it should have been, taking up most of her frame of reference. There should have been other houses with lawns to either side of it but she couldn't see any, as if they weren't quite important enough to show. Everything was perfect and real down to the last detail, including the cracked keystone over the second window to the left of the library.

Except . . .

Alice frowned.

In the real world—or back home, or whatever—the window with the cracked keystone was on the *right* side of the house if you were standing in front and looking at it. A quick ascertaining of other pertinent details further proved her sneaking suspicion: the house had been reversed. Her mother's little kitchen garden could be seen poking out the *left* side of this one.

"Astounding," Alice murmured. Someone else probably would have said *creepy* or *disquieting*, but this was Alice in Wonderland, and everything was amazing.

"Dodo, this is where I live!" she added with excitement.

"Of course," the Dodo said offhandedly, straightening his cuffs. "Very Unlikely it should be here at all."

"Right," Alice said. "I know we're on a mission to unite the Heartlanders, but I would love just a peek inside. I could show you my room!"

The Dodo shrugged. He seemed neither interested nor anxious to go on. Then again, she remembered from her first visit that in Wonderland all things had a habit of leading to the same place. Avoiding her house or going into her house might not have any effect at all on defeating the Queen of Hearts.

Alice practically skipped up to the front door, which tried to sidle out of her grasp once or twice before reluctantly letting her in. It seemed to be just peevish, though, not really set on keeping her out.

"Oh, look!" she cried. "Everything's the same . . . but different!"

At first glance it appeared to be exactly like her real home (in reverse). Beyond the symmetry, however, all other details were slightly askew. Portraits on the wall were occasionally empty of people, as if their subjects had grown bored and wandered off. Many of the smaller inanimate objects—like her mother's favorite vase and a blown-glass candy dish—had little faces and personalities. Alice tried to see what the candies were in Wonderland; in the real world she had eaten all the good ones, and only the licorice were left. But the dish scuttled away from her. It made little tsking sounds that were almost too high-pitched to hear, and that was really the most vexing thing.

"I'm not a child anymore," Alice protested. "I can have as many sweets as I want!"

"Seems like you don't keep your place in very good order," the Dodo chastised. "You should really reprimand it more. Spare the rod, spoil the house, as they say."

"I should do," Alice agreed.

The pianoforte was asleep and its keys unsettlingly warm. The wax fruit in the basket laughed and dissolved under her touch. The fancy carpet slowly revealed scene after scene of distant meadows, other places.

"If the rug at home were really like that, I should never leave the living room!" Alice declared, fascinated. How much her childhood would have changed with the magic views. She might not have done anything else at all.

The downstairs fireplace was unlit and Alice had the distinct feeling that the hearth was yawning every time she turned away. And the . . .

She suddenly turned back to the fireplace, realizing something else was amiss, even for a Reversed, Wonderland House.

There was the little broom for sweeping the cinders, there the scary black iron poker she had not been allowed to touch when she was little. But in place of the little shovel normally used to lift out the coals was a dark green shovel-bird. It stood very still and held its shovel-beak downward the way the real shovel would have pointed. Its dull orange legs were held tight together to imitate the handle and it seemed to suck in its breath to make itself skinnier and more normal-shovel-like.

There was a scratch across its breast and right eye and a bandage just above its right knee.

Alice felt her heart melt.

"Oh, what is it about the eyes?" she asked the Dodo sadly. "The Hatter, your own injury, and this poor fellow here. What does it mean? The Queen of Hearts always seems to be trying to take out your eyes. Why?"

"Why *could* be next, I suppose," the Dodo said thoughtfully, scratching the healing wound on his own brow. "That makes sense. Eyes, Wise, and then she'll go back around and do the Ays, Ease, Owes, and Yous, too."

Alice shook her head disgustedly and turned her attention to the (other) bird.

"Hello. I won't hurt you," she said gently, not holding her hand out for fear of scaring it further.

The shovelbird opened one eye and regarded her blankly.

"Come on, come on," Alice cooed. She reached—slowly—into the pocket of her new outfit and pulled out one of the biscuits from the Castle of Clubs. "Here you go. This is my house, and I'm not going to hurt you."

Slowly the bird took awkward and bobbling steps around the other fireplace tools, untangling itself efficiently if not gracefully. It came to within about a foot of Alice and regarded her for a moment—then shot out its shovel-beak and scooped the biscuit out of her hand, neatly and expertly prying it out of her fingers with its pointed tip. It threw the treat up in the air and let it fall precisely down its throat and into its stomach. Alice could see the shape of the biscuit as it traveled down the inside of its scrawny neck.

"Very good. Mostly. Come with us! The Queen of Clubs has told us that if we stand up for ourselves, en masse, against the Queen of Hearts, she will come to our aid and help overthrow her!"

This was Alice's first rousing speech to get Wonderlandians on her side.

It was not, she reflected, very good.

The creature looked at her sideways, then began to peck at the ground, looking for missed crumbs.

"All right. I suppose you still have no real reason to trust me," Alice sighed. "Well, when we depart I shall still endeavor to take you with me, rather than leaving you here, hiding amongst the ashes. Although . . . isn't it funny . . ." She bit her lip, remembering. "When I was . . . very little . . . I used to wonder what it would be like to hide there myself. I imagined Father mistaking me for the poker and picking me up by the head and poking at the logs with my legs. . . . I must have been very small to imagine that, if I could have fit there. Mrs. Anderbee and my nurse were always scolding me to get away from the fire.

"I wonder if there are any more refugees hiding here, in places where *I* used to hide! Dodo, I'll look in the kitchen, you in the pantry. No—let's make it the other way around. I used to tuck away in the pantry myself and pretend the pies were boats that would take me away to Puddingland."

"There is already a Puddingland," the Dodo pointed out. "Or wait—it's Puddinglane. Or maybe Penny Lane. In my eyes and all that . . ."

"Pudding is in your eyes?" Alice asked.

"Better than pennies," the Dodo answered sagely. "That would mean I was dead."

"Too true." She patted him solicitously. "We wouldn't want that. Come now!"

The copper pots and pans in the kitchen had obviously been gossiping or engaged in some other inappropriate activity, because the moment the two walked in they immediately flew apart from their tight little crowd and tried to rehang themselves on the proper hooks, banging and making a noise so thunderous that Alice had to cover her ears.

Actually, on second glance they seemed to *enjoy* the noise they were making, and didn't look like they were trying to sort themselves out at all.

"Stop that at once!" Alice cried.

This only made them bang and clang even more loudly. Now tinny laughter and minuscule jeers were added to the clamor. One saucier actually paused long enough to stick his thumb to his handle and waggle his fingers provocatively at her.

*"Stop it right now!"* Alice ordered. She popped a biscuit in her mouth and opened her hands, surrounding the pans—at least visually—and then brought her hands together until they almost touched.

The pots and pans and lids shrank, of course, their wails getting higher and higher pitched as they almost disappeared. Alice waited a moment, then opened her hands again. They grew and screamed at her.

She clapped her hands all the way closed.

She waited a moment.

Then she opened them, slowly, and this time the cookware was silent and looked thoroughly chastised.

"*Thank* you," Alice said, a little shortly. Somewhat hangdog, they made their way back to the rack and hung themselves up in the proper position. "I have no issue at all with you socializing—it's your behavior while you did so that was unseemly."

"Quite right, too," the Dodo said. "Keeping an orderly house is the first tenet of civilization. Oh, I found these, hiding in the stockpot."

Huddling in the palm of his wing was a family of mice with ribbons for tails and buttons for eyes and pocket-handkerchief corners for ears. They were calico and shivering miserably.

"Are you fleeing the Heart soldiers?" Alice asked, trying not to squeal with delight. One of the smaller ones, probably a baby of some sort, held up a wee doll and shook it defiantly. The toy was no bigger than the nail of Alice's smallest finger and had what looked like poppy seeds sewn on for eyes. "Oh dear, she's going after toys as small as that?"

The mice nodded fiercely. One of the other children began to cry—presumably because her toy had already been lost to the Queen of Hearts. Reluctantly, her brother held out the doll for her to touch for comfort.

"This is madness," Alice swore.

"We're all mad here," the Dodo said a little sadly, obviously thinking of the Hatter.

"You know," Alice said gently to the crying mousekin, "I used to hide *my* doll—her name was Sophia—in the stockpot. We played hide-and-go-seek, and it was terribly hard pretending not to know where she was. I would try to make myself forget—because *Mathilda* wouldn't hide her. Ever. She was never up for any sort of game, except for charades with family and friends. What a wet blanket she is."

"That's unusual!" the Dodo said, intrigued. "I would have thought in a boring world like yours she would have been a girl, like you."

Alice decided to ignore that. It wasn't likely the Dodo would ever meet Mathilda, so she would never really have to explain it all anyway.

"Come with us, little mice," she offered, trying again. "The Queen of Clubs has promised to help as long as we try to rebel against the Queen of Hearts ourselves. If she sees the entire country is aligned against the bad queen, she will come with troops and save us all."

The parent mice shook their heads and drew their children close.

"Well, please think about it. Here: not a bribe, just a parting gift." She pulled out one of her biscuits and broke it in half, handing over a piece. The adult mice grabbed it with tiny claws like pins.

As they turned away into the pantry, Alice frowned, thinking.

"Dodo, how are all these creatures escaping the Queen of Hearts making their way here? Wouldn't they have to go through Snakes and Ladders first and win it?"

"There are many different ways into the Unlikely." The Dodo shrugged. "But most are tiny."

"Succinct, and yet meaningless," Alice observed. "Oh, look—what a surprise. A mome rath in the pantry."

A bright pink-and-green one, its head tuft a darker pink. It stood out amongst the quietly murmuring pots of jam and old biscuits like a bright chintz-print curtain in the middle of an ancient wood. It did not belong there at all; for even the Wonderland version of her house had colors duller than the rest of the imaginary world.

*This* creature showed no hesitation at all and immediately threw itself into Alice's arms. It was a little shocking, and very furry, and exceptionally soft. She hugged it back, trying to ignore its rather oversized eyes.

"It's not a monster—it's just a terrified little thing," she told herself.

"There, there," she whispered aloud. Should she offer it a biscuit? Did it even have a mouth? Was it rude to offer a biscuit to something that didn't have a mouth? "I didn't only play pretend things in the pantry. I always ran there when I was—when I was sad, or scared. Or felt bad."

Her head swam for a moment with déjà vu. She suddenly felt that she was comforting a much younger Alice, and not a ridiculous little Wonderland creature. The room didn't spin, exactly, but she felt light-headed, like things were shifting behind her eyes, her brain resettling itself for a different reality.

"Dodo," she said quietly, putting a hand to her head. "We are still in Wonderland, are we not?"

"We are where we've been," the Dodo said kindly. "I've always been here. Still am."

"I'm not really *home*, at a different time, am I?" she asked, looking around. For when she didn't look *too* close, the bizarre differences weren't readily apparent, and the movement of normally inanimate objects out the corner of her eyes seemed more like the beginning of dizziness or a fainting spell. "I'm not in the past when I was a little girl—or in the future, when I'm wandering about the rooms, old and mad?"

"You might be old—I don't know how folks age where you're from—but you're certainly mad," the Dodo said soothingly.

"You don't think it's queer that in each place where I've had a memory of hiding—either an object or myself—we find another refugee of the Queen of Hearts?" She knelt down to look the Dodo dead in the eye. "*Specifically* in each place I remember, and nowhere else? As if . . . as if they either knew somehow it's where I hid and felt safe, or . . . they're all in my mind to begin with?"

The Dodo just blinked at her, and for a frosty moment all she saw were blank avian eyes.

"Dodo, please tell me! Are there mome raths in my head?" Alice pleaded. "Do I carry my Nonsense around with me everywhere? Even back in Angleland? Is that what the Cheshire meant? What does it all mean?"

"It means that, with all these good fellows we're finding, we have a great head start on telling everyone about the Great Hearts Uprising!" the Dodo said, patting the little mome rath on its head in a fond but ultimately patronizing manner.

"But, but . . ." Alice fretted. "This is very perplexing. I feel like I'm on the edge of a great precipice, or a sudden expansion of my range of knowledge. Where do I *go* when I am in Wonderland? Or is it just my mind, while my body stays at home—possibly asleep? Does any of it come back *with* me? Literally? Do the little mome raths and calico mice sneak a ride in my . . . mind house here? How is it I forget facts and figures and memories from the world I come from while here, and while I'm over there, Wonderland seems to drift away entirely? For when I'm over there, I almost entirely forget the importance of what is going on *here*."

"That," the Dodo said, "is tragic. That's like paying a painter with a squib instead of a penny."

Alice regarded him steadily. Here she was having an attack of existentialism and all she got was Nonsense.

The Dodo shrugged. "I'm a politician. Talk to a philosopher about these issues—you can usually find them scavenging in the garbage bins. Talk to *me* about caucus races. But I shan't have any constituents at all if the Queen of Hearts takes their toys and murders them."

*What world do I really belong to?* was a question that flitted through the forefront of Alice's mind for only a tenth of the tick of a second hand on a fancy grandfather clock. It was actually irrelevant. Both worlds needed saving.

"I've forgotten what's really important. It's not what's going on my head at all—it's real things happening to real people, in Wonderland *and* Angleland," she said, chastising herself. "I've entirely lost my perspective."

Suddenly she blinked.

*"Perspective!"* she cried aloud.

"No one is answering to that name," the Dodo said, looking around.

"No, listen!" she said excitedly.

*"I have mine and you have yours*
*It's needed in a painting*
*But in the end none agree on*
*the meaning of the thing.*

"The answer is *perspective*! It's a riddle my friend told me. I forget his name."

"And yet you remember the riddle," the Dodo observed.

"Why, that's true, isn't it?" Alice said slowly. "How can I remember that so clearly?"

"You must remember to tell it to the Cheshire when you see him again. He *loves* riddles. More than the Hatter, actually. Now, I think you were going to show me your room?"

"Quite right," Alice said distractedly. She felt the way she did sometimes when a conversation with someone had not gone quite the way it should, and even though she played and replayed the dialogue in her head later she couldn't figure out what had gone wrong, but still felt bad about it. She needed a good sulk or quiet sit by the window, possibly with a kitten.

Who had told her the riddle? He had said it was important. That he depended upon it, or something of the sort.

The weight of this and two worlds fell heavily upon her and her shoulders. So many people depended on her now!

But as she put one hand on the banister, suddenly she felt exactly the opposite.

Not knowing quite how it had begun, Alice found herself slowly floating up the stairs, drifting with purpose, one finger keeping her anchored to the railing.

"Of course," she said in wonder, as if she had only just rediscovered this method of taking the stairs—how could she have ever forgotten? "I must remember to do this when I get home—what a much better way for moving between floors! I'm surprised no one else has started the trend already."

The souvenir etchings of foreign places that hung on the wall animated themselves most pleasingly as she passed them by: a little sailboat in Venice made its way past Saint Mark's; crows circled the onion domes of St. Petersburg while banners snapped in the soundless wind. A salmon leapt and sparkled—in a sepia sort of way—out of a very detailed waterfall.

"I never noticed that before," she observed.

"Lovely, just lovely," the Dodo said, floating behind her. He had on a pair of reading glasses this time, but they balanced on his beak awkwardly, their arms extending the wrong way, out away from his face.

At the top of the stairs was a broom dog who apparently couldn't remain in hiding while there were messes to clean up. His long, whiskery beard and moustache, like those of a very healthy Scottie, made a sort of brush; sweeping his head back and forth allowed him to tidy together a neat little pile of dust (and if he missed something, the other brush, the tiny one at the end of his tail, jotted forward and finished it). Alice had seen one very much like this on her first trip to Wonderland, but that dog had been brown, and this was more ash colored.

Some of his whiskers were bent and broken, but otherwise he seemed all right.

"Hallo there, good boy," Alice said, putting out her hand. Like most Wonderland creatures he was diffident at best; a shaggy ear rose up, leaving his bristles to sway back and forth below, but then he continued sweeping up. "I wish we had you round back home. Then Mrs. Anderbee could have a rest and put her feet up now and then. Perhaps have a cup of tea while you did the parlor. I wonder who you are in Angleland."

As they approached the doorway to her own room, she saw that the shadows inside were slightly off. And though the house was a mishmash of memories and history, Alice immediately grew tense. Something was *wrong* in there. There was something extra. Something alive.

Waiting for her.

Alice took a deep breath and put her hand on what

would have been the Dodo's shoulder had he been a human. He bobbed his head but said nothing.

She stepped over the threshold, the heel of her shoe making rather more noise on the wooden floor than she would have liked.

She expected cards to attack, she expected the executioner dog, she expected many things . . .

. . . but not the quivering lump just beyond the bed, which looked as though someone were doing a poor job of crouching down and hiding behind it.

"Ahem," Alice said, clearing her throat.

The lump rose and grew hesitantly, taking on the form of a rather . . . large . . .

Top hat . . .

# Chapter Twenty-Five

"Hatter!" Alice cried.

The hat rose more, appearing to grow. A face appeared under it: cautious, framed by crazy hair, and finished with a gaping wide mouth that revealed two large buckteeth. His one good eye blinked slowly. In place of the tiny top hat over his injured eye was half a pair of cinder goggles. The mica lens was dark, hiding whatever lay beneath.

"Hatter!" Alice cried again and threw herself over the bed in a most unladylike move. She wrapped her arms around him and squeezed.

"Alice . . . ?" the Hatter said slowly and unsurely, a ghost of a smile beginning to form on his wide mouth.

"What what, Hatter old fellow," the Dodo said. "Good to see you're up and about."

The Hatter came out of his crouch—he had been hunkering down to protect a number of small beasts. Amongst them was a cat the size of an egg, several mome raths, a teakettle with legs, and what was probably a dragon fly: a tiny lizard with outsized eyes and leathery wings, smoking a bit from its tail and mouth.

"Nearly wasn't. Up and about." The Hatter looked down at himself and patted his own shoulders and chest. "Nearly grabbed by those nasty cards. They knocked what remaining Nonsense I had right out me. I'm afraid they might have gotten the others. . . . I haven't seen the Gryphon or Bill, though he *is* very small."

"Bill is fine. He escaped with help from the Rabbit's housekeeper," the Dodo told him.

"But . . . the Dormouse?" Alice asked hesitantly.

In answer to this the Hatter took off his hat. There on his bald pate slept the silly little thing, both his front paws in plaster and paper. The Hatter put his hat back on, as gentle as a mother.

"Oh, Hatter, I'm so relieved. What a terrible time it is," Alice sighed.

"He's a right ready misbegotten toethrower these days, pardon my language," the Hatter muttered. "I shan't be sending him a present at Christmas, I can tell you that."

"But what are you doing here? In my bedroom?"

"Where else would I be?" the Hatter asked curiously. "Safe as houses in your house. Safest in your room."

And if Alice didn't think too much about it, there was a certain sense to it.

"Of course," she said softly, squeezing his shoulder. "Of course you're here, in my—sanctum sanctorum. You always have been. You always will be. You're the Nonsense in my head that mustn't be ignored. You're the piece of me that maddens everyone, my sister the most."

The Hatter gave her a tired smile and said nothing—which might have been the wisest thing he ever said.

"Hatter, I've been to see the Queen of Clubs—"

"Why?" he asked, surprised.

"So we can form an alliance with her and defeat the Queen of Hearts."

"But they are always at War anyway," the Hatter said. "And they're both queens. Why would she help us? And what's to stop her from taking all the toys herself, and taking over Hearts if she invades?"

"Do you have a better idea?" How quickly her feelings had gone from relief at seeing him alive to frustration! "I'm *not* Mary Ann, and *I* don't have any better ideas."

"Does the Queen have all the toys yet? Or is she still gathering them?" the Dodo asked quickly, trying to change the subject.

"Funny you should ask that. We saw *cartloads* of toys being loaded up and hauled off on our way here. Apparently soldiers are going to every house and confiscating toys—and then burning the houses."

"It sounds like maybe she hasn't enough yet. So if she ends Time now, she may not be able to win," Alice said thoughtfully.

"Aha! That is what she is doing? Trying to be the one with the most toys in the end?" the Hatter said, nodding in realization. "She already has lots. Scads. Mountains. But knowing her, she will probably make twice as certain that she has enough, and *then* send the White Rabbit to stop the Great Clock."

"That's very tactical of her," the Dodo said. "I always do that with my halves. When two and two is four, I always say eight, just to be twice as certain."

Alice ignored him. "Hatter, that was surprisingly logical and concise. Well done."

But he began to shiver. "I *told* you they knocked the Nonsense out of me. I'm not myself—no, don't follow up on that one, Dodo. It doesn't look good for me."

And to be sure, he did look a bit pale and wan around the edges. Hungry. *Tall.* Alice was fairly certain that neither sense nor nonsense was a necessity to living healthily in the real world, not in a meat-and-potatoes sort of way—but who knew here? Maybe it was bad for the soul to be lacking in it, and the flesh soon followed.

"Alice . . ." he began softly. "Why did you leave us? When we needed you most?"

"I didn't *want* to, Hatter!" Alice cried. "I wanted to stay and help you—I didn't know what to do! I was terrified but prepared to fight until the end. I had no idea at all that I would be whisked away back to my home. If I *made* it happen somehow, I am dreadfully sorry.

"The first time I left Wonderland I was so, so sad and missing home, and then I was attacked by the Queen of Hearts, and I woke up elsewhere, and I was *glad* to be home. For a while, anyway," she admitted. "But *this* time I had no desire to go home at all! Maybe home just yanked me back, somehow, sensing I was in danger."

"Hatter, old fellow," the Dodo said gently, "this stupid girl came into the Rabbit's own house to rescue me. Surrounded by cards and guards. She is not wanting in will or bravery."

"No, of course not," the Hatter said quickly, but his good eye never left her two blue ones, as if making sure she was still there. "Forgive me. I had supposed that with Mary Ann gone, you would naturally disappear as well."

"I am *not* Mary Ann," Alice growled, almost stomping her foot. "And she didn't *disappear*—she was *murdered.*

Please do not confuse the two. What happened to her was the direct result of an order by the Queen. Do not just chalk it up to the random happenings of Wonderland. And I came back and was nearly killed by a herd of rabid toves and almost lost a game of Snakes and Ladders while trying to get to the Queen of Clubs—which is the best way I thought of to save everyone. I realize my methods are more real-worldy than Wonderland's, but that's all I have to work with!"

"And if we win?" the Hatter asked unexpectedly.

"I beg your pardon?" Alice asked, still fuming but trying to calm down. Oh *why* did comparisons to the poor dead girl upset her so?

"If we win . . . will you stay?" It wasn't quite plaintive; it was genuinely curious. "Forever?"

Alice blinked.

"Why, I . . . I don't know, Hatter."

Things in Wonderland would be different if they won, and she was the reason. If it was anything like last time, they would probably make her a Queen of Something and maybe listen to her now and then.

But . . . what about the real world?

What about Mayor Ramses and the mome raths of the Circle?

And—Mother and Father would miss her. Maybe her sister, too, although perhaps she would be too busy trying to avoid the scandal of having a missing sister to really weep for little Alice.

And that boy . . . there was a *boy*, wasn't there?

And if she won there, in the real world?

If she saved the—whatevers, and defeated Mayor Ramses and . . . well . . . *somethinged* with the boy . . . she wouldn't think about that bit right now . . . would that be winning? Would it be enough that she would never want to return to Wonderland? What if they made her Queen of the World over there? Or even just the Americas? Would that be enough to occupy her ideas and banish thoughts of borogoves and bread-and-butterflies?

"Let's concentrate on defeating the Queen of Hearts right now," Alice said, a little too swiftly. "My personal future is far less important than stopping her from imprisoning and executing innocents, and then ending the world."

"Too true, too true," the Dodo cooed.

"The Queen of Clubs says she will help if there's a mass uprising against the Queen of Hearts. She must see that this is what the people really want. So we must convince the otherwise timid and skittish inhabitants of the realm to come together, face their fears, and resist rather than just running away and hiding—*as welcome as that idea might be*."

Alice addressed this last bit to an umbrella leaning

casually up against the wardrobe, trying to look like an inanimate object rather than the vulture it really was.

The normally spooky, beaked head looked around at her in almost comical chagrin.

"Have you ever had a thought you couldn't catch?" the Hatter asked. "It just . . . skitters around the edges of your mind while you're having an argument with someone, and only later does it turn up and you say to yourself: *yes*, that is what I should have said? 'Where were you when I needed you most, you silly little thought?' "

He nodded, using his chin to point out the various hidden creatures around the room. It was the same as trying to catch the creatures of Wonderland and reason with them, was what he was trying to say.

"Well, until someone comes up with a better plan, this is all we have. We shall just have to try," Alice said firmly, pursing her lips. "And lead by example. Creatures? Wonderlandians? *Les enfants?*" She clapped her hands together the way she had seen foreign governesses do when taking a number of their charges to the park. "Attend me now. It is time to go."

A dozen different Wonderland natives stuck their large-eyed heads out of various hiding places. While Alice wasn't entirely surprised to see a mirrorbird step down off her vanity (fancy and new and not from her real house) or a pencilbird sneak up off her tiny child's desk (gotten rid of years ago), the eighteen-footed raterpillar crawling out from under the bed was a bit of a shock. But the thing that looked a little bit like a garland and a little bit like a string of pom-poms that fluttered through the room on uncertain wings was most surprising of all. Alice was afraid it would tangle up in her hair somehow. It settled itself rather endearingly around the Dodo's shoulders, where he thoughtlessly adjusted it like a muffler and patted one of the yarn baubles on its body.

"Very fetching," Alice said approvingly. "Let us depart; it is time to leave the Unlikely."

And trying to project an aura of unquestionable, calm leadership—again, like a foreign governess—Alice left her room and floated down the stairs, not daring to look back to see if anyone followed.

# Chapter Twenty-Six

She did, however, *hear* the Dodo and Hatter pattering down the stairs behind her; apparently they didn't float, or didn't choose to. And she very much hoped the soft susurrus and mushy cloth sounds that were just on the edge of her hearing were the rest of the small and assorted Wonderlandkind following.

"And what if I throw open the front door," she thought as she reached for the doorknob, "and we are immediately surrounded by Heart cards?"

When she did open it—at a speed somewhere between bravery and caution: too slow for real bravado but too fast to do any actual good should there have been a danger—there was nothing.

Well, not quite nothing. For one thing, the Queen of Clubs' castle was no longer in view. Perhaps it was behind the house now, or perhaps it or the house had hidden itself entirely elsewhere. Whatever the case, the grounds that now spread out below the house were soft and infinite. Rolling hills and friendly trees invited the viewer to walk, no, *run* into their embrace, propelled by half-recalled memories of childhood. The air that blew was sweet, somewhere between bedstraw and the sea. A tiny, jolly train rode over the crests of hills and disappeared, only to reappear again with white puffs of smoke that bubbled up to the sky in the shapes of fish, and whales, and miniature suns.

Alice was at first enthralled and then immediately suspicious.

None of her companions gave the view a second thought, but they all piled up around the doorway—behind her, of course—and looked out at it with their owlish eyes.

"Well," Alice said, trying to sound bright. "Here we go!"

The other not-quite-nothing revealed by the open door was a bright piece of fluff lying in the middle of the walkway, too slim to be the tuft of a buried mome rath. Alice went to pick it up, but it was far heavier than it looked and somehow *caught*—on the scene itself, it seemed.

"Excuse *me*!" a voice cried out in purple indignation.

"Oh!" Alice dropped the furry bit, but it stayed angrily where it was in the air.

And then, of course, the rest of the Cheshire Cat appeared, walking back and forth above the ground with the hauteur only a truly affronted cat could pull off.

"What are you doing out here?" Alice asked, scratching him on the back of his neck. He stretched to better enjoy it, the tip of his tail extending far beyond its supposedly natural limits, the space between the purple stripes increasing to a foot or more. Then it snapped back into a tight coil. "Why aren't you hiding inside with the others?"

"I haven't been invited in," the cat said with cool dignity, suddenly flipping on his back and wearing a top hat, spectacles, and a gentleman's general appearance.

"Lovely hat, Cheshire," the Hatter said from behind Alice.

The cat rolled his eyes. "Of course *he's* here. Before she took off your head she would have to take off your hat, wouldn't she? And that would be difficult. . . ."

The Hatter doffed his hat to reveal the Dormouse. The cat's eyes widened and he leapt at the poor sleeping thing with the yowl and frenzy of a real cat, glasses and hat forgotten.

The Hatter immediately clamped the hat back down on his head and held it there hard, over his ears. The Cheshire screeched to a halt in midair, barely stopping in time to keep from colliding.

"Choose a side, cat," the Hatter growled.

"I dare say, Hatter old boy," the Dodo said, alarmed. "It's just a *little* bit of nonsense. How far gone are you? Ease off!"

"I choose *inside*," the cat said, opening his mouth wide and walking his tail and hind end into it until he entirely disappeared, having swallowed himself.

"No, on the contrary, outside is better." His voice came out of the air, sounding far away and hollow. He reappeared in the air before them, lying contentedly on his side.

Alice took a deep breath to steady herself.

"Cheshire Cat, can you help us? We need to drum up—no," she said hastily, "we need to *encourage* everyone to resist the Queen of Hearts on their own, and then the Queen of Clubs will help stop her."

"And the Queen of Diamonds shall dine on fine sums and the Queen of Spades will call for all ransoms," the Cheshire sang.

"I'm *serious*, cat," Alice said, frowning at the fact that she sounded like the Hatter. "People's lives are at stake."

"Mary Ann tried to rally them to a man, and now she is no more," the cat said thoughtfully, looking at his claws. "What makes you think you can do better than she?"

"I *know* I'm not Mary Ann! But I am trying my hardest! And besides, I bring . . . an outside *perspective* to the whole thing!" she surprised herself by saying.

"Here's a riddle, liddell Alice: then why are you trying to *be* Mary Ann? Why are you pursuing such a complicated plan?"

"Do you have a better idea?" Alice demanded.

"I don't. But I'm a cat, sweetheart." He twirled and flipped around and regarded her with lazy eyes. "Mary Ann and the Rabbit and the Rabbit and Mary Ann. There are always two. Me and . . ."

. . . he grinned and disappeared.

"Bother," Alice said, kicking the dirt he had been floating over. "He always makes me feel itchy and stupid. Come on, you lot. Which way do we go?"

Two of the mome raths, a big and a little one, toddled forward and threw themselves onto the ground, making an arrow.

"Fine," Alice hissed and tried to march with some dignity in that direction.

The landscape changed in just the sort of way Alice now expected; that is, she expected it to change unsettlingly but couldn't of course predict what it would change *into.* Somehow the summery hills faded and the little band entered a dark forest of positively enormous trees—far larger around than those in the Tulgey Wood. The ground rose in humps about their roots. It was so dark on the path that Alice couldn't clearly see what kinds of leaves or branches were overhead; pine, she thought, considering the cylindrical shape of some of the silhouettes she managed to make out. But there was no inkling of dark green or light green or any green at all: this was apparently an autumn forest where the tones were all brown and grey and black and shadow.

Sometimes the trees shivered.

And instead of muted birdcalls and the riffling through leaves by small animals, there were strange, deep-throated mumblings and murmurings. Like a conversation you couldn't quite catch a word of, the sounds drifting maddeningly just at the edge of comprehension.

"Where are we?" Alice asked the Hatter and the Dodo. The smaller creatures followed them like a particolored parade with their own murmurs and snufflings, the broom dog bringing up the rear. It would have been very jolly indeed if the mood in the woods hadn't been so mysterious and grim.

"Still at the edge of the Unlikely, I suppose," the Dodo said, looking around.

"The Droozy Forest, I think," the Hatter said

mournfully. "Shan't make it out of here without a scratch, that's for certain."

At this the Dodo reached over with his big and seemingly buffoonish beak and raked it across the Hatter's left wrist. It left a ragged line of broken white skin and a few pricks of pink blood.

"What was that for?" the Hatter demanded in outrage.

"Now you have a scratch. Now we can leave," the Dodo said simply.

"I really don't know how much more of this I can take," Alice muttered. She was beginning to remember a much younger Alice weeping in the Tulgey Wood, tired of all the nonsense. Could she even *imagine* living here forever? Even if she were queen? Her penchant for nonsense was less than when she was a child, but more than the Hatter could endure right now, and far more than most adult Anglishmen and women would put up with. "I saw a train on the hills—could we take a train to Heartland?"

"Why would we take it there? It belongs here," the Dodo said pointedly.

"Is there a *station* around here?" she asked through gritted teeth.

"I believe so."

"Well, let's get out of these woods as fast as we can and find it," Alice decided. She doubled her speed and walked with her chin in the air, away from the mystery of the whispering trees.

A train; that was something reasonable. And civilized. How badly could Wonderland muck up something so real, so mechanical, so invented by humans?

She thought she saw the path lighten a little before them, as if it were opening up, just past the two argyle oaks. Maybe this was only a small wood, like in a park! Yes, a town park. Then the train station would be nearby, and . . .

. . . Argyle oaks?

Alice stopped. She took a look—a really *good* look—at the trees around her. They all stood in pairs, well matched. The swells at the bottom of each that she had thought were boulders or roots were dully shiny, black, and brown. *And laced.*

The cones and cylinders that sheathed the fat trunks were wool, of course. . . .

"mumble mumble Alice not a chance . . ."

"little upstart, mumble? *Cut her down to size* . . . sssssize . . . size. . . . card cutter will. . . ."

"Hallo!" Alice shouted, trying not to panic. "I can hear you! It's very rude to talk about someone who's *right below your nose*!"

"thinks she's so important . . . irrelevant as a hat on a tove. . . ."

There was faraway grown-up laughter. A pair of stockinged feet in ladies' heels tapped a little up and down as if unable to conceal their mirth at whatever scornful thing was being said.

"I can't tell precisely what you're saying, but I know it's about me!" Alice continued. "And I know it's very impolite. What is that? About a cutter?"

The legs and feet, now that she recognized them as such, were very, very conventional. There wasn't a bright sock or Dormouse hidden amongst them. They were *very* real world.

A horrid thought occurred to Alice: did she actually know these people? She couldn't recognize them, of course, but then again she didn't spend much time admiring people's footwear. "Something I shall strive to correct in the future," she admonished herself.

Then conversations started up again, incomprehensible and quiet and casual, as if everyone was trying to talk over an embarrassing moment. As if *she* was an embarrassment to be quietly ignored by everyone. And hopefully removed.

"Hello! I'm real! I'm right here! Hello!" Alice waved, trying to maintain her anger but feeling queer, like she was fading from the inside out.

"Fancy sensible Alice, talking to the trees," the Dodo said, not unkindly. "Dear girl, the train station is up ahead."

"But—they're talking about me," Alice protested. "I heard them. Didn't you hear them? They were making fun. They said . . . I wasn't important. They were laughing, like I was a joke. . . ."

"Of course they were, dear," the Dodo said soothingly. "Wind in the branches. Let us go, then. Have a butterscotch?"

He held up a tiny hard candy wrapped in paper. Unsure what else to do and feeling very blue, Alice took it.

"Is there any such thing as a card cutter here, Dodo? Is it like a dealer, or someone who just cuts a deck of cards, before a game?" she asked glumly.

"A dealer? Oh no, not at all. The Card Cutter is *terrifying*," the Hatter said, looking pale and serious. "Don't even mention his name! He'll smell it!"

And there, before them, was the station.

# Chapter Twenty-Seven

The ticket booth was made of paper. Printed-page bricks, grey paste from old wet fish wrappings as mortar in between, the signboard DROOZY STATION in rolled newspaper sections. The window had oiled paper to let light in, and the praying mantis who sat there wore a crisp white paper hat.

"Well, step up, step up," she snapped, but not unkindly. "Where's it to be, then?"

"Good afternoon," Alice said, a little distracted. "I'm sorry, I arrived here rather more suddenly than I expected."

"That's the National Railway for you!" the mantis crowed, which was strange, and then blew a little horn in triumph, which was also strange. "Now, will you be going first class or premium?"

"I don't know how much it is," Alice admitted. "How much is a one way, no return, to Heartland?"

The mantis blinked, which was hard, for she had no lashes—or eyelids, for that matter. "The Local-Nine to Heartland is not recommended, for reasons of bloody civil war. Try a different place instead. The park not too far from TulgVapCo station is lovely this time of year, I've heard tell."

"No, I'm afraid it's Heartland," Alice said, putting her hands in her pockets. "One ticket for me and all my . . ."

She turned, but no one stood there except the Hatter, who was now a slightly stooped, middle-aged, very plain Hatter—with a large hat, to be sure, and a prominent nose, but that was all.

". . . and my friend here," she finished lamely.

"Perhaps they've gone ahead," she told herself. "Perhaps they're running to tell all their friends to pass the word along about the Queen of Clubs and how they should rise up against the Queen of Hearts!"

She felt a little sad without the colorful mome raths and the Dodo and the shovelbirds. It was scary to lead them but lonely without them.

"No sale," the mantis said briskly, and reached up to try to slam the oiled paper down.

Without thinking Alice reached up as well. Despite having shorter arms than the giant insect, she managed to grab the ends of the paper window first and rip it away from the ticket seller—to rip it out of the wall entirely, in fact.

"I'll have my ticket to Heartland, thank you very much!" she said, huffing a little. "And so will my friend!"

The mantis made a terrible hissing, clicking noise with her mandibles. Alice stood firm in the face of this terrifying display. She had held one once as a child, and though it was unsettling and surprising how strong the slender and fragile insect's legs were, it had neither bitten nor tried to.

The present mantis finally reached under her desk, ripped two tickets off a roll, and sulkily slammed them down in front of Alice. "No return indeed. I'm on my tea break now. Good day. And good *luck*."

"Charming lady," Alice murmured. She turned and handed her companion his ticket as if he were a child. "Don't lose this, now—or shall I keep it for you? Where did everyone go off to?"

"Away. To . . . rally everyone." The Hatter shrugged, putting his hands in his pockets and falling into step beside her. It seemed like the most natural thing in the world. Hair grew out of the insides of his ears. His striking half goggle had become a frayed-looking eye patch.

"Well, that's good! Just as I thought."

They wandered over to the single track that came out of

the hideous Droozy Forest. A heavy mist lay over the land now, so it was impossible to see the tops of the "trees." Alice hoped it turned to rain and soaked the trousers of whosever legs made the forest.

A train charged in, blasting smoke and screeching to a halt far more unpleasantly than the little choo choo she had seen far away on the hillside. Alice took the Hatter by his arm and made for first class, holding her head high and trying to look like she belonged. She didn't *not* belong, considering that all the other passengers waiting were, in order, a half-empty jam jar, a cow with very long horns, a pair of furred creatures that resembled ducks but for their manes and tails, a small gaggle of eggs with feet, and a woman with a giant crab on her head.

Once she and her family had taken a leisurely boat trip to France and her father had sprung for chaises on the fashionable part of the deck. Alice had watched with amusement as her mother, somewhat surreptitiously, tried to adjust and tie her shawl around her hat the way the rather more glamorous (and younger) wealthy ladies just starting out on the Grand Tour did.

(Mathilda had also seen this and proceeded to lecture her own mother on the sin of vanity.)

Now Alice sort of wished she had a crab to put on her head as well.

They had a nice cozy little compartment to themselves. A kindly old walrus took their tickets and clucked when he saw their destination.

"Ahh, I wouldn't go there given the *choith*, mith. It ain't a thafe plathe for vithiting theeth dayth."

Alice supposed the tusks were why he lisped.

"Thank you," she said politely. "But we have unavoidable business there."

"Well, all hail the Queen of Heart-th," he said unemotionally. She noticed, as he waddled to leave, that amongst the black scrimshaw figures that decorated his tusks, a new and bloodred heart stood out. It made her uncomfortable.

Alice shivered and turned back to her companion. "Dear Hatter, are you feeling all right? It seems as though every last bit of nonsense has been just . . . drained from you."

"That's it, exactly." The Hatter nodded. "I've seen too much and none of it is funny. The Queen of Hearts has ruined the world, or me. You've got to stop her, Alice," he begged. "Please."

"I'm trying, dear Hatter. I'm *trying*." Alice put her hand on his.

Poor man! He was all dried up by the horrors of the reality he experienced. All that was left was sense, and it was aging him terribly.

Was this happening to all of Wonderland?

Was this the future of all its dreams and creatures? Was it too late, even if she prevented the End of Time? Saving the world was one thing. Fixing it was another.

"Here, I'll just go fetch us some tea from the dining car," Alice said, trying to put worry and panic aside. "And maybe a biscuit or two. That should do us worlds of good."

The Hatter nodded morosely and looked out the window.

"Perhaps I can find him a talking tart, or something else," Alice thought as she gracefully wended her way down the swaying aisle into the next car. "The next thing that says Eat Me or Drink Me I'll give *him* instead of taking myself."

She passed all manner of passengers and then the smoking car, which was, literally, smoking. Closed, impenetrable, and grey windows showed nothing of the world outside; and its occupants were betrayed only by a scaly tail or tentacle snaking out the bottom of the door. After that was a baggage car, which narrowed down considerably and which Alice had to turn sidewise to get through. It wasn't so bad in her new Land of Clubs outfit, but it was still a little tight. And then a man stepped out in front of her.

She didn't see him at first because he too was turned sideways; and card thin as he was, practically invisible even in his luxurious velvets and silk.

And ridiculous feather.

"Alice!" he purred, blocking her way forward and angling himself so she was forced into a baggage nook.

"Knave! You . . . disgusting *pig*!" Alice cried, spitting angry. She wished she *could* spit, like she had seen other people do. Of course Mathilda and Alice had not been raised that way at all and Alice was afraid it would come out all wrong if she tried it now.

"Actually, not a pig at all!" she then added, thinking of the toves. "They are at least honest about their alliances and loyalties and affections!"

"Why, Alice," the Knave said, and she honestly couldn't tell if his surprise was genuine or mocking. "Did I break your Heart?"

"You betrayed me and my friends and may have got some of them killed!"

"Oh, is that all," the Knave said, a little disappointed. "It's War, darling."

"It is *not* War!" Alice hissed. "It is an insane tyrant wreaking violence on her own people. And what *you* did was not an act of war—it was an act of cowardice. Going traitor and running to the Queen to reveal the location of the Grunderound condemned dozens of innocent victims without you having to risk yourself at all, or take a single shot yourself! You don't even have the honest awfulness of a regular enlisted man ordered to shoot. You had a choice, and you hid behind the Queen's skirts when the real violence occurred!"

Perhaps the Knave flushed, perhaps he went pale: it was hard to tell behind the shiny finish of the card.

"I'm sure the innocent will be let go," he mumbled.

"Mary Ann was executed, the Hatter was *almost* executed—"

"*They* were enemies of the state! They broke the law. They conspired to overthrow the Queen."

"A mad queen. An *unfit* queen! A queen who was was locking everyone up and torturing them and seizing their property and killing everyone! An insane tyrant!"

"The law is the law, Alice," the Knave said with a smile. "The Queen is the queen. Even in your world there is a queen who rules."

"*My* queen would never attack her own people, or try to bring about the end of the world."

"So she fancies herself a *good* queen, eh? To . . . *everyone*, really?"

Alice regarded him frostily. "Victoria would never take toys from babes. And what about this whole business about the Queen *winning*? I have heard that once she has enough toys, she will bring about the End of Time and therefore the end of the world, and *that* is how she wins. Are you really in favor of that?"

The Knave gave her a brilliant smile. "I'm but a knave,

with no power or say in these things: the pursuits and glories of queens and kings. The game of thrones. Whatever happens, I intend to stay on top until the end."

"What a pleasant philosophy. It allows you to feel no guilt and just float along with whatever those in charge decide, leaving you free from thought or duty beyond the next moment."

The Knave sighed. "What are you even *doing* going back into Heartland?" he asked wearily. "It is the exact wrong place for you to be—you made it out of there, you should *stay* out. There is a price on your head: a thousand tarts and a jack-in-the-box confiscated from one of the auntlions."

"How did you find me?" Alice countered. "Have you been following me?"

"Of *course* I've been following you!" he said, exasperated. His entire countenance of bravado and enthusiasm fell. He simply looked tired—like everyone in Wonderland now. "Initially we thought you were dead, or trampled, or otherwise gone forever after the raid on the Grunderound. When it was obvious you had somehow escaped, the Queen had me find and follow you."

"You couldn't have followed where I had escaped to," Alice said. "You cannot go to Angleland."

"*Some* can. And do."

A narrow panel of window that lit the dark baggage

nook flashed with the changing scenes outside, at one point showing an orchard whose fruits were all shiny black letters sparkling in the sun. Alice had a single glimpse of a pleased-looking rabbit, a brown one, holding up an *E* and getting ready to take a bite.

"But I cannot. I admit that road is closed to me," the Knave finally said. "Be that as it may, I picked up your trail as soon as you returned to our fair land. There is still a price on my own head, you know? The tarts. The stupid, stupid, delicious tarts that I ate in the Forest of Forgetting. I am to repay my misdeed by serving the Queen in whatever way she wants."

"So what now?" Alice asked.

She made herself look in his eyes—his printed, black eyes.

"Now I turn you in," the Knave said—perhaps a little too flatly. Flat as a pressed card. Both were silent for a moment.

"Or maybe I rip you in two," Alice suggested. She had no idea if the new powers she had in Wonderland would work; she had no cookies or drinks left. But her hands twitched, delicate fingers posed to grab card and *tear*.

"Or maybe you call for the Hatter," the Knave said. "Or maybe the conductor. Or, perhaps, you will simply push me out under the door. . . ."

He wasn't mocking her this time; his eye slid to the thin

space under the door from which the roaring sound of the wheels on the track came. He *would* fit.

He was . . . suggesting it.

"Why?" she asked softly.

He shrugged and smiled sadly.

"The next time I see you, I will have to take you in. Listen to me: do not return to Heartland. It will mean your death. The Queen is so furious about you and Mary Ann she would be likely to set everything aside just to hunt you down and punish you. There are those . . . unlike me . . . who do not have a paper heart. They have scissors to rend and cut and destroy."

Alice's eyes widened. Scissors to *cut*?

"You mean the Card Cutter? The Droozy Trees mentioned something about it . . . the Hatter was terrified!"

The Knave shook his head impatiently.

*"Do it,"* he whispered. "Now or never!"

"Hatter . . . ?" she called. *"Hatter!"*

Then she took the Knave by his side and carried him to the door like a piece of mail delivered to the wrong address, when one slips it back through the slot and out. *"Hatter!"*

The Hatter came rushing in just in time to see the Knave get sucked out the car and fly into the fields beyond, picked up by a fresh breeze, turning over and over into the blue sky until he disappeared.

He did *not* arrive in time to see the Knave give Alice a saucy little wave before he went, or the kiss he blew.

"Oh," the Hatter said, surprised but not crestfallen. He saw that Alice was unharmed and safe, and that was enough for him. He had no obvious machismo, nor any desire to be a hero if it was uncalled for. Only when it was needed. Alice rather appreciated that; it was so contrary to all the men and boys she had known (except for her cousin Cuthbert). "You're all right, then. Was that the Knave?"

"It was indeed," Alice said, breathing heavily from her exertions and—whatever else. The new outfit she wore had a much looser corset, which made the process easier and more pleasant, but she wondered about how good it was for supporting her back. "Either he was just information gathering, or there really is a price on my head. Or Mary Ann's head. I'm not sure the Queen can tell the difference—I'm not sure any of you can."

"Oh, that's not fair," the Hatter said reasonably.

"Let us do go get that tea," Alice decided, patting her trousers clean. "I have a feeling it may be a while before we have another chance."

# Chapter Twenty-Eight

The long-faced gentleman behind the counter in the dining car regarded them gravely when Alice ordered two cream teas and a packet of sweets. She realized she hadn't even thought about payment—it was always somehow just handled in Wonderland—and the attendant definitely looked distrustful of the situation.

"What is your affiliation?" he asked carefully around his large teeth, avoiding any hint of a horsey accent. "You don't wear any indication."

"I wasn't aware one needed to when traveling by rail. What is *yours*?"

"The great National Rail, of course." He sniffed through wide nostrils. "It is beyond any *local*, geographic loyalty. I am a citizen of the world. Your tea, miss." He turned his back on her. Alice raised an eyebrow at the Hatter.

"Mind he doesn't introduce you to the biscuits," he whispered. "I know this breed."

"I had no idea Appaloosas were so rude," Alice murmured.

But the fellow didn't say another word, keeping whatever prejudice he had against the pair of travelers to himself while sliding over a tray of biscuits and scones along with a waxed bag of candies that seemed to be shuffling themselves in an attempt to get comfortable for the ride. EAT US was scrawled in clotted cream and underlined in jam—raspberry, it seemed—on the tray.

"Very posh," Alice said with admiration. "Eat up, Hatter old chum! With any luck these will have you feeling like your old self again."

They perched on the stools and she nibbled a scone while the Hatter literally threw everything else into his mouth. Alice just barely managed to keep back the bag of sweets but was delighted to see his maw did seem a little larger and out of proportion compared to a normal human man's. Perhaps he was going to be all right.

But then he took a little flask out of his pocket and carefully metered out a single shining silver drop into the steamy depths of his tea.

"Hatter!" Alice cried in dismay. "And before noon!

"I think," she added, unsure.

"It's all right. It's just mercury," he reassured her. "To feel like myself again."

"But that's poison!"

"Yes, so are arsenic and all the other things the ridiculous women of your world use to keep your complexion perfect," he said with a shrug. "I do this to keep my Madness intact."

"How do you know that? About arsenic and the women of my world?" Alice asked suspiciously. Of course she and Mathilda never did such things; between parents who thought they were perfectly beautiful as they were and simple levelheadedness, the most they ever snuck was (newly—for Mathilda, at least) rouged powder and simple cosmetics.

"Cheshire," the Hatter said with a shrug as if it were the most obvious thing in the world. "He has a friend over there."

Alice sipped her own undoctored tea and wondered.

*"HEARTLAND,"* the walrus cried hours or minutes later, walking through and taking the ticket stubs off the back of the seats. "All idiot-th off to their violent fate."

Before Alice had time to look around and collect her things and then remember that she had no things to collect, the train was quite forgotten and she and the Hatter stood on a platform next to a higgledy-piggledy stack of dishware for a ticket house.

A nicely cobbled road led away from the station . . . bright red and sticky, dripping with blood.

"Alice," the Hatter said, looking faint.

*Everything* the road led to and past was crimson and wet: trees, walls, small churches, postboxes. Alice stepped forward—hesitantly—and knelt down to take a closer look. The Hatter clung to her side.

(Was he perhaps just a little shorter than before the tea? Ungrowing back to his old size? She couldn't be sure.)

"It's only paint," she said, trying to soothe him—but she leaned over to take a sniff, just to double-check. "She has covered absolutely everything in paint."

There were also signs posted *absolutely everywhere* along the road.

HEARTLAND

THE QUEEN OF HEARTS LAND

KEEP OUT UNLESS FEALTY SWORN

ALL TOYS CONFISCATED AT BORDER

TRAITORS WILL BE EXECUTED

UNDOCUMENTED TRAVELERS WILL BE EXECUTED

EVERYONE WILL BE EXECUTED JUST TO BE SAFE

THE WINNINGEST QUEEN EVER

THIS WAY TO GREAT HEARTLAND

THAT WAY FOR LOSERS

HEARTS WILL WIN

"Well, one can't accuse her of being unsure of herself," Alice observed.

"We are going to walk down that road to our death, aren't we," the Hatter said morosely.

"Have a sweet," Alice suggested, holding out the bag and shaking it at him as she would at a small child or a dog. He grumpily took one and ate it and then smiled like a tot who had accidentally picked his favorite flavor.

Alice took the egg out of her pocket and, feeling a little ridiculous, held it up and "showed" it everything, wondered if the Queen of Clubs could see somehow. "This is what is left of the land out here," she narrated as seriously as she could.

"Come on then, Hatter!" she added brightly, stepping carefully onto the road to not get paint on the sides of her shoes. "We're off to change hearts and minds. Remember that: hearts and minds."

"Please don't say that. Don't say *hearts*," the Hatter begged.

---

The area just beyond the train station was desolate and unpopulated, at least as of recently. Scattered across arid fields were the still-burning ruins of what once might have been farmhouses. The smoke that puffed up from these garbage fires made heart shapes that would have been perfect for Valentine's Day had they not been so dreadfully black and oily, dripping down desultorily to their points.

The sun and moon met briefly in the sky and must have had some sort of argument; the moon retreated back the way it had come, even sulkier than before. The sun glowed stronger and more smugly after, and the day grew hot, and the paint on everything dulled and cracked.

"Brings a whole new meaning to 'watching paint dry,' eh?" Alice asked, nudging the Hatter. "Get it? *This* time it is really quite fast."

"Might as well be as fast as a sliggerdoo," the Hatter said sadly. "Might as well be as slow as a Racing Lorikeet."

Alice didn't say anything, afraid of getting her hopes up. But his words were silly and he *had* seemed to shrink a little. And his hat might have been just a touch bigger than before.

The first inhabited hamlet they came to was a tiny farmstead. Only half of the orchards around seemed to have been set on fire, and these smoldered ineffectually anyway. The minuscule houses hunkered down and bowed out like animals against whatever attacked.

"Hello?" Alice called, turning off the main road and onto a dusty path that had been only splattered a bit rather than painted. The dust shrugged off the liquid, as expected; it beaded up and dried in ugly pots and divots.

"Hello?" she cried again. "It's Alice. I'm here to help. The . . . *recoveringly* Mad Hatter is here. Hello? We're not going to hurt you!"

Eventually these constant and vaguely soothing words produced some result: several very strange furry creatures dressed in farmers' duds poked their heads out of doorways, holes, and wells. They were sparklingly golden and almost perfectly round and didn't seem to have any eyes at all. Their large, adorable noses tested the air rapidly like rabbits'.

"GO AWAY!" one cried out, turning toward Alice, having apparently found her by scent or sound. "Leave us to mourn our family and farm in peace."

"There will be no peace for anyone," Alice called back reasonably. "There will *be* no more anyone. Once the Queen of Hearts has a significant pile of toys, she plans on bringing about the End of Time and ending the world."

One of the golden moles howled at this and clutched its baby—which was the tiniest, roundest, cutest thing Alice had ever laid eyes on, and despite the urgency of her mission, her fingers actually itched to hold it.

"No more no more no more," another one cried. "Bring the bandersnatches and dovercoots, but let it be over finally."

"She's speaking the truth," the Hatter said, raising his voice. "She's been to the Grunderound. She's had messages from Mary Ann. In a sense, she was *sent* by Mary Ann."

"Mary Ann?" one of the creatures said softly.

"I bring this," Alice said, pulling the egg out of her pocket. A dozen noses, some whose owners she couldn't even see the rest of, quested at and queried the air excitedly. She turned the club so it was facing them, though she had no idea if they could see it was there—or if they merely hungered for fresh egg. "We have an ally in the Queen of Clubs. If she sees that everyone is opposed to the Queen of Hearts, she will come with her armies and save us."

"And Mary Ann arranged all this?" a different mole—or perhaps one of the first ones, Alice honestly couldn't tell—asked hopefully.

"No, *I* did," Alice said through gritted teeth. "But . . . because Mary Ann summoned me."

The Golden Moles whispered to each other and conferred in a snuffling, whustly way.

"Mary Ann will bring the Queen of Clubs."

"Armies of cards will go to War and we shall be saved."

"We shall be saved and all our toys returned."

"And the End of Time shall *not* come earlier than usual!"

"We hear," a female mole spoke up. At least Alice assumed it was female; its voice was slightly higher and it had a bright blue kerchief knotted neatly around where its neck would have been had it not been such a delightfully round creature.

(Of course, this was Wonderland, and one shouldn't make assumptions.)

"And we feel. We will tell."

"We will tell! Mary Ann and the Bringers of Hope!"

And then, without another word, the creatures all went tail up—although they didn't actually have tails—and snuffled down into whatever earth was closest to them. Alice watched with alarm as their shapes pushed up dirt and zoomed just below the surface faster than she felt was strictly acceptable for underground speed without a pre-made tunnel. If they hadn't been so cute and furry in person they would have been terrifying.

"Just imagine if they traveled like that in Mother's garden and lawn back home," she murmured.

"That went well. I think," she added more loudly.

"In fact they *were* faster than sliggerdoos," the Hatter mused. "But don't expect everyone we meet to be so agreeable."

—

And of course no one else at all was like that, because no two people or groups of people in Wonderland were alike. The next thing they came to was a very tiny, very detailed castle, accurate down to all the loops and the garderobes. Alice walked around it grinning in delight, wishing she had something like it as a little girl. She could easily have crouched and hidden in the bailey—with a good book or two, or maybe a snack—and had her dolls man the battlements.

Comfortably tucked inside the walls were several toddlers armed to the teeth, one with a crown on her head that seemed to be made out of hawthorn switches and paste gems.

Alice tried to make her case as well as she could to such an audience but was cut off immediately.

"WE CAN DEFEND OURSELVES! BE OFF WITH YOU!" one baby—whose nappy dipped precipitously—shrieked.

"But you're just wee little bairns," Alice said, alarmed. "And I see there's a dolly over there in the corner, and a stuffed bear. The Hearts army will seize it all immediately."

"WE ARE PROOF AGAINST THE QUEEN OF HEARTS!" the queen baby screamed. "NO ONE SHALL CONQUER US WHILE THE DOOKIE TOWER STANDS!"

"The—oh, I see. But here, look." Alice brought out the

egg, wondering if it was perhaps a bad idea: if the Queen of Clubs saw these obstreperous babies, perhaps she would assume that more Heartlanders wanted no rescuing. "The Queen of Clubs shall come and save us and protect us if only you will resist, in word if not deed, the Queen of Hearts' plan. You know she intends to destroy the world?"

"WE DO NOT RELY ON FOREIGN ARMIES," the little queen shrieked. "AND NEITHER SHOULD YOU IF YOU HAD ANY SENSE. SAVE YOURSELF, OR SAVE YOUR WORLD YOURSELF. OTHERS ARE FOR NAUGHT BUT CHANGING NAPPIES AND BUYING MILK."

"Well!" Alice said, putting her hands on her hips. "Aren't you a naughty bunch of babies!"

At this the quartet began to scream and cry and shriek louder and grow red in the face. Hurriedly Alice found a dummy in the eastern ramparts and stuck it into the queen's round, howling mouth. The baby shut up immediately but continued to glare at Alice with large, beautiful eyes.

"Told you," the Hatter said as they wandered away.

"Yes, but they were just babies," Alice said, unsure what she meant. "In any case, in fairy tales these things always go in threes, so at our next place we should get a real idea of how things are going to go."

She was silent for a moment as they walked, still brooding on the interaction.

"But really: 'Other people are for changing nappies.' How rude."

"Well, could you imagine a bunch of babies touting the benefits of self-reliance instead?" the Hatter asked. "At best it would be rather ironic, wouldn't you say?"

Alice honestly couldn't tell if that was Nonsense or sense. She was beginning to lose track.

Somewhat foolishly, Alice didn't question how they were able to move so freely down the main road—which was dotted with signs specifically to intimidate people like them—without their actually being hunted or captured. She was Alice. This was Wonderland. And though every place and every person here was different, they were all gifted with a singular lack of an attention span. Alice had no doubts that the Queen, having had the road painted red, had promptly forgotten it.

Instead her thoughts wandered. She wondered if Mary Ann had ever been on this very road before all the terrible things began. If she had, there was a chance that Alice's shoes actually trod in the other girl's footsteps! That was a strange thought. She shivered, imagining ghosts and ghostly tracks disappearing as she erased them with her own—presumably—same-sized feet.

An unexpected squeak came from inside the Hatter's hat. In response to the Dormouse's warning, the Hatter grabbed Alice and the three of them went tumbling off the side of the road together, rolling and imprinting themselves with the terrible paint as they did.

Alice was about to indignantly protest this rough treatment and the ruining of her Land of Clubs outfit (which she was really growing to like) until she saw the cards marching down the road toward them.

But it wasn't just cards this time; there were all sorts of nasty-looking creatures alongside: angular and spined, tall and scrappy, pustule-covered and bulbous—all wearing shiny ruby-red armor that glittered in the sun. One, in a giant helmet sized for his deformed head, sat on the shoulders of a large sad creature with long hair and short tusks. This ox or yeti pulled a caged cart that was full of toys—and several hapless victims as well, who tried to claw their way out of piles of doll arms and miniature trebuchets and lead soldiers.

The Hatter put a hand over Alice's mouth before she could cry out in shock and anger.

The Dormouse stayed awake long enough to lift up the edge of Hatter's hat and give a low, sad whistle at the scene.

One of the rear card guards whipped around, having heard the sound.

The three friends froze.

Alice tried very hard not to close her eyes: if death or capture was coming, she would meet it head-on and ready.

It was difficult.

A long, long moment passed as the entourage moved on down the road, disappearing, and this one clever card stayed behind, searching back and forth across the road, using his spear to prod the bushes.

Seconds ticked by.

The card drew close to where they hid.

Finally he spat and spun around, marching after the rest of his comrades.

Alice and the Hatter shuddered in relief—but the Dormouse was already asleep again.

# Chapter Twenty-Nine

After recovering for a bit the three continued on—but more carefully now, keeping to the edge of the road and remaining much warier. The way soon split, a smaller road leading off to the right. Of course the fork was marked with signs.

ORNITHSIVILLE THIS WAY—LOYALISTS ONLY!

TOYS THAT WAY

Each sign was stamped with the rabbit symbol, hastily and sloppily, so white ink ran down and mixed with the red paint on the wood. It made a rather pretty shade of pink, if you didn't pay attention to the meaning.

"All the way back round again," the Hatter murmured in wonder.

"Ornithsiville! Like from the Greek *ornitho*, meaning *bird*?" Alice cried. "Is that the village where we first saw everyone so craven and beholden to the White Rabbit?"

"Yes," the Hatter sighed, closing his eyes. "It would be madness to go back there, right into the hea—ah, *belly* of the sycophants and Queen loyalists."

"But that is precisely where we should go, to change people's minds," Alice pointed out. "If the Queen of Clubs saw that we rallied *those* cowardly birds, she would be sure to help us!"

"Of course an Alice would say that sort of thing," the Hatter muttered.

But she felt with all her being that this was the right decision, especially since her companion said it was Madness. And that was also what *he* needed right now, more than anything else. Didn't he seem to shrink just a smidgen further?

Also there was the matter of the egg. Nothing in Wonderland made any sense, so perhaps there was no real connection—but it was extremely curious that the Queen of Clubs had chosen to send Alice with an egg, and here she had wound up back in a village of birds.

"I suppose it could have been alligators," Alice murmured to herself. "Or crocodiles."

There was something different about *those* eggs, of course; and of course right now she couldn't remember what it was. Were they soft, unlike chicken eggs, or was it that they were inside out? Gooshy and yellow on the outside? They were opposite of birds' eggs *some*how. . . .

They took the way to Ornithsiville and followed it assiduously, even when it curled around itself and spat them out only a foot over from where they had entered the roundabout.

(This was doubly odd because she was sure there had been no solid road into Ornithsiville when they had come through last time; it seemed to be just plopped in the middle of the country, like everything else in Wonderland.)

In the market a woman was arguing with a man, quietly and furiously, in cheeps and whistles, as he shook a piece of paper at her and raised a Rabbit-stamp threateningly. She had two mewling chicks at her feet. One was mostly human, the other as fuzzy and large-beaked a fledgling as there ever was.

"Here now, leave her alone," Alice said, moving forward and making shooing motions with her hands. The bureaugrackle hopped back. "Can't you see you are upsetting her children?"

"If the Rabbit knew she was hiding a ball along with some extra fine alfalfa sprouts, he would *come* for her children, and her, too!"

"Never mind that; I have an announcement to make that will change everything. Hatter, a hand?"

She went to climb up on the birdbath, but of course the Hatter paid no attention and just began clapping: enthusiastically at no one and nothing in particular.

"How droll," Alice muttered. She was glad to see his Nonsense coming back so strongly, but did it have to be when she needed him? Setting her boot carefully against the marble, she managed to hoist herself up and then balance on the edge with only minimal swaying.

"Good people of Ornithsiville! May I have your attention, please? Hello? Just a moment of your time, that's all I ask! Hi! Over by the fountain here! I have an announcement to make!"

Immediately the birds turned their bright eyes to the plaza center and began to flock toward her. Monocles flashed in the light; top hats were removed so others might see.

"Oh, another bloody politician. I thought they had migrated already," a swallow groaned.

"I heard there is to be punch and pie afterward," a grouse told him knowingly.

Someone set up a stand to distribute flyers and buttons;

Alice couldn't make out the insignia or the slogans. Lemonade was served, which caused a bit of a row because there wound up being no pie at all.

A hundred or more birds were now facing Alice, scratching the ground, preening, and impatiently waiting for her to begin. Although she was high up and out of their immediate reach, she couldn't help being a little flustered by their sharp eyes and sharper beaks. Not a crowd to stick around in should the mood turn ugly. Some of the cocks had truly formidable spurs.

"Ladybirds and game, and men," she called out, "the time of being afraid is over. The time of hiding your toys and paying ridiculous tribute to those in charge is over. The reign of the Queen of Hearts itself is over! If you want it.

"I come bearing great news: the Queen of Clubs will aid us with her forces and liberate—"

". . . liberate us from cards of the Heart, and return all our toys—yes, we've heard all that already," a pinch-beaked goose squonked.

Alice blinked in astonishment.

"And *we* heard it from a Dodo," a short, bushy ground owl said with a great burr of an accent. "Much more reliable source than a human girl, I might add."

"Hatter!" Alice cried out in delight. "They've already been through here, spreading the word! All of our friends!"

"Didn't I say they had gone ahead?" he replied a little peevishly. "Back at the train station when you were bullying that poor mantis?"

"So you're with me? And against the Queen of Hearts?" Alice called out.

"We've been discussing the notion at our committee meetings. There's some question of the seriousness of the claim," a bird yelled back. "Some proof of the Queen of Clubs' intentions would be helpful. Mostly we're with the Dodo. And Mary Ann. Some of us, anyway. She is almost as good as a bird. You should hear her sing."

"But she's . . ." Alice didn't know what to do. This time it wasn't even irritation at the constant mention of Mary Ann. The poor girl was dead. Did she dare tell this crowd? Didn't they know already? Would this dampen their spirits?

"Mary Ann lives on," she said, neither telling the truth nor acknowledging the comment. "But you must work to bring about your own salvation. I know it's been hard having your, ah, toys confiscated, and watching your friends be imprisoned, sometimes tortured, sometimes killed. But no one—no Mary Ann—is going to leap in and save you if you don't try to save yourselves.

"Make your rebellion known and the Queen of Clubs will see and bring in her armies. She will fight the Queen of Hearts and win, freeing you all. But she needs to see you *want* to be liberated. She will not invade to take another queen's domain without recourse."

"Fie on *all* your queens," a brant spoke up, bobbing his head and trying not to squonk in the middle of his speech. "But if Mary Ann says we can save ourselves, we will do it. I've *seen* Mary Ann. Plain as that girl up there on the fountain. Actually, that girl looks ever so much like her, in fact. Never seen no Queen of Clubs. But if she speaks for Mary Ann, I know we're saved."

There were murmurs in the crowd, birds nodding and looking toward Alice and commenting on the similarities. Alice's head spun. They were agreeing to do what she asked only because they thought a dead girl was still alive and asking? Or because Alice somewhat resembled this girl? None of it made any sense. It was all, of course, Nonsense. What was real were treaties and pacts and armies and weapons.

It took someone from the real world to see that. Someone with real-world perspective.

"This is ridiculous," Alice complained down to the Hatter.

"You still don't get it, do you?" the Hatter said with a sigh. "This whole plan is ridiculous. It's not about armies—it's about you. It's *always* been about you, Alice."

"Seems like it's more about Mary Ann," Alice muttered.

But she carefully took the egg out of her pocket and held it up. *That* caught the crowd's attention.

"What's that she's got?"

"An egg? Is it *her* egg?"

"Can human girls lay eggs, too?"

"No, *but they eat them*!"

"Lord sakes! IS SHE GOING TO EAT THAT EGG?"

"What's that on it?"

"Why, it's an egg in the suit of Clubs!"

*"She speaks for the birds!"*

"I'll follow that egg anywhere!"

"Down with the Queen of Hearts! Down with the Queen of Hearts!"

"Hooray for the *Quack of Clubs*!"

*"FREEDOM!"*

As they shouted and Alice held the egg, club side out, a crack appeared in its side.

The crack grew and grew like lightning over a field with a distant horizon, when you can see the whole bolt crackling from end to end. Its points divided and divided and became more cracks until the egg was riddled with them and the shell was more like a jigsaw puzzle than a solid surface.

Suddenly it exploded.

A white owl, adult, fully formed, complete with an accordion neck, took off directly into the sky as if winging its way to the sun. It hovered for a moment high up, sweeping its wings while scoping out the crowd and feeling the wind. Then it swooped away, off in the direction of the Unlikely.

The crowd oohed and aahed and gasped.

"So that's how that works," Alice observed, watching it go.

# Chapter Thirty

"It can't be that easy . . ." she added, tearing her eyes from the sky and resettling them on the crowd. Birds were talking excitedly, arguing viciously, taking great gulps of lemonade, and affixing various pins to their feathers. Some of the brooches were of hearts, some clubs, some rabbits, some funny-looking question marks that looked like they were cut through with an exclamation point. Some, worn by the most decadent, old, or philosophical, showed an image of a clock with the minute hand approaching thirteen.

"Let's go find the Dodo. We must be right behind him," the Hatter said, but whether or not he was responding to her thought she couldn't tell. "I'll bet the Gryphon's with him, too. They both have wings, you know."

"But if the Queen of Clubs is being summoned, or told, by that bird thing, then she will be on her way very soon with her army. Directly to the Queen of Hearts' castle, I presume, to wage war there. We should continue in that direction, spreading word and raising support and then helping the Queen of Clubs any way we can."

"I was afraid you would say something like that," the Hatter moaned.

The two (three with the Dormouse) quietly slipped out the back way of Ornithsiville.

"I very much would like to avoid the Forest of Forgetting," Alice said. "We should go more directly across that checkered plain."

"As you wish," the Hatter sighed.

They drew away from the bird village and closer to the castle, taking Alice's journey backward, and the landscape and environment began to change. Immediately, of course, not with the slow progression of colors and geography one might be used to in a world more like Angleland. And as she walked through this shifting landscape Alice realized she hadn't asked the Hatter to lead, or even troubled about how to get there. All actions and signs—some quite literally—pointed to the Queen of Hearts. That was where the next, hopefully final, confrontation between everyone was to be. So of course Wonderland would take Alice there.

She wondered what it would have been like to grow up as Mary Ann, used to traveling by inevitability. It had taken three visits for Alice to get the hang of it.

The checkered plain came fast and quick but now it was dead and dusty. The red paint had completely coated and dried on the bushes and grass, killing the plants entirely and rendering them into bony, crimson blots on the landscape. The sky was dark with bloody red smoke and the air had a pungent thickness to it. Ugly embers danced in the upper reaches, around and down and only eventually out, like malevolent demons from books in Alice's world. Like nothing at all from Wonderland.

"I don't like the looks of that," the Hatter said despite being unable to turn away.

Alice found herself filled with a sort dread that she had rarely experienced since she was a child: a fear of even greater terror to come, of the future punishment from the *other* parent after the first one has yelled, promising worse later.

She took the Hatter's hand and he squeezed hers back, a little absently, but hard. They walked silently like a very grim Hansel and Gretel into the desolate landscape.

Far too soon they came upon the cause of such rank pollution.

Blocking out the sunlight and sending the land around

them into shadow were giant piles of things smoldering and burning and releasing great oily red billows.

Covering her mouth with her hand and trying to breathe only through her nose, Alice approached the closest heap. She thought they would be toys—which, admittedly, didn't make sense because the Queen had to actually have functioning ones to win (she assumed). But what sense was there in anything now in Heartland?

In fact the things on fire were everything *but* toys. Chairs, bicycles, teakettles, pencils, baby blankets, eyeglasses, plum puddings, lamp glass, bricks, pantaloons, cupboards, snuffboxes, policemen's hats, loaves of day-old raisin bread, saddles, stoops and stairways, leather bags, bonnets, stamps from printing presses . . . everything and anything Alice could name was mounded into these giant, endless piles of burning rubbish.

The Hatter looked and poked at the pile interestedly; even the Dormouse stuck his head out and pointed at a silver teaspoon that shone a bit in the flames. The Hatter dutifully picked it out (wrapping his hand in his muff first) and handed it to his companion, who sighed in delight and promptly went back to sleep, cradling it for warmth.

Rushing around the base of these hills were giant ants pushing soiled red carts. Using some reason or logic or pattern known only to herself, each would reach into a cart, pick up an object—feelers moving about in the air as if receiving signals on what to do—and then fling it onto a particular bonfire.

Suddenly one of the smaller ants began gesticulating wildly with her feelers and arms.

*I got one! I got one!*

Alice put her hands to her temples, not meant to receive that kind of communication. It hurt. The Hatter pulled his hat all the way down over his head.

A dozen other ants rushed over to this crying one, their feelers flurrying.

The ant held up her find: a tiny doll missing its head.

*Rubbish is it rubbish*

*Is it a toy*

*Is it a doll without a head a doll*

*Is it something to play with*

*It is if a brother popped the head off*

*Is it still a game?*

*No matter, look!* the first ant said, triumphantly digging around her cart some more and holding up a tiny thing covered in hair. *Here is the head! It* is *a doll, by any definition! A* toy*!*

*A toy a toy a toy!* all the other ones joined in.

Clacking her mandibles with glee, the ant rushed away, holding the toy aloft.

Immediately the other ants clambered up the side of her cart and began methodically going through the rest of her stuff to see if there was more luck, if there were more toys.

"That's very clever, I suppose," Alice said, taking the Hatter and drawing the two of them back away from the uncomfortably large insects. "Using ants to sort through everything. Like the fairy tale about the princess spreading the sacks of grain out over grass and making a poor suitor try to find them all and refill the sacks—and some friendly ants doing the job for him."

"Certainly, except the headless doll was horrible, and the giant ants are horrible, and *all of this is horrible*."

The Hatter pointed. There was a slowly charring skeleton in one of the piles and Alice couldn't say for certain whether it was a corpse or a model from a scholar's laboratory.

The rubble shifted as something finally collapsed, too charred to hold weight any longer, causing the skeleton to turn slightly, as if it was looking at Alice.

"Oh," Alice said, spinning away and swallowing, trying not to throw up. But as shocked as she was, she was more worried about the Hatter, who looked grim and impassive. He was straightening out again, taller, with a smaller hat and head.

"Ever have a Flying Butterscotch?" she asked quickly.

"No, what's a—"

Alice took out a sweet and lobbed it at his head. It hit the rim of his hat and fell down—right into his open mouth, which he readied just in time.

"To the castle!" Alice said brightly, popping another candy into her own mouth. She closed one eye and moved her hand as if to brush the burning pile away . . . and so it slid into the background improbably and unnoticeably, a trick of the eye made real.

"To the castle!" the Hatter agreed, sucking on the candy and taking her hand again and skipping. Alice was on the point of telling him not to skip with a sweet in his mouth, for he might choke—but wisely decided not to.

(It was good she had kept that packet of sweets. Just like someone had told her—who was it? Always keep a packet of sweets on you? One's life might depend on it? She couldn't quite remember. . . .)

The ants took no notice of them, just as they wouldn't in the real world unless a mischievous younger Alice had put an obstacle in their line of progress: a rock or a bit of honey, say. When the two companions made any effort at all to look at the carts or bits being sorted they both tried to keep their observations light. "That's an unusually shaped ottoman" or "My aunt used to have an eggbeater like that." Otherwise their progress was mostly silent amongst the rubbish heaps except for the clicking sound of the ants.

Then a strange feeling began to come over Alice. A creepy-crawly scared one—and oddly, it had nothing to do with the ants.

She spun around to regard the desolation behind her. It was like being at a fancy, crowded party and something was stepping on her dress. Or was about to.

"What are you doing?" the Hatter demanded the third time she stopped. "You're as nervous as a tove pup in a blanderpatch."

"I feel like we're being followed," Alice admitted, once again turning around and scanning the horizon. The Hatter looked with her, but all they could see were the mindless ants.

"There's nothing behind us at all," the Hatter said.

"That's because your death is in *front* of you," came a whispery dry voice.

Alice spun back around.

There stood a skeleton, closely resembling the skeleton from the burning pile of rubble before: there were char marks on his bones here and there. Perhaps it *had* been him. On a closer look he was strangely angular, with dead geodesic eyes and an upside-down trapezoid for a skull. Also he seemed . . . flat. Thinner than a card even when he curled around to draw his sword, an evil-looking half scissor. The hole where his nose would have been was the only part of him that was curved; it looked like an upside-down heart.

"The Card Cutter," the Hatter whispered, his voice thick with fear.

"Hello," Alice said with a little curtsy. "We're just on our way through, if you don't mind. . . ."

"But I *do* mind," the skeleton said, inching closer. Its flat and bony toes made tiny *clink* sounds against the ground. "I am the evener of odds. I make all games fair. I am the great equalizer. I wipe out cheating advantages. I am here for *you*."

"Whatever for?" Alice demanded, trying to keep her voice from shaking. "I never cheat. Much. Anymore. I'm an adult, not a child."

"You are definitely trying to cheat, little Alice. You are bringing a whole new deck into this game. It's not fair for the Hearts."

"I beg your pardon!" Alice said. "Your Queen has all the weapons, all the soldiers, all the armies, all the power, all the toys—"

"Not all the toys, yet," the skeleton interrupted. "Soon."

"—all the roads and towns and prisons and jails and garrotes against the hapless folk of Heartland, and you accuse *me* of cheating because I want to *even* the odds? By bringing in an equally powerful ally?"

"She was not in the game at the beginning, when the rules were called," the skeleton said, shifting his stance and grip on the scissor half.

"There was never any precise beginning to this madness, and no one ever called out the rules!"

"So you say."

"It sounds to me like you are just rationalizing whatever reason you were sent after me," Alice snapped. "Or you can only do as you are meant to, and the Queen of Hearts somehow twisted the words and rules around to make you think this is the right thing. When really—"

But whatever she was going to say next, probably some handy bit of Alice wisdom, was cut off as the Card Cutter suddenly and silently brought his scissor-scythe down at her head.

The Hatter yanked Alice out of the way.

But not *quite* out of the way.

For one seemingly endless, silent moment she saw a neat triangle of cloth break free from her trousers and drift to and fro toward the ground. A short lock of hair, no more than a comma of blond, followed. Already on the dirt was a scrap of Alice's shoe leather, the precise color and shape of a trimmed nail that has fallen to the floor—but larger.

*"ALICE!"* the Hatter roared, pushing her away again.

Time restarted. The Card Cutter swung, the scissor half this time going *snicker-snack* despite the absence of its opposite twin.

Alice twirled out of the way hysterically, unsure what to do. There had only ever been one real fight between her and Mathilda, and that had involved hair pulling.

"Do something!" the Hatter hissed.

"Unfair—" Alice cried as the scissor half *clanged* down again on the road next to her, temporarily sticking itself between two cobbles. Without a grunt or a huff or any sound at all, the too-thin skeleton bent himself upon freeing it. Alice stumbled up and jabbed her hands in her pockets, but panicking fingers couldn't manage to find the packet of sweets now.

So it really seemed like a good time to—

"Run!" she cried, grabbing the Hatter by the hand. No fighters, they. It was survival, not cowardice.

They barreled down the path around and *past* the skeleton; what little sense Alice kept made her choose to at least run away in the direction of their eventual destination. The

Hatter's legs were much shorter than hers now and he had a hard time trying to keep up—especially with one hand on his gigantic hat.

Although her own heartbeats and breath were loud and fear seemed to make a noise of its own, after a little while Alice couldn't hear anything else at all. The only sounds in the world around her were things crackling and shifting in the burning piles of rubble. There was no hint of pursuit, there was no *swish* of the scissor half.

Alice was torn. On the one hand: Excitement! Had they really evaded their attacker so easily?

And on the other: Unease. Had he let them go because they were heading into the lion's den, as it were? Closer to the castle?

Should they have danced away instead?

But her emotions were quickly settled by a discarded and dirty card blown by the wind; it arced overhead and drifted down in front of her.

The Card Cutter rose up, brandishing his scissor half triumphantly.

Alice and the Hatter stopped their forward momentum just in time.

"You cannot escape equity," the skeleton said with a broad bony grin. "Fairness comes for everyone in the end; everyone becomes food for the worms, equally. This world is almost over. Consider yourselves the lucky forerunners into the next."

Alice turned to run again.

"We cannot escape him," the Hatter hissed madly, teeth chattering with fear. "He can go anywhere—appear anywhere. He cuts down cards wherever they are. He is unstoppable."

"I'm not a card!" Alice cried, both to him and the skeleton.

The skeleton made a mocking little half bow. "Yet you look like you are trying to become a queen; you play in the Queens' Games."

He suddenly lunged forward, twirling his weapon and bringing it horizontal this time, intending to cut the two friends in twain.

The Hatter and Alice ducked.

The top of his giant hat was lopped off.

"My hat!" the Hatter cried, grabbing it on either side of its brim. Alice pushed him out of the path of the skeleton's riposte: having spun all the way around, swooping his weapon out like a scythe, he let it continue its momentum *up* and over his ivory shoulder only to come straight back down on top of the two.

*"Alice!"* the Dormouse cried, popping out the top of the Hatter's sad hat. "The sweets! *EAT THEM!*"

Alice dug desperately into her pockets again—but was so distracted she wound up tripping over her own feet. She stumbled and fell into the dust and dried paint, hitting her head against the Hatter's shoe.

She did manage to pull out a single candy, a licorice, and pop it in her mouth.

Her tongue recoiled from the hated taste. She forced herself to swallow.

Her view of the sky was cut off by a grinning skull: the skeleton took one strangely delicate-seeming foot and kicked the Hatter away from Alice. The poor man went flying.

The Card Cutter raised his scissor half into the air; it sparkled prettily, golden and sharp.

"*You* shut up like a telescope," Alice whispered, holding out her hand and seeming to catch his skull between her thumb and finger. She squeezed them together like she was crushing his head.

There was a terrible sound that must have been bone on bone: grinding and squeaking and sandpaper grit like teeth forced to do something they shouldn't.

Whether the skull became small and fell off its neck, rendering the skeleton deceased; or whether it stayed on but the whole thing was such a drastic and sudden change that the skeleton couldn't cope; or whether whatever it had for a brain or soul shrank into uselessness along with its cranial protection, Alice never found out.

Its arms were still moving, caught in the middle of its last blow, and the scissor half came down squarely into her Heart.

# Chapter Thirty-One

"Alice!" the Hatter cried.

"It's funny," she thought, looking at the scissor half that stuck up out of whatever you called the part of your body that was sort of between the ribs. The fleshy, lumpy, beating bit.

"A Diamond, is that it? Or no, the Spade?" she wondered.

The scissor sort of swayed back and forth and for just a moment looked like it was as thin as the skeleton itself, but of course even so it was pure sharp golden metal.

"Brass, maybe," she decided.

"Vile thing!" the Hatter swore, grabbing it with both his hands—and almost cutting his fingers off in the process.

"No!" Alice started to shout, for though she had little knowledge of medicine, she did have a feeling, or maybe remembered a story, or . . . The point was, one didn't . . .

Whatever it was, it was too late.

The Hatter pulled the scissor out, and with it came great pumps of blood. Real blood, not red paint. It smelled of meat and copper and as it flecked her lips Alice could taste it. The Hatter's eyes widened in shock, and unable to think of anything else, he grabbed his hat and held it over the flow. It didn't work very well without its top.

"Things aren't . . . supposed . . . to hurt . . . in Wonderland . . ." Alice murmured.

"Alice, you have to go home now. Go back to wherever Alices come from," the Hatter begged. "You will die here."

"No!" Alice struggled to sit up. "You'll *all die* here! The world will come to an end! Patch this up—bandage it. . . . It's not going to kill me. . . . I cannot die in Wonderland."

But whatever shock had reduced most of her initial pain took this moment to wear off. A strange sloshing went back and forth through Alice's whole body, half nausea, half heat, half something else.

*Half scissors,* she thought. A bright white light of pain like nothing she had ever experienced before divided her chest from her torso, as if the sharp weapon had relodged itself there.

She cried out, unable to stop herself.

"Alice, go home, that's an order," the Hatter said, saluting her. "Come back as soon as you can. You're no good to us dead."

"Might make a good martyr for the cause . . ." the Dormouse suggested sleepily from the middle of his balding head.

"We already have Mary Ann for that, you heartless rodent," the Hatter said without feeling. "Alice . . . we need *you.* Alice. Only Alice. Alive. Come back to us. Soon . . ."

"I don't know how!" Alice said, feeling blackness come over her. It wasn't pleasant like falling asleep. It was like a thousand delicate crabs had dropped on her slowly from above and were pinching their way into her. Why did her stomach hurt if her arm was nearly cut off? Wait, *was* it her arm?

"Don't . . ." she said, grabbing the Hatter's hand.

She tried to memorize it: the little hairs, some of which were grey, around his knuckles. The dimples of pores where they entered his skin. A tiny scar. An actual fingerprint. All these things, unique to the Hatter, and as real as, as real as . . .

# Chapter Thirty-Two

She came to in an alleyway.

Alice felt strangely encumbered and kicked her legs, trying to get out from underneath the quilts and nooses that held her down . . . and then realized that it was all just her own skirts, pinafores, and various assorted underthings. She had been thinking of her other outfit, her Wonderland one.

"The Hatter! The Hatter's hand!" she cried, trying to remember. It was an older man's hand, still with a little plumpness around the knuckles but thinning out around the bones. "No, no! *Details!*" But her clever brain substituted descriptive words for specific facts, glossing over *exactly* what he looked like with what he probably *should* have looked like. The way any brain will do upon awaking, filling in the forgotten or unimagined bits of dream.

Large hat, crazy hair, large nose, short stature, like a children's illustration in a book of funny poems . . .

"The Card Cutter! We were almost at the castle! We showed the egg to the Ornithsivillians and the Queen of Clubs will come! We almost *won*!"

Two of the children from the Square were standing over her, staring at her worriedly. One was Zara. Alice had no idea what the boy's name was.

"Mistress Alice, are you all right?" the boy asked solicitously. "You're very white."

Things were drifting in and out of focus.

"I need to get back," Alice said, trying to hang on to the feelings she had just a few moments before. Unfortunately all it involved was tremendous pain and then a faintness, with all the cares of the world lifting away from her.

The *Card Cutter*. The burning piles of rubbish. The mad queen. The end of the world . . . the desperation . . .

*Hold on to it, Alice!* she told herself.

She screamed in a very un-Alice way: more of a forced groan made loud as her entire body and soul tried to expel the real world and its sensations that infringed on her mind.

She raked her nails along her arms, leaving long white scratches and trailing pinpricks of blood like pearls. Pain would focus her. Pain would help her remember. . . .

"What are you *doing*?" the boy cried. "STOP IT!"

Zara was more practical and simply reached over with her two strong and chubby hands and grabbed her.

"I'm just trying to remember," Alice said calmly.

"You could tie a string around your finger, maybe," Zara suggested with an insouciant irony that seemed far too young for a girl of seven. Then again, that was how old Alice had been when she spoke back to monsters and creatures from that other world.

Just not adults of this one.

Alice gave her a wan smile. It tasted terrible. She smacked her tongue around somewhat impolitely, trying to dispel whatever it was.

"Your camera's gone," the boy said, picking up her bag and shaking its obvious lightness. He peeped in. "Other stuff is still in there, though."

"My camera?!" she cried in dismay.

Then:

"No, wait, that is not important. The *other* things are more important. An entire world . . ."

"I really think you should go to the doctor," the boy said seriously. "You have had a fit or something."

"No, I'm fine. Perhaps I just fainted and someone came along and saw me and stole my valuables."

But that wasn't precisely true, was it? She had a memory of tripping, and an arm, and not being able to breathe, and an assailant. . . .

"You still have your necklace and ring," the little girl pointed out promptly.

"And your little purse with money in it," the boy said, taking it up and shaking it.

"Someone has mugged me to . . . just take my camera? Why not everything else as well?"

Her arm itched for a moment as she thought about the implications of this. She scratched it idly and then remembered why the injury was there.

"No, no, this is all irrelevant. There are other things to worry about." She rose to her feet, unsteady but determined. "Little darlings, thank you so much for my rescue. If it wouldn't be too much trouble, could I offer a reward for you to see me safely home?"

"No reward," the boy said simply. The girl spat in disgust.

*Aha!* Alice thought. That *is how it's done. I should take note!*

"Can I reimburse you for the task of helping me get there, then, and carrying my bag for me?" she asked politely. "And can you remember all the strange things I may say along the way, if I ask later?"

"Home or *vrach*?" Zara said, rolling her eyes.

"Doctor," the boy translated.

"Home. An extra penny if you don't mention the doctor again," Alice said with a smile.

And actually it was good that they went with her: walking was a little harder than it should have been. Her head was swimming with the remnants of her dream or having fallen; reality moved slowly around her, landscape and objects only slowly catching up to what her body and eyes told her was going on. Sort of the reverse of Wonderland, where the scenery sped up on you. Every time there was a sudden change of altitude, a slope down or a step up, she wobbled and the world spun. The worst was a set of four steps down. At the base of them everything went dizzily blurred and a sharp pain drilled itself into her chest with an intensity so great she began to black out.

"Alice, is that you? *Get away from her at once!*"

Alice jumped at the shouts as an unwanted pair of intruders came over to investigate her decrepitude.

It was, she saw from the light shining painfully off a half dozen buttons like angry little suns, a police officer, and—

"Are you all right? Begone, vermin!"

She closed her eyes. Coney. Of course Coney. *Again*

Coney! Even when she was trying to avoid him, he reappeared in her life. Like . . . almost like . . .

She had it on the tip of her tongue but couldn't quite place it.

"I'm fine," Alice moaned in irritation. "I'm all right. I've just been robbed. . . ."

"You little *thieves*! Officer, take these two away at once! This is the body—the girl, I mean—I told you I saw in the alley! These two must have been stealing her blind while she lay prone!"

"No, no, no." Alice was finally able to pry her eyes open enough to glare at the hateful face of Coney, pale and surrounded by a halo of ridiculously glassy pale hair. "They *found* me. They saved me. Someone knocked me down and they came upon me. . . ."

"A likely story. You're too forgiving, Alice. Officer, search these two at once for the missing camera!" Coney ordered.

The policeman gave the kids a distrusting but mild look. "They're filthy, thieving, foreign gutter rats, to be sure," he said almost regretfully, "but I don't think there's any place on their selves they could *hide* a camera. And why would they stick around after the crime?"

Alice raised an eyebrow at Coney.

"To . . . put you off the scent . . . ?" he asked lamely.

"I am happy you are all right," Zara said with a perfect curtsy, holding her patched but mostly clean pinny in between delicately arranged fingers as she did so. Alice was pretty sure only she—and possibly the police officer—saw the sarcastic sparkle in the girl's eyes as she performed the maneuver.

Brother and sister turned to go.

"But wait—" Alice said, fumbling for her purse. The boy gave a quick, nearly undetectable shake of his head. His eyes flicked to the two men. With a hot lick of shame and anger, Alice understood: giving them money would just encourage Coney to claim they were profiting off her neediness. The policeman would question the children further, prolong the encounter—who knew. It would cause problems. The kids wanted to get out of there as quickly as possible without any more fuss or attention. *"Thank you."*

The siblings ran off, happy to escape.

"I'll see you home," the policeman said, offering her a hand up. "And when you have rested you can make a complete report to us about the theft."

"Take me to my aunt's. It's closer."

"I'll take care of her," Coney told the police officer with a man-to-man smugness. Alice dearly wished she could have done something to him—she couldn't remember quite what, but in Wonderland she could have effected a physically final response.

"Just you take care to come by the station, or I'll have one of my men drop by your house," the officer said—ignoring Coney and his looks. "This is a strange and serious thing. You still have your jewelry, and your purse. The miscreant just wanted the camera. The sooner we can get all the details, the sooner we can apprehend this criminal—and protect other ladies as well."

Alice nodded dully. These were all excellent points and he was only doing his job, but aside from the annoyance of having to acquire a new camera, it was all unimportant. The police officer tipped his cap to her and strode off.

She endured the walk to her aunt's as best she could, putting up with Coney's careful holding of her arm and constant exhortations to lean on him if necessary. It was agony. Fortunately Vivian's house wasn't actually too far, and the relief she felt when she saw its odd, green-painted door was as perfect and complete as lemonade on a hot summer day.

"Thank you," she said politely and succinctly as she opened the door. "I'll be all right now."

"Should I see you in? I really am . . . I really am worried about your health. I hadn't realized it was *you* when I saw your unconscious form on the ground. I just ran and fetched the policeman . . ." He did indeed sound worried, all unctuousness aside.

"No, pray do not come in." She stepped over the threshold and turned around, holding the door half closed between them before delivering her final word.

"I never said that it was my *camera* that had been stolen."

She slammed the door in his face.

With her head still aching she stumbled through the blessedly cool, dim, and for once incense-free interior. Vivian came out, covered in clay and frowning; myopically concerned.

"Alice! You look terrible. Is everything all right?"

"Not at all. I've just been manhandled and mugged by a truly loathsome individual so he could steal my camera . . . for, I assume, some image he thought was captured on the film. *Evidence* of something. But all that was on that plate was a harmless little blue bird. He left behind all the other plates in the bag, because he's an idiot as well as a thief. I must develop them all immediately to see what he was after."

"Alice, that's dreadful! What hap—"

"*But far more importantly,*" Alice interrupted, holding up her hand, "there is a whole fantastic world under siege that I must return to at once. The villain who stole my camera is simply a distraction. I'm beginning to forget what it was all for."

Her aunt stared at her through gradually narrowing eyes, like a lizard overcome with cold.

"You haven't been in my personal things—taken anything from my rosewood cabinet in the studio, for instance?"

"No, Aunt Vivian."

"All right. Just checking. So . . . this camera theft. You aren't hurt—physically—and you don't seem to be overly upset by the crime. Although I must point out your dialogue is just the slightest bit off for . . . normal society. Just a word to the wise. You may indeed want to see a doctor for any lingering effects of your trauma.

"But as for your other concerns—your 'fantastic world,' I mean. Am I to understand that you are upset less about the crime and more because the camera thief is a person from Porlock, interrupting your visit to some sort of private Xanadu?"

"Let's say yes, Aunt Vivian. But if Xanadu were real, and in danger of being destroyed."

"But Xanadu *was* destroyed the moment Coleridge awoke. He never went back."

"I can. I have. I must again."

Vivian was silent for a moment.

"All right. What can I do for you now?" she finally inquired, brisk and businesslike.

"I have promised everyone so much, in both worlds," Alice said with an impatient shake of her arms. "There, I must save the world. Here, I need to develop the film I have left. And I still have to go to the newspaper with that photo of Mrs. Yao. Also, I could use some tea."

"And sandwiches, no doubt," Vivian said, nodding seriously. "I'm on it. Go put on one of the work pinnies and I'll be right back with a plate. I love my brother very much," she added—seemingly without emotion—"but really I do wish you were my own child sometimes."

Alice had a lopsided smile on her face as Vivian strode away. She loved her aunt, too, of course. But there was something more. What she felt was the sort of affection she could only compare to her feelings for the creatures of Wonderland. Love, but also a delight that such creatures should exist in the first place.

And a certain amount of curiosity, she had to admit. There was always some *holding back* with the Wonderland denizens, some further truth or mystery they took their own time revealing. Alice wondered, for a moment, what her aunt's was.

# Chapter Thirty-Three

Of course all the plates she developed wound up displaying only Wonderlandians—at least for Alice. And none of them portended anything good at all.

The first photograph was of Messrs. Tweedledee and Tweedledum. They were, just as Alice had expected, Gilbert and Quagley Ramsbottom. They grinned and held hands and wore Heart badges.

"Of course," Alice muttered. "They look positively gleeful."

The second was of the Dodo. With a giant sheep—a ram—who was weeping.

Alice nearly dropped this one when she picked it up. The Dodo was looking directly at the camera and had his wings out in supplication: *come back.*

"I *will*! Oh, Dodo, I am trying!" she cried.

She fished around in her bag until she found the monocle that she had sort of co-opted from her aunt. Who *was* he, anyway? In this world? There wasn't a lot of help from the background, most of which was blocked out by the giant sheep. It seemed like basic Wonderland scenery . . . a grassy plain, some trees, what looked like a train . . . *There.* Closer in, almost hidden by the ram's girth, was a side table that seemed put there for the posers' extra things so they wouldn't have to hold them. But instead of the Dodo's wig, or one of his telescopes, or a bell for the sheep, there was a pair of gloves with particularly large, ugly leather bows on the wrists. They didn't look *feminine* and *delicate* so much as that they perhaps more properly belonged on a dog's collar.

Alice would have known those gloves anywhere.

"Mathilda . . . ?" she said in wonder.

She sat back, gobsmacked.

The Dodo. Sweet, loyal Dodo. The least nonsensical of all the tea party. Always proper. Always trying to talk politics and caucus races. He had trusted that Alice would come back . . . and walked right into the enemy's hands, knowing she would rescue him. He believed in Alice.

Of course Willard wasn't *really* the Mad Hatter and Mrs. Pogysdunhow was much, much nicer than the Queen of Hearts (probably; she had always been all right to Alice and Mathilda, at least). Headstrewth wasn't at all sheepish, although in some ways he was large and harmless.

The other-world doubles possessed only the shallowest of similarities.

But . . .

What if under all her annoying pastimes and lectures and recriminations Mathilda really did think she was doing the right thing? That she was merely reining in the crazy people? What if her trying to manage Alice's life was because she wanted her to be happy—but *exactly like herself*? It wasn't from a lack of kindness or love, but a lack of imagination. She literally didn't know any other way of being.

*Thoughts for another time,* Alice told herself. It was indeed something to consider, but not when there was a world to save and a mystery to solve.

The last photograph was a nightmare that Alice almost dropped in revulsion.

It was a trio. The Caterpillar, a Scottie dog, and *the March Hare.*

Who was a corpse.

The Caterpillar looked terrified, as if something was about to hit him in the face. The Scottie was screaming, looking at a golden watch at the end of a fob made of beetles.

And the March Hare . . . was stiff, and white, with unseeing dull eyes and his arms crossed over his chest.

Alice let out a wail before she could silence herself.

She *knew* the poor thing was dead. The Hatter had told her that. But that was very different from seeing such ghastly proof.

This was the photograph of Aunt Vivian and the two lawyers. Ivy was the Scottie dog, Alexandros was the March Hare.

Alice wiped the tears that were spilling silently out of her eyes, trying to keep that last thing in mind. The March Hare might have been dead over there, but here he was alive and well. Some part of him remained.

"I must get back," she whispered. "I must avenge him."

Reluctantly she pushed this photo aside.

There was still the mystery of what Coney wanted from her camera. There was nothing incriminating in any of the portraits. She shuffled through all the photographs again and again, trying to see something new.

"How goes it, dear?" Vivian asked, popping her head into the spare room where Alice was investigating her negatives. She had been as good as her word; a three-tiered tea set of sandwiches had already been delivered to and utterly demolished by her niece, not a crumb remaining, as well as two small pots of tea.

"Please tell me what you see here," Alice said tiredly. She held the up the old image of the Queen of Clubs posed with her clubs, now raised high above her head in a warrior's pose.

"Oh my goodness, that's Mrs. Yao and her broken window," Vivian said, putting on her pince-nez. "She is holding up the offending brick—is she not? Oh no, it's a stone. And a note? What does it say? It's too small for these old eyes, and too backward."

"I can't remember precisely. Some rubbish about 'go back home.' I'm taking it to the newspaper. I want everyone to know about it. They've already taken away several children—who I think cannot even write in English—for the crime, falsely and with no evidence. I think if I had the photo enlarged enough, the handwriting might give away the identity of the perpetrator. *Oh* . . ."

Alice suddenly realized the truth.

"*This* is the image the thief wanted to steal! He thought it might incriminate *him*! And he's so stupid he thought it was still in my camera somehow!"

"Brilliant! You're a regular Dupin!" Aunt Vivian cried. "But . . . who knew that you had taken that photograph? Besides Mrs. Yao and yourself, I mean?"

"Only my sister and Headstrewth and . . ." And big sheepy Headstrewth had a big sheepy mouth, though he never really meant any harm with it. "Anyone Headstrewth told, which is probably everyone. Honestly, Aunt Vivian, I'm pretty sure the thief was Richard Coney. He appeared shockingly quickly after I came to—with a policeman in tow, no less—and seemed to already know about the theft."

"Ooooh, lovely," Vivian said with a hard, toothy smile. "Put that photo in the paper and *everyone* will figure it out for him or herself. Whether or not Coney is convicted of the crime, I would say his time in Kexford is over. And maybe Ramsbottom's, too!

"Are you going to the paper now? I could do with a walk. And so could you, by the looks of it. You're as pale as a mushroom from being in the darkroom so long. Let me fetch my hat and walking stick."

One couldn't say no to Aunt Viv; she was a force of nature when she cared to be. What Alice really wanted to do was lie down and sleep for a thousand hours—and hopefully reawaken in Wonderland.

But she rose and tidied her work, and finally summoned up the energy to meet her aunt at the front door—when it burst open and Mr. Willard exploded inside.

"I have done it!" he announced grandly, his pale blue eyes blazing and a shocking grin revealing a set of very square, very even yellow teeth.

"Done *what*, Mr. Willard?" Aunt Vivian asked, coming

in with her hat—one of his creations; there were several birds on it—and a walking stick with a silver wolf's head for the grip.

"Why, what you suggested: I put my name in for mayorship of our fair town!" He gave an extended, exquisite bow.

"Oh! Good show, Mr. Willard, good show indeed!" Aunt Vivian said in surprise. She reached out and pumped his hand vigorously. "I am very, very happy about this turn of events."

"To be sure," Mr. Willard said with a put-on, aristocratic smile. "We need to plan, to politicize, to figure out what our next steps are. Posters, pamphlets, pro-Willard advertisements!"

"Oh, and pins," Aunt Vivian said sagely. "People love the pins."

"Precisely!" Willard agreed, cackling.

"Well, by lovely coincidence it is definitely teatime, so let us away to Hendrick's for a bit of artemisia and some political planning! Dear, do you mind if we walk you to the café and you go the rest of the way yourself?"

"I'll be fine, Aunt Vivian," Alice said with a smile. "I fear no further camera thieves."

"Let us proceed thence," Willard said with a bow, gesturing to the open door. "After you, my lady. May I count on your support in the election?"

"If I could vote, you would absolutely have my vote," Alice said, a little archly. "But you may have my *support*, only if you would promise to help out the children of the Square—in a thoughtful, reasonable fashion."

"But of course!" Willard said indignantly. "And because you asked, it shall go to the top of my list. Along with democratizing the local textile mills and turning over the means of production to the workers."

"Ah, yes, you may need to put a bit of your socialism on the back burner if you want to win," Aunt Vivian said bluntly. "We can discuss this further over drinks."

The three walked out onto the road full of goodwill and some hilarity. Even exhausted and sick about the March Hare, Alice found her mood a trifle lifted.

*I shall just go to the newspaper with the photograph, inform Mr. Katz of poor incarcerated Joshua and his friends, and then I can finally concentrate on going back to Wonderland*, she told herself. *Just like that!*

As they approached what passed for the high street in their small town, the three saw what appeared to be something of a festival going on near the large fountain. A table was set up and clustered around by a crowd of all sorts of people: young, old, children, adults, mill workers, farmers and townspeople. There were brightly colored toy balloons and ribbons and bunting strung about.

*Birds,* for some reason Alice suddenly thought they resembled.

Ramsbottom sat behind the table. His beaming, jocular visage seemed to light on each and every person's face, and his right hand moved faster than a magician's to shake a hearty hello. During this he also somehow managed a quick—and hatefully smug—look over at Alice and her party. Coney was right beside him, handing out pins, looking harried—and a little pale when he saw Alice.

"Mr. Willard," Ramsbottom called out in cheerful aggression. "I heard that you have declared against me. Best of luck."

Mr. Willard started to roll his eyes, but Aunt Vivian hit him on the arm.

"And to you," the hatter added quickly.

"I'm running, too," said a quiet man at a small and lonely table all his own. Alice thought she recognized him from around town—the post office, perhaps.

"I am Mallory Griffle Frundus. My platform is primarily predicated upon a complete and long-overdue overhaul of the metropolitan sewer system and imposing *some* regulation on the out-of-control growth of factories along the river—all while encouraging progress and creating jobs for those now squeezed out of agriculture. Pin?" He held out a blue-and-red rosette with FRUNDUS—FOR US! written on it.

Alice smiled sympathetically. "I'm afraid I am supporting Mr. Willard here, but I will wear your pin, too, if you think it will help."

"Oh, anything would at this point," the man said with good humor. "I'm also having a little breakfast gathering Tuesday, a forum where people can come and discuss the issues important to them. Mostly as it pertains to urban improvements, of course. Sewers, schools, and the like."

"*We're* having a big rally that day, too!" Ramsbottom announced. "A *Pride for England* parade. All citizens from *good* families are welcome. And by 'good' I don't mean wealthy. Solid men of the earth, as you people like to say, are invited—anyone is, as long as they have hearts shaped by centuries of generational love in the nurturing warmth of English soil."

Alice sighed. Really understanding Ramsbottom was like deciphering a riddle. And what she saw at the end of it was more broken windows, hate and fury in the guise of patriotism. How much did those signing his petitions and taking his balloons understand and willfully join in on? How much did they not *quite* understand, but went along with anyway?

"Everyone loves a rally," Coney added half-heartedly.

"I don't think I shall be able to make it," Willard said.

"Loving our fellow man can take many different forms, but this is not one of them."

"Alice, will you come?" Coney asked nervously.

She gave him a look, but before a real answer came out of her mouth, Ramsbottom's grin went even wider.

"I'm afraid it's men only to march, anyway. Women may watch and then clean up, with a bit of punch, of course, provided by my campaign. As it should be in politics in England."

Whether he was referring to women in politics or free punch in politics it was hard to say, but the would-be mayor raised his voice for the last bit and looked to the crowd with an *am I right?* wave of his arms. The crowd responded immediately with cheers; who knew which thing they were cheering, but he had them in the palms of his oily hands.

Alice, Vivian, and the hatter left the square melancholy and disturbed.

"This is bad," Willard said darkly. "Not just for my campaign—but for Kexford in general. It's like he's whipping the masses into some sort of beast of hate. Mrs. Yao will not be the last of the victims of this state-sponsored xenophobia."

"I don't disagree," Aunt Vivian said with worry. "I don't know what to do—even if you don't win as a mayor, there has to be *something*."

"Auntie," Alice said slowly, thinking about what

Ramsbottom had said, especially about women. "Do you think the newspaper will *listen* to me at all? Will it print the photo and story if it's given to them by a woman?"

"Alice," Aunt Vivian said sternly, "it is your photo, and it is Mrs. Yao's story. You're *her* friend. You must stand up for women everywhere by insisting they listen to you."

"But if the point is to get notice and justice for Mrs. Yao, isn't the most important thing that the photograph just gets printed, however it gets there? Isn't *that* what really matters here?"

"Both are good points. In the end, however, you can and must only do what *you* feel is right," Willard said kindly. "Welcome to the world of politics, Alice. In the end, it is all stuff and nonsense."

# Chapter Thirty-Four

"Stuff and Nonsense."

*What a strange—and particular—choice of words,* Alice said to herself.

She considered all the twins of the two worlds: herself and Mary Ann, the Dodo and her sister, the March Hare and Alexandros. . . . Was there more to it than that? Were events, geographies, all of *life* mirrored as well? Did the mayoral race and Ramsbottom's rally somehow have something to do with events or goings-on in Wonderland? Was the Queen of Hearts' insane, murderous game somehow fueling events in Kexford, investing the upcoming election with otherwise dismissible emotions and meaning? If

Ramsbottom won, if the children in the Square continued to be hassled and locked up for crimes they never committed, and Mrs. Yao never received justice . . . was this all because of their doubles?

Or was this just the madness of England?

Or was there an in-between answer: did each world have some sort of effect on the other?

*What if the mad goings-on in England somehow polluted Wonderland?* Alice suddenly wondered.

What if the Queen of Hearts was bitten by whatever bug that made her decide to win the silliest and last of all games—because of what was happening in Kexford?

Also, the Hatter knew about things from this world because the Cheshire Cat had told him—presumably because the Cheshire had been here himself at some point. And the Knave had said some people could go back and forth! Not just Alice. There was some sort of fluidity between the two places; ideas and personalities and even people could sometimes pass through whatever walls normally kept them separated.

Then . . . possibly . . . whatever she did to solve the problems of one world would help the other. Or the reverse: if she failed, it would destroy both.

*It seems terribly unfair*, she thought. *It seems like I've been given a hopeless task, or pieces for a game with no rules at all and a shifting number of opponents, and told that everything depends on my figuring it out and winning.*

How very Wonderland.

As she walked, the street grew busier and more cluttered with shops and offices in what passed for the downtown section of Kexford. Alice watched all the businessmen and servants and people shopping and chatting and waving hello to one another and wished she had someone *she* could talk to. About everything. Someone both logical and a little mad. And perhaps not quite as close and concerned as Aunt Vivian (bless her, though).

Her subconscious already knew what she was thinking and Alice laughed a little at her false naivete. She paused, debating the pros and cons, at a literal crossroads. Then she took a left turn, knowing her mind had been made up a long time ago.

There it was: ALEXANDROS & IVY, BARRISTERS-AT-LAW. Gilt on richly stained wood.

She hesitated just a moment—was anyone looking? Was there going to be a rumor about young, single Alice approaching a law firm by herself? This particular law firm?

She went in.

(And what would Mary Ann have done? Just stood,

helplessly, assuming England would take her to wherever she was needed next?)

The interior was cool and dark with heavily stained wood. Everything smelled of ink and paper and musty books and fresh polish. A secretary, seated at a secretary, leapt up upon her entrance. He was ageless, skinny, perhaps needed to wash his hair, and gave her a look of such dismissal that she very much wanted to pull him by the ear and yell into it the way her neighbor sometimes did with her grandchildren.

"May I help you?" he asked, looking like he had no desire to do any such thing.

"I'm looking for Mr. Katz," she said politely. "I have some business with him."

"Do you have an appointment?"

"I don't," Alice admitted. "But I'm sure he'll see me."

And she was. There might be a veritable hurricane of nonsense flying around, but he had stayed by her at the park and covered her with his jacket. He had given her a riddle. He would see her, as definitely as she would smile upon seeing his rosy cheeks.

"I will check to see if he wishes to be disturbed," the secretary said in such a tone that Alice immediately knew he would most likely go upstairs, pretend to confer, then come back down and tell her sadly that the barrister was busy.

"I'll go myself. It's no problem," Alice said serenely, heading up the stairs with one delicate, gloved hand on the banister.

"No, I must insist—he mustn't be disturbed. . . ." The clerk went to stop her, putting his hand out.

Alice just widened her eyes and paused: that was all. Her meaning was clear enough. You *dare* lay a hand on a lady? And expect to keep your job?

He would not dare.

The man crumpled as visibly as a bachelor's button when the sun goes in.

Alice gave him a frosty nod and continued upstairs. Any incipient panic she had about looking like an idiot once at the top was quickly dispelled: unlike in Wonderland, the doors here were labeled clearly with neat little plaques. She knocked on the one that said MR. A. JOSEPH KATZ, ESQ.

A voice from inside: *"Drat it, Brigsby, I* said *I would go over to Mrs. Bickler's later and . . ."*

The door opened.

"Oh, it's you."

He was startled.

Alice found she had held her breath.

They stood there alone in the upstairs, him on one side of the door, her on the other, this situation arising only because she had decided to come see him. This *moment* only existed because she had sought him out, and that fact hung in the air very palpably. His brown eyes seemed extra wide and deep. She felt her own cheeks start to go as red as his were. The moment dragged on. Neither one of them said anything.

"I have solved your riddle," she finally said. "It's *perspective*."

"Indeed!" His eyes crinkled in relief and merriment. "And have you found that answer helpful? For other things in your life?"

"Yes, but not *entirely* helpful, and not for all things. There are some problems riddles cannot fix, I'm afraid," she said with a sigh. "And I have such a problem. Not a legal matter—a personal quandary, if you will, and I would dearly love an outsider's perspective, if you have a moment."

"For you, I have every single moment, all of them," Katz said frankly. "I'll clear my appointments for the day—for the next week, if you like."

Alice smiled.

"I hope it doesn't take that much time," she said, stepping in.

"I do," Katz said with feeling. Then he grinned. "This is de*light*ful!"

His office was small and well-appointed and full of books. His desk was mostly neat—tidy blotter, expensive but simple pens and inkwells, stacks of papers in neat little piles; the only off thing was the *Kexford Weekly* in an untidy heap in the middle as if it had been thrown there.

"Oh!" Alice said. "That was sort of what I came to see you about."

Katz made a sour face and threw himself into his chair with the strength and lankiness of a young man not quite grown out of childish acrobatics but constrained by the very nice suit he wore. Alice couldn't help noticing how pretty his lips were even when pursed in distaste.

"Is it about 'Ramsbottom's Rally'? They're going to be burning down houses by the end of it, the silly fool," he spat. "Always a good idea to rally up the proletariat with hate and free punch."

"Ah, no, although Aunt Vivian and Mr. Willard are equally concerned as you. I am, too," she added hastily. "I just don't see what can be done about it. It's a free country, Mr. Katz, and Ramsbottom is allowed to have a rally if he wants and has all the permits."

"It's a free country for you and Mr. Coney," Katz agreed. "There are some of us who might find it uncomfortable to continue living in a town where he holds sway."

Alice took this not *quite* as a slap in the face. Here she was showing up wantonly at his door and he was flinging their differences in her face and making her feel bad about it.

"Yes. I suppose I am free. But how did you vote in the last election?" she asked pointedly.

"Why, for Garretty, of course. He . . . Oh." He looked at her in wry amusement. "I see what you did there. You didn't vote, of course. Because you're a woman. Well played, Alice, well played. I am quite justly put in my place."

She smiled. "I think perhaps you've never had an opponent quite like me. At any rate, I came for advice from a friend, not to spar. *This* is why I'm here." She fished the photo of Yao and the stone out of her purse and handed it to him. He had to squint and hold it under the green-shaded lamp to see it clearly.

"I don't understand," Katz admitted immediately.

"Some ruffian threw a stone through Mrs. Yao's window with a nasty note attached—you could read it, if the picture were a bit larger—suggesting she leave town before worse things were done to her shop. She has had to replace the window at her own expense and the police have made no effort to try to catch the true villain. Instead they rounded up a couple of very innocent children from the Square and have them locked up. I thought maybe having this picture in the paper would put a fire under the police, as it were, to find the actual villain, to let the children go . . . or at least I shall wake local sympathy to her plight."

"Hmm, not a bad plan at all," Katz said. "Plus it's a nice advertisement for the tea shop—it would certainly help her business. Alice: 'English white savior to the rescue' again, eh?"

"You're very disagreeable sometimes, Mr. Katz," Alice said, narrowing her eyes at him. "It's not about me at all. It's about my friend, and the children in the Square. I am perfectly willing to not even have a credit to the photo—I am here considering having *you* bring it to the paper, since they may not even accept one from a woman."

"Well, there I think you're wrong. Not about my being disagreeable—I am entirely. I'm a *barrister.* We're always disagreeable. If we agreed all the time there would be no court cases at all.

"I think everyone in Kexford knows Alice, the town photographer, and it would only help to know that you were involved with this. Say . . ." He pulled out a magnifying glass and held it over the photo, frowning. "I still can't entirely read what the note says, but that handwriting looks *awfully* neat and flowing for some random thug without schooling, much less an immigrant from Russia. . . . Just look at the flourishes on the end."

"Yes . . . I'm fairly certain I already know who the miscreant is. The police, with some actual effort, could also figure out who wrote out the note and paid someone else to do the actual dirty work. Probably the same person who stole my camera in an attempt to get the film back."

"Your camera?" Katz asked, blinking. "Someone stole it?"

"Yes, rather mugged me for it. I shall deal with all that shortly."

"Someone *attacked* you?" Katz asked, standing up. "And stole your camera? You seem very calm about the crime that was perpetrated upon your person!"

"There are so many things going on right now, Mr. Katz," Alice said wearily. "As strange as it may sound, it is not my greatest concern. My brains are fine. The camera can be replaced. The perpetrator will be caught. I have other things to attend to. I have a world to—ah, a world *of* other concerns to get back to. Other things need saving more than I do, Mr. Katz."

"Such as what? What could a young woman like you have to worry yourself with—what *other* things?"

"I wish I could tell you. It would ease my mind considerably to share some of these troubles," Alice said with a wan smile. "And afterward you would never speak to me again—you would send me to straight to the madhouse."

"Oh, I doubt that," Katz said, raising an eyebrow. "I mean, we don't need a special house for that. We're all mad here."

Alice looked at him sharply. But he was just smiling his

usual guileless smile . . . with perhaps a bit of extra sparkle in it. She had the urge to curtsy, to take time while she thought of something to say. The moment drew out, and it was rich and full like a slant of late-afternoon sunlight through a dusty window.

"Why isn't your name on the sign outside?" she finally found herself saying, rather stupidly.

"Oh." Katz rolled his eyes. "I am not a partner yet—another six months and another connection with the right solicitor, I think. It's coming, don't you or my mother worry about that. Look, though, I have all the proper paraphernalia!"

He went over to a small wardrobe and with more energy than strictly necessary pulled out a robe and wig with a flourish.

"I even have a mirror to make sure not a whisker is out of place."

He opened the wardrobe all the way and revealed a simple but long looking-glass that showed a slightly warped version of the handsome young man: his jowl pulled out to ridiculous horizontal lengths and his toes disappeared into pinpoints. He grinned and put the wig loosely and lopsidedly on, and the overall effect made Alice laugh—out loud, for the first time in days, in the real world.

"All right, it's a bit of a carnival deal," he admitted,

putting the wig back after making one last face. "But as soon as I'm a full partner I'll get myself a really nice one. And a house," he added quickly.

He looked uncertain—and hopeful—and nervous—and—

And Alice found she was enjoying all of it rather much.

"A *house.* Indeed, Mr. Katz. I hadn't realized they were required for barristers, or solicitors, or even clerks. Along with the uniform, I mean."

Katz flushed but also grinned with good humor.

"Let me take care of your photograph—*and* Mrs. Yao, and the children," he offered. "What's a little more pro bono between friends? Anything that will ease your mind and lighten your troubles would be pleasure for me. And it would allow you to concentrate on your . . . other . . . concerns, whatever they may be. Saving the world."

"Thank you, Mr. Katz," Alice said, standing up and preparing to say goodbye. She was relieved—she felt she really could trust him to do the right thing. But she was also sad the interview was coming to a close. She put out her hand. "But I'm not, ah, saving the world. I just need to . . . need to find a way to . . ."

"To get back to *that world*?" he asked softly.

"I have no idea what you're talking about, Mr. Katz."

But he was pointing at the mirror.

Alice gasped.

Somehow, rather than the dusky and half-lit view of Katz's office that *should* have been reflected, there was instead a scene of a grim but sunlit field: of checkerboard squares, and fires burning, and smoke. . . .

Alice looked back at the barrister and found herself reaching for a camera she no longer had.

Katz shook his head. "You know who I am in that other world, Alice. You don't need a photograph."

"Kat-z," Alice said slowly. "Cheshire Cat!"

He executed a bow, and just as easily she could imagine him disappearing halfway through, or tumbling all the way over in a somersault, or something else ridiculous but graceful.

He didn't, however.

"But how? And how do you—*know* all this?"

Katz shrugged. "How do you travel back and forth so? My other half can, and he comes to visit. He brings me riddles."

"And you give him riddles in return," Alice said slowly, suddenly seeing all her recent interactions with the Cheshire in a whole new light. They had *both* been trying to help her, all along.

In infuriatingly mysterious ways.

"Return to Wonderland," he said, looking her in the eyes. "Save their world. But . . . come back to mine."

"That's rather forward of you, Mr. Cat."

He grinned. But it wasn't *just* like the Cheshire Cat's smile. There was warmth in it, and even love.

"I'm not the single young lady who goes knocking on strange barristers' doors," he pointed out.

"Hmmph," Alice said, sniffing. "Excellent point."

He gave her his hand. She picked up her skirts with her other one and began to step through the mirror—which was all soft and fading, just as she somehow expected.

She stopped before she was all the way through to turn back and look at him.

"Well then, Mr. Katz?"

"Well then," Katz said. He leaned forward and brushed a tendril of hair out of her face. "Good luck, Alice. Remember, time is always on *your* side. Or your wrist, in fact, if you're wearing a watch."

And then she fell backward into Wonderland.

# Forever and Ever Alice

# Chapter Thirty-Five

She didn't so much *plummet* as sort of drop and float at the same time.

*"Flop,"* Alice decided.

Fast and violent but also peaceful and quiet. End over end, head over heels, slowly turning round as though she were a leaf making its leisurely way from a branch to the ground. Her skirts billowed out around her and she was a little sorry to see they were her clothes from Angleland, not the smart suit the Queen of Clubs had given her. Still, the layers of fabric blossomed and fluttered like a pretty flower as she continued her journey downward.

She flapped her arms and tried to spin herself right way up. She kicked her legs to propel herself through the air faster, but to no avail. Gravity took the girl with her own sweet time, like a thistle seed, through low puffy clouds and air pockets of different temperatures, fluttering through flocks of fast-flying birds.

"Geddoutta the right lane, it's for fast fliers and passing only!" an angry goose squonked at her.

Far, far below, like one of those amusing paintings for which you need a magnifying glass to view all the details properly, was a vast board game—*field*—upon which two opponents—*armies*—had drawn up their sides. Literally drawn, though not so much like a picture as from a deck of cards, of course. These soldiers were neatly arrayed into rank and file on either side, but there were dozens upon dozens of other red and black cards patrolling the edges, organizing the support, trying to spy, and checking weapons.

Alice wondered where the Spades and Diamonds were.

"Ah well, adventure for another time, I suppose."

On the side of the red cards, defended by them, were the giant slowly burning piles of rubbish—and one *really* giant hill of toys.

All the toys in the world, it looked like.

There was every kind of dolly: folksy ones with no faces and angelic French porcelain ones whose eyes closed when they were laid down to nap. There were pushcarts and model trains and tiny velocipedes for tots and wagons and hoops and those little wooden ducklings on a rope you pull along whose bills snap open and shut and whose heads nod as they go. There were lawn games like croquet and darts, and many beautiful rocking horses, and tops and marbles and music boxes and jack-in-the-boxes. And there were things that Alice couldn't quite categorize, for they were toys unique to Wonderland and unfettered by English imagination.

And on top of this, grinning horribly and kicking her legs and shaking an evil black and twisted sword above her head with glee, was the Queen of Hearts.

Alice was so immediately filled with rage that she wanted nothing more than to reach down and shake the stupid little card queen until her head popped off like a flower.

"You . . . *stupid* . . . *murdering* . . . little . . . *spoiled brat*!" Alice screamed, thinking of the worst words she could. "I will destroy you!"

She had no plans beyond smashing herself into the nasty little creature from above; even now-Alice had her moments of acting without thinking.

Which is why it was a good thing she had friends.

Sensing something amiss, the Queen of Hearts stopped her laughing. She looked up with big, bulgy eyes that popped even further when she saw what was coming at her from the heavens. Her mouth opened wide, wider, wider still as if she couldn't decide whether to scream or to swallow the approaching danger.

Alice felt her own mouth pull back into a dry grin. All her teeth were exposed.

It wasn't really at the *last* moment; she had quite a good number more feet to go, really, but nearabouts the end something like a violent wind *wooshed* through and seized Alice, knocking her off course and carrying her aside.

(Of course the very angry and frustrated Alice couldn't see the Queen of Hearts' reaction; suffice it to say that the Queen merely looked perplexed for a moment, then took it in stride. "Must have been about to rain cats and dogs, and then the impounder came," she decided—quite reasonably for Wonderland.)

*"No!"* Alice cried. "Let me *go*!"

"Killing yourself and the Queen won't save the world now. Not even killing the Queen and lightly injuring yourself would save the world," came the voice of the thing that had seized her. Alice saw that she was in the grips of four strong claws, two leonine and two eagle-y. But no sooner had she noticed this than they switched directions quickly again and she had to focus on not losing the many sandwiches she had eaten back in Angleland.

Just as her stomach righted itself they were done: the

wind stopped and was she released. Alice tumbled unprettily to the ground, and the Gryphon just stood there for a moment preening a stray spot on his neck without saying a word—he was half lion, after all.

She rose unsteadily to her feet. They were in a tiny wood that jutted out into the battlefield, a strange little peninsula of trees and thicket that felt protected and safe. A small assortment of Wonderland creatures were also there (hiding), including the Hatter, the Dormouse, the Dodo, and Bill.

"Hatter!" Alice cried and ran over and hugged him. "Dodo!" she added just as happily. "Dormouse, Bill," she said, carefully taking their tiny appendages and shaking them delicately but properly. "And Gryphon. Sorry I struggled, but . . ."

"No worries. My rescues are always affronting. It's just the family way."

"I'm so glad you're all safe," Alice said.

"We are not *all* of us," the Hatter said. "But we are glad you've not bled to death, or however you do it in that other world of yours."

"I see the plan worked—the Queen of Clubs is here to save the day!" Alice said, admiring the two armies in the distance. Her royal friend rode a giant, fuzzy creature Alice decided to call a *buzzywhump* for future reference. It was mostly calm but pawed the ground occasionally with its furry front hooves. The Queen wore a black helm with a set of shining black clubs on top and a long black horsehair plume behind. The older accordion-necked owl sat on her shoulder, wearing black feathers for the occasion; his child, or tiny twin, was perched right next to him. The Clubs army was dealt out on either side of the Queen as far as the eye could see, some riding black pigs.

Alice thought it most interesting that the Queen was down in the fray, as opposed to remaining above her army like the Queen of Hearts.

On the other side, Tweedledum and Tweedledee raced round and round the base of the toy pile in opposite directions, singing. They crashed into each other, of course, falling down onto their backsides with their legs kicking into the air. Then they leapt up, rather more adroitly than seemed likely, shook hands, bowed, linked arms, and twirled around each other. Their ruby-colored heart pins glittered in what little light there was.

Alice couldn't decide if their antics were amusing or chilling.

*"Surrender now!"* the Queen of Clubs ordered, raising her club. "You cannot hope to win this game of War."

"What do you mean? *Win?* And win *only* War? I intend to win *all* games! The last one! I shall be the one with the most toys!" the Queen of Hearts shouted back, laughing baldly. She nearly cut herself on her own sinuous black blade with her dramatic antics.

"She *can* win, can't she? The Queen of Clubs, I mean?" Alice asked a trifle nervously. "That's a lot of cards out there. More than enough for a game of War."

"*You* tell *us*," the Dodo said, not unkindly. "You're the one who arranged all this."

"I? Yes I did, but I couldn't be certain exactly how it would turn out . . . and what else was there to do? No one has told me that yet," Alice said a little peevishly. "It was the only solution I could think of that I could effect."

"It doesn't involve *you* at all," the Hatter said cryptically. Or maybe not so cryptically, considering the eyebrow he raised at her like a dueling pistol.

"Why are you even here?" the Queen of Hearts was shouting to the other Queen. "Is it just to witness my excellent royal winning of the last game?"

"We are here to free your people, and to take over whatever worldly possessions and treasures you have as our reward," the Queen of Clubs shouted back (a little too honestly, in Alice's private opinion). "You have betrayed every noble responsibility of being a queen. You have scared, tortured, killed, seized, imprisoned, and stolen from your subjects willy-nilly, without even a warrant or an advertisement in the newspaper about it. You are, in a word, unfit to be queen. Step down willingly and we shan't execute you too much."

At this the Queen of Hearts threw her head back and laughed. "Step down? When I am about to *win*? We'll have one final count, and then it's game over—I win forever!

"Rabbit! Rabbit! Where is the list? How many toys do I have now? Rabbit . . . ?"

The Queen of Hearts looked around, at first in annoyance, and then in complete perplexity. "Knave! Where is that dratted rabbit? He's supposed to be doing the tally for me!"

The Knave, Alice saw, was at the base of the mountain of toys along with several of the Queen's closest advisers (one was the Knave of Accounting—of course he would be in charge of lists of toys). None was the Rabbit, however, and all were shaking their heads and shrugging and denying and looking in general very worried and excitable.

"We shall execute the Rabbit twice as much," the Queen of Clubs announced. "For being a traitor to his own people as well as carrying out your ghastly orders."

But no one was paying attention to her.

The Knave put a reluctant foot on the base of the pile of toys, then gave up any pretense of trying to climb the ramshackle structure at all.

"No one has any idea where he is," he admitted loudly.

*"WHAT?"* the Queen of Hearts shouted, putting a hand to her ear.

*"He's gone AWOL!"* the Knave shouted back.

Then a little thing, something like a vole but with a longer snout and red eyes and webbed feet where its ears might normally have been, scrabbled up to the Knave and whispered something in his ear.

"Apparently he's gone to the Great Clock—*What?*" the Knave demanded in surprise, interrupting himself. He asked a question, quickly and quietly. The thing nodded. "All right. Apparently he's already gone to the Plain of Time, to push the clock forward."

"But that's ridiculous!" the Queen said as thoughtfully as was possible for her. "We haven't done a final tallying. I don't know if I have enough toys yet."

"They're all about to be *mine* anyway," the Queen of Clubs said helpfully.

"And what about the Ticket Master?" the Queen of Hearts' owl called out. "Have you checked against him? He has been collecting toys since the beginning of the last age. He definitely had more jacks than anyone else, acres of them."

"Yes, there's no point in ending the world until we know for certain," the Queen of Hearts agreed. "There may be no point in ending it at all. That rabbit is a traitor! He'll ruin everything! Off with his head!"

*"Surprise attack!"* the Queen of Clubs suddenly yelled.

A black card ran forward and threw himself down in the middle of the battlefield, directly between the two armies. He flipped himself over.

He was a nine.

All the spectators—where had they come from? They were suddenly there in bleachers, *oohing* in impressed surprise. The crowd was a perfect cross section of Wonderland: creatures from the Unlikely and the land of the Clubs were bright-eyed and eager, well-dressed, and passing bags of snacks to one another. Those from Heartland were tired, bloody, sad, wounded, fixed up with bandages and slings and eye patches. But they looked toward the battlefield with hope.

"Odds, odds on the war, on the end of the world, on the number of toys," a genial pig in a cap shouted, walking up and down the aisles waving pound notes in the air.

"I'll take seven to one against the Queen of Clubs," a duck declared, handing over what looked like a small bag of buttons.

"Lemonade, punch, quizzes, and comfits. Biscuits and breaderflies," a woman with a tray of concessions called out.

"We're all going to go with the end of the world in a few moments," the Gryphon reminded her. "No one could possibly finish a bag of comfits in time."

The woman shrugged.

"This is terrible!" Alice cried. "I don't understand! I had solved everything! Oh, *why* is the White Rabbit going ahead to try to end the world if the Queen of Hearts isn't ready?"

"Of all the questions that pertain to this situation, is that really the one that's the most ripe?" the Hatter demanded.

"But the two armies—won't *they* determine the winner? And what about the Rabbit? What do we *do* . . ."

She looked around at their expectant faces, as if she were about to pull a March Hare out of her hat.

"No, what do *I* do," she said slowly. "I am the only one who can get us out of this. That is what you have been saying all along. I just didn't believe it until now. That I had anything to offer Wonderland at all—compared to you natives."

"I told you she wasn't a stupid girl," the Dodo said mildly, stirring his tea. "She just takes a while to get to the right answer. She's slow, that's all. But I think everyone in Angleland must be. Don't be hard on her."

"Where is the Plain of Time?" Alice asked.

"Oh, it's a terrible adventure off," the Gryphon said,

frowning. "First you have to go through the Labyrinth of Shifting Persimmons. Then you must cross the Sinking Sea. If you survive that, there's the land of—"

As he spoke the Dormouse tumbled down from the Hatter's hat with a large iced biscuit, aiming for the Dodo's tea to dunk it.

"Yes yes, *no*," Alice said, seizing the biscuit out of the poor little mouse's hands. She popped it into her own mouth. "Sorry. Seized for emergency measures."

Then she stuck all her fingers together like she was holding a very tiny, very sticky ball—and drew them apart.

Inside the space she created was a scene of a surprisingly serene, if empty and endless, prairie. Stuck in the middle of it was what looked very much like Big Ben, if Big Ben went to thirteen instead of twelve.

"Wish me luck," Alice said, stepping through.

"We're counting on you," the Dodo said, raising his teacup.

"It's one rabbit," Alice said, knowing exactly how stupid she sounded. "How hard can it be?"

# Chapter Thirty-Six

The Plain of Time smelled funny.

"This," Alice said, "is how one can tell it isn't a dream at all but reality: one doesn't remember smells in dreams most of the time."

The air was . . . burning a little? There was nothing precisely she could see, but something definitely reminded her of the scent of *blue*. Sparks. Clean, like before a thunderstorm or after a particularly close lightning strike. The opposite of the smoldering piles of rubbish in Heartland. She felt the hairs on her arms rise and her heart quicken. Something exciting was about to happen.

And yet it didn't look like a place where anything exciting happened, ever; it looked like an African veldt or a flat alpine field that extended endlessly. The grass was low and not green and vibrant emerald like a proper field, but shades of straw and sage. The flowers were delicate and tiny. The shadows were strange because the sun and all the moons stood next to each other in the sky in a kind of a standoff. The sun had fire, of course, but there were at least eight moons in their different phases, and some of the horns looked quite sharp indeed.

The clock tower stood in the middle of the field—or really, it could have been at either corner, at the bottom, or near the top, because the field went on forever, so who could say where the middle was, really? If clocks read the same in this world, it looked like it was about an hour and a half until thirteen o'clock. Whereas through the doorway, the Great Clock had seemed austere and severe ruling over the empty space, up close she saw that it had rosy cheeks and a cheeky smile and eyes that looked left and right with the seconds. Surprisingly friendly for something that could bring about the end of the world.

To the right of her was the White Rabbit.

They caught each other's eyes for a long moment. He wore his little waistcoat. He had his pocket watch (with heart-shaped fob) out but the face seemed to be cracked. The *Rabbit's* face was still and strange and his red eyes held hers with no fear—but also not with the blankness one normally associated with lagomorphs.

It was a pause before the storm, the breath before a tirade, a last moment of peace before the crying began.

Then he slipped the watch into his pocket and—took off.

On all fours, like a rabbit.

"No!" Alice cried and raced after him.

There were many disadvantages for the girl.

For one thing, she was not made for running in the way a rabbit is. The poor dear had only two legs. Also her dress, corset, crinolines, and underskirts were ridiculously confining. (A giant and satisfying *riiiiiiip* could be heard as she opened her stride up just a little more, forcing the pace of legs below her a little faster.) Her shoes were stupid. She was not used to exercise.

She *did* have the fate of a world and panic within her, but whatever drove the Rabbit drove him mercilessly and madly.

Alice was larger than the Rabbit, which was a little bit of an advantage; her steps were three or four times his body length. There was a moment when she felt like she could have, if she just knew how, thrown herself over and on top of him.

But rabbits are made to evade meat eaters; the way they run is tricky and wily. He would suddenly change direction, zigging and zagging with each leap, as confounding and frustrating as any rabbit a child has chased at dusk. It is like they can always predict the straight, boring paths of the house-apes who chase them.

The Rabbit danced around a small boulder; Alice leapt over it.

The Rabbit cleared a trickling not-quite-stream in a single hop, and Alice's leather boot went deep into the mud, becoming stuck there for precious seconds.

The Rabbit suddenly cut right, a perfect ninety degrees right, and Alice tripped over him trying to stop and change her own direction.

She could hear nothing but the Rabbit's hind feet beating the ground like a drum—and her own breathing in her ears, too loud and not enough.

The Rabbit made a mighty jump and landed on the first step of the clock tower. Without so much as a pause he leapt up and up and up, clearing several stairs at a time and never resuming his upright, human stance.

Alice practically fell over the first step, tumbling forward and hitting her hands hard on the fifth and sixth one. She bled but continued her forward and upward motion, all her limbs now out of sync and staggering.

She had to keep going. The world depended on her.

Around and around she followed the Rabbit up the outside of the tower.

She looked for cookies in her pockets. She tried to make a window or a door while trying not to trip.

All too soon—or too late—she was on the walkway that led to the giant hands of the rosy, smiling clockface.

The Rabbit had the hour hand in his paws.

"NO!" Alice cried.

The Rabbit swung hard, and pushed it to thirteen.

"It had to be," the Rabbit said.

The ground—the whole world—began to shake. Alice flung up her arms to try to balance on the narrow walkway.

"*NO!* There has to be another way. There is always another way in Wonderland!" she cried in despair. She grabbed the hour hand herself to pull it back, but it didn't budge. The Rabbit didn't even try to stop her.

As Alice struggled and groaned, her dress stretched and ripped more, this time at the seams of her arms. The cloth shrank up her biceps as it tore, exposing her wrists and forearms.

And also the watch she had won from the Queen of Clubs.

"My watch . . ." she murmured.

What was it someone had said?

*Time is always on* your *side, Alice. Or your wrist, if you're wearing a watch.*

The Rabbit was looking at her curiously but bleakly. The tower began shaking so hard that she stumbled, almost falling off the platform. Strange cracks of purple and black lightning split the sky.

Alice grabbed the knob of the watch with her right hand and pulled.

Everything stopped.

Everything . . .

. . . was . . .

. . . silent.

# Chapter Thirty-Seven

Alice fell forward from momentum, her body already used to the movements of the crumbling world. An ugly black streak of not-lightning froze in the sky; the waxing half-moon was caught in a look of surprise and horror. The Rabbit's eyes were glassy and wide like a taxidermy's.

Alice sobbed, catching her breath. The sound carried strangely across the prairie.

All was still except for her.

She didn't pause to ask *now what.* Perhaps little Alice would have done that.

Ever so carefully she popped open her watch—which also had thirteen numbers on it, each in a different style and font—and tried pushing its hands backward.

Like the one on the tower itself, the hour hand wouldn't budge.

Neither would the minute hand.

Tentatively, holding her breath, Alice tried the second hand.

Success!

She sobbed again, in relief.

She wound the hand backward . . . once . . . twice . . .

. . . and was plucked up through the air, pulled backside-first like the hand of God was playing dolls with her. Her hair waved the wrong way, and despite her body repeating the motions that had led her to where she was now, in reverse her mind wasn't pulled that way. She still *thought* forward and could examine the strange course she and the Rabbit had taken across the field.

Suddenly she stopped with a jerk, half in and out of the window she had created to get to the Plain of Time.

Two minutes and fourteen seconds.

That was as far back as she could go.

Perhaps the window was the end point; perhaps time couldn't travel through it the way it could through local space. She was frozen at the beginning, right before the Rabbit had come up next to her. She could see him hopping toward the tower but just starting to turn toward where she had popped out of nowhere.

"This is an easy fix," she said. But her words sounded

strange and dead, as if they too couldn't travel through time-stopped air.

She made for the Rabbit, taking her belt off. All she would have to do was tie him up when he was frozen like this, and the game would be over.

"No," she told herself, despite the horrid sound of her voice. "No more game metaphors. We're done with that."

But as Alice approached the White Rabbit, the air around her seemed to thicken, like she was pushing against a strong wind. She closed her eyes and dug her feet in but the force grew stronger in response. Soon it was as hard as walking through water or mud. A hollow booming sound emanated every time she forced a foot or a hand forward even an inch, trying to split the air with her fingers.

Finally she ground to a complete stop. She could push no farther. And she was still several feet from the Rabbit.

Well, if she couldn't get to the Rabbit, the obvious answer was just to go to the tower, perhaps with a stick or a stone, and wait for him there, and bop him over the head.

Alas, Time had other ideas.

As she walked farther away from her starting point, once again the air built itself up against her. She was little more than halfway to the Tower before she couldn't budge, even by sliding her feet forward in the dirt a smidgen at a time. The booming sound became unbearable.

"All right, then. I can't stray far from my point of origin, in time *or* geographic locality," she concluded. "I'll just set myself right in front of the Rabbit, as close as I can to him, and grab him when he runs by. He'll be so surprised at my sudden appearance that he will be unable to do anything but continue barreling forward into me. It's a trap that practically sets itself."

She went as close to the Rabbit as she could and walked back and forth in front of him several times, checking the angles, making absolutely sure she was directly in front of his path. No room for error.

Then she hunched down with her hands out like a wicketkeeper in cricket, ready for catching.

She took a deep breath and put a finger on the watch knob.

"Three . . . two . . . one . . . *go*!"

She hit the button.

# Chapter Thirty-Eight

Time restarted.

The White Rabbit started moving—but slowly, as if Time was warming up, stretching.

Suddenly he shot forward.

His sometimes-human eyes saw the girl who had somehow appeared between him and the clock tower. They widened in shock. It was obvious from just that little movement that he had no idea Alice was capable of anything like this—anything at all surprising or dangerous. Alice would remember that later.

But right now she was too busy being confronted with a simple fact of nature. White Rabbits in waistcoats with pocket watches aside, rabbits in general were creatures of the wild with very little brain—but very lots of instinct. He might not have understood *how* Alice got there, but this puzzle meant nothing to the rabbitiness inherent in him.

*Without thinking* he thumped his hind legs to the side and darted around the unexpected obstacle.

Alice cried out in dismay as he whisked by her, his inside leg beating the ground twice in a double thump to make up for the hard right turn. Rabbit fur flew up Alice's nose.

Being human (and a Victorian one at that) the girl had very little instinct and very lots of reason: it took her a precious millisecond or two to process what had happened and then turn and run after him.

Although her plan hadn't worked out the way she had expected, she was at least much, much closer to him than in their previous race. Alice made herself run harder, pumping her arms and legs and running on her toes. It was easy because her dress was already torn.

The Rabbit bounced around the large rock as before; this time she cleared it without pausing.

There was the stream and bog—he leapt straight over it. She wasted a second or two pausing to see what was the best way through so she wouldn't get stuck like last time. There was a tuffet that looked perfect for pushing off from—and it was. Strong and sturdy and springy, it gave her an extra foot or two of lift, which recovered a little of her precious lost yards.

The Rabbit made one human mistake: looking around back at her just as he began to leap up the tower stairs.

Alice threw herself forward to grab him but missed and once again tumbled against the hard stone steps, scraping her palms *and* her shins this time. With a shriek of frustration she pushed herself to her feet and practically crawled up the steps before rightfully regaining her footing.

Despite all her flailing about, she was right behind the Rabbit. By the time the two reached the top, he was once again within grabbing distance.

Without a thought for the danger of the unfenced catwalk and the height they were at, Alice lunged forward and clawed at him.

One finger got a bit of waistcoat; the luckier left hand got what felt like a neck-fold and a little bit of flesh.

But the rabbit thumped and kicked and his hair shed into her fingers; he slipped like a jacket out of her grasp with great clouds of white bunny fur.

He leapt straight up and caught himself on the hour hand of the clock. His weight and momentum were enough to pull it down to thirteen.

The world began to shake.

Alice pulled the knob on her watch. . . .

# Chapter Thirty-Nine

It was something to have the entire world stopped and frozen and to be able to scream as much as she wanted. No one heard and everyone waited for her to be done.

Finally Alice wiped her forehead with her wrist—careful not to nudge the watch. She glared at the dumb rabbit dangling from the hour hand and for just a moment had a vision of him strung up with a brace of other conies over the shoulder of a hunter returning home from a good day's work.

Immediately she felt sorry for that; the White Rabbit was an intelligent being who deserved neither being filled with shot nor being eaten.

Although he *had* decided to end the entire world, killing

everyone in it, and of his own volition! Not even on the Queen of Hearts' orders; he was a would-be mass murderer!

She slowly wound the second hand of her watch widdershins, watching everything carefully in reverse as she was pulled back toward the start: the beginning of the race, the boulder, the bog, the stairs, her falling. . . .

Then she took a moment to breathe and think.

She walked out to the boulder—the air only thickened a little at that distance—and, breaking back multiple nails and scraping her fingertips raw, managed to pull it out of place and turn it on its small side, revealing a hole in the ground. This she covered with grass and rushes.

She dusted off her hands, pleased with her work.

"He's so intent on the clock tower he won't have noticed things in the landscape shifting. He'll just be barreling forward and *pop*—if he doesn't bonk headfirst right into the stone he'll definitely get stuck in the hole, even for a moment."

She smiled, stretched, and got herself ready.

"Three . . . two . . . one . . . *go*!"

She hit the knob.

# Chapter Forty

Time restarted.

The stone *did* catch him off guard.

He almost leapt right into it. At the last minute he tried to change direction but fell back into the hole.

*"Ha!"* Alice cried. "I have you now!"

Like a child's toy—or Bill, pushed out of a chimney—the White Rabbit shot straight back up out of the hole, powered only by the fire of his hind legs. He hung in the air for a moment like a confused balloon and then dropped back down, touching a single left claw onto the top of the upright stone.

He used that to push himself off again, and continued toward the tower.

"Damn!" Alice cried.

She chased.

He ran.

He bounded up the stone steps.

She tripped.

Not quite as badly this time—she didn't even scrape her hands. Merely reddened them.

He leapt for the clock's hands.

"I did it for—" he shouted.

Alice pulled the knob on her watch. Time stopped.

# Chapter Forty-One

Time restarted.

Time restarted.

Time restarted.

Alice added a gash to her forehead, a slightly turned ankle, an abrasion all up her left calf, several puncture wounds to her arms, and embedded grit in her cheek. She lost a boot.

She also lost her bodice trying to rig up a net to ensnare him.

She screamed and kicked and threw stones at the Rabbit. They slowed down as they approached his frozen form and dropped equally slowly to the ground, far out of harm's way.

She stood in her undershirt and corset, covered in mud and sweat and blood, her hair down around her, looking like a witch from *Macbeth*.

She lay back on the grass of the Plain of Time for a while, watching the strange moons and sun and chewing on a stalk of timegrass.

"It's just another stupid Wonderland riddle," she mused. "I can't capture the rabbit. I never could. Not before, not now. That's apparently just not allowed. Alice never gets the White Rabbit.

"So what *can* I do? Just let the world end? Someone told me that time was on my side—I have figured out that part at least, with the watch. But if I can't get the Rabbit, who can? How can I stop him? How can I stop him from getting to the clock and ending the world? What do I have that is unique in solving this? How does *perspective* solve this?"

She regarded the tower, the strange thing out of a child's dream or nightmare. It seemed so harmless with its rosy cheeks and rolling eyes. Even the ancient stone steps could be seen as part of the block tower an imaginative child had built while muttering to herself about Time and rabbits and Snakes and Ladders and games of War and piles of toys and suns and moons and stopping the end of the world. Being a hero. So many different games of childhood all mixed together in the mad mind of a lonely child. All of them old and familiar.

Alice blinked.

"*Perspective.* I don't have the right one!

"You're given a rabbit and a tower and a countdown and think you've got to stop the rabbit. But you're playing the wrong game, Alice," she said, beginning to grin. "Forget the rabbit! The *tower* is the object of this game! Just *GET THERE FIRST!*"

She smiled, rose, and kicked off her other boot. She stretched, and got herself ready, crouching down the way she had seen serious runners do.

"Last one there's a rotten egg," she told the frozen rabbit over her shoulder.

"Three . . . two . . . one . . . *go!*"

She hit the button.

# Chapter Forty-Two

Time restarted.

Alice didn't look left, right, or behind her. She didn't even bother to imagine the surprised look on the White Rabbit's bewhiskered face as she suddenly appeared out of nowhere in front of him, running to the same goal. She ignored him.

She pumped her arms and dug her toes into the soft ground. It was really quite delightful, feeling the two connect with a primal joy she hadn't experienced since she was a young girl at the beach. The earth was pushing her off with each stride, *helping* her spring along to the finish. Her long golden hair streamed out behind her, shedding the dried mud and blood.

For a brief moment something white appeared below and to the right of her, perilously near her feet. It was the Rabbit, pushing faster and harder than ever. He was so close she could have wasted a second and kicked him—out of her way, out of the race.

She didn't.

She concentrated on running and pulled ahead.

She worried for one ecstatic moment as she cleared the bog that she was actually losing precious moments in the air as she hung there below the absurd celestial orbs.

But she landed and went on regardless.

*The steps.*

She was there first. She just had to not—

—fall.

Without thinking she lengthened her legs and leapt. She didn't worry about landing.

And so she touched down seven steps up, and the falling-forward momentum at the end of her jump only propelled her farther along.

Around and around she ran, two, three steps at a time, leaning into the tower and letting her own weight keep her safe.

Alice could hear the tiny stony *thuds* below her of a rabbit's hind feet pounding the grey stone.

She broke out onto the catwalk below the clock's face with a scream of triumph. She swung around to face the

White Rabbit, who tried with one last, valiant bound to leap *over* her and land on the hour hand. Alice punched straight up above her and knocked him into the clock's nose, where the two iron hands were attached.

The Rabbit fell in a crumpled heap at her feet.

"HA!" Alice cried, kneeling down and seizing him. "*I WIN!* The Queen of Hearts loses! The world is safe from your terrible mistress—and your own terrible, terrible acts of villainy!"

The Rabbit was shuddering and shaking. Alice turned him to face her, to make him look her in the eye—and saw that he was sobbing.

"The Queen can't hurt you," she said hesitantly, confused. "Any more than I and my friends will, I mean. She has lost. The world is saved and she will be punished. You will be, too—but in a fair trial."

"Win . . . ?" the White Rabbit moaned. "I never wanted her to *win*. I don't care about winning. I wanted to end it all."

"I beg your pardon?" Alice asked, unsure she heard him properly. Adrenaline and triumph were still raging in her ears and making it hard to understand.

"End it. . . . End her raids, tortures, executions, imprisonments, looting, burning . . . End it all. End the pain. End her reign. End the world where my Mary Ann was killed."

*"You?"* she eventually asked, trying to understand.

"Wanted to destroy the world? You? Not the Queen of Hearts? Coming here to speed up the clock wasn't all a plan of her invention?"

"She wanted to have all the toys when the world ended, whenever it was due," the Rabbit said, pointing miserably at the clock. Tears rolled down the fur on his face, eventually sinking in and matting it down. Without thinking Alice pulled out what remained of her last handkerchief and tried to hand it to him. He didn't even see it. The little, respectable, ridiculous White Rabbit no longer cared about such picayune niceties. For some reason this was more shocking than anything he had said. Alice did her best to wipe away the majority of tears herself as he lay prone in her lap.

"Once she was sure she had the most toys she probably *would* have advanced Time so no one would have a chance to beat her, and win. I don't care. I just want this world to be over, to restart with Mary Ann alive again. Even if I didn't know her, even if we never met again. *She* would be alive. And safe. And no one would be in pain or in prison anymore. Everyone would come back. And maybe even the Queen of Hearts would be reborn as someone better. Who knows?"

Alice's head was whirring.

"This clock doesn't end the world? It . . . restarts it?" she asked.

"It does both, you dim thing. Ends one game and starts the next. Don't you know how games on a timer work? You really are such a dull girl compared to my Mary Ann. Sometimes. But sometimes you outwit the Rabbit . . ." he mused.

Alice put a hand to her temple, exhausted and confused by this revelation, unmindful of the dried sweat and bits of dirt that flaked off as she did so.

*"THREEE CHEERS FOR QUEEN ALICE!"*

Alice leaned over—dangerously—and peeped at the plain below.

There was a small but growing crowd of bedraggled and excited Wonderland creatures, clapping and shouting and leaping up and down and capering about.

"She's saved the world!"

"She beat the Queen of Hearts!"

"She wins!"

"I didn't . . ." Alice began, standing up to address them better. The rabbit was still in her arms, prone, apparently unconcerned with whatever happened next.

Suddenly there was a curious weight on Alice's head.

Cradling the Rabbit with her left hand, she reached up cautiously with her right and found exactly what she expected there: a giant crown, probably golden, heavy and ornate and, from the glints she saw reflected in the clockface, very, very, sparkly. A cape somehow slipped over her shoulders and Alice hoped very sorely that the soft fur at the edges wasn't ermine. She had seen several ermines on this adventure.

The crowd below her was very large now: she could pick out, like shapes in the clouds, the people from the various places she had been: there was a contingent from Ornithsi-ville, mostly dignified but with one enthusiastic cider seller. The Queen of Clubs stood at the head of a fantastic procession, riding her buzzywhump. She smiled broadly at Alice, apparently not at all displeased at her coronation. There was the horse at the head of a train, toasting her with a cup of foul train tea.

Alice's heart leapt when she saw the Hatter, Gryphon, Dodo, and some of the others waving madly at the very base of tower, telling anyone who would listen how *they* knew her *personally*. She waved back, which was now hard with a rabbit in one hand and a scepter in the other.

"Bother!" she swore.

Carefully, being sure not to trip on her cape, she made a long, slow descent from the catwalk. At the base of the steps was a ceremonial float that had been prepared in her honor, complete with a high chair that looked a bit like the clock tower for her to sit in and wave from. It was so rickety she felt far more dizzy and unsafe atop it than she had at the top of the clock tower itself.

The Queen of Hearts was in a cage on a wagon, pouting furiously. At first Alice found it hard to be angry with such a ridiculous creature . . . and then she thought of Mary Ann, and the March Hare, and the Hatter's eye, and all the insanely horrible things the Queen had perpetrated against the good people of Wonderland.

"You are a vile creature," Alice told her coldly. "Without a bit of Nonsense in you. You are directed, cruel, and hateful. You don't deserve to live—more than that, you don't deserve to live in *Wonderland*."

The Queen of Hearts' eyes bulged wider than seemed possible. Of all the things she had expected from Alice, this was very obviously the furthest from it—and worse than anything she could have imagined.

Suddenly two bright, ball-shaped boys popped up between the cage and Alice's float. From their mouths came a grating, wheedly apology sound. Alice's ears nearly crumpled with horror.

"We are sorry, Alice, Alice."

There was Tweedledee.

"Alice, we are *very* sorry."

That was Tweedledum, and he raised his eyebrows at his brother to show how much more sorry he was.

"She took all our toys—"

"But said we should have new ones—"

"Once the world was over," they finished together.

Alice looked at them levelly.

Was it worth pointing out the ridiculousness of what they said?

"Can we sing a song for you?" Tweedledee asked.

"It's a very good one," Tweedledum added eagerly.

They opened their mouths—

"Nope," Alice said, spotting some people in the crowd below she would much rather spend time with. She slipped down the chair and ran over to them, still cradling the White Rabbit. The Hatter regarded the creature with a raised eyebrow.

"I think he is punishing himself enough," Alice admitted. "He wanted to end the world to stop all the terrible things that were going on—and because he didn't want to live without Mary Ann."

"Hmm," the Hatter said thoughtfully.

"But now we're all safe, and the Queen is behind bars, and we can all live happily ever after," Alice said with a grin. Mice and gnats were replacing her outfit—discreetly—with a golden gown, and she didn't even mind.

"Yup! At least for another hour or so," the Gryphon agreed happily.

"Yes, at least for—*What?* What do you mean?"

"The clock," the Hatter said, pointing at it. "This day's almost over. World's about to end."

"Well, we must stop it!" Alice jumped up, putting the catatonic rabbit back on the wagon. "Let's go and move the hands back . . . !"

The Hatter looked at her as if she were Mad. "You can't stop the end of the world. Silly girl. Maybe *you* stole my Nonsense," he added suspiciously.

"But! But! That's terrible! All of this was for nothing!" Alice shouted, feeling panic take over her body, arms and legs.

"Not true at all," said the Cheshire Cat, rubbing against her legs. "You beat the Queen of Hearts. You prevented her from winning. You caught the White Rabbit. You won, you became queen, you stopped all the pain and misery in this world."

"But you only have an hour left!" she shrieked.

"All games end, Alice," the cat said softly. "All dreams get woken from, eventually."

"The same game forever would be *boring*," the Dodo put in. "Even for me."

"Yes, definitely time for something new," the Hatter agreed.

"But I don't want you to . . ." What? Die? Disappear? Restart? "I don't want to say goodbye."

"Then don't," the Gryphon said, shrugging. A forked tongue came out and licked her tears. It was warm and wet like a dog's; not entirely unpleasant.

"But what do we do?" Alice asked plaintively.

"That's up to you now," the Hatter said simply. "You are Queen."

Alice looked around her. All the creatures of Wonderland she had met and saved, she had avoided and fought with, she had sung songs with and run from, all the cards and bandersnatches and mome raths and borogroves and paper people and dragon flies, the animals and birds and insects and people, they all looked at her expectantly.

(The Knave looked at her curiously, toasting her with his cider.)

"I . . ." She thought hard.

What else *was* there to do?

"I . . . declare teatime and Nonsense until the End of Time!"

# Chapter Forty-Three

An ear-deafening roar the likes of which even Wonderland had never heard before went up from the Plain of Time. Everyone danced and shouted and cavorted and jumped and flew. There was cheering and a ticker-tape parade, the pops of some sort of cannon or gun or perhaps champagne, and a walrus band that marched through blowing their tusks. Tea was served all around, from large and small kettles into endless souvenir coronation cups. Trays and trays of EAT ME cookies were distributed. It would not be too much to say it was the largest, happiest, most raucous party anywhere at any Time.

Alice sat on the wagon, dangling her legs over the side, one hand on the slowly recovering Rabbit, the other on the

Cheshire Cat's back. Her scepter was being used to stir some lemon into a cup of tea the size of a church. Her crown was cocked on her head.

She felt very, very strange.

She wanted to cry, but it was obvious that no one else was sad—or wanted anyone sad around them at the party.

"Maybe this time I'll come back as a cobbler," the Hatter was telling a pretty young chicken eagerly. "*That* would be a fun change."

"Not me. I shall be a Dodo, I think," the Dodo mused. "Maybe with a different wig."

"Cheshire," Alice said, suddenly remembering, "You told me that *Mary Ann* was the real hero. You said, 'If you want my advice . . . you'll find her.' "

"And you did," the Cheshire said, bathing his tail. "You found her . . . or a hero . . . or something that led to all of this. Inside of you. Oh, but you have needed so much of my help! I even sent Katz to help you find your way back, through the pond and the old tree. . . ."

Alice sighed, for once not distracted by thoughts of the boy (though it was nice to remember his name). "I wish I could have known Mary Ann. I feel like I've been right behind her, just missing her the whole time, unable to catch her—like the White Rabbit. I was foolish to be jealous of her for so long. . . . It's just that she always seemed to know what she was doing, and everyone loved her for that. She knew who she was and what to do and how to bring about change in her world. It made me feel so useless and unsure of myself. I should have just learned from her. And I suppose I did, in a way.

"I would dearly love to meet her. I suppose . . . with the world beginning again . . . she will come back. Will I ever be able to return here again, Cheshire?"

"A man cannot walk into the same river twice, for later he is not the same man and it is not the same river," the Cheshire answered.

"I am not a man and this is not a river," she said, rolling her eyes. She gestured at her friends, who were now singing, even the Dormouse. "Will they even remember me?"

"Katz will remember you," the Cheshire said with a grin, his body fading in and out of existence. He walked up and down clawingly in her lap like a real cat, albeit one that went invisible. He sighed in contentment as he settled himself down and curled up. "I can't remember a single thing *now*."

And they all lived very very happily until the clock struck thirteen.

# Chapter Forty-Four

Alice woke up slowly.

She was at home in her own bed, and it was morning, late but not too late; there were shafts of pale golden sun on the wall in front of her. She watched it for a while, feeling sad—no, *melancholy*. She did not turn over and try to go back to sleep, however. She just lay awake in silence. Dinah regarded her out of one blearily open eye.

When she finally went downstairs for breakfast no one was there, which was a relief. She sat down and had the first, hot sip of tea all to herself. She closed her eyes and just felt the quiet inside her, the quiet. It wasn't an *empty* feeling. It was a pause, a breath before a birth. It was waiting.

The paper was next to the butter, folded so that the

top of the front page showed: RAMSBOTTOM RALLY TUESDAY NIGHT. Alice shivered. There was something so stark and ominous about the words. They foreshadowed truly dreadful things to come. In this world villains weren't even whimsical—the streets would never run red here with milk paint, but with real blood. Alice was back in the land of no Nonsense *ever*. Possibly *for*ever.

How could she fix *this*? She had saved a whole world—somehow; the details were fading a bit now. But she knew she had managed to do it because she had the advantage of coming from the real world, with a real-world, strategic mind. Here she was just an ordinary citizen of England, no special advantages or perspective whatsoever.

Mathilda came in, and when she saw Alice sitting there, started to open her mouth—and then closed it. She sat down and made her own tea instead, but without the extra clinks and noises that very obviously stated I AM MAKING MY TEA AND NOT TALKING TO YOU—which tactic *both* sisters occasionally employed.

Mathilda shuffled through some letters and then said, very casually, "I don't think Corwin and I will be attending the rally tonight."

Alice blinked, surprised but remaining silent, waiting, gazing at her sister over the rim of her cup.

"It's all a bit . . ." Mathilda squinched her face, looking

for just the right dismissive word. "Ugly. Corwin and I feel very strongly England should take care of its own first, mind you. But those in the Square *are* England's own now. And we should treat them with nothing less than charity."

"Hmm," Alice said, not wanting to say anything to jinx the moment. She nodded, as if this was the logical and proper, the *only,* conclusion to come to.

"And Corwin is especially sorry for ever suggesting we introduce you to Coney," Mathilda added. "He will come around later with his own apology and probably a very large, very ugly gift. Please just nod and take it and do what you will with it later."

Alice smiled. "But why this change of heart for him, all of a sudden?"

"Corwin . . . looks for the best in everyone, perhaps to the point of certain blindness. But even he has no trouble at recognizing criminal behavior."

She held up a copy of the morning *Kexford Weekly*.

There on the front page was the photo of Mrs. Yao. There was even a blowup and a callout of the note she held—the handwriting *very* clear—and a plea for any good citizen who recognized the handwriting to report the miscreant to the police immediately.

The photo was credited to *A*.

Everyone in Kexford would soon figure out who both the perpetrator and the photographer were.

"Actually, I find myself running out of some of that oolong that Mrs. Yao carries," Mathilda added contemplatively. "I may drop by her shop later. She could use the business to help pay for this bit of nonsense."

At no point did Mathilda actually apologize.

Aloud.

But it was enough.

Alice opened her mouth to say something nice and meaningful and sisterly, but what came out was . . .

"Bit of nonsense! *Nonsense* . . . But of course! That's *it*! I *do* have an advantage and perspective different from everyone here! Take *that,* Mary Ann! Mathilda, you're a genius!" She leapt up, kissed her sister on the cheek, and ran out of the room.

"Well," her sister muttered after she had left, "at least someone in this ridiculous family finally recognizes that."

A onetime visit to the esteemed law offices of Alexandros and Ivy was unusual. Twice would have been suspect. So instead Alice went to the Square and grabbed the first child she found—Zara, the one who had found her after her camera was stolen.

"Hello! I need a favor—I need a message sent to a friend. Would you do it for me? I'll pay you for your time," she said, opening her purse.

"It's Katz, isn't it?" the girl said flatly. With neither intrigue nor condemnation.

Alice looked into the eyes of this little girl who was not her, whom she had never been. But there was a spark in her eye, an Alice-spark. Humor and willfulness and curiosity. It just came out differently. The little girl tried not to grin wickedly and mostly succeeded.

"Yes," Alice admitted.

*"Is it a love note?"*

"No. Not yet, anyway. Look, do you want to earn a ha'penny or not?"

"Always," the little girl said promptly. "But can I still earn it if I know where he is, and it's not at his work, and it's a public place where you can meet and talk, but it's very loud, so the two of you won't be heard? *Perfect* for a secret meeting?"

Alice pretended to think for a moment. "Oh, all right. You drive a hard bargain."

"He's at the Samovar right now, reading the news and probably being grumpy."

This was a café run by an Englishman, but with sort of a Russian theme because he loved Russian novels. All the students who could afford it went there to discuss literature, play chess, and toss around revolutionary ideas that they would then forget later, in their cups.

"Thank you kindly! A pleasure doing business with you, Miss Sarah. Here's your reward."

The little girl looked at the big copper coin she was handed in wonder.

"I don't have change for a full penny," she said regretfully.

"Oh no, it's all yours. A ha'penny for the information. Another for your silence."

Zara grinned and curtsied and then ran off, overcome with eagerness to share her fortune with her friends—or at least the news of it.

Katz *was* at the Samovar, but he wasn't reading the news; he was considering a chess problem laid out on the table before him. The pieces were exquisitely carved red and white bone but the board was chalked in on the table by what seemed like a fairly tipsy hand. Katz was frowning at it so intently he didn't see her walk up.

Alice reached out and tipped over the red queen.

"Alice!" Katz cried. His face broke out into a smile that encompassed all of him and made it seem like all days would be sunny forever. Alice wanted to live in that smile. "What a surprise! Twice in one week, and both times unexpected."

She sat down across from him. A quick look around revealed students in robes, students in plain clothes, a few old professors, and even a couple of Aunt Vivian's librarian friends (who looked a little disgusted with the ruckus around them).

"Can I get you some tea?" he offered. "It's terrible."

"Lovely offer, but no thank you."

They were both silent for a moment, but it wasn't as awkward as it was supposed to be.

"Are you really the Cheshire Cat?" she finally asked, softly.

Katz smiled broadly and shrugged maddeningly. "I don't think I *am* him. I know him. He knows me. We are one of a kind in our separate worlds."

"That's a Cheshire answer if I ever heard one," Alice said with a sigh. "Will he remember me if I ever go back? Will any of them?"

"No one could ever forget Alice," Katz said, taking her hands in his.

"Will I—will I see them again?"

"I think it's a fairly good possibility. But who can say? Did you come just to talk to me about that other place, and that other me?" he asked, a little accusingly.

Alice smiled. "No, of course not.

"I came to talk to you about what we could do about Ramsbottom's ridiculous rally."

His hands froze on her own, skeleton-stiff. His jaw

didn't *quite* drop, but did fall a little, along with the rest of his face.

He recovered himself quickly and pulled back from her, releasing her hands and sort of shaking out his shoulders, moving his jaw this way and that to dispel any lingering emotion.

"Oh, of course, of course. Most excellent. I'm interested in hearing any of your ideas. It's going to be a terrible thing, no matter what happens, really . . . you know . . . bad for the community . . . and bad . . . just . . . in general. . . ."

Alice couldn't keep a straight face. She burst out into peals of naughty, hysterical giggles, covering her mouth with one gloved hand as prettily as any coquette—but really afraid of spraying her companion.

"Of course I want to talk to you about *other* things, too, you silly goose! You're as serious and sensitive as—as, well, *I* was when I first went to Wonderland."

He looked confused, his handsome face a funny blank until it relaxed into a rueful smile.

"You . . . I . . . certainly . . ." The barrister was at a loss for words. Then he grinned and indicated her hands. "May I?"

"Of course," Alice said, presenting them. He took them properly this time, clasped them together and kissed them.

"This is going to be difficult," he said, soft and serious. "Your family, my family . . ."

"All amazing and new things *are* difficult," Alice said, squeezing his hands back. "But most turn out to be worth it. And everything else is Nonsense.

"Which, ironically, is actually the other thing I came to talk to you about. . . ."

The day of the rally was grey and a little chilly, a little damp, which might have already tempered spirits some. Mathilda had announced primly that she and Corwin were "going to take a ride in the country with Mother and Father"; they were going to avoid the whole situation entirely. And while it seemed a little cowardly, Alice couldn't entirely blame them.

"I'm afraid we shall miss all the fun," Alice's mother said wistfully.

"Yes, I think I would prefer *anything* to sitting in a bumpy carriage on a cold and wet day with that giant sheep of a man looking at what—fields? Forests? From a distance? I don't think there's even going to be a picnic," Alice's father added mournfully. "And whatever am I going to do with *this* now?"

He pulled out a ridiculous multicolored scarf fringed in gold coins and draped it around his head. "I had such plans!"

Alice was overcome and hugged both her parents at once.

"Corwin is here," Mathilda said, coming into the room and pulling on her hideously ugly brown gloves, the ones with the big bows. Her big man came through the door after only a single knock—rude!—carrying a large box.

"Hello, everyone!" he called genially.

*Really,* Alice thought, wincing, *he would be ever so much more tolerable if he just lowered his voice!*

"This is for you, Alice!" he bawled, shoving the box toward her. Then his face went a little red and his voice *did* lower, uncharacteristically. He even looked at his feet. "I . . . ah . . . we . . . You know, he seemed so . . . but then, of course . . . Butting in where we're not wanted, obviously! Turned out . . . even if they don't prosecute," he finished.

Alice nodded, trying to look serious.

"Thank you. I very much appreciate the apology. More than *any* gift," she said, and opened the box.

Then: *"Oh!"*

"My goodness," her father said, looking over her shoulder.

It was a camera. A top-of-the-line, latest-model version of the one that had been stolen.

"*Thank* you," Alice said again, really this time.

Even Mathilda looked surprised. "Hm," she said,

apparently having still expected something ugly and unuseful. Alice wondered at that: it seemed as though her sister hadn't told him what to get. Whatever faults and prejudices and incorrect views Corwin had, at least he paid attention. He knew what was important to Alice, which meant he knew what was important to Mathilda. Alice might not agree with him on anything, but it was obvious he loved her sister and his heart was in the right place. Even if his mind and his mouth weren't.

Still, holiday conversations would be a struggle from here on out.

Especially when . . . eventually . . . Alice introduced them all to Katz. Then things would get *really* interesting.

At the market Ramsbottom grinned and kept his spirits up like a carnival ringmaster; he even wore a spotless grey tailcoat and top hat with a bright red rose in it, like some sort of showman. His brother was more discreetly dressed, in browns, quietly helping set up the stage and directing crowd management. Coney bipped and bopped around him like the White Rabbit Alice knew him to be.

(Also soon to be as irrelevant as a prone lagomorph.)

Almost everyone from every part of Kexford was assembling for the thing, eyeing the now-empty tables soon to be set with punch and treats—but only *after* everyone paid attention nicely to the things that were to be said. And cheered appropriately.

Alice watched this all from behind a tree.

She wore a little-girl Alice outfit; short dress and ridiculous oversized blue sash, gigantic blue bow in her hair (there were wide, French-style knickers under the dress, so it was all proper). The bright-colored scarf her father had was tied around her wrist. He was there in spirit.

"All ready, darling?" Katz asked, slipping in next to her behind the tree.

She reached out and squeezed his hand excitedly. "This is going to be *brilliant*!"

"I can't imagine this is going to do wonders for my career," Katz said with a sigh, indicating the bright purple-and-white striped union suit he wore under his more proper jacket and boots. An extra bit of the material hung off his back like a tail.

"That's what these are for," Alice pointed out, slipping on her Venetian mask and indicating that he do the same. "Oh look, they're starting. Remember—wait for the signal!"

The crowd had filled out as much as it was going to. Gilbert looked out over them, preening like an Ornithsiville native, sticking his chest out and grinning. Red, white, and blue flags had been handed out to the audience and were being waved most patriotically. Everything looked perfect.

"My friends and fellow countrymen," he bellowed with a grin. "Thank you for joining me! We are gathered here to celebrate government and our glorious England! But not all is perfect in this great nation of ours. Recently there has been a trend of . . ."

*"There they go!"* Alice whispered. "Perfect!"

From the far side of the market came two dancing clowns. They wore matching caps and had their clothing pulled up over upside-down skirt hoops, the resulting effect making them look like giant, perfectly round balls. On their chests each wore a giant pin, one of which said GILBERT and the other of which said QUAGLEY. They held hands high in the air and pirouetted around one another, trying to look serious while balancing on their toes.

The crowd roared in laughter and approval.

The look on Gilbert's face was *not* approval. It was very, very dark.

But he knew his audience.

He put on a game grin and shouted: "All right, yes, very amusing. The hats are a nice touch."

*"I WANT TO BE MAYOR,"* the Gilbert clown shouted.

*"I WANT TO KICK LITTLE CHILDREN IN THEIR PANTS,"* the Quagley clown cried.

*"THEY'RE SO DANGEROUS!"* the Gilbert clown agreed. They nodded, shook hands, and bowed.

"Who are those two?" Katz whispered.

"Friends of Aunt Viv's. Poster painters and onetime performance artists," Alice whispered back. "*NOW!*" she added, shaking the particolored scarf up and down as a signal.

Suddenly, from all around the crowd, children came running: the children from the Square, wearing bright capes and flower crowns and holding bouquets. They threaded in and around everyone in the audience, giving people flowers and tossing handful of candies in the air.

"*FOREIGNERS! GET THEM!*" the Gilbert clown screamed.

"*LOCK UP THE CHILDREN! LOCK THEM UP!*" the Quagley clown cried. The two ran into each other, fell down, and then ran after the children. Poorly.

The audience ate it up. Everyone was laughing.

The real Gilbert was fuming.

He cleared his throat.

"A joke's a joke, but these are serious times, my people—"

"*NOOOOOOO! MY ENGLAND! MY PRECIOUS ENGLAND!*"

This was Aunt Vivian herself, powdered white like a ghost, with ugly red rouge and a black beauty mark (and mask). She was wrapped in layers and layers of old-fashioned dresses, three corsets at least, all black, and trailed a black lace train. She walked on shoes with almost stilt-tall heels and towered above the crowd like a theater monster.

*"BETTER TO DIE A WIDOW THAN LIVE A WOMAN!"* she cried, then swooned into the arms of a sturdy-looking young fellow at the edge of the crowd. His friends whistled and jeered. At first he looked uncertain, but then he got into the spirit of it—and gave her a kiss.

*"OOOH, YOU CHEEKY YOUNG MAN,"* Aunt Viv said, hitting him lightly with her fan.

"KICK THEM OUT! KICK THEM ALL OUT!"

This was a clown policeman with a club made from a giant piece of bread. He pretended to check everyone's identifications. "PAPERS! BIRTH CERTIFICATES! CHRISTENING RECORDS! NEWSPAPER ARTICLES!"

Gilbert and Quagley—the real ones—were now shouting at each other, arguing with very heated-looking faces. They couldn't be heard at all above the din. Coney looked sort of wilted beside them.

"Ready for our grand entrance?" Katz asked.

"Of course!" Alice answered.

And because they were wearing masks and no one could see or know, they kissed.

For the *second* scandalous time.

Then they joined the throngs of other clowns coming

out of hiding, dancing with the audience, playing horns, throwing flower confetti into the air, and generally sowing Nonsense.

"Because, of course, the real world needs some Nonsense, sometimes," Alice had said to Katz at the Samovar, when originally revealing her plan. "Not *all the time* and not *never.* Just enough to remind us when real things get too ridiculous to be borne. And sometimes we have to create that Nonsense ourselves."

"What the real world *needs* is an Alice," Katz had said back to her. "And Wonderland, too."

That was the first time he had kissed her.

Willard came in at the very end of the performance, riding on the shoulders of one of the stronger clowns. He wore nothing too silly beyond a giant red, white, and blue hat he had designed himself. He waved and threw candy and shook hands and kissed babies—both real and clown doll.

And afterward there was punch for all.

# Epilogue

Dear reader, I suppose you have questions. You, unlike the Dodo and the Hatter and the Dormouse, are not content with things just being as they are—you must know the *future*, the *outcomes*, the *reasons*. So I shall give you three answers, and three only, for that is the magic number in fairy stories.

**Question Number Three:**

Was Willard elected mayor, thereby saving the town of Kexford and all its inhabitants forever—or, perhaps, condemning them to life in a humorless town where each worked according to his ability and was given according to his need, forever?

**Answer:**

No, he was not.

However, his bid for the position (and takeover of Ramsbottom's rally) brought to light some of the less palatable beliefs of the other party.

So it was Mallory Griffle Frundus (*Frundus—For Us!*) who was elected. And he did a very good job of making over the town sewer system.

(Even Willard grudgingly approved of his negotiations with the factory owners to get fair wages for their employees in return for some rezoning by the city.)

Once elected, Frundus was asked what he thought about the unruly immigrant children in the Square, and was taken there by certain prejudiced members of the community to observe their foul and disgraceful behavior. He watched the children for a moment, frowned, and then declared:

"You're playing marbles all wrong! Let me show you how we did it when *I* was a lad."

**Question Number Two:**

Did Alice and Katz marry and live happily ever after?

**Answer:**

Yes.

It was difficult—very difficult—at first; neither set of parents approved of the arrangement. But love and gritted teeth won out.

(Also grandchildren. Grandchildren have a way of smoothing out the worst, most cranky old people.)

Katz became a full partner in the law firm; Alice became even more Alice, exhibiting her photographs and touring Europe with him and occasionally Aunt Vivian, who introduced her to such strangely familiar venues as the Cabaret Voltaire. You will not have heard of Alice when reading about the early Dadaist movement, but you can rest assured she was there and played an integral part in their formative years.

**Question Number One:**

Did Alice ever make it back to Wonderland?

**Answer:**

Why, dear reader, I think you already know the answer to that.

*One thing was certain, that the* white *kitten had had nothing to do with it:—it was the black kitten's fault entirely. For the white kitten had been having its face washed by the old cat for the last quarter of an hour (and bearing it pretty well, considering); so you see that it* couldn't *have had any hand in the mischief.*

*Alice was sitting curled up in a corner of the great armchair, her large, round belly finally comfortable now that its tiny occupant had settled for a bit. The kitten had been having a grand game of romps with the ball of worsted Alice had been knitting into a tiny sweater, rolling the ball up and down till it had all come undone again; and there it was, spread over the hearth-rug, all knots and tangles, with the kitten running after its own tail in the middle.*

*'Oh, you wicked little thing!' cried Alice, catching up the kitten, and giving it a little kiss to make it understand that it was in disgrace. 'Really, Dinah ought to have taught you better manners! Now, if you'll only attend, Kitty, and leave my knitting alone, I'll tell you all about Looking-glass House. Everything there is reversed, and the candy runs away from your hand. It's positively delightful.*

*'Oh, how nice it would be if we could only get through into Looking-glass House again! Let's pretend there's a way of getting through into it, somehow. Let's pretend the glass has got all soft like gauze, so that we can get through. Why, it's turning into a sort of mist now, I declare! It'll be easy enough to get through—' She was standing up, leaning on the chimney-piece while she said this, though she hardly knew how she had got there. And certainly the glass* was *beginning to melt away, just like a bright silvery mist. . . .*

# Straight On Till Morning

## A Twisted Tale

LIZ BRASWELL

Disney · HYPERION
Los Angeles • New York

Published by Disney • Hyperion, an imprint of Buena Vista Books, Inc.

For information address Disney • Hyperion, 77 West 66th Street,
New York, New York 10023.

Printed in China
First Hardcover Edition, February 2020
First Paperback Edition, September 2024
1 3 5 7 9 10 8 6 4 2
FAC-031939-24095
Library of Congress Control Number: 2019940035
ISBN 978-1-368-10402-9

Visit disneybooks.com

This book is for my mom and dad, who gave me things I truly love, like ducklings and computers (and not small, obnoxious dogs).

A giant thank you to the best agent in the world: Ginger Clark. You help me see into a bright future—and don't mind tidying up the present.

*—L.B.*

# Prologue

*Somewhere in Never Land . . .*

"Wait, did we look over by the Troll Bridge?"

". . . We did?"

"What about the Tonal Spring?"

"And the beaches around the Shimmering Sea?"

The asker of these questions was a slender young man of indeterminate age—though perhaps if an observer looked him dead in the face she would notice the last pockets of baby fat plumping his cheeks just above the cheekbones. His eyes and mouth and even nose wiggled and puckered with every word and thought in between, like a toddler telling a very important story to his mother. His hair was mussed up and red, his eyebrows a thicker, darker red.

And were his ears just a touch pointed, at the tips?

The one who answered his questions certainly had pointed ears, though the same observer might be hard-pressed to make out any ears—or actual answers—at all. The boy spoke to what appeared to be little more than a golden light that bobbed and sparkled and tinkled like bells. In fact, the whole scene resembled a mesmerist quizzing a pendulum held from a long golden chain, glittering in the sunlight, whose vague swings returned meanings known only to the occultist himself.

But upon looking more closely, one would see that inside the golden bauble was a tiny woman with *very* pointed ears, a serious face, a green dress, and sparkling wings. Her body was like a series of energetic globes, from her golden hair in its messy bun to her hips to the round silver bells that decorated her shoes. Throughout the conversation every part of her was as animated as her friend's face.

"Really? We looked in all those places? Huh. Well, what about . . . here!"

The boy spun suddenly and grabbed the side of a tree, as if to physically move it out of the way. Really, he was just looking behind it. But there was nothing hiding there aside from some brightly colored lichen, a camouflage moss, and a few grazing unicorn beetles.

From this sudden motion and burst of energy to dead exhaustion; the boy slumped, strangely drained by disappointment and exertion. He slid down to the base of the tree, causing at least two of the shining white beetles to flee into higher branches.

The bauble of light glittered aggressively up and down. It jingled angrily.

"I can't anymore, Tink. I'm beat. I just . . . I just don't feel like it."

The fairy—for that is what she was—zoomed closer, concerned. And it was when her light shone its brightest on his countenance that the most unusual detail of an already fey and wondrous scene became apparent. For no matter how intensely she glowed, no matter how perfectly yellow and dazzling the sun in the sky shone, neither source of light managed to produce a shadow off the boy.

The bauble jingled in tones of hope.

"I don't know. We've looked *everywhere.* Twice. Tink, I just don't know where it could be!"

The bauble swayed quietly, pensively. Almost as if the fairy within was in that rarest state of all for fairies: deep thought.

Possibly *bothered* by something.

But the boy, even in his diminished state, still kept his attention permanently fixed on himself. He did not notice.

She jingled once, tentatively.

"Naw, I don't feel like flying. Not right now. I think I'll

just rest here for a while. You go on without me. I could use a nap. Then I'll feel better. I just know it."

The fairy jingled worriedly around his face.

"Just . . . go look without me." He swatted her away like a gnat, sleep already overtaking his body once the decision had been made. "Don't feel like flying . . . anymore. . . ."

He yawned a giant, repulsive yawn, and was soon snoring.

The fairy regarded him silently. She hung in a cool shadow of the generous tree, spun gently by a summery breeze.

They were at the edge of the Quiescent Jungle, which was the friendliest forest in Never Land. The leaves of the trees spanned every shade of golden green, and the creatures who lived there were all harmless and mostly furry. The air smelled like ripening blackberries—although it was not quite the right season—and a whisper of cool moistness hinted at a delightfully icy stream somewhere nearby.

Only a fool would want to leave. Only a genius would choose to nap there.

But Tinker Bell was twitchy. She had a rather dark inkling of where the shadow *could* be, since they had effectively proven where it could *not* be.

And if her friend ever found out that she'd had this inkling all along, he would be very cross with her indeed.

She floated silently over to his face, her golden sparkles illuminating every lash, every freckle, every pore. He blew out through his careless lips, and his breath lifted up the ends of his long, shaggy bangs. She hovered above his pug nose. After debating and biting her own lip, she gave him the tiniest quick fairy kiss on it.

Then she steeled herself and zoomed into the sky like a bee bent on finding its way home after a day of foraging nectar.

But she was not going home.

She was going to look for Peter's shadow in the scariest place of all.

She was going to London.

# London

Yes, it's a scene re-created so often it has become almost a caricature of a trope, but let's go through the process once again anyway because it's necessary, even to this story.

Low clouds do not *blanket* the sky, for that implies coziness and comfort. No, these clouds mask the sky, weigh on the sky, choke the sky. They are strengthened by smoke from below, the trickling-upward effluence of a hundred thousand chimneys that decorate the landscape like unhealthily angular flowers. The slate-and-clay-shingled, higgledy-piggledy rooftops seem to extend forever in an industrial upside-down version of the fairy-tale hills and dales in a children's book with bright pictures and bad perspective. Everything—*everything*—is in shades of gray and black. A great gray river slinks through the city like a tired but friendly snake, hobbled by bridges far less impressive than their names imply.

(Don't believe me? Look up *London Bridge* and gaze at its pictures. An utter disappointment.)

Of course there's Big Ben, the giant clock with equally giant gunmetal and copper hands that an astounding number of fictional characters have wound up standing on at one time or another. Its bells, along with *all* the church bells of the city, toll the hour menacingly with the obvious mournful implication of time passing, death coming, soup's getting cold.

On the cobbled streets below the towers and rooftops, weather has some impact and energy; the almost-rain and morning mist combine to make a wet, stinging atmosphere that has men swirling into greatcoats, nannies bundling up their charges, and mums shouting, "Come out of the garden, you'll catch your death in the fog!" Also many, many umbrellas. So many black umbrellas with the usual spindly frames—like insects or skeletons or whatever—that watching them pass is almost torturously jejune.

There.

*London.*

End of one century, beginning of another.

Got it?

Good.

Halfway between where the umbrellas ended and where the sky should have started, maybe twenty and a half feet below the tallest chimney, was one particular casement window. Gazing out of it was a young woman in an unfashionable pale blue dress. Her hair was a popular shade of brown and her eyes an exquisitely normal blue for that time and place.

At first she looked up at the sky, but it was impossible to make out any shapes in the clouds because of their utter completion, filling the heavens from one end to the other in the same unbroken shade. So she looked down. But the dismal garden below soaked up the wet like a moldy sponge; there were no puddles, no reflections. The tree was sodden.

Nothing in this stolidly real vista was alterable by even the strongest imagination: there was no foothold for pirates, fairies, golden carriages, knights, or even a hint of swashbuckling. Someone from the street had thrown a brown banana skin over the fence, and there it lay, out of place in the English yard, attesting to the banality of global commerce and how it didn't bring with it sultans or magic horses—only bananas.

Wendy sighed and turned from the window. Afternoons were the hardest.

In the mornings she still saw her tutor, and there were chores and writing exercises. After elevenses was a *good improving book* recommended by the bookseller, the one with the handsome nephew.

By then Mrs. Darling had usually either gone to pay visits or was busily engaged in correspondence with her delicate blue pen at her elegant secretary. The gloom never seemed to affect her even if she did stay home all day; she was always gracefully and slowly attending to some task or other: her face; her toilette; her sewing; the little expense book she kept for the house; the pantry; their unpredictable cook, Mary. Wendy used to watch her mother engage in these endless circuits with delight, but that feeling was now tempered with confusion: how could someone remain so serene and glowing while working through the same indoor errands, rainy day in and day out?

Wendy still enjoyed it when Mrs. Darling included her in some of her "feminine rituals," which usually involved the proper application of powders and creams, tips on how to polish her nails, or ideas for sprucing up an old bow. She loved it when they had enough extra house money to go for a fancy tea out at Saxelbrees, just the two of them. Wendy would admire her mother smiling and laughing beneath her many-times-renewed hat, and would think once again that she was the most beautiful mother in the world.

She wondered when she herself would attain that delicate beauty, confidence, and perfection of manner.

But these outings were rare. And anyway, even the most appealing things lost their glamour when held up to the imaginary delights of Never Land.

Wendy turned to her bureau. Normally she tried resisting until the end of the day, as a sort of reward. Like the opera creams her mother secretly indulged in. Mrs. Darling smiled so blissfully while she chewed—she sometimes even popped one before dinner if it was an especially trying day!

Often, when tempted to peek into the drawer too early, Wendy could assuage her longing by pulling out the tiny notebook she always kept with her. It had a very slim blue pencil that perfectly fit down the spine, and was nearly full of her neat, enthusiastic words. Well-thumbed pages were titled with things like "Peter Pan and the Pirates and the Unexpected Zeppelin" or "Peter Pan and Tiger Lily versus the Cyclops of the Cerulean Sea." And she had illustrated "Captain Hook Is Taught a *Timely* Lesson by Peter Pan" with a little picture of a clock she had carefully copied from the mantel, as well as the eyes and nostrils of a fierce crocodile—the rest of whose body she had no hope of depicting accurately, and thus chose to submerge.

But today the words looked bleak and worn, and the empty lines beyond them bleaker still.

Wendy couldn't resist anymore. Not today. Not when everything was so *particularly* gray and dreadful and hopeless.

She slid open the creaky wooden drawer and picked up an inky-soft bundle that lay neatly folded within. It shook out like a spider's web, softer than silk and without the little catchy bits that clung to rough fingers. Its outline deformed easily. Only when she laid it out on the floor completely flat could she coax the shadow into its proper shape: Peter Pan.

Four years ago Nana had torn it from the boy. For four years Wendy had kept it carefully safe in her top drawer, waiting for Peter to come back and claim it.

Michael and John gave up first.

In the beginning they had been even more exultant than she at the discovery; in Michael's case, jumping and crying and generally bouncing off the walls. John had pushed his ridiculous glasses up on his nose and tried to speak in grown-up terms of *actual evidence* and *irrefutable facts* and the like.

But . . .

Weeks turned into months. Into a year. Into four years.

There was no *more* proof, no more evidence, no more sign of a visitor from Never Land. And though the boys kept stealing quick looks at the shadow, Michael soon began to remark that it was "kind of crummy" and "a bit faded" and John muttered darkly about *manifestations of another realm* and *meteorological phenomena.* Somehow, astonishingly, it became just another piece of bric-a-brac, a souvenir from an earlier time or an only slightly more exotic place, like the tiny mosaic mirror Mr. Darling had bought from a man who was traveling back to his home in Kashmir.

But every night since then, Wendy had gone to sleep burning for Never Land. She hoped, the way some questionable but trendy pamphlets suggested, that if she thought about what she desired most of all before she fell asleep, she would dream of it. She drifted off whispering, *Peter, I have your shadow. . . . Peter . . .*

She often woke with a strange golden feeling, like she had just touched the boundaries of Never Land—something about wolves and strange fruit and freedom—but then quickly forgot it; the feeling never stayed.

Wendy rubbed a thumb along the edge of the shadow and shuddered. If she wasn't careful she would begin weeping.

*What had she done wrong?*

What was so repulsive about her that Peter Pan wouldn't return—even for his own shadow?

What about her was so lacking that *no one* from Never Land ever sought her out again?

She dropped the thing back into the drawer and slammed it closed, crushing a knuckle into her mouth to keep from sobbing.

Soon it would be time to prepare tea, and she didn't want her mother commenting about unattractive red splotches on her cheeks or rings under her eyes.

In the afternoon her brothers came home, and things should have been better.

"John, Michael," Wendy said with relief as their boyish humors and exuberance filled the otherwise silent house.

"Greetings, Sister," John said, handing her his hat while pecking her on the cheek with a vaguely sarcastic air. He was bound for a real university someday, perhaps even Oxford, and had already begun effecting the irony and insouciance necessary for a sojourn there. Michael just kicked his boots off willy-nilly and threw his coat on a chair. Of course, other families had maids to deal with such situations, but aside from the Darlings' general lack of excessive funds, Wendy enjoyed the routine.

At least, she used to.

*Tsk*ing mindlessly, she picked up Michael's jacket and smoothed it out, hanging it up properly.

"Wendy, you're a damn fool for not continuing your studies within the sphere of public education," John announced, sounding like someone else.

"It's *heaps* of fun, too," Michael growled, a stormy look on his face. He was a less subtle wielder of sarcasm than his older brother.

"Well, Father said none of the daughters of his clients go—and they are all very respectable girls. And anyway, I have all the time and books I need," she added, a little hollowly. It had seemed like the right choice to decline when her parents had—somewhat reluctantly—presented her with the option of attending one of the newfangled public schools. Why should she spend time cooped up in a crowded institution and be treated like a child when she could have a tutor and then putter about the house, dreaming and keeping things in order like an adult?

"It's dumb. I *hate it.* School and its stupid rules," Michael shouted. " 'If you don't eat yer peas, you can't have yer pudding!' Stupid lunch matron."

"Now, Michael, I'm sure they just want you to have a nutritious, healthy supper," Wendy said, feeling the comfortable role of *mother* easily slide over her with its dulcet tones and indulgent smiles, banishing any uncertain feelings from the moment before.

"Are there any of those French biscuits left?" Michael asked hopefully. "The ones you made?"

"The ones I and *Mother* made? Perhaps. I'll set out some and serve you a nice cup of proper tea while you go upstairs and bathe. And then, if there's time, I'll tell you a story before bed."

"Oh, Wendy and her stories," John said with a smile

and not *quite* a roll of his eyes. "I have too much reading to do. Like *actual* reading. Of *actual* history. Plus, Wendy Darling, I find your tales have a bit of a Freudian bent to them these days. Haven't you noticed? It's all *fathers* and *sons* and *missing mothers. . . .*"

"I'm sure I have no idea what you're talking about," she said frostily. And indeed she didn't. But his tone was nasty enough.

"I want three lumps in my tea! And milk!" Michael called over his shoulder as he stomped out of the room.

"Oh," Wendy said, suddenly remembering. "Mother is supposed to come home from her dinner with Mrs. Cradgeapple early tonight—if you hurry, you may get to say good night to her before you turn in!"

"Oh. Yes. *Mother*," John said thoughtfully. "Haven't seen her in *ages*. Tall lady? About so high? Would absolutely *love* to catch up with the old hen."

"John!" Wendy put her hands on her hips.

"Tootles, Sister. Off to read some more Swiss psychology. You know those Swiss. All chocolate and timepieces and subtext." John made an elaborate bow and pretended to tip the hat that was no longer there.

Once he was gone, Nana, curled up comfortably in her early retirement by the fire, gave Wendy the sort of questioning look that only a really intelligent dog could.

"Yes, I see the muddy tracks they left on the floor," Wendy sighed. "And no, I don't know what to do about them. Boys! They grow up so fast."

Now *that* was an interesting idea.

Never Land was full of children who never grew up—but what about a boy who grew up too fast? Literally. Like . . . hatching out of an egg as a baby and then attaining the height of a man by the end of the day.

"They watched the egg with expectant faces," she murmured, trying it out. "'What's it gonna be?' asked Cubby. 'How should I know?' Peter laughed. 'It'll be something great, though—you can count on that!'"

Yes. That was lovely. She pulled out her little notebook. Now that her brothers no longer cared to hear Wendy's stories, she had to put them *somewhere.*

And maybe, someday, someone would like to hear them again.

Michael came back down dripping wet and yet somehow barely clean—there was still chalk on his neck. He guzzled his tea and madeleines and stomped back upstairs to play with his lead soldiers. John hadn't bothered descending yet, probably caught up in his books about real soldiers being played in the wars of kings.

Wendy sat by herself in the kitchen, regarding the

notebook and the abandoned and untouched tea plates. Madeleines were all the rage right now and it had been wonderful spending the afternoon trying to make them with Mother, but after the first day they had sort of dried out and become a little tasteless. She picked one up and tentatively dipped it in her cooling tea, then nibbled its now soft edge. *Much* better. They almost tasted a little bit like sunshine—like warm, exotic days. . . .

Her mind whirled. Suddenly, she saw a ship bobbing in tropical waters, and herself on a beach. It was another Never Land dream she was remembering—but this one had felt so real! The sailors—pirates—were singing, and Hook was bowing from the waist, as perfect and gallant as John had been awkward and foolish. In the sunlight and open air the captain seemed far less terrifying.

But maybe it was because of the wolf at her side, the one she had befriended so long ago, growling and ready to kill for her. Maybe that was why she was brave.

*A pity you can't stay here . . .* the captain was saying. *That rapscallion utterly abandoned you to such a dismal, gray life in London Town. . . .*

She had frowned. "Do *not* talk about Peter Pan that way. You are a *pirate.* You make people walk the plank and burn their ships."

*And yet never in my most evil and wretched moments*

*would I abandon a lady like yourself to such a fate. He really has no heart, not even a black one like mine.*

"I am *not* abandoned. He left me his shadow," she said, perhaps a little too boastfully.

Hook's eyes widened at that.

*You . . . have . . . his* shadow, *you say?*

Wendy felt her lip quiver a little but stilled it. A mistake?

"It is nothing to you. And I am fine, thank you very much."

*After all those stories you told about him . . . all that time you devoted to enriching his legend . . . and this is how he treats you? By leaving you . . . and making you be caretaker of his* shadow, *no less. . . .*

Wendy in the dream didn't cry. She wouldn't, not in front of a villain like Hook.

Wendy with the madeleine did.

She put her head on her arms and wept herself to sleep.

Hours later she was gently woken by the soft touches and sweet perfume of her mother, who somehow, without actually picking up the nearly grown Wendy, managed to gather her daughter in her arms and gently lead her upstairs.

"What in the blazes is wrong with her?" Mr. Darling growled. "Asleep at the table like a serving wench?"

"Shhh," Mrs. Darling cooed. She gestured with her

hand, making him scoop up the notebook Wendy took with her everywhere.

"Mother," Wendy murmured, waking a little. "Oh, Mother, you look so beautiful."

"Thank you, dear. You're so sweet. . . ."

Mrs. Darling helped her out of her dress and fixed her hair, more shadowy apparition of eyelashes and perfect coif than parent of stuff and substance. Wendy enjoyed being treated like a little girl again. She snuggled into her bed drowsily and heard her parents talk.

"Something's got to be done about her," Mr. Darling swore, shaking the notebook for emphasis. "There's something not quite right about that girl."

"She's just a little . . . blue. She needs a project," Mrs. Darling said. "A boy. Or maybe a charity."

"Charity? How about a Darling charity?" Mr. Darling huffed. "Courtships are all very well and good but require dresses and hats and all sorts of expensive shenanigans. That was always the advantage of Wendy . . . she never wanted the things other girls had."

"No," Mrs. Darling said with a touch of sadness. "She always wanted something . . . else."

And Wendy dreamed quickly forgotten dreams of foreign seas and wolves.

# *In Bocca al Lupo*

Wendy opened her eyes, dreams of hidden cabins and friendly wolves and menacing pirates disappearing into the dim morning grayness. She had absolutely no desire to get up and perform the start-of-day rituals she used to relish: washing her face with fresh, cold water, giving her hair a hundred solid strokes before pinning it back, going through her dresses and deciding which one to wear, which one to mend, which one perhaps to embellish a little.

But despite her whole-body unwillingness to begin this process, routine took over. Habits, especially healthy ones, become easily ingrained in people like Wendy. Without even meaning to she rose and turned and neatened her bed, smoothing the pillow out so it would look pretty and inviting when she went to lie down again that night. She drifted over to the basin of water and splashed her face (without looking in the mirror), ran the brush through her hair (only fifty-seven times), and examined her nails (dispassionately; she decided they didn't need to be buffed).

Moving made her feel better; accomplishing little things gave her dim sparks of satisfaction. Before long she had the boys up and out of bed, a whirlwind of toast and tea and brushing down jackets. Some of the brothers' energy managed to rub off on their sister. And Nana, bless her, tried to help like she used to, holding a spare white cuff in her mouth, waiting patiently and dolorously until one of the passing boys—Michael—grabbed it and patted her in thanks. It all ended when John blew an airy kiss and pulled his reluctant brother after him out the door.

"Goodness," Mrs. Darling said, appearing for a moment in the foyer like a tentative daytime ghost. She was resplendent in her white froth of a nightgown, and prettily covered her mouth for a delicate yawn. "Whatever would I do without you, dear."

She kissed her daughter on the head and Wendy fell to warm pieces under her praise. But then the figment retreated back upstairs to perform her own ablutions and the lower house was released to the normal workaday world. Wendy had toast and tea and settled down for her French lessons with Mademoiselle Gabineau. Not satisfied with her main subject of expertise, Mademoiselle also had strong opinions on history and maths, lecturing angrily—and often incomprehensibly—in her native tongue about the first topic while not letting Wendy give up on the second. "You must keep a house someday, wiz all of ze accounts," she admonished. "And make ze right decreases when knitting a jumper."

Wendy didn't deign to reply, uninterested in either application of maths. She surreptitiously stroked the pages of the tiny notebook in her apron pocket and dreamed of a well-spoken, logical, and utterly evil witch.

The day *seemed* like it was going to progress along the same lines as the one before it, and the one before that, and the one before that—but sometime before tea there were strange noises downstairs, outer doors opening and closing and a deep-throated male voice sounding out.

It was far too early for Mr. Darling to be done with business already. Concerned, Wendy tripped down the stairs as fast as she thought it decorous to do so. Nana waited at the bottom, doing something she rarely engaged in. She was *growling*. Very softly.

"Dear Nana, what is it?" Wendy asked, growing even more nervous. The dog was large but not much of a wolf, and probably too old to do any real damage to an intruder.

"Oh, what a funny thought. 'Not much of a wolf.' Wherever did that come from, I wonder? *Wolves* indeed."

It was just prattle, but talking aloud to herself always made Wendy feel brave. And anyway, if the house was being invaded, it was up to her to defend its inhabitants and silverware.

She stuck out her chin and pushed open the front hall door with a carefully composed look of indignation on her face.

"Now see here, villain—!"

She stopped immediately, presented with a very odd scene.

Mr. Darling *was* home early. It was rare to see him by day in a full suit, coat, and hat; usually when he came home it was dark and he went straight upstairs to change into his slippers and smoking jacket. He held his arms strangely, as if one were broken and he were cradling it with the other. Also unusual was that Mrs. Darling was with him, a gloved hand resting lightly on his shoulder.

Mr. Darling looked utterly confused by his daughter's words, his large, bushy black eyebrows rising nearly to the top of his head.

"Wendy? What in blazes is the reason for that tone? I? A *villain*?"

"Dear, whatever is the matter?" Mrs. Darling asked with an indulgent smile.

"I heard noises—I just thought . . . I'm so glad you're home early today, though, Father! Wait, did you hurt yourself? Did you break your arm? Is that why you're—no, if you had, Dr. Sorello would be here with his treatments and nasty draughts. Is it some sort of holiday? I don't think I had it in my datebook. Is it a birthday? Are the banks closed? Or—no! Oh no, Father. You didn't lose your job, did you? You and Mother look so radiant, that can't be it. Is there other news?"

Mr. Darling looked more and more blown back by the torrent of Wendy's words, as if a wind were physically assaulting him.

"All right, all right," he said, unable to think of anything better to quiet her.

"Wendy, dear, we've brought you something," Mrs. Darling said through soft laughter. "Show her."

Mr. Darling moved his arms and revealed the reason he had been cradling them so carefully.

At first Wendy thought it was a rat, which would explain its size (small), its color (white), and Nana's discomfort (extreme).

But then a fat little pink tongue lolled out of its mouth and large black eyes blinked in excitement. It panted and pawed at Mr. Darling's arms, excited but obviously unsure what it wanted to do. Its little ears, no larger than the corners of a lady's pocket handkerchief, were actually quite huge compared to the thing's head and didn't seem to be able to move very much, as they would have on a German shepherd or Nana.

"Oh," Wendy said, blinking. Her carefully read and reread books of *Manners for English Girls and Boys* had nothing she could draw from for this sort of situation. "Oh. A small dog."

"It's a teacup terrier. Isn't it the most darling thing?" Mrs. Darling said, rubbing her face against its and kissing.

Mr. Darling looked unsettled by this physical display of affection, the dry nose touching the wet one.

"Yes, well, all the girls seem to be into them right now. Carrying them in baskets . . . bows in their fur . . . taking them to the park . . . I don't know. You don't hunt with them, I'm fairly certain. We just thought you could use . . . ah . . . a little friend."

"We were afraid you were getting lonely in this big old drafty house," Mrs. Darling said, taking her daughter's hands and squeezing them.

Wendy, so talkative before, now had nothing to say. Mr. Darling always complained about how *tiny* their house was, endlessly comparing it to those of his business associates and of the managers whose ranks he wanted to someday be among. Mrs. Darling never said anything obviously unkind about their home, but did often refer to it in painfully obvious terms: *adorable, cozy, manageable, charming, doll-sized.*

"Oh . . . yes . . . lonely . . ." Wendy said, seizing on that one point, the one that was most reasonable.

(Nana whuffed indignantly. What was she, a piece of furniture?)

Her parents waited expectantly.

The polite thing to do, Wendy realized, was to walk forward and put a hand out to the tiny dog and let it smell her. She made herself do so.

The teeny puppy snuffled its wet nose all over her hand and seemed to lick—or slurp—her, like a jungle creature from one of her adventure books. Something horrid that ate ants or honey or anything else that required sucking up. It barked several times in a manner that was both strangely too quiet and somehow extremely irritating.

"Thank you, Father," Wendy said, carefully removing her hand as if for the purpose of hugging him. It wasn't entirely a lie; she did indeed want to envelop Mr. Darling's large form and rest her head on his side, smelling his aftershave and his general father-ness. Her mother hugged her on the other side and kissed her on the forehead.

They loved her, that was more than obvious.

They just didn't understand her.

---

Wendy did make an effort to try to see what the puppy could do.

(With Nana watching in stern disapproval.)

It would run into the middle of the room and then wag its tail like it had accomplished something truly incredible.

It would run up into her arms and lick her chin.

It would scamper along next to a ball that Wendy rolled.

It would *not* make any actual attempt to stop the ball, grab the ball, fetch the ball, or do anything with the ball aside from barking at it in that tiny yip that made Wendy want to lean over and say *"Pardon me?"*

Eventually, with two hours until the boys came home, Mother and Father now nowhere to be seen, and nothing else to do, Wendy found an appropriately sized basket, tied a ribbon around it, tucked in Snowball (really, what else could she name it?), put on her coat, and attempted an outing. She left her notebook behind, encumbered with her new pet and umbrella.

Nana also remained inside, aloof and disapproving.

While she felt a little ridiculous, Wendy had to admit that the cold, slightly damp air felt good on her face. *Moisturizing*, her mother would say. *Invigorating*, her father would say. The little dog peeped out of the basket and looked around blankly with no actual interest in hopping out and getting a firsthand sniff of the many wonders they passed. Wendy nodded to other walkers, most of whom regarded Snowball with amusement or delight.

And then, down the path, came the demonic Shesbow twins.

They were clad as was their wont: in similar dresses of different hue, similar hats with different flowers, similar parasols with different tassels. Outfits just alike enough to give a nod to the sisters' ostensible sameness, just a bit off to remind the viewer that they weren't the same person at all.

Wendy froze and considered heading back the other way, as if she had forgotten something. She could see the steely blue of four Shesbow eyes and didn't feel strong under their lantern gazes, especially after the caroling party last Christmas.

But they had spotted her, and she had something interesting to distract them with, so maybe it would be all right. Wendy stuck out her chin and walked forward bravely to meet her fate.

"Miss Darling," Clara said with the beginnings of a coldly amused smile. "It's so lovely to see you out and about in public, especially after—"

"Oh! What is that you have there?" Phoebe cried, spotting the basket.

"Him?" Wendy almost blew it immediately. Was the dog even a him? She hadn't bothered to check. "He's new."

"Oh—oh, how *perfect*," Phoebe simpered, holding out

a delicately curled gloved finger. The puppy obligingly sniffed and she practically screamed with delight.

"He's adorable," Clara said flatly, to the point as always. "When did you get him?"

"Well," Wendy said, stalling. She hated the way that, despite the girls' continually bad treatment of her, she was flushing and eager for any kind word of acceptance. Telling the specifics of the puppy's origin might spoil the chances of that happening. "The house was feeling a bit lonely, don't you know? And I thought, well, what I need is a nice little companion to keep me company and to absolutely indulge."

"Isn't he the *sweetest*," Phoebe cooed.

"I'm gratified to hear you've taken on a project like this," Clara said, tapping her parasol and trying to sound like her grandmother. "Everyone was worried, you know."

"Worried? About me? *Every*one?"

"Oh, please, Wendy. After Christmas it became fairly obvious what your future is. Your brothers will go to university, and you will be stuck helping your parents, and then probably care for your nieces or nephews as their spinster aunt."

"With cats," Phoebe added, not looking away from petting the dog. "You would have cats, of course."

"Quite right, lots of cats."

"People . . . are talking . . . about me? As a spinster?

With—cats?" Wendy's mind was too overcome with this new information to even take offense at it. She was sixteen, for heaven's sake! She had time. She had just moved out of the nursery not that long ago. . . .

And to think of a husband? *Now?* There were so many other things to think about. Balloons and submarines. Airships and pirates. Deepest Africa and farthest Australia. Peter Pan and fairies and mermaids and centaurs . . .

"But now this," Phoebe sighed, throwing her hands up at the dog as if there were no words. "You know, Alice has a little dog, too! Oh, we should all go walking together! Wouldn't that be fun? We could bring a ball, or something like that."

"He could accompany you to one of our teas sometime," Clara said thoughtfully. "We have literary ones, you know. Almost like our own salon."

"I would like that very much," Wendy responded before she could decide whether or not that was true. Or if *she* had even been properly invited at all; it almost sounded like Snowball was really the intended recipient of the offer. Then again—*literary* salon. That was a place for stories!

"You could absolutely meet someone there, perhaps, someday," Phoebe added. "Someone dreamy, who likes dogs, like you."

"It's a project," Clara said, eyes glittering. "Making you

acceptable and finding you a match. But you must promise not to do that thing—not to run off at the mouth the way you do. No one finds that attractive or ladylike."

"No one at all," Phoebe agreed. "You really will end up all alone."

"I don't want to be alone. I have Snowball now," Wendy said, trying to make her thoughts come out the way they were flowing in her head. It didn't seem to be working. "But I couldn't possibly think of a match. Now. And I can't help talking—I like stories, and telling them. And really, isn't there another choice? Besides a match, and spinsters, and cats? Something—else?"

"You're doing it again," Phoebe said kindly. She put a finger to Wendy's mouth. "Shhh."

And then the sisters nodded to each other, in full agreement, full of themselves and very happy.

"I'll send round my card," Clara called as they walked off, arm in arm.

Wendy stood there watching them go and then looked at Snowball, who gazed dimly back.

This could be the beginning of something really big, and quite different. If she could do things properly, her lonely days batting around the house by herself would be over—there would be teas and salons and parties and group dog walks.

And boys.

And dances and happily-ever-afters, where she would attend balls and cotillions, and have a husband and children like Michael and John, and a different, perhaps less lonely old house.

Was that what she wanted?

Was it better or worse than what she had now?

Wendy managed one giant breath.

It was enough to get her home, running and heaving in a most unladylike fashion.

# Ireland

When she burst through the front door, Wendy was for the second time that day surprised by the presence of her parents.

She was a little frazzled, the dog basket dangling on her left elbow while she shook out her umbrella with her right hand, and deep, deep in her own thoughts. She needed time to reflect, to figure out the possibilities resulting from her interaction with the Shesbow twins. This meant journaling. *And* fiction. With her father home from work early and the new dog and everything, it felt like a day out of time, a holiday—so why *not* spend the afternoon writing up her latest ideas for Never Land? She would indulge herself, the same way other girls did with naps, baths, and dresses.

She had been playing with the idea of linking all her stories together somehow, maybe into a novel. . . .

*"Oh,"* she said, blinking at the unexpected sight of her mother sitting at the kitchen table, her father standing over it, both with very, very serious expressions on their faces. Like someone had died.

And there, under her father's hand, was the very notebook she had just been thinking about.

"Mother, Father," she added, feeling something flutter and flop somewhere between her stomach and heart. *A new organ,* she told herself crazily. *One whose sole purpose is to react to the uncomfortable tension in the air.*

"Wendy," Mr. Darling said in his lowest, most managerial voice.

"Darling," Mrs. Darling said. "I think . . . I think we had better talk."

Mr. Darling coughed suddenly, like he was trying not to look nervous.

Wendy had the strange notion of asking if *she* had been let go from the firm.

"You read my notebook," she said instead.

"Yes, and really, darling, your writing is *quite* exquisite," her mother said quickly. "Really. I had no idea you were so talented with words. Your descriptions . . . Your characterizations . . . Mademoiselle Gabineau has never mentioned your facility. At all."

"She is unaware. May I have it, please?" Wendy said, unable to keep her eyes or attention off her book. The little dog waggled frantically in the basket, causing it to swing. She barely felt it.

"The thing is, darling," her mother went on, "the stories themselves are . . . well . . ."

"Oh, enough of this blustering around," Mr. Darling exploded. "They are the product of an infantile mind. The febrile imaginings of a child. I thought you had *done* with all this Peter Pan nonsense years ago! You're *sixteen* now, for heaven's sake, Wendy!"

"It's my fault," Mrs. Darling said apologetically. "I have always indulged my baby girl."

"You haven't changed at all since you were little, Wendy. These silly stories—"

"They aren't silly," Wendy said, offended by the word.

"Well, yes—yes they are, because they aren't real! None of it is *real,* Wendy! Not a deuced thing! And you write them with *yourself* in the stories, like you're some kind of hero, like you're still pretending with your baby brothers! Like you *think* it's all real!"

"I never believed it was—"

But her voice caught in her throat.

She couldn't do it.

She could never knowingly lie about Never Land—she would never betray it that way.

Her parents saw her swallow. They saw her hesitation, her refusal to finish the sentence.

Her mother's head sank toward her chest, and this hurt Wendy most of all.

Mr. Darling cleared his throat again.

"I think you have some growing up to do, Wendy. I think you need to see the world as it is, and what must be done in it to live a full adult life. I think you need a break from these environs and thoughts."

"Father, what are you—"

"The Rennets have a cousin with a country house in Conaught. Their governess had to take a leave of absence on account of her mother passing away," Mrs. Darling said quietly, almost musically. Like delivering the news in operetta format somehow made it less unappealing. "You will join them for several months and care for their five boys."

*"Ireland?"* Wendy cried. "It's . . . a long way off."

It was the first, the only thing she could think to say: she had been looking at a map of the British Isles just the other day to help fill in some descriptive passages of Never Land, and had been drawn to the county's green meadows and hills.

"I know, darling, and I will miss you terribly—" her mother started.

"Now stop there." Mr. Darling held up his hand to silence her. "Brave heart. We're doing this for her own good."

"You're sending me to *Ireland.* You are *exiling* me. To care for a bunch of . . . of . . . nasty little boys I don't even know!"

"Think of it as an adventure! Like in your stories!" Mrs. Darling said brightly. "They could be your Misplaced Boys!"

"*Lost* Boys, Mother. And no, they can't."

"Well, think of it as a nice little excursion from London, then. A vacation, really . . ."

"You're hiring me out to complete strangers hundreds of miles away just because I write stories about Peter Pan?"

It wasn't really a question. It was a reaffirming of the facts as presented to her.

"It's not just about the stories," Mr. Darling said, looking desperately at his wife.

Mrs. Darling raised an eyebrow. She may have been soft in many ways, but Wendy's mother never, ever lied.

"All right, it *is* just about the stories," Mr. Darling sighed. "And I think you could do with a break from each other for a while."

"We will keep the notebook safe here with us while you go," Mrs. Darling said soothingly.

"But they're *my* stories. They're *mine.* They belong to *me*!"

Mr. Darling threw up his hands. "Wendy, they are not the product of a happy, normal girl!"

"No, I suppose *not*," Wendy cried, and she fled upstairs, the basket with the dog still swinging from her arm.

# Wendy Makes a Decision

This at least could be said about Snowball: the little thing curled up on Wendy's neck and breathed his soft wet breath on her cheek while she lay on her bed, dry-eyed and insensate. Nana sat loyally on the floor nearby, perhaps withholding her disdain for the new interloper in view of her mistress's distress.

"Ireland . . ." Wendy finally whispered. "I don't want to go to Ireland.

"Unless . . . *maybe* I would if I got to go in an airship.

"Or if I went by regular ship, while chasing pirates.

"Or if I wasn't alone. If I was brought there by . . .

*"Peter Pan."*

This time hearing her voice aloud didn't make her braver at all.

"Peter Pan," she repeated bitterly.

"*Peter Pan*, who only visited when I couldn't see him. Peter Pan, who left his shadow and never came back for it. Who never came back for *me*."

She turned her head to look out the window, but all she saw was gray. The same gray that was inside her head; the two reached out to each other, like sensing like. Wendy closed her eyes, severing the connection. But it was still gray behind her closed lids.

What had happened?

Somehow her life had gone from heady days of playing games with Michael and John and telling stories about pirates to . . . passing time until they came home. And then there were no more pirates anyway. Something had slipped out of her hands. There would be no pirates of any sort in her future. No fairies, no Peter Pan, no Never Land. Just banishment to another family in another drearily real country. And there? And then back home? The same: social mistakes, misery in a crowd, boys who probably didn't like her anyway.

She sighed and looked at Snowball. "Pretty doggy," she said, giving him a pet. "When they gave you to me they were only trying to make me happy. They really do think this nannying abroad, this . . . . *gothic situation*, would be good for me. But I don't like gothic novels, Snowball. They're dreary.

"I suppose it could have been worse, like an arranged marriage. All right, perhaps that's going a bit far. It's really a bit more Charlotte than Emily. 'A serious introduction to a proper boy,' then."

She carefully moved Snowball so she could give Nana a good petting too.

"I thought *Peter Pan* was the proper boy for me. But all I have is a shadow of him."

She paused for a moment, wondering if that sounded too dramatic.

"But I really did think he was going to come back, Nana. At least to fetch his property. It's his *shadow,* for heaven's sake. What is he doing without it?"

She went to the bureau and opened the drawer and regarded the black non-object that lay there unmoving, darkening the shapes under it.

"He mustn't need it anymore," she said thoughtfully.

"He mustn't *want* it. Anymore," she added after another moment.

Nana let out a sound somewhere between a growl and a chuff. Almost like she knew what Wendy was thinking.

Wendy herself wasn't sure what she was thinking. An idea was just beginning to form in her head—an extremely alien idea, but one that opened a space in the clouds even before it was fully formed, like a sigh that precedes great things.

Things that did *not* include Ireland.

Acquiring these things would be tricky, however.

Apart from maths, nothing in Wendy's life was strictly transactional—though certainly there were times when the boys were younger that she'd had to divide time into five-minute slots so each could have a turn playing with a favorite toy. And, of course, she often overheard Mr. Darling going on about how if Mrs. Darling bought a new hat they wouldn't be able to afford a new tea service—and her mother calmly agreeing, to her father's never-ending surprise (for she was practical underneath her lashes and perfume, and quite good at maths).

But the idea of *worth* . . . of *trade* . . . of something having value to someone else in a way that was useful to *her*, to Wendy . . . this was new, and a little frightening.

Here were the facts: Peter Pan didn't value his shadow anymore, apparently.

But someone else might.

No, scratch that; someone else *did.*

She wouldn't let herself think beyond this. She wouldn't let her mind chatter the way her mouth did, ruining everything. This time she would *do.*

She looked around until she found the perfect thing: a delicate linen and lace envelope for keeping her nightgown in that she had done a pretty job of embroidering. She carefully scooped up the shadow, folded it, and slipped it in.

What else might she need?

A sewing kit, a tiny lady's knife, a muffler, a half dozen extra hairpins, some string and ribbons. She put all this along with the envelope into a worn leather satchel and slipped it under her bed.

Then she took out a pair of stockings and began to darn them, an innocent and useful task should anyone come upon her unexpectedly.

Hours later, Michael and John returned home full of their usual youthful energy and droll remarks. Wendy neither remonstrated them nor laughed softly; her brothers remarked on her distracted nature.

When Mrs. Darling came into the kitchen it was with a tentative step and furtive looks.

"How is your little pet?" she eventually asked.

"What? Oh, he's absolutely adorable," Wendy said, remembering to toss Snowball a tidbit of mutton. For Nana she reserved the bone.

"You can . . . take him with you, you know. To Ireland. He would be a delightful little travel companion."

For a moment, just a moment, Wendy looked at her mother—*really* looked at her, steadily and clearly.

"You would never send the boys away."

The statement fell hard and final and full of more meaning than anything that had ever been said in the kitchen before.

"But they didn't write the . . . fantasies. . . ." her mother said quietly.

Then Mr. Darling came in, loud and blustery, talking up Irish butter and clean country air.

Mother and daughter both ignored him.

Wendy went to bed early that night, claiming fatigue. Since the sun had almost won its daily Sisyphean battle with the weather, the sky was light a long time before the air became heavy enough to subtly infiltrate thoughts with sleep.

"Hook . . ." she whispered, finally drowsing.

"I have his shadow. . . ."

# Ramifications

Wendy woke as the clock tolled midnight. If she had any doubts about the reality of her situation or the rashness of her escape plan, this clarified it all immediately. Of course, midnight: the witching hour.

A foggy memory of instructions whispered to her in dreams guided Wendy's hands through the act of slipping on her boots and lacing them up, of wrapping herself up in a coat and grabbing her satchel.

She tiptoed down the hall, pausing to look into Michael and John's room. They were both peacefully asleep. John's glasses hung precariously from the headboard above him and a book was slipping out of his arms. Michael had fallen unconscious with the force of a tot: immediately and completely, no book, and he hadn't moved from that position at all.

"Goodbye—for a little while, at least," she whispered. "You have your own adventures now. It's my turn this time."

Despite attempting to be a ladylike sister, Wendy knew just as well as the boys where the squeaky stairs were and how to hold on to the banister and silently swing to a more polite step. Mr. Darling was snoring; the house was otherwise silent, and she had a clear path to the back door. . . .

Except for Nana, who sat resolutely in front of it.

"Now, Nana," Wendy whispered. "If you really loved me, you would let me go."

Nana made a sound of doubt in the back of her throat.

"Nana. I am *not* going to Ireland. Michael and John don't need either one of us anymore. You need a safe, warm, loving home and a good fire. I need . . . something else."

Nana's doggy eyebrows raised plaintively. She whimpered a question.

"Well, all right. I'll tell you, so that if anything happens to me you may tell the authorities. I'm making my way to Never Land."

Nana sighed, as if to say *I wish I had never grabbed that shadow.*

Then she slowly stepped aside and gestured at the door with her head: *Well, there it is. Go on.*

"Thank you for understanding," Wendy said, kissing her on the head. "I'm grateful."

She opened the door the smallest crack. *"Able to slip through sideways . . . Wasted away with love and longing,"* she whispered spitefully. "Stupid John and his stupid Ovid."

She drifted down the walk carelessly for a moment, stunned by the night. The moon had come out, and though not dramatically full or a perfect crescent, its three quarters were bright enough to turn the fog and dew and all that had the power to shimmer a bright silver, and everything else—the metal of the streetlamps, the gates, the cracks in the cobbles—a velvety black.

After a moment Wendy recovered from the strange beauty and remembered why she was there. She padded into the street before she could rethink anything and pulled up her hood. "Why didn't I do this earlier?" she marveled. Sneaking out when she wasn't supposed to was its own kind of adventure, its own kind of magic. London was beautiful. It felt like she had the whole city to herself except for a stray cat or two.

Despite never venturing beyond the neighborhood much by herself, she had spent plenty of time with maps, studying them for someday adventures. And as all roads lead to Rome, so too do all the major thoroughfares wind up at the Thames. Names like Vauxhall and Victoria (and Horseferry) sprang from her brain as clearly as if there had been signs in the sky pointing the way.

Besides Lost Boys and pirates, Wendy had occasionally terrified her brothers with stories about Springheel Jack and the half-animal orphan children with catlike eyes who roamed the streets at night. As the minutes wore on she felt her initial bravery dissipate and terror slowly creep down her neck—along with the fog, which was also somehow finding its way under her coat, chilling her to her core.

"If I'm not careful I'm liable to catch a terrible head cold! Perhaps that's *really* why people don't adventure out in London at night," she told herself sternly, chasing away thoughts of crazed, dagger-wielding murderers with a vision of ugly red runny noses and cod-liver oil.

But was it safer to walk down the middle of the street, far from shadowed corners where villains might lurk? Being exposed out in the open meant she would be more easily seen by police or other do-gooders who would try to escort her home.

"My mother is sick and requires this one particular tonic that can only be obtained from the chemist across town," she practiced. "A nasty decoction of elderberries and slippery elm, but it does such wonders for your throat. *No* one else has it. And do you know how hard it is to call for a cab this time of night? In this part of town? *That's* the crime, really."

In less time than she imagined it would take, Wendy

arrived at a promenade that overlooked the mighty Thames. She had never seen it from that particular angle before or at that time of night. On either bank, windows of all the more important buildings glowed with candles or gas lamps or even electric lights behind their icy panes, little tiny yellow auras that lifted her heart.

"I *do* wish I had done this before," she breathed.

Maybe if she had, then things wouldn't have come to *this*. . . .

She bit her lip. A decision had been made; it was time to follow through on it. There was no room for weakness or second thoughts in a hero, and if nothing else, Wendy had to be the hero of her own soul. She found the closest set of stairs down to the river and descended lightly, keeping an eye out for thugs and cutthroats. There was no one around at all—no one visible, anyway—except for a suspicious old man in a broken top hat sucking on a pipe on the opposite bank.

She stood at the edge of the turgid black waters and waited.

A breeze rose, curling the little hairs that strayed from Wendy's chignon. She realized with a start that the air now had the sharp tang of salt. Of the *sea.* The wispy fog that had seemed to follow her from home was now joined by its big brother, which swept down the river like a swift, dark carriage. Thick tendrils preceded it, scraping this way and that just above the water, as if feeling a clear path for the billows that followed. In a very short time Wendy was once again surrounded by gray. She couldn't even see the stairs up to the road.

Everything was still.

And then, emerging out of the darkness like a wraith, a single yellow light bobbed in the inky distance.

Slowly and steadily it grew closer.

Wendy sucked in her breath.

The light resolved into a lantern hung on a yoke. . . .

No, not a yoke—a *prow*!

Incredibly, unbelievably, a silent galleon glided down the Thames toward her. Its sails were furled and its masts as thin and bare as the bones of a broken ribcage rotting on some ancient, forgotten battlefield.

The ship paused improbably in the currents.

Nothing moved in the foggy night but a single black flag rippling in the salty breeze, its skull and crossbones faded and yellow.

Wendy forced herself to stand still, waiting, as motionlessly as she could, her heart pounding loudly in her ears. She had made her decision. She had taken an action. These were the results, and she would deal with them.

"Well, well, well," came a voice from the deck.

Then came the measured *clops* of surprisingly hard and

high-heeled boots on the planks, approaching the railing. Wendy gritted her teeth.

Captain Hook leaned over and grinned at her.

He was exactly and precisely the way she had imagined—*remembered*—him. Long, black, ridiculous curling locks. Probably a wig. Long face, clear of the dissolution of rum but ruined by the joint devils of villainy and insanity. He obviously thought himself a duke in a red-and-gold coat, prim breeches, and mostly spotless stockings. A feather stuck out of his oversized hat; a Jacobean collar throttled his neck. Above his smile was a mustache waxed and styled to within an inch of its—probably dyed—life.

Yet Wendy gulped.

*Seeing* him was different from imagining—remembering—him. He looked utterly absurd, and that was exactly what made him terrifying.

"Ah, Miss Darling. How are you on this fine night?" he called, saluting her with his hook, sharp and golden, the only thing that glittered in the dim light of the solitary lantern.

"Very well, thank you!" Wendy shouted back. Manners stepped in, bless them, when the mind scrambled away to hide. "And you?"

"Oh, I couldn't be better, thank you for asking," he answered with an oily smile. "That is, assuming you have brought what you said you would."

"I have it. I have Peter Pan's shadow here." She took out the satchel and showed it to him.

"Oh, excellent, excellent girl."

Any pretense at politeness, any mockery he exhibited, disappeared entirely as visceral excitement took over. The greed on his face was both reassuring and nauseating. He rubbed his hand and hook together with tangible glee.

"Do we have a deal?" Wendy asked, clearly and loudly.

"Yes, yes, of course. Passage to Never Land. In return for one shadow."

"And *home* again," Wendy pressed. "When I wish to return."

"And passage home again," Hook said impatiently. "Yes, yes. As for when you wish to return, that can be a tricky business. Getting *here* . . . without pixie magic or flight . . . is an uncertain thing. My crew wasn't too keen on the idea to begin with."

"That was the deal. Never Land and home again," Wendy said, pulling the satchel away from his view and making as if to put it back in her coat.

*"Of course, of course,"* Hook said desperately, eyes never leaving the satchel. "Never Land and home again. Without question. Just be aware that we are not some sort of ferry service, Miss Darling. We are *pirates*. With limited magical means. You cannot on a whim decide you've missed

Mummy and Daddy long enough and expect to be transported instantly. These things take time."

"All right, I will take that into due consideration," Wendy said. "Otherwise, promise?"

"Oh, I promise."

"Swear . . . swear by the pirates' code!"

Hook looked exasperated.

Wendy put her hands on her hips.

She knew about boys trying to sneak out of promises. She had two younger brothers. You had to be *very specific* with your orders and wishes, or they were as wily and untrustworthy as evil genies. And what was a pirate, really, but a boy grown, with a real sword and a mustache?

"Swear it," she repeated.

She could have sworn she heard muffled laughter from behind him on the deck.

Hook sighed.

"All right, all right. I *swear* on the pirates' code: I, Captain Hook, promise that in return for Peter Pan's shadow I shall grant Wendy Darling passage to Never Land *and home*—when circumstances allow it."

"All right then," Wendy said, trying to sound surer than she felt. She had just won a battle of wits with a pirate, just like in a story. Why didn't she feel triumphant?

"Come on, men, let's welcome our passenger aboard!"

Hook grinned again at her, a smile that narrowed to points at the corners of his mouth that were as sharp as those at the ends of his mustache, as the end of his hook.

There was a thumping and pounding on the deck. A rope ladder unrolled over the side, bumping and bouncing on its way down, the last step landing neatly at Wendy's feet.

She took a deep breath, set her jaw, and climbed up.

# Wendy Among the Pirates

As might have been guessed from the preceding pages, Wendy hadn't much experience interacting with the world at large; that is, people who weren't her family, shopkeepers, neighbors, or other audience members at the theater. Yet despite this innocence she had an immediate sense that perhaps these pirates were not the nicest people to be left alone with. It was one thing to tell tales of swashbuckling battles and the backstory behind the bosun with the eye patch—and quite another to actually be in their midst.

Captain Hook presented his men with a flourish. They stood neither in neat rows nor at attention—with very little respect at all, actually—and beheld Wendy far too boldly for her liking. One skinny chap with large gold earrings who slouched provocatively to one side actually gave her an appalling wink.

Their clothes were not the bright primary colors of nursery room imagination; they were salt-faded and dull. Their faces weren't merely unshorn and artfully streaked with a daub of tar; they were *grubby*. All shades of skin were dulled with not enough washing. Wendy found her hands twitching, the urge to grab a cloth and scrub them almost overwhelming all other thoughts.

"Men, this is Wendy Darling. Wendy, this is me crew. Crew, she is a *guest* aboard the *Jolly Roger* and I expect you swabs to treat her as such."

"It's bad luck to have a woman aboard," one large old pirate with a red bandanna growled. "Worse than a cat. Brings storms and swells."

"Oh . . . I think it's the *best* sort of luck to have a lass on deck." A man with one eye and a loathsome leer grinned at her disgustingly.

"If any one of you touches her," Captain Hook said with a very false smile, "you'll be feeding the sharks before you can draw your next breath." He leaned on his heels and put his hands on his hips, a movement that threw his splendid jacket back and revealed the twin pistols that were holstered elegantly on his hips.

This made Wendy feel a lot calmer but a little vexed.

What if the pirate was saving her life, or wanted to arm wrestle? What then?

“This whole thing is a bloody waste of time,” a third pirate scoffed. “We should be out attacking ships, looting gold, and plundering treasure!”

“And so we shall. But in the meantime, she has given me something more valuable than all the gold in Never Land,” Hook said airily. “Peter Pan’s *shadow*!”

He unfurled the poor limpid thing and flapped it out to show them. The shadow hung limply from its neck where the pirate held it, struggling only a little.

The pirates looked mostly unhappy at the sight, a smidgen angry, and not just a little uncomfortable. Seeing a shadow hanging there apart from its owner was unnatural and might make the heartiest and blackest soul shiver, but even Wendy could see there was more to it than that.

“And what will that get us?” demanded an orange-haired lout with a northern European accent.

“Why, it will get us P—” Hook paused with a not-very-subtle side-eye at Wendy. “It will get us something we’ve always wanted. Well, something *I* have always wanted. And I am your captain. So it’s what you want, too—or at least it’s in your best interests to want it. And when I have it, we will be done with Never Land and all its silliness forever, and there will be only plundering and loot from here on out. All right?”

There were muttered grumbles of grudging assent.

"For now, I'm putting the shadow in safekeeping, in the trusted hands of Mr. Smee."

At this the pirates looked even *more* uncomfortable—and disgusted. Possibly resigned. They threw up their hands and slowly dispersed, growling and unsatisfied and muttering curses.

"So there you are, my dear," Captain Hook said, bowing to her. "A loathsome lot, to be sure, but you're safe among them while we're on our way to Never Land."

"What time shall we get there, if you please?" Wendy asked politely.

"We don't deal with time or clocks or watches on the *Jolly Roger*, Miss Darling. Except for figuring latitude and longitude. Pirates are free from such civilizing constraints and demonic inventions of man. We have none of those infernal contraptions on *this* ship, I can tell you."

Wendy narrowed her eyes. What a strange thing to say—and there was a strange look behind his bluster. Fear? Could it possibly have been *fear*? He was afraid of something. Something he wasn't telling her.

"All right, well . . . Approximately how *long* will it take to get there? Surely pirates aren't entirely free from the passage of time, what with meals and sleep and the like."

"Oh, you're a very clever girl, aren't you, Miss Darling?

Well, these things aren't precise, but it shouldn't be more than a day or so."

"And how are we to get there?"

Captain Hook gave her a knowing smile. "I suppose if you were with Peter Pan he would say something like *oh, second star on the left,* et cetera, et cetera. And you would fly through the sky, straight to the island of your dreams.

"Alas, my lady, pixie dust and good magic are rather out of a pirate's reach. We had to go a different route, and it nearly cost poor Major Thomas his life. Possibly his soul. It was a bit unclear. Anyway, he's a useless lubber and prone to grog. Not much of a loss there."

Wendy's eyes widened and her hand went to her mouth in dismay, but Hook was already touching his hat to her and spinning away, chuckling over the shadow he held.

Now alone, she looked around the deck nervously. There were no benches or chaise lounges as on a proper transport vessel. Because of the lateness—or the earliness—of the hour, the pirates mostly went belowdecks to their bunks. None of those remaining seemed particularly happy about the strange motion of the ship, gliding along without oars or sails or any human help at all. They occupied themselves with other pirate-y pursuits: five-finger fillet on an upturned barrel, surreptitious sips from leather flasks, shouting over a game that involved rolling with what looked very much like knucklebones instead of dice.

(*And how were those come by?* Wendy wondered.)

She fidgeted with her fingers a bit the way she did at parties, and then decided that the dice throwers seemed the least dangerous.

"My, those are certainly unique implements you're playing with," she ventured.

The pirates just grunted.

"Of course, I don't approve of gambling at all, but Father has a lovely pair of dice that he keeps with his jewelry. They're not . . . bones. At least, I don't think so. I believe they're ivory. Although I suppose that's basically a sort of bone, isn't it?"

The pirates frowned and tried to ignore her.

"They have real pips on them, carved and painted. They really are quite lovely. Of course, I *am* against gambling, and so is Mother. It's not a proper occupation for anyone, even men. But his dice are quite pretty and nice to hold, and they warm up in your hand so. And how do you know which side yours land on? Without pips?"

The pirates stopped their game entirely and stared up at her in exasperation.

"Well, I've never played before," she said, a little defensively. "I'm not asking you to teach me. I'm just wondering. I should have to say no if you asked me, wouldn't I? Seeing as gambling and games of chance are immoral. So please, I'd rather you didn't ask."

"Weren't going to," one of the pirates grumbled. And with that, he swept the dice up into his bag and left her alone with the other players, who gave her nasty looks before they, too, retreated.

Wendy wilted. Life aboard the pirate ship was actually surprisingly similar to a fancy party, the type she hated. With dressed-up girls and boys and men and women and tea and tiny sandwiches and aspic and someone showing off on the piano. No one wanted to talk to her at *those* gatherings, either. It was like Christmas all over again.

She wandered forlornly across the deck and looked out over the railing.

The sky was blank. Fog surrounded the ship and there was no more breeze. It was as if they had reached the middle of the night, the middle of nowhere. Everything stood still except for a few tendrils of Wendy's hair and the black flag. She shivered, pulling her coat more closely around her. She didn't want to be alone. But the five-finger fillet players looked . . . dangerous.

And then Wendy saw salvation.

A lone pirate was sitting cross-legged on the deck, looking squint-eyed and studious, pulling at a string on his pants.

*He was sewing!*

Wendy brightened like the sun. Now *there* was a subject she could feel confident about.

She walked up to the fellow and watched for a moment as he ineffectually stabbed a giant needle into a piece of cloth that he held awkwardly in place on his pants, trying to cover a hole.

"Excuse me, if you don't mind me saying, but I'm afraid you're doing that entirely wrong," Wendy said politely.

The pirate looked up at her, one eye still squinted. She wondered if it was a permanent affliction.

"Well, I ain't got me a seamstress to fix up my fancy pants now, do I?" He cackled. "'What Mother can't do, sons must *makes* do,' as they say."

"Ah—I don't know about that," Wendy said, trying to work the words out in her head and failing. "But if you'll hand it to me, I'll have a go."

The pirate's eyes widened. Without a second thought, he shoved the whole mess over to her, including his pants—which, as his brightly striped knickers attested, he had apparently not been wearing.

"Oh!" Wendy blushed and turned around.

The pirate cackled again. "What, you think I'd stick it with a needle while it's on me own skin? I'm unskilled, not *daft*, ye silly co'. Now settle down. Ye can't see me privates or me bum, and there's them that wear less on washing day round here, so ye'd best get used to it."

"Well!"

Wendy tried to rearrange her shocked expression while busying herself sorting through the mess of cloth. He was right, of course. She was in alien country now: a ship full of uncivilized men. All she could do was act properly, like a decent civilized person, as there was no guarantee that others would.

She settled herself down on a tipped-over quarter cask and smoothed out the pieces. Actually, the pirate had made a very nice, neat little knot to begin with. But that made sense, she supposed. Sailors had to be very good at knots, hadn't they? She bet they would be excellent at macramé, or even crochet, if patiently taught. . . .

Wendy whistled and hummed to herself and felt much better with something familiar in her hands. In a short while the patch was finished and held tightly on by tiny and neat little stitches.

"There, all done. You can see how I—oh!"

There was a crowd around her now. Pirates, speechless and wide-eyed to a man.

"*BLIMEY!* Do mine next!" one said, whipping off his shirt.

"No, me! I got no seat on me trousers!" another begged.

"No! Me next!" whined a third.

"All right, all right now . . ."

She put her hands on her hips, feeling crowded and overwhelmed. It was on the tip of her tongue to say that as long as she was on board, she would do any minor repairs and mending that were needed. Might as well make herself useful, right? That's what she always did: made herself useful, and as a result she was always needed. And liked.

Then again . . .

She had paid her passage on this vessel. A very dear one. She wasn't a scullery maid; she was a customer.

"My jacket's fearful cold when the wind blows—I'll give ye a halfpenny if ye do it first," a fourth pirate said slyly, seeing her hesitate.

The others caught on fast.

"I'll give ye me grog ration! For me pants!"

"I'll give ye a whale-bone needle and carve ye a thimble, if ye like. Can ye *make* things, too? Like a muffler for cold days?"

*Well, that's better,* Wendy decided. *I think.*

Pirates were *very* transactional—and seemed to respect you more if you were as well. In some ways it was rather a windfall: who knew what other supplies she would require for her foray into Never Land? In her dreams and stories there was always just the right-shaped stick or rock or key discovered at the last possible moment. But was the real Never Land like that?

And, of course, the pirates would have to talk to her now.

*Take that, Shesbows!* thought Wendy, very pleased with herself.

There was no sun to mark the passage of time. After her third mending project, Wendy began to grow restless. She asked the hovering pirates the precise o'clock but they all shook their heads.

"Without a sun ye can't use no sundial," one said, pointing to the dark gray wall of fog around the ship. "And Hook don't allow no modrun clocks nor watches nowhere on account of that crocodile what took his hand. It tocks like the clock it swallowed."

*Aha* . . . Now it made sense! She had called the creature Tick-Tock in her own telling of the story. Hook's hand had given the beast a craving for more of the pirate captain, and it followed the *Jolly Roger* everywhere. The noise of the clock it had swallowed always presaged its appearance.

(The boys would shriek with glee when Wendy said things like: "But wait! What was that? Off in the distance? *Tick . . . tock . . . . tick . . . tock.*" "IT'S A CROCODILE!" Young Michael would cry.)

"That thing hasn't been around for years," another pirate said. "Probably dead from indigestion. But Hook, he still thinks it's out there somewhere."

"He can't bear being reminded of it. Thinks the beast is still after 'im," said a third. "Every time he hears a clock it drives him batty."

She wondered what had happened to the crocodile in the real Never Land. She hadn't killed it off in her own stories—yet.

But despite the lack of clocks, lunch came anyway, and blessedly just in time. Wendy's stomach was growling in a most unladylike way. She followed the crew to the mess hall. Each pirate presented his own bowl to the, er, sous chef. It was then filled with glop that might have been a chowder or a mulligatawny. One polite fellow (whose waistcoat Wendy had fixed) offered to give her his own bowl once he was done. She discreetly tried to wipe it out. The tall, slouchy pirate with the two big gold earrings saw this and cackled.

"Have you anything of your own you would like fixed?" Wendy asked him, trying to change the subject and distract attention from her covert actions.

"Oh, I'm plenty handy with a needle and thread," the pirate said, posing for her. And in fact, he was more solidly dressed than the rest. Everything was mostly clean, if not perfect, and unpatched. "I just don't let it get out too much, know what I mean?"

"I suppose I do," Wendy said uncertainly as the pirate winked at her.

"The name's Zane," he said with a bow. "Alodon Zane, at your service."

"Wendy Darling at yours," she said with a curtsy.

*"MISS DARLING, WHAT ARE YOU DOING IN HERE WITH THESE LOUTS?"*

Captain Hook was suddenly filling the door like a bad omen and roaring like an enraged lion. At her dismay and the other pirates' shock, he immediately softened his voice. "My dear, you're a *guest*, not a midshipman. Come dine in my quarters. Mr. Smee will serve us."

Wendy shivered. She *might* have read a few books that were not strictly approved by Father or prescreened by the bookseller. In those typeset pages, she'd had glimpses of the greater world—even if she didn't fully understand it. She knew it was not proper to be alone in the company of a strange man.

"Dinna worry," Zane whispered into her left ear. "He's not . . . I mean, Hook's a lunatic, but he loves decorum. Your maidenhood is safe with him. Not yer throat, maybe. But the rest of you is."

"Thank you?" Wendy whispered back. Then she returned the bowl to the pirate who had provided it. "Thank you, sir, but I suppose I will be dining on the lido deck instead. Your generosity is very much appreciated."

"Oh, yes, me too. Absolutely, ma'am," the pirate blustered, bowing.

Lunch with a pirate captain could have been many things: terrifying, spooky, embattled—even romantic, given the right circumstances.

But in reality, lunch was . . . awkward.

Wendy sat up properly and used her best manners.

Captain Hook bowed and flourished and removed his hat and pulled out a chair for her. The table was a tiny fold-out thing spread with a fancy cloth, silver utensils, and a clever golden candelabrum that was held upright on chains so it didn't tip with the waves. It was all very lovely, and for the first moment Wendy was overcome with the precise perfection of the scene. There was even a spinet piano in the corner of the room.

"I do play, if you're wondering," Hook said, following her eyes. "A bit harder since the . . . well . . . *hook*, but I make do."

They settled down to empty plates.

"Mr. Smee," Hook called politely.

No one came.

"Mr. *Smee*," he said again with a growl—while still smiling at Wendy.

Silence.

"MR. SMEE!" the captain finally cried, slamming his hook down on the table. "Blast that man. He'll be at the grog again, no doubt."

He leapt up and crashed through the door, muttering under his breath.

*"Confounded . . . lazy . . . overpaid . . ."*

Wendy sat stiffly and continued to look around at everything she had already looked at.

Eventually Hook came back, awkwardly carrying a plate of carved beef, a bowl of neeps and tatties, and a beautiful if stale-looking baguette, all cradled in his hand and hook.

Wendy leapt up to help, but he *tsked* her back down and actually quite neatly and deftly laid out the feast.

"Good help is so hard to get," he said apologetically. "I should have had him walk the plank years ago, but we go way back. . . . He's even saved my life a few times. It's like keeping an old dry cow around because you can't bear the look in her eyes."

"Oh," Wendy said uncertainly.

They concentrated on serving themselves in silence. Wendy wondered if this was what having a distant uncle was like—an odd grown-up who didn't know how to interact properly with young people and who often said inappropriate things.

"So I'm curious, Miss Darling," Hook finally began,

with a casual tone so false Wendy's ears practically curled at his words. "Whatever made you come to the rather rash decision to trade Peter Pan's shadow to his greatest enemy in exchange for passage to Never Land?"

Wendy was *about* to interrupt and point out that Hook wasn't Peter Pan's *greatest* enemy. Depending on how you looked at it, Peter Pan's greatest enemy could have been growing up, his own sense of self-importance, or his more immediately dangerous foes: the warlike, winged L'cki, the Fangriders of Upper Hillsdale, or the Cyclops of the Cerulean Sea. Hook was a *recurring* enemy. Not his *greatest* enemy.

Then she thought better of mentioning it.

"Well, you know, he never came back for it. He just left it there," she said airily. Trying to ignore the agency she had in the decision, that what she had done wasn't *right*. That these words were *false*. "What was I supposed to do, keep it around for the rest of my life among my trinkets and bric-a-brac? Hanging after me? You seemed to want it more than he, and I wanted a little holiday. Everyone is happy. Shall I pour you some water, Captain?"

"Thank you, my dear, but I'll stick to this lovely Barolo. A very interesting . . . argument—*justification*, maybe? Now don't look at me like that; it's just us, Miss Darling. But surely you of all people know that Never Land is a bit trickier than that. There is no *holidaying* there, like Blackpool or the South of France. You have made quite the commitment. I can't help but wonder what drove such a pretty, innocent little thing like you to such desperation—abandoning her life and family to leap into the unknown, and trading in her hero's shadow in the process."

Wendy had mixed feelings at these words. On the one hand, they made her sound a little epic.

On the other hand, was her life really that dire? Her family loved her. Nana loved her. Ireland was terrible, but it was for only a short period of time, right? And *safe* . . .

She looked up at the pirate, suspicious. In her stories Captain Hook was always planning, always conniving. He had an angle on everything, even if that angle was stupid and resulted in ridiculous defeats. So what was he driving at now?

"Yes, it shall make a fascinating chapter in my memoirs, won't it?" she said as haughtily as she could, pouring herself another glass of tar-scented water.

"Won't your family miss you—the Mister and Missus Darling?"

"I don't really know how time operates between Never Land and the real world. Perhaps I'll just have been gone a day," she answered carelessly. "Perhaps it will be a blink of an eye. Perhaps this is all now a dream and I will wake when it's over, back in my bed. Either way, Mother and Father have their hands quite full with Michael and John. I daresay they shan't miss me beyond needing to write an embarrassing explanation to a certain family in Ireland. I just hope Nana remembers to feed Snowball.

"But what about you, Captain Hook? What exactly are your plans for Peter's shadow? Are you going to keep it and hold it over his head forever? In return for your . . . hook?"

*"Forever?"* Hook sat back in his chair, looking astonished. "Oh no, no, my girl. I have no desire to continue this endless charade with Peter Pan any longer at all. I have wasted far too much of my life on it. My crew hasn't looted a merchant vessel or stormed a port in years. No, I am done with Never Land. Rather permanently. I think it's high time I put it and Peter behind me. *Rather permanently.*"

"That sounds a bit ominous," Wendy observed.

"It was supposed to. I'm actually quite thrilled by the fact that you will be here as an audience to his and its fate."

"What precisely are you going to do, if I may ask?"

"Well, my dear, unlike the villains in *your* quaint little tales, I am not daft enough to reveal my cunning plans to anyone—a hero or even a bystander like yourself—before carrying them out."

Wendy took some umbrage at the term *bystander*—wasn't she on a pirate ship headed to Never Land of her own volition? Didn't she *invent* much of the world he inhabited?

But there were more pressing issues than her own ego.

"Of course not," she agreed, around a sip of water so she wouldn't choke on her subterfuge. "But surely you couldn't keep such ideas entirely to yourself. Even a great captain like yourself needs help with the dirty work. And perhaps a sympathetic ear."

"Well, you are right there, of course," Hook said, swirling his deep red wine in its glass. "But I have Mr. Smee, who holds all my secrets dearly. He alone is aware of the not so happily-ever-after that awaits all of Never Land.

"And I'll have you know, Miss Darling, I was rather despairing of ever being able to carry out all the details needed for my plans. Your offer of Peter's shadow came like a miracle out of the blue—finally Mr. Smee and I can get to work on it!"

Wendy . . . was, however inadvertently, responsible for setting in motion one of Hook's most murderous schemes? That involved all of Never Land? *Rather permanently?* She swallowed and tried to stay calm.

"Lucky break for you, I suppose," she said casually. "But how *does* it involve Peter's shadow? You couldn't have made all of these plans without knowing for certain you could get it, and—"

"Tut tut," the captain said, shaking a finger at her like a

schoolmarm. "It's highly impolite to question a pirate captain so closely when he has invited you to lunch, don't you know? Terribly bad form."

And Wendy ground her teeth, defeated.

The moment lunch—or whatever it was; the world was still gray and formless—ended, she escaped back to the deck. Her eyes had that dry, crusty feeling of having been open too long from being up too late. How long had it been since she had left the house? It was mad not having clocks or watches around. Despite just eating a rather substantial meal she felt a little light-headed. But not queasy. Even with the rhythmic rocking of the ship, she walked steadily and her stomach remained firmly digesting the surprisingly good repast.

"Lady! Missy! Miss Darling!" A pirate ran up to her, a loop of string in his hands. Two other pirates came reluctantly behind, looking chagrined. One of them cradled a badly bleeding hand.

"My goodness, whatever happened here?"

"Me and these louts was just arguing about the proper play of cat's cradle," the pirate with the string said. "The White Duke here kept flubbing it up."

"I had to cut him," the second pirate admitted, pointing at the wound on the third's hand.

"Can you show us how to do it, proper-like?" the Duke asked, heedless of his injury.

Wendy gave them all a severe look.

"Let me take care of this poor fellow first and *then* see what we can do."

She took the pirate's bloody hand and gently peeled open his fingers for a better look. It wasn't so bad, really—just deep and narrow. All it needed was to be thoroughly cleaned before infection set in. For this they used some pure rum and one of Wendy's precious handkerchiefs. The pirate tried not to swear during her judicious application of the stinging cleanser.

Only then did she take the loop of string and demonstrate the proper sequence of cat's cradle. She even included some of the more difficult variations like the clock tower and the bishop's cap.

Delighted, the pirates clapped her on the back rather harder than she would have liked and strode off, guffawing and chatting like there had never been a row to begin with.

Wendy sighed and shook her head. If all of Never Land's adventures were as easily won as that, she was in for a nice time indeed.

She leaned on the gunwale and looked out. Was it getting lighter? Really this time?

Yes! The rosy fingers of dawn had finally slipped through the fog and gently pulled it apart, separating the tendrils, weakening it.

Wendy watched in fascination. She almost never saw the sunrise except in winter and that was through her window, under the gray sprawl of London Town. Nothing like this. As the sea lightened and the sky began to clear, the two elements resolved themselves into colors unlike anything she was used to: brilliant emerald and deep aquamarine, pellucid azure and shining lapis. It was so storybook perfect she wouldn't have been surprised at all if the sun came out with a great smiley face drawn on it.

"Miss Darling," came a whisper behind her.

Wendy spun around. A cadaverously skinny pirate stood there, the one who had leered at her so loathsomely before. His one eye was narrow and lecherous, his smile thin and frightening.

"I don't believe we've properly met yet. How do you do?" Wendy said, putting out her hand.

"Oh, I do just fine," the pirate growled—and pushed her back up against the railing.

Wendy was caught before she could even figure out what was happening. It took her a moment to find her voice and one more to realize that, despite struggling, she had no ability to fend off this attacker.

"Unhand me!" she cried.

The pirate laughed, his foul-smelling breath nearly asphyxiating her. Wendy screamed.

The pirate leaned over her—

A shot rang out.

So loudly, so close, she felt its hot wind singe her face.

Her attacker looked surprised and then slumped to the deck.

A pool of blood formed under his head. As his body crumpled into a more permanent position, she saw the perfect hole behind his ear where the bullet had gone in.

Wendy knew from stories that this was the time when women screamed and screamed and screamed—and sometimes men, too. But she was just happy to be able to breathe freely again and to have the monster off of her. She felt little of anything except relief.

Hook stood on the deck posed either heroically or demonically, depending on how you read the scene. He had his pistol out and aimed in case the foul miscreant rose again and a curious golden two-cigar holder balanced in his hook. Smoke rose from both cigars as well as the muzzle of his gun.

The rest of the crew appeared as silently as rats (and just as curious) from all parts of the ship, including the crow's nest.

"Miss Darling, are you hurt?" Captain Hook asked, his tone soft and flat.

"No, I don't . . . I'm a little . . ." She touched her mouth and throat, wiping away the grease from the dead man's fingers. *Then* she began to shake. "I'm . . . physically, I'm all fine."

"Mr. Smee, have the crew remove this . . . filth at once," Hook said with a curl of his lip, the gun and cigars still held steady. "And someone bring Miss Darling a draught of something to restore her spirits."

"Oh, I don't . . ." Wendy began. But then again, maybe a drop of something might not be such a bad idea. The shaking had spread to her feet and parts of her body untouched by the villain, and she was having a hard time reining in all the ants she felt crawling on her skin.

Three pirates came forward—none of them named Mr. Smee, Wendy was fairly certain—and unceremoniously dumped the body overboard. A fourth brought a mop and duly began scrubbing the blood and brains away. Two more rushed to her side, one holding a silver-and-crystal decanter and the other a matching cup, both of which looked like they were from Captain Hook's personal stash. Someone held her upright and someone else poured a few drops of a liquid, thick and amber, into the glass. She downed it in one gulp, feeling all eyes on her.

It burned just as she'd imagined it would. Her eyes felt like they were spinning in their sockets.

"Begging your pardon, Cap'n," she heard someone say as she staggered a bit, still trying to collect herself. "But we're back in our proper seas now, Cap'n. And on course for Never Land."

"Thank you, but right now we have more serious things to clear up here," Hook growled. He looked over the crew, into each and every man's eyes. The muzzle of his gun followed closely.

"*This* is how you treat her?" he demanded, his voice carrying across the deck although he didn't shout. "I bring you someone to be your *mother*, and this is how you treat her?"

"Oh," Wendy said, apologies coming to her lips far too easily, the deadly niceties of social convention, the stupidity of being raised by the Darlings. Or maybe it was just the drink. "Most of them were gentlemen. They didn't all treat me badly. It was just that one fellow and—I'm sorry, what?"

She blinked as his words caught up with her brain.

Captain Hook put his arm protectively around her shoulders, careful not to burn her with the cigars. He addressed the men with a tone of great disappointment.

"I bring you a *lady* and a *gentlewoman* to take care of all of you, and this is what you *do*?"

"We would never!" one pirate called out piteously.

"Valentine is a villain, everyone knowed it, he's the worst!" another called out.

"We wuz nice to her! I gave her me own bowl for lunch!"

"She fixed my pants up real good—I'd never harm a hair on her head!"

"WELL, YOU ALMOST LET *THIS* HAPPEN!" Hook roared, firing his pistol in the air.

Wendy winced at the repetition of the loud sound, the ringing in her ears. But it didn't stop her from speaking.

"Excuse me? I'm sorry, I don't believe I quite understand what you're saying," she pressed. "I'm glad to have helped out here and there while aboard, but as someone just said—we're not far from Never Land now. My journey aboard your lovely ship is nearly over. It will soon be time to disembark. I'm not here to be a mother to anyone. I'm here to have adventures."

"And adventures you shall have," Hook promised. "After we leave these cursed waters of Never Land, we shall travel the high seas, plundering and looting along the way, and you shall fix our pants, do our laundry, mend our wounds, and generally take care of us. And probably do a *much* better job than Mr. Smee."

"I shall do nothing of the sort!" Wendy protested, almost stamping her foot. "We had a deal. I bought passage to Never Land for Peter's shadow."

"Yes. And here we are, *almost* arrived." Captain Hook said this politely, but a nasty grin stretched across his face. He indicated the horizon with his gun: far off in the distance was indeed a pale bright line, a glowing golden beach. "That was what you bargained for—and that was *all* you bargained for.

*"I never promised to put you ashore."*

# Tink Among the Salarymen

The way to London was not unknown to fairies; it was just rarely used anymore. Smog was bad for wings and the new machines made for strange dreams in children; fewer and fewer were of the sunny meadows and hidden vales that once captured their imagination.

When Tink appeared in the sky above, it was as if a shy star had worked up the courage to appear among its brighter cousins. She glimmered golden and faint at first . . . and then brighter and nearer . . . but never any larger.

The sound she made as she descended, however, was not the music of the spheres or anything so celestial. It fell somewhere between *angry hornet* and *angry percussionist shaking a rack of bells for the worst ever Christmas concert.*

Below her all of London was gray and rolling and endless

and eternally the same. If she squinted, the little fairy could almost pretend that, instead of houses, the streets were lined with the hives of meerrabbits. Maybe from the wrong side of the savanna, but friendly nonetheless.

The thing was . . . Tinker Bell never actually paid attention when Peter took her on these jaunts. She loved hearing about Peter's babyhood; she loved revisiting his lost home. But she *hated* going to Ugly Wendy's house. She had no idea how Peter had even found the girl and her stupid, snotty little brothers. Somehow the stories that Wendy told of his exploits ad nauseam had reached his pixie ears in a way that was just quintessentially Pan-ish.

It was near Kensington Gardens, wasn't it?

She flew the way she vaguely remembered they used to go, following the Thames and keeping an eye out for pockets of green among the gray, brown, and black.

*Aha*—at last, something familiar! She recognized the updraft that suddenly lifted her high into the sky and made it difficult for someone as light as she to land anywhere. Peter never had any trouble. Once in a great while she clung to his collar while he dove through gusts, and these were the best moments of all.

The sky was just beginning to lighten as Tinker Bell touched down delicately inside a park. She felt some fairy familiarity; magic had not entirely deserted this ancient place. But these fey folk were of earthly origin and she had no time for such riffraff. She was Never Land empyreal—and she had work to do.

As she peeped around the garden gate and up the street, she realized that things looked very different when you were down among the ugly buildings and not high above them. At least it was early and she had the city mostly to herself while she explored. There were only a few humans around this time of the morning.

A solitary girl hurried along, looking over her shoulder every few steps. She was large and ugly—was it Wendy?

Tinker Bell approached her eagerly.

But no, up close it was obvious the girl's dress was shabby and poor and her eyes darted about in fear; they didn't hold steady in dreams.

Toward this not-Wendy girl a pair of men strode broadly. Their voices were loud and their dress obviously fine even to a forest pixie's eyes: great silk and wool capes, shiny top hats slightly askew, walking canes with glittering knobs. Much like foxes and wolves they had obviously been out all night hunting for whatever rarefied things these humans craved—eyeglasses, taxes, creampuffs.

"*EGADS*, is that the dancer from the Moulin Rouge? The one you liked so much?" one of the men said, guffawing, pointing at the human girl.

"Good evening, sirs," she said, pulling her collar close and trying to hurry past them.

The other man put out his hand and stopped her, then looked her up and down.

"No, she's a bad copy. Still . . ."

"Please, sirs, let me go. I'm just on my way home."

"From what nefarious activities, I should like to know," the first man said with a snort. "Would anyone even miss you? At 'home'? All the decent girls have been in bed and asleep for hours now. They're not out wandering the streets at night, looking for trouble."

"I ain't looking for trouble. Just let me go," she pleaded.

Tinker Bell's eyes widened as she watched the man reach out to touch the girl's cheek.

Before she knew what she was doing, the little fairy was suddenly zooming in between the two, pelting pixie dust into the man's eyes.

The reaction was immediate: he howled and clawed at his face like a madman.

His friend drew back in surprise.

The girl saw her chance and ran off, mouthing silent thanks to her mysterious savior. The ball of light now zooming away brightened visibly—thanks to a new believer in fairy magic.

"I can see!" the man moaned, falling to his knees. "I

see too much! The world . . . as it really is . . . the great god Pan . . ."

But Tink was already whisking down the street, that adventure over and forgotten.

There were plenty of helpful street signs in this London—if only she could read. She remembered a big tree at the house; that's how Peter always found it. A big tree in a tiny yard with an unused doghouse below. The windows to the nursery were on level with the highest branches of that tree, so they could perch there and listen. If Peter was especially enamored of the story they would glide silently over to the roof and lie on the slate shingles, half listening, half dreaming.

Some of the street trees were indeed large, grand, and imposing—and sadly penned in, surrounded by cobbles and flagstones. None were in a yard.

Human movement increased as the sun rose. Lamps were doused and people came out; they were sweeping the streets, hurrying into shops, unlocking doors with big keys. Tinker Bell buzzed unseen over everyone's heads, looking out for young women of a certain height.

*Aha! There!*

A young woman in a *very familiar* blue dress entered a bookstore and coughed to get the bookseller's attention. How perfectly Wendy!

Tinker Bell zoomed down to see if she was indeed her; this girl definitely seemed more likely than the first one. All right, her skin looked darker, and her hair, too, but who could tell? Humans were strange. Maybe they changed now and then.

"I have a question about a book. Please," the girl spoke softly.

No, that was definitely not Ugly Wendy. Ugly Wendy wasn't shy when she spoke. She was loud. And to the fairy's ears, strident and pushy.

"My wares are far more refined and intellectual than what will satisfy the likes of you," the shop owner snapped without looking up from his own book. "I doubt you can even read. Where are you from?"

"My parents are from Barbados, sir. I was born in England and am a citizen."

"Hardly. Please leave my premises at once."

"But—"

"Get out. Now. Or I shall summon the constable. Your kind is *not* welcome here."

The girl sighed, shook her head, and left.

Tinker Bell also buzzed off, confused and full of unquiet thoughts. She paused to catch her breath and sort things out—and also to suggest to a couple of nearby mice that they would probably very much enjoy comfy nests made exclusively out of a shop's worth of shredded books. They agreed and scampered off, summoning dozens of their friends.

Wendy *was* a big ugly girl. That was just the truth of the matter. And she took Peter's attention away from Tink, despite being big and ugly.

But . . .

Was this the world she lived in?

Where random men might try to hurt her?

Where even if a girl was polite, people . . . ignored her? Yelled at her? Made fun of her?

Was this why Ugly Wendy stayed inside all the time telling stories to her brothers?

Because it was safe?

Because she could be whatever she wanted?

Maybe her brothers were also ugly, but at least they treated her with respect. . . .

Tinker Bell shook her head, trying to physically beat the thoughts out. They were complicated and negative and felt strangely similar to the ones she had about Peter and convincing him that his shadow wasn't in London. There was something . . . *icky* about them. Like the bad-smelling graklemud you could never completely get off. You always thought you had, but there would be just a tiny bit somewhere and you wouldn't be able to find it and you would stink embarrassingly for days.

She rose into the air to fly her mind clean. She skimmed along the roofs and chimneys and spires of London, spiraling out wider and wider, expanding her search.

Sometime mid-morning, when the tired sun crawled into its work clothes of smoke and mist, Tinker Bell finally found the attic gable she remembered from years before.

But unlike every other time when she and Peter had come to hear stories, the windows were shut and fastened tight.

Tinker Bell frowned and whizzed back and forth. She rapped on the glass angrily with her tiny knuckles.

No one was there.

She zoomed into the garden and up to the kitchen door and knocked, trying to stick her head into the too-small keyhole. She jingled furiously when she got stuck there for a moment.

Then she heard a scratching on the other side, almost like a response to her knocks. She redoubled her efforts, slamming against the wood feetfirst.

The door pulled slowly and laboriously inward and she tumbled into the Darling household.

There were no humans about; only the dog was there. She regarded the fairy with large, woeful eyes. But the little fairy didn't stop to say hello or thank you. She zoomed like an angry hornet from room to room until she found the stairs and zipped up them—and then a second set of stairs when she realized her destination lay on the next floor.

The low thudding steps of Nana came up slowly behind her, as well as a doggy sigh or two.

*Here* was the terrible room. Where Ugly Wendy told her stories to her brothers while Tink and Peter stayed outside looking, listening in. With all of its stupid, ugly, large human tools and bits and pieces littering the room . . . though it seemed there was far less clutter than the last time. She flew chaotically back and forth, over lamps and trunks, into the wardrobe and amongst the clothes, causing dust of both the general and pixie varieties to spray about indiscriminately.

"Woof."

Nana had finally made it to the top of the stairs and sat down on her haunches with resignation, knowing it would do little good to try to physically stop the fairy.

Tinker Bell stopped her buzzing around and hovered in front of the dog, angrily jingling questions.

"Woof . . ." Nana said, rolling her eyes toward the bureau.

Tinker Bell flew into the half-open top drawer so hard she bonked against the back. She might have gotten trapped inside had Nana not put up a massive paw to stop the drawer from closing.

The fairy looked around frantically, lighting up every

corner with her glow. But all of the shadows behaved normally, twisting and shrugging and shrinking and growing with her movements. None were Peter's.

She flew out and glared at the dog.

Nana didn't respond, hearing something with her giant dog ears that even the pixie couldn't at first.

Something horrible was waking. Bones clicked into place as it stretched its feeble limbs . . .

And realized it was all alone.

"Yip! Yipyip yipyip yip!"

Tinker Bell froze. *Another* dog? Where were the humans? Where were Wendy and her two brothers? What was going on here?

She hadn't realized how much she had expected things to be exactly the same as before: three children in the nursery, Nana puttering about, furniture and toys askew. Everything had changed subtly and strangely like a spring after a bad winter, when plants came up where they hadn't before.

Fear began to sneak through her anger.

She jingled tentatively.

In answer, Nana just jerked her head toward the window. Peter's shadow—and Wendy—were somewhere behind the clouds. Beyond London.

Tinker Bell jingled a hesitant question.

"Woof."

Tink's facility with dog speak wasn't perfect.

So there was no way to be certain that Nana had said anything at all about *pirates*.

Right?

Without a second thought Tinker Bell took off as fast as she could, out of the house and into the clouds.

# Interlude: A Dog's View

Some readers might well be curious: was Nana upset at being left home from all these adventures—school, Never Land, doings with pirates and pixies?

No, she was a dog, with dog dreams. Few things made her happier than the stories in her own head when she was hunkered down in front of a warm fire with a full belly.

She *would* have appreciated some gratitude, however, for time well served. Perhaps a nice juicy steak on her birthday and Christmas—and maybe the occasional Tuesday as a welcome surprise.

# Unexpected Help

"I WILL NOT!"

Wendy sat with her arms crossed and legs primly together. Before her was a washtub full of hot salt water, suds, pirate clothes, and stink.

A half dozen half-naked pirates glowered around her, arms also crossed—though some were holding knives in their fists.

"But you're the mother of the ship now," one said—Screaming Byron, whose jacket she had patched. It was only the second or third day and she had already learned most of their names. "The washing's your responsibility."

"Absolutely *not*!" Wendy snapped, glaring at him so violently he almost fell backward. "I already take issue with the whole *idea* of being your mother, but being your *scullery maid* is entirely out of the question! Go find someone else to do your dirty work. My mother's beautiful hands never scrubbed a nasty pair of pirate unmentionables, and neither shall mine!"

The men looked at each other in surprise; apparently this was an idea new to them. Mothers always did the wash, didn't they? But perhaps they hadn't much experience with the type.

One leaned forward with his long knife and actually growled.

"Oh, cut me if you will, Ziggy," Wendy said, rolling her eyes. "*That's* proper behavior toward a mother. Let's ignore the fact that not a single one of you has presented me with a posy, or a badly done but affectionate drawing, or a pretty shell you found, or even a—" She had been about to say *kiss*, but thought better of it at the last moment. "Even the tiniest token of your appreciation. And after I sang you all that lullaby last night!"

The pirates looked, if not exactly chagrined, then at least a little thoughtful.

"We're new at this," the one with green teeth said: T. Jerome Newton. "Ain't never had a mother before. Don't know the rules."

Another—Djareth—cleared his throat. "Well, if you're

not ginna do the wash . . . then just . . . set a nice table tonight then. With folded napkins? Maybe?"

"We'll see," Wendy said levelly.

The pirates shuffled off, muttering, chastised.

Wendy collapsed. It had taken all of her will to remain indignant and cold. Their knives were actually absolutely terrifying, and the pirates' behavior was violent and insane.

"And here I am, *negotiating* with them," she said with a disgusted sigh, kicking the washtub. "They've made me their slave, and I'm telling them I won't do the very worst of the work."

She sighed and picked up the finished clean clothes, folding them. These she dropped into a basket, trying to remember which thing belonged to which pirate so she could place each on the proper hammock and they wouldn't just tear into the pile, throwing things all over the place as was their usual custom.

What a mess.

She had escaped her boring, dismal life in London only to enter an even more dismal one in Never Land! Where were the wishes? Where were the palm trees? Where were the adventures on savage shores?

What to do?

She could see one terrible possible future: one in which she remained with the pirates and became a little hard like them, praising some and castigating others, wrapping them all around her finger until they did her bidding like good little boys. Maybe even to the point of rebelling against their father.

Er, Hook.

There was of course a far more immediate and pressing concern than her eventual career aboard the *Jolly Roger*: the fate of Never Land itself. Hook had definitely implied its—and Peter's—destruction at his hand. Somehow she didn't believe that "rather permanent" meant the decision of never docking on its shores again.

Despite some sly questioning of the newly friendly crew, Wendy received no answers about Hook's plans: the pirates didn't know, nor did they care. They were sick of Never Land and eager to get on with their privateering on other seas. That was all they cared about.

(Which of course begged the question: *What* other seas? She'd never really thought about the rest of this world, beyond the island where Peter and the Lost Boys lived.)

And somehow her handing Peter's shadow to Hook helped him with his plot.

She had to escape, to find help—to find Peter Pan. There was nothing else for it.

But how?

As she carried the basket of clothes toward the hatch

that led belowdecks to the crew's quarters, Hook swooshed by her, all ruffles and coat and double cigars in their fancy golden holder.

"How goes it this morning with you, Mother?" he asked, a sly smile on his face.

Wendy felt a twist of violence in her stomach. It had been bad enough when John and Michael joked about how rarely they saw their own mother and how Wendy had taken her place. It was of course worse when these murderous hooligans called her Mother. But there was something specifically, especially nasty about Hook's use of the word. The way a quarrelsome old husband might say it to his old wife. Not that there was anything *untoward* about it; the captain wasn't at all suggesting anything inappropriate in their relationship.

It was just . . . wrong.

"This morning is going most terribly, Captain Hook. I will organize, fold, and mend the crew's clean clothes. But I will *not* do the washing. I have my limits," she said firmly.

"Ohh, whatever. We can have that done ashore if we must," he said, rolling his eyes as if she were silly for even mentioning it.

"And how are *you* doing this morning?" Wendy asked coldly. "Or, shall I ask, *what* are you doing?"

"Just the usual captainy, piratey things," he said,

whirling his hand in the air. "Trying to figure out the proper route to take . . . with a little spectral help. . . . And then we shall set sail."

Wendy didn't like the sound of that at all. "A little *spectral* help? Do you mean Peter Pan's shadow? What are you doing with it?"

"Miss Darling." He leaned forward and grinned eerily into her face. "If you were so worried about its fate, perhaps you shouldn't have traded it away in a deal with the devil?"

And with that, he spun and strode off, obviously pleased with his answer.

Wendy felt what remaining energy she had drain out through her feet, slide along the planks, and spill overboard.

She sank to the deck, resting her head on the pile of clean clothes, and began to weep.

What had she *done*?

She *knew* it was wrong. She knew it. No good would ever come of trading Pan's shadow. Any arrangement made with Hook and his pirates could never end happily. She had known that in her heart, and still she had done it, desperate to escape to Never Land.

And now it seemed like all of Never Land was going to pay for her rash decision.

"Pirate's life got ye down, love?"

Wendy looked up, wiping her tears. Standing there in a

swaybacked, repugnantly self-assured slouch was Zane.

"I thought I was coming here to have adventures," she said disgustedly, wiping her tears. "Not to be a *slave* to *pirates* for the rest of my life while Never Land is utterly destroyed. I have to get out of here."

"Ah, so many of us look for adventure and wind up as slaves, one way or another," the pirate said philosophically. "When you're young, you think the world will make room for who you are and what you want. . . . And then you find the world of adults is even more limiting than the world of children. With no room for adventure, much less yer own thoughts."

Wendy regarded the pirate curiously. This was the most thoughtful, intelligent thing she had heard on the ship so far.

He laughed quietly at the look on her face. "I'll get ye out," he promised.

"Really?" Wendy asked, surprised out of her usual politeness. "But . . . why?"

"Because some of us always have to escape, to hide in plain sight, to fight with the world to get the adventure we deserve. Ye'd think a pirate would be the freest person in the world, wouldn't you? But even here there are other people's rules to follow. And men don't like what's different—at least not at first, now do they?"

"No, I suppose not," Wendy said thoughtfully. She

wasn't entirely sure what he was driving at. Maybe he didn't want to be a pirate? Maybe he wanted to be something else altogether. What if she and the boys, just by imagining it, had cast him in the roll of buccaneer forever? What if he wanted to be a shepherd, or even a banker? The poignancy of his words struck her heart.

"I might be trapped in the part I play . . . and maybe it's *because* o' that, but I can't stand to see others what are constrained against their will, too. And maybe it'll be a good deed what goes against my own litany of skullduggery.

"But enough o' ruminatin'. The captain's involved in that shadow nonsense and the crew is getting restless. He's promised we're soon back to our villainous ways, so when the tide turns on the morrow we'll be off—or there'll be mutiny, mark my words. You'll have to get out tonight, just before dawn."

"I can't swim," Wendy said, looking doubtfully at the water below. "At least, not very well."

"There's a one-man dinghy for repairs and whatnot I'll toss over the side. But you'll have to slide down the rope to it, and I don't think I could spare more'n one paddle without raising suspicion. If you care enough about your freedom, you'll figure out how to use it right."

"I feel like that is some sort of metaphor you could apply to your own life, sir."

The pirate laughed again, and not at all like a villain.

"Just make sure you're up before the Southern Cross fades from view, and meet me stern side."

"Not that I am not greatly appreciative of all of this," Wendy said politely, "but what is to keep Hook from turning around to look for me? Even if I manage to figure out how to row with one paddle, I daresay it's unlikely I could be on the beach outrunning a crew of angry pirates bereft of their . . . mother."

Zane gave a thin smile. "Oh, don't you worry about that, love. I'll just say, 'What's that? Anyone hear the tickings of a clock?' And Hook will have us speeding out of here like that old dead croc is on his pants. Or he'll *say* it's the croc—but between you and me, I think it's just the sound of time passing that puts the fear of the devil into him. I think he knows somewhere in that musty head of his that his old companion is long gone.

"Anyway, our beloved captain is mostly engaged in other pursuits. You're a pretty thing, and useful, but a thin detail in the calamitous fable of our captain's life. He's after bigger prey."

"Bigger prey?"

"Ain't it obvious? His using the shadow to somehow find and get Peter Pan. Thought we were *done* with that nonsense years ago," Zane said, sighing.

"But what about his first mate, Mr. Smee? It sounds like he's very loyal to Captain Hook. Won't he see through your ruse and try to persuade Hook to chase me?"

At this the pirate just laughed and kept laughing, wandering away and slapping his knee. It wasn't pleasant laughter, and despite the rescue she was being offered, it left Wendy uneasy.

To stay up, she tried a trick she'd read about in a book: she drank several pints of (tar-scented) water just before bedtime.

(This was hard to keep from the pirates, who drank nothing before bed besides their grog ration and whatever flasks they had hidden.)

The crew had made her a private "bedroom" belowdecks among the ship's stores, and to their credit, they hung there a very nice hammock and covered it with whatever they had that passed for cushions. Hook even contributed a tiny fringed velvet pillow that looked more like a jellyfish than something fit for a bed. Wendy contemplated it now, wondering what hapless ship or manor it had been looted from.

She drifted off, almost pleasantly, in the gently rocking hammock.

It didn't seem like any time had passed at all when her eyes snapped open to utter darkness. The terrible, disturbing noises of a ship full of sleeping pirates came from the berths above her: snoring, tossing, turning, talking or whining in their sleep . . . as well as other far more unmentionable noises.

Wendy tipped out of her hammock as quietly as she could, wincing at the creaks from the newly knotted ropes. Then she strapped on her leather satchel (now full of strange bits and bobs and pirate treasures) and climbed the ladder.

The pirate noises reached a crescendo as she pulled herself up onto the gun deck right behind their quarters. Her mind whirled through all the possible scenarios of being caught. She expected a hand to clamp down on her shoulder at any moment, her flight discovered. Although she tiptoed, it was probably unnecessary: the ship rattled and groaned like a haunted mansion as it rode the little nighttime waves. The planks she walked didn't squeak at all.

Shaking and trembling she finally made it out to the main deck, where a great gulp of fresh air and an upside-down bowl of stars were a welcome relief. She studied the sky and finally managed to locate the Southern Cross, which was already fading in the false dawn. *Funny that Never Land skies should be so similar to the real world's,* Wendy thought. Not *London's* skies, of course, for rare was the night that one could see stars through the fog. And that particular constellation was of course absent from northern heavens.

The mizzenmast rose like a great sentinel. She cast a wary eye up to the crow's nest, but it was empty; perhaps the most dreadful pirates on the seas of Never Land didn't need to post a lookout for Royal Navy ships or potential foes. Still, the cockiness (or laziness) of it irked her sense of propriety.

She edged up to the rail and looked down. Directly below her was the balcony that hung off the captain's quarters. While it wouldn't have surprised her at all to see the nearly inhuman Captain Hook awake and smoking his infernal cigars, pondering whatever insanity it was that kept him going, the balcony was blessedly empty.

Far, far below that was the black sea, little white tips of its baby waves playing in the starlight.

"Quietly done, young miss," came a voice from behind her.

She spun around. It was just Zane, but now he was shaking his head.

"That is, I *was* impressed with your sneaking, until it were obvious you had no idea I was here. You'll never survive Never Land if you're not on your guard."

"Survive *Never Land*?" Wendy whispered indignantly. "It's a place of fantasy and imagination. I *lived* Never Land growing up. It is mine as much as yours."

"And how well do you know yourself then, I wonder,"

the pirate said softly. "Anyhow, look." He pulled back a tarp that was lying on the deck, unnoticed amongst the dregs and bits aboard a pirate vessel. A *very tiny* dinghy was revealed. It was more like the coracles children played with at the seaside than a proper boat.

Wendy sucked in her breath but didn't say anything.

The pirate picked up the boat and gave it a surprising throw: it arced out almost like a fishing line before dropping to the water with a very minute splash. It could have been a large fish leaping from the water. Angelic blue phosphorescence dazzled for a moment in a ring around the boat before fading.

"Down you go, lassie," Zane said, pointing to another rope tied to the railing.

Wendy looked at the old frayed-looking rope and the sea far below.

But she was an English girl. She squared her shoulders, took a deep breath, and saluted the pirate.

"Thank you, sir. I shall endeavor to repay your kindness someday."

"Nobody salutes on a pirate ship," he said with disgust. "We're all equals here, except for the captain. More than anywhere else in the world, I might add. You should think about that some, missy. Off you go, then."

He hoisted her up over the railing, making sure her hands were tight around the rope.

Then he let go.

Aside from antics in the nursery and some games when she had gone to school, Wendy's physical activity had been limited to bracing constitutionals around the park. *Fast walks*, in other words. Barring a few morning stretches, her arm strength was delimited by chores.

She was terrified.

But she closed her eyes, wrapped her feet around the rope, and . . . slid.

What it must have looked like from a distance! A tiny, pale girl slipping down a thin rope from a galleon that floated silently on the midnight sea. Her light blue dress ballooned around her like a paper lantern lit from underneath, yet it was not without a certain amount of grace that she made her way to the icy waters below.

Zane had fished the dinghy as close to the ship as possible, so only half of Wendy's skirts got wet as she awkwardly transferred to the tiny boat. The equally tiny paddle was hooked in just under the hull as neat as a child's play set.

She waved once to the figure on the ship high above her; whether he waved back or was even still there at all was impossible to tell against the blackness of the sky.

Wendy gritted her teeth, settled herself on her knees, and began to row.

This was the point where, if she were telling the story to Michael and John, she would say something like this:

*"And so the hero struggled, arms growing weak, a glittering sheen of cold perspiration covering her brow. She felt faint. In the east, rosy-fingered dawn was just brushing the sky, but all else was black: the black vault of heavens above her, the black sea around her, the black distant shore, the thousand slimy things that lived in the murky waters below and occasionally brushed the boat with their black fins.*

*"Countless hours passed.*

*"It was all she could do to keep her eyes fixed on the shore and her strength at the paddle. The terror of being captured and the need to escape drove her through the harrowing gauntlet of exhaustion and fear. Wearily—but triumphantly—she passed through to the other side. Though the task seemed endless, nevertheless she persisted."*

But the real Wendy was growing weak and utterly fatigued. The whole thing seemed less heroic and more like a scene from some farce: she was paddling a prop boat, comedically dipping her oar on one side and then the other, frantic and ceaseless, making no headway along the silken scrim.

Above where the sun would eventually rise, a few decorative clouds swept tentatively past: sleek, long, thin, and dark purple, unlike London clouds. The air itself was somehow lightening, glowing a sort of pale green.

Was time finally passing? Was she actually making headway?

At first Wendy thought she was hallucinating, delirious with exhaustion. But the shoreline *did* seem a little closer. When she let herself turn around once or twice in fear, straining her neck, the pirate ship, too, seemed a little farther away.

After a time, Wendy looked down and saw that the sea was only a couple of feet deep and as clear as drinking water. Despite a thousand different ingrained rules telling her *no* (don't get your feet wet, you will catch cold; don't ruin your skirts in the salt water; don't get your clothes wet *also* because they will become see-through), our hero was fed up with the boat. She slipped her boots off and tied their laces around her neck. She carefully undid her stockings and did the same with these. Then, holding up her skirts, she stepped out into the water.

It wasn't cold at all.

She felt like an idiot standing there in such a lovely current, skirts raised like some sort of fainting milksop from a terrible operetta. So she let them drop and strode to shore, pushing against the water. Little fish she couldn't quite see scooted out of her path.

The sun pushed its way through the purple clouds and its light grew on the beach strangely and organically, starting out weak and white and then ripening strong and yellow. Wendy cast a final glance back. The ship and she—the only two tall things in an endless flat plain of water and shore—seemed to regard each other in wonder. Then she turned from it and stepped onto land. The dry rattle of coconut palms swaying in the distance filled the air when the sound of the ocean began to recede.

Wendy had arrived in Never Land.

# Never Land

The beach sand was crunchy and perfectly golden, like—well, like in a winter Londoner's wildest imagination. Wendy walked inland watching her feet, her toes curling and spreading into the sensual granules. Halfway to where the shore met the jungle was a perfectly picturesque shipwreck. She clambered up it, holding on to the helpfully curvy trunk of a palm tree for balance. With a hand to her forehead, Wendy surveyed her new kingdom.

She was perched at what was obviously the edge of a cove, Pegleg Point just to the south and west of her. Despite its scurrilous reputation the place looked downright pleasant. Tiny waves of sparkling aquamarine lapped at the edges and were probably delightful to splash in. Out of sight to the northeast lay Mermaid Lagoon. Off the shore beyond that would be the nefarious Skull Rock, riddled with caves where pirates hid their loot.

Emptying into the cove was Crocodile Creek, a wide, sparkling rivulet whose source was somewhere in the Black Dragon Mountains (Michael had named them). These were a wild range in the center of the island that grew bleaker and spikier to the northern, or Hyperborean, shore (John had named that). While the closer peaks were green and clear, the farther ones were gray and shrouded in mist and mystery.

And if one followed Crocodile Creek toward these mountains, through the Pernicious Forest and Quiescent Jungle (both John's touch), one eventually came to the Hangman's Tree, hideout for the Lost Boys. But in the very northwesternmost part of the island, there was . . .

There was . . .

Wendy frowned.

She couldn't remember—or she had never described it, or had never dreamed it. Or maybe she had, and then she had forgotten it? There was *something* there, but it was like it was wiped from her memory completely.

Or maybe the reverse—maybe it was unimagined yet. And therefore unexplored.

The sun was a brilliant lemon yellow, the sky a bracing

blue. The sea wind whipped Wendy's hair into an obliging jig.

Her adventure was beginning! Her quest to find Peter Pan and save Never Land!

But, truth be told, *while* she was living the adventure, it didn't feel like one. It felt horrible. Not at all like the stories she made up. Never Land wasn't supposed to be actually dangerous. Never Land wasn't supposed to have murderous grown-ups in it. Pirates shooting each other seemed awfully funny in the context of a bedtime tale, but the blood on the deck had been thick and ugly and she could still hear the way his head had hit the planks. Pirates attacking ladies had never been part of *her* story.

And neither was laundry.

"And that poor pirate," she whispered. "Zane. What was his story? I didn't make it up. . . . What did he mean he was trapped?"

Never Land was not as simple—or as innocent—as it had seemed. Wendy would have to stay on her toes whilst there. But everything *looked* just as bright and sunny and perfect as ever. Her shadow was as black and strong against the sand as a child's drawing, and . . .

Wait, was the shadow crossing her arms?

Wendy looked at her own arms, which were first at her sides, and then snapped to her chest in surprise.

Her shadow still kept her arms crossed. And was now shaking her head as if to chastise.

Then she flexed her hand and curled it into a menacing hook. Shadow puppets without the puppets.

There was no doubt at all what she was trying to say: she was upset with what Wendy had done, selling Peter's shadow. Of course shadow–Wendy was worried about shadow–Peter Pan. Here she was simply free to express it.

"He didn't *want* his shadow," Wendy muttered to herself—and her shadow—for the thousandth time.

She still didn't believe it.

Wendy took a deep breath and straightened her shoulders. Whatever, it was done. She had already dealt with some of the results of her actions and would now see to righting the additional wrongs she had created as a result. She would go find Peter.

She would save Never Land.

And if he was angry with her for what she had done—well, she would deal with it and accept it as fair punishment for her actions.

She hopped off the shipwreck and wandered toward the greenery at the edge of the cove. Trying not to notice or hope that her shadow was coming along and behaving, trying to keep her eyes on the jungle ahead.

A strange structure untangled itself out of the background like a hallucination, not part of the natural landscape.

It was a funny-shaped, almost spherical, green podlike thing woven from living branches of trees and vines. A trellis of flowers hung down over the opening that served as a door.

Wendy was so delighted tears sprang to her eyes.

It was her Imaginary House!

They all had them. Michael wanted his to be like a ship with views of the sea. John had wanted to live like a nomad on the steppes. And Wendy . . . Wendy had wanted something that was part of the natural world itself.

She tentatively stepped forward, almost swooning at the heavy scent of the door flowers. Languorously lighting on them were a few scissorflies, silver and almost perfectly translucent in the glittery sunlight. Their sharp wings made little snickety noises as they fluttered off.

Her shadow made a few half-hearted attempts to drag back, pointing to the jungle. But Wendy ignored her, stepping into the hut.

She was immediately knocked over by a mad, barking thing that leapt at her from the darkness of the shelter.

"Luna!" Wendy cried in joy.

The wolf pup, which she had rescued in one of her earliest stories, stood triumphantly on her chest, drooling very visceral, very stinky dog spit onto her face.

"Oh, Luna! You're *real*!" Wendy hugged the gray-and-white pup as tightly as she could, and it didn't let out a single protest yelp.

Although . . .

"You're a bit bigger than I imagined," Wendy said thoughtfully, sitting up. "I thought you were a puppy."

Indeed, the wolf was approaching *formidable* size, although she was obviously not yet quite full-grown and still had large puppy paws. She was at least four stone and her coat was thick and fluffy. Yet she pranced back and forth like a child, not circling with the sly lope Wendy imagined adult wolves used.

"*You're* not a stupid little lapdog, are you?" Wendy whispered, nuzzling her face into the wolf's fur. Luna chuffed happily and gave her a big wet sloppy lick across the cheek. "Let's see what's inside the house!"

As the cool interior embraced her, she felt a strange shudder of relief and . . . *welcome* was the only way she could describe it. She was home.

The interior was small and cozy; plaited sweet-smelling rush mats softened the floor. The rounded walls made shelves difficult, so macramé ropes hung from the ceiling, cradling halved logs or flat stones that displayed pretty pebbles, several beautiful eggs, and what looked like a teacup made from a coconut. A lantern assembled from translucent pearly shells sat atop a real cherry writing desk, intricately carved and entirely out of place with the rest of the interior.

Wendy picked up one of the pretty pebbles in wonder,

turning it this way and that before putting it into her pocket.

"This is . . . me . . ." she breathed. She had never been there before, but it felt so secure and so right that it couldn't have been anything *but* her home. Her real home. Here there was no slight tension of her back as she waited for footsteps to intrude, for reality to wake her from her dreams; there was nothing here to remind her of previous days, sad *or* happy ones. There were no windows looking out at the gray world of London. There was just peace, and the scent of the mats, and the quiet droning of insects and waves outside.

"Never Land is a . . . mishmash of us. Of me," she said slowly. "It's what we imagine and dream of—including the dreams we can't quite remember."

What an odd thought. "Zane was right. It *is* an island that knows me better than I know myself."

She could easily envision herself falling asleep on the scented mats—adventuring was exhausting work—but she went back outside instead. Luna leapt beside her.

In the bright sunlight her shadow reappeared, jumping and waving her arms and trying to pull herself away from Wendy again.

"We *are* going after Peter Pan. I promise. We'll certainly need him against Hook and whatever he has planned. But I really don't know where to even begin looking for him! I suppose we'll just start. In *that* direction." And with that, she strode resolutely ahead, Luna leaping beside her.

(If she had snuck a look, she might have seen her shadow wag her head back and forth as if making fun of her, then snap back to aping her mistress's movements—if a little slower and more reluctantly than they were actually performed.)

Large-leafed plants at the edge of the jungle reflected the sun rather than soaking it up, their dark green surfaces sparkling white in the sunlight. Some of the smaller ones had *literally* low-hanging fruit, like jewels from a fairy tale. Behind them was an extremely inviting path into the jungle with giant white shells for stepping-stones. And rather than the muggy, disease-filled forests of books that seemed to kill so many explorers, here the air was cool and pleasant and not too moist—although Wendy could hear the distant tinkle of water splashing from a height.

"Oh! Is that the Tonal Springs? Or Diamond Falls?" Wendy wondered breathlessly. "Luna, let's go see!"

She made herself *not* race ahead down the path, but moved at a leisurely, measured pace. Like an adventuress sure of herself but wary of her surroundings.

(And yet, as she wouldn't realize until later, she hadn't thought to grab her stockings or shoes. Those got left in her hut without even a simple goodbye.)

Everywhere she looked, Wendy found another wonder

of Never Land, from the slow camosnails to the gently nodding heads of the fritillary lilies. She smiled, imagining John as he peered over his glasses and the snail faded away into the background in fear—or Michael getting his nose covered in honey-scented lily pollen as he enthusiastically sniffed the pretty flowers.

The path continued, winding around a boulder into a delightful little clearing, sandy but padded here and there with tuffets of emerald green grass and clumps of purple orchids. It was like a desert island version of a perfect English meadow.

"Oh, Luna, isn't it beautiful? Let's go see!"

With the loud *snap* of a horse rider's crop a white vine whipped out across the path at her ankles.

"Oh!" she cried, stumbling forward.

But she didn't fall; another vine shot out across her chest. She bounced jarringly into and then off it. This one, too, was ugly and poisonous white—but also slightly sticky. Her dress got caught and so did her throat, already bruised from the impact.

Another vine whipped behind her so she couldn't fall backward. Couldn't escape.

"What the deuce!" she cried, pulling at the vines. They were tough but stretchy and gave rather than broke under her hands.

More of them—slowly now, like they had all the time in the world—coiled around her wrists and ankles. Their viscous sap itched and burned where she struggled, and it was an unhealthy scarlet color.

*"No grown-ups allowed."*

Out of the clearing stepped the speaker of these words, a strange little fellow indeed. He was short and fat and as clear and crystalline as a blob of molten glass. His head was a misshapen oval on top of his body. A peaked crystal hat sat on his head, and he held a sharp shard of a spear. The only color on him at all was his eyes, strange and tan, like two butterscotch candies pressed into the face of a snowman.

"What?" Wendy asked indignantly, trying to understand the harsh words from the otherwise almost adorable figurine.

*"No grown-ups allowed."*

He turned to face her, but not like a normal person; more like a cross between an owl and some sort of hideous, broken toy. His body didn't move. Instead, his *head* spun smoothly and slowly and farther than it should have until his pupilless eyes locked on hers.

Probably. It was hard to tell what he was looking at.

"I am not a grown-up!" Wendy sputtered. "Let me through!"

*"You are sixteen,"* the guard said tonelessly. *"The time of parties and balls and weddings and husbands has commenced."*

"It has *not* commenced," Wendy said with great dignity. "I'm here in Never Land, aren't I?"

The creature's button eyes didn't move at all but somehow darkened.

*"You should not be here in Never Land.* No grown-ups in Never Land. *No fun killers! No bringers of pain and boredom! GET OUT!"*

Wendy blinked at the ferocity of the ridiculous, strangely terrifying little thing. It leaned forward, bringing the tip of its spear perilously close to her stomach.

Where on earth had it come from? She had never invented any such monster. True, adults *didn't* figure in her stories of Never Land except as incidental characters—pirates and their ilk, villains and foils. Never Land was supposed to be an island of endless fun for children like her and Michael and John, but she had never said anything specifically about prohibiting grown-ups or threatening them with spears.

*"You make the days long. You make the food terrible. You make us go to* school!*"*

Wendy caught her breath in shock, recognizing the tirade. *Michael.* Michael had horrifyingly once told his own father that he hated him—actually hated him—for making him go to school, where the seats were hard and the lessons worse. And for forcing him to eat their mashed peas.

Also, now that she thought about it, the shape of the little creature wasn't unlike something Michael had made out of mud once. *Puppin*, he'd called it.

Yes, this whole scenario felt a bit like Michael, now that she thought about it. A crazed, all-powerful Michael.

"Now, you listen to me—" Wendy began in her best adult voice, as if she were speaking to Michael.

Bad choice.

*"NO MORE LISTENING!"* the thing screeched madly, pushing itself as high and far into Wendy's face as it could. *"YOU GO AWAY NOW. FOREVER. TO FOREVER PLACE!"*

It reached back its arm to hurl the little spear—

But Luna had had enough.

She threw herself at the horrid thing. Her claws made little *tinging* noises as they scraped harmlessly against the crystalline surface. Her teeth slipped from the creature's neck, unable to get a good hold or sink into real flesh.

While the creature was distracted by this Wendy took the opportunity to try to free herself. She rocked back and forth as hard as she could against the vines, pushing her arms and legs out as far as they would go. The tendrils gave just enough for her to be able to slip her right hand out. She immediately reached into her pocket and grabbed the stone she had taken from her hut. Summoning as much *boy-chucking-rocks-in-a-fountain* as she could, Wendy hurled it full-force at the creature's bulbous crystalline stomach.

There was a very satisfying *crack.*

As soon as the tip of the rock hit its "skin," giant ragged cracks appeared from the impact point. These rapidly winnowed out through the rest of its body, growing like Jack Frost on a windowpane—but much, much faster.

The thing's mouth hung open and it dropped its spear. As the fractures spread it waved its arms back and forth helplessly, like a puppet or a windup toy.

When the cracks reached its head and became so numerous that its body was almost opaque, the thing exploded.

Its glittering bits hurled themselves every which way through the dappled sunlight in a beautiful wave of *tinkles* and *pings* one might expect to hear from baby angels playing harps.

Wendy flinched and covered her face. Where a shard hit her skin it immediately melted, running down to the ground with little droplets of her own blood.

"Well," she said uncertainly.

Luna jumped back and forth over the thing's rapidly disappearing body, barking last warnings and triumph.

"Goodness," Wendy added.

She let herself experience one more moment of shock,

then forced herself to focus and work at pulling away the vines. They were unpleasant to touch (and sticky and itchy) but actually not that hard to wrestle out of now that she had one hand free and no distractions. In fact they were strangely like a pair of her mother's hose the three children had once gotten into *massive* amounts of trouble for using to tie up Michael when he was "kidnapped by pirates." Same color, even.

"Hmm . . ." Wendy said thoughtfully.

Then, a little nervously: "I suppose that's the last of them?"

Luna barked, and it *sounded* like an affirmative response, but Wendy couldn't be certain.

"I think it was really going to kill me," Wendy murmured, putting her hand out. The wolf immediately came over and leaned against her friend, sensing her need. "Isn't it funny . . ."

There were a lot of thoughts in Wendy's head, and none of them were actually funny at all. They weren't even clear or formed thoughts; just a mishmash of feelings, misgivings, and the unnamed, fetal beginnings of ideas. Not a situation she was used to: possessing a quiet mess of genesis with no articulation. No pronouncements, aphorisms, or decisions came readily to her tongue.

"Isn't it funny," she tried again. "I thought Captain

Hook would be the only real villain here. I mean, the only one I would bump into, because of the shadow. And here I have run into a villain I didn't even know existed . . . one my brother invented as some sort of protector or savior. It's not really clear what that thing was, is it? But all of *my* stories were perfectly clear and straightforward."

She looked around at the trees and the foliage, the sky and the ground. Things she had brushed by in quick descriptive phrases to the boys—*desert island, tropical plants, venomous but beautiful insects*—were solid in more detail than she could ever imagine, down to the tiny veins on the leaves. Apparently Never Land got "worked on" when she wasn't even talking to the boys . . . they imagined things on their own. Or at least Michael did. To a little child, the idea of *No Grown-Ups Allowed,* to the point of the death, might seem reasonable. Funny, even.

Time passed for the three siblings in London . . . but it didn't in Never Land. Michael's whims and fancies remained the same here while he grew up in London. And these whims seen through older eyes were not harmless. They were diabolical.

"Never Land isn't just a simple place of childhood dreams—because childhood dreams are actually never simple. Oh, I do wish I could write that down in my little notebook."

Her face suddenly constricted into a cartoonish expression of terror as she recalled a younger John, furious at the Shesbow twin who had tweaked his cheek and giggled at his hat and glasses. "Girls shouldn't be allowed to talk at *all*," he had growled at her. "To boys, anyhow."

How had the rest of the conversation gone? Had he made an exception for his sister? Had Wendy laughed and remonstrated him?

More to the point, was there some sort of horrible punishment zone for girls in Never Land devised by the fiendishly clever—but undeveloped—mind of a preadolescent John?

Luna was watching with giant unblinking yellow eyes as Wendy worked out all these things, far more patient than anyone Wendy had ever known.

"We must be on our guard," she said, kissing the wolf on her nose. "This place is tricky. Far trickier than I ever dreamed. The dangers I *expect* are not the only dangers. Who knows what other horrors my little brothers dreamed up? Then again, if Never Land were as simple as my own childish fantasies, it would be no fun at all. Toffee trees and mazes easily solvable by a simple application of *left left right left*. Where's the challenge in that? I *am* sixteen now, whether or not I am an adult. I should expect more!"

Wendy dusted off her dress. The sun had moved slightly

in the sky; ideas and creatures might be eternal in Never Land, but still night came. *Time* still existed. Decisions had to be made. Luna pranced back and forth in front of her, yellow eyes gleaming with excitement. Ready to go.

But where to?

The Mermaid Lagoon. Obviously.

Peter Pan often visited the mermaids in her stories. Maybe she would find him there, or get help from the friendly locals. But also . . .

*Mermaids!*

And they would be *very* helpful in a maritime war waged against apocalyptic pirates.

And maybe along the way Wendy could look for fairies. They were powerful little denizens of Never Land, weren't they? Surely they could use some magic or something against Hook.

(Plus: *fairies!*)

And . . . what about the Lost Boys, by Hangman's Tree? Maybe she should find them first. They would know where Peter was. And they would be terribly useful—how many stories she had written about their battles with the pirates! And how lovely it would be to have a visit, too. All of those clever things Wendy had invented for them, like the slides down to the hideout from hollow trees . . . How marvelous to see it in person, to understand how Never Land had worked out the details. Maybe Peter would even be there already!

She gulped a little at the thought.

Or . . . maybe the Lost Boys later.

Really, the best thing was to round up an army to defend Never Land, wasn't it? She could find Peter and apologize to him—and bring him up to speed on Hook's nefarious plot—later.

"Yes, mermaids first. And then maybe fairies. I wonder where we should go to find them?"

And her question was answered, in true Never Land fashion, as a fairy dove headfirst into Wendy's chest.

# Meanwhile, on the High Seas…

Captain Hook paced back and forth in his cabin predatorily—but not at all like a wolf. More like a military commander with a motive and possibly a bad back. The angry movements and swishing clothes made the captain's quarters seem even tighter than they already were; he filled the space with his plumes, red jacket, and frustration. There was room for nothing else besides his rage. When he was interrupted—rarely—the interrupting pirate stayed outside, unable or unwilling to come in.

"*Talk*, bloody *talk*, and this will all be over!" Hook swore at his prisoner. "Just tell me where Peter Pan is. Once I have him you can go!"

Pan's shadow writhed and shrank before the captain, but didn't answer.

Its lower body was cinched tight with a silken cord, only a little string of shadow sticking out the bottom of the knots—possibly its toe. The rest puffed up and out like a dark genie out of a bottle, though its arms were also stretched and tied. It squirmed and distended itself pitifully in an attempt to get free.

All of the usual sorts of torture had little effect on the thing: discarded implements were strewn around the floor as testament to their uselessness. Knives, pincers, hot brands, tacks through the nails, fingernails drawn across slate boards. He even had a drunk Smee play the concertina, but the terrible music had no effect on the shadow at all.

(It did, however, make the captain want to put his own ears out with his hook.)

The shadow had *some* presence in the real world; otherwise the cord wouldn't have held at all. But the rules that governed it were tricky and, well, Hook wasn't the most logical and thorough practitioner of the scientific method. He grew frustrated often and tantrums came quick.

The captain stewed, rage boiling up quietly behind his eyes and face again.

And then, in the silence of this latest lull, a quiet ticking began. Distant and weak.

Hook's prodigious brows shot up to the top of his forehead.

He dashed out of the cabin, throwing papers and chairs aside, and ran to the railing—nearly knocking a pirate overboard along the way.

*Tick.*

*Tick.*

*Tick.*

He started to let out a sigh of relief. Just some of the rigging snapping against a mast, or . . .

*Tock.*

What passed for Hook's heart almost stopped, clenched in an invisible icy fist.

He staggered away from the railing, hands over his ears so he couldn't hear it anymore.

*Tick.*

*Tock.*

*Tick.*

*Tock.*

"No, no no no no no! Not *now*! It was all coming together!" he cried, rushing up and down the deck in a panic. "I was practically *handed* Peter's shadow. And once I used it to get Peter, I could blow everything the boy loves to smithereens—while he watched! It's the greatest revenge ever planned by any villain *ever*! And I was almost *there*!"

He ran back to the comforting darkness of his cabin and threw the door violently shut behind him.

*"WE ARE RUNNING OUT OF TIME HERE!"* he screeched at the shadow. "*I* am running out of time! Can you hear that? It's the vile croc, come for me! So talk, blast you!"

"Maybe it *can't* talk," Smee suggested from the corner of the room, where he had waited quietly until the captain's fit had passed.

"Of course it can't talk," Hook swore, raising his eyebrows at his first mate's predictable stupidity. "It's a *shadow*. But it could make a sign, or write something. . . . I *gave* it the bloody slate, before I made those dismal noises! It didn't even bother to try."

"Maybe it can't write. Maybe Peter Pan can't write. Can he read?" Smee asked curiously. "Never seen the lad with a book or nothin' . . ."

"Why, that's . . ." Hook paused, thinking. "Actually, that's a very good point, Mr. Smee. The *sadly ignorant* Peter Pan probably can't even write his own name—uneducated lout."

"So maybe he's not worth your time," Mr. Smee hazarded. "Such a useless, adventurous, young, enthusiastic . . . er, I mean *utterly uneducated* boy. A right simpleton. Not much of a nemesis, right? Maybe you should just forget about him, like the crew's been suggesting. Forget about all of Never Land. Just put it behind you. Let's go out and find us a merchant vessel or pillage a seaside town. Right now. Like in the good old days."

*"I won't let Peter get away! I won't let him escape me this time!"*

"But Cap'n. It's a never-ending chase," Mr. Smee pointed out as gently as a mother consoling a child chasing his own shadow. "Oh, sometimes it seems like you get the best of him, but he always gets the best of you in the end, and then he slips away. Maybe it's time to . . . let it go, like? Move on? Wrap up that part of your life and enjoy what's enjoyable now? The sea, the sun, the blood of your enemies . . ."

"But . . . but I *want* him," Hook whispered, lips trembling. "He always gets away from me and it's *not fair*. He took my *hand*. He took the best of me."

"Nawww," Mr. Smee said, patting him on the back. "Not the best of you. Your hook is so useful, ain't it? And shiny. He didn't take nothing away. He gave you a deadly weapon, and a boatload of memories, and a souvenir. Let the lad go. You're the bigger man. You're the only actual *man*, as it were. So maybe it's time you—"

*"WHERE IS PETER?"* Hook roared suddenly, whirling on the shadow, leveling an accusing hook at it.

The thing flung itself backward in fear but did nothing else.

It didn't even shrug, which one would assume even an ignorant, badly behaved, etiquetteless shadow of an uncivilized simpleton could resort to.

Hook's eyes narrowed.

"Maybe you don't know *exactly* where he is. But you have some idea. You're part of him. You even act like him. There is some sort of ley line or force that connects the two of you. If I set you free, you might even fly off yourself, in search of him, lonely in your bodiless state."

The thing bobbed quickly and wretchedly up and down. It tipped its head toward the small porthole window. *Let me go,* it was obviously pleading.

*"AHA!"* Hook said triumphantly. "You *do* have some idea. The direction at least. Now that the two of you are both back in Never Land, you can somehow sense where he is. You couldn't when you were trapped in London."

"Almost like a compass," Mr. Smee said whimsically, chuckling from deep within his large belly. "Always pointing north, in a manner o' speakin'."

"Always pointing—what?" Hook blinked. "Almost like a compass, you say?"

He rubbed his chin thoughtfully.

"Now *that*, Mr. Smee, is an interesting idea. . . ."

# Pernicious Pixies

Wendy stumbled backward. She wasn't hit hard enough to fall down, but the tiny points of the fairy's—feet? Fingers? Head? *Stinger?*—jabbed her right in the middle of her rib cage, knocking the wind out of her. It would probably leave a nasty bruise.

She warily regarded her attacker. The fairy—again, Wendy assumed—was an angry tinkling ball of light with the prettiest girl imaginable inside. Diminutive but . . . *solid,* with a scandalous lack of decorous dress. All she wore was a ragged green shift which barely covered her hips and thighs and breasts and was gathered dangerously over only one shoulder. This was both shocking and delightful; it made the tiny creature resemble statues of ancient nymphs and nereids Wendy had seen. Her hair was even done up in classical style, a goddess-like bun of hair so golden it glowed. Tiny pointed ears curved their way through the few dangling tresses. Her eyes were enormous and not even remotely human: they were far apart and glaring.

The crowning glory was, of course, a pair of delicate iridescent wings sprouting from her back. Their shape was somewhere between butterfly and dragonfly. They were clear as glass and thin as onion skin.

The fairy chimed and jingled angrily, shedding little sparkles of golden light that danced for a bit in the air before drifting down to the ground and fading. Wendy couldn't tell where the girl's lovely tinkling sound was coming from, exactly. At first she thought it was bells on the tiny shoes but close inspection revealed nothing. The chimes, like the dust, seemed to come from her very essence.

"Oh my, I'm so sorry," Wendy breathed, apologizing for her . . . standing? Being? In the way of the beautiful little thing? "Are you all right?"

The tinkling grew more insistent. The fairy bobbed up and down in the air and balled her tiny hands into fists.

She aimed herself at Wendy's chest again and struck her.

Prepared as she was for it this time, the pain was no worse than a bumblebee accidentally knocking into her and then buzzing drowsily off into the sunlight.

"Whatever is the matter?" Wendy asked patiently. "Have I done something wrong? Will you tell me?"

Luna barked once, forefeet planted firmly and defensively.

The fairy suddenly dipped down to the ground. The light emanating from her dimmed.

"What is it?"

The fairy stamped on the dirt and pointed at it.

"Am I trampling your flower?" Wendy asked, stepping back carefully and examining the prints where she had just stood. There were no crushed petals there, just some grass and sand. No dead insects, either.

The fairy gritted her teeth in frustration and flew back up to Wendy. She grabbed a lock of her hair and yanked, hoisting it over her shoulder like the heaviest rope on a ship.

"Ow! Hey! What is it? You merely have to tell me!" Wendy cried, stumbling farther into the clearing, trying to free her hair from the pixie's grasp.

Apparently satisfied, the creature released her grip and dove back down to the ground . . . and walked. Slowly and carefully out over the ground, along . . .

"My shadow," Wendy said slowly.

A sinking feeling came over her.

Her shadow crossed her arms knowingly.

"Not *my* shadow, of course," Wendy said, biting her lip. "Peter Pan's shadow."

The fairy nodded twice, slowly and solidly—no misinterpretation possible.

Wendy sighed. The time of reckoning had come far sooner than she expected. She had hoped for a *little* more time in Never Land before her choices caught up with her. How did this fairy even know about it, really? Wendy thought she would only have to apologize to Peter. Not anyone else.

(Of course she also rather hoped that the imminent doom of Never Land would overshadow any mistakes or transgressions on her part.)

"I don't have it. Anymore."

The fairy's eyes widened. She started to move, uncertainly—perhaps to pull Wendy's hair again, perhaps to shrug: *Why?* Perhaps to make motions to get a fuller explanation . . . but Wendy's guilty conscience was way ahead of her.

"I traded it to Captain Hook in return for my passage here," she said calmly.

Her shadow did a sarcastic little curtsy, as if to say, *Thank you. Now we're getting somewhere.*

The seconds stretched out to infinity as Wendy watched the fairy register what she had said. She could feel the tropical sun on her back, feel the breeze from the sea lift the little hairs off her forehead, smell Luna's clean but doggy fur scent as she waited for a reaction.

When the fairy's eyes had widened further than it seemed possible, she dove at Wendy again.

Here and there and everywhere at once—pinching, pulling, yanking hair, biting.

Wendy covered her face and flung herself around the clearing, trying to get away from the creature without hurting her. It was like being attacked by an angry swarm of bees or a dozen fairies at once.

"Oh! Stop! Please!"

Luna leapt up and bit at the air, snapping and growling and trying to grab the annoying flying thing that was hurting her friend.

As she slapped madly at the air around her, Wendy prayed that neither one of them actually injured the fairy.

Finally Luna's muzzle smacked the creature hard on her tiny behind, and she went tumbling head over feet, straight into a tree. She slid down it, landing in a heap among the roots.

"Oh no, are you all right?" Wendy cried, immediately running over despite the myriad pinches and tiny cuts she had suffered from the attack. She knelt down and cradled the stunned fairy carefully in her hands. The fairy sat up, swaying woozily. Then she leaned over and sank her teeth into Wendy's thumb.

"Now stop that this instant," Wendy said sternly, gripping her a little more tightly around the middle. "Let us try discussing this like adul—ah, like civilized people. I take it you are a friend of Peter's?"

For yet again, this creature—this particular fairy—wasn't one she had invented in her Never Land tales. And she didn't imagine her brothers could have come up with anything like her.

The tiny girl pouted and frowned and crossed her arms sullenly. It was so adorable Wendy had to work very hard not to giggle.

"Well, I'm very sorry about what I did. I'm not proud of it. I messed up," she admitted. "But look here. Your friend Peter *left* his shadow in my bedroom. Ages ago. Four years, in fact."

The fairy blinked at this. Wendy couldn't be sure how intelligent the fairy was; she took quite a bit of time to process this new information, and with surprise.

"Yes! Four years I've kept it safe, free from dust, awaiting Peter's return. Of course, I had every intention of giving it back! I'm not a thief. But he . . . never returned."

The fairy looked uncomfortable. Her eyes darted to the side and she squirmed a little in Wendy's palm.

"For years I waited for him," Wendy continued, trying not to sound *too* sorrowful. She was in the wrong, after all. "Every night I told stories about him, watched the night sky for him. . . . Then they moved me out of the nursery.

Michael and John went to school. I was left all by myself, alone and waiting. And still he never came.

"I grew a bit despondent, I suppose. The boys didn't want to hear my stories anymore. If it wasn't for the shadow I would have begun to think I had imagined every last moment of Never Land. Life was just so dreary and dreich. . . . And then my parents bought me this stupid dog. . . . Not you, Luna," she added before the wolf could even react. Luna wagged her tail happily. "And *then* they decided to send me away to Ireland. *Ireland!* They only want to see me settled down with some nice boy with a nice job at a nice office somewhere, or as a spinster governess in some remote location, and I don't want either of those things. Not yet, anyway."

Despite her anger, the fairy made a questioning tinkle that wasn't too hard to interpret.

"Well, I don't know *what* I really want. I want to see Never Land, obviously," Wendy answered, indicating the world around them. She opened her fingers, loosening her grip on the fairy. "I want adventures. I want . . . I don't know, other things. Certainly not to do laundry aboard a pirate ship for the rest of my life.

"Yes, I'm ashamed of what I did. It was a bad deed. But Peter can't have missed his shadow much, since he never came to get it."

The fairy tinkled angrily at her, rising up off her palm and clenching her tiny hands once again into tiny adorable fists.

"All right, look, before you start again, two things. One, I'm perfectly willing to make amends for what I did," Wendy said, squaring her shoulders. "Whatever it takes. Right now."

Her shadow stood up straight upon hearing this, intrigued.

The fairy frowned at her suspiciously.

"I'm absolutely serious. Also, number two, and potentially far more importantly: either as a result of my actions or alongside of them, Never Land is in trouble. Captain Hook seems like he means to destroy the whole island. We need to stop him—*and* find Peter. He and his shadow are involved somehow. And I will do whatever it takes to accomplish both things."

She meant it. She conjured up images in her head of all sorts of brave Englishmen and realized she couldn't think of a single face. But the idea of dying at sword point or being forced to walk the plank in a dramatic rescue attempt was somehow still easier to swallow than an eternity of serving aboard a pirate ship as a nanny and scullery maid.

The fairy narrowed her eyes, obviously reevaluating the human.

Then she nodded. Once.

Not enthusiastically.

"Shall we go then?" Wendy asked primly. "Last I saw, the pirates were headed north, or what would have been north in England. Up the coast. We need to get some help to stop them, I should think. More of you fairies, perhaps? And mermaids might be helpful. Or we could arrange some sort of boat, one with cannons, I expect, and a willing crew—"

The fairy stamped her foot angrily—then lowered herself back down onto Wendy's hand so the big human girl could actually feel it. She shook her head. She pointed into the jungle.

"I'm sorry, I don't . . ."

The fairy snarled in frustration. Then she made a big show of miming the act of looking for something or someone, hand shielding her eyes from the sun, peering into the distance. She pretended to find the thing and marched very dramatically toward it. She had a whole conversation with this thing, which was now obviously a person, took him by the hand, and pretended to fly off.

Then she and he either battled a small army together or succumbed to St. Vitus's dance; it was hard to tell which.

"Oh—you want to find Peter Pan *first*?" Wendy said, suddenly realizing what it all meant. "Find him and bring him along to get his shadow back from the pirates?"

The fairy nodded excitedly, and for a heartbreaking second looked absolutely delighted that Wendy understood.

"But I don't know how much time Never Land has! And do you even know where he is?"

The fairy shrugged and looked exasperated, throwing her arms out to indicate all of Never Land. Wendy wondered, from the way the fairy was acting, if the two friends had ever been separated before this happened.

In spite of her determination to save their world, Wendy was ashamed to admit her first reaction was *No, let's* not *go find Peter first*—only because then she would have to tell her hero straight off that she had sold his shadow to his enemy. It was one thing to admit wrongdoing to a random fairy, but to the person you've slighted himself—well, that took a different kind of courage. "Perhaps he isn't so useful right now, without his shadow?" she ventured.

The fairy frowned and pointed again.

"But perhaps we should drum up some other help against the pirates first?"

The fairy crossed her arms and closed her eyes haughtily, shaking her head.

"Oh, please," Wendy said. "Even *with* Peter Pan, the two of us can't take on an entire pirate crew. In all my stories about Peter Pan he fights Captain Hook man to man, not against *all* of them."

The fairy turned her head away and sniffed.

Wendy rubbed her head. She hadn't had a lot of experience cajoling people—beyond her father, at least—much less an irrational little creature like this. The thing wouldn't listen to logic or reason.

But of course, she was a fairy. Why *would* she put up with terribly human ideas like logic and reason?

Wendy thought about her mother's gentle arguments with shopkeepers when the Darling account came up a bit short.

"Well, how about this," she said, using her best *reasonable* voice. "Let's do go fetch Peter. But perhaps we should *start* with the Lost Boys? He's always with his crew. So he might be there, or they might know where he is. And if he's *not* there, we can see if they're interested in joining us for our big run-in with the pirates. All right?"

The fairy pouted and looked suspicious, as if she thought Wendy were trying to trick her somehow. But she couldn't find anything obviously wrong with what had been suggested, so she nodded. Reluctantly.

"All right then, let's—"

And the fairy took off like a shot, a golden bauble that zipped high into the air and disappeared.

"All right," Wendy repeated, uncertainly, watching it go.

"I can't fly," she added after another moment.

The clearing was silent except for the chirping of a single insect. It regarded Wendy through what looked like a very tiny pair of spectacles.

"I'll just walk then, I guess." She adjusted her dress and looked at Luna. "Shall we? I think . . . I think the Hangman's Tree is due north of us, and a bit east. We may need to bushwhack. A pity I don't have a machete or some such . . ."

Just as Wendy set foot into the shady, vaguely threatening undergrowth, there came a distant tinkling sound. The bauble of golden light tore back through the sky and stopped suddenly in front of her like a confused meteor. It hovered up and down angrily. Within the glow, the fairy tapped her foot and pointed to the sky.

"I can't fly," Wendy said politely. "I will have to meet you there. It will take me rather longer than you, I should expect."

The fairy looked like she was going to explode in frustration. Her face turned red and her tiny hands became grasping, strained claws. Her shoulders rose up around her neck.

"Ah . . . sorry?"

With a strangled cry, the fairy flew at her. Wendy threw her hands up over her face for protection.

Nothing happened.

When no pinches or bites occurred, she hesitantly lowered her arms.

The fairy was flying in loops and swirls around her, shedding fairy dust as she went. Throwing it at Wendy.

Delighted, the human girl raised her arms up to fully experience what was happening. Delicate golden sparkles floated down and kissed her skin. Where they touched, Wendy felt *lighter*. Tiny pains she hadn't even realized she felt entirely disappeared, and any weariness vanished. She felt rested, energetic, eager, and—*airy*.

"Oh! Fairy dust! Will this help me fly?"

The little fairy crossed her arms and nodded. She looked over Wendy with an appraising eye, perhaps seeing if she had done a good enough job. Then she nodded again, satisfied, and buzzed off into the sky.

Wendy raised her arms. She felt like the wind itself!

Nothing happened.

"All right," she said. "Here I go!"

Did the ends of her hair lift a little, or was that just the breeze?

Sparkles continued to twinkle on her arms for a bit before settling into her skin. She worried: Was there a time limit? Did the magic fade if not used properly?

And with that worry, she felt the earth solidly under her heels again, her full weight bearing down on the soil.

"Oh, oh oh oh," she cried, panicking. "Don't do that, don't think bad thoughts. I don't think the fairy dust likes that. It won't work if I think bad thoughts."

She then had to stop herself from worrying about not flying *because* of worrying and bad thoughts. It made her head a little crazy.

The fairy hovered a good twenty feet up with her arms crossed and an impatient, bored look on her face.

"Sorry," Wendy called as brightly as she could. "Never done this before! Doing my best here!"

The fairy rolled her eyes. Wendy winced. Nothing she did or said seemed to endear her to the pretty little thing at all. She wished she could do something *right*, immediately, the first time.

The fairy dove down and grabbed Wendy's left thumb with both her hands and pulled. Wendy caught her breath, delighted by the tiny, warm touch.

Luna barked. She didn't at all like the unfriendly creature coming too close to her mistress.

Wendy was torn, not wanting to upset the fairy—but not wanting to upset her wolf, either.

"Oh, it's all right, girl," Wendy said, putting her other hand out for Luna. "She's just trying to help."

The wolf pushed her nose into Wendy's palm, licking it and forcing the hand up over her head to encourage scratching behind her ears. Wendy felt a rush of warmth and affection for this friend she only knew from dreams, who loved her so fiercely and unconditionally.

She felt herself lighten.

The fairy also must have felt it somehow, because at that exact same moment she tugged, beating her little wings, trying to fly backward and drag the girl *up*.

Wendy rose onto her toes.

Luna barked again, less worried and more perplexed.

"*Oh!* It's working!" Wendy cried.

In that moment, all of Never Land became everything she had always imagined it would be. She could do anything. The sky was blue, the future full of infinite good.

The fairy still held her hand, obviously trying to keep a skeptical, annoyed look on her face. But her lips moved in a strange duck-billed twist, as if she was working very hard to keep them frowning. Her whole face had lightened, the scowling darkness removed like a storm whisked away by a whimsical and beneficent god. When she impatiently rolled her eyes and twirled her fingers, it wasn't with anger this time; it was encouraging: *Come on, come on! More of that!*

"But . . . more of *what*?" Wendy asked, distracted by the feeling of weightlessness, Luna, and her own thoughts.

The fairy tapped her head then pointed at the human girl and shrugged dramatically.

"What? What was I thinking? Is that what you—yes, it was. Well, I was thinking about flying—no, I was thinking about Luna, actually. What a good girl she is and how wonderful it is that she loves me. . . ."

Wendy's toes left the ground entirely.

"Oh! Oh! It's happy thoughts! I see it now! They make you fly!" she cried, clapping her hands.

And with that, she slipped the surly bonds of the earth and rose slowly, twirling into the sky. The fairy kept one tiny hand on hers, steadying her ascent.

Trees and bushes below her waved in the mild tropical breeze like undersea plants. Wendy wasn't as terrified of the height as she had thought she might be. The change in perspective was a little thrilling, a little startling, but that was all. It was like she merely had nothing to do with the ground anymore.

Luna barked.

"Oh, Luna, I'm all right, I—"

The fairy let go.

Wendy suddenly listed to the left. It was as if the fairy were the only thing anchoring her to the sky. She thrashed wildly, making flailing swimming motions that did little to help. The earth rolled sickeningly below, looming close.

The fairy immediately grabbed her again.

Wendy felt everything . . . *stabilize.* The lightness on

both sides of her evened out and she bobbed steadily again, feeling somehow supported by the air around her.

The fairy waited a moment and gave her a look—*All right? Are you ready?*

Wendy swallowed and nodded.

The fairy—slowly—withdrew her tiny hand, drawing it across Wendy's skin until just a finger touched, and then nothing at all.

Wendy remained steady this time.

She laughed. Out loud, like she hadn't laughed in years—honest, billowing peals of pure joy. Her skirts swished and spread out. Gravity had no effect on her anymore—nothing tugged at her shoulders, feet, neck, mind, ears—she was weightless, untouchable.

Luna barked. But it was a bark of excitement this time, a *wow look at us and you and me and that's all great yes!* bark.

Seeing this, the fairy dipped down and started to sprinkle some dust on her—but the wolf ducked neatly out of the way. She pranced back and forth, her back bending and shimmering in the sunlight. She barked again politely. *No, thank you,* she was obviously saying. *I'll go my own way.*

The fairy shook her head—*Who wouldn't want to fly? Silly thing!*—then buzzed up to Wendy's nose and snapped her fingers imperiously.

"All right, yes, yes," Wendy said, too happy to take

offense. "I'm coming. Forgive me—I've only flown in my dreams before!"

The fairy rolled her eyes and took off toward the gray mountains. More slowly this time.

And Wendy, spreading her arms out to catch the wind, happily followed.

# The Lost Boys

Wendy followed the fairy as best she could without becoming distracted by the details of the landscape below. Some things looked *exactly* as she had imagined them (the savannas of Upper Hillsdale, for instance, and the multilevel pools of the Tonal Springs). But some things were subtly different and others entirely unrecognizable. Far to the northwest was the area she couldn't remember very well: in reality it turned out to be a peninsula shrouded in a heavy gray and viscous fog.

*Maybe it really is masked by the elements because it hasn't been described yet, or used in a story,* Wendy thought.

To the south of that was a strange, balding mound of a hill that was just crying out for an obvious name. Was it

John's invention? Or Michael's? Or . . . someone else's?

*And, wait a moment, what about those* someone elses? *Other children? Besides me and Michael and John?* Wendy suddenly wondered. Did they make up whole areas of the island in their own games? And was there any part of Never Land that was just—itself, not prone to the stories and imaginations of children? Was this fairy with her a *native*, as it were, or the result of some little girl's dream?

Maybe Wendy could get some answers once everything with Hook and the shadow was sorted.

Luna ran far below them, disappearing into the jungles here, reappearing on a trail there, keeping an eye on the two fliers and barking at their shadows.

(Wendy's shadow waved insouciantly at her as she rippled over the treetops and clearings.)

The fairy was already descending toward the center of the island, which wasn't really that big.

Despite the very obviously *non*-temperate flora near the beach, here the Pernicious Forest became solidly northern (if not quite Hyperborean). There were pines and oaks with their surprisingly familiar leaf shapes that spoke of cool, moist shadows below. But these grew alongside palms and vines and exotic flowers and the like, a mishmash of ideas. Spot in the middle of this mess was a scrubby clearing that was just short of terrifying and very long on *creepy*. A giant dead tree stood in the center. Its gnarled, broken-off branches and twigs were like bones grasping at the sky, as if the tree were still fighting its fate a hundred years after its death. What looked too regular to be vines turned out, of course, to be the frayed ends of ropes and nooses, all sizes and shapes. "For all sorts of necks, I suppose," Wendy said thoughtfully.

The grass and weeds around the tree had been trampled into dry brown dust by unknown activity. Standing like sentinels on the cardinal points just outside this circle were other gigantic trees, but these were very much alive. Almost too alive.

Wendy carefully and slowly lowered herself to the ground, wobbling a bit as she went. She was hoping for a perfect, graceful landing like a Russian ballerina *en* one *pointe* but had to settle for a mostly-on-two-flat-feet stumble. She bowed forward with momentum, managing to catch herself before completely tumbling over her own head.

The fairy had disappeared, presumably into the hidden hideout of the Lost Boys.

"Luna?" Wendy called. *"Luna!"*

An answering howl came from somewhere downhill and to the south: the wolf was on her way, but still far.

"All right, I'll see you in a bit!"

She made a barefoot circle of the clearing, the weight of

her dress now feeling strange as it swished against her legs, catching against the little hairs on her skin. She studied the living trees on the perimeter carefully and was quickly rewarded for her efforts: giant knots in their trunks had suspicious black cracks around them. Body-sized holes rose up from their roots with edges that seemed strangely smooth, as if they had been polished by constant use.

"They're not actually hidden that well, are they?" she mused. Anyone, not just clever Wendy, with an eye and a moment's thought could tell there was something off and a little too *frequented* about the area. Did the pirates really never find Peter Pan's hideout? Had they ever actually looked? It brought to mind the idea of when a child plays hide-and-go-seek with his mummy and tries not to giggle while posing behind something too small to adequately camouflage him. The family dog, for instance. Or a small ottoman.

Wendy shrugged and primly stepped through a door, feeling just a *tad* superior.

So she was more than a bit taken aback when the floor fell away mechanically below her and she tumbled, heels over head, down a hard and lumpy ramp.

She landed on an equally hard floor, a mess of dress, hair, and sash, legs splayed and vision spinning. But she could see enough to notice a *very* smug-looking fairy hovering in the air before her, arms crossed.

"Oh! I'm really here! This is Peter Pan's hideout! . . . And yours, too," Wendy added quickly just as the fairy began to frown.

The place was as delightful as she had imagined. The cave under the Hangman's Tree was perfectly dry and smelled mostly fresh—with only the very slight tang of dirty little boys. The ground was even, and, if not neatly swept, then at least covered with an assortment of skins and rugs. One particularly large sheepskin near the firepit had its soft and thick fleece turned upward, showing indentations where it was obviously slept on. Other beds were stashed willy-nilly around the cave: some nestled in hollows made in the walls themselves, some in the cradling arms of gigantic roots that stuck through the ceiling. Some were hammocks hanging from those same roots.

There were a few civilized details, like chairs that looked as though they had been purloined from more modern and elegant domiciles—a red velvet recliner, for instance, which would have been far more at home at Mr. Darling's club than in a cave. *Wherever did that come from?* Wendy wondered. But the rest of the furniture consisted primarily of things like barrels cut in half with moss for cushions, and the stumps of trees with hastily hammered-on backs. Enormous mushrooms made for tables. Some of the lanterns were fungus as well—softly glowing bluish-green "flowers" that spread in delicate clumps just below the ceiling.

"John would just have a field day with those, I'm certain," Wendy said with a smile.

One large barrel was placed under the end of a hollowed-out root to collect rainwater. There were shelves and nooks for the few possessions considered precious by the Lost Boys: piles of gold coins, interesting animal skeletons, shiny crystals, captivating burrs and seedpods. Also more strange detritus of the civilized world: a hinge, a pipe, a knob from a drawer, a spanner, and even a pocket watch.

"Oh, this is all . . . amazing! Not that it couldn't do with a bit of a woman's touch." A proper cauldron could be hung from a chain above the fire for soups and stews, for instance. The rugs could be beaten out a bit. Where was the washtub? And the out-of-place, ornate gold frame that cleverly delineated a window could have used a nice little chintz curtain to keep bright light and prying eyes out.

Oh, she could do so *much* with it! Imagine if it were hers, and all the Lost Boys, too; she would take care of them . . .

. . . like young pirates. . . .

Wendy struggled with that thought. In many of her stories about Never Land, she kept house for Peter and them much like Snow White for the dwarfs. And they revered her and promised to never leave her and always brought back the best little trinkets from their adventures. . . .

An inquisitive tinkling brought her out of her reverie.

"I don't know where they are," Wendy answered, thinking she had guessed the question. "But I'm sure they'll be back soon. . . ."

With an irritated swoop, the fairy grabbed one of her locks and pulled, flying to the far corner of the cave and forcing Wendy to stumble quickly after to avoid any pain.

"You don't have to—oh!"

The fairy let her go and pulled aside a piece of bright gold-and-pink silk hanging on the wall. Behind it was the fairy's own private room.

She had a soft bed of bright green moss with several iridescent feathers for a counterpane. A shelf mushroom served as an actual shelf displaying an assortment of dried flowers and pretty gewgaws the fairy had collected. There was a charming little dining table, somewhat bold in irony: It was the cheery but deadly red-and-white amanita. The wide top was set with an acorn cap bowl and jingle shell charger. In the corner, a beautifully curved, bright green leaf collected drops from somewhere in the celling much like the water barrel did, but this was obviously for discreet fairy bathing. An assortment of tiny buds, rough seeds, and spongy moss were arranged neatly on a piece of gray driftwood nearby to aid in cleansing.

"Oh my," Wendy sighed. "This is the most beautiful flat I have ever seen."

The fairy tried very hard not to look pleased.

"The accessories . . . the flowers . . . the *furniture*. It's all *perfect*."

Maybe the fairy didn't precisely blush, but she did allow a single grudging smile.

Wendy felt her heart leap. They were, despite the fairy's initial hatred, growing closer.

Maybe.

Suddenly the cave resounded with bumps and knocks and disturbing echoes from above. The furniture—fairy *and* full-sized—shook.

"What's that?" Wendy cried. "Are we being attacked?"

The fairy rolled her eyes, once again dismissive of her human companion.

As the first boy's body tumbled into view, Wendy understood: the Lost Boys were home.

They came flying down the tunnels' slides, landed neatly, and unfurled like ferns or strange creatures. These were the lads Peter had rescued from orphanages and the terrible fate of *growing up*. In her stories, Wendy always had them wearing the skins of animals.

And so they did, sort of. The first boy definitely had on a real bearskin, as real as the rug on the floor, and the animal's claws were worn over his hands like gloves. The next one, the tallest, had on the tail of a fox, but he also sported the bright red coat of a traveling salesperson and a red felt hat beaten into two peaks to resemble fox ears.

There was a set of twins with black gloves and black masks plastered directly onto their faces somehow. They also had fluffy striped tails affixed to their gray baggy overalls—which they wore *with no shirts on underneath.* Scandalous, like poor street ruffians. Wendy searched her mind for what animal they could possibly be and finally came up with *raccoon*, a creature from the Americas that was supposed to be terribly smart and devious but quite prim, habituated to washing its hands and food before dining.

The smallest Lost Boy was no more than a toddler. He also wore real fur, a beautiful black-and-white hide with a strangely pungent but not entirely unpleasant smell. Another New World creature: a skunk. They could spray their stink in acidic streams to deter predators. *Very useful defense for one so small and helpless,* Wendy found herself thinking.

Right in the middle of the group, neither the tallest nor the shortest, not the fattest or the skinniest, was an approximation of something that was not quite a rabbit. A long, *very* used dove-gray tailcoat had an equally long black tail with a white tip on the end. A leather headband that held back short brown hair sported two long, floppy gray ears.

"Oh! Hello!" Wendy said, clapping her hands together in delight at all of them.

They looked up at her with a little surprise, but not much more. A shadow hung over them and in their eyes.

"Who's this, Tinker Bell?" the tall fox asked.

The fairy flew down in between them and tinkled and jangled.

"A *Wendy*? What's a Wendy? Oh, *she* is. The Wendy. I get it."

While Wendy was pleased with this introduction, she felt a little slighted. She had loved fairies, always loved fairies. How come the Lost Boys could understand what the fairy said, and she couldn't? And they even knew her *name*!

"Pleased to meet you," Wendy said, very properly holding out her hand.

The fox looked at it.

"I'm Slightly," he said. He couldn't have been more than fifteen, but there was something in his eyes that seemed both older and younger. "I'm the leader when Peter's not around. This is Skipper." He gestured at the rabbit thing, who looked away. "And these are the twins."

The two raccoons bobbed their heads and grinned.

"How d'ya . . ."

". . . do?"

Wendy grinned, charmed by the way they acted in perfect unison.

"Cubby." The bear bowed and growled. He pointed at

the littlest one, standing next to him. "This is Tootles. He don't talk much. He's a baby—but, I mean, a *fierce* baby. Don't scrap with 'im."

The skunk had started to look annoyed and sulky, but then smiled broadly, easily lulled by quick-thought words of praise.

"How do you do," Wendy said, leaning forward to the little skunk. His smell was actually less offensive than what was coming off some of the other ones. She had to resist the urge to crinkle her nose or hide behind a scented glove (which she didn't have, anyway). Slightly seemed to be the only one who bathed at all. His dark skin was free from the permanent layer of grubbiness that covered the rest of them. As with the pirates, Wendy desperately wanted to scrub them with a nice boar-bristle brush, starting with the fierce baby.

Tootles melted under her attention, practically swooning.

"Whatcha doing here, The Wendy?" Cubby asked, displaying a set of teeth pocked by the occasional absent baby tooth.

"I'm here because . . . well . . ."

Any internal struggle she had about confessing her use of Peter's shadow and handing it over to the pirates was immediately cut short as Tinker Bell dove in, literally and figuratively, bouncing up and down and angrily shedding sparkles as she obviously told what she thought was a tale of betrayal and near-murder.

Slightly nodded and said, "Uh-huh," madly understanding everything the fairy jingled.

"Oh . . . so *that's* what happened to his shadow," was all he said when she finished. Then he collapsed contemplatively onto a giant mushroom chair that bowed a little under his weight.

Wendy tried to stave off her anxiety while waiting for his reaction, conclusion, or decision, by running her hands through Tootles's wispy hair.

Meanwhile, Skipper kept staring at *her*, unblinkingly, either in awe or disgust.

"But . . . wait . . ." Slightly finally said, frowning. "There's one part of your story I dinna get, Tink. His shadow was in London the *whole time* and he never thought to look there?"

The fairy began to sway back and forth in the air, her face twisting like a child's between contrived innocence and a brow furrowed in deep thought as she desperately tried to come up with a better answer.

"Oh, Tink," Slightly said, shaking his head. "Did you *keep* him from going back? Were you *jealous* of The Wendy?"

"It's just Wendy," Wendy corrected, unable to stop

herself even as she processed this new information. She looked at the fairy in shock. That pretty thing had been *jealous*? Of *Wendy*? A plain, boring London girl living with her brothers in a nursery, inventing tales of a world more wonderful than their own? Tinker Bell had Peter Pan himself! All Wendy had were stories and his shadow. And the *fairy* was jealous?

"But . . . why?" Slightly pressed, echoing Wendy's thoughts precisely.

The fairy looked taken aback by this honest question.

Then she stuck her tongue out at Wendy, put her hands on her hips, and turned away, fluttering her wings provokingly and buzzing. Skipper shook his head in acute disgust.

"She says it was stupid the way he always made her go to London and sit outside your window," Slightly translated. "And then forced her to listen to *you,* The Ugly Wendy, tell long and boring stories about *her* friend."

"Oh dear," Wendy said, unable to think of anything else.

"That's Tink," the fox boy said with a sigh. "No one gets between her and Peter."

"But I wasn't, I didn't, I couldn't even . . ."

"Aw, don't worry about it. She'll come around," Cubby said, rolling his eyes. *"Girls."*

"Oh, there is so much I must make up for in Never Land, and I haven't been here a day!" Wendy cried. "Starting with you Lost Boys. Slightly, I am deeply sorry for what I have done. Trading in Peter Pan's shadow for passage to Never Land was a base, cowardly thing to do."

"What?" Slightly—and all the other Lost Boys—looked at her in surprise. "Why are you sorry? Wasn't no other way you could get here. Grown-ups ain't allowed. Pretty clever, really. Besides . . . *pirates*, you know? Hook was the one that tricked you. They're the bad guys. They're always scheming to get Peter."

"So you forgive me?" Wendy asked timidly.

"I guess it's Peter's got to do that. You should, um, probably talk to him," Slightly said, but he seemed uncomfortable saying it. He looked over at Skipper, who looked away.

"What? What's going on?" Wendy demanded. "Something is going on. You're not telling me."

"It ain't nothing," Skipper murmured.

"It's just that no one's really talked to Peter . . ."

". . . since he lost his shadow," the twins said.

"He's been real ornery. Gotten way worse lately," Cubby said, rolling his eyes. "No fun at all. Him and Slightly been going at it."

"Going at it?" Wendy asked in shock. "You've been fighting with Peter Pan? Your leader?"

"Peter said it was time for Slightly to get out of Never Land . . ."

". . . because he was growing up," the twins said quietly.

The rest of the Lost Boys looked embarrassed. Like it was something they would rather die than reveal to an outsider.

Slightly frowned and worked his jaw, rapping his fingers on the table in nervous anger.

"Aye. He did. He said I was growing up and there weren't no place for me here anymore."

"But—that's unheard of! No one gets kicked out of the Lost Boys! *Why?* Why did he say that? Was it anything you did at all?"

The fox boy shifted in his chair and then suddenly leapt up, going to look out the window. "I was just getting sick of it . . . you know? I been here the longest. Done it all. 'Go hunting.' 'Talk to the mermaids.' 'Battle the pirates.' 'Raid the L'cki.' 'Get raided by the L'cki.' 'Tease the Cyclops.' It's always the same things."

"He begun to *miss* things," Cubby whispered, like it was too awful to mention aloud. "He thinks he can remember his mother."

"He misses *beds* . . ."

". . . and hard things . . ."

". . . and nurses . . ."

". . . and being indoors all the time!" the twins said in disgust.

"I don't ever," Slightly swore, spinning around. "I don't want any of *those* things. I just . . . I want different things. New things. Aright, and maybe a bed. So what's wrong with that? I just had some ideas about things we could do and Peter just . . . Peter just . . . *laughed* at them."

"*You* look like a mother," Tootles ventured, tugging on Wendy's skirt. The Lost Boys looked at him in surprise.

"Oh, why, thank you, darling," Wendy said, scooping him up—reminding herself to wash her hands thoroughly as soon as she had a chance. The skunk boy snuggled into her soft chest. "So . . . because of this, he threatened to throw you out?"

"Peter don't like change," Slightly said, scowling. "Anything different—unless it's a newer, better game that *he* thought up—is growing up. And bad. So *I'm* bad. And I'm growing up. So I have to go."

"And do all of you agree?" Wendy asked, shifting Tootles onto her hip so she could turn and look each one of the Lost Boys in the eye.

None of them met that look.

"No," Skipper finally said, eyes to the ground.

"We love Slightly," Tootles murmured.

"He's all we got when Peter's not around," Cubby said.

"He's a good . . ."

". . . leader," the twins said.

"Well, I don't suppose it's entirely up to Peter, then, is it?" Wendy said. "Is he the *king* of Never Land?"

"No! No one is!" Slightly swore. "That's the whole point, right? No growing up and no rules and whatever you want and fun all the time. If you *want* fun," he added thoughtfully. "I don't always want fun. And don't freedom mean you get to do what you want, at least sometimes?"

"Absolutely correct. Well, all right then. You will stay if you so desire," Wendy said, carefully putting Tootles back down. "That's sorted. No one is the boss of you here."

"That's it?" Cubby asked, surprised.

Wendy nodded. "Why not? It's Never Land. Do as thou wilt—isn't that the whole of the law here?"

"Huh," Skipper said thoughtfully.

"I don't think it's quite that simple," Slightly said. "At least not between Peter and me."

"Well, I don't think there's much I can do there. The two of you will need to work things out on your own. Just as I need to apologize to him myself. Tinker Bell and I are actually here trying to find Peter and help him get his shadow back. Which may ameliorate his mood a bit, and tone down the tension in your little tête-à-tête."

"Ameliorate . . . ? Tet-a-*what*? You memorize a dictionary or somethin'?" Slightly scoffed, waving his hand at her. "Aw, who would *want* to go back to London?"

"Who indeed," Wendy said dryly. "But listen: besides having Peter's shadow, Hook also has something terrible up his sleeve for all of Never Land. Deadly, and *rather permanent*, as he said."

"What? Like destroying all of Never Land?" Skipper asked.

Tinker Bell nodded.

"But why?" Slightly demanded.

"I have some theories," Wendy said, "but I think it's mostly because he's mad. Anyway, we need to stop him, and I don't think we could defeat the pirates on our own, just the three of us, me and Tinker Bell and Peter. Even with Peter reunited with his shadow. Can we count on you?"

The fairy rolled her eyes and turned her head away with a sniff.

"Aye, of course," Slightly said, sticking out his chin. "Whatever my beef with Peter is, a man needs his shadow. O' *course* we'll go with him to get the pirates and save Never Land!"

"That's the spirit, Slightly!" Cubby cried.

"We'll show those stupid pirates . . ."

". . . and that *stupid*, stupid Captain Hook!" the twins crowed.

"Wonderful," Wendy said warmly. Everything was coming together! She had met the Lost Boys, rallied them to her cause, and now they would come with her, and of course the fairy—*Tinker Bell*—couldn't object. It would be like trying to resist a cheery force of nature, a good-willed waterfall, once they decided to come along. "So where do you think Peter is?"

"Sometimes when he's down he goes to Mermaid Lagoon," Cubby said, rolling his eyes. "Talks with the fishgirls."

"Aye, I'd try there first," Slightly said, nodding.

Wendy tried to quell the quick thumping of her heart. *Mermaids!* First she got to see her fairy—who admittedly was much more hostile than she had imagined, but Wendy was working on that—and now *mermaids*! With glittering scales and flowing hair! Everything was turning out so wonderfully.

"All right then, lead the way!" she cried.

"Ah . . . well . . . you go on ahead," Slightly suggested. "We'll just wait until you bring him up to speed. Once you tell him about what you did, and where his shadow is, and give him some time to . . . you know . . . *react* to that."

"He might be very angry," Cubby said, nodding.

"Or very happy," one of the twins said.

"*Too* very happy," the other one added.

"He might fly off and go by hisself," Skipper mumbled.

"Or fly off the handle—right at you, or Tink. Or Slightly, even."

The fox boy nodded. "I don't know *how* he'll take all this news. You tell him, let him work it out for a bit. I don't want him taking nothing out on me because he ain't got his head on straight. He's sore enough as it is."

"But together we can convince him, or argue with him. And be ready to immediately go get the pirates!" Wendy said desperately. "Power in numbers!"

"'Do as thou wilt,'" Slightly quoted back at her. "We wiln't. Not until Peter's all right with all of this and all of us."

"'All of this' sounds like a terrible idea," Wendy said forlornly.

But the little fairy smiled, looking more than a touch smug.

# The Lost Girls

Luna chose that moment to burst onto the scene.

She had found one of the "secret" doors to the hideout almost immediately and scrambled down—much more elegantly than Wendy. She barked happily, pleased with her entrance and audience.

"Wow! A wolf!" Cubby said in awe.

"He's so fierce!" Skipper sighed.

"*She's* mine," Wendy said proudly, going over to pet her. "And I'm hers."

"That's incredible. She's beautiful," Slightly said, a little jealous but more impressed.

As she ran her hands over the wolf's coat, Wendy saw with dismay it was covered in burrs and mud. Luna panted—a little laboriously—and leaned extra hard against her human friend. It was obvious she was exhausted. Still part puppy, she was too young to realize when she had worn herself out.

Honestly, Wendy was feeling a little done in as well. Flying was hard work. And so was being kidnapped by pirates.

"Poor girl! Well, if we *must* go on alone," she said (a little peevishly; she couldn't help it), "I think we will require a bit of rest and refreshment here first."

The fairy looked outraged and put her hands on her hips. She made a very obvious walking motion with two of her fingers, then pointed to the door. *No. We have to keep going.*

"I'm sorry, *you* might be used to spending most of your day on wing," Wendy said politely, "but while it's glorious sport, like something out of a dream, well, *unlike* a dream, it's a bit exhausting. Like all sports, really. And Luna had to run here on foot. She's had it."

The fairy frowned at Luna and then tossed her head. Like she was saying, *Fine, all right, but only for your wolf. Not for you.*

"You heard her, boys! It's teatime!" Slightly cried.

In a sort of reverse of Snow White's story, the boys ran around gathering what provisions they could like dwarfs desperately making everything nice for their lady guest. The twins quickly filled a basket with berries and fruit. Cubby found a big bowl of nuts. Slightly blew embers into a lovely little fire and put the kettle on (where they had gotten the kettle, a highly decorated affair of blue and gold enamel, was a mystery). Tootles somehow managed to carry and set out a stack of mismatched cups: wood, bone china, and coconut shell. Skipper brought out a pot of golden comb honey.

While this happy chaos was happening, Wendy took the opportunity to approach the fairy alone, in a—very slightly—quieter part of the hideout.

"Tinker Bell?" she ventured. "So that is your name?"

The fairy looked at her in surprise—then grudgingly nodded her head.

"Did you . . . Did you really keep Peter from going to London . . . on purpose?"

Tinker Bell looked away, but she didn't disagree.

Wendy was torn. More than anything she wanted this beautiful little fairy to be her friend, to like her back, to initiate her into the secret world of flowers and fey folk. But she had to know the truth.

"Did you really do it because you were . . . jealous of me?"

Tinker Bell crossed her arms and scowled at her. She jingled something disdainful.

"Of . . . *me*?" Wendy repeated, indicating her torn

dress, her size, her brown hair, her overall very un-fairylike plainness.

Tinker Bell nodded, a little less certainly.

"Well, I think that's very flattering. Perhaps even the highest compliment I've ever been paid—no matter how backhanded. I thank you."

The fairy rolled her eyes. Wendy sighed. She sat down heavily on a barrel.

"If we are being completely honest here, and I feel we should be since we are companions in this strange adventure, then I should tell you straight: I *do* like Peter Pan. I used to worship him, in fact. I used to dream about him, too. I suppose if he had actually come to me, I might have . . . well, who knows. He's all I ever cared about, really, besides Mother and Father and Michael and John and Nana, of course."

Tinker Bell had an *aha!* look on her face, and waggled an accusing finger at the human girl.

"But I never even saw him while I was awake, Tinker Bell," Wendy pointed out. "These thoughts of him were just that—all in my imagination. I am very sorry it upset you to come and listen to my stories. But I was never even aware that you and Peter were there. You have had such amazing, *real* adventures with him here in Never Land. All I ever had was his shadow."

Tinker Bell blinked. It was obviously an entirely new idea for her.

"It was a very naughty thing you did to Peter out of jealousy, Tinker Bell. Preventing him from getting his own shadow . . . And what *I* did was naughty, too, trading that shadow to his enemy to come here. Far more naughty, really. Especially since it seems to have resulted in putting all of Never Land in danger. We *both* have a lot to answer for. Apologies and reparations to make. Together."

The fairy looked outraged at this suggestion of any similarity between them. But then she recovered herself, crossing her arms again. *Go on,* she seemed to say.

"And look, here we are, talking about Peter while he isn't even here at all! In person, or in shadow form!" Wendy said with a laugh. "Is he really the king of Never Land, after all? Invading our conversations and making everything about himself even when he's not present? Hook can't stop talking about him, the Lost Boys are depressed about him, you are constantly jealous around him, and I—well, I sold him out when I couldn't have him. It's ridiculous, really, the effect he has on all our lives.

"Tinker Bell!"

The fairy jumped at the sudden, direct address: Wendy was looking at her sternly, full of purpose, shoulders back and jaw firm.

"You and I must resolve not to discuss him any longer, at least until everything else is settled and we have properly saved Never Land. Surely the two of us have other things we could talk about that don't involve a boy. Other things that warrant our attention. Pirates, flying, the job of getting this shadow back, beating Captain Hook. The adventures *we* have. Our lives. The life of a fairy. The life of a plain human girl. That should be more than enough for many hours of solid conversation. So enough talk about him for now. Are we agreed?"

The fairy looked at her as if it were a weird thing to ask.

And Wendy supposed it was a *bit* odd. Wasn't Peter the very reason they were thrown together in the first place?

But then, as the thought *really* wound its way through her mind, the fairy relaxed. She shook her head from side to side, as if sloshing the idea around and physically measuring it.

Finally, she nodded. She put out her tiny hand.

Wendy grinned, thrilled to have made some headway with the fairy at last.

She very carefully took the tiny hand between her own index finger and thumb and gave it a gentle but solid shake.

"Excellent. This should make our task that much easier, as well as our working together."

Tinker Bell narrowed her eyes at that—maybe the

idea of actively *working together* with the human girl, or at least expressing it out loud, was still a bit much. But she didn't jingle or otherwise comment. Whatever their feelings toward each other or Peter were, they had a job to do.

The tea was filling but strange. Wendy could have done with some proper sandwiches, pastries, or crackers. And she had to sneak the questionable day-old rabbit meat to Luna, who snapped it up discreetly and happily. But she appreciatively drank the strange reddish-brown decoction of leaves and twigs the Lost Boys swore was just like proper tea if you didn't think about it too much. And in truth, it wasn't bad; it just wasn't East India Company Darjeeling. It had a warm, almost cinnamony taste.

Luna had a big bowl of fresh, cold water, and Tootles insisted on having his tea the same way, on the floor. After that and several stale biscuits, plus a little rest (and more tummy rubs than any puppy could really ask for from a hideout full of instantly devoted fans), it was finally time to leave.

Outside the air was as fresh and bracing as Never Land air ever was. A *great* day for flying.

But while the two girls were getting ready to say their goodbyes, Wendy noticed that Skipper kept looking at her strangely—almost in fascination.

"Is there something wrong?" Wendy asked, of course immediately needing to fix whatever problem there was.

"Nuthin'," Skipper said, turning away so she couldn't see his face.

Wendy wasn't the girl at parties who caused boys to blush. But she had seen it happen with others, like at the spring dance when John was caught off guard by a hello from Alice Cotswaldington. He had turned red, turned away, and choked into his punch.

This wasn't that. Skipper didn't seem to be *blushing*, exactly, and there was little wonder or fear in his eyes. He grew nervous under her scrutiny.

"Come on, you can tell me," Wendy prodded. "Is it that you actually want to join me and Tinker Bell? Looking for Peter Pan, I mean?" She tried to keep the hope out of her voice.

"No!" he cried. He immediately looked down and lowered his voice to its usual mumble. "I don't want to see Peter right now. Maybe not even after he's finished being angry or whatever. Maybe not ever."

His voice . . .

It hit Wendy all at once. Skipper's constant staring at her and his reluctance to speak. The especially baggy clothing he wore and soft, almost babyish face he had despite his height. The obvious desire not to be noticed by the new girl while being unable to take his eyes off her.

"Skipper, you're a *girl*!" Wendy exclaimed.

The Lost Boys all turned around at her cry.

Skipper swallowed and hardened her look, but that was all.

"Sort of," Slightly said with a shrug.

"What do you mean, *sort* of?" Wendy demanded.

"She ain't like *you*," Cubby said.

"Not like me? She's *exactly* like me!"

"She doesn't wear . . ." one twin began.

". . . dresses and ribbons," the other one finished.

"She don't talk like you."

"Her hair's short."

"She don't feel like a mother."

"Yes, yes, but those are all just externalities!" Wendy protested. "She and I both have . . ."

Well, nothing that could be said aloud in mixed company.

How old was Skipper? Old enough to be reminded of these things once a month?

Skipper's eyes were tortoiseshell, her eyelashes short and black. Wendy found herself imagining the Lost Boy with long hair in a proper girlish curl down her back, a ribbon round her neck, and a simple but fetching strolling frock . . .

And realized it would have been ridiculous.

This girl was perfectly at ease and comfortable in her

jacket and animal getup. Anything less freeing would have forced her to stand weirdly or made her look like a clown.

"But . . . how are you a Lost Boy?" Wendy finally asked, baffled.

"Always wanted to be one," Skipper answered, voice strong now that she had decided to speak. "I saw Peter come and take boys away from the orphanage. *Only* boys. Everyone knew that. Only *boys* could become Lost Boys. So I became a boy. The nurses forgot. They hated me—they hated who I was when I was a girl. They could barely read, so I changed my name in the books. I was a boy. And then, when Peter came, he took . . . me."

Everyone was quiet during her little speech. As if it were as natural and acceptable an escape plan as selling Peter's shadow.

"But why did you want to leave the home? Did they . . ." Wendy leaned in close and lowered her voice. "Did they hurt you . . . as a girl? Is that why you wanted to leave?"

Skipper gave her a look of shock and revulsion. "*No!* I just wanted to be free. Like all of us. To not have rules and not brush my teeth and hunt and fish and have fun all day. To never grow up. Ever."

"Right on, Skipper!" Cubby cheered. "That's my Lost Boy!"

"But she's not . . ." Wendy started to correct.

Slightly smiled at her confusion.

"She *is* a Lost Boy," he said gently. "One hundred percent. Like all of us."

"But that's the problem," Skipper said sorrowfully. "I'm not *exactly* a boy."

"All right," Wendy said uncertainly. "But . . . if it's always been like this, why are you worried about it *now*?"

Skipper shrugged but looked a little desperate. "Peter don't know. Not really. And Peter wants to kick Slightly out 'cause he wants new things. Peter's *always* talking about silly girls. Stupid girls. There are so many . . . all over Never Land . . . and you in London. . . . And I guess Tink *says* he likes you, but you're not like him, you know?"

Wendy considered this. True: Peter would never ask someone like Wendy to be a Lost Boy. He never did, in fact.

What would happen if she suddenly popped up in his crew?

"I see your point," she said slowly. "I think, however, we can get this all straightened out. No need to worry about it right now. We'll find Peter, retrieve his shadow, beat the pirates, have him make up with Slightly, and . . . then deal with you, however you wish. All right? But we'll wait until things are a bit calmer and he can see things with a clearer head."

Skipper nodded a little unhappily, but she had the

look of a child who has just cried and is in the feeling calm and being mollified stage, tears having been sniffed away. Wendy wondered if the girl ever cried—*had* ever cried in her strange, short life—at least in front of other people.

"But, ahh. . . ." She couldn't stop herself from asking, from leaning in and whispering: "Don't you find it a little . . . bothersome to be with these wild boys all the time?"

For an answer, Skipper opened her mouth and let out a terrifically loud burp.

"*Nice* one, Skip," Slightly said, touching his hat and bowing to her. The rest of the Lost Boys cackled and laughed and cheered and tried to follow suit, with considerably less success.

"Well," Wendy said, trying not to appear flustered or embarrassed, "I suppose that answers that."

"Mermaid Lagoon is that way, when the two of you are ready," Slightly said, pointing to the southeast. "How will you go? There's the path east and south beyond the Tonal Springs, or will you be trying to sail across the Bay of Skull Island?"

"Neither," Wendy said politely—and perhaps just a little smugly. "We'll be taking the *ether*."

And with that, she neatly rose up off her toes and a few feet into the air.

The Lost Boys cheered, crowed, and guffawed at that.

"Tink! You gave an outsider *fairy dust*?" Slightly called in mock outrage. "My my, how far down in the world we have come."

Tinker Bell stuck her tongue out at him. Slightly made a very inappropriate, rude gesture back at her that Wendy had only seen thugs and urchins use. But he was laughing. The fairy tossed her head derisively.

Wendy wondered about their interactions. Tinker Bell had her own room in the Lost Boys' hangout. Yet she seemed to treat them as meanly—or, at least, indifferently—as she did everyone else. For their part, the Lost Boys seemed to not to care what she thought, or they simply accepted that it was just part of her touchy personality. *Maybe it's not just me,* Wendy thought. Maybe the fairy was naturally prickly and bad-tempered to everyone.

But she doubted if Tinker Bell had ever physically attacked a Lost Boy the way she had assaulted *her* back at the clearing with the crystal creature. And she couldn't imagine Skipper acting the way Wendy had, stepping away and apologizing. The Lost Boy probably would have cracked Tinker Bell across the pate for such behavior.

Luna yawned, turning herself around several times before sitting down heavily next to Tootles. The little boy laughed and rubbed his face into her fur. The wolf looked wearily up at Wendy: *Are we* really *taking off again so soon?*

*Just look what a lovely group of playmates we have here. I could use a nap, too. . . .*

"Can we . . ."

". . . keep her?" the twins begged immediately.

"Just for now?"

"She's so tired!"

"Nobody can *keep* her," Wendy said. "She's her own person."

And yet . . . insomuch as Luna was anyone's, she *was* Wendy's. She was Wendy's dream dog, the perfect companion for adventures in Never Land.

But was she a pet?

Perhaps something created in Never Land was never really a Londoner's to begin with.

And the wolf really was just a puppy—a very large, very tired-looking one at that.

"Tinker Bell," Wendy said as casually as she could, relishing the use of the fairy's name and the intimacy it brought, "what do you think about Luna? Perhaps she *is* looking a little exhausted."

Tinker Bell considered the wolf, then nodded slowly. She pointed at the Lost Boys and shrugged: *What better place for a puppy to stay?*

"All right then, goodbye for now," Wendy said, dipping down to give Luna a big hug around her neck and shoulders. The wolf licked her all over.

Then the girl sighed and rose into the air. Tinker Bell followed—a few feet away, of course.

*At least,* Wendy thought, *we two have just had our first completely neutral conversation: no anger, no recriminations, no insult jingles. It is certainly a step.*

She waved at the Lost Boys. "It was lovely meeting all of you."

"See you! Send us a signal as soon as you've sorted stuff out with Peter!" Slightly called.

The Lost Boys leapt and capered and yelled after them. Tootles and the twins broke into a wild twirling circle dance. Skipper gave a shy wave with a half-smile. Cubby howled like a wolf rather than the bear he thought he was. Luna joined in, a great doggy smile on her muzzle.

It was a charming scene—and Wendy dearly hoped that would not be the last she would see of her beloved wolf.

# The Water Girls

Once they were out of the jungle, Tinker Bell chose to hug the curving coast rather than cross the water, which would have been faster. And when Wendy took a detour over the waves to get a closer look at a whale spouting she realized why. The mild breezes that kept her cool on the beach were whipped into much stronger versions of themselves over the ocean. She found herself suddenly pitched out of control by a rogue gust and in danger of being batted out to sea—or of a good dunking.

"A bit too Icarus there," she chastised herself, using her arms to somewhat un-prettily flap her way back to land.

Tinker Bell wisely only skimmed over the shallowest wavelets that encroached on the beach. She dipped a finger into the surface as she went, throwing up a pretty little spray that made rainbows in the golden sunlight. Fish leapt over her wake, flashing silver. Wendy caught her breath at the thoughtless beauty of it all. The fairy didn't care how others perceived what she did—she just *did*. Whatever she wanted. The results were often grace and spectacle.

When Wendy did whatever she wanted, people hated it. Like at parties. Like at Christmas, when she had been so full of the beauty of the season and the festive caroling music that she had made the mistake of enthusiastically telling everyone how a Never Land holiday might be run. Utterly unaware (at first) that not only did the people there not care about the holidays of an imaginary world or its cleverly invented trappings, but also that they were more than a little horrified that these stories came out of the mouth of a sixteen-year-old, and not a child.

(She had also been unaware at the time that her behavior would become the prime topic of jokes and gossip for the next season.)

Back in the reality of Never Land, the dark peaks of the Black Dragon Mountains glowered in the far distance, ominous smoke circling them like a scarf. Gray and brown twists of vapor rolled around each other like serpents, the air so thick it had texture and mass. Everything together fooled the eye into thinking there was an actual dragon—the size of a city—slithering through the landscape.

Maybe after they found Peter Pan and saved Never Land Wendy could explore those mountains and look for real dragons. She wondered how long the fairy dust would last.

It would, of course, be far more fun with someone else along. Even a foul-tempered fairy.

The northern side of the Mermaid Lagoon was a rocky, leisurely half-moon with a strip of jungle clinging to its stony spine. Flickering through green shadows were bright birds in orange, green, and yellow flocks. Here the clean, salty slap of the sea air was replaced by a heavy atmosphere of exotic blooms and ancient, earthy decay.

Tinker Bell headed for a gray ledge studded with palm trees, a hidden platform from which they could survey the water below. She landed silently and then crawled to the edge to peep over the side, keeping her body flat and out of sight from the ground.

Wendy did her best to emulate the fairy but her long skirt kept tangling in her legs. Frustrated and in a huff, she decided it was safe with no one but a girl fairy around to see her and hiked the dress up between her knees. Ignoring Tink's eye roll at her awkward maneuvers, she leaned over the lip of the rock for a look.

A paradisiacal lagoon lay below them. The water was

an unbelievable, unreal turquoise, its surface so still that every feature of the bottom could be admired in magnified detail: colorful pebbles, bright red kelp, fish as pretty and colorful as the jungle birds. A waterfall on the far side fell softly from a height of at least twenty feet. A triple rainbow graced its frothy bottom. Large boulders stuck out of the water at seemingly random intervals, black and sun-warmed and extremely inviting, like they had been placed there on purpose by some ancient giant. And on these were the mermaids.

Wendy gasped at their beauty.

Their tails were all colors of the rainbow, somehow managing not to look tawdry or clownish. Deep royal blue, glittery emerald green, coral red, anemone purple. Slick and wet and as beautifully real as the salmon Wendy's father had once caught on holiday in Scotland. Shining and voluptuously alive.

The mermaids were rather scandalously naked except for a few who wore carefully placed shells and starfish, although their hair did afford some measure of decorum as it trailed down their torsos. Their locks were long and thick and sinuous and mostly the same shades as their tails. Some had very tightly coiled curls, some had braids. Some had decorated their tresses with limpets and bright hibiscus flowers.

Their "human" skins were familiar tones: dark brown to pale white, pink and beige and golden and everything in between. Their eyes were also familiar eye colors but strangely clear and flat. Either depthless or extremely shallow depending on how one stared.

They sang, they brushed their hair, they played in the water. In short, they did everything mythical and magical mermaids were supposed to do, laughing and splashing as they did.

"Oh!" Wendy whispered. "They're—" And then she stopped.

Tinker Bell was giving her a funny look. An unhappy funny look.

The mermaids were beautiful. Indescribably, perfectly beautiful. They glowed and were radiant and seemed to suck up every ray of sun and sparkle of water; Wendy found she had no interest looking anywhere else.

*Sometimes when he's down he goes to Mermaid Lagoon.* Wasn't that what Cubby had said?

Of course, it made sense: just a few moments of *watching* these mysterious beings made Wendy feel light and happy all over. But . . . imagine having to compete with them.

Even if the fairy and Peter Pan weren't—*involved*, romantically, this would have been a hard act to follow.

What kind of girl, even just a friend, wouldn't grow jealous of a crowd of the most extraordinary, delightful creatures on the planet? Ones to whom your best friend turned whenever he was down?

*Stupid girls. There are so many . . . all over Never Land . . . and you in London. . . .* Skipper had said that. Who knew what other sirens populated this island? Selkies? Fairy princesses? Normal princesses? Pirate queens? Dryads? Naiads?

Wendy decided to say nothing about the exquisite beauty of the mermaids.

"Ah, there they are. But I don't see Peter Pan," she said instead, narrowing her eyes and casting her gaze to every obvious shadow and cranny.

Tinker Bell shook her head slowly, thoughtfully.

"Perhaps we should . . ." Wendy's voice trailed off.

The old Wendy would have stood up and marched on down to find out where he had gone, questioning the pretty mermaids closely.

The new Wendy, Never Land Wendy, paused.

She had been held hostage by blackhearted pirates when she had thought she had made a simple deal.

She had nearly been killed when crossing a harmless-looking clearing.

And these beautiful, innocent-looking mermaids, in their

beautiful lagoon—were they actually what they seemed?

Were their teeth just a little sharper than those of their human counterparts?

"Perhaps we should continue to surveil the situation from up here," Wendy said finally, sitting up straight-backed, her legs crossed. She cupped her hands around her mouth.

"Hallo down there! Good afternoon!"

Immediately the mermaids froze. Some dove down into the water. They made esses of their bodies like snakes, keeping their heads above the surface. All fixed her with their large, unblinking wet eyes.

The one on the largest rock alone stayed where she was. She had tightly braided purple locks and gripped the sides of her gray stone with fingers that now seemed a little more clawlike than human.

She relaxed when her eyes found Wendy.

So did all of the other mermaids, as if they all saw her at the same time. As one.

"Don't be afraid!" Wendy called. "I'm not going to hurt you."

"Oh, that's nice," the—leader?—said. Her tail began to swish behind her on the rock, the tip of her fin just touching the water, flipping it so little droplets spit into the air. The other mermaids began slowly moving again as well, treading water or beating their tails. They kept their faces halfway below the surface, however, noses firmly beneath. It was more than a little disturbing. While Wendy knew logically that mermaids could breathe underwater, it seemed very unnatural to hold themselves that way. No bubbles burbled up.

"Humans are *always* trying to catch us," the purple one said, pouting. "Nasty piratesss . . ."

"I'm not a pirate!" Wendy said quickly. "I've just escaped from being their prisoner, in fact."

"Nasty piratesss," another one said, pink-haired, kicking herself above the water for a moment so she could speak, her tail working and sliding.

*A little surprising, because serpents can't speak, of course,* Wendy thought.

Then she wondered what had suddenly made her think of serpents.

"Humans want to steal from us. A lock of our beautiful hair . . ." a red-haired one growled. Her locks weren't merely ginger; they were a flaming, tomato, poppy red. Red as a ladybug or the lips of some inappropriately dressed woman.

"Oh, I wouldn't do that," Wendy promised. "Though your hair *is* beautiful. It's the most beautiful hair I've ever seen."

Tinker Bell rolled her eyes. But the mermaids rolled in the water, smiling and—hissing? They seemed to like what she had said quite a bit.

"We can't see you very well," the purple one called out. "We can't see *your* hair. Our eyes don't work very well above water. Come down so we can see you."

"Yess," a green-haired beauty begged. "So we can see your hair."

"So we can comb it," another said.

"So we can brush it," a third said.

The mermaids swam back and forth in the lagoon, pleading and making dizzying patterns. They were beautiful and plaintive and hypnotizing to watch.

Wendy's heart tugged with a terrible pain. Such a scene had only existed in her wildest, most secret fantasies, ones she hadn't even told her brothers about: How she would make friends with a beautiful mermaid and the two would comb each other's hair, and laugh and sing. And *maybe* the mermaid would make fun of her voice, for Wendy could manage simple hymns and popular songs all right, but she was no siren. And then they would trade combs; Wendy would give the mermaid the silver-handled brush the Darlings had given her for Christmas one year, and the mermaid would give her an ivory comb, or maybe one made from a fish skeleton with tiny white translucent teeth. And they would forever remain friends, and even if they were far apart, they would think of each other every time they brushed their hair.

Wendy wanted nothing more than to lean over and plunge into the water below, to sit on a rock and have them do her hair in proper mermaid style. Long and down and flowing, with a flower or sea star for decoration.

But their enticements were a little overmuch, their teeth a little sharp.

"Oh, I would dearly love to, after I've asked a few questions," Wendy said apologetically.

"What?" the leader called out, putting a hand to her ear. "I'm afraid I can't hear you."

*"I said I have a few questions!"*

The mermaid was silent—all of them were silent. They stared at her without blinking. It was like she had reached a dead end in a game.

Wendy groaned inwardly.

"I will come down to talk to you," she said, regretting every word. "But not to the water's edge. I'm afraid of falling in, you see. I'm not a terribly good swimmer."

She thought it was a good story. But Tinker Bell shook her head and slapped a hand over her face.

There was another ledge just a little bit below the one they sat on that still seemed a safe distance from the water.

Wendy clambered down to it as neatly as she could, trying not to further tear her already ruined dress. Never Land was not easy on one's clothes. Perhaps that's why the little fairy's skirt was all ragged at the hem. If Wendy wasn't careful, she'd wind up in animal skins and purloined gear like the Lost Boys . . . or, heavens forfend, as naked as the mermaids!

Tinker Bell was wary, taking a long, lingering moment before drifting in a lazy spiral down to where Wendy now stood four or five feet above the water. She crossed her arms, upset that they had given in even this much.

But the mermaids leapt and played in joy at this development, swimming up close to and almost under Wendy—and then away again on their backs, like otters.

"What are you *wearing*?"

"Take it *off* this moment!"

"You can't swim in *that*!"

"I do not plan on swimming anytime soon. As I mentioned before, I cannot swim very well," Wendy said primly. "And anyway I . . . *we* . . . came here with rather urgent business. . . ."

"Bah!" The blue-haired mermaid stuck out her lip and splashed water with the tip of her tail so expertly that it hit Wendy squarely in the face.

The mermaids laughed and tittered and dove and flipped.

"Here's to *business*," another one said, hitting her tail even harder on the water. This time Wendy managed to cover her face, but it was a much larger volume of water, drenching her head and her hair. It was a hot day and the water was cool, so it wasn't the most unpleasant thing at first. But the jungle air at the edge of the lagoon was close and her dress stuck to her in clumps now, not likely to dry anytime in the near future.

Her shadow seemed outraged; she shook herself from top to bottom and wrung herself out like a towel, throwing little shadow droplets everywhere.

Tinker Bell peeped out from a large monstera leaf she had managed to duck behind. Her eyes widened in wonder at the giant, salty droplets that ran down her green shield, but then she noticed the sopping wet human girl. She giggled, pointing.

"All right, all right," Wendy said gamely, trying to keep her smile. Her shadow straightened herself out and set herself back in place behind Wendy—but *very* behind Wendy, keeping her as a sort of bulwark against more splashes of shadow water. "Very funny. But really, I'm here for a rather serious quest. You see, Peter Pan has . . ."

"Peter Pan!" the red-haired one sighed, flipping herself onto her back and swimming dreamily across the lagoon.

"That Peter Pan . . ." A green-haired one whistled.

"What do *you* know of Peter Pan?" the purple-haired one still on the rock asked, eyes narrowing.

The pink-haired one swam up close to Wendy, near the bottom of her ledge, listening intently.

"Well, he and I have some things to . . . sort out," Wendy stammered. She didn't want to admit that she was responsible for his shadow now being in the hands of pirates—whom the mermaids obviously feared and hated. And they didn't seem to have a great attention span. It would be difficult to make it all the way to the end, when she explained how she was trying to make reparations for what she had done.

The pink-haired one grinned strangely up at her.

"Yes?" Wendy asked politely.

But the mermaid just fixed her with giant caramel eyes and held up a vine draped over her hands.

"I don't understand," Wendy said. "What—"

Suddenly, the mermaid yanked. The vine snapped taut; the other end clung to a tree that was *behind* Wendy. She was thrown headfirst into the water.

Not the best swimmer even in calm situations, Wendy panicked, throwing her arms over her face as if expecting another splash. She hit the lagoon in the worst sort of tangled position, mouth open as she tried to cry out.

Salt water immediately ran down her throat and up her nose. She coughed and choked and sneezed, flailing her arms around and trying desperately to right herself. Her dress swirled and caught around her legs and waist, tangling her limbs utterly and weighing her down.

Her toes touched the bottom.

This shocked her into thinking again, and she kicked off it toward the surface.

"HELP!" Wendy called out as soon as her mouth was out of the water—instead of breathing, which might have been a better call.

A mermaid took this opportunity to grab her hair and yank her head back.

Wendy's lower half flipped up as her torso bent backward underwater, forcing a river's worth of water up her nose.

She coughed and floundered. Opening her eyes underwater didn't cause any extreme discomfort, although what she *saw* did: the sinuous forms of mermaids cutting back and forth through the current, quick as knives.

She tried to paddle to the surface, old lessons finally kicking in. She pushed her legs hard, hoping to connect with one of the glittering, slick bodies.

Her left foot did, and it was just enough to propel her to the surface.

She didn't waste her chance this time; she sucked in a deep breath of air.

The mermaids leapt and porpoised around her, their

grins hard and white. Their mouths seemed a little wider than they should have been, their teeth even sharper.

One of John's random facts popped into her consciousness: how some sharks had *four rows* of teeth, one inside the other, to more quickly disembowel their prey.

"Tinker Bell!" she cried. "Help!"

The fairy hovered in the air, watching the commotion thoughtfully.

Or . . . could it have been . . . *disinterestedly*?

Slimy, strong hands grabbed Wendy's waist and tugged. Down.

But the mermaid didn't manage to pull her entirely underwater. She had expected the human girl to be as light and lithe as one of them.

So the next mermaid leapt *out* of the water and landed with her hands on Wendy's shoulders, trying to push her down from above.

Once again, this mermaid wasn't strong or heavy enough to do much besides dunk Wendy for a moment. But they were learning. Hands and mouths grabbed at her body and dress, pulling and pushing and trying to drown her with their combined efforts.

"Tinker Bell!" Wendy spluttered.

The fairy, hanging above the lagoon, shook her head slowly.

That was the second to last thing Wendy saw.

The last thing was the fairy flying off, away into the jungle.

Tinker Bell had given up on the human girl and her hopeless situation.

Wendy went under.

# The Drying-Off Girls

Wendy's thoughts as the water closed above her head were a strange mix of things.

Primarily it was panic and survival, her body thrashing and arms circling, mouth shut tight, trying to keep from breathing in the water that was now all around her.

And obviously her mind touched a bit on her rapidly approaching and inevitable death.

But there was also a surprising amount of disappointment. She and Tinker Bell had finally been starting to make a connection, even if it was just over a common goal. The fairy had even given her pixie dust to fly! And then the little thing had revealed herself to be no better than any of the other heartless members of Never Land—pirates, crystal monsters, murderous mermaids. She was utterly selfish, only concerned with her own problems and adventures.

Wendy couldn't hold her breath any longer. She opened her mouth and . . .

The water was suddenly clear of mermaids and the weight holding her down was gone.

She popped to the surface like a child's toy in the bath, free of all hands, tails, mouths, and other impedimenta.

Coughing and spluttering—as quietly as she could—she sucked down great, painful gulps of air.

No one attacked her.

She kicked to the side of the lagoon, muscles screaming. Whatever had happened, she had to get out of the water before the mermaids returned.

She was almost too weak to pull herself up onto the ledge and scraped the sides of her legs raw while scrambling for a good foothold. Once finally up, her muscles and lungs desperately wanted her to lie there and recover. But Wendy forced herself to roll until she was a good arm's length away from the water and clear of any sneaky vines.

She took many amazing breaths while looking up at the sky. It was an intense deep blue and the palm fronds were black against the sun. It was bliss just to be alive. Even the little clouds of gnats hovering around her face didn't bother her. Anyway, they were sort of cute, with what looked like giant red and yellow feathers trailing from their heads and behinds.

Eventually she recovered enough to sit up. Salt water poured indelicately out of her nose and down the back of her throat, burning it even more. Water sloshed in her ears dizzyingly. If she hadn't known better, with the way her head was aching, she would have thought there was salt water up in her brains, too.

The mermaids were all still there, roiling in the water, lashing their tails and whipping up foam, fighting.

*Each other.*

"It's mine!" the purple one cried. She was no longer so queenly or stately upon her boulder throne. She was in the water with the rest of them, wide mouth even wider with toothy glee, holding up what looked like a piece of fruit. Something orangish but elongated like a banana.

"No, it's mine!"

The red-haired one leapt out of the water like a dolphin and snatched it out of her hands.

Two more mermaids dove after her, and so the roiling rebegan.

Tinker Bell hovered out of harm's way above the water, shaking her head disgustedly. She had another piece of fruit in her hands, a small reddish thing rather like an oversized cherry.

Now Wendy understood.

Legends told of how mermaids craved fruit because there was nothing like it in the sea. They would trade pearls and gems and long-lost treasures for a single apple, according to old sea chanteys the boys used to sing.

Tinker Bell had managed to distract the mermaids and make them turn on each other just by pelting them with bananas—like a mean child at the zoo.

"Oh, well done," Wendy tried to say aloud. It came out a rasping whisper. She coughed and more water came out—along with a thin trickle of blood. Nothing serious, she decided, being a practical girl not prone to flights of panic or hypochondria. It wasn't tuberculosis or cancer; it was just the result of her throat being scraped raw. But the taste and feel of it combined with the salt water threatened her already turbulent stomach.

Despite the whisper, Tinker Bell, with her fairy ears, had heard what she had said, or at least caught the tone of it. Her eyes widened in surprise.

"That was very clever. Very, very clever," Wendy said, her voice slowly gaining volume. "Good show."

Tinker Bell—*blushed?* —and gave a timid smile.

The purple-haired mermaid below took the distraction as an opportunity: she leapt high in the air to snatch at the cherry thing the fairy held.

Tinker Bell buzzed straight up out of reach, dropping the fruit as ballast as she went.

The mermaid caught it and laughed with glee.

Wendy glared daggers at the sea creatures as she wrung out her dripping, tangled, sodden hair.

*These* were the majestic beings she had imagined brushing it?

"You're quite *literally* the worst," she growled. "The. Worst."

The purple mermaid took a salacious bite out of the cherry and grinned at her wickedly.

The rest of the mermaids calmed down, the last of the fruit having been torn into several pieces and devoured by the lucky—or most vicious—ones.

"We were just having a little fun," the pink-haired mermaid said with a pout.

"Fun. That's *all*," the green-haired one said, floating on her back.

"We were only trying to drown you," the red-haired one added innocently.

"As I said," Wendy said flatly. *"The worst."*

Tinker Bell flew over to her, careful to avoid the reaching hands of the mermaids. She blanched when she saw the raw skin and sheets of blood on the human girl's legs. Wendy grimaced and ripped off a wide strip of hem from her already bedraggled skirt and carefully dabbed at the wounds. The salt water was, if not sterile, then at least safer than anything coming out of the jungle. Once her legs were clean, she tore the makeshift bandage in two, wrapped one around each leg, and tied them neatly.

"We came here to get your help in finding *your friend*, you know," she said when she was done. "And saving *your land*. We know where Peter Pan's shadow is and came here looking for him so we could get it back. And also—"

But it didn't matter that their entire world was being threatened by psychotic pirates; the mermaids only heard or cared about one thing.

"Peter Pan?"

They paused whatever they were doing at his name, bobbing in the water like floats on a fishing line.

"Why didn't you say you were here for Peter Pan?" one of them asked.

*"I DID!"* Wendy barked angrily, so unlike herself that Tinker Bell blew a couple feet away in surprise. "You were too busy trying to lure me into the water to listen. You horrible, murdering fishwives!"

"We didn't know it was about Peter *Pan*. . . ."

They began to dreamily glide and drift through the water.

"We know he lost his shadow. . . ."

"He hasn't been the same without it. . . ."

"So sad, our Peter!"

"We'll help him get it back. . . ."

"And then he'll be happy again!"

Wendy gritted her teeth, trying to control her temper.

"All right. You can start by telling us where Peter is. We were told he came here."

"He *did*!" the red-haired mermaid said, as serious as any toddler telling an actual truth. "He always comes here when he's sad."

"We cheer him up."

"We . . . make him happy again."

Tinker Bell grew red in the face, literally red, literally glowing, and her wispy brows became thunderheads.

"All right, yes, good, whatever," Wendy said quickly. She didn't want to hear any more, either, honestly. What a little harem he had here in Never Land! "When was that?"

"He came when the first moon was a tiny sickle," the green-haired one said thoughtfully, putting a fetching finger to her lip, deep in thought.

"An ickle-sickle," the red-haired one giggled.

"And he left just two mornings later!"

"No time at all with us, this time," one pouted.

"So *boring* . . ."

"So *sad* . . ."

“All right. Please stop. Tinker Bell, how long ago was that? I’m afraid I’m quite unfamiliar with the phases of the moon here. Moons, I suppose.” For all she knew, time ran backward, or made no sense at all.

Tinker Bell cocked her head, thinking, then jingled four times.

“Four days ago? That’s bad news,” Wendy said grimly. “He could be anywhere by now. Did he mention at all where he was going?”

“Yes,” the purple-haired one said grandly, trying to regain her original poise. “He said he was going to petition . . . the First.”

At this, everything became silent. The mermaids stopped chattering and bobbing. The jungle noises faded into the background. Tinker Bell shuddered. Even the waterfall seemed subdued.

“All right, then, that’s something,” Wendy said, trying to sound bright despite the apparent dire connotations of the mermaid’s words. “And where do we find ‘the First’?”

“Hopefully,” one mermaid said as she turned a lazy barrel roll, “you don’t. And they never find you.”

“Helpful. As always.” Wendy stood up to wring out the rest of her skirts. “Thank you for the information. And who knows? If it turns out to be useful, I may *not* direct the pirates to your lagoon after we’ve dealt with them.”

"Oh! You're so mean!" the pink-haired mermaid cried in dismay.

"*Really?* Are you *kidding* me?" Wendy demanded.

She felt a tiny tap on her hand.

Tinker Bell squeezed her finger and shook her head. *It's not worth it.*

Wendy realized the little fairy was right. If Tinker Bell, who had just as much—if not more—reason to hate these mermaids than Wendy, could walk away, well, so could she.

"Good day," she growled with as much dignity as she could muster. Feeling her dress drip-drop in tatters and streams behind her, her legs scandalously bare but for the bandages that now wrapped them, Wendy marched into the jungle unsure of the direction she was going except that it was *away from the mermaids.* Beside her was someone who might not be her friend yet, but who at least didn't seem to want to kill her.

Which was beginning to seem like a very rare thing indeed in Never Land.

# Meanwhile, on the High Seas . . .

"I thought you said my idea was a good one," Mr. Smee said doubtfully from behind Hook. "I thought you was going to use the shadow like a sextant or compass or whatnot to find Peter."

The captain stood ramrod straight at the wheel, his lower jaw jutted out. That was one thing you could certainly say about Captain Hook—when he was moved by a plan (his own) or an emotion (his own) or a crazy idea suggested by another member of the crew (somehow reinterpreted as his own), his bravery and clarity of purpose surpassed those of the finest storybook hero. His antics might not have made a lot of sense to an outside observer, but he carried them through with the enthusiasm and fearlessness of a toddler who didn't know any better.

Right now the outside observers were his own crew, who pretended to do their tasks while visibly unnerved by the sea changes going on around them. Most gave up and just twiddled their thumbs or daggers, trying to listen in on the captain's plans.

"Yes, but the bloody thing's a *shadow*," Hook said with great disdain. "I can't put a gold needle in its mouth and align it with north, now can I? I need someone else's expertise on the matter. Outside direction on how to filter its essence into compass *form*."

"Yes, Cap'n, I see that, but . . ." Smee swallowed. "Madam *Moreia*?"

"I don't see anyone here with a better idea," Hook said with a sniff. "I don't like the idea too much meself . . . but there's times a villain has got to rely on a little help from his people. His *community*, as it were. Exchange some trade secrets. My expertise is piracy, not black magic. Moreia is conjured out of the darkest fears stupid little children have of old women and their unknown habits. She'll help. Out of professional courtesy, if nothing else."

"Unknown habits?" Zane protested, overhearing. "Everyone normal's got a granny. Smacks of ageism, don't it?"

"Not if it's *specifically* the unknown habits," Major Thomas suggested. "For years I didn't know that the foul-smelling cack me nanna smeared on her rump every morning was anti-wrinkle cream. Thought it was oils decocted from the placentae of unborn babes. So she could fly or sommat."

"What was the recipe?" the Duke asked, trying to sound casual.

"Oh, shut up, you lot. I said *stupid* children, didn't I?" Hook roared. "Who knows why they fear their old neighbors and not rabid dogs or Staphylococcus aureus or stepping out in front of oncoming carriages? Now SHUT UP and let me remember the passage over Soulsucker Reef!"

The heavens turned murky and thin. In patches between strangely resinous clouds, the sky was black with cold, un-glittering stars—despite its being late afternoon. A wind picked up, so hideous and unclean that even the most wretched pirates shuddered and held their noses against the foul stench. Polluted thoughts came with it, and not the usual familiar nightmares of witchery like ravens and cats and curses; these were presages of end-times: battlefields crawling with things no longer quite human, the dead and decaying in piles on the ground to every horizon, the wrenching howl of the last person alive.

Far too quickly for some on board, a rocky island emerged out of the mist. Hook muttered *port port, starboard a bit, keep it steady* to himself, his eyes as cold and unblinking as the alien stars above.

There was a dock on the otherwise empty island. Despite the crew's desperate pleas to weigh anchor farther out, their captain refused.

"You, none of you, would still be here when I was done," was all he would say, without his usual bluster and speechifying. The truth was enough to silence the men.

Ever so carefully, Hook piloted the ship in. Strange apparitions appeared on the dock. Their mouths dripped to the planks and they flickered in and out of view at irregular intervals . . . but they caught the ropes thrown down and tied them neatly to solid-seeming cleats. Soon, for better or worse, the boat was fastened tightly and in no danger of drifting off.

Captain Hook seemed almost jolly as he put on his hat and adjusted his mustache. "You're with me, Smee."

"I was really hoping you wouldn't say that," the other pirate murmured sadly, pulling his own cap down over his ears.

The captain grabbed a jaunty walking stick and sauntered down the gangplank. "I don't think I need to tell you fellows no shore leave here, today," he called over his shoulder.

The island wasn't much more than a single rocky promontory rising up out of the sea like the longest claw of a dying antediluvian beast. On the tip of that claw was Madam Moreia's hut.

"What kind of witch lives on an island?" Smee muttered as they left the dock and clambered up the narrow path that spiraled around the island (allowing the witch several perfect views of approaching visitors). "Shouldn't she be in a nice snug little house in the woods somewhere, luring children in with candy and then eating them?"

"This is the oldest kind of witch, Mr. Smee. If you had any education at all, you would know all about the Greeks and their very, *very* scary witches."

"Guess I'm glad I never got a proper education, then," the other pirate said, looking around woefully.

At the top of the promontory they walked across a precarious bridge to the hut: a gnarled mess of driftwood, strange black vines, and what looked like seaweed or possibly human flesh stretched taut for a roof.

Hook took off his hat and rapped.

"Madam Moreia? It's Hook! Come to visit!"

The door opened of its own accord after a suitably spooky pause.

The inside of the hut was of course much larger than the outside, but so dark and cramped and filled with indistinguishable things that the effect was much less grand than it could have been. A primitive fire burned coals on the floor without a ring or anything around to contain it.

Tending the cauldron suspended above the flames was a bent-over old woman. Her skin was thick with grease and soot. Great ropy locks of hair were mounded on her head until they practically doubled her height. When she turned to fix a pair of milky eyes on her guests, Smee's heart almost stopped.

"Ah, Hook! Such a long time!" she cried, surprisingly merry. "How's my favorite handsome pirate captain?"

"Very well, Moreia, very well," Hook said politely, leaning over and submitting himself to a kiss on the cheek that left a gray lip print.

"You want something, don't you," she said with a sigh. "You never just come to visit. Ah, well, what's to be expected among the evil? Polite behavior? *Niceties?*" She cackled and slurped from the ladle she held. "I'm just cooking up a nice bowl of baby bits. Care for a bowl?"

"None for me, thank you," Hook said, trying to sound regretful. "Maybe Mr. Smee would."

"Who? *Oh.*" The witch looked up and made a big deal of winking at the first mate, although not quite in the right direction. Perhaps because of her cataracts. "What do you want, then? May as well get right down to business, eh?"

"Well, I'm having some *shadow* issues," Hook admitted with a sigh, sitting down in a comfy red-velvet chair whose hard parts were carved from human femurs and tibias.

"Shadows, mm? Tricky business. For mortals."

"Yes, well, it's *Peter Pan's* shadow. So trickier than most, I would say."

"*Peter Pan?* You're still chasing after that wretch? Well, well. Some things never change in Never Land."

"It is what it is." Hook crossed one leg over the other and sniffed with great dignity. "But I had this rather brilliant idea that I could use his shadow—currently in my possession—to lead me *to* him. Like a compass."

Mr. Smee nodded eagerly—then frowned, perhaps remembering where the idea had come from originally. Hook was careful not to look at him.

The witch sucked her tooth, stirring the soup thoughtfully. "Not a compass . . . There's problems with enchanting the shadow down so small. For long periods of time. Especially if you don't plan on staying near the equator. No, a compass won't work. You need something more human-sized. Like . . . a Painopticon."

"What's that?" Hook asked eagerly.

"I think it's the thing you're looking for. The engineering of it escapes me. Was mentioned in one of me books over there."

The witch gestured to a shelf, which had on it things that made even Hook squirm: moldering jars of foul-smelling ointments, shiny black plants that looked more liquid than fiber, cloches protecting half-fleshed skeletons that could have been human or reptile—and which moved a little when not looked at directly. *Also* a set of musty black-bound books, some of which had blinking eyeballs set in their covers.

"Splendid, splendid!" Hook said enthusiastically—concealing his disgust. "How much for the lot?"

"If you were a good fellow, I'd say free—the chaos and pain released by your attempting to use them would certainly make it worthwhile," the witch said with a smile that wasn't entirely unkind. "But since you're one of us, I have to charge. Let me see. . . ."

She waddled back and forth in front of her fire, a giddy, almost childlike look on her face as she tapped her tooth in thought.

Hook fidgeted.

Smee whispered, *"You don't think she'll make us get her more babies, do you, Cap'n?"*

*"Even I have my limits,"* Hook whispered back.

The witch whirled around, and both men jumped like boys caught by a teacher.

"All the rum on your ship!" she declared happily. "Not the grog. The real, pure stuff. Also any cones of sugar. And a silk dressing gown."

"Absolutely," Hook said in relief. "Whatever you like. It is yours."

Moreia rubbed her hands together in excitement. Strange oils came off them but disappeared into dust and smoke before hitting the floor. Smee began to inch toward the exit.

"Oooh, I haven't had a real drink in years. And there's spirits like it, too."

"And you look like a woman who deserves a nice gown to eat your, er, breakfast in," Hook said politely.

The witch cackled. "Oh, the dressing gown is for a bit of a disguise. . . . There's a handsome young merman I rather fancy. And who, I might add, could stand to be taught a lesson or two."

"Well, I'll leave you to your projects," Hook said hastily, standing up.

The witch rolled her eyes and spat. "Least I'm honest about *my* issues. Chasing Pan, indeed. Put your anger at lost youth into violence, I say. Go burn some villages or raid one of the other islands. Become a despot. Keep yourself busy."

"I'll just have what you ordered sent up here by a couple of my men. With some extra goodies for you, of course," Hook said, pushing the door open with his rump and bowing out.

"Oh, you're too kind. I'll have one of my own 'men' bring you the books once I get what I want. I don't suppose I need to tell you there is no way your ship is leaving these waters until you hold up your end of the bargain?"

"And I don't need to tell you that my cannons are aimed at your lovely house on the off chance you don't hold up yours, of course."

"Always a pleasure, Hook." The witch grinned and blew him a kiss.

"For me as well." The captain tipped his hat before setting it on his head and closing the door behind him.

He and Smee stood for a moment in the dismal half-light of the weird island and its foul vapors, breathing deeply in relief.

"That weren't pleasant, if you don't mind me saying so, Cap'n," Smee eventually said.

"No . . . but I wonder," Hook said, thoughtful. "Maybe what we feel now . . . that's how people feel when *they* deal with pirates. I mean, we're frightening, too, aren't we? Killing and looting and looking generally fearsome . . . Isn't that why the heroes always come after us?"

"Never thought about it that way before, Cap'n," Smee admitted, scratching under his hat. "I guess that's why you're the cap'n, Cap'n! Always thinking the deep thoughts and whatnot."

"True," Hook said, nodding. "Too true, Mr. Smee. 'Tis a burden of leadership. You know, I will almost miss her when she's gone, with the rest of Never Land. Poor old witch. Now let's back to the ship. I want to get her the rum and be out of here as soon as we can. And I think it's high time for a bath and a shave. . . . I always feel unclean after dealing with her."

"That's the thing! One bath and shave coming right up, Cap'n, sir!" Mr. Smee said happily.

And the two brightly colored pirates descended the steep spiral path, the only red and blue and gold things for miles around. Hook's feather bobbed jauntily in the air. He even smiled despite the foul breeze.

Soon he would have the shadow showing the way. . . . Peter Pan was as good as gone, along with the rest of Never Land.

# Steps

Tinker Bell's glow lit the dark understory of the jungle with a sprightly—if feeble—twinkling. Whatever triumph Wendy had felt upon surviving the mermaids soon dissipated into the dark, moist, enveloping atmosphere.

She was walking away from creatures she had dreamed of meeting since she was a very little girl.

"Thank you," she said aloud, eventually.

Tinker Bell looked at her.

"For saving me," Wendy elaborated.

Tinker Bell blinked, as if she hadn't thought about it. Wendy watched expressions flit over her face as quick and transparent as the wings of a dragonfly (or a fairy); there was no need for language. The fairy frowned, obviously recalling details of the previous hour. Then an expression of wonder and an unguarded smile appeared: she *did* save Wendy, didn't she? The smile grew into a rosy grin as she remembered her own heroics, a pleased, proud smugness settling over her features.

Finally she looked up at Wendy—as if just remembering that the person she had saved was still there. And perhaps that person was someone she didn't want to like.

She rolled her eyes and shrugged. *No big deal.*

"Well, it meant a lot. To me," Wendy said, refusing to let her companion retreat so easily from the conversation. "I didn't think . . . Well, I didn't think you were going to come back for me. I had thought you left. For good."

The fairy flew up toward Wendy's face, settling inches from her nose. She put her tiny hands on her hips in exasperation.

"Well, really, how was I supposed to know? You've made it quite clear that you don't have the fondest feelings for me. From the moment we first met. You were boxing me about a bit, remember?" She didn't mean to overemphasize her statement, but she couldn't help rubbing her arm where the fairy had pinched her extra viciously.

The fairy looked thoughtful.

"Well, you *did*."

Tinker Bell really was like a child, Wendy decided.

Her intelligence and wisdom *in the moment* were certainly advanced and adultlike. But anything that required reflecting on previous moments or her own past behavior, any consideration of intangible elements like consequences or empathy, was as impossible as the close observation of a distant world. Tinker Bell of earlier in the day was an entirely different creature from afternoon Tinker Bell, alien and divorced from her.

The fairy looked left and right, as if trying to figure a way out of Wendy's rather obvious and telling statement. Then she cocked her head, as if remembering something, and opened her mouth, waggling a finger at the human girl.

"I know, I know! I sold Peter's shadow. I put all of Never Land in danger. I deserve your ire. Which makes it only *more* likely that you would abandon me to be drowned by the mermaids—especially if it looked hopeless." Wendy sighed, feeling the heaviness of the last few days fall solidly on her shoulders. "All I ever wanted was to be friends with a fairy, or a mermaid, and go on an adventure. I didn't mean for all of this to happen. I don't know how many times I can apologize, Tinker Bell.

"Look, I know I said we shouldn't discuss him anymore. . . . But really. Ask yourself. Why do you like Peter Pan?"

The fairy looked up, surprised at the apparent change in conversation.

"Is it because he's different from everyone you would normally spend time with? Is it because he leads you on great adventures? Is it because he draws you out of your pretty, delicate little bedroom and you get to battle pirates with him and do great things?"

Tinker Bell gave a tiny nod.

"*I* liked Peter—the idea of Peter—*for the exact same reasons*. I always dreamed of going on great adventures, of battling pirates, of exploring caves and finding treasures. Because there *are* no adventures or pirates in London. Not for girls, anyway. All of the stories I read are about boys and men. Oh, there are a few, rare female explorers . . . but I am not one of them. I need a little help to get going, do you know what I mean? I don't seem to be able to escape my own bedroom in London without someone giving me a bit of a push. Peter Pan would come and save me from all that dreariness.

"Had I known about you, and how you already had a . . . relationship with Peter, a strong and—perhaps rightfully—jealous one, I would have been much more careful. But I would still want *a* Peter Pan. I would still want adventure. But I would in no way have put myself between you and *the* Peter. Your Peter."

Tinker Bell frowned as she slowly processed these words.

"Really. You needn't have hated me," Wendy said with

a wan smile. "You could have just said something like . . . 'Back off, woman! The fair lad is *mine*!' And then we would have shaken on it. Or whatever it is dumb men do when they come to some dumb manly agreement."

The fairy's mouth tugged to the side in a snarky smile. She knew exactly what Wendy was talking about, the ridiculous gestures of a gender prone to extroversion.

"And then maybe you could have eventually introduced me to some fairy prince. . . ." Wendy said lightly, with a smile. "Just like my mother is always trying to get girls to introduce me to their brothers or cousins or whatever."

At this Tinker Bell frowned and made a little gagging motion, sticking her finger on her tongue.

"No, I suppose there's a reason you spend time with Peter and the Lost Boys, and not males of the fey kind," Wendy said, laughing. "Perhaps they are as boring to you as London boys are to me. Anyway, without Peter—or you—I had to find my way here myself. I didn't understand the cost or consequences. I'm getting my adventure finally, even if it's not exactly the one I wanted. I just wish—I really, really wish—we could travel together more as friends. I'm not your enemy, Tinker Bell. If I had known about you, I would have been your greatest fan."

Tinker Bell was silent. For once her face and body were unreadable, an enigma.

"Anyway, we should probably get going," Wendy finished, a little lamely. She already felt like she had pulled a real Wendy, talking too much, revealing too much, feeling too much. All in the open.

But Tinker Bell still seemed frozen in thought. Almost as if once Wendy had got her thinking about things she had never considered before she couldn't easily give them up, like a cat worrying a toy.

"You should probably lead," Wendy added politely, "Since I have no idea where we are going."

The fairy tipped her head back and took the human in, as if really looking at her for the first time. She paused for a moment in what appeared to be a *new* thought, judging by the spark in her eyes.

"What is it?" Wendy asked.

Tinker Bell opened her mouth. Widely. *Very* widely. Wider than it seemed should have been possible for such a tiny creature. Wendy couldn't help noticing familiar, almost mermaid-ish rows of sharp, perfectly white teeth. Was every resident of Never Land equipped with such weapons? Such mouths? How dangerous *was* this place?

"I don't know what you . . ."

Tinker Bell closed her mouth, then opened it again widely and pointed at Wendy.

"You want me to . . . ?" Wendy asked, opening her own

mouth—but not *quite* as wide as Tinker Bell had. She was a little self-conscious. Mother and Father had always told her to chew with her mouth closed, of course, and ladies didn't yawn or speak while eating, at least not without hiding behind a properly gloved set of fingers.

But she opened up a *little* wider, seeing the fairy's growing impatience and fearing her retribution.

"Ike ish?" she asked.

In answer, the fairy shook her wings and spun—hurling a stream of fairy dust directly onto Wendy's tongue.

# Wendy and the Fairies (Finally!)

What Wendy felt was a spray of something that could only be described as *golden*. Light, effervescent, slightly dry. Fizzy, like the horrible mineral waters Mother sometimes made Father take to aid his digestion. But not with the terrible metallic taste. For the brief moment she could taste anything at all, it was sweet—or no, maybe sour like lemons. No, not that, either—more like sparks from a fire.

All too soon it was gone, down her throat or up her nose or dissipated into her flesh and brain.

A wave crashed through her body starting in her sinuses. She was frozen all over, and then sweating and shuddering, but in the next moment felt like herself again.

"What was—thank you—why did you—"

Tinker Bell jingled.

*Can you understand me?*

"Yes, of course, but what did you just . . . Wait, what?"

Just like that, like nothing at all, everything the fairy said made sense. Like it had always made sense when taken all together: her jingles, her wing flutters, her eye movements . . . The human girl just hadn't been able to understand it before.

"Your . . . dust," Wendy said slowly. "Somehow it allows me to understand you. The way everyone else can."

Tinker Bell shrugged and did a slow spiral in the air, apparently now bored with the conversation. She zoomed up to a palm leaf to examine a bug there: something like the unicorn beetles but with an iridescent rainbow mane that fluttered in the breeze. She jingled quietly and nuzzled it.

"Well, this will make things a lot easier," Wendy said happily. Did the dust allow her to understand just Tinker Bell, or all fairies? What about all the creatures of Never Land? How long would it last? Did it change other parts of her? Was it poisonous? If she had been doused with fairy dust to fly, and imbibed fairy dust to hear fairy language, how much more of her was there to infuse with the substance? Would she become—she secretly hoped—fairy herself?

Magical translating dust aside, she also understood

without anyone saying it that despite this apparent change in their relationship status, the fairy would still not stand for the usual Wendy-barrage of questions. They might be on better terms now, but they weren't bosom companions.

Not yet, at least.

"All right then," Wendy said, patting her dress down and dusting herself off—as best she could—while ordering in her head a careful list of questions she would dole out, slowly, over the course of her time with the fairy. "Where do we find these First?"

Tinker Bell shrugged.

"Oh," Wendy said, perplexed. "But—when they said that thing, about him going to see the First, you looked like you knew of them. You looked, if you don't mind me saying so, worried."

*I am worried.*

"About what? Are they dangerous?"

Tinker Bell swayed this way and that on a whisper-soft breeze so faint she might have summoned it with her own wings.

*The First are . . . the first. The first inhabitants of Never Land. The first spirits of the place. Ancient. They were here before mermaids and pirates and fairies and the dreams of men. They* are *Never Land. Whatever Never Land was when it was born. We are all . . . a result of them, and you.*

Wendy frowned, considering this. The history of Never Land had never occurred to her as a discrete idea before. Never Land was Never Land, a place of infinite happiness and adventure, where anything you could imagine was possible. Did theories like geology, the true age of the Earth, and Mr. Darwin's evolution hold for imaginary lands?

"Where do fairies come from?" she asked, thinking it was the simplest entry into a complicated subject.

*The first laugh of a baby. A special baby. So they say.* Tinker Bell smiled wryly. *We are here, we appear, sometimes there are more of us. I awoke under a leaf, curled up like a drop of dew, complete. Tinker Bell!*

*But . . .* also *we come the usual way.*

She made a face.

"But there *is* a connection between you and the imagination, the *minds* of human beings," Wendy hazarded.

*I guess so.*

"When I tell a story about Never Land to my brothers, am I making it up? Or am I just repeating something, which my inner mind already knows—a story that has already actually happened, in Never Land?"

*Who knows? I don't.*

*Who cares? I don't.*

"But we're talking about the nature of your existence! Your *world's* existence. Doesn't that make you wonder at all?"

*I* am. *You* are. *Everything else is talk.* Tinker Bell jingled, a little impatiently. *What's important is getting Peter's shadow back and figuring out how Captain Hook plans to destroy Never Land.*

"No, no, of course, you're right," Wendy said—but a little distractedly. She did *not* really agree. Details mattered to her. Which hand of Hook's Peter actually cut off, for instance. How many masts the *Jolly Roger* had. The precise workings of an entire world, the rules by which it existed . . . Well, besides soothing her constantly tumbling mind, knowledge was power. The more she knew about Never Land, the safer she was—and the more successful their quest would be. "But—just—what do they look like? The First, I mean?"

*They do not look like men or fairies or mermaids or pirates or animals or insects or fish or plants. They look like nothing—and everything at once.*

Wendy sighed. "All right. I see. But if they're so dangerous and unknowable, why do you think Peter went to see them?"

The fairy looked disgusted at yet another question. But then she thought about it.

*Maybe he thought they could get him a new one.*

"A new . . . shadow? Can the First do that?"

*They are Never Land. Why did I give you the dust to hear if you won't* listen*?*

"All right, all right. But—*would* they do it?"

At this the fairy looked troubled.

*They don't talk or listen to reason . . . or they do things for their own unknowable reasons. Big things. Scary things.*

"So they are opaque and random? Powerful and whimsical? Unknowable, inscrutable, and unpredictable, like an Old Testament sort of god?"

Tinker Bell looked at her for a long moment.

*Sure.*

"Lovely. I suppose we must go then and chase Peter Pan together to the demesne of these terrifying gods of Never Land. How do we go about finding them?"

*Their place of being is never constant for very long. We will need to ask where they were seen last.*

"Oh, dangerous whimsical gods—on something like the *Flying Dutchman.* This gets better and better. So how do we find out where they are?"

*I have been asking the Small Friends, the many-legged companions of the woods. But I think we shall need to seek fairy help.*

The *OOOOOOH!* that Wendy couldn't quite suppress in her throat had to be caught and killed physically with her hands: she clapped them over her mouth and held tight while the sound tried to come out.

Tinker Bell did something that was a like an eye roll

stopped midway, with a *tiny* smile thrown in for good measure.

*Unfortunately, this is not the best place to do it. We're at the edge of the Qqrimal Range in the Pernicious Forest, and things live here that feast upon fairy kind. We tend to avoid this area. And we certainly don't draw attention to ourselves while here by gathering in groups. But hopefully there will be one or two of my kind about, traveling through.*

*Besides predators, my brethren avoid human contact. Hide somewhere and peep out.*

"Absolutely!" Wendy breathed, only a little disappointed not to be involved in actually meeting them. *Watching* fairies up close was still more fairy contact than she'd ever had before . . . even if it didn't seem fair somehow, now that she could understand what they said.

She found a clump of shiny, large-leafed plants and arranged their long canes until her body was hidden from view. There was a nice hole in one of the leaves through which she could spy. The hole was still being worked on by a "Small Friend," a caterpillar with purple scales instead of fur. It looked at Wendy in dubious surprise. Or so Wendy assumed. It was hard to tell with its faceted but depthless golden eyes.

"Excuse me," she whispered. "I'll just be here for a moment."

She was unsure if the fairy dust gave her the ability to communicate with otherwise unspeaking Never Land creatures, but the thing *did* give her a long, hard look before going back to the business of chewing and ignoring.

Tinker Bell, meanwhile, was drifting with purpose up to the highest leafy branches of the jungle. Her light glowed warmly off the leaves below, the droplets seeping off their thick veins, the sweet sap running down the trunks of the trees. It made the whole clearing look . . .

*Well, like it was touched by fairies,* Wendy thought with a smile.

All her life she had looked for fairies in more mundane places, experiencing a rush of hope and warmth whenever a scene even palely imitated the one before her now. Candles at Christmas, fireflies in the park, flickering lamps in teahouses. The sparkling leaded glass windows of a sweets shop on winter afternoons when dusk came at four. A febrile, glowing crisscross of threads on a rotten log her cousin had once shown her out in the country: fox fire, magical mushrooms.

And here it was, for real! Tinker Bell was performing what appeared be a slow and majestic dance. First, she moved to specific points in the air around her, perhaps north, south, east, and west, twirling a little at each stop. Then she flew back to the center and made a strange bowing motion, keeping her tiny feet daintily together and putting her arms out gracefully like a swan. As she completed each movement, fairy dust fell from her wings in glittering, languorous trails, hanging in the air just long enough to form shapes. She started the dance over again, faster this time.

And again even faster. Her trail of sparkles almost resolved into a picture, crisscrossed lines constantly flowing slowly down like drips of luminous paint.

Wendy felt a bit like John, overwhelmed with a desire to try to reduce and explain and thereby translate the magic. But she also felt a lot like Michael, with an *almost* overwhelming urge to break free from her hiding place and see it up close, to feel the sparkles on her nose, to run a hand through the sigils not for the purpose of destruction but from a hapless, joyful desire to be part of it all.

Tinker Bell finally stopped, breathing heavily.

Wendy held her own breath.

And then . . .

Out of the darkness . . .

An answering glow.

# The Never Land Empyreal

Like a firefly in the mists or fish from the darkest deep, the light came bobbling through the jungle gloom. This one was tinged orange like the last ember of a really good fire. Wendy felt warm all over just looking at it.

The tiny ball of light soon resolved into another fairy. She had darker skin than Tinker Bell's that was orangey red at the tips of her ears—which were a little longer than the other fairy's, and more pointed. Her hair was hard to focus on, more foam or spirit than actual strands: a cloud of dark reddish brown that had ribbons dividing it into two big puffs, each the size of her head. She wore a simple poncho belted around the middle—but it was hemmed nicely and not ragged like Tinker Bell's. The belt was prettily tooled and had an intricate metal-and-gem buckle that

Wendy desperately wanted a closer look at (with a magnifying glass).

*Well, I didn't even know you knew the Call.*

If Wendy had expected some sort of intricate fairy greeting ritual, she was more than taken aback by the new fairy's *very* casual tone.

Tinker Bell opened her mouth, and Wendy waited, wincing, for her usual intemperate response.

Instead, the fairy took a deep breath.

*I know the Call, sister. I am fairy.*

*Really? I haven't seen you at any of the midseason fetes, or the blossom gatherings, or the acorn hunts, or . . .*

*I don't like crowds.*

*You don't seem to like much of what it means to be fairy.*

More and more was revealed about Wendy's temperamental little friend! Fairies were apparently gregarious—social creatures, like people. Or horses. Not the lonely solitary haunters of hills and isolated groves Wendy had imagined, who came together for the rare dance around a ring of mushrooms.

But Tinker Bell obviously shunned the company of others like herself, preferring the company of a few giant humans like Peter Pan.

*I need help.* Tinker Bell put out her arms in supplication, trying to change the subject.

I'll *say,* the other fairy retorted with a raised eyebrow.

Then: *I was hoping this was a Friends Invite; I don't usually travel so far into the Pernicious Forest. It's dangerous—there are qqrimals around here, you know. I'll bet you don't even have any nectar or cake to offer a weary fellow traveler, do you?*

Tinker Bell shook her head morosely, looking at the ground.

Wendy started to fumble around in her bag. Along with her hastily thrown-together belongings, she was sure there was a packet of throat lozenges, maybe a mint pillow or two. Then she remembered her main directive: to stay hidden. She couldn't help out her little companion even if she wanted to. Reluctantly, she settled back down.

A third glow appeared during this awkward silence; it zipped along more definitively through the gloom and then stopped in the space next to the two fairies, revealing itself to be a fairy prince.

All right, perhaps it was just a male fairy.

But either way Wendy was thrown. He was *devastatingly* handsome.

He had bark-brown skin and high cheekbones and a broad chest—and he sported a neatly folded kilt and sash that did little to cover said chest. His head was shorn and his ears were extremely long, tapering to filaments that waved gently as he spoke. A weapon like a sword hung from his waist, hilt-less and slender and golden.

Even at his diminutive size, he radiated confidence, martial skills, and a general calmness that spoke to all the best characteristics of a leader of men *or* fairies.

*Oh, it's Tinker Bell! What a surprise. And hello, Berryloon.*

He was polite enough to Tinker Bell, but he bowed to the other girl.

*It's more than a little dangerous for the three of us to be gathered together here like this—every qqrimal in the area will sense our presence. What's the emergency?*

*I don't know, ask* her, Berryloon snorted, tilting her head at Tinker Bell.

*I have to find the First. Have either of you seen them, or heard about them lately?*

Both the fairies looked shocked at her question.

*What is this about?* the boy fairy asked seriously. *Are you in trouble?*

Tinker Bell looked a little cagey. *No—not me.*

*Who then?*

*Peter Pan has lost his shadow, and seeks them out for help.*

Berryloon burst out laughing. The male fairy just looked greatly disappointed. Wendy cringed, feeling like the look was directed at her as well.

*Bell, let the boy to his own fate,* he suggested, putting a hand on her shoulder in a brotherly fashion. *For how long are you going to keep rescuing and following after that big ugly human?*

*He's not human!* Tinker Bell responded angrily, so angrily that she put her hands on her hips and her backside lifted up as her wings buzzed.

*All right, calm down, he's not . . . exactly . . . human,* the boy said soothingly—while giving Berryloon an eye roll. *But his friends are. Tinker Bell, if he's such a great* not-*human adventurer, he can take care of himself. And* you *can come with us to the Pinkpetal Harvest!*

*Oooh!* Berryloon—well, *squeaked* would be the closest approximation to the way she jingled. She spun and grabbed the boy fairy's hands. *Me too! Let's be partners! We could even trio, if little miss boring wings here will come. . . .*

As nasty as it sounded, Wendy could tell that Berryloon was making a real effort to reach out to Tinker Bell. The offer was genuine despite her tone, whatever it all meant.

Tinker Bell shook her head. *I have to find Peter. I know where his shadow is—it's with the pirates. And they're planning to destroy all of Never Land! Peter needs to hear about this before he reaches the First and makes some sort of terrible bargain. Or mistake. And then we'll go after Captain Hook and stop him.*

*Planning to destroy all of Never Land,* Berryloon sneered. *Uh-huh.*

The boy fairy sighed, shaking his head. *It sounds like just another round of games between Peter and the pirates. But all right, Bell. A comrade of mine saw the demesne of the First appear on the northwestern corner of the island, at the base of the Chanting Peninsula, east of the Shimmering Sea.*

*Thank you,* Tinker Bell said with relief, and gave him a little bow.

*Good luck, weirdo,* Berryloon said with a toss of her head. *Guess we'll see you next time you need something, or you finally tire of the company you keep. Shall we?*

Hand in hand, she and the boy fairy rose perfectly in tandem, more gracefully than the most skilled ballerinas Wendy had ever seen, more smoothly than any ice-skaters.

And then—just before they disappeared into the depths of the jungle darkness as little bobbing glows, the boy fairy turned and winked.

Directly at Wendy.

She fell back, overcome by the direct, smiling gaze of the tiny man-at-arms.

Strange thoughts popped into her head: shrinking, or growing, clinging to a boy as he rode up into the air on the winds, his dragonfly wings beating strongly behind them.

Breathless, she staggered out of her hiding place, feeling a trifle disconnected from things.

Seeing Tinker Bell knocked sense back into her. The little fairy was hanging in the air like an old toy tied to a string to amuse a baby or a cat but then forgotten: she twisted a little right and then left as the breeze nudged her. Her gaze was fixed on the disappearing lights of her "friends."

Poor Tinker Bell!

How entirely wrong Wendy had gotten her! What she had *thought* was fairy affectation—artfully ragged dress, tousled hair in a messy bun, snobby and antisocial behavior—was not *de rigueur* for fairies at all. The other two seemed to spend all of their time at parties and gatherings. They both had neatly tailored apparel complete with perfect, high-fashion little accessories. Tink cared less about her appearance than whatever quest she was currently on, whatever fun she was having, whatever the Lost Boys and Peter were up to, whatever her own mischief involved.

Oh yes, Tinker Bell did appreciate the finer things, like her delicate little bedroom. But on her own terms and, most importantly, on her own. She didn't fit in with other fairies. And *they* obviously had issues with her chosen way of life.

No wonder she was so enamored of Peter Pan. She finally had a companion like herself. And of course she would be jealous and unwilling to share—without him, she might be alone.

"Tinker Bell?" Wendy said softly.

The fairy spun around in the air, obviously not having heard her approach. Her eyes were filled with brightness and wet. She shook her head to physically remove any traces of emotion and crossed her arms resolutely.

"Tinker Bell, I . . ."

Wendy bit her lip. The sort of person who abandoned her extremely cozy people to live a wild life with an unapproved-of boy, a girl who wore tatters and didn't care . . . well, she wouldn't be the sort of girl eager to discuss her feelings. She was obviously already embarrassed by what the human girl had witnessed.

"I feel like we should get started on our way to this Enchanted Peninsula, shouldn't we?"

Tinker Bell let out an audible sigh, relieved at the direction Wendy's statement had gone.

*Chanting. Not* "Enchanted." *You'll understand when we get there.*

"All right then. Let's—"

And that's when the creature leapt from the bush, grabbing Tinker Bell out of the air.

# The Qqrimal

It was all predator. Sleek and slinky and black and lithe. Its paws had claws, long curled half-moons that easily ripped through the fairy's dress and closed around her waist.

Without thinking, Wendy threw herself at it, grasping at the beast with her own hands, naked, pink, and clawless.

One would suppose that after her experiences in Never Land she might stop and think twice about engaging a strange creature, an unknown entity who might have had any number of unpredictable and magical attacks. But the thing's closest approximation to any London beast was *cat*; an angry, starving alley cat. Fierce but not indomitable. Wendy had her share of experiences with those, ranging from pulling them off hapless songbirds to begging her parents to let her keep one.

And in fact, the twin mirrors on the front of its snub face could have been mistaken for cat's eyes with a light shining into them.

"Down!" Wendy cried imperiously.

Her hands closed tightly around its middle—but it didn't yowl as she expected. It dropped the fairy in shock . . . then sort of *thinned out* between Wendy's fingers. The creature slid through them like oil, dripped to the ground, and reformed into a weaselly, mink-like critter.

"Ugh!" Wendy looked at her hands. But they were clean and all she had actually felt was the soft fur one would expect.

With barely a pause the creature found Tinker Bell and again leapt on her.

The little fairy was a bit stunned and shaken up by its first attack; she was still on the ground and stumbling.

She emitted exactly half a jingle-wail before it had body-slammed her, smashing her straight down into the ground.

"I said, get *off*!" Wendy cried. She grabbed the first stick she saw and—though usually opposed to violence toward animals—whacked the qqrimal as hard as she could on its side.

It rolled out of the way but kept its claws around Tinker Bell, the fairy close to its belly.

Then it jumped upright on its four paws and—laughed?

"You—you—" Wendy stammered, indignant.

It really was. The horrible thing *was* laughing at her, chuckling and warbling. It bent its head and licked Tinker Bell with an ugly gray forked tongue. It smacked its mouth.

Wendy brought the stick down as hard as she could on its head.

It easily leapt out of her reach, landing on the side of a tree. From this new perch it chuffed one more time back at Wendy before scuttling up like a lizard into its branches.

"No!" Wendy dropped her stick and grabbed the trunk of the tree. "Come back! Come down here this *instant*!"

She shook the tree as hard as she could, expecting disappointment. But the tree was a slender tropical thing whose body was far more lithe and pliable than its London counterparts. It swayed easily under her efforts, and its long leafy fronds clattered and clashed satisfyingly.

The creature fell and hit the ground with an equally satisfying *whomp*.

"Tink!" Wendy grabbed the creature's tail to yank it off the fairy.

Only—its tail slid into nothing in her hands. Overpowered by the momentum she had created with nothing to balance it, Wendy fell back onto her bum.

The creature looked back at her and chuffed again.

Faint jingling sounds could be heard (pitifully) from under its stomach.

The qqrimal waggled its tail at Wendy and took off into the forest. Tinker Bell dangled from its mouth; the poor fairy jingled desperately as it disappeared into the bushes.

"No!" Wendy got up and ran after it as fast as she could. Flying was out of the question—she wasn't an expert and the understory of the jungle was far too dense for her to even consider it.

And she already had a late start; the smaller, more lithe carnivore easily leapt over obstacles and slunk under them.

Wendy also jumped over fallen trees and ducked under canopies of vines, trying to keep the thing in her sights—but she was much, much slower. The qqrimal was black as shadow and made almost no noise as it flowed on the forest floor, just a pitter-patter and occasional chuff.

She burst out into a hot clearing, an empty hilltop whose dry pinnacle could support little life. The sun beat down like a physical force. It was no longer a happy lemon; it was a blazing ball of fire. Wendy spun around, looking for signs of the qqrimal. But the ground was dried and cracked mud that recorded no footprints. The edges around the outside of the clearing were staffed by half-dead, yellowed trees that all looked the same.

There was no hint of the creature.

*"TINK?"* Wendy cried. "Tink?

"No," she murmured, turning and turning.

"No!" she cried again, and her voice fell flat and quiet in the thick fetid air.

"TINKER BELL!" she screamed.

But the jungle was silent.

# A Shadow (of a) Doubt

There was a very thin line between panic and giving up.

Wendy was filled with rage and terror—but also a split second away from collapsing onto the ground and weeping. And that would be the end of everything.

If she just started running—in the wrong direction—she would merely *continue* in the wrong direction and get farther and farther from the creature and the fairy.

If she retraced her steps looking for clues, she would be wasting time.

The image came to her mind ruthlessly unbidden: the black, formless creature biting down on the fairy's midriff; the resulting terrible *crunch*.

"TINKER BELL!" she screamed until her voice cracked.

Nothing.

Wendy choked back a sob and pulled at her hair. What to do? What would a hero do? What would Peter Pan do? What could *she* do? Where was the terribly clever deus ex machina or plot device that she would write for her own heroes?

What sort of nightmare creature *was* that thing—that qqrimal—anyway?

At least the crystalline guardian from before had made some sort of sense, pulled out of Michael's angry toddlerhood and a doll he had made out of clay. This animal was far too precise, too detailed for his young mind. And John would never have imagined something so horrible and vicious. Secretly he loved fairies as much as Wendy and delighted in designing the twig and acorn contraptions they used to simplify their forest tasks.

"What sort of child would come up with a carnivorous beast that *eats* fairies? That hunts and devours and tears them apart?" she wailed.

But of course there were other children besides the Darlings who believed in Never Land.

Children who . . . delighted in the destruction of fairies? Who hated beauty?

Or who didn't believe beauty was possible? That only ugliness and horror survived?

What kind of children were they—what were their lives like?

Wendy shivered.

"What do I do?" she whispered. What *could* she do, when there were monsters like these and worse roaming the fairy-tale world she had thought was safe?

That was when she noticed her shadow.

The black shape was doing the equivalent of jumping up and down—elongating and contracting, still connected to Wendy's feet. She waved her arms frantically, trying to get Wendy's attention.

"What? What is it?"

The shadow bent down and pulled at her feet. Then she stretched her arms, making a flying gesture, and pointed into the woods.

"What do you—oh, you want me to release you? So you can go look for Tinker Bell?"

The shadow nodded vigorously.

"You think you can find her?"

The shadow nodded again.

"But even if you find her—how can you help her until I get there?"

The shadow shook her head: *no time.* She pointed at their feet again.

"Oh. I suppose there isn't much of a choice, really, is there?"

The shadow nodded vigorously.

Wendy bent down, unsure what to do exactly. She placed her hands on her left foot and made as if to untie a boot.

Something . . . *gave.*

It felt like something untied from her belly and slid out through her feet. A wave of nausea washed over her, leaving her enervated. Everything, even standing, suddenly seemed exhausting.

It wasn't a simple thing to release one's shadow, Wendy realized. It wasn't all fun and games and a funny quest to reunite with it. The shadow—in Never Land, at least—contained something besides a lack of light and mimicry of movements. Some very visceral part of Wendy was in her shadow. And when she let go . . .

"You *will* come back to me, after you find her, right?" she asked before reaching for her other foot.

The shadow shrugged and shook her head.

*No time.*

No time to stop and think. No time to consider the ramifications.

"For Tinker Bell," Wendy told herself sternly and untied her right foot.

The shadow shot off out of the clearing, into the woods.

Wendy slumped to the ground.

Her energy and strength weren't *all* gone, she figured out after a few silent moments. She could still move and still stand up with a little effort. It was more like she didn't really care to.

"It's like I have the chills, or a cold, but of the soul," she said aloud to cheer herself up. "Nothing so *very* serious. Manageable. Peter has done without a shadow for four years. Certainly I can go an hour."

She did a few stretches and was satisfied with the way her body responded. Weakly, but up to the task if pressed.

She just hoped her shadow was going to do what she said—what Wendy *assumed* she was saying. That she would go find Tinker Bell before it was too late and somehow signal to Wendy. After all, despite whatever influence Never Land had, she was still Wendy's shadow. The shade of a good, well-meaning, honest girl must be a little good herself.

Unless all of Wendy's worst behaviors were contained in her shadow.

Like her betrayal of Peter Pan . . .

Wendy had a few long minutes of pondering these oppressive thoughts. But before she even thought it was possible there came a strange and ominous crashing in the woods. As if something was being flailed wildly back and forth. Thrown into the bushes, picked up, and thrown again.

And was that—was there the faintest jingle?

"Tinker Bell!"

Wendy made her feet move in the direction the sounds were coming from as quickly as she could manage.

She often had to stop, pause to listen, run the wrong way for a moment, trip over a plant, then turn the *right* way again (at least seven times), the way all heroes do when chasing through the woods on a rescue mission.

Like all good heroes she eventually found her quarry. But the scene made no sense at all when she first came upon it.

The qqrimal seemed to be throwing *itself* around violently. It growled, shook its head, leapt headfirst into a tree, then flowed down its trunk—and then began the whole thing over again. Like a dog with hydrophobia.

Tinker Bell was still clutched in its paws.

Wendy crept up quietly—but it didn't seem to see her at all.

When she accidentally stepped on a twig and snapped it, *then* the creature leapt up, alert.

Looking the wrong way.

Carefully, unsure what was going on, Wendy came up behind it as silently as she could, as close as she could.

She grabbed it by the nape of its neck.

Swinging it around quickly before it could flow out of her grasp, she seized its stomach with her other hand. She had to keep tossing it from hold to hold so it couldn't use its tricky thinning-out powers to escape.

The thing yowled and growled and hissed and batted out with his hind legs. It snapped is jaws wildly in all the wrong directions.

Something strange was going on with its mirror eyes. They looked dull and unseeing.

Wendy tore Tinker Bell out of its grasp and then slammed the qqrimal into the ground. Perhaps harder than was strictly necessary.

"Tink—are you all right?" She held the crumpled and bruised little fairy up for a better look.

Tinker Bell nodded woefully. She was bleeding, but not from the giant punctures Wendy had expected from the creature's claws. More like scratches from being shaken around while in its grasp.

*It was taking me back to its lair. They don't like . . .* fresh *fairy meat.*

"Oh!" Wendy said, swallowing.

The qqrimal stood up woozily, swaying and sick.

A black mist—no, *shadow!*—peeled itself off its face.

Wendy's shadow had covered its eyes, using herself as a mask!

The animal shook its head and blinked its eyes, back to their normal shiny silver. It gave Wendy a wounded, irritated look.

Wendy, pulling a Tinker Bell, stuck her tongue out at it.

The qqrimal leapt away into the underbrush and

disappeared as fast as it could—this time without a single snarky chuff.

Wendy's shadow triumphantly unfolded herself and stood tall, hands on hips. Her toes touched Wendy's and the human girl could feel energy and strength pour back into her.

"That was very clever!" Wendy crowed. "You blinded him! Oh, very clever indeed!"

The shadow bowed.

Then she saluted.

And then she took off.

Disappeared into the woods like the qqrimal, but high: into the branches of the canopy layer.

Wendy stumbled but didn't quite fall.

"I suppose I should have expected that," she muttered. "No one helps for free around here."

Tinker Bell, despite her wounds, looked up at the human girl with pity and concern.

*That was brave and noble, giving up your shadow for me. Thank you.*

"Well, what else was there to do, really?" Wendy asked, a little more tiredly than she wanted.

*After the way I treated you—*

"I mean, that's a fair point," Wendy said with a faint smile. "You're welcome."

*I don't deserve it.*

*You can't go back to London now.*

"What?" the human girl asked, startled.

(Well, that was interesting, at least: she could still feel panic, though muted, in her shadowless state.)

*You can't return home without your shadow.*

"But why? Peter left his own shadow in London. And he returned here!"

*Peter is almost pixie. You are entirely human. Shadows are different here. They are less of a . . . requirement than they are in London. The rules of your world are very strict about that sort of thing.*

*I'm sorry.*

"But I didn't *want* to go back to London," Wendy protested.

It was a little bit of a lie: she had always thought she would return, otherwise she wouldn't have insisted on a return ticket from the pirates.

And now that it looked like that option was taken away, she was suddenly a lot more concerned about it.

Never see Michael and John again?

Mother and Father?

Nana?

Even the evil old Shesbow twins, the smokestacks, the roofs, the clouds?

Tinker Bell seemed to read her mind. *You gave up a lot for me. More than you knew.*

"Well, I can't think about any of that now," Wendy told Tinker Bell—and herself—firmly. "Before anything else, we must rescue *Peter's* shadow and save Never Land. I can't go home until everyone here is safe. So let us continue to make our way to the En—no, the *Chanting* Peninsula. Are you well enough to travel?"

Tinker Bell looked at her with wonder. She nodded once.

"And is it very far away? Because—I'm afraid to admit it, but I'm a bit done in. All these adventures really wear a girl out. I'm dying to sleep." Wendy was very, *very* shaky in fact, but she ground her teeth and tried to sound as blasé as possible. The loss of her shadow made all of her aches and pains and tiredness worse—the exact opposite of the fairy dust.

*Sleep on the way. That's what we do.*

And although the idea of tiny winged creatures sleeping high in the sky with clouds for their cushions was positively delightful, Wendy couldn't see herself doing it without heading directly into a thunderhead, or a cliff, or the mouth of some sort of horrid Never Land creature.

"Oh, Tinker Bell, I don't think I could. I'd be terrified of falling, or smashing into something."

Tinker Bell smiled. *Go to sleep. I'll watch you.*

"Are you certain? I won't be afraid if you really will keep an eye on me. Sorry about being such a terrible burden. Big ugly human and all. Utterly useless."

Tinker Bell opened her mouth and out came great peals of strange, jingly laughter. Then she grabbed Wendy's hand and pulled her aloft, into the darkening sky.

# The First

The next few hours were strange.

Or maybe it was a day, or a half day, or two. . . .

A glorious sunset performed its final bows across Never Land. Dark purple clouds rolled out along a horizon edged in fiery orange so bright it was like looking into the depths of a blacksmith's forge. The first stars were entering with some confusion into the not-quite-black sky. It was delightful to see them floating in a sea of turquoise ether.

"How often do they get to do that?" Wendy wondered aloud tiredly.

Tinker Bell kept rising up and up into the sky and then pausing, then dipping down, then going sideways—and then repeating the whole procedure. Wendy had just summoned enough energy to ask her what she was doing when, with a bright look of satisfaction, the fairy apparently found whatever she was looking for and dragged the human girl through the air to her.

*Aha!*

Wendy suddenly realized what the invisible object of her friend's search was: a calm thermal wind. It was so large and encompassing that when she slipped into its embrace the howling breezes of the upper airs immediately became silent, as if in the presence of a king. Here it was surprisingly warm and scented with things that didn't seem to come from the jungles of Never Land: exotic but somehow familiar, like Mrs. Darling's perfume when she kissed her daughter before going out.

Wendy had no trouble at all curling up on this invisible bed, and sleep came quick despite the confusing scenes she saw between languorous blinks. Instead of crisp sheets, comforting fire, and downy quilt, she saw nothing but empty space, sharp mountains, and trees a thousand feet below. But not even these could keep her from unconsciousness.

She drifted, literally and figuratively, the whole night, Tinker Bell always close by. One time the little creature took a sit-down *on* her, lying back on the big girl's shoulder and watching the stars. Wendy remained silent and as still as she could, reluctant to disturb her.

Eventually, the fairy woke Wendy with a tug on her ear—back to her usual naughty tricks. But as the human girl started, indignant, she saw that the sun was close to rising. More importantly, the fairy held a rather ridiculously sized rubyfruit to break her fast with. These were the fruits that heroes stranded on a desert island in Wendy's stories always hoped to find to quench their thirst and save themselves from starvation.

Wendy sat up as best she could on nothing.

"Thank you, that's most kind." She took the rubyfruit and popped off the stem like she had in dreams. It fell neatly into ten perfect, juicy sections. "Would you like one?"

Tinker Bell shrugged nonchalantly but took a section and immediately sank her face into its pale, creamy flesh, tearing out mouthfuls while somehow managing not to get any juice on her face. A delicate, civilized little beast.

It was rather funny when Wendy thought about it. Despite Tinker Bell giving Wendy the gift of understanding fairy tongue, they had just had an entire conversation without the fairy speaking a single word. In fact, most of Tink's communicating still seemed to be in gestures, facial expressions, and body movements. They weren't just affectations or simply to enhance understanding for those who couldn't decipher jingles; this was really just how Tinker Bell spoke. When she had to she could be as articulate and verbose as anyone else—including other fairies, who spoke clearly and wordily and whose hands didn't move at all during discourse (like well-trained boarding school ladies). Tinker Bell's meaning was wrapped up in movement; she *was* energy and gesture.

Wendy ate another piece of fruit and turned to watch the east. She wasn't normally fond of sunrises because she was barely awake when they occurred and because they signaled the end of the peaceful quiet of the house. Others rose at that time, and Wendy had to deal with the various personalities and problems of the day that were outside her own head. Sunrises were never spectacular in London, anyway: just a yellowish lightening of the fog, or, on a really clear day in autumn, a brightening of rare blue sky somewhere behind all the rooftops. Perhaps in some neighborhood east of the Darlings' house, east of their street, east of the park, east and east and east, maybe *someone* at the edge of London saw the sun come up properly, from behind something natural like the sea or a forest edge. But no one else did.

Now two days in a row Wendy got to witness the real thing, Never Land–style. First came the strange false dawn that presaged the sun's appearance, like the hopeful breath of an audience before a famous chanteuse steps out onto stage.

Taking its own time, the lemony Never Land sun finally

rose—and surprisingly hot for the morning, its first rays hitting Wendy's skin with an almost tangible pressure.

Through all this, the air and the sunlight, came a strange vibration.

At first Wendy's brain almost dismissed it, thoughtlessly categorizing the repeated drone as "waves crashing on a shore." But the girls weren't low enough to hear any waves—and they weren't over a beach at all. So her mind tried to resolve the sounds into words or hums: *ommm, nam-nam-nam-nam ommmmm* and strings of only slightly more complicated sounds.

Tinker Bell saw her frowning and smiled.

*Chanting Peninsula,* she jingled. *Get it?*

"Oh! Yes! Not 'Enchanted'! The whole peninsula . . . *chants*. That's amazing! But what is it that makes the sounds, specifically?"

Tinker Bell shrugged, no longer interested in the question or the subject. She pulled Wendy's sleeve and pointed down: directly beneath them was the recognizable forest of Never Land, and there, just beyond it, was . . . a blank wall.

Clouds, gray and white and eggshell and beige and every not-quite-color in between drifted over each other in unhealthy layers. Fingers of mist spun out almost purposefully, ensnaring a tree or a rock and then using that anchor to crawl along farther. Yet in other places the mist stretched thin and snapped away from wherever it was before, revealing seemingly untouched foliage and landscape beneath it. Wendy wasn't sure what she expected—dead land? Changed, unfamiliar objects?—but was nevertheless surprised the magical fog moved on without altering anything in its wake. It didn't *look* harmless.

Inside the mist itself, however, something seemed not quite right. There were hints of pale brown or orange, with ochre . . . some surface that reflected light not from the sun that was now twinkling over Never Land; a different star perhaps, dun-colored and morose. Wendy shivered. The pirates were frightening, the crystal guardian was murderous, and the mermaids were surprisingly hostile, but this . . . this was a hint of the completely unknowable. And far, far more terrifying.

Tinker Bell pointed down and began to descend, spiraling like a drill.

"But why?" Wendy asked, coming somewhat clumsily after her, skirts flying up into her face as she desperately tried to hold them against her thighs. "Can't we just skim low under the fog, and search for Peter that way?"

*One does not simply fly into the Land of the First.*

"I don't suppose it should have been that easy," Wendy said with a sigh. She landed fairly elegantly and slowly—she thought—touching her tippy-toes down to the ground first the way Tinker Bell did. The two girls reluctantly regarded the strange, unwholesome smog before them as it coiled around itself like the intertwined bodies of mythic serpents. Jörmungandr or perhaps Ouroboros.

Though Wendy could not have possibly known it, the fairy and the human had the exact same expression on their faces: wonder, distrust, false bravery.

Tinker Bell tentatively reached a tiny, bauble-decorated toe into the mist—and then quickly pulled it out.

"I don't want to suggest anything untoward," Wendy said after a full moment's hesitation, "but, since you said one shouldn't fly here, well, if you don't think it's beneath you, perhaps you wouldn't object to sitting—*riding* rather, on my shoulder? That way we will be on equal footing, together, with whatever comes at us. Also you wouldn't be lost, or stepped on, or . . ."

But the fairy was already zooming up to her neck. She perched daintily on the crook of Wendy's shoulder and held on to a lock of brown hair—but less like reins and more for balance and possible security. She did not tug.

"Very well then," Wendy said, lifting her chin and trying to muster bravado and dignity appropriate to the moment—and to disguise how tickled she was at the closeness of the fairy, despite their circumstances. She could just feel the tiniest weight on her skin and the occasional brief heat of a speck of fairy dust.

Together, they entered the mists.

The first thing that struck Wendy was how it felt nothing at all like she had expected. The clouds were neither damp, nor moist, nor cold. They were *hot,* and somehow drier than the land around them. Yet they didn't smell of smoke or smog or anything burning.

Strange noises streamed past her ear: whispers she couldn't quite make out, the distant echo of something very large pounding off in the distance. A rhythmic beat whose direction she couldn't put her finger on.

Then the flat yellow, white, and gray entirely surrounded her, masking the world. There was no distance or perspective. She closed her eyes and tried to put her feet in the same direction she had been heading. There was nothing else to do. And since nothing was *touching* her, there was no immediate threat to worry about.

After some period of time she couldn't quite keep track of, the whispers quieted. She opened her eyes. Like tears after a good cry, the mists quickly dried and disappeared—or perhaps they rose up, joining the uncolored sky to make a complete dome of gray and beige around everything.

They stood in what appeared to be very much a desert.

Wendy, of course, had never seen one in real life but had read enough adventure novels and explorer's narratives to recognize one when she saw it. Sadly, the ground was not quite as dramatic as the sands of Egypt were described; not an endless ocean of dunes and ripples, solid waves and particulate shores. There *was* sand, but it was gritty white here and streaked with yellow there, broken up with a band of gray beyond that, and red, red, red where the far-off ruby cliffs seemed to dissolve under their own weight into the floor of the planet.

There were also rocks strewn about everywhere untidily. Tiny rocks like pebbles, large rocks like you might build a wall out of, but in all the wrong shapes and colors. Perfectly black rounded rocks scattered randomly among the rest for no good reason. Countless flat, flaking red rocks that made more sense in the red-tinged landscape.

Keeping close to the ground were strange little plants. And though Wendy generally didn't like imposing subjective opinions on defenseless inanimate objects, they were quite ugly. Thorny, narrow-twigged, bunched up tight, and miserly with leaves of dull colors. Some of them looked dead but apparently weren't. There wasn't a single "normal" cactus among them. No barrels with spikes, no tall ones with rounded branches like letters from another language.

Disappointing.

And then there were tall strange boulders that stood by themselves, spires or pinnacles dotting the landscape like bowling pins set up by a giant toddler. They were higher than buildings but narrow, their bodies striped with layers of red and white and tan like half-sucked peppermint canes a hundred years old and yellowed with age.

A dead wind blew so dry it burned Wendy's nostrils. Sand got in her eyes and it wasn't even normal *sand*, the pretty round and faceted jewels of a good English beach. It was more like dust, tiny slippery flakes that soon found their way into every crease and crevice of her clothes and person.

As for the rest of the land, from her squinted eyes Wendy saw . . . *farther* than she ever had. Her brain hurt trying to make some sort of sense of the images it received. At home even outside the city there were always houses blocking the view, and trees, and hills; every couple of miles something like a hedge cut off one's view of the rest of the world. Here she could see for what appeared to be fifty miles in every direction, maybe a hundred, with no real end but for the ability of her eyes.

She felt dizzy, utterly exposed under such a huge, bright, dead sky and endless flat desert, with its weird chess-like rock figures, its unmeasurable walls of red rock and distant plateaus. There was nothing else; she herself was nothing.

She didn't even have her shadow.

Wendy collapsed to her knees, overcome by it all.

*Careful!* Tinker Bell exhorted, buzzing up off her shoulder for a moment before remembering not to fly. *You're going to get all sticky and mucky.*

"Mucky?" Wendy asked huskily. "Are you joking? Tinker Bell, are you feeling all right? Is the heat getting to you?"

*Heat? It's cold and nasty and wet with all the mud bubbling up everywhere!*

"Mud?" Wendy looked around. "All I see is desert, miles and miles of empty desert. What do you see?"

The fairy shifted uncomfortably on her shoulder. *I just told you. Mud. A whole world of it. A giant flat. Dead. World. Mud bubbling up. Nothing.*

"I wonder which one of us is right," Wendy murmured. "Do you think it's some sort of trap, some way of disguising themselves? Of keeping us from finding them and Peter? An illusion . . . like fairy glamour?"

*They are the most powerful beings in Never Land. They* are *Never Land,* Tinker Bell jingled darkly. *No need for illusion.*

"How does this place usually appear? Have you seen it before?"

*Those who return never say. And no.*

"Well." Wendy bit her lip. Even words spoken aloud here sounded thin and dead and useless. "If it's real at all, at least what I can see, from where I stand, there is no sign of Peter anywhere. Or anything living. You?"

*Nothing. Mud.*

"Hmm. Hold on then. We'll walk a bit, and see if we see anything or anyone. Let's just take a good look at where we started so we can remember. . . ."

She forced herself back up on her feet and looked behind them. To her relief, the air—or reality—seemed to ripple; shreds of white and gray blew aside and the desert petered out. Glimpses of the dark green jungle peeped from beyond.

"Well, good," she said, turning back the way they were headed. "We can always return. We shall mark our place with those three rocks there, and—oh!"

Not twenty feet from them, where there was nothing but scrub before, stood a giant monolith. A red-and-orange jagged-edged hoodoo reaching high into the sky. Its top was worn into three strange and slightly bulbous shapes. With just a little imagination Wendy could make out heads and maybe faces—blank, primordial ones.

*"Tinker Bell,"* she whispered. *"What do you see?"*

*Mud welling up. Bubbling up into three ugly mud statues. Sweating and bleeding and oozing mud.*

Wendy was only a little relieved that she and her friend were both seeing different versions of what appeared to be the same thing. The stone effigy in front of her was terrifying in every way: in its size, silence, and sudden appearance.

**Why are you here?**

Nothing spoke. Nothing that looked like a head or a

face moved. No *sound* emerged, and yet the words reverberated across the dead landscape, echoing and unmistakable. There could be no doubt where it came from.

"If you please . . ." Wendy dropped into a small curtsy. "We're here in search of our friend, Peter Pan. Have you seen him?"

Silence.

Terrible, dreadful silence. It, too, echoed, blanketing the desert with a deadly finality.

Wendy waited and waited.

The dry wind blew past her ear. She felt Tinker Bell grow tense, tiny fingernails digging into her skin. Not urging her to do anything. Just nervous.

"I'm sorry," she began again after a while. "Peter Pan. Have you seen him? He's about my size, and wears green. . . ."

**Peter Pan was here. Now he is gone.**

"Ah. Do you know when he left? Or where he went to? Did you give him a new shadow?"

One question too many.

Despite the lack of change in the landscape, Wendy could feel its impatience.

**The problems of the boy are not our concern. We sent him away. Why are you here. You are not from Never Land. You are—older.**

"I beg your forgiveness if I am too old to be allowed here," Wendy said, immediately lowering her head. "I shall leave as soon as I help my friend here find *her* friend, and help him get his shadow back, and defeat the pirates with whatever they are planning."

There was a strange un-noise, as if the air were shaking.

**Age is no rule of ours. It is a law created by you humans from the other side. We make no laws. We make no rules. We just *are*. It is humans who seek to name and regulate and shape this land to their ridiculous whims. Our world is crystallizing to the point of permanence, thanks to your ridiculous dreaming.**

"I . . . don't understand. . . ."

**Once we and the world were one. We *were* the world. Then humans came. Their dreams were simple at first. But soon came the rules and the laws and the ideas and the suppositions and the feelings and the wishes and the decisions and the hopes. With each one another mountain hardened and another sea narrowed into a river. Now you have your Never Land. And because children's dreams are the strongest, their dreams rule the world. Everywhere except for here, where we still rule. We, the First of this world.**

"Oh, but isn't it all rather lovely?" Wendy asked. "Fairies and mermaids—despite their vicious tendencies—and dragons and flying and moonlit beaches? You have an amazing, beautiful world here. Never Land exists the way it does as a result of all that innocent childhood dreaming . . . all of their most magical and creative thoughts before they grow up and it slips away. . . ."

**INSOLENT!**

**Wendy Darling you *know***

**You know you and your brothers are not the only ones who dream**

Wendy was forced to her knees by the strength of the words. She covered her ears despite not actually hearing anything.

When she managed to look up again, the rock formation had changed. There was something about it that *looked* different, and it appeared to be looming over her more.

**Some children are so twisted by hate from others they can dream of nothing but hate.**

**Some children dream of going through a day without being whipped or beaten.**

**Some children dream of nothing more than a full meal. They smile in their sleep as their minds conjure something that would fill their bellies if it were only real.**

**Some dream that their parents are still alive, or at least that their ghosts come to visit.**

**Some dream of still being able to play with their friends and go to school although they no longer can.**

***This* Never Land you see is the Never Land you and your brothers are used to. There are other parts of Never Land you never see, with no fairies or mermaids. Only dishes of food and clean water and kindness. Or beasts so horrible you would die upon viewing them.**

Silence filled the space in Wendy's ears and mind when the First finished speaking. Her heart paused.

*Other . . . children's dreams . . .*

"The qqrimal," she murmured.

But that wasn't *her* fault. Was it? These other children weren't part of *her* Never Land, her world—were they? They weren't part of the London where she and John and Michael played in the nursery with Nana and cufflinks and perfume and Mr. and Mrs. Darling and tea and rain.

But . . . of course they were.

Wendy knew that.

She just didn't like to think about it.

They were out there somewhere, at the edges or hidden in plain sight. Orphans, beggars, children with bruises, girls whose parents really did force them into arranged marriages—without even the choice of going to Ireland instead.

Some of them may even have dreamed of a life where

*all* they had to worry about was growing lonely and old in a large house, where there was food and heat every day.

Why else would they have dreamed up a Peter Pan to rescue them?

"I . . . I just never even thought about that before."

The First didn't say anything.

"I'm sorry. I didn't—I still don't know how Never Land works. Or . . . my world, either, I suppose."

**How much do you *care* about your world? Or this one? The mad pirate will destroy all of Never Land rather than simply quit it, once he has Peter Pan in his clutches to watch it all and weep.**

"Yes, that's why I'm here. But I don't see what I or my world has to do with—"

**Hook is the villain and star of so many of your tales. He was birthed from the tides of your world. And he will destroy ours.**

"I didn't mean to . . . They were just stories. . . . But *you* can stop him, can't you?"

**We cannot stop this, because of your world's hold over ours. He is of your making.**

"What do you want me to *do*?" Wendy cried desperately. "I'll do it! Whatever you ask!"

Nothing. Silence.

Normally she was not a girl prone to perspiring—she

never moved much faster than a brisk walk, and remained inside on the hottest days. Now she felt sweat break out across her brow and uncomfortably under her arms.

But it wasn't from the desert heat.

"Should I leave now?" she asked.

Maybe she and the fairy should just go. Maybe the First were done with them. But it felt wrong to turn her back on these creatures, whatever they were, and walk away . . . rather like turning one's back on a king or queen. Were *they* done with her?

"Please. I'm sorry. I was so stupid. Never Land is a learning experience," she ventured, nervousness and sweat coalescing into words that just poured out of her mouth. "I came for adventure—perhaps wrongfully—and it's far more complicated than the place I dreamed of. Pirates who don't seem to want to be pirates, girls who have to hide their true selves to come here, monsters who only eat fairies, mermaids who will fight each other tooth and claw over an apple . . . And Hook. And *I* am responsible for his doomsday visions?"

**Never Land is a reflection of your world.**

Wendy jumped. She had no longer been expecting a response, much less one so calm.

**Are things broken here? Save this world. Then go back to your own broken world and fix it. Perhaps we shall be mended as well.**

"Me? Fix the *entire* world? I can't even fix my own situation at home! That's why I came here!"

**Is escape to Never Land your only recourse for being made to grow up, for being sent away? For disagreeing with your parents? Is there nothing else you could do? For yourself? For others like you? For others *un*like you?**

This was not how Wendy expected the conversation to go. After her outburst, she expected irritation from the strange beings and maybe a boulder or two hurled at her for perceived insolence. Being squashed would have made more sense than these strange questions.

"I'm just . . . I'm no one. I can't do anything. I can't even disobey my father."

**Perhaps you should see if that really is true.**

**Go quickly. Time is running out for Never Land and for Peter.**

There was a pause and a ripple in the atmosphere that Wendy realized meant a change in mood.

**Goodbye, human not grown-up not child not hero not villain. Goodbye, pixie not pixie not human.**

Wendy blinked and the monolith was gone. The others behind it in the landscape had also rearranged. There seemed to be fewer.

She let out a breath, not even realizing she had been holding it.

Tinker Bell decided that it was safe to flitter, and zoomed around like a nervous bee—keeping *very* close to her big friend.

"That was . . . very interesting. Educational."

She finally found the right word.

*"Terrifying."*

Tinker Bell nodded, swallowing.

"We really have to get out of here and find Peter and get Hook. Immediately. When even the gods of a world are worried about its destruction, well—it's serious indeed. And I know you think it's better to find Peter first and then deal with his shadow and the pirates, but perhaps we really should go after the pirates now? I think we'll find them more easily at this point. What do you think? Tink?"

But the little fairy wasn't paying attention. She tugged on Wendy's hair and pointed back the way they had come.

Wendy looked, very reluctantly. Afraid of what would be there—or rather, what wouldn't.

And she was right.

Never Land was entirely gone. The desert extended for a hundred miles in all directions, seamless and complete.

# The Desert

"No," Wendy said softly.

Even though she had predicted it, even though now she could see the truth with her own eyes, she still fell down the long-familiar tunnel of childishness: wishing that what just happened hadn't. Denying with her full being that the vase had tipped and smashed, that the terrible thing just said had come out of her own mouth, that the soufflé had fallen moments before she served it to Mother and Father.

That she and Tinker Bell were stranded, cut off from the rest of Never Land, in what looked like an infinite desert.

Wendy carefully stepped back to the point she had mentally marked before, knowing full well it might be important later. Three red stones in increasing size were lined up like a fallen desert sandman. A scrubby little black and matte turquoise bush with two pom-pom-like appendages grew nearby. There were her footprints coming out of nowhere. Beginning the journey. She bent over, trying to feel a hint of moist air, of cool sea breeze, of pungent jungle funk.

But of course there was nothing.

Tinker Bell zipped around back and forth above Wendy, trying to see what she was seeing. Then she flew a little farther out, to the left and right and front and back with the neat, almost unnatural motions of a dragonfly hunting. Actually, she *was* hunting. For a way out.

"Anything?" Wendy asked, trying to keep the hope out of her voice.

Tinker Bell shrugged, shook her head, and jingled sadly.

"Maybe . . . Look, I know you don't want to disrespect this place, but the First seem to have abandoned us to our fates. For now. Maybe it would be all right if you just flew up—really high—into the air? And looked around?"

Tinker Bell nodded reluctantly.

She took a big, dramatic breath and rose into the pale sky. Wendy had to shade her eyes with her hand to see the fairy at all against the brightness. High, higher still, higher than a kite. Eventually she disappeared.

While Wendy knew her friend's invisibility was just a

trick of distance and the limitation of her own eyesight, she couldn't help fretting. She shuffled her feet and bit her lip until the fairy reappeared, falling down on the exact same path she had taken up with the inevitability and determination of an acorn freed from its twig. Wendy held out her hand, and the tiny girl landed on it with obvious gratitude.

"Anything?"

Tinker Bell shook her head, looking perplexed. She pointed: north, east, south, west, or whatever passed for them in this strange land. She put a hand to her head, much like Wendy had when watching for her, and mimed looking far out in each direction, frowning and squinting. Then she shrugged again.

"It just goes on and on, in every direction?"

*Forever. Just that big muddy plateau in front of us—that is the only feature in any distance.*

"But . . . we *saw* boundaries to it when we flew down," Wendy protested, not arguing with her friend so much as with reality. "It wasn't so big, this area. It only covered a tiny portion of the island."

Tinker Bell gave her a look.

"All right, all right, I know we're not dealing with normal forces here." Wendy sighed. "After telling us that we need to save Never Land, and soon, the First abandoned and trapped us here. One can only assume they think we can find our way out. It's some sort of test.

"So let's think about this logically. Their demesne seems to continue forever. It's all outside, beyond us. But where did the First go? I don't see any of those monoliths—er, I guess you would see mud piles—in any direction *far away* from us. They are only in the middle distance. So perhaps . . . perhaps there is someplace *inward* they go. Or *downward.* Yes, that seems rather backward and Never Land-y. What do you think, Tinker Bell?"

The fairy shrugged and nodded, pursing her lips. Like*: sure, sounds as good as anything at this point.*

"All right then, let's head over to those cliffs over there. Maybe there's a secret canyon that burrows deep into their lair. Race you!" Wendy raised her arms to fly.

Nothing happened.

"Up now! Happy thoughts!"

Her feet remained firmly planted on the ground.

Tinker Bell frowned.

"Oh dear," Wendy said.

The fairy spiraled up and down around the human girl, practically smothering her with fairy dust. Much of it was blown away on the harsh, hot breeze: thousands of sparkles spreading across the arid landscape in a cloud that grew taller and taller and more spread out as it dissipated into the air. "What a waste," Wendy sighed.

She thought of all good things. Candy floss, the first scent of lilacs in the spring, a really nice day in the shade of the backyard tree with her notebook, Nana under her hand.

Still nothing happened.

"Either I'm terrified to the core of my soul by this place," Wendy said thoughtfully, "or I can't borrow your fairy magic here."

Tinker Bell shook her head sorrowfully and patted her on the hand.

"Well then, onward anyway!"

Wendy straightened her back, gave Tinker Bell (and herself) a reassuring nod, and began marching toward the cliffs. That's what Englishmen did. They pushed up their sleeves, gritted their teeth, and did what needed to be done. Out in the midday sun, if need be. Like mad dogs.

And so went she.

It was hard going in the strange sand. There were occasional patches of slick white rock, flat as a tabletop and much easier to walk on. But these didn't always line up the way she was heading; often she had to walk along one until its end and then stumble in the sand until the next one. Any plant she accidentally dragged her legs against left scrapes of both kinds: harmless little white-lined reminders and truly defensive strikes, deep angry red welts.

Wendy was sweating profusely now although it evaporated immediately in the dry air. This caused her some confusion until she finally figured out where the potential rivulets of sweat were disappearing to. Which brought up another worry. In her stories dehydration was much less threatening: *"And they couldn't find water anywhere on the deserted island, not even a coconut palm to climb and crack the fruits thereof and drink the sweet nectar. And so the heroes wandered and thirsted and dreamed of lemonade. . . ."* And of course, Peter Pan and the Lost Boys eventually found something like a washed-up cask of cider or a hidden spring.

Here there were no trees at all, and it seemed very unlikely without Moses to find a spring in the middle of the desert. Lack of water was going to be a real problem, real soon.

Not to mention hunger . . .

She looked askance at her little friend, who was flying beside her with an equal look of determination. Her teensy brow was a bit dewy and smeared with dust, but it didn't seem like she was in any real discomfort.

It was hard to tell if time passed at all in that strange land. The cliffs and mesas did seem to grow closer—very slowly—but the light didn't change at all. Wendy noticed with fascination that the shadows of this land chose their angle and size with no particular logic. A stone might have a long shadow lying to the area she thought of as "east," as if the sun were setting somewhere to the west, while the bush next to it might have a barely-there black circle clinging to its twiggy skirts like it was high noon. Perhaps that was why Peter was drawn here; the First might have some sort of strange affinity to shadows and shadow magic.

Tinker Bell's shadow yawned and stretched and pointed here and there, but honestly, the little fairy moved too quickly herself for the difference between them to be that noticeable.

Unlike Wendy's lack of shadow, which was *very* noticeable. The ground looked bleak and empty beneath her. She found she missed even the shadow's not quite appropriate behavior, like when she grew distracted and did something Wendy wasn't doing. She wondered if the shadow was out looking for Peter. Did she also grow weak without contact with her mistress? Did she *need* Wendy? And once they found Peter and reunited him with his shadow—would her shadow follow suit?

Or would her shadow prefer to stay in Never Land, where she was free to do as she pleased, rather than return to London and a life of just copying Wendy's every movement? Would Wendy be able to convince her to go home with her?

She found herself missing deeply the cold and wet weather of that city. It was vastly preferable to the oven they were in now.

Minutes or hours passed. Wendy fretted and swore quietly to herself. Time was ticking away and they were no closer to stopping Hook, his nefarious plans now confirmed by the First.

"What sort of lunatic destroys *everything* when he can't win?" she growled. Perhaps it was her fault, as a storyteller. Perhaps recurring villains grew sick of their own recurrence.

Wendy tried not to brush back the hair that wound up in her eyes because then she would get red streaks from the ubiquitous dust in it and all over her face. Tinker Bell had plucked a tiny, thick leaf and tried to hold it as an umbrella above her head—perhaps to keep herself dry in whatever the landscape was doing in her vision. But no matter which way she tilted it she seemed unsatisfed with the results. Eventually she let it drop—but only after taking a tentative bite out of its flesh.

The look on her face was all that was needed to stop Wendy from launching into a lecture on the danger of unknown plants and their possible toxicity. The fairy wasted precious spit getting all of it—and the taste—out of her mouth.

Finally they arrived at the skirts of the red cliffs. Here giant slopes of rock that looked like they used to be part of the mountains finally succumbed to time and melted into piles of sand and rubble. Amongst their folds were multiple canyons twisting and leading deep into the plateau. Wendy picked a likely one and pointed. Tinker Bell nodded. They plunged ahead.

"So . . . Tinker Bell . . ." Wendy ventured after they had walked for a bit. "Your little—pardon me—your fairy friends back there . . . What were their names? Berryloon and . . . ?"

*Thorn.*

"Thorn. Yes, that suits the fellow quite well. *Thorn.* Like with his sword, stabbing."

Tinker Bell narrowed her eyes suspiciously.

Wendy slipped down a treacherous patch of slick rock covered in fine gravel. More of her skirt tore. Without even thinking this time, she simply ripped off the ragged piece and tied it around her middle like a belt.

"Cuts quite a figure, doesn't he? I mean, his apparel was most immodest—but he wore it well. Didn't he?"

Tinker Bell buzzed over to hang in Wendy's face.

*Oh my phlox. You* like *him.*

"Like?" Wendy said indignantly. "I hardly know the boy. I was just saying how handsome he was, and well-spoken, and his ears were *very* elegant."

*You like Thorn.*

Whatever the fairy was saying from then on grew incomprehensible as she lapsed into great peals of jingly laughter that echoed off the canyon walls. She actually held her belly and guffawed, wasting quantities of sparkling fairy dust on the sand below. This only irritated Wendy further. She had just grown used to flying and was now more than a little peeved that her power was gone.

"All right, all right, no need to be all gossipy and schoolgirlish about it."

*It's just . . .* Thorn. *He's so* dull. *And you're so* big.

"I was only making conversation," Wendy said grumpily.

*Oh, I'm just teasing,* the little fairy said, patting her hand, eyes wide with mock apology. *When we get out of here and rescue Peter's shadow, we can go find him in the fairy realms and you can tell him your true feelings.*

*Or I will, if you can't.*

"Don't you dare!" Wendy cried.

Tinker Bell wiped a tear of laughter out of her eye. *Kidding! I wouldn't unless you asked me to. It's just so weird.*

"I don't see why it's strange. But let me just make sure I am clear about this, so we don't get into trouble again: *you* don't . . . ah . . . *like* him?"

Tinker Bell made a sick face. Then she thought about it. Really thought about it. Then she shrugged*: nope.*

"You only have eyes for Peter Pan, don't you?" Wendy asked softly.

Tinker Bell nodded woefully.

"All right, well, we're not going to discuss him. But what about that other girl? Berryloon or whatever? She acted like she knew you very well. Are you friends?"

Tinker Bell frowned and made a sour face, like she would have spit if she had been less ladylike. Or perhaps had any spit to waste.

"Ah, so you know each other well, but aren't friends. There are girls like that in my neighborhood—the demonic Shesbow twins, as I call them. Mother and Father are always trying to make me spend time with them. Frankly, I'd rather be alone. Alone, hungry, thirsty, hot, and exhausted, really."

Tinker Bell nodded vigorously.

"Fairies . . . spend a lot of time . . . *together,* don't they?"

Tinker Bell rolled her eyes.

*Fetes. Balls. Parties. Moon viewings. New moon festivals. Farmers markets. Pollen whispers. Nectar-ines.*

"I should very much like to see a fairy Nectar-ine," Wendy said wistfully. "But I'm sure I probably wouldn't want to attend many, if I *were* a fairy. Like the parties and dances in London. I never know what to say that's appropriate, and everyone thinks I talk too much and I'm odd and . . . I don't know. Immature. Childish. Strange?"

Tinker Bell nodded meaninfully. But her eyes were focused elsewhere, on an incident, on the past.

"I guess neither you *nor* I have had many female friends—any, really?"

Tinker Bell slowly shook her head.

"What about that Lost Boy—er, girl? Skipper?"

Tinker Bell shrugged. *Lost Boys. You know. They're friends . . . but not* friends.

"I do understand," Wendy said with a sigh. "There are booksellers' nephews and vendors at the market . . . but no bosom companions."

Tinker Bell looked down at her chest, frowning.

"Ah, I mean, very close friends. You know, someone you can tell secrets to, who will always love you no matter what stupid thing you say or do."

*Or will always be there to save you, no matter how mean you've been.*

And for once, Wendy had the sense to just nod and smile and not say anything.

Ahead the canyon opened up wide and flat as it traveled into the heart of the mesa. *Inviting.* Strangely clear of even the hardiest scrubby plants, almost paved in alternating ribbons of soft silt and packed sand. Very easy to walk on. Tiny polished pebbles congregated in delta formations in the middle of the path and along the edges.

"Peculiar," Wendy said softly. "Almost like the bottom of a stream, without a stream on it. Yes, that's exactly what it's like. Like we're walking in a stream that isn't here. What do *you* see?"

Tinker Bell shrugged. *Mud . . . You're walking on flat rocks just above the mud. Your feet are getting filthy.*

"Well, whatever it is, sounds like a road to me. Let's take it."

Tinker Bell nodded. One very suspicious rock guarded the entrance of this new path, a boulder perched on a pedestal with a strangely intelligent look about it. Much, much smaller than the monoliths that had dotted the desert earlier, or the one that had spoken to them. Still . . .

The way gently twisted and turned, the high stony walls above them copying its movements in folds and wrinkles. But the rocks, the sands, the scattered plants, the strange shadows—they all looked more or less exactly the same no matter where they were. There was no discernible feeling of progress.

This was more walking than Wendy had ever done at once, and all without her shadow. At some point she realized she could barely feel her legs. Sometimes when she put her foot down she misjudged the distance and stepped bone-jarringly hard on the ground. Sometimes she felt the world tilt.

The inside of her mouth was rough and painful like sandpaper, but she feared spitting the dust out—afraid of losing any fluid at all, since they'd had nothing to eat or drink since eating that rubyfruit.

And while Wendy didn't like spending too much time dwelling on functions of the body, it had been a very long time since she had last needed to use the loo.

"Tinker Bell, I think I need a break," she finally admitted.

The fairy nodded glumly. Her hair was limp and her wings drooped, and she didn't jingle. They found a large shadow (cast from who knew what object) to collapse in.

"I think this might be a kind of an oubliette," Wendy admitted after they had both sat there silently for a moment. "A trick of the First. There's no end or escape. I put these things into stories now and then—paths which look useful but lead nowhere."

Tinker Bell nodded reluctantly. She had come to the same conclusion.

"This is *so frustrating*!" Wendy suddenly shrieked, using a last bit of energy to kick the canyon wall. "We can't be here—we have to be out there, saving Never Land!"

The fairy was silent.

"You haven't said anything at all about the danger your whole *world* is in," Wendy pointed out, somewhere between curious and peevish.

*Without Peter—*

"It's like you don't have a world anyway. Yes, I understand." Wendy sighed and put a very careful finger on the fairy's hand. "I'm terribly sorry. About him, and everything. But I'm not sorry we're together. Imagine if you had to face this alone!"

Tinker Bell shuddered. She looked up at Wendy with something approaching chagrin.

*I'm very glad you're with me. And not just because you saved me.*

"Those First, eh?" Wendy said wryly, trying to keep her humor. "Nice gods, those lot."

Tinker Bell was silent, neither agreeing nor disagreeing. Then she frowned.

"What? What is it?"

*They said, "Is there nothing else you could do? For yourself? Perhaps you should see if that is really true."*

"They were talking about whether I could change anything back in *London*. If I could fix our world, and therefore make changes here."

*But . . . then they said goodbye and left us here. And* you *said this could be a test. What if they meant perhaps you should see if you can change anything or figure out anything* here, *first?*

"Oh," Wendy said, and she thought about it.

Once she quieted her initial immediate objections the idea sort of tasted right. Like something that would happen in an adventure story. The villains who turn out not to be villains at all, really, just helpers on the hero's path to heroism. What seems like a serious setback is actually a test to see if the hero is worthy enough to proceed with the rest of her quest.

Basic storytelling, really.

"Maybe . . . maybe you're right. If I can get us out of here, I can find Peter and get his shadow back. And If I can do *that,* surely I can save Never Land!"

Tinker Bell nodded vigorously.

"Only . . ." Wendy's face fell. "Only I've never really done anything *real.* Solved any *real* problems or puzzles. What could I possibly do? There are no obvious riddles to solve here. This isn't a labyrinth. There isn't even an actual villain to test my strength against. All my skills are imaginary. And all my real talents are useless. . . . Mend a skirt? Run a house? Stare out the window, dreaming? Which do you think would help us here?"

*Dreaming.*

*You can tell stories.*

"Oh please—that's nothing. Anyone can tell stories."

*No. Stop it. You told stories so wonderful that Peter Pan came to listen—to stories about himself! Your telling stories invited Never Land into your home.*

Wendy blinked. "I . . . suppose that's true. I never considered it that way before. If I hadn't told the stories about Peter Pan, Peter Pan wouldn't have come . . . which is an odd thought in itself. But if he hadn't come, he wouldn't have lost his shadow and left it. And then *I* wouldn't have traded it to Hook to come here. What a strange series of events! It's all because I tell stories.

"But how does this help us now? I can't just make up a story about us escaping here and have it come true."

The fairy looked at her thoughtfully. *What happens in your world, the dreams of your world, affects* our *world. And we are in the Land of the First, the origin and heart of Never Land.*

"Oh, I see what you're saying. My stories change and shape Never Land—and other children's do, too. So perhaps *here* I could directly alter it, myself?"

Tinker Bell shrugged: *why not?*

"It's worth a try!" Wendy said, growing excited. "Let's see. What can I come up with . . . ? All right. Here goes.

"Once upon a time, there were two girls lost in a desert that went on and on forever, one fairy and one human. They seemed to have no means of escape, but then . . . a giant friendly bird, a Never Bird, flew down out of the sky and took them on her back, safely returning them to the Pernicious Forest and Never Land proper!"

Wendy waited expectantly.

Nothing happened.

Although she hadn't completely believed that something would happen in response to her words, she still felt an almost overwhelming sense of disappointment at the completeness of the *nothing* that happened. Not even a random sparrow appeared in the dusty canyon.

*That's not a story,* Tinker Bell said dryly. *That's a wish.*

Wendy started to argue and then actually thought about what the fairy had said. True: although it had a beginning, middle, and end, there was no character change—no character interaction at all, really. There was no setup, no grand description of the scenery, nothing. She should know better! She spent so much of her spare time writing. . . .

Wendy looked at the strange, washed-out path they were on and began to imagine.

"You know, once upon a time this was a thriving, fast-moving river," she said almost conversationally. "It was all sorts of different colors—clear white to the bottom, red from the sand of the cliffs, green with life and fish. Where it splashed out of its banks, lush grass and trees grew.

"But then one day, far north of here, a powerful warlord fell in love with a beautiful maiden who did not love him back. For she loved another, a young farmer who lived on the other side of the river—"

*Farmer?* Tinker Bell interrupted skeptically.

"Shush. This is *my* story. And I always thought farmers were rather dashing and romantic figures in their own way. Especially the Scottish ones. Anyway: The warlord grew angry and swore that the maiden would never see her lover again. He used his incredible strength—from years of rampaging and pillaging—and picked up the river and tied it in a knot. The waters stopped flowing to the south and dried up, turning the once lovely river valley, the very one in which we sit, into just another dead path through the desert.

"The knot was so clever and complex that the maiden and the farmer could not figure out how to untie it, even had they the strength. So they each got a little boat—well, hers was actually rather magnificent because she was a warrior princess, as it happens, with a golden prow and silken cushions. His was more fitting to his station, of course.

"But back to the story. Every day they rowed toward each other but could never find a way to meet, for no matter what path they chose the water kept them apart. The princess had her wisest witches and most wily wizards use their magic to try to help her cross. On the back of a clockwork crocodile, through a tunnel made from the breath of mermaids. . . . None of it worked, of course. And so the maiden and the farmer kept trying, and failing, and wept at their fate.

"All who saw them pitied the poor lovers and cried with them. Year after year the tears fell, adding to the volume—and the saltiness—of the river that divided the princess from the farmer.

"And then one day the tears were just too much for the river to hold. It overflowed its banks and burst the knot—*pop! pop! pop!*—straightening itself out like a snake waking up.

"Not completely, however," Wendy added as a quick aside. "The bumps in the knots became a series of tiny islands and beautiful, rich ponds and lakes known as the Maiden's Tears."

*Why not the Farmer's Tears?*

"Excellent point. They were known as the Farmer's Tears, and made for quite good irrigation. The two lovers, united at last, left their boats in the river and met in the middle of the water on one of the new islands, and that is where they built their house and lived happily for the rest of their lives."

Was it her imagination, or was a breeze picking up?

Was there a shimmer in the sky, a difference beginning in the otherwise flat white sheen?

*All right,* the fairy said, interrupting. *But . . .*

"Just wait. This happened *so far north* that it took *weeks* before the river joyfully managed to come all the way back down to the desert, greeting its old, lost friends and watering the sands around it. Careful, Tinker Bell. Come over here."

Wendy stood and took her friend by the hand, pulling her into the air and moving both of them farther up the side of the gully. She couldn't have said how she knew, but with a calm assuredness like nothing she had ever felt before, she was utterly unsurprised when a strange noise began somewhere up in the canyon.

A crashing, booming, terrifying sound.

Tinker Bell just had time to tightly grab Wendy's finger when a ten-foot wall of water came hurtling down the ravine. It foamed and roiled in all the colors Wendy had described, red and white and green. Rainbow-sparkling fish leapt along its crest, riding it with apparent joy.

Tinker Bell swooped up backward in surprise and delight. Wendy grinned.

The river crashed up against the bank nearest them, careened off it and continued, splashing the two girls. It was like when a hundred children run down the street, out of school for the day and well aware that the marionette performer was back in the square; all violence and speed and good nature and excitement and *force,* bouncing off the gates and fences and alleys of London, un-slowed and untroubled by any accidental crashes.

"The river eventually found its way back to the sea, and settled with great relief into its old banks and beds," Wendy continued, feeling that things should calm down a *little* bit. "Once again it divided Never Land, but never as permanently as when it was in knots."

*It's great we have water now,* Tinker Bell said, *but how does this help us? You can't swim—we've seen that.*

Wendy shook her head at her friend and made a *tch tch* sound.

"Don't you remember the story? The two lovers stayed on the island in the middle, and *left their boats in the river*."

Tinker Bell opened her mouth, about to ask another question, when the boats in question came bumping slowly around the bend.

They looked a little out of place in the desert, drifting along the base of the high umber walls. The farmer's boat was a tiny wood-and-hide thing that could have been mistaken for a pile of driftwood. It was made for quick jaunts close to the land, for poking about ponds and lakes. Not for going down the rocky rapids of a canyon wash.

The warrior maiden's boat was far more intriguing. It was all dark wood, beautifully bent and fitted together with the complexity of a true seafaring vessel. Intricate gilded carvings covered the prow. The gunwale was painted a bright, cheery blue. A pole stood up in the back for steering. While there were no cushions left—they looked like they had been ripped out by the incredibly rough journey—the benches looked comfortable enough.

Tinker Bell clapped and jingled her approval.

The boat seemed to sense their need and nosed its way through the back current over to their bank.

"Shall we?" Wendy asked, trying not to sound too pleased with herself. "After you."

Tinker Bell gave a little bow in the air, and Wendy

returned it with a curtsy and a flourish. Then the fairy flew delicately to the fore bench and sat. On the bench next to her was a carelessly left, beautiful gem-encrusted dagger that hung on a useful necklace. Tinker Bell gave her friend a look.

"Oh yes. She also left her necklace behind, the one her mother gave her for protection," Wendy said, reaching in and putting it on. "All right, it's not really part of the story—but it seems like a weapon would be useful for me to have, don't you agree?"

She carefully held the side of the boat as it tipped a little with her weight, then settled herself in the back with the pole. She had done some punting on a visit to see her mother's cousin up in Oxford but wasn't entirely sure what use that skill would be in a river that was the topological opposite of a sleepy English canal.

A strange *tick tick tock* noise could be heard just above the sound of the rushing water, growing as it came closer.

Tinker Bell looked left and right, trying to find the source of it as Wendy experimentally maneuvered the pole. When the fairy finally figured out what the noise was, she squeaked, jingled desperately, and flew back to desperately squeeze her friend's arm.

But Wendy already knew what it was.

It was a *beautiful* gold-and-steel crocodile. Four yards

long from tip to tail. It skimmed the water, its black nose and glass eyes just sticking out of the surface, its sparkling, mechanical tail swishing back and forth rhythmically. It smiled at the girls with clear crystal teeth.

"Oh yes, that's the clockwork crocodile. Now free from its previous task, the toy beast sought its way downstream to find other people in need of help. And, I daresay, we might have use of a clockwork crocodile somewhere along the way—against pirates, maybe? One *particular* crocodile-fearing pirate?"

Tinker Bell stared at her friend in newly discovered admiration—and the teensiest bit of horror.

*You've changed, girl.*

Wendy smiled as she pushed the boat away from the bank.

There was more to her than just manners and wishing, as her little fairy friend had pointed out. A whole world of Never Land was inside Wendy . . . with beasts as well as fairies.

# The Ride and the Rain

The beautiful little boat began its journey slowly, bumping along the bank until Wendy managed to push them away from shore. The steering pole had a well-hewn and polished handle that fit in her hands perfectly. She couldn't have imagined a better designed piece of equipment. Which was intellectually amusing since some part of her mind *must* have actually imagined or designed it. Of course, she hadn't really visualized every detail of the entire boat; she had just said *boat*, royal boat, and figured there would be gold and blue and fancy things on it and comfy seats. And regal-looking equipment, like this pole. But not specifically the pole she was holding. Which inevitably led to the question: Who or what *did* provide the details? When she invented the story, who filled in the missing bits? Was that just how the magic of Never Land worked?

But this was a deep thought for another time. She had to work the pole around and around with all her strength before finally getting out to the middle of the newly reinvigorated river. The little boat bobbed in place for a moment as if discussing matters with the waters around it, spinning a little as it found a good place to join, and then—it took off.

Wendy squealed with delight as they rushed along with the waves. Tinker Bell also squealed, but with terror, and held on to the seat for dear life. Then she looked over at Wendy and saw her laughing, and the fairy reassessed the dangers. Very slowly she began to smile.

"Yeehaw!" Wendy shouted as they rose up with a swell and then crashed down with a belly-flopping *smash*, spraying water into the sky with bright rainbows. The droplets were small and cool and very refreshing. Her parched skin soaked them up gratefully. She licked her lips: cold, clear, and lightly mineral.

Fish leapt in arcs before the bow of the boat, their scales glittering in the sunlight. The canyon walls raced by. Between her triumph at figuring out how to escape the First and the speed of the river and the water and the day, Wendy was almost overcome with joy.

"I had *no idea* boating could be such fun!" she cried to Tinker Bell. "It's almost like flying!"

Tinker Bell gave a definitive headshake to this. *No.* But Wendy just laughed.

She did worry a little whether the whole plan would really work, if they could really get out of the demesne of the First or if they would just ride the river forever.

But then the landscape around them began to change—slowly. Perhaps indicating that they were getting back to Never Land proper.

The thick red walls of stone that rose into the sky on the left and right of them fell away, too busy with the eternal task of crumbling into piles of dust to bother with the riverbanks any longer. And while there was still the occasional tor or small rocky hill, the buttes and hoodoos and columns and pedestals and other exotic formations grew far less frequent.

Just before these features disappeared entirely, two final ones appeared on opposite sides of the river. These were unbelievably massive, so tall that Wendy couldn't see their tops. Striped layers of red and white and black alternated with each other up and into forever.

She had the strange urge to salute as they passed between these two guardians. Both girls, fey and human, remained silent and still until the columns were far behind. Even the boat seemed to slow for a bit.

After that the land grew greener by stages. Tall, gracefully curving trees with branches like umbrellas marked the edge of the jungle. Canyon walls back in the desert were recalled in living format here as massive gray trunks of trees, barriers of thick foliage, and unbelievably substantial skeins of vines. The calls of monkeys or parrots or other Never Land creatures echoed hauntingly from the tops of emerald hillocks. Far in the distance they could once again just make out the toothy shapes of the Black Dragon Mountains.

Wendy never imagined she could be so relieved to see *jungle*. Or hills, for that matter, even if they were covered in exotic plants. The desert had been fascinating but she never wanted to be somewhere that flat again. It was so exposed—she had felt like a speck peered at by God through an infinite microscope. Now she could relax and breathe again with leaves between her and the sky.

*Where does the river lead?* Tinker Bell asked curiously.

"Why, to the sea, of course," Wendy said with bravado. Things had worked out well so far—why shouldn't it continue to do exactly what she predicted? "It feeds into the cove from the western side of the Pernicious Forest, skirting the Quiescent Jungle."

Tinker Bell looked around a little thoughtfully.

*I wonder how all this new water will affect everything.*

"Whatever do you mean?"

*When you fly, you are aware of these things—air weight, rising, falling, moisture, winds. . . . Remember your tumbling back there, over the ocean?*

"Oh yes," Wendy said with a blush. "But that was the ocean. *This* is just a river. I'm sure it will all work itself out."

Tinker Bell pointed.

Up ahead things grew cloudy.

Literally.

As the two girls watched the jungle began to disappear. Hills and vales faded—but not from supernatural causes. This time it wasn't the First playing tricks with geography; this was real mist and real fog. The world was blurred by something thicker than air but thinner than real rain. This swirled madly as stray breezes gathered considerable speed over the tops of the trees, rushing toward the river. Clouds of all sorts were pulled from across the heavens into the maelstrom: puffy white Never Land specials, thunderheads from the Black Dragon Mountains, mackerel-backs and mare's tails from someplace inland that must have been a bit like England.

"My goodness . . ."

Wendy had never seen anything like it. Whatever was happening was fascinating and hypnotic—and deeply unnerving on a very basic level. She felt the touch of terror that all animals experience when they instinctively know something is wrong with the world around them. When the weather goes south.

There was a giant *crack*. A moment later Wendy realized it wasn't the sound of thunder. It was the sound of thousands of gallons of water spilling out of the sky all at once. Giant, hot raindrops hurt as they hit her head and eyes; the percussion of them pounding the river was deafening.

"We need to get to land!" Wendy cried out, once again grabbing the pole and pushing. Tinker Bell nodded vigorously and started to fly up but quickly realized there was nothing she could do. Each drop was the size of her head; already her wings looked crushed at the tips.

She hid under the bench.

Wendy wrestled with the pole, dress and slip plastered against her body by the torrents of rain. Water streamed into her eyes whenever she tried to look up and see where they were going. Eventually she surrendered to the greater power of nature and just pushed as hard as she could, blind, hoping it was toward the eastern shoreline. The wind worked the surface of the river into a rippling frenzy; the boat spun on its hull like a compass, twisting every direction.

She finally felt the keel of the boat touch soft, sandy bottom. Wendy leapt out. The water was freezing, all thoughts of the desert washed away along with its red dust and sweat. She gritted her teeth and yanked on the boat, dragging it out of the river and as far up the bank as she could manage. It wouldn't do to leave such a pretty, well-made thing to drift out into the ocean or smash itself to bits on the rocks. And it might come in useful later. Things had a way of doing that in adventure stories.

Besides, it was the first boat Wendy had ever made.

"Tink! Come with me!" She held out her left hand. Without a single protest jingle, Tinker Bell zoomed like a well-trained bee out from under the bench and into her friend's palm. Closing her fingers gently over the fairy, Wendy put her head down and ran into the forest.

The noise of the rain was considerably louder here. Giant drops hit giant leaves with *splats* that reverberated like ancient drums. Just breathing was tricky in the constant deluge; Wendy came close to choking several times as she took in gasps of rain along with air.

Tinker Bell's glow peeped out of the cracks between Wendy's fingers.

*Find a trufualuff tree,* she jingled moistly. *Like at the Lost Boys' hideout. They're hollow to their roots.*

Wendy looked for one as best she could, since she didn't perfectly remember those trees and botany was not her strong suit.

There were no edges or shadows in the jungle, just a dark, twilighty gray that made shapes and distances difficult to judge. She stumbled to avoid nearly invisible, deep black pools that were home to playful but spiny seven-legged carapaced things that leapt and splashed in high arcs between them. The whole exercise was exhausting.

Finally, Wendy saw a tree with a comfortingly wide trunk and giant knobby roots. Although she had a fair idea this was their goal, it was confirmed by an intense jingling and shaking of her fairy-holding hand. And there it was, at the base of the trunk: a triangular-shaped hole framed by several intersecting roots. Just wide enough for Wendy to slip through, if she held her breath and twisted herself round like a cork.

"Go take a look," she suggested, opening up her hand. Tinker Bell obligingly buzzed out and down into the hole. Fairy glow flickered and bobbled like a candle in a lantern as she zipped around inside the tree. She reappeared at the entrance and nodded vigorously.

*"Great,"* Wendy said, a little ironically. "A dry hole under a tree. Even more exciting than seeing a jungle again. What a day."

Glad there was no around to see, she awkwardly stuck one foot into the hole, dangling until it touched a hard-ish surface, then squeezed her other foot in place next to it. Spinning slowly with her hands above her head, she ducked down until she disappeared, a genie shrinking into a bottle.

The little cave wasn't half as bad as she expected: it was dry, didn't smell too musty, and didn't contain any fetid animal refuse. If she pulled her knees up there was even room to sit or curl around herself and sleep if she needed to. Rather than feeling claustrophobic because of the weight of the tree above them, Wendy felt safe under the roots that laced together to make their ceiling.

"On the whole, a very acceptable, ah, *hole*," Wendy said approvingly. "If I were a rabbit I should very much like to live in a place like this, permanently."

*We're just here until the rain stops. Then we have to go find Peter,* Tinker Bell jingled, a little anxiously.

"And save the world, don't forget. We have no idea where the pirates are, or exactly what they intend to do. And the First said that time was running out." Wendy sighed and put her hand out without thinking to comfort the little fairy.

Without thinking, the little fairy climbed up onto it.

"I can't even tell how much time has passed since we first entered the Land of the First. Do you have any idea?"

Tinker Bell looked thoughtful, then shrugged and shook her head, jingling meaninglessly.

"I wonder if time passes differently there. Like in fairy tales. No disrespect," she added quickly. "Was the time we spent there like centuries out here? As if we were asleep, or under a fairy spell having the time of our lives, while time passed out here? No . . . that doesn't feel right. I think it's the reverse. And that makes more Never Land sense, really: time passing slower for the dwellers in the infinite beginnings of the world. Oh, I do like the sound of that, don't you? I just came up with it. 'Dwellers in the infinite beginnings of the world.' I should write that down."

She went to take out her journal before remembering that her parents still had it. Worse than that: she realized that her bag was gone. When had she lost it? When the mermaids tried to drown her? When she slept in the air on the way to the First? Clambering around the rocks in the desert? The river journey? She couldn't even remember the last time she had seen it.

"Well, I suppose the pirates' gold buttons and thimbles will *not* become useful later in the story, as originally suggested," she said sadly. "Nothing in Never Land seems to stick around for very long. I must remember when packing up for my next adventure to choose a bigger, sturdier satchel. A solid waxed canvas one, maybe, that goes over my shoulders with tight straps, like a soldier's."

Tinker Bell pouted sympathetically but distractedly, still watching the rain.

"We'll fly as soon as it calms down a bit," Wendy promised. Glumly, she watched her friend's shadow squeeze droplets out of her wings—and the emptiness of the space on the wall where Wendy's own shadow should have been. She sighed and tried to think happier thoughts.

"This is a bit like a tiny version of the Lost Boys' hideout, isn't it? I really liked their home, actually—it could just do with a bit of a woman's touch."

Tinker Bell turned away from the rain and nodded vigorously. Like it was a subject she had thought about often.

"I used to dream of being a sort of a den mother to the Lost Boys, you know. Keeping the house neat, maybe sewing a rug and curtains, mending their rather disreputable clothes . . . Being useful and loved and happy, and surrounded by a passel of adoring children. But children grow up . . . or at least, they're supposed to. In my world, like my brothers. And I think I've tried all that anyway and I'm a bit done."

It was funny . . . she had finally come to Never Land—but for entirely different reasons now. Not because she was a girl who wanted to take care of others and find a place for herself; because she was a human who wanted adventure and quests and a reason for getting up in the morning and a purpose in life. To escape the role and future others wanted for her.

Could her life in London have been different in such a way that she wouldn't *want* to flee to Never Land? She wasn't as brave and strong-willed as those women who went to deepest Africa and the outback of Australia, leaving their families and taunting their detractors.

(Also, she didn't have the money. The world opened up for everyone, girls especially, if there was money. Most of those adventurers were heiresses. Wendy basically ran the Darling household and knew firsthand the cost of clinging to respectable middle class. There was no money for jaunts to the Outer Hebrides, much less Africa.)

So what *would* make Wendy happy? That she could do—in London?

Tinker Bell was looking at her curiously. Time apparently passed outside Wendy's head even as ideas and feelings ran around for what seemed like forever inside it. Like time in the realm of the First and Never Land.

"Sorry, lost in my thoughts. Don't want to be a mother for the Lost Boys anymore, basically. But it *would* be fun to redecorate their hideout. Like your lovely little apartment. Oh, I just adored it!"

Tinker Bell smiled prettily, no modesty or self-deprecation at all.

"If I had a flat of my own, I'd set up a little house for you when you visited, a bit like your place now," Wendy said dreamily, wrapping her arms around her knees. "There's a fancy toy store downtown with the most cunning little furniture for dolls. . . . Tufted sofas and real Persian rugs the size of my hand. They even have tiny pewter dishes and the loveliest little porcelain claw-foot bathtub with a real miniature India-rubber stopper!"

Tinker Bell's eyes widened farther with each item listed.

"I've never much played with dolls, but I always loved looking in the window of that shop. I could make tiny beeswax candles with cotton thread wicks to put in the tiny silver candelabra they sell—they're almost like jewelry, they're so tiny and sparkling and delicate! Imagine if they really worked. Well, I don't suppose you need a candle at night when *you're* getting ready for bed—you carry yours around with you all the time."

Tinker Bell looked around at her glow and smiled smugly.

"Well, anyway, I'd have everything else all set up for you. You *will* come visit? When this is all over? And I return home?"

Despite the newfound (though mild) desire to return to London, the idea of the *end* of her adventure came down on Wendy hard, as solid as the dreaded end of a perfect summer day—or eventual end of life itself. She looked down at her ragged, dripping dress in wonder. She had been kidnapped, beaten around, almost drowned, nearly trapped in a desert for all eternity . . . and yet the thought of it all being over was terrifying.

The thought of never seeing Tinker Bell again . . . after they finally began to get to know each other . . .

The little fairy was frowning, but not angrily. It seemed like she was considering a thought that was so new and alien to her that she automatically distrusted it.

*Me and Peter, you mean? Us come visit you? Come* inside?

"You needn't bring Peter, if it makes you uncomfortable. It's funny, I came all the way to Never Land and haven't even actually met the boy yet. And I've still had lots of adventures. But it could just be . . . *you*, you know. I would miss you so terribly. You could take an afternoon. We could have tea, like my mother does with ladies she likes. I confess I've never liked the idea of tea out with anyone besides Mother before. Because I don't have any close friends—and because it's really a little silly. Flower plates and talk of the weather and only one lump of sugar. I'm supposedly a young woman and I still think tea tastes awful without at least two . . . but I have to put on a good show for the boys. Act like an adult, you know, set an example."

Tinker Bell was nodding, obviously a little perplexed as Wendy chattered on, too nervous about her heartfelt admission to do anything besides babble about inconsequential things afterwards. Belittling and dismissing her own deep feelings. As always.

The little fairy put a hand on her thumb and patted it.

*I think I would like that. But we'll see.*

"All right, plans for the future, better to concentrate on the now, eh?" Wendy said, shaking her head free of silly thoughts of fairies coming to a London bedsit to visit an aging spinster. "Let's keep an eye on the rain, and leave the moment it lets up."

And the drops fell, and time passed, the two girls from different worlds sat in companionable silence.

# Meanwhile, on the High Seas . . .

The sun shone its absolute hardest. The sky it sailed in was a pure balmy blue, empty but for the occasional harmless puffy cloud and the impressive but subtextually unimportant albatross.

(This was Never Land. It was a giant white bird, distinguished from the smaller white birds—seagulls—only by size and call.)

The sea below stretched far and smooth in every direction, green as a precious gem. In London someone would point out how one can see the earth's curvature at sea after only twelve miles, but this was Never Land and nobody cared. The horizon *did* curve gently, and little wispy clouds would flock to it at sunrise and sunset for a perfect viewing.

That was what geometry and distances were for in Never Land.

A jolly pirate ship flew over the waves. Its sails puffed out like a giant wind child was blowing on them. Its skull-and-crossbones flag snapped merrily in the wind.

The whole scene practically screamed *adventure* and *shenanigans*, as in Never Land it should.

But something was wrong.

The crew on the deck was neither swabbing reluctantly nor singing lustily. There were no sea chanteys being belted out or harmonicas or pipes being played. No one was *avast*-ing, or *something*-ing the mainsail, or trying to figure out how to spell *fo'c'sle*. They sat or stood uncomfortably, resting on their mops, unable to play mumbly-pegs, mindlessly hauling rope, end over end beyond its seeming use.

All eyes were directed to the front of the ship, where the reader's should be, too.

The prow of the *Jolly Roger,* a ship well-known to fans of Never Land awake or asleep, was decorated with a giant skull, as on its flag. But its famous figurehead was eclipsed now by a newer, more intricate, and far more terrifying decoration: a giant cage of golden wire and evil pointy bits that was suspended precariously over the water.

Captive inside was a squirming splotch of blackness that didn't quite resolve into focus. It deformed and swelled and shrank and stretched but somehow never managed to ooze out of the wickedly sharp pincers that held it in place. Four of them, sharper than Sleeping Beauty's spindle, were set around the thing at points of the compass. Each dug deeply into the material of Peter Pan's shadow. Four more were set in points indicating places only known to Captain Hook, Mr. Smee, and perhaps the shadow itself.

Its skin rippled around the barbs like a horse's flesh when a fly lands on a sore.

The shadow hunkered down, trying to become as small as it would be underfoot at noon on the equator; to virtually disappear, and thereby free itself of the points. But somehow it remained stuck. Long, thin, sickly strands of shadow ran from the barbs back to its center, refusing to snap free. The shade would vibrate for a few moments—like a hideous spider prevaricating in the middle of its web—before reforming itself and trying something new.

But for long periods in between it would give up and resolve itself into a version of Peter Pan, albeit a horribly distorted one. In terrible irony it put its arms out as if it were Peter: flying free, banking and turning on the wind.

Pulleys and wires under the cage attached to the pincers would then twist and squeak and groan, almost in ridicule of the normal creak of a ship's ropes and rigging. These wires ran through guides and eventually connected to the captain's wheel. When the shadow banked, so did the ship.

That the shadow was in unspeakable amounts of pain wasn't even a question. Sometimes its shrieks actually bordered on the audible. No pirate slept through the night comfortably even with bellies full of purloined grog and bits of cloth stuffed into ears and kerchiefs wrapped around weary heads. Even when the cries couldn't be heard, its torment could be *felt* thrumming throughout the ship.

The crew, already an unhealthy lot, looked even sicker than usual.

"Smooth sailing today," the Duke observed reluctantly, afraid—like all of them—to break the streak.

"Ain't right," Djareth mumbled.

"Go talk to 'im, go talk again," Screaming Byron told Zane.

The tall, skinny pirate spat in response to this, but without conviction.

"Go on then," Ziggy pushed. "You drew the short straw. You have to."

"Likely as kill me as reason with me," Zane sighed. "But better to be dead than caught in this misery forever."

He sauntered over to the captain's quarters and knocked. An irritated voice growled from within.

*"Mr. Smee, could you get that?"*

*"SMEE! Where the deuce did you get to?"*

*"Dash it all, do I have to do everything meself. . . ."*

"COME IN!" the captain finally roared.

Zane swallowed and took a last look back at the crew. They all gave him unconvincing grins and thumbs-up. He sighed and opened the door. He would rather have done many things, including face a fleet of sharks with just a bowie knife, rather than enter the dark, unwholesome hold of his captain.

Hook looked as resplendent as ever in the ridiculous red frock coat that Zane sorely coveted. But his face was an unhealthy pink, glowing and perspiring from something unnatural—certainly nothing wholesome and clean like working the masts, counting loot, or cutting a throat.

"Begging your pardon, Cap'n," Zane began, trying to remain polite—something he wasn't much used to.

"Ah! Alodon. *You* would appreciate this, out of the whole crew. I've come up with some tweaks to the Painopticon that not only enhance its effectiveness, but also add some very stylish flourishes."

Zane licked his dry lips and leaned over the table where Hook gestured. Apparently the captain had been scribbling away with a beautiful swan's feather pen on a sheet of parchment, his fury and passion betrayed by the untidy spots of ink all over his sketch. None of it made any sort of sense except for the flourishes Hook had described, which were drawn as neatly and intricately as an architect's diagram.

"Er, lovely, Cap'n."

Zane let his eyes roam over the rest of the desk, which was covered with black leather-bound books, scrolls written in what appeared to be Greek, and one particularly hideous tome labeled *The Necronomicon*.

"I knew you would like it." Hook grinned smugly and chomped down on the upper cigar of the twin cigarillo holder he sported.

"Yes, Cap'n. Amazing, Cap'n. So the boys were kind of wondering when . . . ah . . . all this would be over? It's a lovely spring day, sir, and we've got a cracking breeze. Perfect weather for despoiling a port or two."

"Yes, yes, I know, I feel it, too, Zane," Hook said with a sigh, looking nostalgic. "This sort of air reminds me of when I was a young man, skewering a few of the queen's finest. But you know, work first, play later."

The pirate was on the one hand relieved by this answer from the intemperate Hook. He had *expected* to be fired upon, or stabbed—or worse, to sit through one of the screaming, incoherent lectures the captain of the *Jolly Roger* so enjoyed.

On the other hand, the seemingly random tempers of Hook were actually quite predictable. This behavior was not, and therefore terrifying.

Knowing he was dangerously tweaking the crazy, Zane

nevertheless persisted. He had drawn the short straw, after all, and pirates did keep to their code.

"Ahh . . . and what work would that be, Cap'n?"

"Why, finding Peter Pan, of course!" Hook said, laughing at his crew member's idiocy. "Once we have him I can put my final plans into action. He must be there to watch the destruction of Never Land, of course. I mean, if we're short on time I could just . . . leave him to his and everyone else's fate. But that would be missing the point, wouldn't it? It would be revenge, but lacking finesse. Anyway, one way or another, after that we'll be free to do whatever we want. Maybe we'll upset the power structure in a small Caribbean island nation. That might be a nice change, eh? A little civil war and *revolución* for the masses? Roast some pigs, party like it's 1699?"

"That sounds lovely, Cap'n. It's just that the crew . . . well, this . . . *work* of capturing Pan seems to be dragging out a bit. . . ."

He continued quickly, seeing the look on Hook's face.

"*And* this whole involvement ye have here with shadows and black magic—it ain't right, sir. It ain't right or wholesome. That's the way of witches and sea sorcerers. We none of us signed up for a sea sorcerer as a captain, sir."

He swallowed but held steady. That was the truth, plain and simple.

"Ah, well, I suppose I could see your issue with that," Hook relented, tapping his chin thoughtfully with his hook. "But shadows—what can you do? There is no other way to deal with them other than black magic. They are . . . literally . . . black.

"But you're right about things dragging out a little long. Time's a ticking, Zane. You can practically hear it. That foul beast of a crocodile is nearly upon me. We don't have forever, you know. The sooner we get this done the sooner we can move on with our lives. I have to rid the world of Peter Pan and his silly Never Land friends before we can all be free."

Zane sighed.

The captain of the *Jolly Roger* was somehow both more reasonable and more insane than ever. There was nothing that could be done besides mutiny—and who was going to try a mutiny against a psychotic, hooked captain who now knew black magic and had captured the power of a shadow?

"What if," the pirate begged, "what if we went after some *other* annoying lad—one of the other Lost Boys, maybe? Or someone else entirely? Someone close and easy to grab? Then you can do whatever you want to Never Land and we'll all be on our way."

Hook laughed. "Well, what would be the point of that? This is *revenge,* Alodon. Peter Pan must see what happens to everything he loves and perhaps just die on his own—of a broken heart."

Zane ground his back teeth in frustration.

He tried a different course.

"You know . . . some would say your chasing after Pan isn't actually about revenge, sir."

"Oh? What else would it be, then?" the captain growled, holding up his hook. Despite his growing lunacy, he kept it regularly sharpened and polished; it glittered even in the low light of the lantern.

"Well, some would say—not me, necessarily, Cap'n—but *some* might say it's less about revenge and more about . . . well . . . chasing your own youth, sir."

Hook stared at him. In the dim hold, the two regarded each other silently for a long, awkward moment.

"What in blazes is that supposed to mean?" the captain finally demanded.

"Well, it's like this, Cap'n. Peter's young and adventurous and can fly, sir. And you can't never catch him, he's always receding from you, as it were, sir. Like youth. And also, he cut off your hand, which *might* could be looked at as representative of the end of your prowess with a sword, and—"

*"OH, SHUT YOUR BLOODY NONSENSE UP!"* Hook roared, standing up and throwing the desk over. As the books tumbled and he pulled out his flintlock, Zane felt

a strange sense of relief. This was the sort of ending he expected.

"I ought to shoot you in the head, you insane, Freudian dimwit," Hook growled. "We're only Jungians on this boat, you know. I can see all this focus on Peter Pan has made you a bit loony."

"*Me . . . ?* Loony? Focused on Peter Pan . . . ?"

But Hook wasn't even paying attention.

"Well, maybe we could all use a break," he said with an air of *giving up*. "A bit of R & R might do you and the crew some good. And, as it happens, although Peter's shadow is leading us almost directly south, I have a bit of an errand to get done first, at Skull Island."

Zane's face lit up. "Skull Island! The boys'll love that! We can dig up some casks we hid there, have a right party. That'll get you back to feeling yourself, sir."

"Yes, well, I suppose you and the crew can have an evening. *I* need to work. To prepare for my final showdown with Peter. . . ."

Hook's eyes flicked to a pile in the corner. It was almost indistinguishable from the other pirate bric-a-brac he chose to collect: pianofortes, urns, snuffboxes, an evil-looking and sinuous black dagger. But there were several tightly capped quarter-casks with what looked like three *X*s stamped on their sides, and a pile of rope or fuse.

There was also what looked like a broken-up clock.

Hook saw the surprise on Zane's face.

"Oh yes, I know. Usually I hate the dratted things. But it's just one last clock," the captain mused quietly. "*The* last clock. For Skull Island."

"All right, Cap'n. Whatever. I'll go tell the crew about landing at the island. They'll be happy to hear it."

But Hook was already picking up the desk and frowning at his drawings.

"If you see Mr. Smee, send him in here. That rascal's been missing all morning and I haven't had my tea yet."

Zane sighed again, shook his head, and prepared to deliver the tiny bit of good news to the crew.

# The Thysolits

The sky above the jungle grew darker and lighter at the same time, shades exchanging depth and brightness. It took Wendy a moment of watching through the hole in the tree to realize what was happening: the storm was clearing up, the clouds were dissipating and leaving a streaky just-washed sky. A *night* sky, bright with stars and a moon that hadn't risen yet. Or moon*s*. Still inky; the world lay in shadow.

"Well, this is rather beautiful," Wendy said, pushing her way up and out of their den. The forest looked like it was covered in pixie dust—and transformed in other indescribably mysterious ways as well. A very *un*-tropical and refreshing breeze blew. The air smelled delightful and fresh;

there was no heavy undercurrent of the rot or foul sweetness that usually permeated the forest floor.

Winged things began to come out of their hiding places. Giant birds flapped heavily overhead like geese (if geese had four wings). Night singers, invisible in their slick black feathers, called out to each other tentatively. Insects began to chirp and *scrtch*.

One particularly wondrous Never Land creature hummed up right in front of Wendy. It looked like a very, very, *very* large carpenter bee . . . if that bee had a thorax the size and shape of a wine glass. Its wings, strangely geometric and crystalline, looked too small to be able to lift such a load. A pair of long legs hung out in front mirrored by a pair of tiny feelers above. Large faceted eyes stared dumbly ahead.

As Wendy watched, its bulb-thorax flickered and slowly lit up.

Not like a fire or an electric light, but more dimly, and sort of black-and-white, like a photograph.

Deep within this glow images began to appear.

A hazy blur resolved itself into a mermaid—perhaps even one of those Wendy had encountered—brushing her hair in the lagoon. Again and again and again. The little play looped around to the beginning again like a circle of yarn in cat's cradle. Sometimes it went in reverse and the mermaid's hair fell up in strokes.

Tinker Bell was rising in the night air along with the other creatures, stretching and looking a little grumpy. She was not, by any account, a nocturnal fairy.

"Tinker Bell! What *is* this creature?"

The insect flew very slowly and Wendy was able to move around it, regarding the thing from every angle. Also like a carpenter bee it seemed more interested in hovering than actually going anywhere with purpose or direction.

Tinker Bell made a bored, disgusted face.

*It's a thysolit. They're stupid. Barely alive. Dangerous.*

"Oh! Dangerous!" Wendy backed away from it immediately. The amount of poison in a stinger from a thorax that size would be enough to kill an army.

*No, not like that,* Tinker Bell said, yawning. *They . . . suck you in. Not you. Not everyone. Those who pay too much attention. Poison the mind, not the body. If you're that kind of person. And if you rouse a whole colony they get you.*

"But I won't get stung?"

*No.*

As if to illustrate, Tinker Bell approached another one of them that was just taking off from the ground and threw herself against it, hard. The insect fell to the side, confused, then shook itself and continued on its original path.

"Oh . . ." Wendy approached closely to see if it was all right—then peered at its images. These were of the same lagoon, but a different part of it. No mermaids, just lapping water and what might have been the fin of a fish about to surface, again and again and again.

More thysolits rose, buzzing drowsily and drifting into the sky like silky seedpods. Wendy walked among them, enchanted.

"But what is going on with their—derrieres? What are they showing?"

*Anything. A moment of time from somewhere in Never Land. They collect them. Usually they're only a few hours old.*

The next one Wendy saw had a monkey swinging from vine to vine across a high stream that fell down into the lagoon. The one after that showed Hangman's Tree.

"Oh, look, Tinker Bell! It's the hideout!"

And in fact, another one had a loop of the Lost Boys themselves (and Luna), sitting around the table and eating a plum pudding they had gotten from who knows where.

The next thysolit showed a placid beach, a scurrying crab. The next one showed an empty sea. . . .

*"And the pirates!"* Wendy cried as the *Jolly Roger* came riding quickly through the waves.

Tinker Bell jingled impatiently. *So? We should go! They are probably looking for Peter!!*

"No, wait," Wendy said, twirling around and searching all the other bees. "It seems like these creatures fly in clusters. Like they gather their *moments* together. There's always a number of the scenes that take place at the same spot. If we can find all the ones related to *this* moment, maybe we can see where the pirates are, or what they are up to!"

Tinker Bell thought about that for only a second before nodding. She began to zoom around the creatures, checking their sides with as much grace and care as an American cowboy searching the flanks of his herd for the right brand.

That is, not very delicately.

Wendy was still a little hesitant about just grabbing and handling the insects. She resorted to glimpsing and ducking and weaving and saying *excuse me* when the situation warranted a gentle pushing-out-of-the-way. Dozens of them were now aloft. Their lights blinked on slowly, one by one, like stars coming out in a hazy summer night.

Some of their scenes took a moment to figure out: one was the black eye of a large animal, blinking; in another, a set of children who *weren't* the Lost Boys danced and cavorted on a hilltop, ribbons round their heads and streamers flowing from their hands and toes.

Tinker Bell jingled loudly and excitedly. Wendy looked up and saw that the fairy was steering a bee from behind, flying it toward her friend.

This one showed a close-up of the prow of the *Jolly*

*Roger*. While the view wasn't far enough back to give them any geographical information, what it did show was interesting—and disturbing. It looked as though the pirates had hung a sort of cage off the front of the ship. The thing was extremely nasty-looking, covered on the insides with spikes and barbs and other horrid implements.

And inside this cage was a dark, oily figure that could only have been Peter's shadow.

Watching over it was Hook, unmistakable even at that distance in his bright red coat.

"What are they doing? It looks like they're torturing him!" Wendy took the bee into her hands without thinking, trying to get a better look. She had to resist shaking it to see if that would help.

*What is the cage for? Why are they suspending it over the water?*

"I don't know—is it to threaten the shadow with drowning, I wonder? Or are they . . . are they using him somehow to *power* the ship? Or maybe . . ." She spun around, letting that thysolit go and running back to where Tinker Bell had first found it. Now she batted the creatures carelessly in her zeal to find the right one. "Let's see . . . water, more water, no. Oh—I know that face," she said, seeing a surprised and angry-looking pirate in one, as if the bee had almost knocked him in the nose. "Ziggy. Interesting fellow. Sewed a patch on for him, sort of a lightning-shaped one. Look—a beach! With rocks! Tinker Bell, does this look familiar to you at all?"

Tinker Bell watched the rolling waves and strangely shaped boulders rewind and replay. She shrugged.

*That could be anywhere on the eastern coast. If the thysolit is following the boat or the pirates, though, they are heading south.*

Wendy frowned. "Why? Do they know where they are going? Did they somehow get the shadow to tell them where Peter is, do you think? Is that why they are torturing him?"

Tinker Bell shrugged again. But her brow was furrowed with worry. She made a little flying-off gesture with her fingers: *we should go.*

"Yes, of course. Peter's shadow is in more peril than ever—and Never Land as well. Let's be off." And Wendy turned to launch herself into the air.

But . . .

A thysolit drifted by with an unusually dreary image in its thorax. Almost entirely black-and-white and grainy, the interior of a dull house. Somehow the room seemed both vacant and cramped at the same time. There was an un-set table. Two ghostly figures sat at it. One looked like he was about to say something—but didn't.

"Michael! John!" Wendy cried.

She grabbed the next closest bee and peered desperately into its bulb. A misty view of the street the Darlings lived on, at dusk or dawn, empty of people.

"Tinker Bell! You said these thysolits only gathered moments in Never Land. How are they showing me London?"

She caught another one, her fear of the supposedly dangerous things now entirely gone as she tried to find another view of home.

*Wendy . . .* Tinker Bell jingled warningly. *We have to go. Stop. This is what they do.*

"But Michael and John! They looked so sad! Do you think they miss me? How much time has passed there since I left? Oh, do let me find just one more. . . ."

As she searched among the bees for more images of her brothers, she was vaguely aware of the insects' growing numbers. The air was filled with the pleasant hum of their ridiculous little wings. It was hard to see anything now, much less take a close look at their behinds.

*Wendy!* Tinker Bell jingled. *Your brothers are fine! They're distracting you! Poisoning your mind!*

"Don't be silly. I feel fine. Oh, look, it's the Shesbow household," Wendy said, turning another thysolit over in her hand. "What are they up to? Piano lessons? Funny, looking in on someone's house without them even knowing it. It's like being a peeping tom, one second at a time. I wonder if Mr. Crenshaw's house is here, too. . . . I would so love to see what he's up to."

*Wendy!*

Struggling, Tinker Bell wove her way through the tightening mass of bees. She grabbed the human girl's arm and yanked it. *This is exactly what happens. You get caught. You humans—too interested in what you can't see for yourself. You fill your heads with too much . . . noise.*

"Too much *news*, you mean," Wendy corrected. "Look! There's parliament. Oh my goodness, they're all arguing! Whatever do you think it is? Taxes or something to do with Europe? Wait, is that a view of Paris? I've always wanted to see Paris."

Wendy reached out for a bee with the Eiffel Tower flashing on and off in its thorax like a strange warning beacon.

It flew just out of her reach. She lunged too far—

But didn't fall.

Instead she found herself drifting softly several feet above the ground.

It wasn't the fairy dust; she wasn't concentrating on floating or flying or anything else but grabbing at the bee.

In some ways it was a far stranger phenomenon that held her aloft: her legs and body were now entirely supported by the soft, furry thysolits.

But she was only vaguely aware of this.

*WENDY! COME!* Tinker Bell jingled anxiously.

The dazed girl had finally managed to get hold of the bee she wanted. It was warm and plummy in her hands, comforting, not at all dangerous or disobedient.

(A bit like that stupid little dog her parents had given her—but quieter and far more pleasant.)

The smell of honey filled the air, sweet and soothing. The cityscape of Paris in miniature was enchanting. Everything was lovely.

Eventually done gazing at the Eiffel Tower, Wendy looked up. She was a little surprised to see that she was in a sort of nest or cocoon made out of the bodies of hundreds of thysolits. They ignored their unwary passenger as they droned and flew to whatever their eventual nighttime destination was, taking her with them.

The frustrated jingles of Tinker Bell were soft and fading as the little fairy tried to force her way in from the outside.

"Ah, excuse me?" Wendy addressed the bees, leaning forward. Those making up her "seat" underneath shifted themselves obligingly to better support her new position. "I don't mean to be rude, but my friend would like to come, too. . . ."

The thysolits in front of her turned themselves slightly so she could see all of their thoraxes—all of their moments—neatly lined up. Paris . . . the Shesbow twins . . . St. Petersburg . . . New York City! The bookseller's nephew . . . *Thorn* . . .

The smell of honey grew stronger.

"Oh, look," Wendy said. "Look at it all! It's like a thousand little plays . . . just for me. . . ."

Every once in a while, as if somehow sensing she had finished watching a scene, a thysolit would gracefully exit its place and another would come to fill in with a new image or scene.

"How thoughtful of them . . ." Wendy said dreamily. "I can just sit here and watch . . . don't have to lift a finger. . . .

*"OUCH!"*

Finally, having shoved her way through the wall of bees and apparently out of options, Tinker Bell had resorted to the last trick of fairies. She sank her sharp little teeth into Wendy's arm, forcefully enough to summon bright drops of blood.

"Tinker Bell, you . . . !"

But the pain cleared her head; the smell of blood was stronger than honey. Wendy took a fresh look at the scene around her through slightly more wakeful eyes.

Thysolits. Everywhere. Completely caging her.

"I'm surrounded by a bunch of bees with pictures in their bottoms. And they've kidnapped me," she said slowly.

Tinker Bell decided an extra little nip would drive the point home.

Wendy didn't even really react, thoughtlessly scratching at both wounds.

"Yes, you told me so. I really could have sat here forever, trying to satisfy my curiosity. And they would have kept finding something else to pique my interest, to make me continue. . . . And I would have been lost. A subtle kind of poison indeed. They promise to show you the world but just sort of hypnotize you instead while life goes on without you. What would they have done with me ultimately, do you think?"

Tinker Bell shrugged. *Something not good?*

"As succinct and correct as always. Shall we?"

Concentrating on flying the normal way—Ha, normal! As if flying had been a normal thing a week ago!—Wendy tried to part the bees like a curtain. Tinker Bell didn't bother with such niceties, kicking them in their rear ends and punching them in their eyes. Which actually seemed to be a better tactic, because the thysolits resisted Wendy's efforts utterly, pushing back with a force she didn't believe insects should have.

"Let me out!" she cried, finally also resorting to kicks.

The wall of bees opened—and then enveloped her leg, covering it with their combined weight. This threw her awkwardly off-balance; she flailed and swayed and swung her arms, trying to regain herself.

Concentrating and tipping only a little, she managed to draw her little dagger from its necklace sheath.

"Don't make me use this!"

No reaction. She might as well have been talking to a bunch of . . . well, bees.

Feeling a little guilty about the violence, Wendy swept her arm out with the knife held diagonally, her thumb on its top, like she was sawing off a strip of old cloth. The blade slipped harmlessly in between the first thysolits, who moved slowly out of its way . . . and then caught and sank into the bodies of those who couldn't or wouldn't escape.

The result was immediate: a black and amber ichor began to pour out of the torn bee bodies. The smell of honey became overwhelming. And sickening.

The humming changed; it was no longer drowsy but growling and angry.

The swarm turned and dove at her face.

Wendy screamed. She tried to knock them away, now using her dagger like a badminton racquet. But they didn't bounce away lightly like a shuttlecock. Every time she injured one, it *stuck* on the dagger—like thick honey—and she had to shake it loose before defending herself from another one.

"Tinker Bell! Are you all right? How are you doing?"

The jingles that came back to her were angry and loud but otherwise unintelligible.

The things were now bludgeoning Wendy's body hard enough to leave bruises.

"Let's just push our way through—maybe we can outpace them!"

Wendy covered her face with her arms, and, pointing her dagger before her, flew upward *into* the thick of the swarm. Hopefully where they least expected her to go.

She burst into the clear night air, shedding bees like ugly raindrops.

Tinker Bell zoomed through the path she had made and appeared by her side, disheveled and a little scratched. But red with anger and ready to go.

"Come on, this way!" Wendy pointed south, because that was the way the pirate ship had been heading. At least she thought it was south—she was turned around from the bees and there were no points of reference from which to take her bearings. Ursa Major didn't look quite right and there were no moons at all.

The two girls spread their arms and took off into the wind . . . and then Wendy looked behind her.

The swarm had caught on to their escape plans. Like a strange yellow-and-orange tornado, they crowded together and rushed at the two girls.

"Back this way!" Wendy cried, pointing. Tinker Bell nodded, understanding immediately.

They dove *under* the swarm.

Momentum—and insect stupidity—continued to carry the bees forward, now the wrong way, *away* from the two girls.

But it wasn't very long before they righted themselves and were in pursuit again.

"All right. Hide in the clouds?" Wendy suggested. But there were none now. The storm had finished and it was a perfectly clear night, not a wisp in sight.

*I don't think we can outrun them,* Tinker Bell jingled sadly. *This is why they're so dangerous—they're relentless. Once the colony is on the warpath, they will never let up.*

"Surely there must be some escape . . ." Wendy said, looking around desperately for a mountain or a cave or some other sort of answer to present itself.

*This isn't London. You can't escape Never Land the way you could escape your life in the city.*

"I feel like we should revisit this theme later, and less ironically," Wendy muttered. "Also: *Ouch.* All right. I suppose it's . . . fisticuffs, then?"

She tried to ready herself for the clash, putting her arms up the way she imagined a boxer might, but with her dagger out.

The bees came, their hum and bodies filling the sky to the horizon.

"They never actually *sting*," Wendy reminded herself bravely. They just had numbers and mass.

That didn't stop it from being utterly terrifying when they hit.

They slammed into her all over her body. She could barely get a breath in between their blows, which came like a massive, fuzzy hailstorm. Their droning drowned all her thoughts.

She tried her badminton strategy again, using the length of her arm and dagger together as one weapon, connecting with as many bees as she could with each blow.

This was moderately successful, at least for knocking them away—if not actually killing them.

Still they kept coming.

One clocked her in the head so badly she saw stars. She fell, spiraling to earth.

Only Tinker Bell's quick response and tiny hands on hers guided Wendy back into remembering which way was up.

A hundred, a *thousand* bees were waiting for her when she returned to battle.

Her arm throbbed. Her left eye swelled almost shut. Her stomach ached from the angry purple bruises that now covered it. Without her shadow, Wendy's reserves were depleted quickly.

And they just kept coming.

Every time she thought they had done enough, that she and Tinker Bell had killed *enough* of the creatures, they would try to fly away—only to be pursued twice as angrily by the remainders. They never gave up.

Hit, block, hit, drop.

Hit, block, hit, drop.

It was clear: there was no escaping, no flying away, no resting, no stopping for a breath, no doing *anything* else until the last bee was gone.

Wendy dispatched the thysolits one after another without thought, sending their waning lights and broken bodies down to earth. The whole thing was less like a heroic battle than scullery work: endlessly scrubbing and scrubbing a room of dirt and grime that would, given the chance, kill her.

She couldn't turn her attention away long enough for a glance at Tinker Bell. She heard encouraging jingles now and then and knew the fairy was doing the best she could, maybe one thysolit for every dozen or two of her own. Eventually exhaustion wore even the terror whisper-thin.

She lost her fear of falling and dying.

The stars wheeled overhead in a way that made little sense. The moon (moons) never rose. Nothing Wendy had ever done in her life, not the most menial, boring household task, had ever lasted this long. Or required such continual strength: acid burned in her muscles as she lifted her arm, hit, dropped her arm, lifted, hit, and dropped. . . .

She barely noticed when there were only a dozen thysolits left. She had begun to sink slowly groundward, losing whatever it was that kept her afloat with the fairy dust.

"I . . . can't . . . fly . . . Tinker Bell. . . ."

The little fairy grabbed her by the hand—while kicking a bee hard in its mandibles. Her touch helped but didn't stop the fall. So she guided Wendy's descent into the little boat, where the human girl crumpled into a ball. Tinker Bell defended her there, valiantly trying to drive off the last few bees.

One final thought occurred to Wendy before she passed out: *They don't talk about* this *in adventures.*

*That being a hero is just work . . . and boring work . . . endless work . . . nothing more . . .*

# Meanwhile, in Another World...

But what of the family Wendy left behind? *Does* time pass in the real world as it does in Never Land? As it does in the Land of the First? How exactly are the two worlds (three worlds) connected? If it's teatime in Never Land, what hour is it on the east coast of the Americas? What does Wendy's father mean when he says, "It's gin-and-tonic time *somewhere* in this great, bloody world," and what exactly are cocktails? Does Wendy's family miss her?

We shall indulge the reader with the answer to exactly two of these questions, even as we indulge the author in a bit of fourth wall breakage.

In the empty, somewhat dark house of the Darlings, it was raining outside. John and Michael burst through the door with the endless energy and boundless enthusiasm of two young men, the elder of whom had just aced a botany exam and the younger of whom had toast and treacle for lunch as a special treat from the headmaster. Also there were puddles: Michael was soaking. John was trim and dry from the top of his ridiculous hat down to his spats, for he had a large umbrella given to him at Christmastime that he took with him everywhere and called Bella.

("Bella the *umbrella*, isn't that just perfect?" And maybe it was, the first twelve times. After that, even Wendy began to grow cross.)

"Wendy, we're home!" John called.

"Where's the tea? I can't smell tea," Michael said a little plaintively.

"You can't *smell* tea being made."

"I can smell the steam, it's all warm and moist and lovely," Michael snapped. "And I can hear the whistle. And if she or the cook has made buns, I can smell those, too."

"Neither hearing a whistle nor smelling buns has anything to do with smelling *tea*," John pointed out with the wise air of someone much older—and more often than not a pain in the thorax.

"I guess we shall have to make it ourselves," Michael said, completely ignoring his brother's freely given wisdom, as he often did. He poked cautiously at the stove and looked around for the box of matches. Lack of Wendy and how-to knowledge were only temporary impediments to teatime, not permanent ones.

"But where could she be?" John asked, now sounding plaintive himself.

Old Nana finally made it into the kitchen by this point. She had been slumbering in front of the fire in one of the upstairs rooms, happily dreaming of lying in front of a fire. She chuffed, demanding the sort of greeting an elder doyenne of the household deserved.

"Nana." Michael hugged her, and the dog didn't mind his wet and muddy paws—the same as Michael never minded hers back when she, too, was of puddle-jumping age. "Have you seen Wendy?"

Nana sighed. If the two boys had been a little more observant of her large, expressive brown eyes, they would have realized she was saying something to the extent of, *Oh, here we go again. You're not going to bother even trying to understand what I'm about to say, but I will try to tell you anyway, because that is what good dogs do.*

She walked over to the kitchen door, sat down pointedly, looked out the window, and barked once.

"She's gone out," Michael hazarded.

Nana sighed a moist pant of relief.

"Wendy? Gone out at teatime? Most suspicious. That's not like her at all."

"Maybe she has gone out to buy us special treats and got caught in the rain," Michael said hopefully.

"It's *London*, Michael. No one ever 'gets caught in the rain.' It rains all the bloody time here." John started off saying it amusingly, like his father would, but trailed off into something somewhere between wistful and bitter. For the slightest moment, a world had flashed in front of his eyes, a memory of bright sun and blue sea that wasn't a real memory at all, but a memory of imagination. There was a palm tree and the smell of coconuts.

Without being able to read his brother's mind and yet somehow sensing the mood behind it, Michael took the sort of cerebral right turn that babes sometimes manage when their too-learned betters cannot.

"We should get treats for Wendy sometime," he ventured, not coming to quite the right conclusion (but not the wrong one, either).

"Yes, we should," John said uncertainly. The two sat down at the un-set table, and the older boy's mind went the way the younger one's couldn't, wondering, perhaps, if it was too late for something like treats to rectify a situation they had been stupidly unaware of—despite how traces of it were pressed into every dark corner of the house, making itself widely known, and permanent, and sad.

---

When Mr. Darling returned home for a light supper before going to his study to get even more work done and Mrs. Darling finished her book club/charity drive/sherry session with the Tevvervilles and Miss Pontescue, the two entered to a half-lit house and an uninspired supper. Wendy rarely cooked unless it was a special occasion, but *every* occasion had her mark upon it. An extra garnish, a pretty bouquet, a little menu she had written out.

But this night the table was set minimally, napkins thrown down on chairs. The lamps weren't trimmed. The leftover roast, plopped in the middle of the table for anyone to steal or any mouse to nibble, was mostly cold. John and Michael sat glumly in their seats, politely waiting for their parents, not even bothering to sneak an early morsel. John had a book he wasn't reading.

"Boys." Mrs. Darling kissed them each on the head. "Where is Wendy?"

"No idea, Mother," Michael said. "She hasn't been here for hours."

"Oh." Mrs. Darling looked at Mr. Darling.

"Oh." Mr. Darling looked flummoxed. Wendy was never not where she was supposed to be when she was supposed to be there. "Has there . . . has there been a break-in?"

"Has someone stolen Wendy?" John asked, with a sneer and the touch of irony that often bloomed in an overbright boy with two mediocre parents. "Is that what you're asking?"

Mr. Darling frowned. His eldest son had reined in his tone at the last minute, couching it in what sounded like genuine surprise. Darling fruffled for a moment, feeling like he was being made fun of somehow, but couldn't quite put his finger on it. He wanted to be angry.

But Wendy . . .

Mrs. Darling, ever practical, was looking around the foyer. "Her umbrella is here, though her jacket is gone. She couldn't have gone out, or at least not far."

"I go outside without an umbrella all the time," Michael said.

"If there was fun to be had, you would go out without your own shadow," John said waspishly, rolling his eyes.

The two boys looked at each other, realizing the same thing at the same time.

*"The shadow,"* Michael whispered.

*"It's not real,"* John reminded him, also whispering.

*"We should check."*

"We'll go look upstairs one more time, Mother," John said loudly as the two boys hurried away from the table. "I . . . pray she doesn't have a fever and lie collapsed, insensate, somewhere."

"That's a bit much," Michael muttered, realizing with a wisdom beyond his years that he would be saying very similar things to his older brother for the rest of their lives. Nevertheless, united in this mission they raced upstairs together into the old nursery, which was now John and Michael's room. It had been repainted, of course, and had a new chair and extra wardrobe, and a neat line drawn down the middle in chalk past which Michael's lead soldiers were not allowed to march.

The old bureau was still there and still had some of Wendy's old things in it: once-favorite toys, bits and bobs, sewing notions. The top drawer was stuck, as always happened in damp weather; John had to wrestle with it up and down until it finally flew open, sending him backward to land on his bum.

Michael ran forward to look in.

"It's not there!" he said in awe, rustling around the drawer, ignoring the pin and needle pricks from the untidy pincushion. John rose up behind him without the usual complaints that should have come from such a pratfall enacted on his serious, scholarly body. He, too, poked around, albeit more hesitantly. But there were no extra shadows to be found—nor even the silken bag and wrapper she sometimes kept it in.

"Was it ever really there?" Michael finally asked, in perfect innocence.

"I don't know," John admitted.

On the one hand, Mr. Darling didn't want a scandal that could jeopardize his position in society or at the firm. On the other hand, neither he nor Mrs. Darling was entirely immune to the stories of Spring-Heeled Jack and the dreary, mysterious gray fogs of a London spring. The police were quietly notified, though the Darlings were quietly notified back that young unwed girls had a tendency to show up again hale and hearty, if often wed, or at least with child. Since there were no signs of violence, no known enemies, and no bodies floating Ophelia-like down the Thames recently, the police weren't concerned.

Mrs. Darling didn't believe it was a boy, at least a boy they knew; whether or not she was the *best* mother (as John and Michael and Wendy believed), she was good enough to know her daughter. Wendy, being a strange kitten, was not interested in any boys that way, except for maybe the bookstore owner's nephew.

"She'll come back. It's all probably just to avoid being sent to Ire—" Mr. Darling began.

Too late he saw Mrs. Darling's panicked eyes and shaking head.

"Sent to—to *Ireland*?" John asked sharply. "You were going to send Wendy to *Ireland*?"

"Why? For how long?" Michael demanded.

"We just felt like your sister needed a little break," their mother said gently.

"Rid her head of fairy stories, the nonsense she continually writes down in that notebook of hers," Mr. Darling blustered, angry at being caught out, angry that he ever had to hide anything.

"You wanted to send her to Ireland to rid her head of fairy stories," John said. "Let me just get this straight: the land of the *daoine sídhe* and the *bean sídthe* and the *pookah*?"

"Now look here, John—"

"You're sending Wendy *away* because of her stories?" Michael shouted. "Did you take her notebook? Did you *read* it?"

"Michael, we're her parents. We have every right to read—"

"But then you know! You *know* she's ever so much better than Beatrix Potter and Robert Louis Stevenson!"

"But those are . . ." Mrs. Darling began. Maybe even she wasn't sure what *those* were.

Something went out of Mr. Darling.

He collapsed onto a chair, head in his hands.

And so the Darling house continued on in a state of uncertainty and gloom. No one would admit a mistake or a problem, but the problem presented itself readily whenever there was a button to be mended, or Nana sighed, or meal after meal was silent and somehow unsatisfying. Despite the cook and the scullery maid the house seemed darker and dirtier. Groceries weren't bought, objects were misplaced, clothing grew ugly. No one hugged Mr. Darling in that special way daughters did; no one fell speechless at Mrs. Darling's dress or asked to use her perfume.

And no one wrote stories anymore.

There, you see? Everyone was perfectly miserable, and for each day that passed in the real world, a day passed in Never Land, more or less. Though you probably have guessed that already because of the business of Peter's shadow going missing for so long. But tell me this, since you're such a clever reader: If Wendy ever *does* arrive back home, changed or unchanged from her adventures, will life go on as before? Do you really think that's possible?

The Darlings were beginning to think not.

# Pan

Night slowly rolled into morning as the boat drifted down the last length of the new river. The sun was warm, the rain was gone, there were no maniacal mermaids, tyrannical pirates, unknowable gods, crystalline guards, or tricksy thysolits. . . . Despite their pressing quest, Wendy found herself relishing the quietude. If life back in London were as fraught and dangerous as in Never Land, she shouldn't have minded the quiet in-between days so much. A giant house with nothing to do seemed almost inviting after such travails.

Tinker Bell did not seem to be enjoying the lull in action. She had grabbed the prow of the boat and flew hard, trying to drag it through the water faster. Wendy laughed not unkindly at the look of fierce determination on the fairy's face and the tiny muscles popping out along her arms and base of her wings. A few sparkles of fairy dust sweated off.

The water grew shallow and spread into a silver delta, sculpting the soft sand into a thousand scales. The banks on either side became dunes. Once again Wendy was on a beach facing the sea.

Tinker Bell flew high up to get a better view, letting the boat go. It continued on, neither slower nor faster without her help.

"I wish you wouldn't get your hopes up about Peter," Wendy began carefully. "We still have no idea at all where he is, nor any way to find him. Hook should be our main concern now. We'll have to—"

But Tinker Bell dove down and grabbed her hand violently. She pointed across the sand. The fairy's eyes were the widest Wendy had ever seen, so wide they threatened to consume her face.

There, lying nonchalantly in the curve of a coconut tree, was Peter Pan.

"Oh," Wendy said, her mouth making the perfect shape of the letter she spoke.

He was unmistakable. Slender, clad in bright leafy green. Soft shoes with pointed tips. Soft hat with a red feather sticking jauntily out the back. Swooping nose.

Auburn hair and extremely distinctive eyebrows. Dagger dangling from a thin belt.

He let one hand trail languorously toward the ground and seemed to be conducting some sort of invisible orchestra with the other. His eyes were closed.

He was *so* Peter Pan it was ridiculous. He was realer than real. In brighter colors than Wendy ever imagined and far greater detail. Just like a dream but *more.*

"But how . . . ?"

They had been chasing his ghost all over Never Land and he wound up exactly where they were headed?

Tinker Bell was smiling devilishly.

*Part of your magic. The stories. Part of his magic. Peter Pan.*

Then she zoomed off to see him, abandoning Wendy and the boat.

Wendy struggled with a foot that was asleep and a boat that was tippy, only clumsily managing to disembark.

She started to haul the boat onto the beach—and then thought better of it. In Never Land one seemed to be stripped of everything: bags, modern possessions, decent clothing, ideas. Nothing material remained with anyone for long.

"Just look at what the Lost Boys wore and sat on, and what happened with Luna," she murmured.

Found and then lost again. Even her own shadow.

If they needed transport someplace else, they would improvise. Wasn't that what Peter always did in her stories?

Wendy pushed the boat back into the slow current and slapped it playfully on what would have been its flank.

"You go and help someone else now. You're free—of me, at least."

She watched it float away, so pretty and blue and gold like a toy, until it was safely far out in the sea. . . .

And pretended she wasn't trying to delay meeting her hero.

With a sigh she turned and began to head for him (and Tink). She watched the prints her feet made in the sand and the trailing threads and tatters of her dress dancing around her freckled legs. Not the way she had imagined she would be dressed when she met Peter. Not that she really ever had imagined clothing in the adventures. Only the accessories: a stylish cap, a sharp sword. Everything else was ignored or assumed to be the usual; Wendy in a light blue dress, probably.

A shadow—*her* shadow!—danced over the sand to her feet, daintily touching them with her own toes. Wendy felt a surge of completeness, of warmth and solidity. Some exhaustion faded away.

She kicked her feet, spraying sand and shadow sand at her shade.

Her shadow sputtered in surprise.

"Oh, you're back. Lovely to see you again," Wendy said dryly.

The shadow pointed at Peter excitedly.

"Yes, I know. We found him. Ourselves. No thanks to you. You didn't even come get us once *you* found him. Fat lot of good you are."

And with that, Wendy ignored her shadow, walking with great dignity toward the palms where her friends were.

(I'm afraid, dear reader, you can't see how the shadow reacted to this, for Wendy very steadfastly ignored her—literally refusing to see her. And since we are living this story in Wendy's point of view, you shall have to resort to your own imagination to decide what the shadow did.)

Peter Pan sat up and looked at Wendy.

The time had come to admit her wrongdoing and take her comeuppance. To begin the next part of her quest, where together the three of them would save Never Land.

She stuck her chin out and marched up to him.

Upon closer inspection she realized how small the boy was. Not tiny, but slender and no taller than she. Maybe even shorter. His face was *very* boyish—he hadn't lost all the baby fat from his cheekbones yet, and his teeth were suspiciously small . . . like his adult teeth hadn't come in yet.

Wendy swallowed, remembering the near-romantic thoughts she used to have of him. The eager young lad looking up at her now couldn't have been more than twelve or thirteen in London years. His eyes, though feral and dark, seemed somehow younger than John's.

"Hello, you must be Peter Pan." Wendy covered her mixed feelings and nervousness with accent and politeness. She did not curtsy.

"Tink here was just telling me you were going to help me find my shadow!" Peter said with a grin of undiluted happiness. His teeth sparkled and his eyes crinkled in joy.

All misgivings and reluctance disappeared. Wendy was immediately swept up by his energy. She would do *anything* with him—she could tell he was the most fun person in the whole world. His games would be the *best*.

"I can see you're having trouble with *your* shadow, too," he went on to say, smirking at Wendy's. She risked a look—the shadow was pouting, arms crossed.

"Well . . . wolves and shadows," Wendy said nonchalantly. "They have their own minds and motives. What can you do?"

"Ain't that the truth," Peter said with a sigh. Wendy felt her heart skip. He was *commiserating* with her! They were *bonding*! "'Cause say what you want about them, but it's hard not having a shadow, you know. It really tires you right out. I was just taking a lie down here, on account of my continual exhaustion and the pains."

"Pains?"

Tinker Bell and Wendy looked at each other, worried.

"Oh, stomachaches and heart aches, like I've eaten too much from the snacky tree," Peter said airily, dismissing it. "But ha, Wendy! I can't believe it! I used to come and hear your stories . . . and here you are, helping me! On this beach, no less!"

"Of course. But . . . what *are* you doing on this beach?" Wendy asked, curiosity getting the better of her—and her apology.

"Looking for my shadow, silly! Didn't I just say I was missing it?" he said with disgust.

It was approaching noon, and they were close enough to whatever passed for an equator that nothing had a shadow, except for the puffed heads of the palms directly over their roots.

And Wendy, of course, whose shadow sulked away from her on a sandy mound.

"But . . . there aren't any shadows here at all. . . ."

"Exactly! So mine would stand out, right? I'd see him immediately!" Peter crowed in triumph.

Wendy looked helplessly at Tinker Bell, unable to think of a response to this lunacy. The fairy, who had been looking up at Peter with wide eyes a moment before, a delicate hand on his, gave her a little shrug: *what can you do*?

"Peter, I *know* where your shadow is," Wendy said quickly, before something else stopped her from admitting the truth. "I had it. In London. I traded it for passage to Never Land."

And Peter Pan, for perhaps the first time in his existence, was silenced.

Tinker Bell gave Wendy a nod and a tiny smile, pleased at her friend's brave admission.

"You . . . had it?" he finally said, trying to work it out. "In . . . London?"

Wendy nodded. "You left it there. The last time you came, I suppose you surprised or upset Nana, our dog. She tried to bite you but grabbed your shadow instead, and I'm afraid she rather ripped it off of you. She didn't mean to, really. She's a good dog. She was just trying to protect us. I kept it all these years—folded carefully in a drawer, waiting for you to come back and fetch it."

"I remember now!" Peter leapt up, twirling, laughing and crowing. "That *was* the last place I saw him! Gosh,

I haven't been back to London at all since then! I haven't gone back at all, not even to look! That's strange, I searched everywhere else. I *should* have looked there. But Tink kept telling me . . . Tink kept telling me . . ."

He frowned.

Tinker Bell swallowed.

Wendy bit her lip.

"Tink," Peter said, eyes glowing with rage and suspicion. "Why did you keep telling me it wasn't there? That I shouldn't bother looking in London, or ever going back? Didn't you *want* me to find my shadow?"

Tinker Bell wrung her hands and swayed back and forth miserably.

*I didn't want you seeing Wendy again.*

"Wendy?" Peter demanded, confused out of his anger. "Why? What's wrong with Wendy? Is she—is she evil?"

*No! She—I was jealous.*

"What? *Jealous?* Of some silly girl?"

"I beg your pardon," Wendy said, her eyebrows rising.

Tinker Bell nodded woefully.

"And you were so jealous that you were all right with me going without a shadow for the rest of my life? What kind of friend *are* you, Tink?"

"She didn't *know* I had the shadow," Wendy interrupted quickly, seeing the flames in his eyes. "Not really. In fact, she came to London of her own accord to look for it, but I had already left for Never Land."

"Well, *thank you* for that," he spat, looking wrathfully at the fairy. "It's been like . . . hundreds of moons since I lost it! You're the worst, Tink."

The little fairy collapsed into a crumpled ball of wings and arms and legs and began to weep.

"Oh!" Wendy cried, scooping her up. "She made a mistake, Peter. She's trying to make up for it. She did it because she loves you. And didn't want to lose you."

*"Loves . . . ?"* Peter asked, sounding sick.

He stuck his head close to the teary-eyed fairy.

"Is this true, Tinker Bell? Do you . . . *love* me?"

The fairy nodded, sparkling tears still spilling out of her eyes.

"Well, that's all nuts," he swore, sitting back on his heels.

"Shh, don't cry, it's all right," Wendy murmured. The fairy tears stung and burned. For only a moment, but it was still a little unnerving. "Just give him a few minutes."

"And I don't mean nuts just about the love—*blech*—business," Peter continued, stomping up the beach, then spinning around and stomping back. "It's nuts and bananas that you say that you care about me and then wait *forever* to go get my shadow!

"Tinker Bell, you're *banished*! For *treason*!"

"Oh no, stop it! She did the wrong thing for the right reasons," Wendy snapped. Which was incredibly strange, because here was the hero of her dreams and she was talking to him like she would Michael or John when they were being silly. "Don't go about banishing her or whatever. Accept her apology and move on—we're wasting precious time. There are other things going on besides reuniting you with your shadow.

"Hook is planning to destroy Never Land as some sort of doomsday farewell gesture—he was just waiting to capture you before he carried it out."

"Oh? All of Never Land? Destroyed?" Peter asked, surprised. "That's huge. All right then. Tink, you're forgiven."

His switch from red-faced anger to forgiveness was so abrupt—and apparently free from reflection—that Wendy felt seasick.

*I'm sorry,* Tinker Bell jingled through a gap in Wendy's fingers. Golden light spilled out around her apologetic face. She looked like a tiny Renaissance saint.

"Apology accepted," Peter said, nodding officiously. "Don't do it again."

*I never will.* She said it with such warmth Wendy could feel it on her fingers.

"Now then, what's this about Hook wanting to destroy

Never Land?" Peter asked. "I mean, he's evil, but he's not *insane.* Well, all right. He's insane. But not *that* insane. If he destroys Never Land, where will he go?"

"Right out of my stories forever," Wendy said. "Along with the rest of you."

Tinker Bell shivered.

"Well, it all seems crazy to me. So how does he plan on doing it?"

"I don't know—I don't have any of the details beyond the fact that it has something to do with getting you first, maybe by using your shadow to lure you in. It's like he wants to punish you and erase his past at the same time. And," she added quickly, making herself say it again, clearly and aloud, "it's *my* fault he has the shadow. Because as I said, I traded it *to him* to come here."

"Hm." Peter looked her up and down as if seeing her for the first time. Reevaluating. "Yes, you are a bit old to come to Never Land the normal way. Plus, you're a girl."

"A silly one, I'm told," she said archly.

"Exactly. At least, you were when I first started visiting you. Now you're like . . . a silly young woman. Pretty clever, using my shadow as payment for passage. Even if it wasn't yours."

"Thank you?" Wendy said uncertainly.

"So wait—let me get this straight. You gave the shadow

I left behind to my enemy? Crazy old codfish whose hand I took, who's been after me ever since?"

"Ah . . . yes? Yes. I did. I did that." She cleared her throat. "I did the worst possible thing, and I'm so sorry, Peter, you don't know how—"

But she was interrupted by a loud crowing, a resounding *cock-a-doodle-do* from Peter's wide mouth.

He was grinning and spinning, hands on his hips, laughing, dancing.

"I get to fight the *pirates* for it!" he sang. "I get to battle old Codfish to get my shadow back! Oh, I've been meaning to give him another hook! This is a *perfect* opportunity! Well done, Wendy! You're brilliant!"

He grabbed her hands and spun her around, causing Tinker Bell to go flying head over heels through the air and then land with a hard *thump* on the sand.

Wendy should have been over the moon that the legendary Peter Pan was delighted by her antics and was now dancing with her. She should have felt a happiness and satisfaction in her heart that she had never known before. Rather than earning his scorn or hatred, she had *impressed* her hero. It was a glorious, greedy feeling. One that Peter Pan particularly inspired; she could see herself doing anything to recapture that feeling, to make him feel that way about her again and again—if he couldn't feel about her any other way.

But . . .

She looked over to where Tinker Bell had landed. The fairy was a little stunned and a little rumpled and glaring furiously.

At *Wendy*.

Not Peter.

If her eyes had been coals, they would have lit what was left of Wendy's dress on fire.

Wendy quickly dropped Peter's hand.

"Well, yes, but I'm still sorry. The shadow was never mine to trade. It was terribly selfish of me."

"Oh, it's all fine," Peter said, waving his hands at her. "C'mon! Let's go get the pirates!"

He turned and went to dive into the air, but paused on the ground in a ridiculous tiptoe pose.

"Little help here, Tink?" he asked.

The fairy shook her head forcefully, crossing her arms and pouting.

Wendy felt weariness descend upon her. *This* was the sticking point? *This* was where their quest ended? Despite the evolution of her and Tinker Bell's friendship, Tinker Bell remained very much a fairy: prone to sudden passions, savage angers, swift tears, and whatever one moment demanded but the next moment forgot.

Just like Peter Pan.

Just like characters in story after story who never change because you don't want them to. You want them to stay the same forever, like you wished your best friends or your relationship with your mother would.

Wendy watched the two of them bicker with a strange mixture of feelings. They were both like children. Wendy wasn't really, not anymore. Despite living in her parents' house and taking on tasks like Mother in a game of pretend and dreaming out the window and making up stories no one wanted to listen to. She had started to want other things, even if she couldn't name them yet, and had grown tired of her current life.

But was that change so terrible, really?

Would it be better to stay in Never Land forever and never change?

To be the same talky, nervous Wendy forever? To always have the same desire to make others like her by taking care of them? To always be the same lonely girl who never fit in any world? To always dream and never *do*?

Sometimes stories needed to be pushed along. Things needed to happen. People needed to accomplish things. And as long as Peter and Tink were somewhere in the world, never changing, and Wendy knew that, she would be happy with whatever happened to her. As someone who changed in the course of a story.

As someone who *changed* the course of a story.

"Actually, she's right," she said, her wonderful, storytelling mind coming up with a useful plan that would make everyone happy—and behave.

"I mean, you should still give him the fairy dust, but he should really *stay where he is*. The pirates have been running all over the seas looking for him—it would be much easier to work this out by just having them come to us, don't you think?"

Peter and Tinker Bell frowned almost identically in confusion.

"I've said this before: I really don't think the three of us can go up against the pirates all by ourselves. I'm not that handy with a sword—a real one. I'm sure Tinker Bell can be quite dangerous in her own way. But as someone who has been actually captive to those seafaring hoodlums, I don't know how much good fairy dust does against gunpowder and savage bloodlust."

"I don't need help!" Peter protested. "All I need is to be able to fly! I can take on old Hook by myself!"

"But can you, I wonder . . ." Wendy said thoughtfully. "I think I'm beginning to figure this all out. You've been tired and weak without your shadow, just like I was. And now Hook *has* your shadow, in a cage. A nasty one. And you were talking about strange pains and aches. . . . I think

Hook is getting to you through your own shadow. Maybe he can't kill you directly, but he can hurt *it* and affect *you.*"

This gave Peter pause.

"A cage? He has my shadow in a cage?"

"I'm afraid so. With all sorts of nasty barbs and pincers inside."

Tinker Bell watched Peter closely for his decision. As he considered this information, he unthinkingly offered the fairy his hand up.

She grinned from ear to pointed ear.

"I don't like this. I don't like this at all," he swore. "Using my *shadow.* That's against the rules. That's bad form. So I guess what you're saying is that I need a crew. An army. All right then, to the Lost Boys! Yeah! Together we'll all save Never Land! Let's go get 'em!" He made to fly again.

"You should stay here," Wendy said, "remember? We decided that a moment ago? Even assuming you're back to yourself enough to fly, Tinker Bell would be fastest. She'll fly there, and you and I will . . ."

Tinker Bell narrowed her eyes at Wendy.

"I mean . . . *I'll go.* Yes, that's best," Wendy said, correcting herself quickly. "Tinker Bell can stay here and look after you. If that's all right? I'll just need very precise directions. And some more fairy dust, if you don't mind. For me *and* Peter."

Tinker Bell closed her eyes and bowed politely—*of course. For you.*

She flew up in a dainty spiral around Peter, gracefully whisking showers of golden sparks over him. Peter laughed in delight.

She threw the dust over her shoulder without looking at Wendy, getting her in the face. Not out of spite—it was just that the fairy's eyes were still on Peter.

"I'm not sure this relationship is very good for either one of you," Wendy muttered, wiping dust off her nose. No one paid her any attention.

"It's easy to get there," Peter said. He squatted down and pulled out his dagger to draw a map in the sand. "We're here, at Pegleg Point. Then hang right at Blind Man's Bluff. Then follow the river up—"

"Sorry, which river?" Wendy asked, trying to understand. All she saw were vague lines and gashes and one sinuous, perhaps watery, track.

"Whaddayamean, *which* river?" Peter said, laughing. He pushed his hat from the back so it dipped down over his face. "There's only *one* river in Never Land."

Tinker Bell jingled, shaking her head.

"There's two now," Wendy said. "I made one."

For perhaps the second time in his existence, Peter Pan was shocked into silence.

"When we were with the First," she continued primly, trying—sort of—not to be smug. Had Peter ever created anything from nothing in Never Land? Anything so grand?

"You went to the *First*?" Peter Pan gulped.

"The mermaids told us you went there to see about obtaining a new shadow."

"I did! Good-for-nothing jerks," he growled, kicking sand over his map. "They wouldn't even let me in. I had to walk the whole way and *they wouldn't let me in*! Told me to deal with 'my own piddling issues.' *Me!* Peter Pan! I'm practically the *king* of Never Land."

Wendy turned this declaration over in her mind. How often did Peter say things like this? How often did he act like that? How true was it? No wonder Slightly was chafing a bit.

"Well, consider yourself lucky, perhaps. They tried to trap us there—we very nearly could have spent eternity in a desert maze, trying to find our way out."

"I can't even believe you went there to begin with," he said, turning to Tinker Bell. "Tink? That was incredibly dangerous. You know, for someone who isn't me. You really did that? You went in there . . . for me?"

Tinker Bell nodded shyly.

"Huh. That's some powerful stuff there." He scratched his chin. "L—uh, whatever is you feel, I mean."

*Wouldn't you do the same for me?* Tinker Bell asked, the tips of her wings quivering.

Wendy felt her heart stop. She waited as anxiously as her friend for the answer.

"Yeah, of course," the boy said, shaking his head in disgust. "But that's not 'cause of love, that's 'cause we're buddies. You're my first mate. You're the most important member of my crew. I wouldn't let anything happen to you, ever."

Tinker Bell clasped her hands in delight and looked at him with shining eyes. He smiled and patted her on the head.

"Good enough," Wendy decided.

"Whatever river you choose, Hangman's Tree is here." He put an X on the ground.

*Can you remember from when we went there before?* Tinker Bell asked. *It's southeast of the Black Dragon Mountains, about halfway to the coast. In a round clearing, like a fire or a meteor cleared it out.*

"Thank you, Tinker Bell," Wendy said. "That was very precise and clear."

"Did you name it?" Peter asked suddenly.

"Name what?"

"The river! Did you name it yet?"

He was deadly serious.

"No—I don't suppose I have," Wendy said. "Hadn't we better—"

"We absolutely had better!"

Peter put a finger to his chin, thinking.

Tinker Bell furrowed her brow, trying to come up with something.

Wendy looked at both of them in exasperation. They didn't have time for this.

Peter's eyes lit up and he opened his mouth.

"How about—"

"We are *not* calling it the River Pan," Wendy interrupted.

"I wasn't," Peter said peevishly. "I was going to call it the River Peter."

Tinker Bell giggled, sparkles of dust falling around her.

"No. How about . . . the First River? *You* should like that. It makes sense, but it makes absolutely no sense at all. It's just Never Land's style."

"The First River! It's the River of the First . . . but it's *not really* the *first river*! I love it!" He clapped her on the back—rather a little too hard, and she fell forward.

*But what if the pirates get here before you get back? What if Hook gets to Peter before we're ready?* Tinker Bell asked.

"What about your fairy friends? Can you ask them to help? To at least—keep you company?" Wendy asked. "To keep an eye out?"

The little fairy gave her a nearly uncomprehending look.

"I know you aren't the closest with them, really, but this is an emergency. You're in serious need. All of Never Land is in trouble. Thorn might come—he seems a decent sort."

Tinker bell tossed her head and began to jingle something contemptuously.

*"Don't,"* Wendy interrupted. "Don't let your ego get in the way of protecting yourself and Peter."

*"I don't need protecting by fairies!"* Peter squawked indignantly.

Wendy and Tinker Bell ignored him.

Finally, the fairy nodded. *All right. For Peter.*

"Good," Wendy said with a sigh. "Well look, I should head out. Stay *here*," she ordered, standing up and readying herself to go. "Tinker Bell, take care of him. Make sure he doesn't leave. But if the pirates appear, fly—if you can—into the jungle and hide."

Tinker Bell saluted her smartly.

But Peter just stood there gazing at her, mouth agape.

Wendy looked down at herself; she hadn't even realized how heroic a pose she struck. From her shadow—which took this opportunity to actually behave—she realized how she appeared: powerful, strong . . . with a scandalously short tunic cinched around her waist and improvised leggings that showed a prodigious amount of her newly tanned skin. Her hair was down around her shoulders. She bet she was the spitting image of an Amazon, short a bow.

"Gosh, Wendy, you sure look different from when I first saw you," Peter mumbled.

Tinker Bell put her hands on her hips and started to jingle.

"Well, I must be off," Wendy said quickly. "Bye!"

And she took off into the air, like Nike, triumphant.

# And She Flew

Wendy fell backward into the sky a little more rapidly than she intended. It felt like a dream she'd had once or twice: suddenly being pulled up into the air, snatched out of a narrative, away from monsters or loved ones.

Her heart jumped at the unnatural movement but she didn't stop.

Barreling forward, she stuck her arms out and—*there.* Her fingertips brushed against the steady warm wind that Tinker Bell looked for when they had great distances to fly. It streamed almost directly due north, so she would have to get off it and take a right at some point, but it would ease the journey somewhat.

She banked into the thermal, feeling important. For the first time in her life she was on a quest where people needed her for real things—for *survival*, not for a popped button or an emergency trip to the market for some dinner veg. If she failed it would mean disaster for her friends and all of Never Land.

And what precisely would Hook do if she failed? If he succeeded in catching Peter? How would he end Never Land *rather permanently*? Would he use dark powers to call up a titanic storm and sink it like Atlantis? Could Peter's shadow have something to do with that? Would he somehow rain down fire and lava?

Well, Wendy didn't intend to find out. She stretched and frowned, flying a little faster.

Was that her shadow down there, also gliding? Rippling over the trees?

Feh! She wouldn't look. At least now she *could* return to London.

And speaking of . . .

What would *she* do, once Hook was defeated?

(As he must be.)

Wendy had wanted adventure; now she had gotten herself one. She could go back home and live the rest of her life on recollections from the past several days, spooning out carefully meted measures of memory to live on when existence grew dull. She could write an entire book on what had happened. She could actually try to get it published and watch with amusement as readers drank up her "fantasy." Or she could just keep it in her notebook, to be taken out and read to eventual children in her life.

She could stay in Never Land forever. . . .

No, that didn't feel right. She *had* grown up a little. And, like Slightly, she chafed at some of the unchanging and arbitrary aspects of Never Land.

Maybe Peter Pan *was* king of the island in his own way. They were similar, or maybe even dependent on each other, just in the same way Never Land was dependent on London—and the rest of the world.

So the real question was: What could Wendy *do* with her life? Back in the real world? What lay in between *household* and *mermaids*? What would give her adventure (of the London sort) and challenges, and a change for the better for both worlds?

*John* knew that he could choose between being a doctor, banker, academic, or barrister. Even shipping, if he had any ability that way (he didn't). These were known, potential futures.

But despite all her reading Wendy hadn't been exposed in any real way to the idea that there were any possibilities for her at all beyond *unhappy spinster* or *unhappy housewife.*

These were odd thoughts, and uncomfortable ones. She felt a little stirring of self-recrimination: Why hadn't she even *thought* things like this before? Why hadn't she even noticed the invisible prison she was in?

"Because," she told herself gently, "I've never been able to fly before."

Below her Never Land unrolled in shades of green except for the misty, unavailable area to the northwest. Wendy gave that place a salute.

The First had said there were people whose idea of Never Land meant a single warm meal for the day. There were girls who weren't held back by well-meaning parents or society, but by poverty or *genuinely* terrible parents who treated them like possessions to trade. There were girls who had no chance simply because of the color of their skin.

*Sometimes stories needed to be pushed along. Things needed to happen.* People *were needed to* do *things.*

Sometimes whole societies needed to be pushed along in the right direction.

The landscape below changed and the Black Dragon Mountains came into view, as blurry and smoggy as ever. It was time to turn east. Wendy felt her heart clench. She so wanted to see the mountains—and a real dragon. She wondered if maybe she would have time to dip by on her way back from talking with the Lost Boys. Just a peep.

She sighed and banked right. Probably not. It would be something for her to dream about later, to wonder about and imagine on dark days.

# Meanwhile, on the High Seas…

Hook took long and precise military steps up and down the deck, his back straight as a knife blade while he inspected each cannon and musket, sword and dagger. Everything had to be *perfect.*

The pirates, more used to going into battle by the seat of their pants, were a little unprepared for such a military-style drill—and completely unfamiliar with the particulars.

Screaming Byron, for instance, had thought he had done a very nice job polishing the cannonballs at his station, and presented them to the captain with a bow and a proud smile.

Hook just stared at him.

"What good is a *shiny cannonball?*" he finally roared. "Is the barrel of the machine cleaned out? Are your powder cartridges stacked, dry, and ready to go? Is your friction primer up to snuff? In short, will your cannon actually *fire* your very pretty and shiny cannonball when it is loaded?"

"I think it looks very nice," Smee said sympathetically, upon seeing the poor pirate's downcast look.

"We're looking at the *final battle* here," Hook reminded Byron, leaning forward so he could look the other pirate dead in the eye. "Our very last run-in ever with Peter Pan and the Lost Boys. We want to look good, absolutely, but we also want to *finish* it for good. I want their bodies washing up on the shore, bloodied and broken. *All* of them. And I want Peter Pan to see it. Do you hear me?"

"Loud and clear," the pirate said, brightening a little at the mention of blood.

And maybe *final battle.*

Hook glowered: no one in his idiotic crew shared his passion for defeating their worst enemy once and for all. They only seemed to look forward to getting it over with and moving on to whatever fun activity was planned afterward. They were short on imagination and education; they had no taste for refined concepts like *nemeses* and *life conflicts* and *guiding principles.*

(They might also all have still been in recovery mode after their shenanigans at Skull Island. The entire crew but Hook and Smee dragged and stumbled a bit.)

No matter. Whatever it took to drive them to victory.

"Mr. Smee, take a note: I need you to go back and recheck cannon crews one, two, and six. They didn't pass muster. Also, have the Duke unlock the stockroom and distribute as many bullets and shells as needed. My personal stash of purloined weaponry will be available for general use, except of course these flintlocks on me belt. I want every man armed and ready."

"Oh, they'll like that, Cap'n. That'll get them in the spirit! Bullets and muskets! Right away, Cap'n!" Mr. Smee doffed his cap and ran off to deliver the news.

Hook twirled his mustache for a moment, enjoying himself utterly. *This* was what it meant to be a pirate captain! To be on top of everything, awash in the excitement before a battle!

Wait? What was that?

That sound . . .

He grabbed the nearest pirate—Djareth—by the earring.

"Do you hear that?" he demanded.

The pirate, wide-eyed, tried to shake his head and shrug.

"*THE TICKING!* Can you not hear it, you villainous fool? The sound of the crocodile approaching!"

"N-no, Cap'n," Djareth stuttered. "Nothing, Cap'n!"

"Bah!"

Hook threw him aside. Of course, when he listened, it was silent now: wherever the beast was, it must have gone beneath the waves.

But it was close.

Hook stalked to the prow. A rope had been hung across the decking between the chart room and the railing along with a hastily painted sign that read NO ADMITTANCE. The words could, of course, just have been gibberish; few of the pirates could read. It was the angry red paint that got their attention.

Zane was on watch. He sat on a stool looking vaguely green, like a reluctant landlubber on a transatlantic voyage. This despite the fact that the wind was up and the ship cut through the waves as beautifully as a knife through a kidney. No, it was *what* he watched: the shadow in its golden prison of bars and sharp picks, the way its blackness recoiled in ripples away from those picks.

"Any change in the prisoner, Alodon?"

"No, Cap'n. He ain't moved an inch. Looks like he even gave up on the whole escaping-himself thing. He's just been man-shaped. Peter-shaped. The whole time. Pointing the same way."

"Hmm." Hook stroked his chin and frowned. The shadow had been pointing that way more or less directly for the last day. It only wavered a little, when the ship had to curve around a bit of coast or shoals, but always returned to face the same way.

The captain made his way back to the chart room. Zane apparently decided that was as good as a dismissal, or an order to follow, and hastily went after him, getting away from the unnatural scene as quickly as he could.

The cool darkness of the cabin caressed Hook's tortured brow. He bent over the table that held the map of Never Land with the help of two pressed-glass prisms, a bronze astrolabe, and a perfect skull. A little pewter model of the *Jolly Roger* stood in for the real one. He did some quick calculations for latitude and longitude. The breeze had remained steady; he pushed the little ship along, down and around the corner of Never Land. Then he took a ruler and tried to predict the route.

"No, it's the same, look at that," Hook said thoughtfully. "If this is all correct, Peter Pan has been in Pegleg Point for two days now—unmoving. I wonder why. That dratted boy can never stay still for more than a moment at a time."

"Maybe he can't fly, Cap'n?" Zane suggested. "That without his shadow, he lost some of his power, or the pixie dust don't work or somethin'?"

"True, true," Hook said, turning it over in his head. "But even if he couldn't *fly*, the boy could still *run,* if the notion took him. No, something else is going on."

"Maybe he's resting. Or sick. Or pining for the fjords. Or . . . captured!"

"But by whom? The First were last spotted on the exact opposite end of the island. The L'cki haven't been heard from in fortnights. The Fangriders of Upper Hillsdale swore they wouldn't bother with him again until they got their numbers back up. It's festival season for the Ragnarosti—they make peace with the deuced fairies and have those terrible musical concerts that go on forever. With the stupid flower crowns and ceremonial kombucha. No . . . it must be a trick. Something he's planning.

"I know, it's an *ambush*!"

He pounded his fists down on the table in realization. But he was smiling.

"Uh, Cap'n . . . ?" Zane asked, worried.

"Don't you see? *I've figured it out.* His ambush! I got it! Ha ha! Peter Pan can't get the best of *me*!"

"But what do we do then, Cap'n?" the other pirate asked carefully. "Surprise him? Go around the island the other way? Sneak in through the back side of the lagoon? Uh, *is* there a back side of the lagoon?"

"No, there isn't, Zane. No . . . I think I may try something else. Go present your flintlocks to Mr. Smee for inspection and see about making any requests from the artillery storeroom. And I need someone else keeping an eye on the prisoner. Someone a bit more . . . proactive, and less squeamish. You know who I mean, Zane. The one who was recently reunited with us."

"Uh, yes, Cap'n. Right away, Cap'n."

Zane shivered as he escaped the room, but Hook didn't notice or care. The moment the other pirate was gone he pulled out one of the black leather books obtained from Madam Moreia. Along with theories on how to capture and remove a person's shadow, there were passages in the book that discussed the connection that remained between them even after the two were separated. The bond between person and shadow was deep and possibly continued through the spirit plane. For if a person was hurt or weakened dramatically—say, an arm cut off—wasn't it true that the shadow was also affected?

So logically it followed the reverse was true, too. And now that Hook had the Painopticon . . .

A smile grew on his face, a genuine, devilish one complete with an evil gleam in his eye.

Finally Captain Hook was going to win. *Really* win against Peter Pan.

And after?

Skull Island.

# Peter Pan and Tink

Tinker Bell performed the fairy call for aid as quickly as she could, just above the tree line at the edge of the forest. Then she zoomed back to where Peter lay talking to himself—and then to her, when he noticed she was back.

"I just can't wait until the pirates are here, Tink," he said in a tone only he could master authentically: dreamy and excited at the same time, wistful and full of resolve. "I'll show Hook. I'll show that stinky old codfish. This time, I'll finish him but good, and . . . ohhh!"

Suddenly he convulsed in pain. He fell, hard, to the sand.

Tinker Bell flew backward up into the air to take him in all at once: Was it a poisonous snake? A spiderphyl?

Something else she could beat back with fairy rage?

But . . . no. She could see nothing.

"Tink? Tink?" Peter cried, squirming and writhing in the dust. His eyes were screwed shut in torment.

She landed on his chest, put a hand on his face.

*What? What is it? What hurts?!*

He opened his eyes and tried to focus them on her, but they were glazed and unwilling to do his bidding.

"Tink, it burns! It's like . . . it's like something inside of me is being pulled—*outside* of me. Something is reaching up into me and is pulling my heart into knots . . . but it's not my heart . . . it's my . . . I don't know what it is. Oh, Tink, it feels terrible. I don't know what it is. I can't see it. I can't fight it. Tink! Help me!"

The fairy buzzed back and forth, helpless and angry. She thought about what she had seen on the thysolit thorax, the pirate ship and the cage. Wendy was right: whatever was happening to Peter must have something to do with the shadow. Something Hook was *doing* to the shadow.

She flew as high into the sky as she could and looked for the pirate ship at sea, Wendy in the jungle. There were no signs of either.

*Hurry!* she jingled loudly, knowing no one could hear her.

"Tink—where are you? Oh! Please! Tink! Come back!"

She returned to Peter, frustrated and powerless to do anything.

"Don't leave me, Tink. Wendy and the Lost Boys will be here soon. The Lost Boys will come. They'll help me out. They're the best. Even Slightly. He just wants . . . he just wants . . . Ohhhhhh!"

He spasmed, contracting over his stomach again.

"Tink! Where are you? Tink!"

Peter put his hand up to feel for her like a blind man. The little fairy took his thumb and squeezed as hard as she could. His face was pale and glittering with translucent beads of sweat. His breath came in thin-sounding rasps.

Tinker Bell hesitantly leaned over. She kissed him ever so gently on the lower lip.

A fairy kiss, invisible and seemingly ephemeral, whose effects and existence would last as long as pixie dust.

Perhaps his breathing eased. Perhaps he looked a trifle more peaceful, despite his eyes rolling beneath their lids.

She wondered what it meant, the touch of human lips on her own—if *it* left any trace on *her.*

*Hurry, Wendy,* she jingled.

# The Lost Boys

Wendy found the trufualuffs and the clearing with Hangman's Tree in the middle of it fairly easily. Were men ever actually hanged from the nooses that dangled from its branches? She had never given it much thought when telling stories to the boys. . . .

Her landing was far more graceful than the first time there. Also more prepared for the slide down this time, she managed to use some pixie dust power at the bottom of the ramp to pop back up on her feet like a jack-in-the-box, immediately and somewhat unbelievably.

Luna, who had been lounging near the fire, leapt up joyfully and stuffed her nose into Wendy's hand.

"Good girl! Miss me? I've had the most extraordinary adventures. What's it been like here?"

The Lost Boys, figures of her tales of swashbuckling adventures under their leader, Peter Pan, seemed to be having a rare quiet moment. The older ones, Slightly, Skipper, and Cubby, were reclined in various supine positions on different furniture stand-ins: mushrooms, ledges, roots. The twins were playing some sort of game like jacks which involved swiping the *other* person's jacks. They looked almost demonic with their quick movements and shiny white teeth bared in grins that contrasted starkly with their black masks. Tootles had what looked like a bright pink dormouse that he was petting and whispering baby-nothings to.

"Wendy!" He put the dormouse in his pocket and smashed into her, wrapping his arms around her legs, squeezing in next to Luna.

"Did you find Peter or his shadow?" Slightly asked, hopping down from his root.

"I—we—found Peter, yes. Can I have this?" Wendy asked, suddenly distracted by the honeycomb on the table mushroom. She couldn't remember the last time she had eaten.

"I was saving it for—" Cubby began.

"Thank you," Wendy said, for the first time in her life being a little rude. And why not? Everyone else in Never Land was. She couldn't be expected to civilize an entire island of barbarians. "I'll just take a piece."

She broke it in two and immediately shoved half into her mouth, closing her eyes at the glorious golden deliciousness. It tasted like summer and flowers and something exotic. When she opened her eyes Slightly was regarding her with an amused expression.

"That's lovely," she added primly, not even bothering to look for a napkin. She wiped her mouth with the back of her hand. "Even without a bit of toast. Anyway, yes, we found Peter. He's at Pegleg Point with Tinker Bell. Seems a bit peaked. As for his shadow, Hook still has it and is doing something unspeakable to it, maybe using it to find Peter. Hook wants Peter in hand—excuse me, hook and hand—before he destroys Never Land so that Peter is forced to watch it. Or something. According to the First. Pretty over-the-top villainy there. Anyway, it's only a matter of time before the pirates reach him and Tinker Bell. Our job is to lure the pirates in, grab the shadow, and return it to Peter."

The boys—and girl—all stared at her.

"Maybe *she* should be the new leader," Skipper ventured.

Slightly raised a foxish eyebrow. "D'you mean to tell me you plan on using Peter as bait to catch old Codfish?"

"Yes. I'm just going to grab one of these apricots here. Before we go. Maybe three."

She wished she had a bag to tuck them into instead of

being forced to pop them all into her mouth at once. She was so hungry and they were so good there was a danger of the juice spilling from her lips and running down her cheeks. Which, again, would not have caused much of a scene in the den of the Lost Boys, but she wanted to keep up *some* appearances.

"Did you—did you talk to Peter?" Skipper asked in a low voice. "About me?"

"Or me?" Slightly added. "Is everything all right again between us?"

Wendy almost choked. "All of Never Land is in *danger*. Did you miss that part? I have left Peter tended by a tiny fairy while a pirate ship is coming after him. I've been nearly drowned by mermaids, fought off thysolits, escaped the realm of the First, and flown *all over* this bloody island. Somehow, during all of that, I may have neglected to launch into an invective against misogyny or a monograph about the necessary skills of a great leader. We don't have a lot of time here, is what I'm trying to say. Do you think you could get over your personal grievances and come to his and all of Never Land's aid? Are the Lost Boys really going to sit around while everything is destroyed around them?"

"Of course we'll help," Slightly said, pulling out his rapier and brandishing it. "That was never a question!"

"We'd never abandon Peter if he was in trouble,"

Skipper mumbled as she put one hand on her scimitar, the other on her bow. "Whatever our problems are."

"For Peter!" the twins said together, drawing the little knives that hung from their waists. "And Never Land!"

"LET ME AT THOSE PIRATES," Cubby roared, pushing up his sleeves and baring his meaty fists.

Tootles just narrowed his eyes and growled.

"Well, I'm glad to hear that," Wendy said. "I'm going to fly ahead and see how they're doing. How long do you think it will take you to get there?"

"Forced march?" one twin asked.

"Several hours," the other answered.

Wendy began to open her mouth, feeling her panic grow.

"We could use the tunnels through the Cenotaph Caves," Skipper suggested quickly, seeing her look.

"Just what I was thinking," Slightly said with a frown. "They lead right into the back of the cove. And maybe we could ask the Elephant Wheels for help. Let's say four hours, max. Depends on the cooperation of the various parties involved."

"All right, well, I suppose that sounds feasible," Wendy said uncertainly. Elephant Wheels seemed interesting. The other . . . perhaps a little dangerous. She worried about Tootles. "Pegleg Point, by the three clustered palms. If we're not there, it's because we're hiding in the jungle from the pirates, who have already arrived."

"Aye, aye, madam!" Slightly said with a bow, doffing his cap.

"Hmm. You're doing this all in a dress," Skipper observed.

"Not much of one, really," Wendy said with a smile.

"To arms, men—ah, mates!" Slightly cried, raising up his rapier.

"TO ARMS!" they all shouted.

The fox boy threw back his head and howled. The rest of the Lost Boys joined in, each in his or her own way, crowing, barking, screaming, roaring.

"Yes, well, all right," Wendy said. She gave Luna another good solid scratching on her head. "You make sure they find me. And remember where they are going."

Luna barked once.

Wendy wished the wolf could meet Nana; she felt somehow sure they would get along splendidly.

# To Arms

The heroine appeared above the jungle like a tatter on the breeze.

Wendy had become just another one of the strange Never Land flying creatures, she realized; had anyone, even her own parents, looked up and seen her—well, they wouldn't have *seen* her. They would have seen a tanned, lanky fairy thing without wings, in strips and bandages of once-blue cotton, performing some unknown task within the realms of the magical island. And considering how many denizens she had interacted with—and almost grown comfortable with—she thought she was also well on her way to being accepted by the *natives* as just another weird flying creature.

Well, maybe not by the First. They were rather cranky about all the newcomers and dreamers who changed their world.

(Who could blame them, really?)

Although she *had* figured out their trap, so maybe that accorded her a smidgen of respect.

But unlike the endlessly cheerful and vicious full-time residents of Never Land, Wendy had hollows around her eyes from the constant flying, fighting, running, bleeding, strategizing, and worrying.

Peter's shape could easily be distinguished among three palm trees on the beach. A tiny golden glow shone against one of the harsh, tree-shaped shadows.

Wendy *tried* not thinking of herself as a ragged facsimile of a Greek god, but she did land as she imagined one might: delicately, cloth whipping around her, arms raised. Not for balance, but for *effect*.

Immediately, the golden glow zipped up and around her madly.

*Peter is hurting somehow! They're doing something to him or his shadow, like you said they would!*

Wendy now saw that what had at first looked like a lazy, reclining Peter was actually a taut-faced, wan Peter, collapsed into his own skin somehow. He shivered on the burning beach but had sweated through his shirt as if he were in the grip of a great fever. Sometimes he grimaced, eyes closed, and clenched his stomach.

"Oh my goodness," Wendy cried, rushing over and laying a hand on his brow. Tinker Bell didn't even object. He *wasn't* burning up—in fact, he was a little clammy.

*Did you find them? Are they coming?*

"Yes, though I'm afraid it will be a few hours before they get here. Are you managing to get any liquids into him?"

Tinker Bell nodded, pointing to a leaf she had been using for just that. A puddle of pink juice lay along its veins.

"Good. Well, that's something."

Wendy slowly collapsed on the sand next to them, exhausted and worried. The hard bark of the palm against her back felt like heaven, or at least something far softer than it actually was. She wiggled a bit to scare off any unicorn beetles—an opalescent one fell glittering to the sand, and without thinking, she scooped it up and placed it back on the tree next to her.

(Her shadow stood up against the palm trunk, watching Peter with worry.)

*They're taking the Cenotaph Caves?* Tinker Bell jingled.

"Um, yes. Do remind me to ask you about what those are sometime. Has Peter been like this the whole time I've been gone?"

"Wendy—you're back," the ailing boy murmured,

rousing a little upon hearing his name. Then his dreamy smile crumpled in a rictus of hurt.

*Those terrible pirates!* Tinker Bell wail-jingled.

"Well, we shall give them what for directly," Wendy promised, summoning brightness into her features.

The three settled in to wait for the pirates—or the Lost Boys, whoever came first.

The sun beat down hard until it hurt to have the tiniest bit of skin exposed beyond the shadow of the palm trees. Waves of heat danced like spirits between the sand and the sea, the latter of which lapped appealingly against the shore and seemed endlessly far away. Hurdy-gurdy gnats droned and riffed their unending calls.

Wendy reached out and squeezed Peter's hand whenever he went through a particularly bad bout of whatever was happening to him. Tinker Bell brought nectar, or sap, or—really, Wendy didn't want to think about the alternatives; beetle milk?—and carefully poured it into his mouth. But silence reigned over all of them; even the fairy's jingles were absent.

Wendy watched her shadow for a bit: she sat at the base of the tree, also apparently trying to keep cool.

"Really. Fat lot of good it did, you running off like that before," she murmured. "We've all wound up back at precisely the same place. *Again.*"

Her shadow shrugged. *Maybe* looking a little sheepish. Then she stood up, straight and proud—not sorry at all.

Tinker Bell raised an eyebrow at Wendy.

*Are you actually yelling at your own shadow?*

"But what good did she do?" Wendy demanded, feeling a little childish.

*She rescued me.*

"All right, yes, but then . . . after . . . She could have been a help, or . . . I was so tired. . . ."

*And yet here we are. You won. You beat the thysolits* and *the First. We found Peter.*

"But—"

*You're different now. Maybe she is, too, in Never Land. Maybe drop it?*

Of course Wendy was different. She was beat up and in tatters, although sometimes she had flashes of feeling heroic. That was something. She considered the black shape standing tall on the sand, her arms crossed. Maybe . . . her shadow wanted a chance to feel heroic, too?

"Maybe that's right," Wendy said slowly. "I've wanted an adventure my whole life—of course it follows that my shadow would, too. I suppose shadows have their own minds in Never Land. I'm not your master, merely your . . . I don't know, solid object. *Home*, maybe?"

The shadow nodded eagerly.

"Whatever you are, I need you and you need me. And we all will most certainly need your help to rescue Peter's shadow. So would you mind staying around at least until we get to the happily-ever-afters? I'll wager you have a better insight into how to aid a fellow shadow in distress than we do."

She reached out her hand and tried to place it on her shadow's. It didn't really work, but the shadow patted the air near where the flesh-and-blood hand was.

Tinker Bell sighed in relief.

And then, finally, something happened.

Tink was high in the sky on one of her lookout missions when she came diving back down like an angry bee (or thysolit).

*I see them—the pirates! They're not far off, rounding Bloody Neck.*

"We should move into the jungle," Wendy said, getting up. Tinker Bell looked skeptical. "Don't worry! I told the Lost Boys that's what we would do if Hook came first. We'll keep an eye on the beach in case they look for us there instead."

Mollified, Tinker Bell fluttered around Peter's face, trying to wake him up.

"Tinker Bell?" he asked softly. "I was just dreaming about you. . . ."

The fairy's face blushed in surprise—and pleasure—but that didn't stop her from planting herself on Peter's chest and gently slapping his chin.

*Get up. The pirates are coming. We don't have reinforcements yet.*

"I don't need no—"

Peter tried to stand up. Instead, he spun on his feet, falling back toward the sand. But Wendy was there to right him.

"No, there you go, easy now," she said, throwing one of his arms around her shoulders. "Let's just take it one step at a time."

Despite his slender build, it was still hard going for the two across the sand. Wendy tried not to imagine baby turtles making their ungainly way to the safety of the sea as predators swooped and salivated overhead. All three of them were terribly exposed—but to what, she wasn't sure. "If pirates can keep shadows as hostages and bees can steal bits of time," Wendy murmured to herself, "who knows what other horrible things in Never Land are on the side of evil?"

When the moist air of the jungle finally hit her nose and lungs Wendy nearly collapsed in relief.

"Here, sit down, and we can keep an eye on the beach," Wendy said, settling Peter on a soft tuffet of ferns which she hoped weren't carnivorous or itchy. Tinker Bell just hovered back and forth around her beloved Peter, not saying anything, so Wendy assumed they were fine.

There was a rubyfruit bush close by covered in the voluptuous red fruit. They were small and not quite the right color yet, but still fairly juicy. She cracked one open and tried giving a piece to Peter.

"Bleh! It's not ripe!" he cried, spitting it out.

"Stop being such a baby. It's all we have right now."

"Feh." He opened his mouth reluctantly to be fed more.

"You're welcome," Wendy said dryly.

Tinker Bell tugged on her sleeve, pointing into the jungle.

"Is it the Lost Boys?" Wendy asked with excitement.

But bouncing slowly through the bushes with great determination was a strange—and familiar— amber glow. It quickly resolved itself into Thorn, who landed and strode through the leaves like a fearless king and giant.

*You came!*

"You came!" Wendy cried at the same time. Then she blushed—she wasn't supposed to have known about the other fairy.

He gave her a knowing smile and the slightest wisp of a bow.

*Someone gave the Call of Aid. Only someone with no honor at all would fail to respond.*

Tinker Bell looked at the empty air around him and raised an eyebrow skeptically.

*None of our kin will reveal themselves near humans, Tinker Bell. You know you are the exception. And you* also *know the Call is for the aid of fairies—not humans. You don't seem to be in trouble, so I can only assume it is your friend Peter again, and perhaps this mighty warrior human here?*

Wendy didn't think she had it in her to react to a man's—no matter how tiny he might be—blandishments. But certainly *mighty warrior* wasn't the normal sort of pretty pap fed to girls? And it sounded genuine. *That* was why she felt a blush, she decided. And exhaustion accounted for her weakened knees.

*The pirates are coming for him,* Tinker Bell said. *In his state, they will surely get him this time.*

*I believe Peter "got" Hook last time and left him without a hand,* Thorn countered. *Turnabout's fair play, wouldn't you say?*

"Yes, but this time they are coming for all of Never Land," Wendy interrupted as politely as she could. "No, they really are. It's not just another one of Peter and Hook's games. The First confirmed it. Once he has Peter, his plan is to destroy everything as a sort of payback, and then leave."

*What? That's mad!* Thorn jingled, horrified.

"I don't disagree."

Peter suddenly crumpled up, whimpering and breathing

too quickly to be able to cry out. Wendy grabbed his hand and squeezed. Tinker Bell looked bleakly at Thorn.

*See? They have his shadow captured in a strange golden cage on their ship. I think they're torturing it somehow. Hurting Peter.*

*Black magic?* The warrior fairy frowned. The tips of his long brown ears seemed to quiver in thought, or maybe it was a stray breeze. His hand brushed the hilt of his sword, almost thoughtlessly. *That's . . . new. And disturbing. Hook really is out of control. Peter may be a nuisance at times, but he's no blackguard. At times he has even done favors for us. All right, Tinker Bell, and Madam—*

"Miss," Wendy interrupted. "But you can call me Wendy."

*Wendy, then, although it is a meaningless name,* he said, bowing. *Better you were named Windy, Mistress of the Winds. And what in blazes happened to you? Since I last caught sight of you—yes, I saw you hiding in the bushes—it looks like you've been through hell.*

*She helped me escape a trap of the First,* Tinker Bell said proudly. *And fought off an entire colony of thysolits.*

Wendy was gratified to see his honey-brown eyes widen in surprise.

*I knew you had the bearing of a warrior, but . . . the First captured you? And you escaped? Truly?*

Wendy gave a slightly ironic curtsy.

"Aww, quit all your palavering and chitchat," Peter moaned. His complexion had brightened a little and his whole countenance had improved—whether it was the rubyfruit, moving to the jungle, something finally *happening*, or all three, it was hard to say. "When do my boys come? Is there any sign of them yet?"

*They should be here soon,* Tinker Bell promised, fluttering over to soothe him. She even made little jingly cooing noises.

Thorn watched this, then sighed and looked over at Wendy: *what can you do?* Wendy couldn't help smiling. She didn't feel like she was betraying her friend; the boy fairy wasn't being snarky or obnoxious. More *resigned*, like a big brother. And she was relieved to see someone shared her feelings about Tinker Bell's obsessive relationship with Peter.

"Do you know, there's a rather popular—though scandalous—story called 'The Great God Pan,'" she ventured, desperate to keep their conversation going, "by a fellow named Arthur Machen. His Pan *is* an actual blackguard. . . ."

*I'd rather hear the stories of your escape from the First and then the thysolits, Windy.*

"Quiet!" the less godly Pan ordered.

Wendy turned, about to give him a piece of her

mind—then saw the expression on his face. He was serious for once. The the tips of his ears twitched, like a dog's in its sleep or a cat's when it isn't paying attention to you. Thorn frowned, also listening.

*I hear it, too.*

Wendy, the only one without pixie hearing, turned and cocked her head and strained.

After a few moments she finally caught the faintest sound of twigs cracking and something crashing through the underbrush. She grabbed her dagger.

"It's the Lost Boys!" Peter cried with delight. He leapt up, his cheeks growing rosy with excitement. "They've come!"

Luna came crashing through the underbrush first, leaping exultantly into Wendy.

"Good girl. How are you, girl?" Wendy hugged the wolf, wondering who was getting more dirt and mud on whom.

Now even *she* could hear the Lost Boys' approach: they were marching, singing some sort of military song—familiar in tune, the original lyrics replaced with something rude and unrepeatable. When they broke into the small clearing where Wendy, Thorn, Tink, and Peter waited, it was with glad eyes and weary triumph.

They were all streaked with blood and makeup. Skipper made for a particularly scary whatever rodent she was with dark blue woad streaks above her eyes and on each cheekbone. Slightly's jacket was stained with unsettlingly large dark brown splotches and his arm was bandaged with a strip of leather over gauze. But he also had a new necklace with the face of a hideous demon or god on it. The twins had new weapons to go with their slings: short, elaborately carved batons. Cubby and Tootles alone looked more or less the same, with just a few rips in their outfits and blue dots on their faces.

Wendy made a mental note to ask them about their adventures later. When she had tossed around *bloody* and *blood* and *terrible wound* in her stories (or, say, the idea of losing a hand in battle), she hadn't really thought about it. She had even basked in the praise when Michael and John said she could tell a good story "unlike most girls" one full of violence and victory. But now that she was viewing the real thing and had experienced some fighting herself she found her zeal for the lurid somewhat tempered. She wondered about the strange wound on Slightly's arm.

"Well then, Slightly," Peter said, straightening himself up and regarding the other boy gravely.

"Well then, Peter," Slightly said back, trying not to sound wary.

The tension between the two of them was more palpable—and uncomfortable—than the humidity in the jungle.

"Looks like you've had a bit of an adventure," Peter said, nodding at Slightly's arm.

"The caves are still inhabited, don't you know."

"You showed 'em who's who, though, right?"

"Oh, we showed them all right!"

Slightly couldn't resist grinning, the whites of his teeth glistening like a real fox's.

The smile was infectious: Peter smiled back proudly.

"I'm awfully glad you made it, Slightly. I'm not in top form at all. Things would be pretty grim without you all here to help me against the pirates," Peter admitted.

"Well, things would be pretty grim without you around ever again," Slightly said softly.

Peter opened his mouth to say something else, but then Tootles broke in excitedly.

*"We fought! And won!"* he cried, pushing his way into the middle of the two older boys.

Peter grinned and swept him up into the air. "Of course you did! You're the best fighters a captain could ever want!"

But he looked at Slightly as he said it.

The fox boy smiled back.

Then all the tension was gone, and everyone was talking and shouting excitedly about what had happened and where Peter's shadow was and what the plan was next.

Peter looked grim. "Fact is, men, it could go down at

any time. Hook's got my shadow and he's been holding it prisoner, torturing it. And when he does that, it hurts *me.* They're rounding the Bloody Neck, or were a little while ago, and should be here any moment. They plan to get all of us, me first. Then all of Never Land. We need to be ready."

"We need to come up with a plan," Wendy added.

"All right then!" Peter said. "All together now—fairies, Lost Boys, Wendy, and me! Let's *do this*!"

*Look, the pirates,* Tinker Bell jingled nervously.

And there it was: riding a fair wind from the west, the *Jolly Roger* swept into view, its ghastly flag—and Peter's shadow—snapping in the breeze.

# A Plan Comes Together

The Lost Boys and Wendy immediately crouched down behind the bushes. The two fairies hid their glow behind a tree and peeped out.

The ship came near enough to the beach that Hook could clearly be seen in his blazing red jacket marching up and down the deck, gesticulating and shouting orders. Pirates scurried everywhere frantically, dropping anchor and readying the skiffs.

"What is *that*?" Slightly whispered in horror. He pointed at the glinting golden cage and the black formless mass within.

"That's my shadow," Peter growled.

"That's why you haven't had any . . . attacks in the last few minutes," Wendy realized. "Hook has been too busy making preparations for landing to pay attention to your shadow."

*That is an ugly desecration of nature,* Thorn said in disgust. *I half thought you were wrong. That no one, not even pirates, would consider such a thing. My apologies. Anyone who would do this is capable of anything—including wiping out Never Land.*

Hook suddenly stopped and pulled out a spyglass, aiming it at the shore.

The little group immediately hunkered down behind the bushes again.

"Should we wait until they're all in the smaller boats?" Slightly asked. "They'll be easy pickings for Skipper with—uh, *his* bow, and the twins with their slings."

*I cannot fly well over the water,* Thorn said. *For us, it would be best to wait until they've landed.*

"I don't know how much good I could do," Wendy admitted. "Even on land. A bunch of bees without stingers is one thing—a bunch of pirates with swords . . . Well, I could try. . . ."

*Me too!* Tinker Bell put in. *I'm not a warrior like Thorn, but any good I do would have to be on land.*

The pirates had begun boarding the skiffs and lowering them down. There were at least a dozen of the men, all armed to the teeth.

Hook remained behind on the ship, one booted foot

up on the railing, a triumphant leer polluting his face as he watched his men row toward the beach.

Peter's face darkened.

"Here's what I think we should do," Wendy said. "When Caesar was invading Gaul, he—"

*"HOOOOOOOOOOOK!"* Peter cried, and flew out of the jungle, knife drawn.

"Oh," Wendy said, too stunned to do much else.

"You heard the captain!" Slightly shouted, shaking his sword. "HOOK! AND THE PIRATES!"

"HOOK AND THE PIRATES!"

The Lost Boys ran screaming out of the jungle, Thorn zipping reluctantly after them.

And the final battle between the pirates and the Lost Boys began.

# A Battle on Land and Sea

The Lost Boys (and Luna) broke out of the jungle and ran screaming down the beach just as the first skiff touched shore. The pirates, undaunted, leapt out of their boats into the water, cutlasses and muskets drawn. They, too, screamed.

For one dizzying moment it was as strange and pretty as a picture: a small army of boys (and one girl) dressed like animals, wielding archaic weapons, their faces in masks or painted with ancient Celtic stripes, making for gaily dressed pirates in eye patches and bright bandannas and golden rings. Wendy knew that image would remain emblazoned on her mind for the rest of her days.

Peter had flown up and over everyone's heads, making

straight for the pirate ship and the few who remained aboard. Well, really, for *one* who remained aboard: Hook.

Peter seemed entirely recovered, but Wendy knew that as long as his shadow was still in captivity his current vigor was only temporary. And it was very suspicious that Hook stayed back when his men were going to fight his most hated enemy—he didn't even have his flintlocks out. He also wasn't overseeing the cannon fire. And he couldn't possibly shout orders from the deck loudly enough for anyone on shore to hear. So what was he doing?

Tinker Bell had, of course, zipped after Peter, knocking a pirate's hat off as she went. The enraged man (the Duke, Wendy was pretty sure) turned and shot wildly into the air after her, singeing the hair and possibly the ear of the pirate next to him. That pirate—Major Thomas—responded by laughing and then backhanding the Duke.

Thorn swooped right up to the first pirate he encountered and sank his blade deep into the flesh behind the man's right knee. Screaming Byron did exactly what one would expect him to do: he let out a high-pitched wail that hardly seemed possible from such a large, sturdy-looking fellow. Then he immediately collapsed onto the sand, unable to stand on that leg any longer.

The fairy immediately wiped his blade and moved to the next pirate without pause.

Wendy watched in disbelief and admiration. He, of course, *looked* like a little warrior. But in her rather prejudiced, giant human-sized head, she had assumed he could do no real damage.

"That will teach me to judge a book by its cover," she murmured.

And maybe that meant *she* could help, too.

Wendy took a deep breath, grasped her dagger, and marched out onto the beach.

But where to go? What to do? The scene was utter chaos. The twins had surrounded T. Jerome Newton and were taking turns smashing him in the stomach and back with their batons. Skipper had planted herself a little farther up the beach and was taking careful aim with her bow at the pirates on the periphery, the ones who hadn't quite made the beachhead yet. Wendy saw one go down with an arrow through his right shoulder. He fell *out* of the water and back into the boat. Slightly was in the middle of a rather amazing duel with Djareth, sword and scimitar flashing in the sun, Luna biting at the pirate's feet. Cubby was roaring and swinging his claymore at several pirates who were closing in on him.

"That's where I am needed! Cubby, I am coming!" Wendy cried and ran forward to help. She tried not to think about whether she would actually *cut* or *slice* one of the pirates; she figured instinct would take over at the last minute and she would do whatever was necessary for the sake of her friend.

"AAAAAAAAAI!" she yelled—more for herself than with any real intention of putting terror into her enemy's heart—and aimed at a pirate whose name she couldn't remember, the one with the blue bandanna. She raised her dagger, thinking to get him in the neck maybe—

Wait, could she really do that? Could she *slice into the artery* of someone—even if it was someone who had held her captive—from the *back*, like a coward? What if he bled on her? What if . . .

Sheathing her dagger, she flipped into the air, and—with the help of fairy dust—spiraled down feetfirst, planting both as hard as she could into the small of his back.

"Take *that*, dread villain!"

With a distinct *oof*, the pirate fell facedown into the sand.

Because fairy dust was merely magical and didn't completely negate the laws of physics, Wendy *kept* falling, her beautiful attack almost ruined by a sprawling somersault over the pirate's head. She landed, straddle-legged and a little confused, sand now in every fold of her clothes.

"That was *brilliant*, Wendy!" Slightly called, saluting her from across the beach before spinning to riposte an attack by a new pirate he was fighting.

"You saved me," Cubby said, smiling dreamily as he used the flat of his giant claymore to knock his remaining attacker into the dust.

"But Wendy," one twin cried, makeup running down his face and pooling around his mask.

"Get *up*!" the other one, equally askew, urged.

Wendy staggered to her feet, feeling it was a bit much to ask of her right then. Hadn't she just taken out a pirate? Her body had been through a great deal over the past few days; she was broken like a doll. And where was Tinker Bell? Somehow this all would have seemed easier with her friend nearby.

*Aha:* she was still on the ship. Peter and Hook were crossing swords amongst the rigging. Peter balanced on the bowsprit, slashing down at the pirate captain. Hook held his hook behind his back and skillfully parried *up*. Neither one of them seemed in a haste to end the fight. Tinker Bell floated and buzzed around them, making the occasional jab at Hook.

Wendy couldn't see all the details, of course, but her mind filled in Peter's grand smile and sparkling eyes. Such a small boy, really, to be fighting so carelessly against such an evil, nasty, experienced, and *large* pirate (with guns and hooks). Yet that was not the impression the scene gave. He looked like the living embodiment of fearlessness, of seizing whatever the moment brought and assuming it would all work out somehow.

Wendy found that besides admiration she felt more than a touch of envy. He was everything that she, a girl so otherwise full of words and worries and doubts, wanted to *be*.

"But really!" she scolded herself. "Here I am, still thinking and observing and watching, when really I should be rejoining the fight!"

*There.* One of the twins was down on the ground, nursing his wrist. The other was backed up against a tree, trying to avoid being run through by Ziggy. Wendy began to push off into the air, but suddenly there were strong arms around her, holding her to the ground instead.

"*NO!* Unhand me, villain!"

She tried to bring her blade back down behind her, slashing wildly. "I'll cut you!"

"That was a short trip from Wendy words to prison patois," a voice spoke dryly in her ear. It was Zane, who despite his slender look had tautly muscled arms and rock-like, immovable shoulders.

"I'll not serve you again!" she cried. "I'd rather die!"

She wasn't sure if this was entirely true, but she was enraged at being unable to move, and anyway, she really did hate laundry.

"I'm not capturing ye, I'm saving ye, ye daft molly," the pirate said, exasperated. He dragged her to a tree, flinging her thoughtlessly upside down, face-first, into the sand in front of it. It was an extremely unbecoming, awkward, and most of all embarrassing position to be in—made worse when she realized he had done it so he could bind her wrists and legs.

"You brute! You villainous cur!"

He worked quickly and methodically, ignoring her words as well as her kicking legs while they were still free.

When he was done, he picked her up like a sack and sat her back down properly at the base of the tree.

"You don't belong in this fight," he said. "You have your reasons to hate Hook, but you're going to get yourself killed."

"No one ever dies in these battles," Wendy scoffed. "None of the good guys do."

Zane's look turned dark. "Hook is serious this time—he's completely mad. He means to do away with the Lost Boys for good. And Peter Pan, and everyone else."

"But . . . the Lost Boys . . . they're children!"

"They're children who chose to fight pirates," Zane pointed out. "They're children who cut the hand off a pirate and left him with one hand, one hook, no sanity, and a death wish for the entire world. Believe you me, I don't want to be wasting none of me time with this here folderol. I want to be out on the open sea, shooting down cargo vessels and looting them, then maybe take a month or two in some island port with coconut rum and time to think things over in the sun."

He took her dagger and threw it into the jungle. "The faster this is all over, the faster we can set sail and leave Never Land forever."

"Yes! *Forever!* Hook intends on destroying it after he's done with Peter!"

"Aye. Seems a bit much," he said with a shrug.

"But do you have any idea how he intends to kill everyone?"

"Not a whit. We're carrying some extra powder—or were. Maybe that has something to do with it. Who knows."

"Oh, you're useless. Why are you even saving me?" Wendy demanded. "*I'm* a child who chose to fight pirates."

"Oh, you're not a child anymore, lassie." Zane chuckled. "And you'd be no help to either side in a fight, eitherways."

He gave her a sparkling gold-doubloon grin and then went running back to the battle.

Wendy fumed. It would be so easy to sit there and watch the battle. No one would blame her: she was tied up. And Zane was right. She didn't really know how to fight—not humans, anyway.

"No help to either side," she muttered. "I'll—I'll show them!"

Struggling, she stood up. She twisted and turned wildly, trying to loosen the stiff old ropes he had tied her with. They wouldn't give an inch. Zane was, of course, an expert at knots. She had no idea where to start looking for her pretty dagger in the forest, and as far as she could tell, no one on the beach had conveniently dropped one for her to use. It seemed rather unreasonable to push herself into a fight and demand to be set free: *Mind loaning me your sword for a moment? And you, pirate, would you mind holding off attacking for that moment?*

She looked at her shadow, who was also tied up and struggling. Apparently sticking to her host had some distinct disadvantages—like sharing her fate while they were attached.

Wendy screamed in frustration. For once, she was *here*, in Never Land, not just narrating the story. And she still couldn't do anything! And Peter and Hook . . .

Wait. There *was* one thing she could do, she realized. She could still fly. Maybe there would be something on the ship she could use. It was full of pointy and jabby things. And then she could set about rescuing Peter's shadow, or snooping around the ship for a hint of Hook's plans.

Wendy grinned and took off into the air—

And immediately began rolling and flailing, her head grinding into the sand while her legs whirled around above her like a pinwheel. Somehow flying required more balance and use of her arms and legs than she had thought.

Stretching, curling up, and then keeping herself very still, Wendy finally managed to move forward. Very awkwardly. Like a caterpillar with all of its little legs bound together, inching along in an undignified fashion. Sometimes as little as a foot above the sand and in constant danger of plowing into it face-first. But she took it slowly and did her best to sneak around the fight, to not draw too much attention to herself.

(Though a twin saw her and nearly lost his ear as he stared, transfixed.)

When she made it to the edge of the water Wendy came in a bit too low. A wave crashed into her face, temporarily blinding her. It took her a bit to reorient herself and then swayingly cross the rest of the way to the ship. Finally, like a bobbing harbor seal, she popped up over the side of the *Jolly Roger* to surveil the scene.

There was the sword fight, of course. Blades flashing in the sun, the scrape of steel on steel.

"I'll get you yet, Peter Pan!" Hook cried, grinning.

"Just try it, you ridiculous codfish!" Peter taunted. He danced on top of the ship's wheel, causing it to spin.

Tinker Bell, hovering nearby, caught sight of Wendy.

*"No—shh,"* Wendy mouthed. She jerked her head toward the prow of the ship, where the golden cage was. *"Meet me there!"*

Tinker Bell nodded and flew off.

Wendy followed, throwing herself over the railing and skidding to a painful halt on her knees, elbows, and chin.

The fairy immediately began to work on her ropes.

"They're very tight," Wendy whispered. "I don't think you have the strength. Maybe you can find a knife or a—"

But the bonds fell away.

Tinker Bell gave a smug little smile.

"Well! That's rather useful," Wendy said, bending over to release her shadow.

The shadow jumped and stretched in her newfound freedom and then slid into the cage, to Peter's shadow.

"Do what you can—see if you can release him," Wendy said. "Meanwhile, Tink and I will—"

But a pirate stepped out from behind the chart room and loomed menacingly over her.

"You didn't think Hook would have left this *unguarded*, did you?" he growled. His skin was pale and torn; his breath reeked of rot.

It was Valentine.

"But . . . you're dead!" Wendy breathed in horror.

"Oh, the dead don't always stay dead in Never Land," he sneered, his mouth full of rotting black and golden teeth. "Not when they're pirates. Not when Davy Jones's locker is full."

He aimed his musket at her belly.

"Not sure the same holds for the likes of *ye*, however."

He began to pull the trigger—

Wendy screamed.

"Wendy!" Peter cried, catching sight of her. "Blackguard! Don't you dare! Don't you dare lay a finger on her!"

"Valentine, lower your weapon," Hook ordered, joining the group with solid, sure smacks of his bootheels. "Miss Darling! Isn't this a nice surprise. Now you can witness my triumph—and Peter Pan's utter defeat. I was just enjoying one last bout with my old nemesis here before getting on with things."

"Defeat? Why, you old codfish, you . . ."

Hook ignored him.

"Valentine? Adjust the machine—to the limit, please."

The pirate grinned. Keeping the gun trained on Wendy with his right hand, he reached out his left to a greasy golden knob on the cage. Peter's shadow shivered and shrank and expanded in dismay, knowing what was to come.

The pirate spun the knob all the way to the left.

The shadow snapped into a thousand quivering tendrils

of pain. It vibrated and shook and trembled so fiercely that the air around it turned black. A strange not-noise—the opposite of noise?—filled the air as it screamed, almost breaking Wendy's eardrums.

Peter fell to the deck, unconscious.

Tinker Bell jingle-screamed.

"And that," Hook said with a smile, "is the end of Peter Pan."

# A Plan Comes Together . . . No, *Really* This Time

The few remaining pirates on the *Jolly Roger* surrounded Wendy, Tinker Bell, and the prone form of Peter lying on the ground.

"SURRENDER!" Hook bellowed toward the shore. *"Lost Boys, we have your Peter Pan!"*

The fighting paused as both pirate and Lost Boy alike stopped to figure out what the captain was shouting. It was hard to hear over the waves and wind.

"I have him!" Hook gestured dramatically at Peter—whom no one could see, hidden as he was on the deck behind the railing—and his shadow in the cage, which made no real sense if you didn't know what you were looking at beforehand.

*"I have Peter Pan!"* he tried again.

Nothing. Those on the beach shrugged and looked at each other in confusion.

Frustrated at the lack of response on shore, Hook reached down and grabbed Peter's shirt, holding him aloft and shaking him so all could see. The boy sagged like a badly made scarecrow, pale and limp.

It was a shocking display.

After all, Peter really was just a boy, and Hook was not a small man. The pirate had no trouble at all tossing his unconscious body about. The strangeness of it—of him manhandling the usually energetic and scrappy Pan—must have gotten even to Hook. His face slipped for just a moment in wonder, as if he was thinking, *"This is all of it? This is my prize?"* And maybe there was just a touch of disappointment, like that of a child who has finally and triumphantly caught a dragonfly, only to open his hands and realize he has killed it in the process.

On the beach there were collective wails and gasps. Even the pirates seemed a little surprised. Wendy was pretty sure she saw Zane blink and gawp before rousing himself and grabbing Cubby, thrusting the boy's hands behind his back. Then the rest of the pirates rounded up the dejected Lost Boys with exaggerated movements, ropes, and whips.

Hook seemed to get over whatever momentary lapse of

joy he had experienced and now leered and grinned and pranced about, dropping Peter's body into Valentine's waiting arms.

"That's right," the captain chortled. "Get them all—it's over now, over *forever*!"

The pirates tied the Lost Boys into a kind of chain and forced them onto the skiffs.

Thorn, aloft and uncaptured, jingled—but it was untranslatable, even for Wendy.

Wendy looked at her shadow. She was wrapped around Peter's, trying to comfort or free him—with little effect. Tinker Bell tried to wrap herself around Peter's flesh and blood body; Valentine kept waving her away.

Wendy Darling didn't normally consider herself someone who surveyed a situation, immediately understood what was going on, and then reacted in a timely and appropriate manner. She was a dreamy, thoughtful girl, slow to decide and act.

But a week was a long time in Never Land.

Without bothering to warn her, Wendy grabbed Tinker Bell and took off.

The little fairy fought and bit and scratched and made noises that were far more terrifying than jingles. Wendy kept her fist shut tight.

Did she feel like a coward, bombing away from the

pirate ship like a bee martin after its prey? Not really. Soon the ship would be full of pirates and weapons and guns, and Hook's attention would inevitably turn to her. It was only while he was gloating that she had a chance to escape—and from the belated *pop pop pop* sounds behind her, it was clear that though it had taken everyone a moment to notice her absence, the use of guns was not forbidden against potential Pan accomplices.

"We need to get away and regroup," she told Tinker Bell. "There's nothing we could have done back there."

The little fairy jingled furiously.

"No, I don't think I *could* have pulled Peter from either Hook or Valentine—I'm not that strong, Tink. I already tried to fight off Valentine when he was *alive* and I failed. And this is all assuming I could fly holding Peter and not drop him in the water, drowning him."

*She's right, Tinker Bell,* Thorn said, flying up beside them—as Wendy knew he would, even without a word or a signal. *I'm no coward. The odds were entirely against us. We need to strategize and come back again and hit them hard.*

Tinker Bell jingled something translatable—but unprintable.

Wendy skimmed along the water and the beach, keeping a wide swath between them and the pirates in the skiffs (and their captives).

"Wendy!" The twins cried together, spotting her. But it wasn't a cry of despair; it was a cheer. They were *glad* one of their number had escaped—and could maybe return to free them.

Slightly also caught her eye as she passed, but didn't say anything. Hope shone brightly on his face, and it spoke for his silence.

Wendy was also full of hope: she hoped she didn't disappoint him.

She flew above the jungle a little before finding a good place to break through the canopy. Curling herself into a ball, she plummeted to the ground through dense leaves and twigs, remembering to stick her feet out at the last minute.

The moment she opened her hand, Tinker Bell shot out and dove at her face.

"Please stop," Wendy said, as patiently as she could manage. But it came out the way she felt: weary, and maybe, like Hook, just a bit disappointed. Did her little friend *never* see the ramifications of actions? Never think a few moves ahead? Never grasp how ridiculous she was being? Wendy suddenly thought of Zane, and his perfunctory removal of her at the battle. He, too, was only trying to save a life.

Tinker Bell must have finally seen or understood what passed through Wendy's mind. She drooped.

*Easy, little sister,* Thorn jingled, coming close to the other fairy. *We will come up with something. It isn't over yet.*

Wendy felt a rush of affection for him that had nothing to do with his physiognomy or his manner. He understood why she did what she did, and he understood that Tinker Bell needed to be appeased. He was useful, kind, and like-minded. Good qualities to have in a friend.

"All right," Wendy said, sitting down at the base of a tree. "Let's see what our options are. Peter is out of the game—and possibly in real danger. While he's hostage I doubt the Lost Boys are going to try to escape. Even Slightly wouldn't risk it. And now that Hook has Peter, all of his little pieces are in place. We don't know how long before he sets into motion his plan to destroy Never Land.

"And we're the only ones who can save it. Of all the inhabitants of Never Land I've met, none of them—literally none of them—would ally with us. Or me, rather. Not the terrible mermaids or the unknowable First. Certainly not the mindless and devouring thysolits. I doubt the Cenotaph cave-dwellers would lend a hand and I have no idea what the Elephant Wheels are."

*They keep to themselves, on the Lost Roads,* Thorn said, which was both helpful and not at all. Wendy decided to file that with the now *very* long list of things to look into if she had more time in Never Land.

"Well, that leaves us and the fairies, then. And you have said they won't fight on our side?"

*Unfortunately, we have no actual proof of Hook's plans. After seeing the blasphemous doings of Captain Hook, it might be possible to rally the Great Army to our side. But it would require a meeting at the Allthing, and just the scheduling of that is a bear.*

"Oh, cripes, this is *impossible*!" Wendy tore off a piece of a plant and threw it at the ground. She had almost said *hopeless*. "We have *nothing*."

*We have you,* Tinker Bell jingled softly.

Wendy gave her a weak smile. "Thank you, but I don't see what I can bring to the table, other than a belated ability to fly and a dagger I seem to have lost."

*You have your stories.*

"But, Tink, those powers only worked in the realm of the First—where the stories and the land of Never Land haven't solidified or *set* yet. It doesn't work out here. Any stories I tell would just be stories."

*Then we can be the powers* for *you. You tell the stories, and we will* make *them come true.*

Tinker Bell's eyes were so wide and she sounded so sincere that Wendy felt like she was drowning in her friend's trust. She snuck a look at Thorn. He gave a slight nod. She wasn't sure if it meant *yes, we will*, or *yes, you can,* but either way it was an endorsement. For some reason he didn't think Tinker Bell was being ridiculous.

"Okay," Wendy said slowly. "But how—"

*We need to take out Captain Hook,* said the warrior fairy. *Without a leader, the pirates will collapse into chaos.*

"Agreed," Wendy said. "A queen for a queen, like in chess. I don't think they're loyal enough to mount a revenge or rescue. There seemed to be some difference of opinion about what pirates are supposed to do even when I was aboard—and getting Peter Pan wasn't high on the list for most of them."

Just then, a ragged black shape slithered through the underbrush toward them.

Tinker Bell leapt up, jingling in fright—but it was only Wendy's shadow.

"Ah! Good of you to join us," Wendy said, patting the ground next to herself. The shadow obligingly slid over and slipped into Wendy's shape. "Any luck with Peter's shadow?"

The shadow shook her head, then held her hand out and rocked it from side to side.

"You think you could help him escape? With more time?"

The shadow shrugged and nodded desperately. *Maybe* or *I have to* or *what else can we do?*

"All right. We were just talking about the pirates and their leader, and how they are not that devoted to their beloved captain. So there's somehow *killing* Hook, somehow *capturing* him, or somehow *disabling* him. And should it be the second two—as I rather hope—we will need the Lost Boys free and ready to battle the pirates if they do put up a resistance. Tinker Bell, when you released me from my ropes before—could you do that for all of them?"

*Not from a distance. It isn't magic, it's . . . fairy knowing. Knots and traps are in our blood.*

"I think that may still count as magic, to humans at least. But in any case, be clear: you have to actually touch the ropes."

*Yes.* Thorn cut in. *And we shine.*

"Well, of course you do. You're the best."

*No,* shine.

Thorn flew up in front of her and glowed so brilliantly she had to shade her eyes.

"Right, right," she said, feeling a little breathless that he was so close. "Not exactly a covert mission, I get it. But what if you could zip around and—I don't know—maybe *give* them something to cut their own bonds with? Drop something in their hands and fly away quickly? Maybe a knife, or a sharp shell?"

*Yes, but someone may still see us. And how will that help, since as you said the Lost Boys won't rise up if their leader is in trouble?*

"I think I'm getting there," Wendy said, trying not to let her heart quicken as it sensed her brain's ideas. Trying not to *hope* or *believe.* "I think you actually nailed it when you said *stories.* Hook certainly loves to talk—to hear himself talk, to hear himself tell stories. He has told stories in his head all his life about Peter and losing his hand. And crocodiles and clocks and time. It's what worked him up into this crazy obsession. I think stories—or plays—are the thing to 'catch the conscience of the king.'"

She sat back, feeling very clever.

The two fairies looked at her, uncomprehending.

*"Shakespeare,"* Wendy said, disappointed no one got the reference. *"Hamlet."*

*Oh! We know* A Midsummer's Night Dream, Thorn said proudly. *I'm in it, sometimes.*

Tinker Bell shot him an annoyed look.

"All right, the point is that, like Peter, Hook loves hearing about himself. You know, they really are a lot alike, if you stop to think about it. . . . Anyway, the tale needs to be big and dramatic, just like Hook. Something that will distract him to pieces. I don't think it would take much to push him over the edge right now. Besides stories, *I* have a clockwork crocodile. Which, unlike my satchel, pirate treasure, or boat, really *will* turn out to be useful at the end of my adventure.

"And, finally, I have . . . myself."

Tinker Bell jingled curiously.

"Why, I'm giving myself up, Tink. I'm going to trade myself for Peter."

# Wendy

While she walked out on the hot sand Wendy imagined herself strolling primly down the avenue with a parasol on her shoulder and a smug little Wendy smile on her face. As if she were going out to market or the bookstore when the demonic Shesbow twins were known to be about, thus requiring her to be extra prim and have an extra-smug smile as first lines of defense.

In reality, of course, it was not an ancient cobbled street she trod, and her pinafore had long since disappeared. Instead, she wore a tunic made of rags bleached white from the sun and salt water, her arms and legs and face darkened by the same powers.

And maybe—just maybe—her smile was less smug and a trifle more sardonic now.

Her shadow behaved like any well-behaved shadow would, copying her precisely. Although, of course, *her* smile was hidden.

The pirate ship lay on the water as pretty and perfect as a ship in a bottle. For a dizzying moment Wendy played with the idea that it *was* a ship in a bottle, that she was standing in her father's study, mouthing words to imaginary heroes and villains as the toll of too much time alone and lack of outside voices finally grew too great.

But her father didn't have a ship in a bottle.

And Wendy had scratches all over that itched terribly—boring, annoying little details that she would never normally imagine or narrate in a story.

External proof aside, internally she had changed as well. Permanently and deeply. She didn't need to see her scars to know that they were real.

She kept walking, right into the water, until it was up to her calves.

"Captain Hook," she called out, waving politely. "Captain Hook? May I have a word?"

Whatever was happening on the ship paused; all attention was directed to her by the antlike pirates and villains.

Hook, ever dramatic and unable to resist a cue, complied.

"WENDY DARLING!" he shouted, his voice a trifle

less unctuous than usual because he had to shout. "I WONDERED WHERE YOU RAN OFF TO."

She curtsied.

"I'M AFRAID WE'RE RATHER BUSY AT THE MOMENT, BUT I WOULD LOVE TO CATCH UP FOR A CHAT JUST AFTER I'VE REVIVED YOUR GOOD FRIEND PAN HERE LONG ENOUGH FOR HIM TO WATCH THE NEXT PHASE OF THE PLAN. IF THERE'S TIME BEFORE YOU'RE ALL WIPED OUT, OF COURSE."

"I've come to give myself up," Wendy shouted.

*"WHAT?"*

"I've come to give myself up. To offer myself in trade for Peter Pan."

The red-coated, black-wigged effigy stood stock-still on the ship for a moment. Then Hook threw back his shoulders and bent double, guffawing heartily.

"AND WHAT DO I CARE ABOUT YOU, WENDY DARLING? I HAVE PETER PAN. I DON'T *WANT* YOU."

"But do you *want* Peter Pan? Really?"

"WANT? PETER PAN? MISS DARLING, HAVE YOU BEEN PAYING ATTENTION TO ANYTHING OUTSIDE YOUR OWN LOVELY HEAD WHILE YOU'VE BEEN HERE?"

"Of course I have, and I come with a warning. . . ." And here she lowered her voice, just a little, letting the wind take it where it would. She recounted the various stories of her time in Never Land, occasionally raising her voice just up to the level it was before, only letting key and cryptic phrases be carried across to the ship. "METAPHORICALLY SPEAKING, OF COURSE . . . NO LESS THAN AN ARMY . . . SURPRISED TO FIND . . ."

The red pirate-ant in the distance grew frustrated. She could imagine exactly what he was saying: *What the deuce? Can anyone hear? What is that dashed girl going on about?*

". . . INEVITABLE," she finished.

"YOU STAY RIGHT THERE, MISS DARLING," Hook ordered, face red with impatience. "I DON'T KNOW WHAT THE BLAZES YOU'RE UP TO, BUT YOU WILL COME ABOARD MY SHIP AND WE WILL RESOLVE THIS—*DISTRACTION*—IMMEDIATELY!"

Wendy curtsied again.

Tinker Bell hadn't understood this part of the plan—why Wendy couldn't just fly up to the ship and proceed from there. But Thorn did. It was all about playing a part, and gaining trust, and making Hook feel like *he* was the one making the decisions. The warrior fairy didn't put it quite that way, of course; he didn't think that way. He spoke in terms of *subverting the enemy's expectations* and *letting the trap draw itself closed.*

Wendy waited there as serenely as she could while the pirates lowered down one dinghy and two men—*only two!* She was insulted. Neither of them was Zane. They were nothing but tertiary characters, thugs whose names she hadn't bothered to learn when she was on board. They looked dangerous and unimaginative.

(Though one gave a kind of apology before tying her hands behind her back.

"No matter," she said. "It's improper, but understandable.")

She kept her spine straight and chin up, like a figurehead in the prow of the dinghy as they rowed back to the ship that had started all her adventures.

The deck was already quite crowded with prisoners and pirates. Members of the crew mumbled greetings to her with downcast eyes; the Lost Boys regarded her curiously. Hook stomped over, impatient and furious.

"Now hurry up with this foolishness, Miss Darling," he said, thrusting his face into hers. "You wanted to trade yourself for Peter Pan—which is ridiculous, ask anyone here. You're no Peter Pan, not half his worth to me. And anyway, I've captured you quite handily and made no sorts of promises to let you go, so you haven't even anything left to trade with. I've got you fair and square there, Miss Darling."

"Not half his *worth* . . . ?" Wendy started to object before getting control of herself.

The sun sparkled brightly on the sea, but something glinted in the rigging that didn't quite belong there. Possibly the head of a fairy peeping out to see how things were progressing.

*"WELL!"* she said dramatically, making sure everyone's eyes were on her. "Captain Hook, now that you *have* Peter Pan, what do you intend to do with him?"

She addressed him like a mother to a child with a song sparrow, or frog, or fox kit, or any other inappropriate pet. Patiently, like she wanted him to work out the ridiculousness of it all himself.

The pirates—and the Lost Boys—looked over at Hook with interest.

"What am I going to *do* with him?" Hook demanded. "Why, I'm going to exact revenge on him for what he did to me!" He shook his hook for emphasis.

"So . . . you're going to cut off his hand."

Hook's—and everyone else's—eyes drifted involuntarily to the unconscious Peter, pale and motionless. Defenseless. Wendy risked a quick look at his shadow: it lay limp in the cage, like the umbra of an unwound pile of string. She made the minutest nod toward it.

Her own shadow silently detached, rippling over the planks of the deck like a centipede. Again she felt the strange inside-out pain, the hollowness that pulsed along her limbs and torso.

A zip of light—Tinker Bell had also used the distraction when everyone was focused on Peter to get to the Lost Boys.

"I'm going to teach him a lesson he'll never forget!" Hook cried. "That all of Never Land will never forget! I'll make him watch as his beloved world is destroyed. And then I'll have him *walk the plank*—without any flying, or rescuing mermaids, or whatnot. Or maybe I'll execute him myself. One shot to the head."

He pulled out his pistol and aimed it menacingly at Wendy.

"You would really kill *Peter Pan*? Your archnemesis. Your greatest enemy. Your sole reason for living these days, it seems."

"Yes, well, maybe I'll find other reasons once he's gone," Hook said thoughtfully, looking at his pistol and frowning at a smudge on it. "Perhaps once again I'll be able to enjoy the simple pleasures in life: raiding a port town, attacking a merchant vessel and stealing its gold, a bit of plunder here, a bit of pillage there. . . ."

"Now you're talking!" Zane said encouragingly.

An amber glimmer swooped over the other side of the ship and disappeared among the prisoners. One pirate suddenly turned, having thought he saw something strange out the corner of his eye.

"But . . . you two have *fought each other forever,*" Wendy said loudly, stepping forward—and drawing all attention to herself again.

Hook frowned and cocked the hammer on his flintlock with an ominous click.

Wendy shrugged as best she could with her hands tied to indicate no threat was intended. She continued to walk around Peter's body and Hook, appearing to think about both of them while blocking the pirates' view of the Lost Boys and any fairy goings-on.

"Hook and Peter, Peter and Hook, always battling it out on the seas or in secret hideaways. . . . You're so archetypal, so famous, so *ever-present* in Never Land that everyone knows your legendary exploits. Both here and in the nurseries of London, where stories of you are told to frighten little children."

Hook gave a modest dip of his head.

"And that's the beauty of the two of you. Peter Pan, always young and full of life. Captain Hook, scurrilous sea dog and villain of the tale. *Blast you, Peter Pan! I'll get you next time!* You're equal, you're opposite. You *can't* get rid of one or the other. Not forever. It's balance. Nothing ever changes here in Never Land.

"Or . . . does it?"

She frowned, as if puzzled.

"Everyone knows the story of the time he cut your hand off. So there must have been a time *before* you had your hook."

The captain looked at his hook with something like surprise.

"It was a long time ago . . ." he said, almost as if he was having trouble remembering.

"But it's still a change."

The pirates looked at each other, confused. Even the Lost Boys looked uncertain of where she was going with this. Slightly alone seemed to be concentrating on something else—but the minute wiggles of his shoulders hinted it was probably because he was trying to cut himself free.

"There have been other changes, too," she added, trying to think of something else to say. She had lost her train of thought—what else could she mention that would keep Hook interested? Where was she going with this all?

She began to panic. Maybe she *couldn't* pull this off. Maybe she was actually terrible at weaving stories on the spot that captured everyone's attention.

"I grow tired of your very obvious delaying tactics, Miss Darling," Hook growled. "What *changes*? How do they relate to *me*?"

Slightly's arm spasmed; he had probably just cut his way through the last of his bonds.

Valentine noticed this movement and frowned, pushing his way forward to look.

"There are so many . . . unexpected things . . ." Wendy babbled, trying to find something that worked. "Not just from children's imaginations . . . Never Land itself is making changes. . . ."

"*I* have!" Skipper suddenly stood up—awkwardly, arms behind her back. "I mean, I *am* a change!"

Everyone turned to stare at the Lost Boy. She stood terrified and defiant.

Wendy's heart nearly broke with gratitude.

"Skipper, tell them who you are," she said gently.

"Explain yourself," Hook ordered, aiming the pistol at her.

*"I'm a girl."*

Her giant animal ears were already off, thrown back over her shoulders, making her look more human. There was nothing more she could do—no taking down of her hair, no revealing a corset, no obvious sign to indicate what she said was true.

"I'm a girl," she said more loudly, when she saw everyone's confusion. "I just cut my hair. And stuff."

"A Lost Boy who's a . . . girl?" Captain Hook said incredulously.

Zane's eyes were wide with interest; his face acquired a light that Wendy hadn't seen in it before.

"Aye, a girl," Skipper said a little more defensively, and stuck her chin out.

"A girl . . . *what*?" Ziggy asked.

Everyone looked at the pirate.

"What?" he demanded. He pointed at the rest of the Lost Boys. "That one's a fox, that's a bear, easy enough to see. What in the bloody deuce are *you* supposed to be? A girl *what*?"

"Ah . . . a bilby?" Skipper cleared her throat and spoke more forcefully: "A bilby."

The pirates looked at her blankly, in silence.

The Lost Boy grew red and shifted on her feet, now uncomfortable with all the attention.

"A marsupial. Kind of like a hare, but with a long nose and tail," Slightly explained helpfully.

"Oh! You mean like a bandicoot?" Djareth said, recognition dawning on his face.

"Exactly."

"They're highly endangered, you know," Screaming Byron told Zane.

"All right, all right," Hook said impatiently. "This is certainly a bizarre turn of events, but what has any of this to do with whatever *warning* you said you were giving me? What has this to do with changes?"

"The warning is about precisely this; it's about *change*, Hook," Wendy said. "It comes slow to Never Land, but still it comes. A girl Lost Boy, for instance. And surely you've heard about the squabbles between Slightly and Peter?"

"Of course," Hook said with a sniff, looking exactly like a schoolboy who has been left out of a good gossip but desperately doesn't want anyone to know. "Who hasn't?"

"Well, then it must have confounded you as much as everyone else! The inseparable Lost Boys! Peter's endlessly brave and loyal crew! With leadership issues! Power struggles! *And* one of them is a girl!"

"I still don't see what this has to do with—"

"Things are changing, Captain Hook. Never Land is changing. Slowly. It is settling in, *aging*.

"And, it is obvious—*you are as well*."

Silence blanketed the ship. The pirates looked aghast.

"Now see here, Miss Darling," Hook said with a lilt in his voice as if it were all a joke—but his voice was shaky, and he raised the pistol to her.

"Everyone knows why you *started* chasing Pan, the youthful, adventurous, dashing young fellow—"

"It's because he took my hand! He's our greatest enemy! Isn't that right, men?" Hook demanded.

The pirates muttered and shook their heads.

"All right," Hook allowed. "Perhaps he's *my* greatest enemy. He's my nemesis. He's my final opponent. He's my—"

"*He's your youth*, Cap'n! Everybody knows it!" the Duke finally exploded.

"What?" Hook roared. "Not this nonsense again!"

"He *is.* Your youth," Zane said tiredly. "Get it through yer thick skull. You've been chasing him all over Never Land and the seas between the worlds because you think you can recapture it. And him."

"Stuff and nonsense!" Hook said, shaking himself all over and resettling himself. "He's an irritation, a thorn in my side, a veritable pain in my—"

"And when you had your famous confrontation with him, finally," Wendy interrupted, "*he took your hand and fed it to the crocodile.* The tick-tock croc, Hook. The one whose very sound puts a thrill of fear up your spine, reminding you of time passing."

Hook again glanced involuntarily at his hook.

"What will Peter take next time?" Wendy asked, stepping closer, speaking more softly. "If you don't finish him off?"

The pirates were silent, all eyes fixed on her and their captain.

(A bouncing glow shot over to another Lost Boy.)

Peter let out the slightest puff of a groan and twitched.

Wendy's shadow must have roused his shadow, but Wendy didn't dare risk a look over to see.

"There are people like me, all over the world, telling the story of the deadly Captain Hook and how he is . . . *changing*. Bits of him slowly hacked off, going gray, unable to take a single ship or port anymore . . . Not even wanting to! All he can think about is this one small boy and his island home. This *boy*. This slip of a thing you wouldn't have thought twice about making walk the plank and being done with years ago. He's gotten into your mind and skull, subverting your every thought and happy moment."

"It's true," Hook moaned. "I haven't had a moment's peace since the appearance of Peter Pan."

"What has it done to you, Captain?" Wendy whispered.

"But I *have* Peter Pan now!" He backed up toward the mast, waving his pistol wildly. "It's all over. I'll finish him and get rid of Never Land—then I'll get it all back. My peace of mind, my life . . . I can go back to being a real pirate!"

"But is it too late, I wonder?" Wendy said thoughtfully. "Peter has already used up every moment of your time. Time passes, even in Never Land. You can practically *hear* the ticktock of the hours as they pass. . . . Listen. . . ."

*Tick.*

*Tick.*

Everyone on the *Jolly Roger* grew perfectly silent and strained their ears.

*Tick.*

*Tock.*

Hook's eyes practically rolled up into his head, the whites showing all around.

*Tick*

*Tock.*

*Tick*

*Tock.*

"Yes, that is the sound of time, Hook," Wendy said. "Ages passing, even here, and taking you with them. . . ."

"*No.* NO!" Hook shrieked. "That's the crocodile! No! He has my hand! He's coming for the rest of me!"

"Crocodile, clocks, life, time, it doesn't matter, Hook. It's coming for you. Whether or not you kill Peter Pan."

The clockwork crocodile surfaced, spines gleaming in the dying scarlet light of the day. It circled the ship, snapping its jaws and slapping its tail.

Several pirates looked over the side at it and blanched.

"I really thought it were dead," T. Jerome Newton whispered.

*"SMEE! IT'S COME FOR ME!"* Hook cried, sliding down against the mast until he was crumpled at the base. "SMEE! HELP ME! HELP!"

Wendy waited, unsure how to deal with a potential rescue.

None came.

“Smee . . . Please . . . can’t you *do* something?” Hook moaned, beginning to cry. “Get it away. I *have* Pan. I won! Get the crocodile away. He can’t get me anymore, really, can he, Smee?”

Slightly leapt up, throwing his bonds dramatically aside and striking a heroic pose.

“To arms, men—and Skipper! We must overpower our captors!”

The Lost Boys leapt up right behind him.

The pirates . . .

Did nothing.

“Don’t bother,” Zane said, sighing. “I think, as they say, we’re done here.”

# Endings

"What?" Slightly asked, taken aback—and not a little disappointed.

"It's over, Lost Boys. You won. All right? Is that what you want to hear?" Zane looked at his captain and shook his head sadly.

The clockwork crocodile had taken a turn closer to the boat and its ticking grew louder. Hook buried his head, whimpering into his knees, continued calling for Mr. Smee. Wendy reached over and gently took the pistol out of his grip. He didn't even try to resist.

"Who *is* this Smee I keep hearing about?" she asked curiously.

"There *is* no Smee," Djareth spat. "Didn't you get that, love?"

"I beg your pardon?"

"Aye, no Smee at all," Zane said, patting Hook on the shoulder. "Never has been. There've been others—that giant rabbit, Barney . . . Remember that one, mates?"

"Aye, that was right cuckoo, that one." Ziggy nodded sagely.

"Oh . . . my. I thought Mr. Smee was like . . . a first mate, or yeoman, or cabin boy, or something," Wendy said in wonder. "I did think it was odd I was never properly introduced."

"Our old captain here hasn't been right for years . . . maybe he never was." Zane shrugged. "Thanks to Peter Pan, or not. Anyway, you've won. We were on the point of mutiny anyway, if you want to know."

They made a strange pair: the crumpled, pale Peter, whose eyelids were just beginning to flutter, hat tipped back—and next to him his nemesis, hunched over, shivering, black wig askew.

"This raises a lot *more* questions about Never Land," Wendy murmured.

Slightly had directed the Lost Boys over to the golden cage. The moment the knobs were all reset and the gate swung open, the two shadows shot out together like captive birds set free.

Wendy watched the shadows, now elongated by the low, failing red light, enjoying their last moments that day together hand in hand, swooping and soaring over the water before merging into the dusk.

She smiled, lost in thoughts of other possibilities, other stories: where she was younger, Tinker Bell didn't mind, and she and Peter wound up together.

In reality, Tinker Bell nervously hovered over Peter. He rubbed a hand over his brow and tried to sit up.

"Wha-what happened?" he asked, somehow sounding both imperious and demanding despite the weakness of his voice.

"We won!" Slightly said, kneeling down to pat his hand. "All thanks to Wendy here, and Tink, and this brave fellow, Thorn."

Thorn bobbed demurely next to Wendy.

"But where's my shadow?" Peter asked, looking around. "I still don't have it!"

"He will be back, I promise," Wendy said. "He's just taking a little jaunt. But he has a good keeper this time. Shadows have their own minds in Never Land, and deserve some freedom, I think."

"Well, then, it doesn't seem like a victory to me," Peter Pan said peevishly. "The whole point was to get my shadow back."

Tinker Bell's eyes widened. She flew in close and *pinched his cheek.*

*And save Never Land, you acorn!*

"Aw, I'm just kidding, Tink," Peter said, waving her away and laughing. "I couldn't have asked for a better rescue. You all did amazing without me. I guess I taught you really well."

Wendy rolled her eyes. Tinker Bell gave Peter a kiss on the nose. Slightly laughed and bumped knuckles with him.

*"You* think *you've won,"* Hook whispered. "All of you standing around congratulating yourselves on a job well done. Well, you haven't won. Peter was supposed to watch all of you die. Everyone and everything he loves. But if I can't have Pan, no one can. Time comes for everyone, eh, Wendy? Tick . . . tock . . . *Boom!*"

He lapsed into a fit of psychotic giggles.

"What do you mean, exactly?" Wendy asked softly, addressing the captain the way she used to her great uncle.

"Goodbye, dear," Hook hissed. "You'd be safer if you had stayed in London. Safe as *houses.* Here you'll be quite exploded."

*It sounds like an incendiary,* Thorn jingled.

"It's a bomb!" Peter Pan exclaimed, standing up. Color was coming back into his face. "That's how he's going to destroy Never Land! He tried to blow up the hideout once—remember? It was attached to a clock!"

"Oh, that was a good adventure, that one," one of the pirates said with nostalgia. "*That* one almost worked."

"There was a clock in the chart room," Zane said. "And powder. Makes sense."

"A bomb to blow up all of Never Land?" Wendy demanded. "It would have to be huge! Where is this bomb, Hook?"

"I'll never tell—*never*," Hook said, holding a finger up to his lips. "We'll all go together!"

"We've got to find it. All of us," Slightly said. "Right now. Who knows when he set it to go off?"

"We'll set sail right now and search the coastlines," Zane said grimly. "With the right wind, we can make quick work of all the perimeters."

"I'll check the most explody places," Peter Pan said. "The volcanoes and the geysers. Those would be *great* places to hide a bomb."

*I'll rally the fairies,* Thorn said.

*Yes, yes!* Tinker Bell jingled. *We can cover all of the jungles if we spread out.*

"We'll take the caves around the mountains," Slightly offered. "And the tunnels, all the places underground where it's possible to hide a giant bomb."

Wendy watched the unlikely group before her—Lost Boys and pirates, fairies and shadows—work together to excitedly plan how they were going to save the world.

She cleared her throat.

*"Gentlemen!"* she shouted.

Everyone stopped talking.

"And ladies," she added. "And those who haven't made a decision one way or the other, or have chosen not to choose. This is *Captain Hook* we're talking about here. A pirate. He is not exactly over-imbued with imagination, or unpredictable. No disrespect intended."

Slightly, Peter Pan, Tinker Bell, Thorn, and Zane looked at each other, a little chagrined.

"Skull Island," they all said or jingled at the same time.

"We just stopped there afore coming here," Zane added, scratching his head. "For something or other secretive."

*"Really,"* Wendy said, crossing her arms and shaking her head. "The *deuce* you say."

"That's where the bomb is!" Peter Pan cried. "I'll go at once!"

*I'm going with you!* Tinker Bell jingled.

"And me as well," Wendy said. She turned to Thorn. "You should come, too, since you know about these kinds of things."

*I don't think I'm needed right now,* he said with a wise smile. *Or wanted. I'll still rally the fairies—just in case. Go save Never Land, Wendy.*

"All right . . ." She *wanted* to lean over and kiss him—on the cheek, of course. She had a feeling they might not see each other after this. But however overwhelming the urge, she was afraid it would terrify him. So she kissed her hand and blew it at him gently instead.

At first he looked surprised at the gesture—and then he grinned.

*I will see you again someday, Windy Wendy. If not in Never Land or London, then somewhere else heroes go.*

Wendy sighed and looked away. Tinker Bell was giving her the side-eye.

"What? Mind your business."

The little fairy grinned wickedly, and the three leapt up into the sky.

# Skull Island

"There it is!" Peter cried.

As clear as a print in a child's book, there was the tiny island: a gray stone skull rising out of the sea as if the rest of a giant gray skeleton lurked in the depths below it. While the formation couldn't possibly have been natural—nothing in Never Land *was* strictly natural—perhaps it arose organically, having felt a need in stories for a spooky landmark. Or maybe it was built and carved by ancient peoples who never truly existed, only appearing in convenient side notes to explain how the island came about. Whatever the case, pirates needed it, and here it was. . . .

Although it was a bit different from when Wendy had told her own stories of Never Land to Michael and John.

The eye sockets, nose, and mouth, previously open and accessible to boats, mermaids, and pirates (and seagulls and ravens picking the bones of those murdered there) were all sealed up. Quickly and sloppily, in true pirate fashion. Boards crisscrossed the sockets with no plan or finesse. Half-hammered nails stuck out. Bricks and stones were piled up in awkward slants to fill in gaps. Cement or spackle had been slapped on the edges like a poor plumber's job.

"He's closed off all the entryways!" Peter said in dismay, pulling up to a stop in midair.

Tinker Bell flitted back and forth worriedly.

Wendy wasn't *quite* skilled enough to do either of those things, so she had to content herself with drifting to and fro over as narrow an area as she could manage.

Peter flew up to an eye socket to investigate more closely. Despite the slapdash appearance, the job was pretty solid. He couldn't pull out any of the stones or boards, or break up the cement.

"No good." He swore, kicking at the island. "That's a pickle."

*I can slip in,* Tinker Bell said, pointing. *There.*

The childish, potty-humored pirates had left a chink in the nose hole toward the bottom left. Some extra cement had been guided to pool around the base to give the appearance of snot.

"Tinker Bell, do you even know how to disarm a bomb?" Wendy asked.

*Pirates are unencumbered with imagination, as a wise lady once said,* Tinker Bell jingled with a wan smile. *Hook tried this before. . . . Easy-peasy!*

"Aw, Tink can do anything," Peter said, waving his hand. "She's a *tinker.* This ain't nothing to her."

"Be careful," Wendy pleaded. "Even defused it's dangerous."

Tinker Bell gave her a quick kiss on the cheek, then snapped to attention in front of Peter, touching her hand to her brow. Then she dove into the nose hole.

"Huh, that's funny," Peter said. "She gave *you* a kiss and *me* a salute."

But that was all he said, and he seemed merely to be puzzled by it, neither offended nor amused.

Wendy fretted while they waited: What if Tink couldn't defuse the bomb? What if, failing, she brought the bomb outside so the three could figure it out together? Wendy didn't know how to defuse a bomb—did Peter? What if they couldn't? What would they do with it?

Meanwhile, Peter whistled, checked his nails, made little churches and people with his fingers, stretched out in the air on his back.

At one point he sat up and noticed his shadow on the

rocks below, reinvigorated by the bright light of the two moons. Wendy's shadow was playing cat's cradle with her friend, using a shadow piece of string from somewhere.

*"Hey,"* Peter said, a little vexed.

Shadow Peter turned to look at him, which of course was no more than a shifting of flat black shapes. But even Wendy could feel the look he gave the solid Peter. *Really? You want to start this again?*

"As you were," Peter said quickly. "You could ask us if *we* wanted to play, though."

This was such a ridiculous and impossible idea that everyone just ignored it.

And then the bomb went off.

It was a noise like nothing Wendy had ever heard before, an earsplitting sound preceded by a blast of air so strong it knocked her back like a carriage pulled by eight panicking horses. Somehow Peter flung himself around her and wrapped her body with his.

The two were thrown, the world went black.

# Flotsam and Jetsam

She must have only been out for a moment or two, but when Wendy came to she found the world a topsy-turvy place that made no sense. It was almost perfectly silent, for one thing; noises like rocks falling and gulls screaming sounded almost hollow, as if very, very far away. Dust and grit poured from her lashes as she tried to make sense of gravity, light, and pain, all of which were coming at her from strange angles.

Peter Pan was lying next to her, one arm still thrown protectively over her waist.

"Peter," she whispered. Even that sounded wrong; she felt the vibrations in her throat but couldn't hear the words.

Wincing at the extreme, *wrong* pain in her back, she managed with great difficulty to push herself onto her elbows and knees.

"Peter, wake up."

She gasped at how bloody he was; a thousand lacerations covered him from forehead to feet. After a panicked moment of wiping it off—with his own soft hat—she was relieved to see they were just tiny divots and scrapes from the grit and scree shot out by the explosion. No wound seemed especially deep.

"Where's Tink?" he murmured. At least, that's what it looked like his lips said.

"I don't know!"

"I can't hear you," he said accusingly.

"The explosion." She touched her ears, then waved to the black and windy sky.

"I can't hear you!" Peter shouted.

*This* Wendy could hear a little, which was a relief. She forced herself to stand up. Her back was a throbbing mass of pain—but it obeyed her will, albeit reluctantly. No permanent damage except for maybe a cracked rib. No tingling in her feet. She was all right, though the crimson streak in the corner of her right eye was a little worrisome.

*"TINK!"* she shouted as loudly as she could, unsure how loud it really was.

The landscape was much changed in the last five minutes. Skull Island was almost entirely gone. What Wendy stood on were its remains: a whole new atoll of big, ugly chunks of gray rock, some of which were still rolling and shifting into place like knucklebones. Dust had risen up and nearly blocked out the moons and stars, diffusing their light strangely and, turning the sky the same sort of monochrome white she associated with the First. A wind had sprung up and the water was an ugly shade of lead.

"TINK!" she screamed.

"Tinker Bell!" Peter yelled, and this time Wendy thought she heard him. He shot into the air, darting back and forth over the sea in the same random, unorganized way Tinker Bell would have. Wendy struggled to fly, buffeted about by the winds and very, very unsteady. She coughed and spat up sand and blood.

"Tinker Bell!"

In snippets and wisps sound was coming back, but it was confusing and snarled. Somehow the noises made her want to vomit. She gagged and ordered her stomach to settle.

"Tink! TINKER BELL!" Peter Pan called again.

A faint shadow appeared over Wendy's vision. *This is it*, she thought; she was going to pass out again.

Then it blinked away and everything was light . . . and then it was dark again. On and off, like a signal.

Confused, Wendy put her hands up between her face and the sky.

Her shadow appeared on her palm, shrinking quickly to fit. She had been trying to get Wendy's attention! She pointed and waved her arms toward what might have been north. Wendy dropped her hands and the shadow fell to the sea, just visible in the dim light. The shadow skittered across the water, still pointing. Peter's was close behind.

"Peter!" Wendy shouted.

Whether he was less injured or his pixie ears healed faster, Peter Pan heard her immediately. He looked to where she pointed and flew after the shadows.

The four skimmed together over the surface of the sea.

And there she was: a glittering lump of golden hair and wings, floating lackluster on the foam.

Peter scooped up the tiny fairy and landed on the closest pile of rocks. He gently lowered her down and cleared the water and silt off her face.

But Tinker Bell wasn't breathing. And she wasn't glowing.

"Don't die, Tinker Bell!" Peter begged. "Don't go out! Tink! You mean more to me than anything!"

"Come on, Tink," Wendy begged. "You can make it. I know you can. I believe in you. I believe in you and fairies and Never Land. I know you wouldn't leave me or Peter Pan or this world. Please, Tinker Bell. I believe in you."

Silence.

And then . . . the faintest of jingles.

*No, Wendy.*

*I believe in* you.

# Endings Again

The pirates sailed away to resume wholesome—well, normal—pirate activities. Zane promised to find a nice tropical port where they would deposit Hook, along with enough gold for a comfortable house and a caretaker. Which was, perhaps, more than the violent, insane captain deserved—but then again, the bomb hadn't really worked all that well after all, and it did nicely set him up for recovering and returning for revenge when he was needed again.

Captain Zane saluted Peter Pan and declared their enmity at an end, but said that he and the crew would cheerfully resume aggressions any time Peter wanted to interfere with their operations. The boy politely offered the same.

The pirate then shook Wendy's hand. "It was a pleasure knowing you, Miss Darling. You . . . brought change. And as you said, change comes to all things. Even Never Land. It was high time."

He turned to Skipper.

"Should you be looking for . . . other employment, my ship is an open and welcoming place to *anyone* who wants to loot and plunder, no matter what they look like, who they snog, or how they dress. As long as you're into murder and burnin', these days we keep an open mind on the *Jolly Roger.*"

Skipper cracked one of her small sideways smiles.

"Thanks, Captain. Maybe someday I'll take you up on it."

And so the pirates sailed away, the *Jolly Roger* growing smaller and smaller until it disappeared into the horizon.

On the white sands of the tropical beach now remained only the Lost Boys (and Luna), Peter Pan, Wendy, Tinker Bell, and everyone's shadows.

It was how Wendy had once imagined a perfect end of an adventurous day . . . and yet entirely different. Peter Pan was covered in ugly wounds. Tink sat slumped on his shoulder, not quite recovered enough to fly. The Lost Boys looked less lost and more real under this Never Land sun, pores and hair and dirt and scratches and eyes and smiles and all.

"Now then, what's this about you being a *girl*, Skipper?" Peter Pan demanded.

Skipper shrugged.

"She is what she is," said Slightly.

"You wouldn't have taken me if I wasn't a boy," she pointed out.

"But it's the Lost *Boys*," Peter said, exasperated.

"Maybe it shouldn't be," Slightly said. "Maybe it shouldn't be *Boys*. Or *Girls*. Maybe it should be *Lost People*."

"Lost *People* . . . ?" Peter repeated, a little distastefully.

"Maybe it shouldn't be *Lost*." Cubby spoke up unexpectedly. "You *found* us, Peter. We're *found*."

"Found People," Slightly said, nodding, "I like that."

"I like it, too," Skipper agreed.

Slightly and Peter stared at each other for a long, silent moment.

Finally, Peter rolled his eyes.

"Lost Boys, Found People, Tiny Bunnies—I don't care what you call yourselves. I just don't ever want to be fighting with you again. I *missed* you guys. I don't know if it was arguing with you or losing my shadow that made me more sick. And I know it was at least half my fault.

"You've, ah, you've grown into quite the position of leader—under my wise tutelage," Peter added, putting his arm around Slightly. "I definitely think it's high time we gave you more responsibility over this little ragtag group of heroes."

Now it was Slightly's turn to roll his eyes, but he did it with a smile.

"Bring it in, Peter," he ordered.

And the two boys hugged and made up.

Tinker Bell disentangled herself from Peter and slipped down his arm. Wendy put out hers and Tink landed on it as gracefully as a ballerina.

*What will* you *do now?*

"I think . . . I've been thinking about this a lot, Tinker Bell. And I think because you are wiser than you let on—when you're not distracted by boys—you can probably guess what it is."

The fairy pulled a face.

*You're returning to stinky London.*

"Yes, I'm afraid I am," Wendy sighed. "Just like in all those terrible stories I said I would never, ever tell or write. The ones English authors love so much, about experiencing magic and wonder as a child and then giving it all up and putting it away to become an adult and take on responsibilities and children and a job—and all that somehow making it all right.

"But I cannot forget what the First said, about how Never Land is a reflection of London, my world. My world has a lot of problems. And not only is it unfair to foist them upon this unfinished, innocent world, it's unfair to ignore them by staying here and pretending they don't exist.

"Somewhere right now a toothless old grandfather is shivering in a poorhouse, starving and without visitors.

Somewhere an orphan—who *wasn't* rescued by Peter—is being beaten by a harsh nurse or sold as a slave to a factory owner. And everywhere in the world, girls have little ability to make their voices heard, or the power to change things. I think about the way *I* changed things in the Land of the First . . . and here, with your and Thorn's help . . . and I wonder if I can use a little of that magic at home.

"I've had the best adventure a girl could ever want—and that is more than I ever dreamed was possible."

*But . . . I'll miss you.*

"I can't even think about it, Tinker Bell. It hurts dreadfully. You're the best friend I ever had. I feel like I'm cutting off a part of me. Forever."

The little fairy drooped, and she was a sad sight indeed: tattered wings, trembling lips, limp hair out of its messy bun and draping her like an old cloak.

Then she looked up.

*Maybe just one last adventure? For goodbye?*

"I'd dearly love to see a dragon," Wendy said eagerly. "I didn't get to do that."

The two girls smiled, and gently touched scratched-up, bruised hands.

# Epilogue

In one of the less pleasant—but eminently affordable—neighborhoods of London was the in/famous flat of Ms. Wendy Darling.

Her apartment was modest but large enough for Wendy, her books, and gatherings of like-minded people. There was hot running water, electric lamps, and a private entrance. Every room had windows. There was a dining area large enough to serve as the nexus for organizing protests, staging letter-writing campaigns, publishing pamphlets, planning speeches, strategizing actions, and occasionally even feeding unannounced hordes of supporters who dropped by.

And none of them said Wendy talked too much. Some came from a hundred miles away just to hear her speak.

(Even Mr. and Mrs. Darling came over to attend her

speeches. They were mostly embarrassed and *very* slightly proud, but more than anything else *surprised* by this enterprise of their eldest, dreamiest child.)

(Michael and John were absolutely on their sister's side about changing the world and voting rights for women, even to the point of marching with her—but that might have been partially due to the number of passionate ladies attracted to the cause.)

Wendy looked mostly the same as an adult; her only nod to the passage of time was the decision to keep her hair up in a messy bun modeled after a dear friend's style. She also found that her years of dreaming had either left her myopic or caused her to let it go unnoticed for a long time. She now sported a pair of glasses very similar to John's.

(These were removed when fisticuffs were expected, as when she joined a number of ladies of Caribbean descent at Saxelbrees Café and Salon for a peaceful sit-in. Tea was an English right, regardless of race, color, or creed.)

This particular evening, all was quiet; constituents and suffragettes and equal-rights advocates and rabble-rousers had all been ordered out. Wendy was indulging herself in a pastime with which even her closest confidants were unacquainted.

First she set the kitchen table with a pretty cloth and her best un-chipped tea service.

Next to this she carefully placed another tea set—but this one was *tiny*: so dainty and perfect that an outside observer would have blinked in astonishment. For Wendy Darling was gifted, passionate, forgiving, and talkative, but not cracked in the head or prone to strange hobbies. And she did *not* have any cats.

(Or dogs. Nana had passed on peacefully. Snowball was happily adopted by Phoebe Shesbow.)

"Oh, I've forgotten a spoon, and a fork for the cake," Wendy realized. She ran up the cramped flight of stairs that led to a dormer. Her neatly made bed was nestled under a brilliantly large pair of windows that looked out on the sky. Next to it was a rickety nightstand that supported a tall stack of pamphlets, chapbooks, and monographs. And next to *that* was a chest, on top of which was a very large dollhouse decorated with every conceivable realistic detail.

("You never played with dolls as a child, Wendy," Michael had pointed out upon seeing it. Perhaps with a touch of envy.

"Maybe this is just a physical manifestation of your reframing the desire for a child, the natural impulse of which has been subverted by mannish occupations?"

John was very fond of modern psychology.

This sort of thing was usually answered with a disappointed look from Wendy—and sometimes a slap.)

It was a work in progress. If Wendy had a little extra money for herself it went to things like having an exactly 1:12-scale Chesterfield sofa made to her specifications and upholstered in real leather with tiny covered buttons decorating the tufts.

If she had a little extra *time* for herself—even rarer—she tatted miniature antimacassars out of single-strand silk, or rolled tiny real beeswax tapers. Teensy gas and oil lamps she hadn't quite worked out yet without teensy explosions.

She carefully opened the miniature china cabinet in the pantry and used the tip of her pinky to pull out a dainty silver spoon and matching fork. It was part of a brilliant charm set she had seen in a jeweler's shop.

(She had received *very* funny looks from the jeweler when she had asked him to pull open the jump ring and separate the eating implements off it.)

She hurried back downstairs, laid the spoon and fork next to the cup, and put the kettle on the hob.

Then she proceeded to wait.

It looked like madness: a famous suffragette sitting at an empty table with two very different-sized saucers laid in front of her.

And if one managed to peep into the mind of Wendy Darling—well, that too might look like a bit of madness.

It had been ten years since she had reappeared in the garden of the Darling household, practically naked and covered with injuries, all of which the Darlings managed to keep a secret.

She was not sent to Ireland.

Those ten years had been full of hard decisions, harder work, and fights with her family and friends and even strangers on the street as her notoriety grew. There were small victories, large setbacks, and of course the endless, tiring, and unglamorous work that no one tells you about when you decide to change the world. Boring stuff like writing letters, keeping accounts, assigning funds, constantly reminding people to show up, and politely pursuing them to hold them to whatever promises they made. Usually about funds.

By the end of most days, her writing arm would ache like she had been battling thysolits the whole time.

But she kept herself going with hopes and dreams, with memories of severe deserts and voices that couldn't be heard. Nothing she did, she reminded herself, was more dangerous than battling pirates—or more terrible than doing their laundry.

And on certain nights, when it *felt* right, when the moon was friendly and she didn't recognize all the stars, she set out two cups of tea and waited.

And waited.

Of course, things happened at a different pace in Never Land, even if the years matched up. Peter Pan was a hard boy to keep in line. Promises over there could be put off for years when the promiser thought only an afternoon had slipped by.

"I have so much to tell her," Wendy said to herself. "The protest outside of parliament where they hit me with that rotten tomato . . . and then that funny tree I saw growing at the botanical gardens that reminded me so much of rubyfruit!"

The mantel clock in the other room (humorously decorated with a TIME TO CHANGE sign penned by one of her friends) continued to ticktock.

As midnight approached, Wendy sighed and stood up to clear the dishes. Again.

At midnight oh one, a golden glow appeared in her kitchen window.

Upon seeing it, Wendy's face also glowed.

"Tinker Bell!" she sighed, and opened the door.